I listened to my phone, heard the distant ring.
"Come on, come on," I mumbled.

No answer. I called Todd's number. The mob guys
were crossing the parking lot toward the back door,
and the cops were hustling out of the vans toward the
corner, splitting up to go in the front and back doors at
the same time.

Cops always park too far away.

Todd's phone was ringing, and ringing, and the
answering service picked up. I hung up and tried the
upstairs phone in the club, the phone in the room behind the mirror. The mob guys had just gotten to the
door, the cops were almost at the corner of the building, and my battery died.

The gangsters plunged through the door just as the
cops came around and broke into a run, and that's the
moment I stopped thinking.

I should've driven away. I should've stayed put. I
should've done anything except what I did, but Nature
took over and I went to protect my mate. The wheels in
my head spun out, tires smoking.

I dropped the phone and reached under my seat
for the snub-nosed S&W .38, opened the door and
stepped out with Joe Pantoliano's voice in my head for
no good reason at all.

Time of your life, eh kid?

Also by the Author

The Heresy Series
By The Sword
Friends Like These
The Kettle Black
After The Flesh
The Camel's Back

The Icarus Trilogy
In Shining Armor
A Mind Diseased
Thy Neighbor's Wife

Comedy Adventure

Saga of the Beverage Men
The Prince of Foxes
Navarre

Memoirs of a Swine
St. Lucy's Eyes
Just Plain Trouble
This Little Piggy
A Bad Husband
No Good Deed
An Empty fist

Nonfiction

Variety Is the Spice
A Thousand Words
The Hero Mindset

HERESY

VOLUMES I ~ V

ALEXANDER FERRAR

HERESY

Copyright © 2008 by Alexander Ferrar

ISBN: 9798575204299

Published by Bunbury
First edition: June 2008
Second edition: May 2009
Third edition: September 2010
Fourth edition: November 2020

Cover art and design by Oliver Clozoff

A Note on the Text

The words herein were set in Champak, the font in which were first printed the ghastly revelations of the mad Arab Fahred Ibrahim al ibn Gabah, to whom the dark Truths were revealed during interviews with ghouls and frequenters of moonlit graveyards, and the ink in which these words were composed is of the black ichor secreted by the most tenebrous of krakens as they battled in the Abyss with the mindless larvae of the Elder Gods. Except for the parts that were set in Times New Roman.

www.alexferrar.com

This collection of novels is dedicated to
Blanche and Louis Tancredi

FRIENDS
LIKE
THESE

I

Dear Diary,

I awoke on the ceiling of my bedroom, and lay there for a long time before dragging myself down the wall to the nightstand where breakfast lay. Between the alarm clock and a mashed pack of Marlboros, my hand mirror waited with two lines cut and ready.

This morning—or afternoon, whatever—my little hitter was already in place beside the two perfect, beautiful, snow-white lines, just waiting. Funny, I can't remember to set my alarm clock, but I always always always have coke ready the night before.

I had my little eye-opener and made my way to the bathroom, where the unforgiving mirror lurked. The girl I saw had been beautiful the night before. The girl I saw now had hickeys on her neck and breasts, as black and terrible as the bags underneath her eyes. Smeared mascara like a psychedelic raccoon and—Christ—a pimple. The taste of my own mouth made me sick. My ears rang, my eyes burned. I could smell the frozen chicken pot pie I'd put in the microwave and forgotten about, again. I used to promise myself that if I could just get through today, tonight would be different from last night. Now, I don't even bother anymore. I don't waste my time trying to remember where the hickeys came from or whose stains those were in my sheets. I looked at the back of my hand, the fingernails painted silver, and scratched at a new cigarette burn. I don't remember doing it, but I don't really care either. Aside from that and a few other scars and blemishes, great body, low mileage.

I leaned in close to the mirror, looking deep into my pale gray eyes, and kissed my reflection, leaving the whore-red lipstick kiss mark there and stepping into the tub. The shower I took was long and hot, but not long enough. I swallowed as much water as I could, holding the shakes at bay until I could get that first redeeming drink. I knew without having to check that I was out of B-12s and painkillers, but the shower helped. I have thirteen shampoos and conditioners in my bathroom, and I used them all as an excuse to spend an hour under the stream, trying to soak my dehydrated brain before it cracked. My hair, fiery red and extending to the small of my back, will probably thank me for it.

While drying off I heard my phone ring, and ignored it until I heard whoever it was hang up on my answering machine. Christ, I hate that. My cell phone went off next, followed by my pager, but I

1

was doing my makeup. I found my watch, a man's silver Fossil I took from somebody's bedroom floor when he was asleep. It was two-thirty. Shit. I had to be somewhere, but I couldn't for the life of me remember where or who or what my agenda was for that day.

I spent a few minutes picking out a pair of tight black pin-striped pants and a collared white shirt with the tails in front that you tie in a knot, exposing my washboard and belly button ring. The phone rang again, but I was strapping my heels on.

Whoever it was hung up on the machine again.   Shit! I hate that.

I lit a cigarette with a silver trench lighter I got from somebody at some time or other, and was putting my cell phone in my purse when it rang again, startling me. I checked the caller ID—it was my day job.

"Hello?"

"It's about time you got up," Cedric snarled.

"I beg your pardon?"

"Knock it off, Simone. I've been calling all day."

"I've been out."

"My ass. Meet us around the corner." The line went dead.

Oh yeah, that's where I was supposed to be. The outfit I'd just finished putting on was not going to work too well for the job I'd have to do, but I felt like making life hard for that big spook, so I went out the way I was. I stopped at the mirror on the wall by my apartment's front door and brushed a wayward strand of hair behind my ear. I was twenty-three, but I looked five years older. An old woman, but still a hottie. I winked at myself and went out the door. Damn, it was bright out. I slid on my Audrey Hepburn over-sized designer shades and went to work.

I have, by far, the coolest car in the world. It's a 1970 Mach I, silver—of course—with two white racing stripes, black leather interior, Kenwood system, and a place under the driver's seat for my snub-nosed S&W .38 that Cedric still hasn't found. I've fired it in anger twice, but haven't killed anybody yet.

The way I got the car was sheer genius on my part.

It was the pride and joy of an ex-fiancé, the fourth one of seven, but hey, who's counting? He'd spent a summer working on it with his dad, who he hated. It was the only thing that brought them together One night while he was at work I drove it out of the parking lot of the restaurant he cooked in, took it to the apartment we shared, and cleaned out anything worth my time. I took his TV, VCR, DVD, laptop computer, and broke all the CDs I wasn't interested in. Trust me, he had it coming.

By the time he discovered the car missing it was legally mine. On a sheet of loose-leaf paper I wrote out that he gave me the car as a gift, using the VIN, and signed his name to it. My sister and her boyfriend signed as witnesses, and a trick of mine was more than happy to notarize it. A lawyer I was fucking told me how to do it. When my ex called the cops on me, they laughed at him. I racked my brains trying to come up with a tag number that would define me as a person, identify me to other drivers. 6UL-DV8 was already taken. I ended up with NI-4-NI, and that suits me well enough.

Now I was pulling that sweet sweet car into the parking space outside of my friend Casey's apartment. No, not friend, *acquaintance*. Let's make that clear. He was already at the door, his stupid grin wide under unblinking, blood-shot eyes. He was smoking sherm. Right out in the open. What a waste of life, I thought. I'm not going to miss him. I got out and hugged him, going inside. He tried to kiss me on the cheek, but got my ear as I brushed passed him.

"Sorry to drop in on you like this, sweetie."

"No problem, no problem, always time for you," he stammered. "Want a hit?" he asked, offering me his cigarette. It had been soaked in embalming fluid the way da niggaz do.

"No thanks," I said.

The apartment was a pigsty and reeked of a cacophony of different smells. Casey, dressed like a beatnik though he didn't know what they were, claimed to be a writer who'd climbed out of his ivory tower and onto the parapet for his inspiration —whatever the hell that means—but the fact is he was a slob and a burnout. Things lived and thrived in his apartment, especially in the corners of his bathroom, that might evolve into intelligent beings and drive him out if he left them alone too long.

"I'm in a hell of a rush, you know how it is."

"Of course, of course, no problem. Hey, you want to come by later and party?" he asked. It was pathetic.

"Sure. I'd love to." That's what I always said. "I need a lot of H, sweetie, can you help me out?"

"Yeah, of course, yeah, yeah. Sure, no problem. I got heroin coming out my ears this week. How much?"

"Twenty." I hadn't shot up in almost a year. I didn't plan to ever again.

"For you?"

"And a couple of girlfriends, yeah."

"Mmmm."

"You want me to bring them, too?"

"Hell yeah, I do. Bring whoever you want. I've got an open-door policy, you know that." He produced and counted out twenty little bags of powder, and I paid him, kissing him on the cheek. Why not? It was the last time he'd touch a girl for years. I left.

I drove out of the parking lot and watched a white van follow me at a respectable distance once I got on the road. I smiled.

"This guy walks into church and gets into the confession box," I said. "The priest on the other side of the screen greets him and he says 'Forgive me, Father, I have been with a loose woman,' and the priest asks 'Was it Kate Hennessy?' and the guy says 'No.' 'Was it Sarah Blanchet?' The guy says 'No', again. 'How about Betty Grimes?' The guy says, 'Father, I cannot say.' The priest says all right, gives him ten Hail Marys and the guy walks out of the church. Outside, his friend asks, 'Well? What did you get?' The guy says, 'Three good leads.'"

I drove the rest of the way in silence.

I met Cedric and the others at a dead end in the middle of nowhere, the white van bringing up the rear. Cedric was a big, burly black cop who thought he knew everything.

"Sugar, that joke was old when I was young," he rumbled.

They went to work, searching the car in case I'd stashed some of the buy, undoing the wire from my chest, and inspecting the evidence. Cedric's partner was this married white guy named Tom who couldn't keep his eyes off of me. I entertained the possibility of sleeping with him and blackmailing him later, but cops can be sick bastards sometimes and there's no telling what they'll do. They re-played the tape in the van, and it crinkled loudly where it had once suffered a miscarriage in a faulty player.

Someday cops will make the switch to CDs and their snitch recordings will actually have a decent fidelity. When that day comes, we'll *all* be screwed. But it won't happen. They spend too much on my fee to foot that bill.

I made seven hundred dollars, cash. Thirty pieces of silver. For ten minute's worth of work. A lot of snitches glamorize it, thinking of themselves as law enforcement officers, but I try not to.

I went to a bar for lunch. Rick, the bartender, had to be gay. He just *had* to be. But he was all the time talking about the girl he didn't hit it off with the night before. Every time I saw him he'd smile and tell me all about the lousy date last night. Today was no exception.

"Hey, Rick. You got a margarita back there for me?"

"Yessum, Miss Scahlett."

"How's life treating ya?" I asked, sliding onto a barstool. I took out a cigarette and he lit it for me and mixed my drink.

"Well, the usual. I had a date last night," he sighed.

"Oh?" I asked, raising my eyebrows as if surprised and interested.

"Yeah, but she was a nutcase."

"Really."

"Oh yeah, check this out. Traffic was bad, so I was a little late picking her up, right? Well, she kept giving me grief about it, joking around, I thought. Here you go, cutie."

"Thank you." I took a big healthy gulp of my drink.

"At dinner, she'd keep making remarks, until finally I said—get this—'Are you going to punish me and get it over with or just keep complaining?' I said 'If it'll make you feel better just hit me so we can have our dinner in peace.' And you know what?"

"What?"

"She busted my lip right there at the table."

"Noooo."

"Yes. I couldn't believe it. Look, see this scab? Then she's all like, 'Oh poor baby, let me kiss it better', and she leans over and we're making out in the booth." I shook my head slowly in exaggerated wonder.

"The waitress comes over and she's like, *ahem*, right? And we look up and we've got my blood all over both our mouths. It was disgusting."

I nodded agreement while sipping my drink. "So you're not going to see her again?"

"Hell, no."

"It's a shame. Sounds like a match made in Heaven."

"Ha." Yep, he had some sugar in his tank, all right.

I drained my glass and he had another one ready for me.

"You dancing tonight?" he asked. I nodded.

"When are you going to give that up, get a decent job?"

"The minute I meet another rich sucker," I replied seriously. He tried to pretend I was kidding.

He had to be gay.

He *had* to be.

I had coke and weed, but I wanted a roll for Friday night and knew I'd be out of money by then, so I went by my friend Todd's place.

Todd was more than just a drug dealer. He was an *alchemist*. He had studied in college and put what he'd learned to use in much more profitable ways than had been expected of him. He told me that Charles Darwin believed plants were fully conscious life forms. Luther Burbank tried to communicate with them. And George Washington Carver actually developed relationships with them, and made huge scientific advances with what they told him.

Sir Jagadis Chandra Bose proved that they responded to the tone of voice when spoken to. Walter Cronkite did a show on Temple Buell College's project, where three plants were isolated, two of them listening to music, one in silence. The quiet atmosphere only allowed the plant to grow normally. Seventies acid rock killed the second plant, and soothing sitar music had the third plant growing at a tremendous rate.

Todd used this discovery in his closet. While every other amateur college horticulturist rigged up UV lamps and hosed Miracle-Gro to get their pot plants to spring up, all he did was sit it next to a small cassette player, running Eastern mood music in a continuous loop. The result was astounding. Todd Ferguson now had a greenhouse out in Royal Palm with massive cannabis trees of the most potent weed I've ever smoked.

Besides that, he made his own designer drugs, the highest quality that I know of. Where he does it, he won't tell me, and it's probably a good idea that he doesn't.

This guy I'd never sell out to Cedric, though. He had been my buddy for years, and we'd slept together at *least* five times. I think. Five or six. But hey, who's counting? I could go into a long description of him, but it wouldn't be necessary. Just picture the kind of guy who would be named Todd and there you are. If he didn't consider himself above it he could model underwear for the rest of his life. I hate to sound like I'm hung up on cars, but once you know what he drives, you pretty much have his personality pegged. It's a 1950 Plymouth Deluxe, blue in the front, fading into a purple rear, and where you'd expect hotrod flames —lavender octopus tentacles. Diamond cut chrome Dayton wheels and that immaculately white stripe on the tires. Purple fuzzy dice, too. It takes a brass set to drive a car like that.

We could never go out. He was the brother I never had.

He had a fabulous apartment. Black leather furniture, a great steel and glass Dia bar with chrome and black leather stools, fully loaded: miniature still, draft tower, stocked with topshelf bottles. A ridiculously expensive, classy and dignified stereo system. Framed prints on the walls: Ruth Orkin's "American Girl in Italy," Robert Doisneau's "Le Baiser de l'Hôtel de Ville" with the French couple kissing outside their hotel, and a gigantic one of an old Buddhist monk "immolating" himself—apparently a nice way of saying "burning himself alive." The bald-headed guy is sitting down in a public place, middle of Saigon in broad daylight, next to a tank of gasoline with fire coming off of him like a giant flag blowing in the wind. I'd seen a cropped version of it on the cover of Rage's first album, but the full image is much more disturbing.

Todd said that the guy was doing it to protest the Vietnamese government's persecution of Buddhists, and ask the US military for help. The date printed at the bottom was June 11, 1963. I think we went over there to fight not too long after that, but don't quote me on it. History was never my strong suit. Todd told me his reason for having this horrible shit hanging up in his apartment was to remind him what kind of sacrifices people are willing to make for what they believe in, when most of us over here in the States don't even give anything up for Lent anymore (I am the exception, of course. One year I gave up chastity, sobriety, and shame, and I didn't just last all the way until Easter—I kept going strong and haven't looked back since!)

Todd's wrought iron coffee table had all these books laid out on its spotless glass surface. He was one of the few people I knew who read. He was the *only* person I knew who had a collection of first editions. Reading is not my cup of tea, really. The last book I read was *The Rum Diary*, and that's because I was in jail and had nothing better to do. I'm not sure what it was that made Todd and me click, since we had almost nothing in common. He understood me, I guess, without judging me, and never fell in love with me.

He was bare-chested, smoking a clove cigarette, the black kind with the gold band around it, when I let myself in, dropped my purse on the couch and kissed him on the cheek.

"Speak of the devil," he laughed.

"What?"

"I was just telling Layla about you."

"Who's Lay—" I broke off, finding myself staring at the most beautiful girl I'd ever seen, standing in the bedroom doorway in a rumpled man's Versace shirt, her bare legs and cleavage striking, her long blonde hair in sexy disarray, her stunning green eyes sizing me up. My breath was caught in my throat, held there by a mixture of surprise and sudden jealousy.

In another situation I would have wanted her, maybe have even gone all gooey the way I sometimes (rarely) do, but right now I was speechless with envy. She was so much better looking than me it was criminal—blasphemous, even. And she'd had my Todd.

The bitch.

"So you're the spitfire." She looked me up and down the same way I did her. "Todd's description didn't do you justice."

"I'm Sam," I said, recovering myself, lighting a cigarette just to be doing something.

"For Samantha?"

I shook my head. "Simone."

"Pretty."

"Layla, Simone, Simone, Layla," Todd said, smiling. "My dear, what can I do for you?"

"I, uh, I could come back."

Layla was naked beneath that shirt.

"Nonsense, take a load off. Want a drink?"

"Of course." I sat on the couch, ash falling ignored from my cigarette onto the carpet, while Todd in all his golden boy perfection went to his bar and fixed three Cuba Librés.

"I had a favor to ask you," I said, trying not to look at Layla. Was she going to get dressed or what? She was in the same place, and I could feel her eyes on me with wry amusement.

"Your wish is my command."

I looked sideways at Layla; she took the hint and vanished into the bedroom.

"I didn't know if I could speak freely in front of her. I need a roll or two for Friday. Oh! And some painkillers. Those big ones."

"No sweat, babes. Look in the candy dish."

I lifted the lid of a beautiful crystal candy dish filled with a multicolored galaxy of pills. There were Xanax bars, Oxycontins, Methaqualone, Dilaudids, Halcyons, Demerol, Dexedrine, Lortabs, and every variety of Ecstasy I could think of, even a few Flintstone vitamins—purple Dinos, mostly—spiked with God knows what. I selected two Tweetie Birds and some Oxys and put them in my cigarette pack for safe-keeping. Todd came over with his drink and mine.

I thanked him, handed him two twenties, and drank, wondering if she was better in bed than me.

She reappeared wearing a pair of jeans that were second skin, Todd's shirt untucked, barefoot with her gold-painted toenails. She'd brushed her hair and, without any makeup, was gorgeous. I don't know what she'd done to me, what spell she'd cast, but I might hold that body in my arms forever and still hunger for it. It would never be enough to own her, to lock her away where no one but me could ever see her.

I wanted to *be* her.

Her skin was the color of teak, her hair sun-bleached blonde and golden-brown. She drank and I envied the rim of the glass that touched those perfect lips.

The bitch.

She sat next to me and smelled wonderful. I had no idea I felt the way I did about Todd until Miss Perfect washed ashore standing in a clam-shell, or however she'd shown up. I felt myself growing hot and embarrassed beside her, and was grateful for the drink.

"What's today?" she asked. "Thursday?"

"Yep," I replied. "All day, too."

She smiled. "Tomorrow night my boyfriend's club is having its grand opening. I'd love for you to be there. Todd's told me so much about you."

I've never in my life been more confused.

"I'll see if I can fit you in," I said, trying to be cool and feeling inadequate for the first time since puberty.

She laughed. "See that you do. It's the new place downtown. Rabbit's named it after me. Layla, on Clematis Street."

"Rabbit?" I asked.

"His real name's Warren. I don't know why everyone calls him

Rabbit, and he refuses to tell me. It suits him, though."

"He's crazy enough about you that his new club is named after you, yet you're here with Todd." My hypocritical accusation was completely unfounded, and we all knew it. I had behaved the same way countless times. Layla smiled again and touched my knee.

"I can't wait for you to meet him," she said.

Todd wore a look I had trouble placing. I think 'enigmatic' was what he was going for, but I don't really know what that means.

"You've talked me into it," I replied finally. I finished my drink in one long draught, set it down on the coffee table next to an empty coaster, and stood, holding out my hand.

"I have to be running along now, though. Nice meeting you."

"Pleasure's mine," she answered, shaking my hand firmly.

Bitch.

I grabbed my purse, thanked Todd, hugged him just to hug him in front of her, and left. Before the door shut behind me I heard her say, "You're right, she *is* hot."

As far as I'm concerned, we're all animals. Just because we elevate ourselves above our station doesn't mean our actions aren't dictated by the same natural urges as those in the wild. Perhaps I'm stealing a little bit of philosophy from an ex of mine, the one I relieved of his car, but hey, screw him. Our behavior is so close to the beasts I see on the nature shows that it seems obvious that we are in a jungle of our own, scratching and clawing every day for a meal and a lair or simply to stay alive, and we have the right to do so by any goddamn means necessary.

When I go to a nightclub I see hundreds of people looking for a mate, choosing one based on colorful plumage and the skill of their mating dance. If two males become rivals for one female, the solution is brutal and bloody. In more boring human circles a male is chosen by his nest and ability to support and defend his young. That said, I watch animals fight and kill whoever stands in their way, for whatever reason they see fit.

However I can justify it, it comes down to this:

What you won't do, I will.

Some of the girls I work with call themselves exotic dancers so they don't sound so much like whores. I, however, am a stripper.

My ex also pointed out to me that not only are we the only living things that hide their natural forms, we're the only ones who'd pay for the privilege of seeing them revealed. I show my body to men and women who can't attract mates, and sometimes I let them mate with me if I'm drunk or broke enough. I cater to the losers of my species, and I do this at Diabolique, almost every night.

No other girl here would have the balls to dance naked to White Zombie, and if any tried, none could pull it off with the savage sexuality I can. Under the lights, I look nothing like I really do. My teeth and eyes glow spectrally from the ultraviolets, and the red ones are there to hide zits and track marks, bruises and scars. What you see is not even close to what you get.

With everyone else, I watch herds of lonely men staring with half-closed eyes, thinking about their second drink when they're only half-finished with the first, but when I take the stage the place comes to life. All eyes are wide and riveted to me and me alone. Feet tap, heads nod, crotches swell, and the wallets come open.

"Gentlemen, the beat goes on," the DJ said. "And I'm sure you'll all give a warm Diabolique welcome to Scarlet coming to the stage in just a moment." That's my cue.

I was locking up my stuff backstage in the dressing room when Ginger asked me if I had any coke. She was skinny, on the waifish side, with a vacant stare that gave the impression she only saw ten feet ahead. She had a ton of makeup on her arms to cover the angry red trainspots, but it was a pitiful attempt. She'd rob you blind and not even remember the next day.

"Sorry, honey. If I could afford coke would I be here right now?"

"Yeah, getting money to buy more."

"That's a nice outfit," I said, nodding at her lacy white 'I'm really a virgin' g-string and top. She tried to smile.

"Why don't you draw up a will," I told her. "So when you O.D. and drop dead that cute little ensemble goes to me?"

I left her standing there, staring stupidly, and walked out into the lights, the music, and the money.

Dear Diary,

I had to get something to eat today. I felt sour and ragged, and had to take a handful of aspirins just to get out the door. I remember nothing about last night after taking a break, having a few drinks, and recording my day backstage.

I'm not trying to remember either.

I went to the diner around the corner, and slid into a booth in the back where I could hide from the day. A waitress about my age brought coffee and the newspaper, her face made up with a paint roller and her eyes done in thick black Egyptian style. Christ, I thought. You'll *always* be a waitress in a greasy spoon.

I found the comics section, discarding the rest of the paper, which is pretty much useless to me. I did my best to ignore the Family Circus, which isn't easy. I am superstitious to the point of obsession, and firmly believe that even looking at that cartoon will ruin my whole day, but it has a kind of magnetism. Like a repulsive toad. Or a car accident. The rest of my old favorites had stopped being funny years ago, but I read them anyway, feeling guilty for some reason. Fuck! This shit really pisses me off. There's no more Calvin & Hobbes, but there's the fucking Family Circus. And that hillbilly bullshit Snuffy Smith that has never, ever been funny. Ever.

All the good stuff is gone, except Sherman's Lagoon and Non Sequitur, which this paper doesn't even carry. But those stupidass ones, they'll outlast cockroaches. We'll have a nuclear holocaust not even roaches will be alive, aliens will land here eons from now and the entire face of the Earth will be a barren wasteland, but a scrap of newspaper will blow along in the wind like a tumbleweed and they'll pick it up and read the Family Circus.

Where's my fucking coffee?

See, that's the problem with the world today. All the shit in the rest of the newspaper, death, war, famine, disease, poverty, AIDS, well whoop-a-dee-shit. That's nothing compared to a hangover morning— afternoon, whatever—and a stupid bitch waitress thinks she's Nefer-frickin-titi can't bring me another cup of coffee like she says she's going to. Oh, thank you, Pharaoh. It's about goddamned time. It's not like I have all day here, you know.

On the next page of the newspaper between the TV listings and Bridge tips I found my horoscope. CANCER: Stars predict adventure, romance, and an exciting new avenue opening today, but tread lightly. Maintain a clear head and level footing.

12

Tell me something I don't know.

I struggled through scrambled eggs, hash browns, and bacon, irritated with my body that it had to inconvenience me with this stupid ritual. I had several hundred dollars on me, but I didn't tip that dumb-looking waitress a penny. I don't see her earning anything. She told me three times to put my cigarette out.

The bitch.

Todd called me while I was shopping, telling me where to go and when, and the rest of my day was boring until then. By eleven p.m. I was walking toward Layla, scowling at the line to get in. It didn't look like much from the outside, but hey, you can't judge a book. Todd was standing outside talking to a gigantic doorman in a decent suit when he saw me and waved. Everyone looked me up and down as I swaggered right past the long line to the door, the doorman already opening the red velvet rope and stepping inside.

I knew girls were waiting to bitch at their boyfriends for staring at my ass in tight black leather jeans while secretly envying me for fitting into them. My matching leather halter top left nothing to the imagination either. Todd grinned.

"I expected you to be fashionably late," he said.

"I was going to be, but I lost track of time."

He kissed my cheek and escorted me inside.

The place was huge. The walls of the first floor were orange-yellow rag roll with old-fashioned torches flaming angrily. Fire hazard. Oh, no wait, they were fake. Some kind of lights that looked like flames. Statues of faux marble, Grecian warriors and Venus de Milos stood as sentries flanking crimson couches with jaguar skin throw pillows. Red velvet curtains hung here and there for semi-privacy. The dance floor was gigantic and easily accessible from all sides, with the obligatory dais set aside for VIPs. There were bars everywhere. Cages hung suspended from the rafters, presumably for go-go girls. The DJ, a semi-celebrity, was a green-haired black man called Enigro.

Two flights led upstairs, the balcony obscured from below by the frenzy of colored lights. Barmaids in catsuits bore trays of drinks with swift efficiency. My breath hissed out between my teeth, and Todd pointed to a sofa beside a marble statue of Bacchus.

We made our way there and sat, stretching out and crossing our legs on the primitive art coffee table. A barmaid arrived out of thin air with a tray of drinks, a Zombie for me, Tom Collins for Todd, and four shots of liquid heroin.

"Are the bartenders psychic, or what?" I asked. The girl smiled.

"Mr. Haggerty sends these with his compliments," she said.

"Mr. Haggerty?"

"Rabbit," Todd said, tipping her handsomely.

"He asks that you wait to do the shots with him," she said before disappearing into the crowd. I watched her go, picturing myself in her outfit. I'd look good in that, too, I thought. There were fountains in remote corners, light glowing from under their frothing tumult, illuminating the walls with a rippling glimmer that combined with the flickering torchlight, out of reach of the stabbing colored beams. Grecian columns supported the balcony, and here and there gargoyles leered at the crowd.

"Like it?" Todd asked, expelling a cloud of fragrant smoke.

"I've never seen anything like it,"

"That's the idea." We clinked glasses and drank.

"Who is this Rabbit guy? How do you know him?"

"I've been running in bigger circles," he said.

"Is that all you're going to tell me?"

"For now." I spotted Layla, looking fabulous, at the same moment she spotted us. She tugged on somebody's elbow and that somebody turned with his eyebrows raised questioningly. She gestured towards us with a jerk of her chin and he followed her gaze, locking eyes with me.

So this is Rabbit.

He was on the short side, in a black leather jacket with lapels like a suitcoat, black trousers and shoes, and an emerald shirt I found out later would match his eyes. He looked like every pretty boy movie star, with the hair and the angelic good looks and the affected scowl. He smiled a crooked smile and came with her across the dance floor, moving through the play of lights.

Up close his nose had been broken, but not too badly, and a few shiny purple scars marred his bronzed complexion. His teeth were way too white. Layla beamed at us as they drew near.

"Rabbit, this is Simone."

"Sam," I said, taking his hand.

"Simone," she corrected me.

Rabbit had the firm grip of a man who'd reminded himself to make it so. "Pleased to meet you."

"Why Rabbit?" I asked, trying my luck.

"A hundred corny reasons," he said evasively.

"Any good reasons?"

"Just one. May I tropose a poast?" He lifted two of the shot glasses and handed one to Layla. We all raised ours in salute as he toasted.

"To evil," he said.

We drank.

And drank.

Everybody who was anybody was at Layla's grand opening, and it was, without a doubt, the best club ever. Rabbit had designed everything and had a hand in much of the actual construction. The floor plan was, according to him, planned so that no one would have to squeeze uncomfortably past inconsiderate crowds, and no one could catch fire or start a fight. Every eventuality had been planned for. No one had to shout for a drink or have it spilled by a jostling drunkard. Rabbit was very proud of his place, and he let it show.

He was charming. *God*, he was charming.

He was self-assured and articulate, and didn't seem to ever be without a drink. He was having a great time showing off his enterprise and telling jokes and smiling his crooked smile.

I can't imagine what it was about him I didn't like.

He had this expression, sort of a facial catch phrase, of "Who, me?" when he said something off-color or pinched his girlfriend's ass. He did it a lot the more he drank. I still couldn't figure out why I was there, though. Rabbit wasn't flirting with me. He didn't seem interested in me at all aside from conversation.

Layla, on the other hand…

She dragged me out onto the floor after another shot, her eyes locked on mine as we danced. I could not help remembering my ex's animal theory as we moved sensuously to a hauntingly familiar song. Every motion was a display of perfect curves to entice and inflame. She closed her eyes and sang along and suddenly I realized I was dancing to a techno version of Eric Clapton's famous song, no doubt mixed for this occasion. The club glowed around me with the magic of drunkenness, that frivolous, adventurous feeling that anything could happen, and probably would. Bright, loud flashes of color played on her face and body. She was close to me, so close that I could feel her breath, our bodies moving within inches of each other but never touching. She opened her eyes, and I kissed her.

The look she gave me was a slap in the face. She was gone an instant later, leaving me standing there stupidly ashamed, stared at by the nameless dancing people around me. I fled. Not to the ladies' room, not to the exit, but straight to the bar. I quickly lit a cigarette, took a long steadying drag, and ordered another Zombie in a quavering voice.

The hand that held the cigarette was trembling. God, I'm such an idiot.

My drink arrived, and was set down empty a moment later. Only then did I go to hide in the ladies'. It was empty, thankfully. No big black woman on a stool by the sink, no chattering girls fussing over makeup or boys. I went to the mirror and took a long look at myself. I was drunk. Not too drunk but not sober. Deep breath, calm, control. I was fine.

I leaned across the counter and kissed my reflection.

Then I saw them.

Slim brown feet in heels, gold-painted toenails. The fog in my head cleared instantly. Had she heard me? Did she know it was me? It took one look to know she wasn't sitting down behind the locked stall door. What was she doing? I went into the stall next to her, sat down, going through the motions so as not to arouse suspicion. A few courtesy flushes for authenticity.

She took a deep breath, let it out in a sigh, and opened her stall. Through the crack of the door I watched her go to the mirror and compose herself. Breath mint, perfume, then notice the kiss in front of her. From where I sat it rested on the cheek of her reflection. She stared at it a moment, and then at herself. She took another deep breath.

"Here goes," she murmured, and walked out.

My cigarette was an inch of dead ash by now, forgotten in my hand. I dropped it into the toilet, flushed, and put myself back together. Freshened up, and armed with a new cigarette, I steeled myself to go out and make as dignified an exit as possible. Outside the bathroom door was a statue of Cupid, obviously mocking me. I gave him the finger.

I moved uncertainly through jostling crowds of laughing people and splashing fountains towards the front, and was intercepted by Rabbit. He smiled pleasantly and leaned in close to shout something I couldn't hear, taking me by the hand to a table upstairs past a bouncer and a velvet rope.

Right in front of us, Todd was selling pills in the shadows. He'd just set up business, right there in the open, and his customers were unashamedly buying and taking. Without a care in the world. Christ, there was even a *menu*, with "Our Prices Are Insane!" at the top and "Each Sold Separately" across the bottom.

I looked questioningly at Rabbit, who gave me his look.

Who, me?

He leaned across the long table and took a tab from Todd's box, holding it out to me.

"Fancy one?" he asked. I shrugged, smiled, and he suddenly became solemn and rigid, holding the pill up before me.

"Body of Christ," he said, and I bent my head, taking it onto the tip of my tongue. He signaled to some unseen barmaid to bring another round, and asked me for a cigarette.

"Todd's cloves are getting tiresome," he said.

"Don't you have your own cigarettes?" I asked.

"I don't smoke." He grinned impishly. "I just want to look cool."

He didn't take himself seriously. That's what I liked about him. It was all an act, though, a front. That's what I didn't like. He was role playing almost. He was a beta or a gamma male trying to fake being an alpha. And what was the story with his girlfriend?

"Give me a jump off yours," he said, and lit the cigarette I'd given him with the smoldering tip of mine. "Sam, are you having a good time tonight?" I nodded. "You like this place?" he asked for about the tenth time.

"Of course."

"Todd here tells me a lot about you. Says you're a very popular girl and you know a lot of good people." Um, I'm a stripper, and I know a lot of druggies. "Maybe you'd like to tell the right people about this place."

"I don't think you'd need me for publicity," I said.

"That's not what I mean. This part of the club, here, is for the real party. That out there is for the rabble. Get me?"

I nodded slowly.

"This is where friends of mine and Todd's will come, and, hopefully, friends of yours. Friends who know how to keep a secret, and enjoy spending money. This up here is the real party, the secret party, out of sight of the public eye. A *real* VIP section."

He led me away from the table and met a girl with our drinks. He thanked her and toasted with me to evil. We watched each other's eyes over the rims of our glasses.

"You can expect a healthy cut for your trouble," he said. "And you don't have to dance for anybody."

We walked past black leather couches, their occupants somewhere between second and third base. On each coffee table was a vase with one dozen red roses. Lines were cut and waiting on some, joints were burning forgotten on others. It looked like the party I wanted to be invited to.

Rabbit flashed his crooked grin at me.

"What do you say, Sam? We in bed together or what?"

Dear Diary,

I went to visit my evil twin today.

Salomé and I can only be told apart by our hands; mine have shiny pink cigarette burns on them, and hers are smooth and Palmolive soft. We grew up sharing everything, but somewhere in our early adolescence we began competing viciously, like two big monsters duking it out over Tokyo for world domination.

We'd sleep with each other's boyfriends and dump them cruelly. We'd set each other up and see how well we could weasel ourselves out of bad situations. We were the flies in each other's ointment, the thorns in each other's sides. We drove each other to more daring exploits, setting new standards for audacity.

I loved her fiercely.

She was tuning her guitar on the sofa when I walked into her apartment, and her boyfriend Chad was doing her dishes. Without looking up at me she said "Hey Sam," and moved over to make room for me. Chad smiled from the kitchen area and I laughed at him. All Sal had to say was Jump.

"She got you doing her laundry, too?" I asked. He looked embarrassed.

"I just finished," he said. Women like Salomé are a masochist's dream.

I took a cigarette out of the pack on the coffee table and she lit it for me, still looking at her strings, and asked what was going on. I blew a stream of smoke at her and she blew it back.

"Went to this new place downtown last night," I told her.

"Oh?"

"Yeah. Got offered a job."

"It's a whorehouse?"

"No, it's a club."

"A gentleman's club?"

I ignored her. "Ever hear of a guy called Warren Haggerty?"

She frowned and thought for a moment.

"No."

"Little guy? Calls himself Rabbit?"

"I've heard of a guy named Rabbit, but I've never seen him. Sells something or other. Blow or something. Why?"

"He's the guy who wants me to work for him."

"Doing what?"

"Public relations."

"Is that what they're calling it now?"

"Funny. It's a great club, Sal. You know all of those speak-easies from Prohibition that had secret rooms in the back selling liquor? It's like that, only it's a drug den. You go there, you buy whatever you want, you don't have to hide anything, and you don't have to worry about getting busted. My job would be spreading the word to cool party people, like, say, you."

"I'm flattered."

"You should be. Come tonight, here's an upstairs pass. You can even bring your lapdog." Chad pretended not to hear me.

Salomé finally looked up and I was staring into a mirror.

"What does this guy want to pay you?"

"Depends on how well business is. If enough people come in buying dope, the place'll be a gold mine. You should see it, Sal. Waitresses come by with joints for five dollars, blunts for ten. The coke is practically uncut, I've tried it. The rolls are like what you used to get years ago, the good stuff. Champagne, heroin, even ni-trous. They got armed guards everywhere and doctors just in case. You present your pass at the foot of the stairs, pay the cover at the top, and there's one of those mirrors on the way up with people on the other side that are watching. They make sure nobody's a narc gets in. I guess they know who the undercover guys are somehow. The club downstairs is pretty cool, too."

"Sounds like Rabbit's watched too many movies."

"Probably has. He does act like he's in a movie sometimes."

In the kitchen, Chad finished the dishes and turned on the dishwasher.

"Have you had breakfast?" Salomé asked.

"No."

"Good. Chad, honey, pour us a couple drinks, okay?"

Salomé showed me her latest: a self-portrait, and an alien land-scape. She had talent. In her still-lifes, you could really *feel* the inher-ent rage in those pears and grapes. The portrait was not of her as Salomé Brennan, but a confusion of veins, organs, tissue, and nerves. Not a living soul but an organism, an elaboration of carbon. It was beautiful. The landscape was a sunset over the wilderness of an imaginary planet.

"You remember all those painting shows we used to watch?" she asked. "The weird guy with the afro and his happy little trees?"

"Bob Ross," I said, nodding.

"He would do these beautiful landscapes. Trees, bushes, meandering streams, birds that you could almost hear singing, and a little shack right there in the middle of it, ruining the whole thing. There was always Man's intrusion spoiling the serenity of Nature. A derelict house, a sagging wooden fence, a half-sunken rowboat."

"Yeahhh…" I couldn't see where she was going with this.

"Well, here," she said, pointing to her painting. "No one can ever detract from the natural beauty of the wild. No developers will bulldoze these alien trees to make room for a space cruiser launch pad or put up a strip mall for tentacled, bug-eyed slime consumers."

I blinked at her.

"What were you smoking when you came up with this crap?"

"Opium," she said, taking me seriously. "Have you painted recently?"

"Not in a while," I sighed. "Nothing will come to me."

"Have you even tried?"

"Well, no."

"Figures."

"I need a muse. Something to inspire me."

"I'll tell you one thing, sis. Nobody ever painted a masterpiece while strung out on coke."

"Are you finished, Mother?"

She drained her glass, the ice cubes sliding and rattling together against her teeth. Smiling at me, she licked her lips.

"Yep."

Times like these, when my mind is reawakened, I am painfully aware of what I used to be. I certainly wasn't always a drunken whore. If someone had told me back in high school that I would be, I'd have laughed. See, I used to have a brain, and I used to enjoy using it. I remember reading and learning and *thinking* so long ago that it seems like someone else's life.

I used to know who Sappho, Clio, Calliope, Erato, and Euterpe were. And Messalina, the first wife of Claudius Caesar, back when Jesus was a man instead of a vague reassurance. Messalina, who competed with a notorious Sicilian prostitute in the world's first spectated fuckathon, and won. History's fun when it's all evil, conniving bitches and heroes instead of dates, treaties, and discoveries to be memorized in time for quizzes and then forgotten.

Livia, Dido, Thalia, Urania. I used to imagine outdoing them in everything they were remembered for, so that I could be remembered also. But instead, I'm a stripper. I'm a narc. I'm a whore. I'm a drunk, and my brain, long-since atrophied, gathers another layer of cobwebs every day.

In the car, I called Todd's number on my cell phone. It rang, and rang, and rang, and finally his voicemail came on. I hung up.

I went by my lawyer's office, Crabbe Malfoy Goyle & Goniff, to see Burt Goniff, who represented me in numerous cases. I was his best contact for cocaine and high-class prostitutes. It was one of those back-scratching arrangements—you get mine and I'll get yours. The secretary asked if I had an appointment and belatedly realized who I was. I remembered her from a party last year when she'd done a line of coke off of my stomach. Those crazy office parties.

"Miss Brennan, if you'll take a seat, Mr. Goniff will be out in a minute or two." Her hair was up in a bun, her glasses on, her skirt long and prudish, and she wore one of those scarves you usually see on real estate ladies. It was her Legal-type disguise.

Goniff looked just as bland and uninteresting with his gray suit and balding shiny skull when he came out, extending his hand stiffly. He had a mustache and smelled like coffee.

"Miss Brennan, a pleasant surprise. Come in, come in."

He ushered me into his diploma-bedecked office and I told him all about Layla and the second floor. He was sure not to say anything compromising, incriminating, or legally whatever during the conversation, but his eyes gleamed.

"It sounds positively Roman," he said. I nodded, while on the inside I was rolling my eyes. I handed him a stack of passes and didn't have to caution him about discretion.

"Is there prostitution involved as well?" he asked.

"I'll look into that and get back to you."

I went to my doctor next, the one who illegally prescribed all manner of psychotropic drugs and painkillers to me, as long as I didn't show the pictures I had to his wife. They were fine examples of my sister's skill as a photographer (photographess, whatever) and my skill as a contortionist.

Enough said.

He told me he and his wife would love to come to Layla sometime.

I told the mayor's two sons while I was in bed with them, and they promised to spread the word. In fact, the only people I didn't tell were the strippers I knew were addicts, and Cedric. One of the cardinal rules is that you don't trust a junkie with beans, because they spill them at the drop of a hat. I filed Cedric away for a rainy day. I wouldn't need him for a while, but if things ever went sour again the way they always do, I'd have that card to play.

My sister would tell everybody else for me, so I could take the rest of the day off. I passed the college campus and saw a blood drive sign on the sidewalk. My stomach was rumbling, so I turned in and found the two big vans with the tables outside. I filled out the forms, signed my name, and stuffed myself with pizza and cookies. When a nurse interrupted my feast to take my donation she asked the preliminary questions.

"Have you gotten any tattoos or piercings in the past twelve months?" she asked eventually. I stuck out my tongue, displaying the stud I've had for the past three years.

"Yeah, just this."

"I'm sorry, you can't donate any blood today," she said.

"Darn."

I went to the tanning bed, aerobics class, and the beauty parlor to get ready for tonight. I had both Tweeties left and a few bucks to spare, and when I called Todd again he told me to be at the club with bells on, whatever the hell that meant. I wore my Catholic schoolgirl slut outfit.

Rabbit sat on a stool at the closest bar to the door and I sauntered up to him.

"Simone!" he laughed when he saw me, and swiveled around on his stool, patting his thigh like he wanted me to sit down on it. "Come tell Daddy what you want for Christmas."

I snorted a giggle, and he asked me if I'd made up my mind about his proposition. I ate both rolls with the drink he slid toward me.

"You'll see when the people come in," I said.

He laughed, then looked me up and down.

"Love the outfit."

"Yeah, it's a big hit with the marks at the titty bars."

He made a face, then caught himself. I asked what he had

against strip clubs and he pretended he didn't mind them at all, but I knew he was lying. He'd put his foot in his mouth without even opening it first.

"Look, Warren, I see plenty wrong with what I do, but it's there and nothing will change that, so I'm cashing in on it. I'm not going to be on the losing side."

"You can't be on the losing side, Sam. You're a woman."

"What?"

"Some other time." He excused himself and went off somewhere.

I got a drink and chatted with Enigro until people started coming in. By midnight, the place was packed to crushing, and they couldn't take the money fast enough. Goniff had told some of his clients and they'd come with the bankrolls from robberies and fenced goods, dying to spend.

Salomé had told all of her friends and Chad had told all of his. She was the only one not in attendance. We had guys with glowsticks doing their light show for people "blowing up" in every corner, and I sat for one of them to get lime green trails flashing around my face in time with the music, like time-lapses of cities at night with the long red streaks made by the tail lights of cars. People kept coming in. Todd was sold out of rolls in one hour. Layla was avoiding me.

I caught Rabbit at a quarter past two.

"Dear, my attorney wants to know if horizontal refreshment is available. I told him I'd ask."

"Tell him never to come back here again," he snapped.

He stopped me when I turned to go, reconsidering.

"Tell him, not at the present time."

I rolled my ass off, charged one hit Simone Tax of every joint I came to, and drank champagne all night long. I danced in one of the cages, my school-girl Oxford shirt coming off to howls of lust and approval. I almost forgot to put it back on when I climbed out. Todd appeared out of nowhere and reminded me.

I don't know what I'd do without him.

He took me to a couch upstairs, carrying me like a baby in his arms, and is currently getting me another drink as I write this, recording the beautiful moment for posterity. I'm sinking into the couch, melting. I can feel the lights knifing through me, and the music strokes my skin with feathery fingers. I can't seem to decide who I'm in love with tonight.

Everybody. I felt wave after blissful invisible wave crash into me.

Oh, my God. Here comes Layla.

Dear Diary,

Her eyes were dancing the way mine must have been. I'd put my diary away two seconds before she climbed on the sofa, pushing me gently onto my back and lying on top of me, her perfect red lips meeting mine. Fireworks exploded behind my tightly-shut eyes as her winterfresh tongue slid into my mouth, finding and writhing with mine. Her hand parted the unbuttoned opening of my shirt, raising goosebumps all over me as she lightly stroked my breast.

The drug and my passion were overwhelming me, and all I could do was lie there and kiss her back. Her hand slid down and found its way under my short plaid skirt, questing fingers scrambling to get under the line of my g-string and I gasped, my back arching, my toes curling, my eyes rolling back.

I lay there, chest heaving, for a long time it seemed before I realized she'd stopped. I opened my eyes.

A waitress was handing her a joint and lighting it for her. She took a few hits, bringing it to life, and passed it to me. I caught up with my breathing and took the joint, hitting it twice, and sat up, passing it back and trying to kiss her.

She gently put her hand on me, stopping me, and we smoked in silence, the music still touching me. Shadowy figures moved about us in jumping slow-motion, illuminated by flashing colored strobe light. I looked down the crowd toward the next couch over, at the two couples writhing like a many-armed monster, their moans and gasps of pleasure going unheard but not unseen.

I jumped as a sudden excruciatingly wonderful feeling engulfed me from behind, and went limp with ecstasy. I weakly turned my head and saw Layla stroking my bare back down my spine with an ice cube. I don't know when my shirt had come off or where the ice bucket had come from, but I didn't care after the bottle of champagne came open, the fragrant sparkling foam fountaining out and splashing onto me, running down my shoulder over my breasts and stomach. The ice cube traced a coldly burning circle around my nipple, hardening it, and made its way slowly and meanderingly down over my washboard abs. I lifted the waist of my skirt away from my stomach and Layla's hand slid in. I writhed in tense pleasure as the rapidly melting cube came closer and achingly closer, and screamed as her cold fingers slipped inside me. I savagely tore my skirt and g-string away and sank back against her, melting into her oblivious to the howls of shadowy spectators. My back arched as

26

her fingers searched for and found me, stroking clumsily with inexperience but still racking me with frozen waves of ecstasy.

For some reason an image popped into my head, Joe Pantoliano standing on a front lawn with a teenaged Tom Cruise, Guido the killer pimp in *Risky Business* saying "Time of your life, eh kid?" I tried to laugh but moaned instead, shivering all over.

Layla's hands turned me, Layla's head came down and forward, Layla's lips and tongue kept the champagne from going to waste. For a moment, I saw Todd watching me, and then he was gone.

I awoke groggily, blinking against the glare of the house lights, with a blanket over me. Somehow I knew that it was the afternoon of a bright and sticky day. A pint glass of water sat on the coffee table, looking pure and enticing. I drank it down in one greedy go, looking around for more. My head throbbed.

I heard voices. I crawled off of the couch, realizing I was naked except for my long white stockings, and went slowly to the railing of the balcony, peering through the bars down on Rabbit, Todd, and Layla.

"I can't believe it," Rabbit was saying. "We made a fortune. We'll break even in six months at this rate, and from there we'll all be millionaires this time next year."

"You're a genius, baby," Layla said, kissing him.

"Everybody have a good time last night?" he asked.

"You even have to ask?" Todd said. "How's Sleeping Beauty?"

"Still watching her eyelids."

"She did a good job, wouldn't you say?"

"Yes, I would say. Here, this is for her trouble." Rabbit handed something I couldn't see to Todd, and their heads all turned to the front of the club. "Can I help you?"

"Yeah," said one of the two huge men who approached. "We understand you have quite a little enterprise here."

"I'm proud of it."

"Our associate would like to be proud, too."

"And he is…"

"Zack Scalisi, you may have heard of him."

The two goons were now point blank with my friends. Rabbit looked thoughtfully upwards, as if trying to place the name. He was being unjustifiably cocky with these two men who dwarfed him easily. Finally, he shook his head.

"Doesn't ring a bell."

"Something's gonna start ringing—" the other goon threatened.

"Listen, listen," the first interrupted. "We're reasonable, hear us out."

"Sure, want a drink?"

"No. We don't need a drink."

"Care to sit down?"

"We're fine right here." It was a command. "Mr. Scalisi wants a cut of your profits, and also to employ a minimum of ten girls as escorts, whose earnings will be—"

"You gonna break my legs?"

"What?"

"Are you going to break my legs or burn the club down or what, when I refuse?"

The other goon stepped forward angrily, but the first one held him back, playing Good Cop or Good Mob Guy or whatever.

"Yunno, we're tryin' to be reasonable here, sport. Yeah, your little place might just burn down without our protection, or worse."

"Gee whiz, that breaks my heart," Rabbit said sadly, then blinked as if he came to his senses. "Waitaminute, no, it doesn't."

I think the guy playing Bad Cop was genuinely mad now. Good Cop seemed to have a hell of a time trying to hold him back, seeing the whole game start to roll downhill.

While they were putting on the charade I guess they expected a captive audience, people who'd just stand there and be intimidated, but instead...I must have blinked, because I'm not sure what happened next. The second guy reeled back, clutching his eyes and screaming, and Rabbit leaped on the first. Todd lunged forward, knocking away the gun the screaming man had pulled, and suddenly both goons were lying still on the ground.

Rabbit didn't even hesitate.

"Layla, get Jimmy and Blue Tick in here on the quick and have them bring the truck around. Todd, help me with Vinnie and Vito here." Layla dashed to the rear of the club out of sight, and the two men bent over the bodies I could only assume were dead. I crawled back to the sofa, pulled the blanket over my head and went back to sleep.

Dear Diary,

I am so in love. It's been a few days since I last wrote, because I simply haven't found the time. Layla and I have been inseparable. We spend the days, while Rabbit is out, making love and lying in bed holding each other. She says I'm the first girl she's been with, but she's always been curious. I can't believe it. When she touches me and kisses me she feels so natural, so comfortable.

She told me today that I'm what was missing from her life.

I've shown her so many new things, exploring every inch of her beautiful brown body, kissing her all over the way I've ached to since the moment I first laid eyes on her. She's fascinated with my body and doing things to it that she'd only done to herself, sharing that deeply personal part of herself with me.

Yesterday as we lay naked in the sunbeams on her bed she painted my toenails silver for me, and I painted hers gold. The taste of her when we make love is sweeter than honey, and I can't get enough. We went shopping for toys that afternoon, so I could show her new things I'm not going to write down.

We went surfing and I couldn't concentrate, wanting to look good in front of her but unable to keep my eyes off of her. I am convinced that the only thing more beautiful than her naked body is her face when she laughs in the sunshine. We've dined at the most romantic restaurants, hiding together from the world in booths, sitting next to each other, always touching, feeding each other morsels with our fingers. We kiss like newlyweds, deeply and constantly.

At her apartment I blew the dust off of my paint set and set up an easel in the bedroom. Layla stretched out lazily on the rumpled sateen sheets, her long blonde hair cascading over her naked brown body, and I painted her in all her splendor. I hadn't lost my touch yet, but I could never do her justice.

The man at the shop looked at us when we took it to be framed, and he frowned but said nothing.

And the nights we spend at the club, with Todd and Rabbit, dancing until dawn. Rabbit joked last night that I'm taking her away from him, but it's no joke. She's mine now, all mine. The fact that I have to share her with anyone—I won't think about it.

We got matching tattoos today, a Celtic design with the words *fighte fuaighte*, "woven into and through each other". I've never been as in love as I am now.

She's awakened the capacity to care for someone that I'd forgotten I even had. When Salomé and I stopped being one I've felt like half a person. Layla fills that hole in me.

We've been apart for half a day now, the longest we've been apart since I can remember. It sucks, but we must keep up a pretense of mere friendship in front of Rabbit. My life before Layla is a blur. I feel giddy and smile for no reason. I ache to hold and kiss her again.

Dear Diary,

We're all getting rich. The days are golden and wonderful, the nights are bright with flashing lights and magic. Champagne, Ecstasy, and Layla; how lucky could I be? I hope this never ends. Ever.

Dear Diary,

A fire started at the club last night. Rabbit said it was probably a careless cigarette fallen behind the couch cushions, but one look at his face and I knew it wasn't so. He's scared and angry. More angry than scared, but scared nonetheless. I remembered the two guys who came to visit us that day, unsure of whether they were a half-forgotten dream or a disturbing reality.

Todd says we're making money hand over fist and some people might be taking notice. Security is tight as a drum. No one gets upstairs without being screened and Layla supervises all the money that comes out of that end. Rabbit handles everything else. People in the downstairs sometimes get curious when they are turned away at the stairs, but there is enough down there to keep them occupied. Almost overnight, Layla has become the most popular club in the area. Celebrity DJs make guest appearances once a week.

I haven't even considered dancing at Diabolique in forever.

I am forced to share Layla with Rabbit sometimes; he loves her fiercely and craves her attention, but I am content with the idyllic times we spend together.

I got to see a different side of him the other day. When was it? I dunno. The other day. I haven't kept up with my diary writing lately, but it was between Layla and me becoming serious and Now.

What happened, Rabbit found out one of the bartenders was ripping off customers. Brian—that's his name—would make all the drinks without alcohol. Now, ripping off customers in bars is nothing new; when they fill up your glass with ice they only have to pour in a little bit to make the glass look full, which is why I demand only three ice cubes per drink. But this guy… Christ, the balls on him! I mean, the *nerve* of this guy!

Say you order a screwdriver. Brian has this little jigger of vodka set aside out of sight, and when you order your screwdriver, he pours you a glass of orange juice, dips his finger in the vodka, and wipes the rim of the glass with it. When you take a drink, your lips touch the vodka first, you taste the vodka first, and you think you taste vodka in the orange juice when it comes right behind it. You just bought an eight dollar glass of orange juice—from *concentrate*, no less.

Of course, no one ever saw him doing this at the bar. That's why bars are designed the way they are. All of the customers' drinks are mixed below their line of sight so that they can be gypped every whicha way; but, as it turns out, Rabbit didn't know about that. And, looking over the balcony rail at just the right time, Rabbit saw.

Rabbit got mad.

And I found out what those go-go girl cages were really for.

Imagine the pillory, or the stocks, or the cage in a medieval town square, where petty criminals are locked up on public display, their charges read to the people, and the public is then allowed to do pretty much whatever they want to those guys. In Rabbit's club, if you make an ass out of yourself, pick a fight, or commit any number of infractions, you have to sit locked in a cage until closing time.

And this is the real treat: you get to see all the people looking for mates in their pretty plumage, doing their mating dances, show exactly how close to animals they are. Civilization turns to savagery at any opportunity.

Rabbit and the bartender had a little talk after the night was over, and Brian came to realize he'd be better off working someplace else, and it'd be best if he left with no hard feelings. And that was it. Brian was a first floor worker, who knew basically nothing about what goes on upstairs so we don't have to worry about him informing to the police for revenge. The second storey workers, however, the ones who do know something worth telling, wouldn't be lucky enough to just get fired. Rabbit said that, and I had a feeling he wasn't kidding.

Dear Diary,

Three men in suits came to visit us at the club this evening, while we were having a quiet drink at one of the bars downstairs before the night got started. I recognized the one who took the helm as spokesman. I slept with him once for a thousand dollars.

His name was Ray Valanga, and, man, he was an asshole. A big whale-boned beast of a man, he would've gone far if the Mafia was what it used to be. His two bodyguards I remembered from that night long ago.

I had been genuinely afraid for the first time in my life. I went to Valanga's hotel room with this other stripper who called herself Illiana, and it took both of us and everything we had to satisfy him. At one point I had to bite down on my fist to keep from screaming, that's how big he was and how fierce. Illiana took him in the back-door and bled like a stuck pig. Howling in agony, she managed to get away from him, but he was close to orgasm and frustrated.

When she resisted him he slapped her and she was stupid enough to slap him back. I cowered against the headboard, frozen, watching him beat her savagely to death. The corner he backed her into was awash with blood, and when he came back to bed he was spattered with it.

He didn't have to say a word.

I turned around and presented my ass to him. Through tear-soaked eyes I stared at Illiana on the floor, her face a scarlet ruin from which two dead eyes stared whitely. In the end, Valanga dismounted, satisfied, and sent me away. I staggered from the hotel one thousand dollars richer, but took eight stitches.

Now this man was standing before us with his two silent henchmen, and I felt a pain in my guts as if he were inside me again.

"Two men came to see you the other day," Valanga said.

"The fire marshal and...?" Rabbit said cockily.

Valanga rolled his eyes and reached behind him, taking the .9mm his white-haired bodyguard held out.

"Where are they?"

"They came, said their peace, and they left."

"Oh, they left, huh? Hmmm. How, exactly?"

"The same way they came in, dragging their knuckles."

Valanga's face darkened, and the gun came up.

"I'm gonna ask you one more fucking time."

The hard metallic slide of a 12-gauge shotgun pump racked

back and forward spun him around, and we were all staring at Jimmy and Tick, the cavalry.

"I wouldn't, if I were you," Jimmy said. He, like the man at his side, was a huge muscle with a head on top, and that's all. They were bodybuilder thugs, juiced up all the time on God-knows-what.

When Rabbit stood between them he looked like the loud-mouthed kid with the two giant brothers.

Valanga looked back at us. "You're an idiot. You're a dead man."

"Who's going to come looking for you?" Rabbit asked. "I'll save him the trip."

"You'll be skinned alive," Ray snarled.

Rabbit laughed. "Not in *your* lifetime."

We took them into a secret room I didn't know about, which was obviously a lab. This was where Ecstasy is made, in rooms like this. Todd wasn't kidding. He *had* been moving in bigger circles.

Jimmy and Tick handcuffed Ray and the white-haired guy to huge pipes coming out of the wall, and strapped the other one to a lab counter, on his back. Rabbit spoke calmly.

"Allow me to introduce you gentlemen to *my* associate, Blue Tick. Tick has been my good friend for a long time, and I owe him a favor. I'm going to return that favor, now. Tick, knock yourself out."

Blue Tick took an ax from behind a cabinet.

"You ladies might want to step outside," he said.

"I'd like to stay if that's all right," Layla said, surprising me.

"Suit yourself, Miss." Such manners. Rabbit turned to Valanga.

"The money I make belongs to me," he said. "The way I make it and spend it is up to me and me alone. When people like you try to take what's mine I think about bullies everywhere and I...you know what? Gimme that ax, Tick."

He took the ax and swung a flashing overhand chop into the man's chest, cracking his ribcage open, spattering blood in a red mist, ripping a horrible scream up out of his victim. Again, and again, and again he struck, hacking into the chest and stomach until the hoarse screams died away in a sickening gurgle.

Todd watched with an ashen-faced horror, his eyes wide and scared, and I could only assume I looked the same. It was Layla who surprised me. She stared unflinching at the gore on the counter, like one accustomed to such things. Ropes of intestine and chunks of splintered bone and viscera oozed from the ghastly wounds as Jimmy and Tick removed the corpse.

"What's going to happen to me?" Rabbit asked, his face measled with spots of blood. "I'm gonna be skinned alive? What do you think's gonna happen to you?"

Tick wound up and punched Valanga in the jaw, his blow backed by the full weight of his massive shoulders, knocking him out cold. Thus they were able to uncuff him and put him on the counter, tied down spread-eagled, without any trouble. Blue Tick held up his hands surgeon-style, and in a solemn voice said "Scalpel?" Rabbit stifled a laugh and handed him the ax. Valanga was still out cold.

They brought him around by chopping off his foot.

His left hand followed, followed by his other foot, followed by his other hand. Blue Tick paused to wipe blood out of his eyes.

"I've always wanted to do this," he said, and continued.

His legs came off at the knees, followed by his arms at the elbows, followed by the torso all around, and Ray Valanga never once cried out. His eyes were wide and tears rolled down his quivering cheeks, and I could hear his teeth crunching and snapping off as he ground them in agony, but he never made a sound.

A stench filled the room, overpowering the acrid reek of the blood that ran in rivers down the counter. We held our noses, but kept watching.

Finally, Blue Tick heaved the ax high over his head and brought it down on Valanga's throat, his head jumping free on an arching fountain of blood.

Jimmy stooped and picked it up by the hair. Incredibly, the eyes were still darting wildly about the room, making contact with each of ours one by one. Rabbit stepped forward and stared deep into those wide eyes, watching for the moment when the light of life would go out, making himself the last thing Valanga ever saw.

Rabbit let the other guy go, giving him the severed head to take back to his boss. Before he went, Jimmy thought to take his driver's license, so we'd know who he was and where he lived "in case we decided to kill his children and eat them." Ernesto Carcotti left with the head bundled up in his jacket, with immediate plans to change his residence.

"Now what?" Jimmy asked. "We can't just wait for a third

friendly visit, can we? They're going to come in here and blow us all up."

Rabbit was silent for a long time. Todd went to the bar and poured himself a shot with shaky hands. He downed it and had another. I thought he was made of harder stuff than that. Oh well.

"I love this place," Rabbit said quietly. "I've always wanted a place like this. I went through hell to get where I am and now I'm going to lose it all."

Layla went to him, but he waved her off.

"They can't blow it up," he said, brightening. "If we burn it down first."

We all blinked at him.

"What?" Layla asked.

"We'll burn it down ourselves so no one gets hurt, collect the insurance, and start a *real* underground club. One that's never in the same place twice. An elusive, and *exclusive*, super-secret underground rave."

"That's the stupidest thing I've ever heard."

"Is that why they call you Rabbit?" Todd asked. "Because you're hare-brained?"

Rabbit ignored him, continuing excitedly. "It will be totally anonymous-looking from the outside. Like an abandoned warehouse or something. With blacked-out windows. We'll call it the Darkside." His tone had the confident finality that only he could muster. To this little man with the movie star hair and calculatedly disarming smile, anything was possible.

"No," Layla said. "We won't."

"We'll need to hire some chick to talk on a PA system, do the countdown, warn everybody in a calm voice if the self-destruct mechanism gets activated. You know, like the bad guys always have at their secret headquarters."

"Dude. We are not going to have a self-destruct mechanism."

"Why not? It could be fun!"

"Dude."

"Okay, no we're not going to *really* have one, but we should have a chick updating us over a PA, saying shit like *The missiles will be launched in t-minus one minute and counting!* This is during our off-hours, you know, when we're setting up. Because why *not?* I mean, what's the point of going to all this trouble to be a criminal master-mind and start the Darkside in the first place if—"

"No," Layla said firmly. "We won't."

Rabbit's manic notion quickly evaporated, as such things inevitably must, and he settled into a despondent gloom. I called my evil twin on my cell phone, sitting on "Our Couch" with a martini.

"I told you never to call here again!" Salomé shouted into the phone, and the line went dead. I dialed again.

"What! What do you want? I don't have time for this shit!"

"Hey, sis."

"Oh, uh, hey."

"Man trouble?"

"No, why do you ask?"

"Just a hunch. What'd he do, forget to mow the lawn?"

"A minor rebellion. I think I've nipped it in the bud, though."

"Congratulations. Keep up the good work."

"Yeah, medals and promotions all around. So what's up?"

"Oh, nothing much. The usual. Just torturing and murdering mob guys. All in a day's work."

"Elaborate, please?"

"I'll get into it later. Do you remember a guy named Scalisi?"

"What am I? A fucking Who's Who?"

"It's important, Sal. Zack Scalisi."

"I slept with him last Saturday."

"What!"

"You mean Zack Scalisi the wannabe gangster, right? Killed his dad so he could take over the business and is a hopeless failure?"

"Uh, could be. You slept with him?"

"Yeah, Shadow and I, you know, the colored girl? We went to a party and entertained him for the night. Good party."

"You have fun?"

"It was a joke. He was so coked up he could barely fuck. I still got paid though. And after he passed out finally I had this other guy Ray come in and ride us both on the bed right there where Scalisi was sleeping. Now *that* was worth my time."

"Ray Valanga?"

"Yeah, you know him?"

"Uh, no."

"Whatever. So I hear this little club of yours is blowing up."

"Yeah, we're doing okay."

"What's wrong, Sam?" her tone dropped, indicating the official end of small talk and bullshit. I felt myself sink heavily.

I told her everything I could get away with saying on the phone. And she listened attentively, prompting me when I got off track, and finishing my sentences when I could not.

She was supportive—not one smartass comment from the peanut gallery—and she was just about to give me her opinions and advice when Todd appeared in the corner of my eye with a fresh martini. I took it without looking at him, told my sister I had to run, and hung up, tossing the phone carelessly onto the couch beside me.

"Strange days," Todd said. I ignored him.

"You okay?" he asked. I shrugged. I needed to talk to someone, but not him. He's been getting jealous of me taking Layla away, and it showed. Or was it over Layla taking me? Hard to tell. But he *had* been acting different lately. I wasn't as upset about Valanga's execution as I thought I'd be, and Todd was genuinely shaken up—the first time I've ever seen him so. To be honest, I was more worried about Layla. She seemed, as much as I hate to say it, *interested*.

She even gave Jimmy and Tick detailed instructions on where to dispose of the bodies. She insisted they be put in such and such a dumpster at such and such a time. I realized Todd was saying something to me as I drained my first martini and plucked the olive out of the second one, popping it into my mouth. Bitter. I chewed thoughtfully and stared off into space until I dimly realized Enigro was spinning records and people were beginning to drift in. I went downstairs with my martini and sat at a bar, chain smoking.

I didn't get any time with Layla at all that night. She was all over the place, doing this and that with a quiet efficiency, always shouting into someone's ear over the music and being shouted at back. I didn't drink that much, just sitting on a barstool with my cigarette, ignoring the men and women who came up to me with their bright, colorful plumage and pick-up lines.

"Hey, baby. You got any German in you?"

"No."

"Want some?"

I wonder if hot chicks in bars on other planets have to listen to this shit.

"Honey, I got the F, the C, and the K. All I need is U."

"You believe in love at first sight? Or do I have to walk by again?"

Does crap like this work on other girls? Or just in soft core porn flicks?

I never took my eyes off Layla, flitting around like a humming-bird. It was strange, watching her from afar. Her long golden hair was braided into two cute girlie pigtails and she had tied the tails and opened the buttons of the Hawaiian shirt I gave her, showing the cleavage of her perfect brown breasts. I'd worn that shirt home one night from a party, having mysteriously lost my own.

I adored her. I worshipped her. I lusted after her to the point of obsession. I stared at her and smiled faintly.

I love you, Layla.

I want to marry you, Layla.

"I'll show you mine if you show me yours."

I turned to the dipshit grinning next to me. He had one of those stupid and ratty-looking goatees minus the mustache, and his hair was gelled up like a platinum-blond porcupine. I looked him up and down, openly unimpressed, and flicked an ash on his fish-scale shirt.

"If I showed you mine you wouldn't know what to do with it."

I turned back to Layla in the distance, the lights playing on her body, her ass perfect in those tight, tight jeans.

"What're you, a dyke or something?"

I thought for a moment, staring at my girlfriend's ass, a faint smile touching my lips, and nodded slowly.

"Yeah. I guess I am."

I finally caught up with her and touched her lightly, stroking her with my fingertips and asked if we could get away for a little while tonight. She shook her head.

"Sorry, Simone. I have to be up early tomorrow." She seemed distracted. "My gynecologist says I'm due for a look under the hood."

I nodded. Personally, I can't stand OB/GYNs. Wait around for an hour in the lobby reading last year's copies of Vaginal Digest and GyneWorld, before climbing into those cold and humiliating things, putting my feet in the stirrups and letting a clammy-handed pervert have his way with me. No thanks.

"And after that I have a bunch of errands to run," she said.

"Uh-huh. Okay. Well...I'll see you tomorrow night, I guess."

"You all right?"

"Oh, yeah, of course. Uh, bye."

"Bye."

I walked out, feeling scared and not knowing why.

It's funny, when you're in love and your lover's not around, that you find yourself with nowhere to go and nothing to do. Your favorite bar is empty, your favorite show is boring, the whole world becomes bland and tasteless until you're together again. You cannot even get drunk.

I went to the cemetery.

There's nothing quite like a cemetery at night. The crickets chirp and night birds chatter in the swaying boughs of gnarled trees, the leaves rustle in soughing breezes, and with the right kind of ears, you can almost hear the talons of a zombie scratching and clawing its way through the lid of its coffin and through six feet of dirt and worms to get you. The jumping shadows of swaying trees in the moonlight are those of shambling corpses with their rotting flesh hanging from their bones by bits of tendon, concealed by the tatters of funeral tuxedos and soiled gowns.

I sat on a large gothic stone, lit a cigarette and stared out over a sea of skeletal crosses. No matter how many times I come here, I never ever *ever* get to see zombies. No ghosts, either. No incubi, no succubi, vampires, werewolves, or ghouls. Not even so much as a witch. What a boring place the world is.

What I can never understand is why there aren't cemeteries all over the place. Everybody dies, so why are there only a few hundred graves here? Where are the rest of us?

My sister says we're made into baloney.

I dabbed the back of my hand with the orange glowing ember of my cigarette, and watched the skin pucker like a coffee ring on a newspaper.

Someday an undertaker will count the burns on me—shiny pink and purple circles of stretched and shiny scar tissue, and wonder what I was thinking. He might sleep with my cold and rubbery lifeless body, and I wonder if I'd mind. I wonder if I'll ever get to be a zombie or a vampire after I'm dead.

I hope so.

I took a final drag, mashed the cigarette out on my wrist and flicked the butt away into the darkness.

Dear Diary,

This morning I awoke early and stared at the two lines waiting beside the alarm clock. I'm not sure what I was feeling—a strange emotion that I couldn't place. I didn't want any coke.

I got out of bed, cleaned myself up, ordered a pizza, and set up my easel. Next to my paints, brushes, and ashtray, I set the strip of lovebird photo booth pictures Layla and I had taken at the mall the other day. My base colors were down and the general idea had taken shape by the time breakfast arrived. My pizza had every meat topping there is.

Fuck vegetables.

The day I start eating "healthy" foods is the day they strap me into a hospital bed and feed me through a tube, and I've got at *least* ten more years before that happens. I remember the conversation with Layla when she asked what I had against vegetables, and I made her doubt my sanity.

"I'm a vegetable rights activist," I told her.

"You're a what?" she asked, blinking her lovely eyes.

"Scientists have measured a pulse that all plants have, a regularity (Todd told me about this), and showed how every time you pick a flower or pull a leaf the pulse jumps as if the plant were screaming. Think about it: the flower of a plant contains the stamen and sex pistils— the reproductive organs. How would you feel if somebody came along and ripped your pussy out and gave it to his sweetheart for Valentine's Day?" I took another bite of my veal scallopine. "Also, pancake syrup. What is that but the blood of a tree? Pretty barbaric wouldn't you say?"

"You know all this, yet you were a stripper?"

"Botany doesn't really float my boat," I said, chewing.

"So, if you feel so bad about plants being alive and having a, uh, consciousness, I guess, why do you eat meat then?"

"Because an animal can either defend itself or run away. It has a chance. But a broccoli, on the other hand, is just sitting there, minding its own business, not bothering anybody."

"You're eating veal, baby. That's a poor baby cow."

"Yeah, well. Fuck it. It was dead before I got here. Besides, if God didn't want us to eat animals, He wouldn't have made them out of meat. There was this bitch going off on me once because I was wearing my leather pants and a leather jacket, saying that was two poor cows I was strutting around in. But I had her, the dumbass, because the top she was wearing was made of silk. So I point that out. I ask her what she's wearing and she goes *silk,* like she was something special. Real haughty. So I remind her of how much stuff out of the asses of bugs is used to make just a bolt of silk. Hundreds of millions of poor exploited bugs, while I'm wearing two dead cows. And it was purple, too. Where did she think purple dye comes from? Murex mollusks. Been doing it since the Phoenicians. And it takes thousands of murex to make just an ounce of purple dye.

"And speaking of millions of dead bugs, carmine comes from one place on this planet, and one place only. A pregnant cochineal. When a female cochineal bug gets knocked up, and you squash it, you get one drop of carmine. So if a couple thousand of them get knocked up, and you grind the whole lot of 'em into a pulp, you get a tube of lipstick." I raised an eyebrow at Layla for emphasis. "I've got dead bugs on my face to make me look pretty."

"You're sick, Simone. You're brain damaged and living in a world of make-believe." She spoke in her overly serious mock don't-be-a-fool tone.

"Wanna bite?" I asked, extending a forkful of succulent veal and pasta. She smiled and leaned forward, lips parting.

Now I dabbed burnt sienna over those lips, munching on a slice of Meat Lover's. My painting was a forest scene, shafts of late afternoon sunlight spearing through the foliage in the background, and in the foreground, two trees growing together. Juxtaposed with the twisting trunks were the bodies of women—Layla and I in each other's arms. Vines and morning glory creepers crawled over the brown bark of our skin, and birds sang in our leafy hair.

While I hate to blow my own trumpet, it was impossible when I was finished to tell where the exposed knuckle-like roots ended and the shapely legs began. Purple blossoms starred the supple curves, the soft swell of full breasts, and their vines became lost in the tangle of branches and hanging aerial roots. Long dribbles of golden sap coursed down suggestively, like wax trails on a candle, above orange disks of bracket fungus.

The trees I'd seen in the graveyard last night. In the light of the moon as it slowly set, I thought they looked like two women locked together in a lover's embrace.

I signed it "Scarlet," my stage name, and stood back to stare at it. I had found my muse at last.

For lack of anything better to do, I made crack in my kitchen. I cooked the coke and baking soda with Cherry 7up so they'd be pink, and put them with the pipe in my drawer that had almost a year of cobwebs and dust on it.

The drawer also contained my smack rig and all kinds of drug paraphernalia odds and ends. My brass whippet cracker that has been cross-threaded for years but I've never thrown away, next to three worn-out psychedelic punchbowl balloons, and the aluminum cracker I'd bought and never used. The little pipe I got at Lollapalooza when I was a kid with the striped stem in red, yellow, and black, like a coral snake.

Or was it a king snake? How's the rhyme go? Red and yellow, kill a fellow; red and black, something something.

My roach clip. My combination roach clip and piercing tool. Boy, that invention was somebody's stroke of genius. My dead Zippo collection. An ancient Vick's Inhaler, blackened by a lighter to sharpen the sniff. Nothing like burnt plastic to clear out the sinuses.

A handful of capsules filled with THC. Boil your weed until the jelly rises to the top, scrape it out and into emptied gelcaps. Swallow them and half an hour later you're stoned immaculate—splendid for breaking the ice at parties. No incriminating stench, no sore throat, no bad breath...well, your eyes still go bloodshot, but one outta four ain't bad. I'd sold them for five dollars apiece.

All of these were completely useless to me now. I shut the drawer.

I wandered listlessly around my apartment in search of something else to do. My photo album sat on an end table, filled with pictures of moments, people, and whole eras of my life that I only half-remembered. I had no pictures of Layla to put in there, just the lovebird photos, and that was too poor a monument to do her justice.

I tallied and appraised everything in my lair, possessions accumulated through deceit and treachery, and realized I didn't really care about anything I owned. I hadn't worked for so much as a toothpick. Half of everything I owned I earned while naked, and the rest of it I stole.

That used to make me proud.

I resolved to paint with a vengeance from that moment on, to sell art professionally, at least one painting a day, and make something of myself. After all, you can't keep titty dancing once they start to sag, and you can't steal a house. I resolved to turn my life around, about-face, new leaf. Trippy art, and surrealism that maybe could be hung on the walls at Layla and bought by party people, right there on the spot. I could've slapped my forehead. Drunk, stoned, and rolling swine with money should have an art gallery of their very own! Why not?

I'm a genius.

I set up another canvas and threw myself into a club scene with a cute candy-raver blowing up on the dance floor. A multi-colored radiance exploded from her, lifting her feet up off of the floor, arching her backward, the glow of ecstasy gleaming out of her eyes, ears, and gasping mouth.

A few more like this and I think I'll really have a chance.

I went to the mall and bought myself a dress. I call this "retail therapy."

It was black and white, but it looked gray from far away because of the close-knit Fendi Fs all over it, coming together like yin yangs. It had a slit up one side all the way to the hip, and exposed cleavage almost to the belly button, tied at the waist with a sash. The deep v-neck had revers, or whatever they're called, with the print reversed, a black field with white Fs forming taikihs. And I bought a brand new pair of heels to go with it, black, with the straps like a ribcage across the top. This was the kind of outfit you wore nothing underneath, and I didn't.

I met Cedric ten months ago—or was it twelve? I was facing charges of Drunk and Disorderly, Possession, and Battery on a LEO (3 counts), and was offered fifteen years. Offered. That's what they were "offering" me, and I made what they call a "counter offer." I offered them the guy I'd gotten the dope from. My charge was reduced to Criminal Mischief, I did six months paper and went into detox, and that was the start of a beautiful friendship. As soon as I was street legal, I began my glamorous double life as a ruthless, treacherous, scandalous bitch. I sold my soul and never looked back.

Now, as I came out of the mall toward my sweet sweet sweet 1970 Mach 1 with the racing stripes I stopped, my eyes going wide behind my Audrey Hepburn oversized shades. Detective Tom and Cedric leaned against my car—*my* car—with their arms folded and feet crossed as if they were cool or something.

"Howdy, Miss Scahlet." What a schmuck.

"Do I know you?" I asked. They were wearing their shields on their belts.

"You'd better be glad you do, young lady."

"C'mon, Simone," Tom said. "We won't bite."

I looked around nervously, saw no one else in the parking lot, and advanced, my keys out. I got to the rear of the car, opened the trunk, and spoke to them under cover of the lid, placing my bags in and pretending to arrange them.

"Anything you want to tell us about that bar you work at?"

"Yeah. Tomorrow's Ladies' Night."

"You like your new boss? What's his name, Haggerty?"

"He's okay." Jesus. I was terrified.

"We're gonna bust that place wide open, with or without you," Cedric said, and I relaxed. That meant he could only do it *with* me. He had nothing but hearsay, which isn't worth the paper it's printed on.

"There's nothing to bust that I know about." I slammed the lid shut.

"You want us to tell you about your boss? I guarantee you don't know his story." Tom was trying to look stern and serious.

"I don't know your story either. Look, I've gone straight. I got a good job, and I'm out of that old life for good. If you think anything's going on under the table at Layla, somebody's lying to you."

"You're right. Somebody is."

"Last chance, Simone," Cedric said quietly. "Are you in or out?"

I looked at him for along time, trying to stare him down before realizing we were both wearing shades and it wouldn't happen.

"I'm out."

They sighed and rocked themselves forward off of the car, stepping away to let me pass. Unlocking and opening my door, I let it swing into the side of the car parked next to me. Cedric snorted and shook his head, frowning. Tom smiled.

I got in and rolled down my window, deliberately ignoring my seatbelt. Cedric stepped forward and leaned in, trying again.

"Haggerty's a killer, Simone. A cold-blooded murderer—"

The blast of Rage Against The Machine on my stereo cut him off as I started the car, startling him. I pointed to my ear and mouthed the words "I can't hear you." He looked tired. He looked very tired and resigned as he backed away from my window.

I drove away and didn't look back once.

When I got on the Interstate headed back toward my apartment a convertible with two surfer guys pulled up alongside me. They grinned at me and arched their eyebrows. I sped up a little. They sped up, too. I turned the stereo off.

Taking a hair-tie off of the gearshift, I pulled my hair back so the wind wouldn't whip it in my face. With a little smile I turned to the two surfers, blew them a kiss, and punched it.

My car leaped forward with a roar, the startled bronze faces vanishing from my window. Surging past them and wrenching the wheel, I cut them off, watching them swerve in the rearview.

While they were distracted I sped up to hide in front of a cluster of cars ahead of us. There weren't many cars up ahead, only a handful sporadically Christmas-treeing the lanes, disappearing one by one over a hill in the distance. I had enough time to light a cigarette before the convertible found me, the two guys trying to shout something at me, their words lost in the wind between us.

I mashed the pedal and felt a rush of excitement as the lines in the road became dots beneath me. They followed, right on my tail. My ponytail whipped around in the roaring wind and stung my cheeks, dancing madly, but I bared my teeth and ignored it.

My cigarette in one hand, the other clamped white-knuckled on the steering wheel, I came swiftly up on the first of the cars ahead, scaring the shit out of its driver. I jerked the wheel and jumped into the other lane along its left, flying past it, coming right up on the ass of the blue sedan with the station wagon right next to it. With another jerk I cut across the highway in front of the first car, narrowly missing it with my tail and the station wagon with my front end.

My heart was in my throat, pounding against the backs of my eyes almost, choking me. The car behind me slammed on its brakes with a smoking screech and juked sideways, almost skidding off the pavement into the grassy swail.

The convertible was still there. I scowled at it in the rearview, then gasped in sudden horror as the trunk of a Volvo loomed in front of me. I cut the wheel sharply again, missing the car by a coat of paint, shooting in front of the wagon and the sedan now, over-correcting and sliding back toward the Volvo. The poofy-haired woman in the Volvo gaped wide-eyed at me in the flashing instant before she swerved to get away from me and sideswiped a parked police car, red and blue lights filling that window and my brain in a sudden moment of dreamlike quiet before the loud, crashing, glass-shattering impact.

Where the hell did that come from?

The cop with his Smokey the Bear hat stood beside a white compact, writing up a ticket and he screamed *"Shit!"* just before the oncoming fender glanced his hip and sent him flying, the ticket paper—white, with the pink and yellow carbons— flying out of his hand along with somebody else's driver's license, registration, and proof of insurance, swirling in the rocky air-wake like confetti.

I looked straight ahead, weaved lightning-quick between five cars that flashed past me in blurs of color, surged up the small hill and launched myself into the air. I may have only come a foot or so off the road, but the jumping-stomached weightlessness felt like "Houston, we have lift off!" and I was jolted violently when my tires touched down on the pavement on the other side. Behind me, closer than they appeared in the mirrors, were plumes of roiling black smoke from a four-car pileup.

The lane was clear ahead of me. I stomped the pedal to the floor and was gone.

Dear Diary,

I can't believe this shit! That bitch! I'm going to kill her!

Dear Diary,

When I went to the club tonight, wearing the new dress with the Fendi Fs like yin yangs, I found Rabbit sitting on one of the red couches next to the statue of Mars, Grecian helmet on, leaning with one hip cocked, his weight resting on the haft of his spear. He was staring quietly into the frothing turmoil of a wish-fountain, the shimmering turquoise light rising out of it playing in ripples on his face.

He looked lost.

I lit two cigarettes and sauntered over, handing him one. He took it silently, nodding thanks. I didn't see Layla anywhere.

"Why the long face, Warren?" I asked, knowing he hated that name.

"Just thinking," he muttered, shaking his head slowly.

"I know what you mean. I get depressed when I start thinking, too." I plopped down on the couch next to him and crooked my finger at a barmaid. She came obediently over, and I winked at Rabbit. "That's why I try not to do it."

"Yes, Miss Brennan?" the barmaid asked.

"That's Queen Brennan to you, wench. Fetch us six liquid heroins and two Dragon Pisses. Oh, do you want anything, Rabbit?"

"Nah, I'll just have a sip of one of yours."

"Fine. Make it snappy, young lady, and this crisp new one dollar bill will be all yours," I said generously.

"Yes, Your Majesty," the girl said. She even curtsied before leaving.

"I like that girl," I laughed. "She's fun."

"She has to be. She works for me."

"Where's Layla?"

"Dunno. Haven't seen her all day." He sounded miserable.

"Ahhh. Is that why you're so down in the dumps?"

"That and this annoying little Mafia problem. I've got my soldiers all over the place, but I'm still a little worried. Do you think they'll try anything tonight, Sam?"

"We'll see. Don't worry, honey. If they do, I'll protect you."

"Promise?"

"Cross my heart."

"That's a lovely dress, by the way," he said, as if just noticing.

"Isn't it, though? I just got it today."

We chit-chatted about the little things for a while until the drinks came, and after we'd split the six shots down the middle the conversation gradually turned to life, love, and the important stuff. Rabbit, when candid, was surprisingly bright and sensitive. He had an informed opinion on just about everything, and said some of the sweetest things, revealing a brain and a heart I had until now assumed were just as small and black as my own.

"I'm curious about something," I asked eventually.

"Okay, but we'll have to hurry. Layla might show up at any minute."

"Oh, please. I have a serious question."

"Shucks. Oh, well."

"Yeah, you should be so lucky. Right. Remember when I told you my lawyer was asking about, um, girls for rent? And you got really mad?"

"Mm-hmm." He was eyeing me warily.

"What is it exactly you have against it? I mean, it *is* the world's oldest profession, after all."

"Pshaw! Oldest profession, my ass."

"Well, yunno, that's what they *say*. But I mean, if everybody involved in the act is happy, why's it illegal, and why do you hate it?"

"All right, I'll tell you. First of all, I don't give a damn what's illegal because legal/illegal doesn't necessarily mean right/wrong. I kill people, which is illegal, but the people I kill deserve it, so it's right. And besides, they say something like five hundred-something people are dying every second. Committing suicide, having heart attacks, getting splattered in car wrecks, while at the same time a thousand new dipshits are being born. That's five hundred people gained, and most of them are going to turn out to be assholes. As overpopulated as the world is right now, they can't be worth much. Greater supply, far lower value. One or two more stepping off the planet here and there can't make too much of a difference.

"I also torture and maim, because some of these sonsabitches have it coming. They need to suffer more than the ones who just die. It's not wrong. But it's legal to screw people out of their money if you do it right, which is wrong. Least in my book, anyway.

"But prostitution, now, you say it doesn't hurt anybody. Illegal, but not wrong. Well, I say it hurts everybody. It's the circumvention of a basic and essential law of nature: only the fittest survive. Natural selection. Only the most worthy in the herd should be allowed to reproduce. But whores sell the opportunity to those unable to earn it, allowing underachievers and the undeserving to make more people like them, thus lowering our collective value even more, because the entire species is affected by a new pollution in the gene pool.

"Christ, that's deep."

"Of course it is. I am the Great Warren, who sees and knows all. And since you got me started, it pisses me off that women, for thousands of years used to be tending their babies and twirling flax and feeding fires, actually doing something worth doing, but now they're automatically assigned the right to diamond rings, held doors, free dinners on every date, pumpkins-turned-sportscars—"

"What?" I asked.

"Cinderella."

"Pumpkins?"

"Mm-hmm. Notice how that story's been turned around? Used to be, Cinderella put up with her cunt stepsisters and did all the work around the house without bitching, and she ended up getting the prince because he was looking for a real woman instead of some thoroughbred, gossiping, uptown whore. But now, instead of being rewarded for hard work, unselfishness, good values and all that jazz, almost every woman feels like she's being cheated out of her prince that she ought to get just because she's got a cha-cha. The power is now in the hands of the wicked stepsisters!

"Think about it, what do men do with all their money? They work hard to earn their money back from women just so that they can spend it on other women! These days, if you're not Prince Charming, you have to at least be Santa Claus."

"Remember who you're talking to, slick."

"Hmm?"

"This is a bandwagon I'm not about to jump on. I like this system just fine."

"…Oh yeah. Bitch."

After the drinks were drained, replaced, and drained again, he explained the nature of the universe to me. He said it came to him one night when he was tripping on shroom tea, and he'd wandered away from his party into the darkness shrouding a cold and windy golf course.

The little flag sticking out of the seventh hole was flapping madly, and the thin pole was bent sharply in the howling wind. As he looked up at the few stars visible through the grumbling clouds, a forked shaft of jagged blue lightning split the sky with a deafening crack. Like a child staring in wide-eyed wonder, Rabbit watched shaft after angry shaft spear the darkness.

He said it was the play of summer lightning and the thought that he was standing on a rock spinning around a ball of flaming gas that made him realize the true nature of the universe.

"Remember chemistry class in high school," he said.

"I didn't take one."

"Oh, well, pretend you did. Remember atoms?"

"Yeah."

"You remember protons, electrons, and neutrons?"

"Vaguely."

"Well, an atom can be visualized as a football field, with a tiny pea in the very center. That pea is the nucleus, and three types of subatomic particles orbit it, in varying—"

"Yeah, I remember that."

"Okay. Now picture our solar system. Huge, gigantic, with the tiny sun right in the middle…"

"And planets orbiting it."

"Yep. Electrons—like Earth—zipping around the nucleus, with a positive charge. Lightning. Electricity. Life. Us. Our nervous system runs on electric synapses, you know, which proves that we are connected to the world around us on a much more complex scale. They say you'll score higher on an IQ test during a thunderstorm than you will on a calm day. I think we exist on a tiny subatomic particle, making up an atom, making up a molecule, making up a cell, making up something so fucking big it'll drive you batshit to imagine it."

"And each of us is made up of a billion, gajillion universes?"

"Uh-huh. And it goes on forever, both ways, bigger and bigger, and smaller and smaller. It was the lightning that made me think of it, because our own nervous systems operate on electric signals. If we have tiny versions of lightning within ourselves, we must be more a part of our world than we think we are. And this also explains astrology. You know that most horoscopes are bullshit because they're made up on the spot, but amazingly, the ones that are based on actual study of the stars can be dead on. And what is never wrong is the description of peoples' personalities in the Zodiac. Just like there are six original storylines and anything else is just a variation, there are only twelve basic categories a person can fall into, and they are mapped out in the patterns in the sky, the cycles of other atoms and their twinkling nuclei. And since they follow a regular pattern, at least from our parallax, just like all of *our* atoms are arranged in a pattern—our genetic coding we call DNA—then the code that applies to us up there in the night sky that we call the Zodiac can't just be a coincidence. It must be the DNA pattern of whatever it is we're all a part of. You smell what I'm cookin', Sam?"

"I think so."

"Good, because this supports the belief that there is no "chaos," that everything in the universe has an underlying order. And it also supports the theory of universal expansion, because just like there is electricity inside everything, there are spirals."

"*What?*"

"Spirals! Look at pictures taken of galaxies. They are in spiral shapes. Our solar system is in the Western Spiral arm of the Milky Way. Ever see a picture of a hurricane moving on the Weather Channel? Hurricanes and galaxies both look like eddies in flowing water or displaced fog. Well, galaxies are shaped that way because there are eddies in the universal flow.

"And you'll see these spirals everywhere. A seashell. A leaf. The back of someone's head—you see a man with short hair, look at the back of his head and tell me his hair doesn't grow in a spiral out from his parietal bone. I promise you, once you see it, you start seeing spirals everywhere you look. You'll start doodling them on cocktail napkins, and pointing them out to strangers. The truth doesn't set you free, Simone. The truth drives you nuts!

"Scary, isn't it?" He was grinning.

"No," I said, thinking about it. "It's comforting. It's a relief, kind of, to think of it that way. It means I'm not really that important, and nothing I do can really be as bad as it seems."

His crooked grin widened. He was turning into Rabbit again.

"So what do you think our atom is a part of?" I asked.

His grin vanished, but somehow remained. It was odd. Like a Cheshire Cat, he could smile even with the solemn expression he wore now. He signaled for the barmaid to hit us again, and leaned in close to me. He looked shiftily to both sides to make sure no one was listening, and whispered conspiratorially.

"A big red crayon."

I blinked at him.

"And if some kid ever eats it, we're *screwed.*"

It felt like my face burst, that's how hard I laughed. I laughed until a deep stitch screamed in my side. It wasn't what he said so much as how he said it. Like he wasn't kidding. I managed to choke out the words, "You're out of your fucking *mind!*" and he sat back indignantly with that look on his face—who, me?—and I laughed even harder. Our drinks arrived.

The music started, the people came, and I got drunk.

With Rabbit's nervousness in mind, I did everything I could to keep him smiling, and we danced and laughed together for hours. I could see now what Layla saw in him, and—ooh, speak of the devil.

Layla came striding through the lights toward me with a strange smile on her face. My God, she looked wonderful. She dutifully kissed Rabbit and leaned in close to me, shouting to be heard.

"How did you get here so fast?"

"What?"

"How did you get here so fast?"

"The hell are you talking about?"

"Find us a drink, honey," Rabbit said, and she was gone. He looked worried again, and shouted to me.

"I think she's cheating on me, Sam."

I froze. The pained look on his face made me feel awful.

"Really?" I asked stupidly.

"Yeah. I suspect unauthorized use of my coital unit by another operator. I think she's cheating on me with Todd."

I relaxed, even smiled, which confused him. Yeah, she *had* been sleeping with Todd, but that was history. Ancient history.

"No, Warren. I promise you she's not."

"How do you know?"

"Trust me on this, honey. I know."

"Promise?"

"Cross my heart."

Layla cornered me by the statue of Cupid on my way out of the ladies' room and took my face in her hands, kissing me deeply.

"Simone, I'm going to buy you a trophy with a big red heart on it," she said. "You are so incredible." She kissed me again.

"What's gotten into you?" I asked, touching her breast. Her hand slipped into my dress and she replied, her voice breathy.

"You've always been great, don't get me wrong, but to-night...tonight...oh my *God!* That thing you did still has me tin-gling!"

"What the fuck are you talking about?"

She stared at me, bewildered, stammering.

"Are you okay, baby?"

"Top of the world, why?"

"You hit your head or something?"

"No. *Why?*"

"Because we had the best sex ever, the best I've ever had in my entire life tonight, and you're acting like it never happened."

It was my turn to be confused, bewildered, stammering.

"I...we...this is the first time I've seen you."

"Simone, come on. You know I don't like games."

"Then why are you playing one?"

"Damn it, what's going on? I just left your apartment—"

She's never been to my apartment. I painted her at her place. I slept with her at her place or Rabbit's. I—wait a minute.

"Where's my apartment, Layla?" I asked, my throat closing.

"Uh...what? Why?"

"Tell me. Tell me where you just came from."

"Your place. Your apartment on the beach."

I don't have an apartment by the beach.

I don't have an apartment anywhere near the beach.

But Salomé does.

I turned and kicked the ladies' room door open, slamming it against the tile wall and stormed in, shaking. Two girls were talking at the mirror while doing their makeup, and they looked up, startled. I saw my red-faced reflection twisted into a snarl of pain and rage as I ran at it, tears streaming, fists clenched. They managed to get out of the way before I leaped and shattered the mirror with one punch, splitting the skin of my knuckles on the glass. The mirror fell in a thousand pieces and broke into a million more.

With my bloody hand I swept the row of perfumes off the counter and they exploded on the tiles in a splash of colored glass and alcohol. The bathroom immediately stank of too many fra-grances. The two girls stared in dumbfounded shock and horror, but that was nothing compared to the look on Layla's face when I turned on her. Her face had turned a ghostly white. She trembled, her eyes wide, her mouth agape. She stood distorted in my tear-filled eyes, with no idea of what she'd done or how badly she'd broken my heart. I could feel my guts wrenching, my face burning, beside which the pain in my hand was nothing.

"You bitch! You cunt! The best you ever had, huh?"

"Baby, what's wrong with you?" She was terrified.

"You fucking idiot, I can't believe how fucking stupid you are!"

"What are you talking about?" she screamed.

"You make me sick!"

I stormed past her, choking the words out, shrinking away from the hand she tried to grab me with.

I've lain here in bed with this bottle for three hours now, listening to the phone ring and Layla cry on my answering machine. It's hard not to pick up a phone, but not as hard as it is to drink yourself to sleep when your heart is broken.

"Baby, whatever it is I did to you, whatever I said, I'm so sorry. Please pick up the phone. Please."

I took another long pull, and this stuff doesn't even taste like tequila anymore. She was sobbing uncontrollably now.

"Simone, please. I love you. I love you so much and you're killing me. And you won't even tell me *why!* Baby…Sam…"

I couldn't take any more. I lurched up off of the bed, picked up the phone, hung up on her, and left the phone off the hook as I staggered to the bathroom, throwing up the whole way there.

Dear Diary,

I awoke in the bathtub with the shower raining freezing water on me. It was so cold I could barely breathe, but in an odd way it was rather pleasant. My dress was in a pile at my feet, soaking wet.

I tried to lift myself up, but a lightning bolt of pain lanced through my head and I collapsed, crying out.

"Good morning, princess." The words came from far away. "Take these." The hand of God came down from Heaven through the rain and stuffed three huge pills into my weakly opened mouth. I turned my head upward with my jaw hanging slack, gulping down draughts of cold water. Painkillers. Big ones.

"Thank you," I mumbled, choking them down.

"Don't mention it," he said tenderly. My head throbbed horribly.

"I hurt."

"I know." He reached down and caressed my cheek.

"You're going to be fine," was the last thing I heard.

I awoke again on the couch in my living room, dry now, with a pillow under my head and a blanket over me. On the coffee table was a tall glass of water with two more of the giant painkillers beside it. The TV was on, and there was something in my hair.

It took a second to realize that it wasn't a pillow but a lap, Todd's lap, and the thing in my hair was his hand, absently caressing me. On the screen, a long-haired Schwarzenegger was reaching for an egg-shaped red jewel and dripping sweat onto the cheek of a gigantic sleeping serpent, awakening it.

"Welcome back," Todd said, smiling down at me.

"I'm hungry," was all I could manage.

"What a surprise."

I suddenly remembered vomiting all over the place, puking up things I hadn't even eaten.

"Oh, shit. I've got a mess to clean up."

"I took care of it."

"You did? When?"

"Layla asked me to come check on you. You'd left the door wide open."

"Is that so? Did she ask you to undress me, too?"

"No, you did that on your own. I found you naked in the tub with vomit all over your nice new dress, balled up on the floor."

It took a long time for me to speak again. I lay there, very still, watching Arnold fight the huge snake, his Asian buddy pincushioning it with arrows while he hacked it into kabobs with his broadsword.

I almost didn't realize I was crying softly.

"Thank you, Todd."

"Shhh. You'd do the same for me. You want some pizza?"

"Yeah, I got leftovers in the fridge."

"Okay, lift your head." I moved so he could get up, and when he did I noticed he'd bandaged my hand as well.

"Todd?" I asked, a little scared. The tears were coming faster now.

"Yes, Sam?"

"I think I hurt my baby last night."

I waited for him to say Layla was all right, but he didn't.

I wrote a long letter and took it by Layla's apartment, intending to slip it under the door, but as I stood there fanning my face with it, I reconsidered. She wasn't at home, so I took my (silver) lock-picking set out of my purse and was inside in under a minute. I knew I shouldn't be there, but it was a nice feeling, being there when she wasn't. The Moby CD I'd bought her was in the stereo, and I hit PLAY, then wandered around to find the best place to put the letter.

I put it on the coffee table, then changed my mind and stuck it to the fridge with a magnet, then changed my mind again and took it into the bathroom to set near the mirror.

I left a little lipstick kiss on the mirror for her, gathered up her dirty clothes and buried my face in them, smelling her. I carried them to the washing machine, hugging them to myself, and sorted them out, washing her whites first.

Then I did her dishes.

Then I wandered into her bedroom. On her vanity I was startled to find three 8x10 black and white photos of us together, taken from a distance. Walking together, holding hands. Kissing in the park on a bench with a blur of pigeons flying around us. Sitting on our surfboards in the ocean, laughing, waiting for the next set to come in.

Wedged in the corner of the mirror was another, the two of us feeding each other bites of our dinners at a restaurant table.

What the hell?

I opened my purse to get a cigarette and realized I'd left the pack out in the car. Looking around, I found one of hers on her nightstand, a pack with the top open and the gold Zippo I'd given her sitting on top of it. I went over to it and picked it up.

It was heavier than it should have been. I opened it…

And found myself staring at a small, black, mini tape recorder and a high-powered tiny microphone.

Dear Diary,

I drove slowly and aimlessly for hours, rolling past the park, looking at the bench I'd been photographed sitting at. I stopped at the very spot, judging from the angle the picture'd been taken, and realized there was no way I could ever have spotted the cameraman. That thought made me paranoid as hell.

And Layla had seemed so calm, so natural, acting in love with me while somebody was happily clicking away. I flashed back to the first night at the club, in the bathroom after I'd tried to kiss her, and realized what she was doing behind that stall door. I knew because I'd been there, too.

She was taking off her wire, just in case she ended up naked later.

I have never felt this empty in my entire life.

Dear Diary,

I went to the club tonight, not sure whether I was going to confront Layla, expose her, or break down and cry. Rabbit greeted me upstairs with a kiss on the cheek.

"Did you hear what happened last night?" he asked.

"If I did, I've forgotten it." I did not want to hear this.

"Two girls got in a fight over some guy in the bathroom. Broke the mirror, smashed all the perfumes, wrecked the place. Layla broke it up, and was just in time, too. Said when she came in they were covered in blood, on the verge of killing each other."

"You don't say." Hmmm, interesting.

"Yeah. The things people will do over love, eh?"

"Are they okay? The two girls?"

"One's jaw was broken. Both of their eyes were swollen shut. I called them an ambulance and made the guy they were fighting over pay for the new mirror. He had the nerve to say he didn't even know what we were talking about. But it all worked out."

"Christ," I muttered. I noticed Layla talking to Todd.

"Look, I've got to get back to work. I'll talk to you later."

I watched Rabbit go off to talk to Blue Tick, who was bulging out of his suit. This place was going to come crashing down around them soon, and I felt sick about it.

I loved this place, and had gotten very close to Rabbit. Todd would go up, too, and he really didn't deserve to. I had to choose between them and her. The next few minutes would make up my mind. I took two glasses of champagne and went to Layla.

Todd saw me coming and gestured with a jerk of his chin. Layla turned to look who it was, and her face turned to stone. Todd tactfully excused himself.

Layla met me halfway. I handed her one of the flutes and toasted with her—to evil, of course—and drained my drink.

"I'm going to say something," Layla told me. "And if you interrupt me I'm going to break your goddamned head."

I opened my mouth and she put a finger to my lips.

"Don't say a fucking word." And she meant it.

I nodded, and she led me over to Our Couch.

"Now, I don't know what got into you last night, but I'm willing to forgive you on one condition: you never, ever act that way again. You scared me half to death, and I've never cried that hard in my life. I beat the hell out of two girls who didn't do anything, and I would've killed them if Tick hadn't come in and stopped me. Now, he covered for both of us with Rabbit, so you owe him.

"Simone," her eyes were very cold and serious, now. "I love you. I love you very much and I'm not going to lose what we have over whatever stupid problem you had last night. Whatever may happen, I want you to know that I never lied to you. Not once. There's something I may need to tell you someday down the road, but this isn't the time or the place."

She twisted the gold ring off of her finger and took my hand, slipping it on next to the silver one I wear. Her eyes were shining with tears, but she did not let them fall. Her voice quavered slightly.

"I need you to go to the liquor store for me," she said quietly. "We're almost out of vermouth. Promise me you'll go."

I stared at her. She was trembling slightly, holding my hand.

"I need you to go immediately. Right now."

"Vermouth, huh?"

"Yeah."

"The only store open this late is clear across town."

"I know."

All at once, I understood. But she had no idea I knew. I looked for Todd and found him talking with Rabbit not too far away. I watched them for a long moment and felt terrible for them, but I swallowed hard and nodded. I looked back into Layla's eyes.

"I love you, too."

I kissed her quickly and walked away.

Downstairs, I asked one of the bartenders, just to be sure, how we were doing in the vermouth department. He checked and said Fine.

I left, making my way through the press of bodies to the door. I moved like I do in dreams, when I'm trying to run from the demons and my legs turn to rubber.

Outside, I saw everything as if for the first time. It was a beautiful night, and I tried to tell myself that what happened here on this part of the planet, this electron, didn't matter one bit in the grand scheme of things. The fate of this club and my friends wouldn't affect the giant red crayon in the slightest.

I walked down the sidewalk to the corner and saw the white vans—four of them—lurking in wait. I went past them, pretending not to even notice, made a right, made another right, and walked to the parking lot behind the strip of bars and stores where my car was parked.

The key in my hand shook so badly I could barely unlock my door, and when I got in I just sat there, motionless. I could see the back door of the club, the one the cops would kick open. That door was guarded heavily, but the cops already knew that and were prepared. I found myself frozen, unable to drive away. The pilot operating my brain kept revving the engine but going nowhere.

Something, God maybe, made me turn and glance out the window at another window, the passenger side front window of a black Cherokee, and the guy racking the slide of a .9mm behind it. The same way you'd notice an ant, and one second later realize there are ten thousand of them, I realized that the Cherokee had five guys in it, and the one parked next to them had six, and all of them had guns.

And the first one I had seen was Ernesto Carcotti.

My veins filled with ice. I looked away sharply, terrified that they might see me, and fished my cell phone out of my purse. Now it was my turn to get Layla out of there. My throat was closing up as I fumbled with the tiny buttons. The display said my battery was low. Fuck! I hit Layla's number anyway.

The Cherokees opened up, all doors at once, all occupants stepping out in unison. I looked up the way toward the white vans and saw the side doors sliding open. From where they were neither group could see the other yet. You've got to be kidding me.

I listened to my phone, heard the distant ring.

"Come on, come one," I mumbled.

No answer. Fuck. I called Todd's number. The mob guys were crossing the parking lot toward the back door, and the cops were hustling out of the vans toward the corner, splitting up to go in the front and back doors at the same time.

Cops always park too far away.

Todd's phone was ringing, and ringing, and the answering service picked up. Fuck. I hung up and tried the upstairs phone in the club, the phone in the room behind the mirror. The mob guys had just gotten to the door, the cops were almost at the corner of the building, and my battery died.

Fuck!

The gangsters plunged through the door just as the cops came around and broke into a run, and that's the moment I stopped thinking. I should've driven away. I should've stayed put. I

64

should've done anything except what I did, but Nature took over and I went to protect my mate. The wheels in my head spun out, tires smoking.

I dropped the phone and reached under my seat for the snub-nosed S&W .38, opened the door and stepped out with Joe Pantoliano's voice in my head for no good reason at all.

Time of your life, eh kid?

All I could hear outside the club was the faint music from within and the pounding of my own heart roaring in my ears. Then it came faintly, the loud flat bangs like a loose shutter banging in the wind against a haunted house. On the other side of that door was chaos. For those inside the world had become sudden death, screaming, blood, and terror. The crowd had turned in just a few short seconds from a reveling throng to a stampeding herd of screaming animals trampling one another in the blind urge to escape.

Just inside the back door lay the slumped bodies of the guards, and beyond them, in the surreally incongruous music and lights, figures jumped and fell in a ghastly dance of death, their bodies flung this way and that by the bullets ripping through them.

The assassins had come in shooting, scattering as the guards posted elsewhere returned fire, and the cops had run into the middle of it all, drenched in garish electric light.

In the jumping slow motion of a strobe light, colored shadows dove for cover or reeled drunkenly, staggering a few steps before collapsing in the tangle of twitching limbs. One wrong step in either direction meant the difference, and some poor lower-echelon clubber went down spinning. More than one faucet sprayed tall fan-shaped geysers of tap water from behind the bars, the lines of bottles exploding in succession on the counters, and statues shattered, dismembered.

The thunder of gunshots rang in my ears as I made my way along the edge of the wall, the .38 shaking in my hand. It was like a war zone, with three enemies firing on each other, and the bystanders were cut down between them. Men and women in their colorful plumage who escaped the stray rounds were crushed underfoot and against the walls and bars, desperate to reach the doors ahead.

The lights and music went out all at once, either Rabbit or Enigro thinking on his feet. The only light now was blacklight, and all of our men wore black. The only things visible on them were dandruff and cigarette ashes. The cops were now floating disembodied signs: POLICE in bold block letters, and anyone else who glowed was fair game. The trippy molten metal design of my dress stood out like a sore thumb in the darkness.

Figures.

The air stank of blood and gunsmoke, was choked with screams and fear. I dove behind an overturned table, landing on a dead man in a trench coat beneath it, just as two rounds pockmarked the wall above me, showering me with bits of plaster that a moment before would've been my skull and brain. Another shot nearby, and I was showered with long stemmed roses, water, and shattered glass.

I grabbed ahold of the coat's sleeves and tugged the corpse's arms out of it. It was black crocodile leather. I've always wanted one of those, only with a sash you would tie across the waist instead of a— something punched a hole through the table and sheared off a lock of my hair.

I slipped the coat on and buttoned it, making myself invisible, rose, and ran as fast as I could toward the stairs. Ricochets whined like banshees, the echoes rolling back, and the bright purple afterimage blotches of gunfire hung before my eyes in triple exposures. In my entire life I've never felt so alive. A thrill was roaring through me that my racing heart could barely keep up with.

"Tick!" I shouted. "Blue Tick!" A figure on the stairs who would've shot me called back, "Sam?" and then I was beside him.

"Where's Layla?"

"Rabbit's upstairs!" It was Jimmy, the other one.

"Yeah, but where's Layla?"

His head jerked backwards and I was sprayed with something warm and sticky. I turned and fired, missing whoever was behind us, stopped and took Jimmy's shotgun.

I passed the mirror on the way up the stairs and out of habit glanced into it. At the top I went to the out-of-order pay phone on the wall, lifted the handset and punched in 6-6-6, opening the secret door.

Inside, down the steps, Rabbit was shouting into a CB, giving orders to his soldiers, and people I didn't recognize were doing things frantically that I couldn't make out. Rabbit looked up and gasped.

"Christ! Sam's hit! Reuben, fix Sam, quick!"

Reuben was one of our doctors, who looked on any given day like he could use one himself. He rose and came toward me.

"No, I'm okay!" I called, trying to be heard over the confusion. "It's Jimmy's blood!"

A pained look came over Rabbit's face.

"Where's Layla?" I asked urgently.

"In the lab." He may have said something else, but I didn't wait around to hear it. I bolted back through the door, not even bothering to close it this time, and was right out in the open when I saw the yellowish flashlight beams of cops coming up the stairs behind me. I dropped to the floor and played possum, terrified. Seeing the blood on my face, they ignored me and stepped over me to get to the secret door, already knowing where to look.

Shots rang out from inside the room, and the cops shrank back from the door, flattening themselves against the wall. There were four of them. I whipped Jimmy's sawed-off 12-gauge around and pulled the trigger. It bucked in my hands and one of the cops screamed, collapsing. The other three turned and fired over my head. I racked the pump and blew another one's head clean off. Then, I could barely believe it, Rabbit came flying out of the door with two pistols, turning over in midair and landing on his back, sliding across the floor and firing again and again and again, killing the remaining two, just like in the movies.

I cannot describe how it feels to shoot someone. The power that surges through you when you end a person's life, and all you have to do is move one finger, it's a pure unholy joy. There is no word for how good it feels, not in any language. Rabbit summed it up without words though, when he rolled over and looked at me, both of us on the floor with smoking guns in our hands, and flashed that crooked grin at me.

"We've got to stop meeting like this," he said.

The lab was downstairs, on the far side of a sea of corpses, the darkness split by muzzle-flashes washing the walls like strobe light. My ears rang from the closeness of deafening explosions, and the club was dreamlike with the haze of gunsmoke. I strained my eyes, drowned in blindness, and saw in one flashing instant a man with a gun straining his own eyes looking for someone to kill.

Plunged back into darkness, I aimed at where he was and

squeezed. The .38 jumped in my hand and spat a roaring tongue of flame, and in its flash I saw the man recoil, screaming. I got up to run for the lab and tripped over a body, falling onto the blood-slippery floor. I landed with one hand on a dead man's face, one finger on his rubbery nose, another feeling his bushy eyebrows, and the rest in the bloody pulp of an exit wound. My shotgun went spinning away into the darkness, but it wasn't important anymore when I looked back and saw Layla lying there, eyes bulging, gasping on the floor like a fish in the bottom of a boat. Rabbit was suddenly at my side, his cool finally shaken.

He gripped my arm and hissed at me through his clenched teeth, his fingers vise-tight, but shaking.

"Get her out of here. Meet up with me at the apartment—no, the docks. Go to the docks where my boat is. Take Reuben."

"I can't carry her."

Layla convulsed and we both stared down at her, stricken. She was clutching her stomach, with snakes of blood running down her hands from between her fingers.

Rabbit pried her hands away and tore her shirt open, panicking, then froze and stared stupidly at the black wire taped to her quaking belly, running up into the small microphone in her bra. Her eyes, if it were possible, went even wider, and flashed to me. Rabbit's mouth gaped as realization fell upon him like a ton of bricks.

It seemed that for a moment the thunderclaps of gunfire were very far away, and the whining bullets stopped whizzing over our heads. We three were all there was of the world. Automatic weapons spitting numberless bullets became whispers like the buzzing of flies on a battlefield.

A look of sick horror crept into Rabbit's eyes, like he'd been slugged in the gut. His whole world was falling apart around him, and now he knew who his Judas was. His wet eyes hardened, narrowed to white hot slits of rage, then widened as I pressed the business end of my .38 to the side of his head and cocked the hammer.

There was the devil, then. No more crooked grin, no more Who, me? Just bloodshot, white-knuckled, purple-faced hatred, foam seething through his teeth, clenched so tight that blood bubbled from his snarling lips. Suddenly his was the face that went with the voice in your head, the one that tells you to take a flying leap off the ledge of a high place. The face just beneath the surface of your consciousness that leers and laughs and screams and urges you to

Go on, do it, put the gun in your mouth. My flesh crawled. I swallowed hard.

I wound my arm back and swung the pistol hard against the side of his head, felt something crunch and saw his eyes go glassy and sightless in that split second before his face hit the floor. I gathered Layla up and ran with her in my arms like a child. I don't know how I could carry her, just that I had to, and I did. Breathing a silent prayer, I bolted across the dance floor, ducking my head as if it would help, with bullets flying past me every step of the way. The long black trench coat hid me, but could not conceal Layla's long, flowing hair, shimmering in the blacklight. More than once I tripped over a dead or dying body and stumbled, expecting a round of hot lead to knock me off my feet, but somehow I got to the back door. I threw my whole weight against it, turning to shield my Layla, and the door burst open, throwing me out into the night.

I got to my car, managed to open the passenger door and stuffed Layla inside, belatedly realizing my gun was still in my hand. I slammed the door and jumped, sliding across the hood on my ass to get to the driver's side, turned the key that I'd left in the ignition and peeled out, almost crashing into a Forerunner.

Fishtailing, tires squealing, I had to jerk the wheel sharply to avoid a honking confusion of cars—the stampeding herd now congesting the streets—and sped through the maze of traffic to the other end of the parking lot.

Layla was still clutching her belly, doubled over in the seat with her knees drawn up in a fetal position. There was blood everywhere. I almost didn't realize I'd been screaming the whole time.

The night was alive with red and blue light, and people stood staring, or crying, or holding each other on the sidewalk when I screeched out onto the street. I floored it and left the horror and carnage in a cloud of rubber smoke.

The crosshatch pattern of the pistol's grip was etched redly in the palm of my hand, with a little circle and a slanted line from the flat-head screw on my lifeline. I stared at it stupidly, and at the anemic blue tendrils of cigarette smoke curling away into the night from the Marlboro I held in that trembling hand.

An elderly woman with blue poodle hair stood outside the front entrance of Good Samaritan Hospital, smoking with me, staring at the splatters of scarlet on my trippy molten metal dress. The night was very quiet for the first time in hours.

"My granddaughter's having a baby," the old woman said, trying to start a conversation.

"I'm sorry to hear it." I couldn't muster much sympathy.

"Why?" she asked, taken by surprise. Fucking old people.

"Look, my girlfriend's been shot. I'm in no mood for a chit-chat."

Her eyes widened a moment, then she smiled strangely and drew on her cigarette, a menthol by the smell of it. She blew a cloud at me and chuckled dryly, her voice sounding like the crunch of dead leaves.

"I was a lesbian once. For about an hour."

I looked at her, startled. She was very, very old.

"That was a long time ago," she said. I nodded slowly.

"I suppose I was about your age. We all do wild things when we're young. We can't get away with them once we grow up."

"How old is your granddaughter?" I asked, warming to her.

"About that age. She doesn't have a husband. Of course, neither did her mother." She said the last with a tone of regret.

We smoked in silence for a while.

I listened to distant sirens and looked at my hand again. Still there. I didn't let go of the pistol after shooting out of the window at somebody stopped at a green light, blocking my way. Startled the hell out of him, but it got him moving. I held onto it until we screeched to a halt outside the hospital and Layla flew forward into the dashboard. Then I was carrying-dragging her into the lobby, trailing bright red slashes of blood on the linoleum and screaming for a doctor.

I looked at the old woman.

"About what age did you settle down?" I asked.

She sighed. "If you want to know when you should…"

She pointed with the two fingers holding her cigarette at the blood all over my dress, nodding gravely.

"Now would probably be a good time."

She dropped her cigarette onto the concrete and ground it out with the toe of her shoe, winked at me, and shuffled back inside.

Fucking old people.

The doctors told me to go home, so I eventually did. In the car at a stoplight I opened my silver cigarette case and took out a black-paper rolled reefer. I put "Jar of Flies" into the CD player and lit the joint with the car lighter, listening to Layne Staley wail about how much it sucks to be strung out. Sitting there, watching the traffic light sway in the wind and getting high, I decided something. It wasn't a moment of weakness, a relapse, a whim, or anything like that. It was a level-headed, well-thought-out decision, made by a sound and able mature mind. I decided to get back on heroin as soon as possible.

Dear Diary,

How do you cure a Polish heroin addict?

Give him a plastic spoon.

I don't know about the rest of the world, but when I come down from H I feel dirty. Like a sap-sticky tree-climbing dirty, and itchy like I've been rolling in the grass.

It's the quinine that makes you itch, but it's also responsible for that initial rush, so I guess you have to live with it. The only way I can describe it is as a slow, sensual massage on the inside, like gentle angel hands caressing your very soul.

I spent all the money I had with me on as much Black Tar as I could get, and that was no small amount.

Back at my apartment, I dug out my spoon and rig, and shot myself to the moon. My favorite song to shoot up to is "Times Of Trouble" by Temple of the Dog, that comforting voice crooning "When the spoon is hot, and the needle's sharp, and you drift away (something something something) and your baw-deeee shaaaaakes," that's when I'm prepping my rig and tying off, usually with a condom for a tourniquet, and the song bursts with this soulful emotion at the same time the magnificent glory of heroin courses up my arm towards my heart....

God, why did I ever stop doing this?

The phone rang.

I wasn't asleep, but I wasn't really awake, either. In any case, I didn't answer it. The machine picked up, and Salomé's voice greeted me as if she hadn't slept with my girlfriend the other day and everything was fine.

The bitch.

"Well, Sam, I found out about your friend Rabbit finally. He's a real winner. Right up your alley. All the soap in the world won't wash the blood off this guy's hands."

Tell me something I don't know.

"I'm coming over this afternoon," she said. "You'd better be in."

Beep.

It seemed like I closed my eyes for one second and opened them, looking up into Salomé's gray eyes as she gently shook me. It was early evening, the orange sun coming through the blinds painting bars of light on my bedroom wall and the side of her face. She smiled.

"Rise and shine, Sam. Have you had breakfast?"

"No. Give me a cigarette."

She put a Marlboro Red between my chapped lips and lit it with the trench lighter from my nightstand. She plucked at the clotted blood-crusty fabric of my dress and *tsk*ed at me.

"You know, they make pads for this kind of thing."

"Get bent." I took a long, satisfying drag.

"I'll fix us something to eat," she said, walking out.

I propped myself up on my elbows and blinked the sleep out of my eyes. I felt awful. Nothing new.

Taking the cigarette into the bathroom with me and slipping the dress down into a pile at my feet, I stared at the whore-red lipstick kiss that I'd never washed off. My whole world had changed and changed again since that day, and here I was looking at the same girl in the mirror. Shit.

Baggy black eyes, bloodshot and empty, face drawn and haggard. Purplish bruises on my chest and arms. Track marks on my thigh because the veins in my arms are collapsed.

"I'm so tired of this shit."

"What?" Salomé called from the kitchen.

"I said I look like shit!" I called back.

"Ha! Quit flattering yourself. You don't look *that* good."

I knew I could count on her.

I splashed some cold water on my face and made my gums bleed with the toothbrush.

Stumbling naked back to the bedroom, I could smell cantaloupe and knew Sal was fixing *prosciutto e melone*. The prosciutto had gone forgotten in the fridge for I don't know how long, but that stuff never goes bad.

I came back out in cutoffs and a sports bra. Sal was on the couch in front of the TV with a plate of salt-and-peppered melon wrapped in prosciutto, about twenty bite-sized morsels. There was one of those stupid "reality shows" on.

"I think MTV was a lot cooler back when they played music videos," she said, shaking her head at two arguing drag queens. I sat beside her and leaned back with my feet on the table.

"Hungry?" she asked.

"Not yet."

We watched the stupid drag queens get in the most pathetic

"cat fight" we'd ever seen, while bystanders cheered them on.

"So, why do they call him 'Rabbit'?" I asked quietly.

We decided it would be a good idea if I crashed at her place for a few days, and packed up my necessities. A few outfits, my dance stuff, and my nest egg—almost seven thousand accumulated in a couple of weeks (or was it months?) at the club. I was going to need a job again soon.

"Is Chad still around?" I asked.

"Chad who?"

We took both our cars to her place and got high together watching "The Simpsons." She hadn't done heroin in a long time, and couldn't pass up Black Tar. It is a rare treat to see my evil twin let her guard down, stop being the tough one, and I enjoy spending time with her alone. She put my hair into cornrows while we caught up on each other's adventures. Apparently, she'd been even busier than me. She always was the crazy one.

I realized how much I missed the way we were as little girls, the fun we had. Of course, that's probably just the smack talking. She showed me her latest paintings, a series of abstracts depicting emotions.

"Rage" was beautiful, a confusion of crimson, yellow, and orange slashes that looked just like the haze that swims across your eyes before you go berserk.

"Envy" was, of course, green. There were pale tendrils of what looked like smoke rising in wisps from an ashtray, but could have been hate seething up into the blotchy darker greens that almost resembled a shadowy forest.

"Despair" was the predictable deep blues and purples.

"I'm feeling plenty of this lately," I said.

"Hmmm. Are you going to fill me in, ever?"

I thought a moment. I decided not to mention the fight I had with Layla, since we never got mad over that kind of thing. We got even, instead.

"My girlfriend got shot last night. At the club when it was raided by cops *and* Zack Scalisi's people."

"Jesus Christ," she whispered. "The hell did you get yourself into?" I saw genuine concern in her eyes.

"We, uh…we chopped Ray Valanga into fourteen pieces and sent the head back to his boss."

Sal whistled through her teeth and shook her head. "And you're hiding from Rabbit because…?"

"Don't worry about it. That's a whole other headache."

"So what are you going to do?"

"The only thing I can do. Go back to Diabolique and start dancing again before I spend all my money. I'm gonna try to stay ahead of the game this time."

"You ain't going to manage if you're shooting up."

"Sssssshit, I know. I wish it didn't have to end this way, Sal. I was having the time of my life."

"Don't waste your time on regret. It'll get you nowhere."

"You want another hit?"

"Nah."

"I do."

"It's a free country."

I cooked up another spoonful and had to shoot it in my foot because the rest of my veins were tired. That beautiful feeling washed over me and I fell back, hitting the couch cushions and melting into them.

After a long time I was dimly aware of Salomé sitting across the coffee table from me at an easel. Glancing at me with two brushes held in her teeth, dabbing on a canvas with a third. I wanted to protest, tell her she didn't dare paint me like this, but I couldn't move, and the thought faded anyway.

Sal had the new Tool CD on, and Maynard was howling a note that seemed to last forever.

Blasphemy never sounded so good.

I closed my eyes and was swallowed up into oblivion.

I stared at my own face, still and pale and lifeless, the face my sister painted, not noticing that I'd left my body. I looked at what I'd become, lying limp as a rag doll on a leather couch with a needle in my foot.

The sliding glass doors were open, the hanging vinyl blinds rattling in the salty sea wind. I moved out onto the balcony.

Three stories down, the scraggly grass was struggling to live in the white sand and pulverized shells, prevailing where it didn't belong. Ahead was the Atlantic Ocean, a blue abyss where all manner of life lived and fought and died, as oblivious of me as I was of them.

And, according to Warren Haggerty, every grain of sand on the beach or drop of water in that ocean contained an infinite number of universes, each of them containing an infinite number of galaxies, solar systems, planets, people, plants, butterflies and red-ass monkeys.

How many planets were in my body now?

Somewhere down there, a tiny little alien was looking up at his night sky and wondering what was out there. I wonder what he'd say if he knew it was just me, high on smack, too much of a pussy to face life sober.

Disgusted, I moved back into the apartment where Salomé was having a cigarette, just starting to realize my body wasn't breathing.

I startled the shit out of her, bolting upright suddenly and tearing the syringe out of my foot, throwing it across the room. I snatched Salomé's cigarette and sucked on it like a starving baby at its mother's tit. The sensation of my heart kicking back on was dizzying and sparks danced in my eyes. The awareness of life all around me, carrying on with or without me, was unnerving enough to start beads of sweat trickling down my forehead.

Salomé sat stunned in her swiveling office chair, staring at me, her fingers still in the attitude of holding the cigarette I had taken. I ignored her as I tried to calm myself. A small glob of paint dropped off the end of the paintbrush she held in her other hand, falling to splatter unnoticed on the floor.

"Yunno something, Sal?" I asked eventually.

She raised her eyebrows at me inquiringly.

"It's about time I grew up."

I rose from the couch unsteadily and walked around the coffee table to the easel. The painting was almost finished, and by any standards, it was brilliant. The blue-black of the bruises on my limbs contrasted with the small red track marks, and the skin was pale and sickly. The bright cornrows on the black leather couch, plus the sports bra and tiny cutoff jeans also helped the red-white-and-blue theme.

The syringe needed work, and my finger and toenails had not been painted silver yet. Aside from that, it was disturbing enough to be very good. I was determined then never to be seen this way again, by anyone.

"I'm going to Diabolique tonight," I said.

"Getting your old job back?"

"Hell no. You don't see animals paying to see each other get naked. You don't see dogs looking at pictures of cats."

She frowned and shook her head to clear it.

"What?"

"Never mind. I'm going to sell off all my dance stuff, and the rest of the H, if I can. I've got no use for it anymore."

"This I've got to see," she said.

"You want to come? Good, you can drive me."

I took a shower, put on simple jeans, a t-shirt, and sneakers, and hid the heroin in my dance bag, buried under my outfits and various stacks and heels. I almost didn't recognize myself in the mirror as I put on the barest minimum of makeup.

I decided to stop by at the hospital with flowers for Layla after going to Diabolique, and decided on orchids. Lots of orchids.

"We're taking your car," Salomé said. "I always wanted to drive it."

"Sure, just give me a minute to record my day."

"I'm glad I don't keep a diary," she muttered. "Why have all that evidence written down in one place? Too dangerous."

"Maybe someday I'll turn it into a book."

"Yeah, like anyone'll want to read your abortion of a life."

Dear Diary,

On the radio, Filter shrieked a eulogy to the guy who blew his brains out at the podium at a press conference. It was the swing remix and we made sure all of downtown heard it. My car stereo is capable of volume levels exceeding "excessive." I have rattled the windows at the Wendy's drive-thru. If they'd parked my Mustang outside of Noriega's fortress during that siege in the Eighties, he'd have shot himself in the mouth. Heads turned on the sidewalk as we passed.

Old people gave us the finger.

We pulled into the parking lot at Diabolique in front of the mural of Betty Page, larger than life in her devil suit. I left the heroin in the secret gun compartment under my back seat, and brought the dance bag in with me.

Inside, the muscle-head bouncer whose name I've never bothered to learn did a double-take when we walked through the door. "I didn't know this town was big enough for two of you," he said.

We both ignored him, since speaking to lowly bouncers is beneath us even when they *don't* say stupid things. Salomé went to the bar and seated herself, getting the bartender to light her cigarette while I went into the back with my dance bag.

There were three girls I'd never spoken to doing their makeup and "powdering their noses." They looked up and suddenly the atmosphere changed.

There was an almost tangible anger at my intrusion. I always knew that they were jealous, treacherous, conniving bitches, but what stripper isn't? This wasn't like them, though.

"So, you're back, huh?" a voice behind me asked.

I turned, and was startled to see good ol' Ginger standing there in a black leather bustier, studded collar, g-string, and stiletto boots. No small change from the white lacy virgin look. But it was more than that. It was in her eyes and the way she stood there as if she considered herself my equal.

"Is Godiva around?" I asked.

"Nah. She got saved and doesn't dance anymore. Does ministry at that old church around the corner now. You come to take your crown back?"

Apparently, she'd somehow become the star of the show while I was gone, and didn't look happy about stepping back down. I'd have to put the bitch in her place if I was coming back to work, but since I wasn't, I just smiled.

"Nah, come to hang up my gloves, too. I'm selling everything. My two-pieces, stacks, and a little somethin-somethin' for whoever's needing. Good shit, too. Interested?"

"What, you got saved too?"

"Something like that."

She eyed the duffel bag for a moment. "You got that little silver outfit still?"

"Yeah, I got everything in here."

"I liked that one."

"Funny, so do all the marks who come in here. Want it?"

She seemed to think a minute, but I knew her better.

"C'mon out to my car, Scarlet. Too many eyes here."

I didn't miss this life, where you had to keep an eye out for anything at all times. A stripper would steal the fillings out of your teeth if you got too drunk, or the skirt off your ass if you looked away too long. One couldn't even do a deal in front of others, because you can never let a girl know what you've gotten out of it.

I followed Ginger out into the bar where Salomé was talking to some guy. She glanced over and saw me pass. I tried to tell her telepathically to watch my back, and crossed the room to the front door.

Ginger turned and said something into the bouncer's ear, and I went past her through the door into the evening. Working my cigarette pack out of my jeans with my free hand I turned my back to the breeze. I got a Red between my lips and was in the middle of lighting it when I noticed a car pull into the lot. An old car. A 1950 Chevy Deluxe.

Something exploded against my head and I hit the sidewalk, scraping the shit out of my elbow and forehead. A bright light danced in my eyes and I tasted blood. Something else hit me hard in the jaw and catapulted me up and backward against the grille of my own car. I fought the darkness that tried to swallow me, my brain reeling drunkenly, and opened my eyes.

Ginger's leg came up and her boot slammed into my face. My nose exploded in blood, my eyes filled with water and I screamed. I could feel my nose lying against my cheek and then that fucking boot hit my stomach just right, making me puke all over the front of my shirt and double up on the concrete. I heard her laughing at me.

"You like that, you dog's cunt?"

I opened my eyes. Behind Ginger was Salomé, smiling.

"Sal…" I groaned, spitting blood and vomit.

Ginger turned and saw my sister standing there.

"The fuck?" It took her way too long to realize we were twins.

Sal stooped and picked up my cigarette.

"Don't mind me," she said, taking a drag. "She can take care of herself."

Ginger hesitated, then cautiously kicked me in the head again, as if unsure of herself now. When she saw that she'd provoked no reaction she smiled wickedly and went to field goal my head. I rolled out of the way just in time, but was still in too much pain to fight back.

If only that bitch hadn't stole me. *Fuck!*

I caught something out of the corner of my eye. Lavender octopus tentacles passing into and out of sight between my car and the one next to it. The crack of the door appeared and stopped. Oh shit. Ohhhhh shit.

Ginger turned, distracted by the car. I saw the door open and a black-shoed, black-trousered leg step out. I looked up at Sal, calmly smoking my cigarette. The sounds echoed in my head, car doors clicking open and then softly chunking closed.

"Hey Sam," I heard Todd's voice say. I shut my eyes. Footsteps approached, two sets, and then I heard Rabbit's voice.

"We've been looking for you everywhere."

"I just bonded out of jail, in case you were interested," Todd said. "Seems somebody we know works for the police."

"So, how've you been?" Rabbit asked, sounding too friendly.

"You'll never guess who I met in jail," Todd said. "This guy named Casey. You know anybody named Casey, Sam?"

I opened my eyes, swallowing hard. They were looking at Salomé. They were standing right there, Todd on one side of her, and Rabbit's four hundred dollar shoes right in front of me. They were looking at Salomé. Not me.

"This guy says he knows you. Told me all kinds of things. Very interesting stuff, Sam. You want to guess what he said?"

Salomé very calmly looked at her watch and was about to say something when I saw Rabbit's hand reach behind his back, up under his Alfani black leather jacket with the lapels like a suit coat, and reappear holding a James Bond Walther PPK with obligatory silencer

"Wait! She's my twin sister! She's innocent!"

At least, that's what I meant to say.

My mouth just wouldn't make the words. Red and yellow strings dangled from my swollen lips, dripping from my face. My head throbbed.

I reached out and touched Rabbit's leg, but he didn't seem to notice. I was choked, out of breath, my throat tight with fear, and the words came out as little more than a wet croak. But maybe a little part of me didn't want to stop him. Maybe a little part of me wanted her to die instead of me.

Then I panicked.

"Wait!" I screamed, just as the arm extended and Sal turned to run, her eyes full of terror like a mere mortal's.

Click!

My sister's body jerked half around.

Clickclickclickclickclick her chest exploded as bullets tore through her, ripping her insides apart and splattering them on the side of the building. Ejected shell casings rained down and clattered on the concrete in front of me. Salomé's body twisted in the air, scattering flying ropes of blood, and fell.

Her eyes were on mine when her head hit the sidewalk hard enough to fracture her skull, but she didn't even blink. She just stared at me with her dead gray eyes.

I heard Rabbit mutter "Sorry, honey. Wrong place, wrong time."

Click! And Ginger crumpled against the wall and slid to her knees, leaving a slash of blood and brains on Betty Page's thigh, then fell forward onto her face in front of me. One of her eyes was a gushing socket, and the other just stared out at nothing. I puked again.

"Whoa, hey! Watch the shoes!"

"Jesus, she's in a world of hurt," Todd said.

"That's her problem."

"Put her out of her misery?"

"Nah, I just did her enough of a favor."

Their footsteps receded, the car doors opened and shut, and I spared one glance as the tentacles appeared again and vanished. The engine roared and they were gone.

I crawled on my belly, slowly and painfully, leaving a trail of blood and vomit like some kind of ghastly slug. It took an eternity to get to Salomé's side and dig her cell phone out of her purse. I flipped it open and tried to focus my eyes on it, punching the buttons. It rang distantly.

"Nine-one-one, what's your emergency?"

My mouth was full of blood.

I garbled pathetically.

The bitch hung up on me.

I dialed again. I punched the wrong buttons and had to try a third time.

"Nine-one-one, what's your emergency?"

"Ambulance!" I shouted.

"What's your location please?"

"Trace the goddamn call!"

I dropped the phone and collapsed. I don't know how long I lay there.

It may have only been minutes, but when every second takes an hour to tick by a minute seems like forever. It occurred to me eventually that them tracing a cell phone wouldn't lead anyone here, but a Good Samaritan-type loser coming out of the door went back in to call the police for me. After finding the phone again and turning it off, I tried to put my nose back on, but it hurt so bad I cried. Years of coke and crystal meth had left me with a deviated septum, so my beautiful nose was just a shapeless bloody mass.

Sal was making little gurgling noises, gas bubbling up through the holes in her body. Her eyes looked like bullet-holes in thick glass, spidery-gray cracks radiating from the oblivion black of her pupils. I wept like a little girl.

I awoke in the glaring sterile whiteness of a hospital room. A nurse with a kindly face was bending over me, gently shaking my shoulder. She had crow's feet and a big nose, but her voice was soft and caring. I felt very, very stoned.

"Rise and shine, sleepy-head."

I smiled weakly.

"We need to know your name and if you have insurance."

"Where's my sister?" I asked, struggling to speak. I could see how swollen my own face was in corners of my eyes, and my voice sounded thick.

"Oh dear, was one of them your sister?"

82

Tears welled in my eyes. The nurse looked sad for me.

"Both of the other girls had passed on before we got there. I'm sorry. The police will want to speak to you about that when you're feeling better. In the meantime, you might have to have some reconstructive surgery. I'm so sorry. They hurt you pretty bad."

I stared at my reflection in her speckled blue eyes, trying to make out just how bad it really was. Finally, I answered, my voice cracking as fresh tears started streaming down.

"My driver's license was in my purse along with my insurance card. There's a picture of me and my sister in there you can use. I'm the pretty one."

"Okay, sweetie. We have the number of a nice detective who's holding onto that stuff. It was a crime scene, you know. But we'll get it. What is your name, dear?"

"Salomé Brennan."

"Oh, that's pretty."

"Could you find out what room Layla Magiera is in for me?"

"Who?"

"I brought her in the other night. Saturday. Gun shot wound."

"Oh dear. So, this is a regular thing for you?"

"What?"

"Girls getting shot. What kind of trouble are you into?"

"The big kind."

She looked away, checked my IV just to be doing something, and looked back.

"Maybe I should tell you about Jesus Christ," she said.

My sister's insurance would pay for everything, so I signed everything the hospital gave me to sign and let them put my face back together. I don't know how long I was there. I also, for sentimental reasons, paid to have my sister buried in the cemetery I sometimes haunted. It was her money I used to do it anyway, so I figured I might as well show her some measure of respect.

A detective came and asked me about the shooting, and who beat me, and I told him all about me and Ginger. But when we got to the shootings all I did was shrug.

"I assume it was a drive-by, or something."

"No, the shots were point-blank."

"I'm sorry. I didn't see who it was."

"How can you not have seen it? They killed your sister."

"I know." You fucking retard. Master of the obvious, we got here.

"Or were you too whacked out on smack to see straight?"

"What?"

"What?" he mimicked my voice with a wide-eyed innocent expression.

"Who the fuck do you think you're talking to?" I demanded.

"A junkie stripper. Am I wrong?"

"I quit all that."

"Uh-huh, right. That's why you've got track marks on your leg."

"Are you going to arrest me?"

"For being an addict?"

"Yeah."

"No."

"Then get the fuck out of my room."

I put my hand on my forehead, stroked the mummy wrappings that covered my face, feeling dizzy. He was still standing there, a tiny smile curving his lips. It occurred to me that maybe I'd seen him somewhere before. Most likely down at the pig station during booking for one thing or another. I know I knew that smile.

"So, you're telling me there's no way you can identify the shooters? Even by voice?"

I was about to scream at him, but my irritation left abruptly, like a record skipping inside my head. What did he say? I looked at him a moment, trying to read his mind.

"What are you afraid of? You think they'll come get you if you finger them? We can protect you, you know."

"Why did you say 'they' just now? Why did you say 'shooters'?"

He frowned. I smiled.

"Why do you think it was more than one? And why do you think they spoke?" I could see him stutter in his mind, trying to backtrack. Then he grinned wide, shaking his head.

"When's the real detective going to show up?" I asked. He put on that wide-eyed innocent look again, mock indignant. Who, me?

"Are you suggesting that I am not who I say I am?"

"You didn't even show me a badge, did you?"

"Shucks. Now I have to kill you." He winked.

"You tell who sent you that he may have saved my life. They showed up in the nick of time and I'm grateful. Even if I did see

84

who pulled the trigger and sent my whore sister to Hell, I'd never tell. You tell him that, Detective."

"You're all right, you know that?"

"Yeah, I do." And you're not a bad bartender.

I asked them time and again where Layla was and they either didn't bother coming back or said she'd never been here. I got hysterical eventually, having lost my patience reminding them that I'd come in screaming with her in my arms. Half carrying, half dragging her along, crimson smears of her blood all over me and on the floor.

Finally my Jesus-freak nurse came in and sat with me. Her eyes were very kind and her voice very gentle. She took my hand and I prepared myself to hear of Layla's death. My throat closed and my stomach soured.

"I think the girl you're looking for is one we had in here for a few days. Pretty thing, a blonde girl."

"Yeah, a day or two before I got here."

"See, the problem was you gave us the wrong name."

"What do you—" Oh yeah. Duhhh.

Layla wasn't her name. Of course it wasn't.

"She was taken by some people to another hospital, where they're taking care of her. But I'm not allowed to say where."

"Please. It's very important. Please."

"I'm sorry, I can't. But she's gonna be all right."

"At least tell me her name, then. Please. Her real name."

"I wish I could. I'm sorry." She left.

At least I knew she was alive, unless the nurse just said that to comfort me. Doubtful. My Layla— or whatever her name was—had made it. At least I had that much. No face, no sister, no job, no girlfriend, but at least she was alive. At least she was still on this planet somewhere.

And that was a start.

The mummy wrappings came off a few days later. The look on my nurse's face as she watched, her eyes lighting up like a child's when the Christmas lights come on, let me know better than a mirror could that I was gorgeous again. Then the mirror, and I saw myself as I'd been before drugs had taken their toll. Clean slate.

Warren Haggerty's head was as good as mine.

II

Dear Diary,

Today I moved all the stuff from my apartment into my sister's, told the landlord about "my" death, and collected the back rent. In my new digs, I sat back on the couch and looked around slowly, mentally redecorating. I'd have to leave things, for the most part, the way they were.

Taking over her life would be a lot easier if she'd kept a diary, but I could do without. At least she had a calendar, every square of which was filled up with scribbles, except for the day she died. The rest of the pertinent information I got from the seventy-something messages on her answering machine. I did a quick study, and by nightfall the only way to tell I wasn't Salomé Brennan was the pattern of pink scars on the back of my left hand. And the fact that I couldn't play the guitar worth a damn.

I made a tally of all the paintings, unframed in the closet, that were now mine to take credit for. I could even finish my portrait and see myself as I was the day I died. I had money, enough not to struggle, and now I had a career. Provided there was a market for shit like this.

The phone rang. Debating whether to answer it, I realized that eventually I'd have to, so I did.

"Domino's Pizza," I said cheerfully.

"Ha. Where you been?" a man's voice asked.

"The hospital. Where've *you* been?"

"The *hospital?* Why, what happened?"

He sounded genuinely upset.

"My sister got me beaten up by someone who thought I was her. Pretty bad. I just got out today."

"Jesus fuck!"

"Yeah, that's about how I felt about it, too. So, what's up?"

"Well, I was worried. You're never home, never answering the phone, so I thought, yunno, something *happened* to you. You weren't even at the jail so I've just been sitting here worrying about you. And here you were seriously hurt and I had no way of knowing and—"

"You could've tried the hospitals."

"Oh. Well, yeah, I could've. I guess."

"No big deal. I'm here."

86

"Look, Mama, I'm sorry about what happened that day—"

"Don't worry about it. I've forgotten the whole thing."

"Really?"

"Look, will you do something for me? I need to be pampered. I've had a real rough time. I need you right now a lot more than I need to hold a grudge, okay?"

"Yeah…" I could hear him, whoever he was, swell with joy.

"I want you to come over, as quick as you can. Bring a nice movie we can curl up on the couch together and ignore."

I could tell he wasn't used to Sal treating him this way at all. She always did a great job breaking boys in. Now this guy would be willing to bathe me with his tongue if I asked him to, and I probably would. He stuttered something in the affirmative and I hung up, pleased with myself.

In the closet I browsed the wealth of lingerie my sister had owned. Bargello, point de gaze, fimbria, furbelow, appliquéd lace, plicated selvage. Leather. Rubber. Spikes.

Mmmm. What kind of mood was I in?

To be honest, I didn't want handcuffs, whips, dildos, oils, or anything like that. I just wanted a good old-fashioned *fuck*. Something I've gone without for a very long time.

I couldn't wait.

An hour or so later Chad showed up with some girly movie and a pizza with crab and shrimp on it. From the word Go he was fawning all over me, always touching me possessively, always kissing up to me. It made me sick.

Good pizza, though. Mozzarella and cheddar and some kind of weird sauce that wasn't tomato or seafood. I ate almost all of it, I was so starved for real food. I'd gone so long being fed through a little needle in my arm that I might even have eaten vegetables if I'd had to.

Right now I was comparing this Chad guy to food, and he was rating somewhere around broccoli when I wanted a hot red steak.

He was attractive, sure, almost handsome, but whatever he had in looks was undermined by his total absence of dignity and pride. No matter how badly I wanted it, I wouldn't stoop to being ridden by this sniveling yes-man. Before I knew it, I was playing the same game with him that Sal was. I finished the last bite of my pizza, washed it down with a gulp of red wine he'd brought me, and rose, eyeing him with open contempt.

"So *that's* the way you came to see me?" I sneered.

He was wearing jeans and a t-shirt. A t-shirt, for Chrissake. A green-eyed pink piranha snarled on the left breast at the words "Hot Tuna." He was a surfer, too, apparently. He couldn't possibly be any good.

"What's wrong?" he asked, paling somewhat.

How pathetic. He could feel my approval of him slipping away and his body language registered anguish.

"You're taking me out tonight, and we're going someplace where you can't get in dressed like that. *Capisce?*"

"But I thought you wanted to be pampered," he whined.

"Have you ever known me to be pampered lying down?"

He could find no adequate answer, since there was none other than "Get lost, bitch" and he had a snowball's chance in Hell of mustering that kind of courage. Dipshit. Salomé must have really treated her men like stepdogs.

Eager little puppy that he was, he immediately came up with a way to please me. His eyes lit up.

"Mama, there's a great place now. You'll love it. It's never in the same location twice, and you have to be on a list to get in. You can bring one guest." He paused to emphasize how impressed I should be with: "I'm on the list."

"Really."

"Yeah. I've been there a few times, and it's even cooler than your sister's club was before it got busted. You know how the upstairs at Layla was? Well, the whole entire place is like that, only better. Much, much better."

"Really."

"Yeah, you'll love it, I promise."

"What's it called?" I asked, though I already knew.

"The Darkside," he said.

Sal had a great skirt suit in her closet, gray, that I wore with lacy white lingerie underneath, stockings and garter belt, like that hit woman in a movie I saw once. Only she didn't have fiery-red cornrows.

Chad had left and came back dressed appropriately, and since he'd mentioned a metal detector at the Darkside's front entrance I decided to leave my .38 at home. I was doing my war paint in the bathroom when Chad let himself in, calling for me, receiving no answer. My lipstick was infinitely more important than acknowledging him. When I came out of the bathroom he whistled and said I looked incredible, this sycophantic grin on his face.

"I know," I said smugly. "Light me a cigarette."

I found a large silver crucifix and chain and fastened it around my neck, filling the space between the lapels of the suit jacket. The lace just barely concealed what needed covering in order to be called clothing, and the cross was the finishing touch. I got my heels on, took the proffered cigarette, and looked at him for the first time.

Khakis, red button-down half opened, white ribbed undershirt, black belt, black shoes, black hair, black leather jacket. While it looked a little like a uniform, it wasn't bad. It needed its own finishing touch, though. I approached, took his chin between my forefinger and thumb, turned his head slightly, and kissed him on the cheek.

Stepping back, I looked at him now with my trademark on him—the whore red lipstick kiss— and smiled.

"Perfect."

We pulled into a parking lot four miles east of the middle of nowhere, in front of a warehouse. There were only twenty or thirty other cars there, but the night was young, and I wanted Rabbit to see me himself. When we stepped out into the twilight I frowned at the warehouse. No sign. No door man. No nothing. No way to tell what the building contained from its outside appearance. We walked around the side to a little door and Chad knocked once, a sharp rap that echoed out here in the silence.

A moment passed, and I noticed a security camera staring at us suspiciously from above. I looked up into the eye and blew it a kiss. The door opened and I was looking up at Blue Tick's baffled face. I smiled sweetly.

"Somebody said there was a party out here."

Tick looked at Chad, who showed him his ID. Shining his Mag-lite on the card, Tick inspected Chad and compared the faces, handed the card back and spoke into his CB.

"Chad Alvarez. F660-010-75-245-0."

He paused and looked at me strangely, then added "And guest."

A voice on the CB crackled something back at him. He nodded. Stepping aside, he held the door for us and we walked through a metal detector with an anti-bug system into a dark antechamber, where a girl took eighty dollars from Chad— forty for the both of us—pretty steep, but that was expected. She directed us to a door nearby, from which faint House music drifted, and we opened it.

The noise hit us in the face like a bucket of cold water, blasting through the doorway into the apparently sound-proofed room. Two guards stood on either hand, just inside, in black on black. I looked back at Tick, who was watching me as he raised his CB to speak into it again.

Chad took my hand and led me into the Darkside, into black velvet hangings, iron-railed walkways and black light. There were things hanging from the ceiling or perched in alcoves that glowed eerily in the fluorescents, and I reached up to touch one when it jerked and snarled its horrible demon face, dropping onto me. I shrieked and tripped over myself trying to get away, falling onto my ass with this shrilly squealing *thing* clawing at my face.

Chad grabbed it, tearing it off of me, and flung it away into the darkness where it sprouted wings and was gone. A glowing trail faded away in its wake.

"What the fuck was that! What the fuck was that thing!"

"A bat, Mama," Chad said soothingly.

"A *what?*"

"A bat. An albino bat."

"A fucking *bat?* What the fuck are bats doing in here?"

"I don't know, but when you're rolling they look really cool."

"It almost fucking ate me!"

"You were fine," he laughed. "It was just scared, is all."

"It was scared? *It* was scared? I'm about to have a fucking heart attack! Are there fucking *wolves* in here too?"

"No, but plenty of snakes."

"Snakes!"

"Big ones, too. Pythons. They glow real pretty just like the bats do. But you're not allowed to touch them."

He gave me a hand up, dusted me off even though I was fine, and led me through the shadows to the light. Nobody was dancing yet, but there were at least sixty or seventy people at the bar or around the dance floor. I recognized Enigro in the DJ booth, his green hair like a beacon.

The place was huge, with the black couches and roses from

Layla, but now instead of Grecian statues was something out of an H.R. Giger catalogue. Paintings of alien or robot women—or both—getting it on with each other, the "Passage" series with plumbing stuff that looked like vaginas, nightmarish landscapes. Hooks. Big meat hooks dangling from chains here and there. Huge spider webs made of chains. From where we stood we could see a maze of black panels in the distance, like cubicle walls, that had a dais at the center. Rabbit's sense of humor. People stumbling around trying to find their way to the VIP section, getting lost, drunk or rolling.

We made a bee-line for the bar where Detective Whatshisname looked up and recognized me.

Startled, but seeming pleasantly surprised, he came over and smiled, lighting my cigarette.

"You look great," he said.

"Thanks. They managed to put me back together again."

I felt a hand touch my shoulder and turned. I never knew the guy's name, but I was friendly with him and he liked me.

"Someone would like to say hello to you," he said.

I left Chad at the bar with instructions to negotiate the purchase of class A narcotics, and margaritas. Following the guard to a ladder, part of a camouflaged scaffold that had gone unnoticed until now, we climbed to a series of catwalks. Tier upon tier of them, crisscrossing, honeycombed the entire warehouse. Safety nets were strung beneath every other one.

The bottom tier had four catwalks converging on a central hub, and in that hub stood Todd Ferguson.

The guard motioned for me to go on alone, and I did, warily. I knew Todd had heard about my twin sister, so I shouldn't be worried. But I was.

"So you're the evil twin," he called. He eyed me appraisingly, then grinned. "There's a resemblance all right, but no one could ever confuse you with Sam."

"And you are...?" I was now face to face with him.

"I was a friend of your sister's. I'm sorry to hear about what happened." His expression was one of genuine concern.

"That makes one of us," I said, startling him.

"What do you mean?"

"That bitch had been a thorn in my ass all my life."

"Is that a fact?" He was amused now, enjoying this.

"It is. So, what can I do for you?"

"Nothing special. Just wanted to welcome you here, offer my condolences, and ask you how you knew about this place."

"Ahh, Sam probably never told you that most of your upstairs clientele came from me. My lawyer friends, my doctor friends, my *banker* friends. So of course I'd know where you went when you moved."

"No, I don't think Sam ever mentioned that. So, what else you know about us that we don't?"

"You'd be surprised. I have her diary."

"What?"

"You heard me."

"Her diary."

"As in 'little book she wrote everything down in.' *Everything.*"

"Is this blackmail?" he asked, his smile gone, his eyes cold.

"Of course not. Think of it more as a resumé."

"What?"

"I want a job."

"You want a job?"

"I want a job."

He blinked at me slowly, then looked around as if trying to locate a hidden camera. It gave me time to consider my next tack.

"Part of my job would be telling you how to find Zack Scalisi, whom I have entertained on several occasions."

His eyes went wide. Poor Todd never had that much of a poker face. He fumbled in his pocket for a clove and I lit it for him.

"Do you remember that night on the beach, you and I went night surfing with some of your friends, and we fucked in the water and we both got stung by a jellyfish?"

The cigarette fell as his mouth dropped open, spraying a shower of sparks on the steel mesh of the catwalk.

"Oopsie," I said, bending down to retrieve it. I stood and took a drag, tasting tea leaves, and blew the smoke at him.

"See? Everything's in that diary. Truly an interesting read."

"Go have yourself a drink or twelve," he said, rallying himself. "I need to talk this over with someone."

"Yeah, say hi to Rabbit for me."

Chad was leaning at the bar, trying not to look like his date had run off somewhere and left him all alone. A margarita was sitting on the bar next to a black plate with eight white lines cut. His own drink was one gulp short of empty, his expression pretty much the same. I joined him and took a drink, startled by how good it was. Chad gestured to the bartender/detective that he wanted another round, and swallowed the last of his.

"Smile, sunbeam," I said, nudging him in the ribs.

"We're too early," he muttered, frowning at the small cliques of people.

"Well, I wanted to talk to somebody."

"Somebody, huh?" He looked hurt, resentful for some reason.

"All right, what's eating you, Gilbert?"

"Was it the same somebody from last time?"

"What last time?"

"You know." I didn't. Shit. I knew this would happen. I winged it.

"Oh, *that*. Are you still whining about that? I'd forgotten by now."

"Funny, I thought you were gonna remember her for the rest of your life. That's what you said, wasn't it? The finest thing on earth since you?"

"Oh, her. I was thinking of someone else."

"What? You mean there was more than one?"

"Calm down there, baby. I'm having fun."

"You're something else, you know that?"

"I've heard." I picked up the dollar roll from the coke plate.

"Hold my hair for me, sweetie," I asked.

He gathered up my dangling cornrows and held them out of the way while I did two of the lines.

Mmmm. Good stuff. I gave him the roll.

"No," I said, while he took his turn. "I was up there talking to a guy who might give me Simone's job here. He's talking it over with the boss man right now. Relax, honey."

"That's the third nice thing you've called me in under a minute," he said, sniffing the stray grains up and straightening.

"So?"

"So, who are you and what have you done with my girlfriend?"

I laughed and took the roll from him, giving him my hair again.

"I killed her and stole her identity."

"Good. I like you a lot better."

After about an hour, we were sitting on a couch with our

drinks, talking. The table had roses just like at Layla, but white this time, glowing in the blacklights the way the bats and snakes were. Spilled cocaine, too, was pretty easy to find.

I had wanted to try and go through the maze, just for the hell of it, but Chad said it was impossible. That's what really piqued my curiosity, and I was determined to do it at some point that night. Perhaps I'd take some X first.

Rabbit appeared suddenly, startling the shit out of me, but I think I disguised it pretty well. He looked very different, his hair dyed black and artificially graying at his temples. He'd grown a goatee and dyed it also, salt and pepper. His face and hands (and I wondered what else) were considerably darkened by skin pigment, like what body-builders use for the after pictures of supplement ads—along with oil and vertically lined backdrops to enhance the difference. A casual observer would have been fooled.

"Miss Brennan, I presume?" he bowed slightly.

"That's Queen Brennan to you, peasant."

"Ha! You're Simone's sister, all right. And I recognize you," he said, turning to Chad. "You come here often, don't you?"

"Yeah, I used to go to Layla since it opened. The best club I'd ever seen, apart from this one."

If anyone liked flattery, it was Rabbit. The little psycho thrived on it.

"Care to join us?" I asked, moving over to make room on the couch, patting a seat cushion next to me. A barmaid was coming over with more drinks.

"Oh, no, I couldn't. Way too busy."

"Lies. Sit down. I have heard all about you, yunno."

"Really? Good things, I hope."

"Oh no, not at all."

The barmaid set our drinks down and I got her attention.

"Excuse me, could you bring one more for the Badger, or Star-nose Mole, or whatever this guy's name is?"

She turned uncertainly to her boss.

"They're having margaritas, Mr. Haggerty."

"Mmm, no. I think we'll have a bottle of Dom. We still have some, don't we? Or did Whatsher-name drink it all?"

"We still have some, sir."

"Good. Thank you, Tracy." She scurried off, and I patted the couch next to me again, inviting Rabbit to sit. He did.

94

"So what's your name, now? Salami?"

"Salomé."

"Sa-lo-may?"

"Yes. Close enough. And you're Weasel."

"Rabbit. What kind of a name is Salami?"

"It's from the Bible. Salomé was a dancing girl who made Herod cut off John the Baptist's head and bring it to her on a plate at this party."

"Is that so?"

"Uh-huh. Is it true they call you Rabbit because of *Cool Hand Luke*? Ya got rabbit in yer blood?"

He grinned his crooked grin at me. "That's part of it."

"Or because you fuck like one?"

"What I do in the bedroom, stays in the bedroom."

"And if you do it in the kitchen?"

He laughed. I offered him the plate of coke, our second.

"Don't ever touch the stuff," he said.

"You're kidding."

"Hell, no. That shit's poison. If you want to stay in business, you can't risk being loyal to anything but your business. Not a woman, not a drug, not anything. But knock yourself out."

"I will, thank you. So, do you even roll at your own club?"

"Of course not. I have to be in control at all times in case something goes wrong."

"That's terrible."

"Not really. I love being alert and in charge. If anything happens, I can take care of it immediately. I sure can't trust anyone else to do it."

"I heard that."

"So, Salomé, I was wondering if you and I could talk privately."

"Sure. Get lost, Chad."

My pseudo-date hesitated momentarily, and much to Rabbit's amazement, sighed heavily, got up, and left with his drink.

"What's on your mind, Rabbit?" I asked. He laughed, unable to believe his eyes, and I allowed myself a little smirk.

"You sure are something!" he said.

"Yeah, I've been accused of that before."

He laughed some more, then: "Todd says you have a proposition."

"Maybe."

"Well, hum a few bars."

"Okay. First of all, my sister was going out with your woman, who was undercover for DEA, FBI, I dunno. Somebody. Point is, she found out and kept it from you. Now the narc is in a hospital under protective custody. Only I can find out where. Second, there's a guy named Scalisi that I hear you don't like. Again, only I can tell you where to find him. And third, I can expand your drug trade expo-fucking-nentially."

"Go on."

"I just want to take over my late sister's job."

"Uh-huh. And I know this isn't a trap how?"

"I'll cross my heart on it."

"Oh, sure. That's good enough for me."

"Uh, all right. I'll be willing to kill somebody if that'll convince you. A cop! I can't kill a cop if I'm a cop, right?"

"Er, no. They frown on that."

"Perfect! Bring me a cop and I'll shoot him in the face."

"No, if you'd shoot just anybody, you'd probably shoot me."

"I wouldn't shoot anybody. I was kidding."

"Well, I hope so. Killing people is illegal here."

"That didn't stop you from chopping up Ray Valanga."

"Uh-huh. Hmmm. You read that in Simone's diary, also?"

"Yep."

"I'd like to see that diary."

"So would a lot of people."

"I don't like those kinds of things written about me."

"Rabs, we're getting away from the important stuff. Remember that when the police—and your bartender over there—questioned me about the shooting at Diabolique, I told them I saw nothing. If I was going to say anything to anyone, that was the time. But, like I said before: you may have saved my life. My sister stood there and watched an enemy of hers kick the shit out of me, thinking I was her. The cunt that was beating me was so whacked out of her mind that she was capable of anything. Now my enemy is dead, and so is the bitch that made my life hell since we were little girls. I owe you, and if anyone knows how to return a favor, it's me, so don't worry about that stupid book anymore."

Our bottle of champagne arrived in a bucket of ice with two flutes. Tracy opened the bottle skillfully and poured our drinks, asking Mr. Haggerty if there'd be anything else.

"No, thank you, cutie." He dismissed her with a wave of his hand and we clinked glasses. The *tink!* of the flutes rang over the music playing, and we drank without toasting Evil. We drank in silence until our glasses were empty and he refilled them.

"Got a cigarette, Red?" he asked.

I gave him one, got one for myself, and we lit them at the same time from one flame in a kind of weird kiss. I watched him smoke thoughtfully.

Looking away, I noticed Chad watching us from the bar, seething with jealousy. I winked at him to reassure him, and his hunched shoulders relaxed—almost melted.

"Tell me about your drug plan," Rabbit said.

"Okay. You make MDMA, which is great, and your weed and coke are top notch. But your heroin leaves room for improvement."

"I haven't gotten any complaints."

"No, because it's good. But I can make it great. See, you serve China White, while I have Black Tar. Also, I can show you how to make tons of things you can add to your menu."

"Such as?"

"DMT, for starters."

"Who?"

"Dimethyltryptamine."

"Oh."

"Made it from the alkaloid crystal psilocybin."

"As in psilocybic mushrooms?"

"Yep. Sell it in a shroom cocktail. I've got a recipe that's pretty good. Make it at the bar, sell it as a Mushroom Cloud."

"I like it. What else?"

"Well, there's a wide variety of natural things that produce different kinds of trips. Add extracts of them to your Ecstasy to make new kinds of rolls. Call 'em Trolls. Stuff like belladonna. Morning glory seeds. The milky sweat secreted on the backs of bufo toads. Angel trumpets."

"Where will I get these things?"

"You won't, I will. I know the Rainbow People."

"The who?"

"The Rainbow People. They live in the woods of rural Florida. Modern-day hippies, living off of the bark of trees and trading natural drugs to people like me for canned food, pizza, and supplies. I give them stuff like soap, lighter fluid, pork n' beans, and they gather all the right stuff for me."

"Cool."

"Yeah. They're the nicest people you will ever meet. I lived with them for a little while once, when I was on the run for something. But bathing in rivers and eating tree bark isn't really my idea of the good life."

"I hear you."

"I can also show you how to make geltabs."

"I know how to make geltabs."

"Not like these, you don't. My way has two variations: killer visuals and mindfuck, and killer visuals with almost no disorientation at all. You can function reasonably well without missing out on great hallucinations. It'll sell like hotcakes."

"Okay, what else?"

"Crack."

"Hell no. No way I'm going to get mixed up in that."

"Hold on, hear me out. I can make regular crack, which'll get people addicted and hand over everything they own, but gradually over a period of time. I can also make you a kind of supercrack with ammonia, that will knock you on your ass, and when you get up you'll give me the deed to your house for a bag of it. We'll be millionaires in two nights with the clientele you've got."

"No. Fuck no. Anyone who deals in crack is going to the deepest pit in Hell. I'm not interested."

"Suit yourself."

"But the rest of what you say sounds good. I especially like the Trolls. With all the varieties of X we have, adding different kinds of hallucinogens would probably start a whole new league of drugs. Mix n' match. We could come out with all kinds of things. We've got K and GHB to experiment with also. Trolls...did you make that up yourself?"

"Yeah," I lied.

Rabbit went off to attend to his duties and I went to Chad's restless side at the bar, bringing the rest of the coke with me. House music and lights are not something you can sit still and talk around for very long, so we did up the last of the coke and went out onto the floor. Whatever his faults, Chad was a great dancer. The strobe light pummeled my eyes, stabbing the blackness with thrusts of white. Figures moving in its eerie flash went jerking by, vanishing, and reappearing.

The club was filling up, and I saw many of the old familiar faces from Layla. My lawyer, of course, and his secretary made an appearance. I couldn't say hello to them because I was my sister now, but they didn't notice me anyway. The secretary looked so much better out of her disguise. Hair down and limbs sparkling with glitter, she looked incongruous to Burt Goniff, attorney at law, who still looked like a lawyer even in his party clothes.

Must've been the comb-over.

I went back to the bar for some tequila and asked Jason the detective/bartender how to get up into the VIP. He laughed and said you had to find your way. Good luck. Bringing the shots over to Chad, I told him we were going into the maze. After downing his shot, it seemed like a great idea.

Some people were stumbling out of it just as we got there.

"Do *not* go in there," a drunk woman warned us. We pushed past them and followed the black panel walls—about ten feet high, or so—to the first intersection. Taking the left branch brought us to a turn, then another, then a four-way split. There were some people straight ahead, so we joined them, curious about their weird behavior. They were stooping, straightening, swaying, making stupid faces, and laughing hysterically.

Coming up next to them, we found that certain areas in the maze had those goofy carnival fun-house mirrors that made you fat, skinny, or both, and if you were drunk enough, or high, this was the source of limitless entertainment. We left them to it.

Continuing on, taking random turns, we came upon four girls kissing and sucking on one very lucky guy. Catching sight of his face, I was surprised he was so ugly. Chad chuckled when he saw my face wrinkle up with disgust.

"He must make them laugh or something."

"Or he's rich," I said, slightly more cynical, but probably right.

No matter where we went, we were walking in circles. If we doubled back and took a different route, we'd inevitably run into the same mirror or make-out session. Chad was right. The damned thing was impossible. Somehow, finding our way back out was rather easy. Regardless, the feeling of being lost stuck with me as we wandered back out into the club.

Those damned bats were everywhere, glowing eerily, unable to sit still because the music was deafening. Flitting this way and that in the lights, they looked like ghosts with nothing to haunt. Screw DEA and ATF, if PETA ever caught wind of this, the place would go down in flames. While I watched them, something else startled me.

People high above us were leaping from the catwalks and falling into the safety nets, rolling around helplessly. It looked like fun. They were shouting things at the dancers below that went unheard, and tussling playfully with one another.

Rabbit came up behind me, tapping my left shoulder while standing on my right side so I looked like an idiot turning this way and that. I gave him a shove and he laughed at me.

"Couldn't find your way, huh?" he asked.

"What, the maze? No, how do you get to the end?"

"It's a secret."

"You dick. And what's going on up there?"

"Oh, those nets? They're great, you should try them. You can't take drinks up on the catwalks because we don't want people pouring them on anyone below, but go up there and jump, you only fall about twenty feet, tops, but it's fun. Last week, we had a couple got busy up there, fucking doggy-style right above the dance floor, and they just *went to town*. People were cheering them on and we put a spotlight on them. Luckily, the guy didn't pull out and shoot it on anybody. That could've gotten ugly."

"Yeah, I'll say. You put all this together today?"

"Yep. And we'll take it all down tomorrow. We close at about noon, dismantle everything, and we're gone."

"Sounds like too much trouble."

"Maybe. But I'm not going to have a repeat of what happened to my last club."

That's what you think.

"We've got bug detectors on the front entrance, so if anyone comes in wearing a recording device of any kind, an alarm goes off. There's a separate one for guns, and the whole thing is sound-proof so you can't hear anything from the outside. Security's so tight that nothing can go wrong."

"You wanna knock on wood, Rabbit? Might be a good idea."

"Nah, I'm tempting Fate. Living dangerously."

"Lemme ask you something."

"Shoot."

"Did you and Simone ever fuck?"

"No..."

"I'm surprised. You're just her type."

I looked toward the dance floor and did a double-take. She looked away. For a second I had locked eyes with a girl and felt something pass between us, but it was probably just the coke playing tricks on me.

She was hot, though. Curly dark hair, almost vampire-white skin, what looked from here like slanted almond eyes, and an incredible body. She was dressed in black go-go boots and a short iridescent purple dress, its Celtic knotwork design glimmering as she danced.

God *damn*, she was gorgeous.

I turned to Chad and told him to get some X.

"Do I look like I'm made of money?"

I think he startled himself more than me, and I watched him cringe the tiniest bit, biting the words back. He and Rabbit both looked like they expected me to go batshit, but I was pleased that he had said No to me. Where Salomé would've beaten him down with a severe tongue-lashing, I smiled and decided to undo her training. Chad had been a pet long enough.

"You're right, lover. I'll get it."

He, like Todd, looked around for the hidden camera. Bewildered, but pleased, he seemed like he might start fawning all over me like he did before. Determined not to let it happen, I assumed a stern look.

"You've definitely got to stand up for yourself more often. I expect a good spanking when we get home."

I sauntered off to the bar, hearing Rabbit bust a gut laughing behind me. I had decided to build Chad's confidence, and I was going to start tonight.

At the bar I got three tabs of Biohazard, this variety of Ecstasy that makes me exceptionally horny. Hell if I know why they call it that, because when you think about it, making someone horny is the opposite of being hazardous for Bio. Reminds me of this gay pride thing I went to, called the Rhythm of Life. As much as I like practicing homosexuality, I can't help but notice that it is very much *against* the rhythm of life, since no babies are ever going to come out of it.

Speaking of which...that girl was looking at me again. I went around the square of the bar without taking my eyes off of hers. She stopped dancing and came toward me. There was something haunt-ingly familiar about her, but I was sure I'd never seen her before. No, I knew her. I definitely knew her, but it was dark, and I'd been drinking.

Face to face, I held up one of the tabs and she took it like a communion wafer, her lips parting, tongue coming out just the tini-est bit. I opened my mouth to speak, but she put a finger to my lips to shush me. Her eyes were pale, pale blue, with a dark ring around the outside, strikingly beautiful. Her skin was even whiter up close.

She leaned in close and put her warm cheek against mine, her plum-colored, drowning victim lips parting to whisper in my ear.

"In one hour, meet me in the maze."

Usually, I'm the one that gives the orders.

I blinked, and she was gone. I stared stupidly into space, una-ble to convince myself that what just happened really had happened. Was she even real? She'd vanished without a trace. I took my tab, and went back to Chad to give him his.

An hour later, the world shook. Shuddering waves of ecstasy crashed into and through me and there was no way to conceal what I was feeling. I felt my body fill with a tingling joy and my feet were no longer on the floor. I'd overcome gravity in a matter of seconds. I looked at my watch, and felt myself getting wet. It was about that time.

I walked slowly, with as much dignity as I could muster, away from Chad without saying a word. No one was near the maze, the majority of the people dancing on the floor and the bar or making out on the couches. I glanced up at the people on the catwalks and falling into the nets and gasped, my eyes arrested by the play of lights.

With an effort, I remembered my mission and kept walking, feeling the dampness between my thighs and trying not to smile. I entered the maze cautiously, stumbling somewhat. I had no idea where she'd be. My nipples got rock hard with anticipation. I took the same corridor as the last time, on a hunch.

"Marco!" I called out, giggling. "Maaaaaarco!"

"Polo!" I heard faintly. My heart quickened.

"Marco?"

"Polo!"

It came from the right, on the other side of the wall. I hurried to the bend, turned, and searched for another corridor that led toward her voice.

"Marco!"

"Polo!"

I turned sharply and ran toward it, taking a wrong turn, doubling back and finding the right one. I passed the row of mirrors and checked my reflections. Damn, I looked strange. No time for that. One turn after another, frantic choice after frustrated, frantic choice. I felt shivers go through me.

"Marco!"

No answer.

"Marco?"

I turned a corner.

There she was.

We didn't say a word, just came together, our mouths open, and I took her hot pink tongue between my lips and sucked on it like it was a small cock. Her hands and mine were busy, fumbling and caressing, raising goosebumps on each other, kissing fiercely. She unbuttoned my suit jacket and exposed the white lace underneath. I slipped one of the straps of her dress off her shoulder and pulled the fabric down over the swell of a pale breast. Her coral-pink nipple stood at attention as I cupped her breast and kneaded it.

She broke away from my lips and kissed my neck, her hot tongue like fire, her breath hard and fast on my throat, as her hands slid into my jacket and down my hips, thighs, under the hem of my skirt and back up again. My short gray skirt climbed with her soft hands, and I felt cool air touch me where I was dripping like candle wax, hot down the insides of my thighs.

I felt her stiffen and I broke away, looking behind me. Rabbit was standing there, eyes wide. There was a thick bulge down the leg of his black trousers, and I was surprised he was so big. I went to him in a few quick steps and put my hand in his movie star hair, ruffling it, my other hand lightly stroking him. I felt him jump at my touch, throbbing. I took him by the hand and led him over to the girl. She was wide-eyed and doubtful, but I kissed her hesitation away.

"Rabbit," I sighed. "Show us how to get in the VIP."

He didn't answer right away, so I reached down and pulled his zipper open. He didn't wear any underwear, and my hand found him trapped down one leg of his pants. I repeated myself.

"Back this way," he said. I pulled my hand out and gestured for him to lead on. Taking the girl's arm, we followed him through the dark halls to the spot where the ugly guy had been getting his, and he looked back at me with a cunning smile.

Pushing hard on one of the panels, it swung inwards, revealing a secret passage. He ushered us through, closing the panel behind him. The VIP dais was right there, with steps leading up to two couches and a small private bar.

We hurried up the steps. The whole club could see us where we were, but that was part of the fun. I grabbed Rabbit's belt and pulled him by it toward a couch. The girl waited there, and when we got to her I turned my back to Rabbit and pulled him against me.

I could feel him, now readjusted in his pants, pressing through the fabric against me. I grabbed the girl and pulled her to my lips. Smothering each other with fierce, hot kisses, our hands found their way to each other's panties, finding them wet and peeling them away from burning mounds and small thatches of hair. Her fingers brushed my lips and my back arched sharply, an animal groan bursting from me.

Rabbit's lips tugged gently on my earlobe, then traced the ridges of my ear, making all of my small hairs stand on end. As I fumbled under the girl's dress, my other hand snaked behind me and into Rabbit's open fly, forcing him away from me as I found his hot throbbing cock.

I pulled it free and dug into the other girl at the same time, feeling both rock violently in my hands. Their grips on me tightened. She thrust her hips forward, trying to take my fingers in further. I delved deeper and curled my fingers back, finding the velvety wetness of her G-spot.

She gasped, and I pushed her gently down onto the couch, pulling Rabbit after me. The girl's hand freed my breasts from my lingerie, and her lips and tongue found my nipples, teething and sucking hungrily, as the fingers of her other hand brushed against me under my skirt.

I pushed her dress down over her high, firm white breasts, which shuddered with her heaving breaths, and slid my jacket off my shoulders.

The lights danced on her skin and in her curly black hair, a slight frown creasing her forehead, her mouth open. I definitely know her from somewhere.

Rabbit was one of those men who kept growing, swollen and purple and angry-looking by now. It burned against me, and I wanted so badly to put him in, but this was such a sweet torture for all three of us. I felt his hands, gripping my ass, slide around beneath me, his questing fingers coming closer, until he'd found my anus. I clenched my jaw, baring my teeth, hoping he'd do it, hoping he'd slip in.

And he did. Waves of ecstasy coursed through me, the drug taking me places sex alone never can. Slippery with my juices, his finger slid into me easily and I rode it, vaguely noticing his other hand making its way to the girl's ass, concealed by her bunched-up dress. Her breasts were high and perfect, bouncing against mine. My lips were on hers, our mouths open, but we weren't kissing, just moaning and gasping, breath hot and sweet.

Her tongue snaked out briefly to touch mine, but it took too much effort to kiss for long. She choked back a scream of pleasure, her whole body shivering as wetness spurted out of her, soaking Rabbit's cock and trousers, making him even more slippery. She put her arms around me, holding me tightly as she rode the waves of her orgasm, crying out as she clung to me.

Tears streamed from her eyelids, scrunched tight under thin scowling dark brows, warm and salty, coursing down her cheek and mine into the corners of our mouths. Shuddering violently, she melted out of my grasp, sliding off of Rabbit and onto the floor of the dais. Gasping, exhausted, she lay there with one hand on her quivering breasts and another on her wet thigh, her dress bunched up around her midriff.

Meeting Rabbit's eyes, I realized a part of me had been crazy about him since the moment we'd met. I couldn't feel this way about someone I had to kill, but the drug and the moment conspired against me. I rocked my hips forward, grinding myself along his swollen shaft to the purple head, and then backwards, slipping him into me.

I was close, and we found a rhythm together that made me explode in under a minute, crying out as the girl had done. The tension in me broke and I felt something heavy lift off of me, an unbearable tingling swallowing me as it spread from my womb to my head, and down my legs to my curling toes. Oh God, I'd forgotten what a good man was like.

I glanced down at the girl, watching me with those pale, pale eyes, breathing heavily. Her belly was exposed; hard, washboard abs, like mine, but with two strange scars. One, seeming to be a tattoo removal of a circular design around her belly button, and the other. A gunshot wound.

Her left hand opened, revealing a small folded square of paper, which tumbled from her delicate fingers to the floor. The image blurred as my eyes filled with tears. I shut them tightly.

After a short time I opened my eyes, and the girl was gone.

All that was left of her was the piece of paper. I reached down and unfolded it, reading.

"I never stopped loving you."

It was signed, "Madeleine."

Chad was nowhere to be found. Oh well.

I guess my plan had gone belly-up when the entire population of the Darkside saw me riding the notorious proprietor and getting filled out like an application form. My head was still fuzzy, all my thoughts still inside out as I got some iced water from the bar. I drank it down in one go, letting the ice cubes rattle out of the glass and into my rearranged lingerie. Burning cold trails slid over me, pooling in my waist. I was enchanted by the lights and the white bats wheeling overhead.

I went to the bathroom to vomit, and when I was finished, cleaned up and refreshed, I came back out and danced the rest of the night away.

Dear Diary,

Rabbit drove me home himself—in a black convertible Jaguar XK8 that made me feel like a princess. He held my hand the whole way. We were sticky in the bright sun from sex and partying all night, and behind his extra pair of Oakleys my eyes were dark and puffy. He walked me to the door of my new apartment and kissed me for a whole hour before saying goodbye.

I'd taken one of the white roses with me as a souvenir, along with Madeleine's note and Rabbit's promise to call me in a few days. I also had instructions to get as much of what I could from the Rainbow People as possible.

Now, in my new living room, with Moby on the stereo to drown out my ears' ringing, I compared the pictures in my mind. Long blonde hair, perfect tan, green eyes. And I knew Layla wore contacts. Now, long, curly black hair, pale skin, blue eyes. No contacts. Okay, her eyes really were pale blue. And the tan was artificial. And the hair, that was easy. But the nose was different, the lips fuller, the eyes somewhat slanted with an Oriental fold.

Not impossible. It could've all been done at that other hospital. You can fake your skin, hair, face and eyes, but you couldn't fake the look in those eyes when they were locked on mine. That was my Layla.

A map to the Rainbow People's camp was in the apartment along with a list of who requested what. For the most part, they wanted soap, douche, hygiene stuff that wouldn't pollute the river they bathed in, and a new can opener—theirs was finally falling apart. I decided to pick up a new bong and pack of lighters also, just to be nice.

I knew they grew their own weed out there, but I was sure they'd appreciate some good KB. The last of mine was for them. Just in case I could use them again, I crushed all of my crack rocks and dusted the buds with them, so their favors in the future would come cheap. Oh, you liked that weed I brought? Want more? Okay, let's talk business.

They'd never smoke crack willingly, but if I managed to hook them, me being their only source, I'd be their god.

Goddess, whatever.

They also wanted a new whippet cracker, because theirs was cross-threaded like my brass one, so I donated my aluminum one, along with the balloons that would outlast cockroaches, they were so strong.

I'm going shopping now.

Dear Diary,

Christ, those people are weird. I just got back, and can't even begin to express how grateful I am for modern conveniences. Air conditioning, for example. And there is no substitute for a roof over my head, and a couch to sit my ass on. Those people are out of their fucking minds.

But I got the shrooms, tons of them, and the angel trumpets, toad sweat, scarlet datura seeds, *devil* trumpets, deadly nightshade, and morning glory seeds. I felt like a botanist with all this crap in my car. Out of curiosity, I had to try one of the new psychedelics. As instructed, I squeezed the pungent black juice out of an angel trumpet bud into a shot glass. The Rainbow guy that showed me how to take them, either drinking the juice or just sucking on a small piece of a leaf, told me to only have a little bit. But, fuck him. What the hell did he know? I pinched my nose shut and choked the sap down, then brushed my teeth twice to wash out the taste.

Now, even a long history of using hallucinogens is a poor indoctrination of each new trip. There's the waiting for the drug to hit, the disappointment and suspicion of being gypped right before it *does* hit, that we usually think of as the worst part. The anticipation. The doubt. But we're always wrong.

I sat down in front of the TV, found the remote, which Sal had Velcro-stuck to the underside of the coffee table, and flipped through the channels. Half an hour later, all the furniture was getting sucked into the television and my head was splitting apart (but in a good way). Um, that doesn't make any sense if you're not tripping, does it? Okay, the chairs and couch and coffee table were all stuck in a frozen-in-time permanent state of *just starting* to move; they were always right about to start sliding across the floor, but hadn't yet. Almost like the way things spin when you're way too drunk, not really spinning but shooting across your vision and reappearing from right back where they started with no apparent way of getting there…but not. God, it was wonderful.

I was paralyzed, giggling deliriously, for several hours, then just staring about the room in awe.

There were neon patterns, rippling across every surface, that fascinated me, spreading toward me on the sofa shore and breaking at my feet with the queerest whispering.

Glittering stalactites of wire-thin ice curled down, broke off like inverted family trees, fuzzy and hazy at first, but when I squinted and blinked to see if they were real they reproduced, sharp, thin, and unimaginably many. I felt as if, when I got too close to the TV and saw that all the colors and images were made up of red, blue, and green pixels, then backed up again to see what they created, that I had actually stepped back away from the *world* and saw the much more complicated design. No, a better way to explain it: the fabric of reality had switched to paisley.

I was goggle-eyed, smoking a cigarette that wasn't there, staring in wonder at infinite fractals ...and dorsal fins sawing through the surface of the light blue carpet.

Damn, I thought, what will they think of next?

Finally, when I could walk again, still in a world outside of comfortable recognition but no longer trapped in a walled-off section of my mind, I went out onto the beach, enchanted by the rhythm of the ocean. There weren't any waves to speak of, but I couldn't resist going in. I ignored the impulse to just tear off my clothes and run in naked, and got a bikini. I spent several hours just frolicking like a little girl.

I needed it.

Being a grown-up is way too much trouble.

Dear Diary,

I had passed out before dark and slept until almost the next evening. I dreamed, not of a fluffy white bunny, but of a large hare, black as soot. Not a cute little rabbit, but the dangerous kind that'll run until there's nowhere else to go, then turn on you with claws and fangs and James Bond-style Walther PPK. Its bright green eyes glowed with savage cunning.

A howling wind came sweeping into the woods, stirring up fallen leaves. Red and gold autumn ones, brittle brown dead ones, the wet kind with pungent fungus and silvery trails where slugs had recently passed, and supple, healthy green ones ripped from the branches. They cartwheeled with a sibilant rustling, then leaped into a swirling dance. The hare hunkered down into a wary crouch, his long ears laid back, his eyes narrowed.

The leaves spun into a climbing, swirling column, the weight of the wind pressing tall grass and bushes flat. One of the black ears twitched forward as more clouds of hissing leaves swept tumbling in like a swarm of bats. Every leaf and flower petal in the forest was stripped, even the bracts, leaving trees and bushes naked and skeletal. The crunching and crackling frenzy of swirling leaves suddenly tightened, as if squeezed by invisible hands, and all of the leaves crushed at once into powder and were flung out into drifting clouds of dust.

Rabbit turned and saw me, his eyes bright and accusing. There was nowhere in his forest left to hide, and somehow it was my fault. As if I was the one who had run through the woods slinging Agent Orange on all the foliage.

I could hear the barking of dogs, somehow knowing that they were police dogs, and they were getting closer. Fast. I'd brought them. I'd told them where to find the hare, and in their blind ferocity they were going to tear apart anything they found when they got here. Including me.

Rabbit bolted. I tried to follow, but I moved as though wading through muck. Terror consumed me, and I slowed to a stop. I watched as the black hare vanished into the naked brambles and thorn thickets, and turned around slowly. The savage growling was all around me. I saw wicked angry eyes, slavering fangs, a wide semicircle of snarling devil faces. Cedric stepped out from behind a tree, grinning wide, gleaming white teeth in a black face. I'd never noticed he had yellow eyes before. Yellow irises, and the piss-yellow of

111

jaundice staining the whites around them.

His partner, Tom, was behind me, massaging his crotch. There were wires all over me, like black vines, or the tentacles of man-o-war. Then they were real tentacles, writhing obscenely, wriggling all over me with a sickening sucking sound.

Lavender octopus tentacles. Todd's skeleton, covered in moss, mold, and small white snails, peered up at me from the barren dirt.

"You know a guy named Casey, Sam?"

Salomé's dead body, bloated and half-rotten, with maggots squirming in the hollow of her cheek, sat up suddenly from somewhere. She was about to say something, but her jawbone fell off, dangling from her face by a shred of tendon. She pointed instead, a whore-red acrylic nail on her bony finger.

I looked, and a stage with a stripper on it, way out here in the woods, somehow didn't look out of place. The dancer was a wrinkled, stooped-over hag with a dowager hump. Toothless, skin hanging in mottled folds and marbleized by varicose veins, eyes rheumy, tits sagging. Only a few wispy hairs on her head. Red ones.

Her capering was pathetic to watch, her smile stinking of decay, her raspy voice trying to talk dirty to a world that wasn't listening.

The dogs turned back at Cedric's command and trotted back the way they had come. Before vanishing with them, I heard Tom do the worst Strother Martin imitation ever.

"That boy must have rabbit in his blood."

A bunch of fragmented images followed, an incoherent collage that I didn't remember upon waking. I was roused by the insistent ringing of my cell phone, and moaned groggily at the intrusion.

"Hello?"

"Miss Brennan? This is Detective Cedric Neely of the Palm Beach County Sheriff's—"

"I gave at the office."

Click.

It was Fight Night at Roxy's, the night they set up a boxing ring on the dance floor and men line up to beat the shit out of each other. There was no betting, no pot to win, and no trophy; just bragging rights and the honor of winning a fair fight in front of hundreds of hot young women. Sometimes girls fought, too, and the crowd went wild

Todd called me up and asked if I'd accompany him, and I couldn't resist, especially when I heard Rabbit was getting in the ring. Maybe I would, too. Just in case I did, I wore my black leather outfit so I could move and still look good.

The place was packed when we got there. The event seemed to draw a slightly older crowd, not so many twenty-ones as on every other night. These people were mostly my age to forty. People with real jobs and family-type stress coming to work off their aggression. Occasionally, you'd get some real bad-ass, like a guard from down at the jailhouse on Gun Club, or a kickboxer, but most of the time it was the you's and me's who'd had too many drinks and wanted to show off.

Todd and I sat at our table, drinking Long Islands, while Rabbit vaulted nimbly over the ropes and into the ring. He looked ridiculous with those gloves and helmet on, in his black jeans and wifebeater. He was just so *short*. Flyweight, they called him. He didn't have toothpick arms, like I'd suspected. He was not particularly muscular, not by my standards, but he didn't have one ounce of fat on him, so all of the muscles, bones, and sinew stood out in sharp relief. Sort of like Bruce Lee, I guess.

When his opponent in blue came forward to punch gloves and hear the Marquis of Queensbury Rules, the guy was at least forty pounds heavier. Everybody was snickering at the sight. The guy behind me said 'Man, that dude won't even bust a grape!' Even I was smiling at little, expecting to see my sister's murderer get his ass handed to him.

What I saw was astounding.

The lights went out, the spotlights came on.

Ding!

They ran at each other, the big guy winding up with his right, when Rabbit *leaped* at him, high enough to clear his shoulder. Startled, guard down as he screeched to a halt, I could see his eyes go wide an instant before Rabbit's red Everlast slammed into them. All his weight was behind that punch, and the man in blue spun and staggered all the way back to hang in the ropes.

A shout went up from the entire crowd. Rabbit retreated a step while the bigger man steadied himself, and then he was on him, his gloves just flashes of red. The blue helmet was battered this way and that until the whole body went limp. The knees buckled, and he collapsed like a rag doll.

I caught one glimpse of Rabbit's eyes as he turned away and walked arrogantly back to his corner, and I swear I saw the devil in them.

The ref (really one of the bouncers) was talking to the man who'd gotten up, wobbling slightly. I saw the blue headgear nod, and the ref shouted something to both of them. Blue charged across the ring like a mad bull, and at the last minute, the cold blooded Rabbit sidestepped easily and ducked the swing, jabbing the exposed flank. Rising, he swung straight from the shoulder and nailed Blue under the ear.

The bigger man staggered. Pushing one shoulder, Rabbit spun the man around to face him and started whaling on him, punishing him brutally. Before he could yell Give, I saw Rabbit wind up with a right labeled TNT and knock him off his feet.

The crowd went wild. With a cocky, casual wave, Rabbit acknowledged their thunderous applause and went to his corner, leaning on the ropes and taking a drag from the cigarette Tick held for him. Todd laughed at this.

"Cheeky bastard."

I still couldn't believe my eyes. I flashed back to the time I saw him come flying out of a door, turning around in midair to blow away three cops and have his one-liner ready. For such a little guy, he was larger than life.

He had just taken another drag when Blue stood firmly, nodded to the ref and punched his gloves together. Rabbit strode to the center of the ring, put his guard up, and blew smoke at his opponent.

Blue lunged, unloosing a barrage Rabbit was hard put to repel. The smack of the gloves as he blocked was loud enough to be heard over the low roar of the crowd. Step by step, he was forced back. Turning, so as not to get himself backed into a corner, he let the guy pound his gloves and forearms for almost a minute. Until.

Until he abruptly jumped backwards and Blue overextended himself, stumbling from the force of the punch he'd thrown, and in a blur of red, Rabbit's left knocked a mist of blood from the guy's mouth. The blue head snapped back and the feet stumbled. Rabbit waited. Blue shook his head, clearing it, and gestured with his arms that he was through.

Half laughing, half cheering, the people roared their approval. I found myself on my feet, screaming Rabbit's name, my face flushed,

Todd had one eyebrow raised at me, grinning. I couldn't blame him. I was acting like such a girly-girl, but damn, I couldn't help it. Something about that guy had me all light-headed, watching him beat the shit out of another man without even breaking a sweat.

And that look in his eyes, like he was toying with him the whole time. I remembered how he'd held my hand, how he'd kissed me so tenderly. A man who could be so sweet and so cruel—*and* rich, was the kind of man I wanted to make more of. He embodied everything I considered worthy in a mate, at least from a Survival of the Fittest standpoint. Too bad I had to kill the fucker.

Both fighters had left the ring, and the DJ was calling for more brave souls. My face was hot, and now I finally understood why some women fan themselves around a real man. I finished my drink instead.

Rabbit appeared at our table not long after, accepting handshakes, compliments, and slaps on the back. Girls were watching him, grinning, and discussing him amongst themselves. I don't know why, but I bristled with jealousy. Surprising them— and him—I grabbed him by the hair and kissed him roughly. He kissed me back, and didn't even wince when I bit his lip hard enough to draw blood.

He chuckled instead, with that look in his eyes, like we'd gotten past all the Who, me? and one-liners and his true nature was naked in front of me. Here was a man who could chop a human being apart with an ax, kill three cops and smile like a kid, and shoot two women to death in public.

Here was a man who could escape from the police three times and vanish like smoke. Legend has it that once he got out of a pair of cuffs, kicked out a squad car window, outran the arresting officer, and charmed the police dogs that came tracking him. The two German Shepherds were found sitting docilely in a suburban backyard with happy idiotic grins on their "relentlessly obedient" faces.

They said he would never be taken alive, and I believed it. He wouldn't break for me no matter what I did, and he'd never bend over for anybody.

He also had the flashy plumage, sturdy nest, and skilled dance that made a mate eligible. I wiped the blood off of his lip.

"You're my hero," I said playfully.

"Yeah, that was pretty impressive, wasn't it?"

"Modesty."

"Never heard of it."

I took him by the hand and led him to the other dance floor, making sure everybody saw me with him. Yeah, look at me, all you painted little porcelain dolls. You fair-weather girls who whine like beebee-shot puppies when you break a nail. You couldn't handle a man like this.

Rabbit made a gesture like Sorry, ladies, as we passed the flocks of girlie-girls. I wished I could fuck him right there in front of their envy-green faces, just to rub their noses in it, but this was Roxy, not the Darkside.

The other dance floor was upstairs, the one we had to go to in place of the main one. It was smaller, but big enough. Like Rabbit in a way, I thought with a smirk. We passed a girl with pale eyes and paler skin, long blue-black hair—gorgeous, but I didn't have time for that kind of thing anymore.

We went back to Rabbit's when the bar had closed. He lived on a yacht, a fifty-one foot Rybovich, with all the fishing stuff chopped off. No tuna tower, outriggers, or fighting chair, and it looked much nicer that way. It was tasteful, which bordered on freakish in the marina where it was docked, surrounded by garish extravagance. A flawless white, with perfect teak and mahogany, and the name Capriole in gold on the transom. Beneath that, "Ibiza, España."

"What's that mean?" I asked, while he pulled on the stern line.

"Capriole? It's a trick horses do. In battle, war-horses can leap into the air and kick with their hind legs to kill foot soldiers."

"And you named your boat that?"

"There are other reasons."

Removing our shoes, he helped me aboard and let us inside. The salon was beautiful, again, designed with simplicity that was old-fashioned and unassuming. I would have preferred something gauche and modern, but hey, one man's meat...

Turning on subtle hidden lights, he crossed to a kitchenette, opened a bottle of red wine that was waiting in a small locker. As he retrieved two wine glasses, his other hand found a remote control and switched on one of those really cool Sharper Image stereos that cost as much as my car.

"What's this?" I asked, as Bob Marley asked if I could be loved.

116

"What's what?" Rabbit turned with two full glasses. I was pointing at a nasty-looking statue about a foot tall. An idol. Almost like a tiki statue, carved from an upside-down small tree, his head a big snarling root with irregular horns branching out. I would say he was anatomically correct, but he wasn't. He was anatomically ridiculous. He was sitting like a cat, lips puckered to receive a kiss, eyes half-closed as if in rapture, with this enormous *thing* protruding from between his legs. Man, it was ugly.

"Oh, that's Kothulga, god of depravity."

"Really. That's disgusting."

"His four-prong yang? Well, Satan's dick has many heads."

"Cool."

"I know. Thirsty?" He handed me one of the glasses. Chianti.

We talked for hours after that, about everything. Our childhoods, our first times, what we considered the deep dark secrets in our seriously checkered lives, the stupid stories from a long time ago before we became who we are now. Rabbit had been into everything at one time or another. He'd trained dogs for pit-fighting, smuggled guns and drugs from South America, learned kyoko-shin-kai in Brazil from a one-hundred-seven-year-old man, and spoke four languages other than English.

"I learned Spanish, Portuguese, French, and Italian so I could communicate with any branch of the underworld I had to. French is the *lingua franca* from Morocco to Chad, and is a second language in some parts of Asia, so I can do business almost anywhere. That's why the name Rabbit. I can run anywhere I have to, if I have to."

"Have you ever had to?"

"Yeah, I just got back."

"From where?"

"It's not important."

"Your name's not Warren Haggerty, is it?" I asked.   He shook his head, pouring us each another glass.

"Of all the names you could've picked, why Warren?"

"Let me ask you. Would you change your name to Esther?"

"No."

"Wilma?"

"No."

"Peggy?"

"Hell no."

"Right, if you were going to give yourself a new name, you'd pick something cool, like, Salomé."

"Thanks."

"But if I wanted you to think my fake name was my real name I'd tell you it was something no one would ever change it to. Like Barry, or Dwight. Or Warren."

"Or Irving."

"Ha! Not if you paid me."

"So, that's how you hide? By being common?"

"Actually, the best way to do it is to be boring, but there'll be time enough for that in the grave. Be overlooked. Standing out is that last thing you want to do. My traveling disguise? Not a beard, not a suit, just rumpled t-shirt, jeans, maybe a college sweater. Pair of glasses, five o'clock shadow, and a baseball cap. Christ, everybody looks like that. Or, better yet, one of those stupid looking fanny-packs, and Birkenstocks."

"Ha! Not if you paid me."

"I know, but that's what you have to do, look like someone you'd never want to be. A nobody. Once, though, I screwed up. Going through the airport dressed like that, forgetting I was wearing a six-thousand dollar watch."

"Oops."

"Yeah. It looked really, really wrong on me. Like I'd stolen it. See, it's stupid stuff like that that arouses suspicion. I should've been wearing a Swatch or a Timex."

He spoke knowledgeably about all kinds of cool things. How to catch and kill a snake to eat it. Leave your hat on the ground and hide behind a tree, the snake'll smell the sweat from your head and slither under it for the warmth. Then you chop its head off. He knew a little something about everything.

Wooooo! Holy *shit!* How the hell do I describe what just happened? It was like those cartoons when the main character visits the mad scientist, and he walks into the lab where all kinds of bottles and alembics and retorts and glass whatevers are cooking up potions—weird glass shit that bends things all around when you look through them. That's what happened all of a sudden. His face looked like he'd walked behind the mad scientist's glass alchemy stuff and took a second to peer at me through it. His skull elongated, one eye swelling up huge, jiggling for an instant before snapping elastically back into place. It startled me, but I guess it was a souvenir from my Angel Trumpets trip. Good thing it's only affect-

118

ing me this way, I thought, and not fucking up my judgement at all.

Wooo! There it goes again!

Not unfamiliar with this stuff, and knowing it was only in my head, I managed to cover it rather well, and forced myself to stay in the conversation.

"Say something to me in French," I said. He looked at me. He spoke gently, sensually, the only way you *can* speak French. I melted when I heard it.

"*Vos lobes d'oreille ressemblent à poisson des têtes.*"

"Wow. What's that mean?"

"I'll tell you someday."

"Mmm, tell me something else."

He grinned evilly. "*Je veux vous manger.*"

"Ooh."

"*Je veux vous manger de vos orteils a votre tête.*"

"Oooooh. Say something in Italian."

"*In Taormina, non ci è orizzonte.*"

"That's pretty."

"Yeah. 'In Taormina, there is no horizon.' When I was in Sicily, I went to this town that was halfway up a mountain, overlooking the Ionian Sea, called Taormina. When I looked out at the sea, it was a perfect blue that matched the cloudless sky, and they just faded into each other. There was no horizon at all, just a clear, hazy blue. To me that meant there was nowhere else in the world to go. When I finally stopped wandering, I would end up in that beautiful town. I just had a few more things to do and see before then."

"And what are you going to do then, once you've settled down there?"

"Marry a pretty Sicilian girl, have ten kids, grow old."

"Really?"

"Of course. What else is there?"

"What about all the adventure? What about the party?"

"You have to grow up someday, Red. All this, running from the cops, Interpol, dealing drugs and having shoot-outs, that's all kid stuff. I just want to have the time of my life before I become a husband and father, so I have it all out of my system. I don't want to have a houseful of teenagers when I decide Oh, I never got to sleep in a cave or piss on a cop car. Then I'll have a midlife crisis and hurt my wife and fuck up my kids and ruin everything. Not me."

"So, what else do you have to do? What's left?"

"Hmm. Uhhh…well, I want to be a guest star on "The Simpsons," fight in the Kumi Te, eat a fifty-ounce steak in one sitting, kill an anaconda or a bear without a gun, probably a bear, and…let's see—"

"I get the picture. So, what all have you done so far?"

"Ain't telling. Whoops, we need another bottle."

He got up for the third time and went to the decorative wine locker while I lit us two cigarettes. The salon door was open enough for the smoke to ventilate, and no mosquitoes were coming in. I checked my watch and was startled to see that the sun would come up soon.

I was suddenly very tired. I put both cigarettes in the ashtray and was asleep before Rabbit turned around.

My cell phone woke me up. I was lying on the salon couch with a pillow under my head, and Rabbit was reading an old leather-bound book, drinking a Corona, and smoking one of my cigarettes. I fumbled groggily for the stupid phone and answered it, burying my face back in the pillow.

"Mmmh, hello?"

"Wake up."

I did, instantly.

"Yeah?" I sat up, and Rabbit pretended not to notice my tension.

"Good morning, Simone."

"Hey."

"We can either talk about this stupid game you're playing, or we can forget all about it and talk about the game *I* want to play."

"I'm listening."

"Yeah, I'll bet you are. I want to meet you today at the church. We've got an awful lot to talk about."

"What time?" I asked, locking eyes with Rabbit.

"Three o'clock. You have two hours."

Click.

I dropped the phone on the carpet and got myself a cigarette.

"Who was that?" Rabbit asked as if he didn't care.

"This fuckin' spook who wants me to sell you out to him."

He just stared at me.

Rabbit had all the spy shit you could possibly want. What he brought with us was an eaves-dropper and a camera with an insanely powerful telescopic lens. An Acho unidirectional micro-dish, it could pick up everything we said up to five hundred yards away. At least, that's what he told me.

We left immediately, taking both of our cars, and I led him to the church. I pointed out the spot where we usually met, only I didn't tell him anything about the Usually. I told him my sister and I both knew Cedric, but she was the one who did the back-scratching, the informing.

"The back-*stabbing*'s more like it," he muttered.

After surveying the scene, he told me he'd park his car somewhere and come back on foot, finding a suitable vantage point. The cops would almost definitely be early, so he'd be extra early, and he instructed me to be late. Wanted to pick up anything they'd bitch about or mention in casual conversation, I supposed. That idea made me a little nervous, but I shrugged it off.

I went by the apartment, got Sal's car instead of mine, and had breakfast at the pizza place where Chad had gotten that crab and shrimp thing. I tried this barbequed chicken one, which was disgusting, and one with a bunch of fruits on it, which was even *more* disgusting, and finally ended up at the Wendy's next door, eating a burger.

At twenty past three I pulled into the parking lot of Saint Ignatius, which was crowded with casuarinas and Spanish bayonets, hidden from the street. They were parked around the back, by the fenced-in playground. I couldn't see any sign of Rabbit, but I hadn't expected to.

Cedric was scowling, which wasn't a surprise, and the rest of them looked varying degrees of pissed. I parked and went up to them arrogantly, putting on a show for my man without any means to back it up.

"I'm looking for the church bake sale. Am I in the right place?"

"You got a fucking watch, Simone. Can't you tell time?"

"My name's Salomé, for the record."

"Yeah, whatever. You can drop your stupid–ass charade now. Do you want getback for your sister? You know you can't do it on your own. Why don't you leave it to people who know what they're doing?"

"You think I don't know what I'm doing?"

121

"We're the professionals," Tom said. Dipshit.

"Professionals built the Titanic," I told him. "Amateurs built the Ark."

"Ha! What do you know about that?" Cedric grumbled.

"Plenty. Lemme tell you about Jesus."

"Shut the fuck up."

"Okay, discussion's over," I said haughtily, turning around to go.

"Don't walk away from me, you little tramp!"

I spun around, my face hot. Cedric's snarling face was all I could see, the son of a bitch, god-damned spook.

"You forget who you're talking to? You're still just a crack-smoking junkie whore, and a snitch to boot. You're nothing. You're a dime a dozen. You think there's a shortage of white-trash bitches? You think anyone'll cry if I lock you up for everything I've got you on? You even think whoever you're fucking now will post bond for your sorry for-sale ass? Hell no! They'll just move on to the next trashy slut they find in a bar. Now, you either saddle up and ride with us, or I'll put you up the road where you can eat all the pussy your little ol' heart desires. Make up your mind right now."

I stared at him, feeling sick. That rocking boat feeling from last night came back, and I found myself shifting my weight nervously from one foot to the other. Dizzy. There was something in my throat. For a second, there was something in my eye, too, but I couldn't give him the satisfaction of seeing how much his words had stung.

"What do you say, you little cock tease?"

He tapped the gold badge he wore on his belt.

"Tease this. Come on, I fucking dare you."

I looked around at the bushes, hoping to Christ I wouldn't see Rabbit. I couldn't believe he'd heard all that. I couldn't believe he'd seen Cedric cut me down like this. My lip was trembling, and I was terrified I couldn't stop it. I both saw and felt a kind of dancing glitter. The parking lot rocked and swooped drunkenly, and I could feel my stomach drop out of me. I looked at Cedric's face, seeing it at the end of a darkly shimmering tunnel.

"Look," he said, softening. "All you have to do is ID Haggerty, get him on tape, and you can go back to peddling your cunt and sticking needles in your ass. I know a smackhead downtown who's horny and holding, so I'll even give him your number, let you get a little somethin'."

My throat was closing up. Cedric's face blurred.

"Tell us where the next party will be."

"I don't know." It came out a whisper; I didn't trust myself to speak aloud. But Cedric heard me.

"Then find out. Blow whoever you have to. But find out. Today."

I shut my eyes, and the tears squeezed out, streaking down my cheeks like drips of hot candle wax.

"We know you know Haggerty. We know your sister was shot by him, and we know what you're trying to do. If you take away our prize, you know you'll fry. Kill him on your own, if that's what you're thinking, and you'll go to the electric chair. Keep hanging out with him, and you'll either do time or get yourself killed. Drop out of the game, and I'll send you up for trafficking and prostitution, guaranteed."

My eyes stayed shut tight. The sonofabitch, the fucker. I tried to become invisible, to disappear and teleport away. I felt myself swaying pathetically, vertigo swallowing me. Rabbit, I thought, please don't be listening. God, don't let that spy-thing work. God, just strike me dead right here.

"Look at me when I'm talking to you!"

I looked. I wished I hadn't, but I did. And there they were, all grinning at me except Cedric, whose eyes weren't yellow after all. *Oh yeah, go on and laugh at me, you fucking pigs.*

"I'll call you tomorrow," I said quietly.

"I bet you will, sugar." He chuckled. "I bet you will."

"I won't know where the club'll be until that day they set everything up. But I'll find out what I can."

"Good girl. You may go now."

I heard the rest of them snickering as I turned and went unsteadily back to the car, shaken and ashamed. The most awful part of what Cedric had said was that it was all true, and I knew it.

Dear Diary,

Todd and Rabbit came by the apartment later, while I was watching TV and drinking Crown Royal straight from its heart-shaped bottle. An MTV cartoon was on, which I was watching only out of mild curiosity. Some cyborg punk show, kind of like Aeon Flux in a futuristic shootout.

"Hey, Red," Rabbit said, stopping in front of the TV. "What's this?"

"Bionic Dyke."

"What?"

"Bionic Dyke vs. the Cannibal Pirate Skanks. It's new."

"It's gotta be."

"I've seen it," Todd said, plopping down beside me. "She's got this chain gun she calls her Vulcan gat, and her arch-nemesis is the evil Space Cooze. It's not that bad."

"That's the stupidest thing I've ever heard," Rabbit said, shocked.

"There's a lot worse stuff on."

"That's even more disturbing. It's stuff like this that keeps me from buying a TV."

Bionic Dyke was crouched behind a pile of bullet-riddled corpses, rounds whizzing over her head and smacking into her barricade with wet *thunks*. Good stuff for kids to watch. Of course, the only other things on were a Muppets version of the Tuesday Night Fights—and watching Oscar de la Grouch stick n' move wasn't really my cup of tea—and the news.

And fuck the news.

"Drink?" I asked.

"Yes, it is." Todd always said that. I got two highball glasses with ice while Rabbit shut the TV off in disgust.

Todd had a large manila envelope, from which he was removing a bunch of what looked like eight-by-tens, laying them out on the table. I went back to them with the glasses and saw my face on the picture closest to me.

"Damn, that was quick. Here." I handed them their drinks after filling them up while Rabbit explained that his camera was digital, and Todd's computer had printed them out within minutes with much better than photographic quality. He'd taken the pictures from the top of a pine tree, and even the tears streaking down my face were visible in startling detail.

"My Acho screwed up a little, and I didn't get to hear the whole conversation," Rabbit told me, but I knew he was lying. And he knew I knew, but it was nice of him to say it.

"We have the addresses of Cedric Neely, Tom Baker, and all the others pictured here. All of them will be visited tonight, exactly midnight. It seemed like an appropriate time, since we were synchronizing the attacks. Might as well do it right, eh?"

I couldn't believe my ears. How had they gotten all this together?

"Easy," Rabbit said. "I'm a genius. Got a cigarette?"

"Do you *ever* buy your own?"

"I don't smoke."

Todd handed him a clove, saying, "We thought you'd appreciate coming along for the expedition on Clovis' house."

"Cedric's?"

"Whatever."

"Got a gun?" Rabbit asked.

"Uhhh, my sister's."

"Pppbfthh! That pea-shooter? You want a real gun?"

"Like what?"

"A MAC-10."

"Ooh, they're nice."

Rabbit told me to wear black, which I thought was common sense, until he had to point out that leather pants was *not* the way to go. Too hot, for starters. And blood was a real bitch to get out of them. And you can't sneak up on anybody with them. So I ended up in black jeans, sweater, and shoes—the Doc Marten combat boots I hadn't worn in years.

One of the guards drove us out to a street off Haverhill at eleven-thirty, and we parked in a quiet cul-de-sac, then hopped fences and stole quietly through bushes and backyards. Many times my clothes were snagged on bougainvillea thorns or the fangs of wire on poorly cut chain-link fences, and it took Rabbit's restraining hand once to keep me from crying out when a blade of Spanish bayonet stabbed through my jeans. This is not a woman's work. At all.

A huge Rottweiler came at us at once, but Rabbit braced himself and let it bite his clenched fist. With his other hand gripping the back of its head, he swung it and broke its neck in one savage wrench. It made a sound like a tree limb snapping off, and the dog just went limp. He shook it off of him and waved us on, his gloved hand covered with blood and drool. He dragged Rover into the bushes and caught up.

Two houses after that, the guard unzipped a duffel bag he carried, full of bundles—three MAC-10s with huge suppressors wrapped in dark beach towels. Rabbit handed me mine, showed me silently how to shoot it, and we started across the yard toward the sleeping one-story house. My heart was pounding hard enough through the arteries in my throat to choke me. This voice in my head was screaming *No, don't do it! Don't go in there! Run! Just throw the gun down and run!* It was so loud I kept glancing at Rabbit and the guard, thinking all my thoughts were on the air. Every step on the grass seemed loud enough to wake the people sleeping inside, but the house was as still as death when we got to the back door.

The guard picked the lock even quicker that I could've, and quietly prized the door open.

It yawned inward and Rabbit nudged me gently. Oh, fuck no, don't make me go first. But I did. The house was full of the regular house noises, the ghost sounds that terrify you even if you belong there, even if you have a fucking machine gun. We crept in like cat-shadows.

The house had a simple layout: living room/ dining room area, open from the front door to the back. On our right, a kitchen and a door to the garage where the lawnmower no doubt sat with cob-webs, judging from the mangy look of the yard we'd just crossed. To the left, the two bedrooms and bath of the doomed Family Neely.

Detective and Mrs. Cedric Neely had two sons who, unfortu-nately, might die tonight. The guard slipped into the boys' room. One of them apparently had sleep apnea, and the rest of them would have to have had become deep sleepers in order to get any rest at all. Hopefully, they'd sleep right through becoming orphans.

Rabbit carefully opened the parents' bedroom door, and re-vealed Cedric in boxer shorts with a .45. We froze.

"Down on the floor," he ordered. Behind him, a black woman in a huge "I'm With Stupid" t-shirt was kneeling on the bed, wide-eyed, with a cordless phone in her hand, ready to dial. Rabbit's body tensed ever so slightly.

"I will shoot you in your fucking face if you don't drop *now.*"

"Everyone's calm," Rabbit said soothingly.

"On the floor. Hands behind your head."

I heard the beeps of Mrs. Neely dialing nine-eleven.

Rabbit started to lower into a crouch, slowly.

"Red," he said.

It was almost like we had planned it telepathically, the way it happened. Like the lunge of a striking serpent, Rabbit leaped sideways, back into the living room. At the same instant, I dove the other way, onto the cold tiles and sliding fuzzy mat in the bathroom. I scrambled into the bathtub where stray bullets might not find me.

The darkness was lit by the strobe-light of muzzle flashes and the hard, flat pops of suppressed machine gun fire, a low chattering, the crash of a heavy body flung against furniture. The scream of a woman. The wails of rudely awakened children. I shut my eyes and clutched the gun to my chest, rocking and praying without words.

The woman's cries were cut short by another burst, and then there was only the two boys.

Another burst, and all was quiet.

This same scene was being played out in six other homes.

I don't know how long I lay there before I was prodded by a warm gun barrel. Looking up, I saw a dark figure, black against the gray, staring down at me.

"Your sister was a lot tougher than you, Red."

His voice was calm, but its undercoating was contempt. He turned and walked off, saying over his shoulder, "Let's go."

I got out of the tub and stumbled after him.

The guard was sloshing gasoline from two containers he must've brought in the duffel bag all over the bed and floor of the kids' room, dragging a trail into the parents' room. I followed Rabbit out the back door. The lights were on in the neighbors' windows, nosy people roused by the screaming, and I could hear distant sirens coming closer. The guard came out, and we started hopping fences.

We moved quietly, but with haste, and no one saw us. By the time the sirens passed us, lighting up the night with red and blue flashes, the house was engulfed in flames. We could see the orange glow of it all the way at the low wall we started from. The houses in the quiet cul-de-sac slept on, oblivious.

Dear Diary,

Today the talk of the town was the simultaneous executions of seven narcotics detectives and their families, and the burning of their homes. Organized crime was suspected (duh), and possibly a drug ring (really?). No mention of who, though. The police were confident that the swine responsible would be found and brought to justice, so rest easy, America.

I turned my horticulture specimens over to Rabbit's lab guys, identifying them, and providing the recipe for geltabs. Combat for Rats. Nasal allergy inhalant, frozen. Water. Windex. And the correct amounts, boiling time, and storage instructions. It took hours.

I watched them distill the extracts from the plants and seeds, bubbling juices flowing down the long Pinocchio noses of glass retorts into receivers like a Mad Scientist's lab, the mad scientists themselves adding one drop of belladonna to the tablets of X in one cookie sheet, and one drop of angel trumpet to each tablet in another. The tablets in the first batch were engraved with the symbol of the Decepticons, dyed purple, and the others were stamped with the eight-arrow symbol for Chaos. A fan was turned on to dry them before they'd have a chance to dissolve.

That's how we made the first Trolls. If there's anything I can take credit for in my life, I had a hand in the manufacture of a possibly great new drug.

They brewed a tea out of the shrooms that you could tell yourself tasted like apple cider, and it almost would, until you remembered it was really fungus. Add Everclear and you have a Mushroom Cloud. Add tequila and you have a Diesel. Add Bacardi 151, and you have Fahrenheit 151. They made cocktails out of Special K, also. That's K for ketamine, a fun anesthetic for surgeries like cataract removal or other operations where you have to be fully conscious. It's an analogue of PCP, as opposed to a digital, I guess. I don't know what that term means, but that's what I was told by my pharmacist buddy.

What you do is boil the liquid ketamine hydrochloride and evaporate the water, then harvest the crystals left behind. Used properly, it kills pain and induces temporary paralysis while not interfering with basic reflexes like breathing. Used popularly, it distorts the user's perceptions, causes minor hallucinations, out of body experiences, a floating sensation, and the gullibility to see great meaning in mindlessly repetitive techno songs with unimaginative

128

lyrics.

Once, dancing at Roxy's, I was in a K-hole and thought I was moving in slow motion, so I sped up a bit. An eternity or a moment later, I was sure I'd slowed down again and, afraid of broadcasting to everyone around that I was drugged up, I danced even faster than before.

It kept happening, me slowing down and speeding up, until I noticed everyone near me was staring. Catching my reflection in the wall mirror, I almost died of shame and horror.

I'd been thrashing around like a lunatic the whole time, damn near throwing out my back or dislocating something, that's how fast I was.

The audience erupted in fitful laughter, but rather than flee the scene and hide in a drink somewhere, I laughed along with them and kept on dancing. In a nutshell, that's Special K, and Todd's chemists mixed many a fine cocktail with it as the main ingredient. Banshee, for example, with Blue Curaçao and some other shit. Astrolabe, a shot with Bacardi, champagne, and I forget what else.

The chemists, like Rabbit, were uninterested in the new supercrack. Something about not burning your meal ticket.

I had talked to Rabbit the other night about possibly showing my paintings at the club, and upon describing them, I think I had his interest hooked. I brought them along with the stuff I got from the Rainbow People, and lined them up on the floor against a wall. Rabbit and Todd appraised them.

They especially liked one I'd done of myself, covered in slime, bursting from a cocoon. Symbolizing rebirth. Their favorites, though, were the ones Salomé had done. Which was disappointing.

That is, until they got to the one I did of Layla.

The two of them just stared, revisiting each graceful curve of her exquisite brown body. Rabbit, the duped and betrayed lover, and Todd, who stole her from him and in turn lost her to me. No matter what she'd done or who she really was, they had still kept a place in themselves for her, apart from anything staining. I could see that they both had a Layla-shaped hole in their hearts.

"How did you paint this?" Todd asked. "How did you know this girl?"

"I didn't. That one my sister did, along with the lesbian trees."

"You can't sell this one." Rabbit's voice was hollow, his eyes somewhere else. "Not to some stranger who didn't know her."

We were all silent; they introspective, and I feigning ignorance.

Finally, "You give me this one and, yeah, we'll sell your stuff. No commission or anything. You said Simone painted this?"

I hesitated, then, "Yeah."

"So it's no loss to you. That a deal?"

"Sure."

"I like this alien landscape you did."

"Thanks."

The next step was to get Zack Scalisi.

The problem was that I had to wait for him to contact me, and variables like that are unacceptable. I am not the "fucking Who's Who" that my sister was, unfortunately, and while I'd done a quick study of what I could find in her apartment, I didn't have the confidence in that knowledge that I needed.

I went to the bar I used to frequent, and was greeted by a whistle. Rick, ever faithful in his praise of me, told me I looked great. And the cornrows worked marvelously for me. Had to be gay.

Had to be.

"Thanks, Rick. You got a Long Island back there for me?"

"I'll rummage around and see what I can find." He went about mixing my drink, happy as always. "Haven't seen you in a while. You been away or something?"

"I've been busy. Got myself a job."

"Really! Nothing legal, I hope."

"Actually, yes. Public Relations. I'm legit now."

"Well, dip me in chocolate. How's it been going for you?"

I made a snort-sigh of exhaustion.

"Yeah, I'll bet," he said. "But isn't it so much more rewarding to do something worthwhile? You were way too good for that stuff you used to do. You know that."

"Mm-hmm. So, what about you?"

"Ah, well. Same old, same old. Had a date last night."

"I figured as much."

"Yeah, but she was nice this time. Real pretty, too."

"Do tell."

"Hair long and dark and curly, just the way I like it. She's a white girl, but she's got these Chinese-type eyes. Beautiful blue Chinese eyes. You never saw a girl this pretty."

130

My eyes got hard and cold, but he didn't notice. He was still measuring liquor into my glass and smiling fondly.

"Pale, though, like she lives underground. Not a sickly pale, but a creamy white. And she's smart, too. Very smart. Here you go, sweetie." He placed my drink in front of me, and I absently stirred it with a straw, clinking the ice.

"I met her at Fight Night, and she was all upset because she saw her boyfriend with her girlfriend. So I had a drink with her and comforted her, and told her obviously her life was way too complicated. She needed to simplify it."

"Did you two get simple together?" I asked, irritable.

"Oh, no. We just talked. Then, we met for an early dinner last night and talked some more. She's holding a lot back, but I'm hoping she'll open up to me. We're meeting again tonight."

"Oh, yeah? Where?"

"We're going to see a movie, then have dinner at that new seafood place right by the theatre. You know the place I mean?"

"Uh-huh. What're you seeing?"

"Oh, something with Brad Pitt. You know how girls are about that guy. It's probably gonna be some chick-flick."

Yeah, right. I know you were the one who chose it. You want to see Brad Pitt more than she does. Maybe you'll get to see his butt, Ricky. Better keep your fingers crossed.

"I heard about that movie. I think you see his butt in it."

"Really?"

"Oh yeah, and if you don't blink, supposedly you can see part of his sack. That's just what I heard, though."

"Well, I'll get her to tell me when it's over."

"What, don't you want to see it?"

"Not particularly."

"You sure?"

"Positive."

"Suit yourself. What's the lucky lady's name?"

"Laney."

"Laney?"

"Yeah, it's short for Madeleine."

"Pretty."

We talked for a while, about this and that. Todd called and interrupted, wanting to go out tonight, but I told him I had plans.

131

Recon, I called it, and he laughed. He wished me luck, and I told him I'd probably need it.

I drank some more, Rick having an occasional shot with me. Finally, I had to go home and prepare. Grabbing a quick bite to eat on the way, I drove carefully back to the beach. For some stupid reason, driving drunk during the day is a lot harder than at night. Could be the traffic. Or that annoying sun that's with you everywhere you go.

At home, I took the cornrows out of my hair, showered, and dressed in a simple shirt and jeans. The air got thick and heavy, smelling like rain coming. A storm would break within the hour. Great. I took Sal's car because it wasn't as noticeable as mine. She used to call it her Inconspicucar.

I miss her.

Badly.

But I try not to think about it.

I sat in that rainy parking lot for an hour and a half, deciding that surveillance was the shittiest job in the world. Boring boring boring. Shit, this is boring.

Finally, a car pulled up in front of the theatre and let a girl out, who scampered into the shelter over the ticket booth. The chivalrous driver then circled around to find a parking space. It was hard to tell if the girl buying the tickets was Madeleine/ Layla/Whatever her name was.

I waited.

Eventually, the driver settled for a spot way in the back, and had to run, splashing in puddles right past me. Yeah, it was Rick, and judging from the way he ran, yep, he had some sugar in his tank, all right. If he ever got her into bed she'd break him in half.

He joined her, shook himself, and held the door for her.

I got out, locked my door, and ran in the cold, pelting rain to buy my own ticket.

"One for the Brad Pitt movie, please."

"Which one?" the gum-chewing black girl asked.

I looked up at the marquee. You're kidding me.

"Brad Pitt's in a fricking Star Wars movie?"

"Yeah. He's Han Solo and Princess Leia's son, grown up."

"Jesus Christmas."

"Yeah, that's what I thought. But it's real good. He gets lured over to the Dark Side of the Force and kills Luke, who's like, an old man now."

"What's the other one?"

"Oh, romantic comedy or something."

Bingo.

"Yeah, that's the one."

"Six dollars."

I paid her and went in, going through the whole pre-movie ceremony with the popcorn and Pepsi and ticket tearing. I eventually found the movie and got a seat, straining my eyes to see the cute couple. I couldn't find them anywhere, so I just watched the movie.

It sucked.

Dinner at that seafood place sucked, too.

Normally, I try not to eat anything with more than four legs. Just kind of a personal policy. Well, the waiter recommended this crab dinner with something, I dunno, plankton? I don't know what the hell it was, but the waiter said it was really good.

He lied, the fucker.

So I ended up eating that and a fish of some kind, smoking two packs of cigarettes and drinking glass after glass of white wine. Watching Rick and Madeleine talking, smiling, but never laughing, and certainly not feeding each other morsels of Shrimp Whatever.

She looked very different, but still gorgeous. I couldn't decide how to feel about that. Rabbit had reawakened something in me, but I couldn't be sure what it was. I was either feeling that Chinese-food love that fills you so completely, until an hour goes by and you want someone else, or the natural urges of a female who's found an ideal mate. Man, those nature shows were screwing me up. As far as mating and reproducing strong, healthy young was concerned, I could never do better than Rabbit. As far as satisfying my nesting and survival instinct, again, I couldn't do better. Same with my high standards for sexual prowess, fashion sense, and courtesy.

Reason, however, warned me of two glaringly obvious but overlookable facts. One, he'd killed my sister while trying to kill me. And two, his whole charming personality was a façade, concealing the cold-blooded ferocity of a fucking maniac. Aside from that, god *damn* I was crazy about him.

I doted on him the way Chad had doted on me.

And here I was, spying on the girl I thought I'd marry. Men are right. We *are* crazy. Or was it stupid? Or was it both?

I compromised and decided it was both, shrugging slightly and watching Madeleine over the rim of my glass as I drank. Since meeting her, I've dined at all the finest restaurants, danced in the finest clubs, and—shit. They were asking for their check. Where the hell was my waiter?

I couldn't let them leave before me and risk being spotted. I had to be in my car already when they got to theirs. If I just walked out, they might see me when the waiter magically appeared to stop me, as he surely would. A waitress was coming down their aisle with a tray of drinks, and a plan leaped, full-grown, into my head.

I plucked the straw out of my untouched water glass and broke off a piece of my crab's claw. With the skill of a school cafeteria spitball champion, I put the armed straw to my lips, calculated the lead on my target, took a sharp breath, and fired. The chunk of hard shell flew straight across the tables and low-walled divider to strike, stinging, just under the poor girl's eye as she passed the couple. With a short squeal, she jumped and the tray fumbled in her hands, sloshing beverages all over the three of them. I got up and went looking for my waiter.

I found him quickly, told him I had to run, and handed him three twenties and a ten to cover my bill. With one glance back at my quarry, I saw them heading angrily to the restrooms to towel off. I was out the door and into the rain before they had a chance to see me.

I followed them to a hotel, where she hugged him and got out. I parked and ran in after her. An apartment or a motel would've been perfect, but no, she had to disappear into a hotel. Figures. I knew she'd go straight to the bar though. After that movie, that crappy dinner, and having sodas and beer rained on her, who wouldn't?

Of course, I was right.

She was signing a Cuba Libré to her room, and the bartender said "Enjoy, Miss Vega." Apparently, Madeleine Vega didn't go to the Warren Haggerty School of Name Invention. I kind of liked the sound of Laney Vega, though. It was cute.

I went to the front desk.

"Excuse me," I said to the bald man in his burgundy suit with gold braid. "I'm here to see Madeleine Vega. She's in 13G, right?"

134

"Just a moment. I'll check." He hummed something while he consulted his computer. "No, 17D."

"Really? Huh."

"Well, they sound alike." He was nodding sympathetically.

I thanked him and went up in the elevator. The floor was deserted when I got there. No chambermaids or anything. I found door 17 and, looking around cautiously, picked the lock in no time. This must've been the only hotel in the area without keycards. I was in.

Rain was drumming on the huge windows, running in snakes down the glass. I checked the closet first. Aha! Clothes. Just as I suspected. I tried all the drawers, too, finding a camera, her wire and recorder, and a .45 with three spare clips. And a stack of black and white glossy 8 x 10s.

Rabbit helping me onto the Capriole.

Rabbit and I talking in the salon.

Rabbit high in the crotch of a tree.

Me crying like a schoolgirl, inches from Cedric's snarling face.

Me in black on a mangy lawn, a MAC-10 held in both hands.

Oh shit.

There were dozens of them. Rabbit and Blue Tick. Rabbit and Todd. Rabbit and Blue Tick and Todd and me. And plenty of just me. Some of me asleep in bed, shot through the slits of my window blinds. Some of me naked.

I had to destroy these. I was in a panic. Who knew how many copies there might be? She could keep the naked ones, something to touch herself to over there on the bed, but the rest could send me straight to hell. I snatched them all up out of the drawer and jumped at the loud click of the door unlocking.

The photos slid from my nerveless fingers to the carpeted floor.

There was nowhere to run.

The door opened and there she was.

We stared at each other with the same stupid deer-in-the-headlights look on our faces.

She looked at the pictures on the floor. I stepped back from them, and our eyes met again. For a long time there was nothing but the drumming of the rain outside and her pale blue eyes.

"There's vodka in the minibar," she said finally.

135

"Okay." My voice sounded like a little girl's.

She walked past me, watching the floor, brushing her wet curly hair out of her face and sitting down on the bed. I watched her get a cigarette from a pack in the nightstand. I watched her light it with a match, striking it on a hotel matchbook. Then she watched me standing there like an idiot.

"So, if you're thirsty," she said, "There's vodka in the minibar."

"I'm fine."

"Then sit down."

I went to the writing table and sat at the ugly-cushioned chair in front of it, locating an ashtray and lighting a cigarette of my own. We watched each other some more.

"So…" I said awkwardly.

"So, you're Rabbit's girl, now?" Her tone wasn't accusing, but the statement was. I didn't know how to answer it.

"I like your new look."

"Thanks. So, you're Rabbit's girl, now?"

"I don't know what I am. Who are you?"

"You want to lay all your cards on the table? If you do, so'll I. Then we can talk about what to do."

"What's your real name?"

"Audrey Gray."

"Hi."

"Hello. Are you fucking him?"

"No. Yes. Well, just that one time."

"Well, stay the hell away from him. I don't know how many times I can get you away when my people are coming in."

"And I don't know how many times I can be there to get you to the hospital."

"Thank you, by the way."

"You're welcome."

"What the fuck were you doing at Cedric Neely's house?"

"I didn't fire a shot. I swear."

"Do you think that'll matter to a judge? They kind of frown on killing cops and their families."

"How many other people know?"

"Just me. For now."

"I wish we could go back to the way things were before."

"I was a DEA agent then, too."

"Oh, is that who you work for?"

136

She blew out a stream of smoke and watched it swirl away.

"What are you going to do about me?" I asked.

"Nothing, if you stay away from Rabbit."

"And if I don't?"

"I'll break your goddamned head."

"I miss you."

"I miss you more."

"Here's a couple hundred bucks, let's call room service."

"Hungry?"

"No, thirsty. And that little bottle of vodka ain't gonna fly."

"I wanted to be an actress," she said, pouring another drink. "I was good, too. Did a bunch of stage plays, musicals, and Shakespeare—I was Caterina in "The Taming of the Shrew," that was my favorite, and Ophelia and Juliet and Viola. So I went to LA to become a star. I met all kinds of people. Brad Pitt, I met him once and saw him in a movie tonight. Not his best, but it was the writer's fault. He's a great guy. Funny, man, you never met anyone so funny."

"I don't think I saw you in anything," I told her.

"That's because I wasn't in anything. I walked off my first job because I was disgusted with all the immature, whiny assholes that the whole world seems to adore. They've always got some stupid problem that's more important to them than getting the job done."

"You quit because of that?"

"Damn right I did. And right out there on the street, I saw two cars screech around the corner with guys leaning out of the windows, firing AK-47s at one another. This one guy in the first car, his chest exploded as bullets tore him apart right in front of me.

"His gun was still firing as he fell back, hanging from the window by his legs, which were, I guess, pinned under a seat. An old woman and a couple with a baby stroller got sprayed. It was horrible, the way their bodies jerked as they were hit."

"Did the baby get hurt?"

"It got killed."

"Oh." Outside, the rain had stopped, and the moon came out.

"Then somebody shot the tires out from under the second car and the first car got away. The pieces of shit in the disabled car had to abandon ship, and they just started shooting people down as they ran. That's when I made up my mind."

"To become a narc?"

"To start really acting. Acting for a purpose. Pretending to be someone else so that I could change this fucked-up world and put a stop to innocent people being killed in the street."

I couldn't think of anything to say. I became a narc just to get off the hook. Where she had noble intentions, I was just a junkie selling my ass for a spoon or a dime rock. It put the world sharply into perspective, and I didn't like what I saw.

"Were you always acting with me?" I asked, just to say something.

"In the beginning, yeah. I had a job to do."

"When did you stop?"

"I think you know."

I thought about it, stepping out of my own shoes and looking at this from a different angle. She reacted to my scene in a bathroom by almost beating two innocent girls to death. Instead of knocking on my door in the middle of the night for a joyful, teary-eyed reunion and violent sex, she's being a peeping-tom, stalking me and withholding evidence from her bosses. I think she's losing her mind maybe. It's romantic, in a creepy kind of way.

"I've been wondering," I said. "If Rabbit's so careful, how'd you find him this time?"

"Ha! You won't believe this. We were alerted by a flower shop. We told all the area florists to report anyone who placed an order for a shitload of roses. When the guy came to pick them up, we followed him. Now we're waiting to see..." She caught herself, then shrugged. "Funny, though. We ended up finding him with plant penises."

We talked some more about life and how no matter who you think you are, or where you're going, it's amazing when you end up the furthest thing from it. And the things you're sure are what make up the Good Life turn out to be the quickest ways to a bad death.

I left after a little while, and drove to Rabbit's marina. This time I made sure I wasn't followed, and I found him in the cockpit, drinking a beer, reading a book, and listening to Bob Marley tell him not to worry.

He looked up and smiled. I took off my shoes, stepped onto the boat, and took his book away from him. I led him inside, down below to his stateroom, and made love to him all night long.

When we'd finished, and he fell asleep with his arms around

me, I made my decision.

Dear Diary,

Marmalade called on my cell phone, asking if I was interested in a gig. That's what we called it, as if we were in a band or something. What she meant was, let's go dance naked at a party and then perform sexual favors for money. She called me Shambleau, Salomé's stage name, and I couldn't imagine what it meant. Something French, I guess.

"Where and when?" I asked.

"Tonight. Remember that guy Ray whose head got chopped off? His boss. You know, the cokehead who can't get it up."

"Scalisi?"

"Yeah, him. He asked for you specifically."

"Of course he did." He did?

"Yeah, well, are you in or not?"

"You know I am."

"Cool. They'll pick us up at Pussycats around ten."

"I'll be there." I hung up and told Rabbit, who lay beside me. His eyes got small and hungry, like an animal's.

"I remember one summer we spent in Tennessee with my aunt and uncle, who play bluegrass in a band. My sister and I took these beebee guns out into the woods to shoot squirrels and stuff. We rigged up this trap, a cage, and went off popping birds out of trees. When we got back to the trap, there was this terrified little rabbit in it. A gray one, about this big." I held my hands a foot apart.

"We took him back to the farm and tacked him spread-eagled on the barn wall with a staple gun. He was shivering and struggling against those thick staples, and we backed up twenty feet and used him for target practice. He screamed. God, I can still hear him screaming. The ears we shot up like Swiss cheese, but the beebees wouldn't go more than a quarter inch into his body. He was covered in blood, screaming in terror and pain, blood streaking in little rivers down the side of the barn by the time we ran out of ammo.

"We let him go. That was the first day of our vacation. A month and a half later we caught a rabbit in our trap, and my sister looked at me like "You thinking what I'm thinking?" We got closer, and it was just staring at us. Then, somehow, it recognized us, our scent or something. It went crazy, snarling and clawing frantically at the cage, trying to get us. It was all deformed, one eye milky white, with tattered ears and mangy, pockmarked fur. There were these nasty little dents all over it, like beebee wounds. There was no doubt it was the same rabbit, growling and spitting, berserk in that cage. It hadn't occurred to me what would happen to it after we let it go. I hadn't given it a second thought."

"What did you do?" he asked.

"Well, my sister laughs and says, 'He came back for more, let's do it again!' But I just took the rifle and shot him in the head. I've never felt that bad, either before or since. But that's what got me started loving those nature shows. The idea of a little bunny rabbit remembering its tormentors and wanting revenge. That's what I think of when I think of you, that crazy rabbit attacking the cage, glaring at us with its one good eye."

"How old were you then?"

"My sister and I were six years old."

"I remind you of rodent you once tortured?"

"Don't take it the wrong way."

"Gee, how could I?"

We still hadn't gotten out of bed yet. He lay on his belly and I straddled him, massaging his back and rambling on. We'd made love again and again and again, pausing only to rest and talk awhile, toying with each other's bodies until we were ready. I was one step away from worshipping him. I eventually noticed something that somehow didn't surprise me; he had these scars on his tool that I think mean he'd had surgery done on it. So that was another fake thing about him. He hadn't been born with that gigantic dong, but I guess it doesn't matter because he has it now.

In the back of my mind was a tiny dark compartment where I'd stored Agent Audrey Gray. I had sweet memories of someone I had loved, but they were like half-forgotten dreams. The woman I remembered was an illusion, and a threat to my new happiness. Now that I'd gotten my head on straight and found myself a proper mate, I could not imagine letting any harm come to him. I didn't know what to do about Audrey, but I didn't want her hurt either. If it came right down to one or the other, though, I was in Rabbit's corner and would do whatever I had to do to protect him.

"I love you," I said, without thinking.

There was a silence, then: "Good."

We made love again, but he seemed somewhere else.

Ten pounds' worth of trolls had been made by Rabbit's chemists, and five thousand geltabs, and gallons of psilocybic tea. If every dose was sold, every employee and soldier could retire comfortably and Rabbit would be a multimillionaire with what remained. All we needed was the patience and the time.

Todd took the goods and loaded them up into a U-Haul truck. He had them packaged inside old television sets he'd found at pawn shops. Opening up the shells, he took out everything except the backing behind the screens and stuffed the packages inside, plus free-weights for realism. The weed, coke, and smack were all vacuum-sealed, wrapped in scented fabric softener, contact-taped, and boxed up in cardboard, gift-wrapped again using the same process. No dog in the world could smell through that, and Rabbit guaranteed that claim with a drug dog of his own.

Then, taking the chemists with him, Todd drove out of my life forever. I was told he was relocating to a new area to await further instructions. I heard something about Miami, but nothing that would hold up in court, so I just assumed I'd see him when I saw him.

I was too busy thinking about the long way I'd come, and the long way I was going to go. I was never going to dance naked again, except maybe for Rabbit. I was never going to lie down with another stranger. For the first time in five years, the future looked bright.

I remembered my dream and refused to end up a toothless old hag on a stage in a titty bar. Rabbit didn't know it yet, but I was going with him to Sicily. I was going to Taormina, where the sea melted into the sky, and nothing on Earth was going to stand in my way.

Dear Diary,

Sometimes I think about what almost was, and I sit down and stare at my reflection in the nickel-plating of my .38, as shiny as surgical steel, trying to think of a reason not to put the barrel in my mouth and pull the trigger. I think about an ambitious, feisty red-head posing for the covers of Cosmo, Maxim, Stuff, and a dozen others, on her way to becoming a high-fashion runway model. I remember walking the beam in front of a full-length mirror, practicing in the living room of my apartment. Lead with the pelvis. Toe, heel, toe, heel, toe, heel, stop, give 'em that Scarlet look that made men and women alike into putty, turn, and toe-heel-toe-heel back. I remember the practice becoming reality.

I remember being in Donna Karan, Yves Saint Laurent, Christian Dior, Paris in January, Milan in March through June, then back to Paris for July. Tokyo in October.

I remember laughing when I found out Ralph Lauren's real name was Lifshitz.

Elizabeth Arden was born Florence Nightingale Graham, and Eve Arden was Eunice Quedens.

Even Yves Saint Laurent was né Henri Donat Mathieu. Whatever their names really were, their merest whim affected economies all over the world. A sheep in Scotland, a silkworm in China, and a cotton-picking Hindu in India all felt the weight of some designer's pen stroke on a scribbled page.

And I was a part of all that. I went to the parties, I kissed up to the photographers, and I put out to whoever I had to. I became a princess.

And then my sister handed me a needle.

Less than a year later, no more Mediterranean cruises. No more limos. No more flashing cameras.

Now it was a brass pole on a wooden stage, groping hands, glassy eyes, and thirty-dollar lap dances. Lying to myself when I say I don't mind. Lying to myself when I say that I like it. It's easier to swallow if you chase it with tequila. It's easier to live with if I can't quite remember.

Was I in love with Rabbit?

Probably not.

Infatuated?

Maybe. But after I thought about it enough, I realized that he was my one ticket out of this day to day existence. And that's all it was: I wasn't alive, I just existed. And that ain't no kind of life. If I hadn't met him and gotten involved with Layla and the club and this whole big mess, I probably would have blown my brains out one night. Either out of utter despair or the simple curiosity about Death.

Would I get to be a ghost? Would I get to haunt somebody? Only one way to find out.

But now I had Rabbit.

It was Rabbit, or nothing, and if Audrey Gray did her job, it would be nothing. I steeled myself to be the cold-blooded and ruthless pragmatist my evil twin had been. It was the only way.

"Rabbit," I said, touching his arm. "I have an idea."

He kissed me lightly and I got out of his sweet sweet Jag, swinging my dance bag over my shoulder by the straps and walking my walk toward Pussycats. Inside, Marmalade was at the bar talking to these two white guys, her smile gleaming against her chocolate skin.

Her chemically straightened hair was many shades of blonde, and her fine features were almost as beautiful as my own. She was smiling broadly as if the conversation was fascinating, and her hand toyed with the lapel of one man's jacket.

I sat down at a table by the stage, allowing Marmalade to work whatever she was planning. A woman who looked like she'd been working here way too long came by to take my drink order, and I paid way too much for a Jack n' Coke. The girl dancing stared vacantly ahead with her plastic smile frozen in place. There's only so long you can hold a smile before it's just gums and teeth, and to me that always looked like lunacy. I'm glad I don't work here.

I watched the Snarl gyrate and run her fingers through her long, brown curly hair. She had small, perky breasts and freckles. Not unattractive, but not gorgeous by any stretch. She strutted toward a group of five guys sitting at the rail, leading with the pelvis, toe-heel, toe-heel in her clear plastic stacks, and teased her g-string down with two suggestive fingers.

Two of the guys elbowed a blushing third, laughing at his shy protests. A fourth stood up with feigned dignity, as if there was a proper way to approach titty dancers and he knew all about it.

Slipping a green bill, folded lengthwise, into the girl's garter, he let his hand linger on her thigh as he said something he thought was slick into her ear. She smiled coyly, then backed away and rolled her eyes when she thought he wasn't looking. The other guys laughed at him while he tried to brush it off.

I looked away at three guys playing Cutthroat on a pool table, cigarette smoke hanging in drifts under the Budweiser lamp, making the colored balls shine with a hazy glare. The boyfriends of the dancers, no doubt. They weren't normally allowed in because they get drunk and jealous and cause trouble when their girlfriends do a lap dance or spend too much time in the champagne room. But they were always there, either shooting pool or drinking alone in the far corner. I don't know why they come. If they care at all, it makes them miserable.

My drink came. It tasted like shit, so I drank it quickly and ordered a Corona instead, sat back and sucked on my wedge of lime to wash out the aftertaste. Snarl unhooked the clasp of her g-string and the garment fell away. She had what Salomé called "an open-faced roast beef sandwich," just a mess of nasty, ragged-out flappy snatch. I could tell from where I sat that she'd gotten a lot of mileage out of that thing. She could be the poster-child for chastity. I envisioned a closeup of her vagina, all purple-gray and overused, with the warning in bold: It Could Happen To You! Girls like her didn't plan on living to thirty anyway.

I turned to check on Marmalade, just in time to see her slip her mark's wallet out of his jacket pocket as her other hand found his crotch. The other guy was looking at Snarl and didn't see his friend stiffen, shut his eyes, and smile. The wallet was in her purse before I realized it, and she patted the guy's cheek and excused herself.

Sidestepping a barmaid and weaving between customers, she made her way to the backstage door. I followed.

I found her at her locker, counting a fat wad of—wouldn't you know it?—ones. I leaned heavily on the row of lockers, making a loud bang on the peeling-painted metal and startled her. She jumped and cursed, dropping a few bills.

"Nice pull," I told her.

"Don't you *ever* do that to me again! Girl, I'll knock you out!"

"How much did you get?"

"Not enough. When did you get here?"

"I've been here, maybe two songs."

"You ready for tonight?" she asked, picking up her fallen money.

"You know it."

She looked over her shoulder, saw the room empty except for the two of us, and asked conspiratorially: "Wanna bump?"

I grinned. "You talked me into it."

We went over to the counter where we do our makeup, and she shook a few clumps of meth out of a pink nickle bag.

"Got a straw?" she asked as I dug my little stainless steel hitter out of my purse. I handed it to her with a "Ta da!"

Taking it, she bent over the counter, holding her blonde tresses out of the way, just as the door came flying open.

"Ooh, whatcha doing?"

I turned and saw Snarl looking at us like she caught us red-handed. Hands in the cookie jar.

"You guys tyin' one on, there?"

"Get lost," Marmalade said, snorting up a little bit.

"Well, pardon me, then. I guess I *won't* warn you about the two guys who're looking for you out there."

"Ask me if I care." Marmalade put the little bag away.

"Okay, I'll just go tell them I found you." She took a step toward the door and hesitated, as if we were going to say, "No, wait!" and was disappointed when we didn't. I took the hitter and tooted the remains of the powder. Uncertainly, Snarl watched us as we checked our makeup in the long mirror. We ignored her.

"Uh, hey." We stopped and looked at her. "You, uh…you got any more?" We shook our heads, and she shrugged. Grabbing our dance bags, we pushed past her and went out the door. In the bar's tricky light, I couldn't see the two guys, but Marmalade spotted the guy we were to meet.

"There he is," she said.

"Who?"

"Whatshisname. Carcotti."

My blood ran cold as I found his face in the crowd. His eyes met mine and I could tell he recognized me even from there. I think I saw him smile. Now I saw it all at once, what kind of a party we were really going to. I hesitated only a moment, then followed Marmalade.

My fear was gradually replaced by the assurance that whatever awaited me in the next hour or so, the joke was gonna be on the other guys. The confidence might've just been the meth up my nose, though. I smiled back at Ernesto Carcotti, remembering the look on his face when Blue Tick handed him Ray Valanga's head. He wanted to kill me just for being in that room.

We passed the stage where another girl was riding the brass pole, and the two angry white guys appeared out of nowhere. The guy in the jacket grabbed Marmalade's arm and yanked her to him, growling into her startled face.

"Give me my fucking wallet, you cunt!"

Bouncers hurried toward us, pushing people roughly aside.

"What wallet?"

"What wallet? My wallet you took just now—"

A bouncer tackled him, and all three of them went down. Two others arrived and went to dogpile, but the guy's friend pulled a knife and waved them back with it.

"All he wants is his wallet, and we'll go," he said.

"Put that knife away and fight like a man!"

"Three on one is fighting like a man?"

In a blur of speed, a shape crashed into him from behind and they flew together into a table, shattering it and the empty glasses it held, scattering chairs and bystanders.

A bloodcurdling scream cut the noise of the bar. The bouncer flopped over onto his back, the knife between his ribs, his fingers clawing at it.

Marmalade was up and running, pushing through the gaping crowd, and I was right behind her. At the door, as calm as you please, Carcotti escorted us outside.

That's how quickly things can happen. No matter how many times I see a stupid situation suddenly become a crime scene, I never quite see it coming. I knew that bouncer would probably die, and the guy and his friend would go to prison because only Marmalade and I knew the truth. All over a handful of ones.

A limousine, black, waited for us outside, and a thin man with pockmarks opened the back door for us. We swung our dance bags into the car and followed them. Carcotti got in behind us and Craterface shut the door. I hadn't been inside one of these in…too long.

"That was an adventure," Carcotti said. "I'm so glad you called attention to yourselves like that."

"Mistaken identity," Marmalade said.

"If you hadn't gotten out of there tonight it would be a real disappointment."

"Tell me about it," I muttered. The car started and Craterface drove us out of the parking lot. I couldn't even see where Rabbit's people were, but I knew they were right behind us, somewhere.

Ernesto Carcotti opened a compartment that contained small liquor bottles—fifths, mostly—and selected a bottle of Tuaca.

"Appetizer?" he asked.

It took about twenty minutes to get where we were going, and I passed the time drinking and watching Marmalade blow our host for a C-note. The whole time her blonde head bobbed in his lap, he never took his eyes off me. I'd look out the window at other cars, people trying to see through our blackened glass, and when I'd look back he'd still be watching me with his dark eyes.

When we finally pulled into a lonely driveway I was sufficiently spooked, unconsciously glancing around to see if a car would drive by with Rabbit in it, or Blue Tick, or anything to reassure me. But, as in the churchyard, there was no sign of them. All there was in front of that haunted-looking house was a chorus of chirping crickets in the trees to cover the sound of my heartbeat. With Craterface holding the door, we stepped out with our dance bags and allowed Carcotti to walk us to the house's portico entrance.

The front door opened, and another big wop welcomed us inside. I didn't hear any music, or talking, or anything to suggest a party. It was all quiet. We walked with echoing footsteps down a hall to a large room with a plastic drop cloth covering the hardwood floor.

On a large L-shaped couch, smoking cigars, eight men sat waiting. In the middle of the room was a gibbet, the kind they use in S&M/D&S for sexual torture, complete with manacles. A young man with longish hair and a weasel face blew a row of smoke rings and pointed at me with his cigar.

"Is that her?" He wore one of those gaudy Versace silk shirts that only nouveau riche ever wear. It was blue with some kind of gold...stuff on it. Christ, it was ugly.

"Yeah," Carcotti said. "It's her."

"Good job," the young man said to Marmalade. "I sure don't recognize her. Been through so many of them."

I looked at Marmalade, who winked at me. A Judas wink.

"You said I'd get ten grand for bringing her," she said.

"I lied."

The guy who answered the door knocked us both to the floor with a hard shove. Marmalade cried out as she was dragged to the gibbet, and even though they were roughly cuffing my hands behind my back I could hardly suppress a smile. She looked just like that little gray rabbit Sal and I stapled to the barn as she was chained spread-eagled to the black wooden beams. She screamed pleas and threats until they stuck a red rubber ball gag into her mouth and fastened it to her head with a leather thong. Now all she made were muffled squeals. They cuffed my feet together too, and then fastened both sets of cuffs together, hog-tie fashion.

"This is how we're gonna play it," Zack Scalisi said. "You're going to see I mean business, then we're going to talk about your little friend. If you cooperate, and tell us everything you know, where to find him, how his business runs, how much merchandise he has, and where he keeps it, we'll rape you, then shoot you in the head."

"And when I don't tell you a goddamned thing?"

"Then we'll do to you everything we do to this nigger until you do talk. Then we'll all rape you and cut you up with a hand saw. Take your pick."

Since Rabbit was going to kick the door in any minute, I could afford to be cocky. I looked at Marmalade, her eyes wide with terror, limbs straining against the manacles.

Serves you right, you fucking turncoat.

"You know, your boy Ray shit all over himself when we killed him." I craned my neck to look up at Carcotti. "And this guy pissed his pants just watching it."

Ernesto Carcotti didn't say anything. Instead, he unzipped his fly and pulled his dick out of his trousers. I shut my eyes and ducked my head back down, flinched when the warm piss hit the back of my neck. Rivers of it soaked my hair and ran down over my face, into my eyes no matter how tightly I scrunched them together, into the corners of my mouth no matter how hard I pursed my lips. That harsh ammonia smell stung even more than my pride. I had to choke back my cry of rage, so no more piss would get in my mouth.

That fucker! That cocksucking wop motherfucker! He pissed all over my back, too, and it went on forever. The roars of laughter and the sound of piss drumming on the drop cloth like rain were all I could hear. I don't think I've ever been that fucking embarrassed.

When he was finally done, I shook myself as much as I could, but it didn't help much. At least I'd have the last laugh. I felt them drag me by one of my feet to the middle of the room and prop me up in the most uncomfortable position ever, right in front of Marmalade so I could look into her terrified eyes. My tears and rapid blinking washed much of the piss out of my own eyes, but they still stung like a bitch. I spat the taste out, wanting to throw up, but refusing to give them the satisfaction. They'd finally stopped laughing.

One of the guys got up from the couch and walked to the gibbet. With one hand, he tore Marmalade's yellow spaghetti-strap shirt off, exposing her large brown breasts, and mashed the smoking end of his cigar into one of her nipples. She bucked and wailed, but there was nothing she could do but cry. Her tormentor pulled a pair of pliers out of his back pocket and clamped them hard on her other nipple. Twisting fiercely, he got her very still and quiet for a moment, holding her leaning sideways and shaking with agony. He twisted it back the other way, and her whole body convulsed, shuddering.

With a savage wrench, he tore it off of her breast, spattering me with her blood. She let out a bloodcurdling shriek and the men on the couch all clapped their hands. The applause went on until Marmalade's cries dwindled to low, pathetic whimpering.

Then, another guy came forward with an electric eggbeater trailing a long orange extension cord. Replacing the pliers, the first man withdrew and opened a straight razor. Deftly, he cut the short-short blue-jean cutoffs off of her and backed away.

"Hey, pay attention!" the guy with the eggbeater said. He slapped her twice, and she weakly stared at him.

"I was gonna make a joke about being pussy-whipped, but I decided it'd be in bad taste."

Crouching, he put the stainless steel whisk somewhere she didn't want it, and squeezed the trigger.

Treacherous bitch that she was, nobody deserved this. Her horrible thrashing threatened to pull the entire gibbet down. I'll remember her muffled screams for the rest of my life. When Rabbit finally showed up, *if* he ever showed up, I would personally put the mercy bullet into her head. The pieces of shit on the couch cheered and whistled and howled.

I cried for her. She lured me here to my death and I cried for her. And Zack Scalisi bust a gut laughing.

One of them opened a door to the backyard, and another turned on a large fan to blow out the smell that was coming. Someone had a can of lighter fluid and he squeezed it, spraying a thin stream all over Marmalade's quaking brown body. He sparked his lighter, and touched the little tongue of flame to her thigh. A wave of blue and yellow fire washed over her and I shut my eyes.

I put myself far, far away where I couldn't hear her. I thought of a town halfway up a cliff in the Mediterranean, where the sea melted into the sky. I thought of a warm salty breeze and the roar of the surf, and Rabbit playing in the water with our children. But I could imagine I was on the moon and still hear Marmalade scream.

A long time later, Zack Scalisi asked me if I had anything to tell him.

"Yes," I said. He waited. I stalled long enough for a shout to cut the silence and the chatter of machine gun fire, but it never came. "Yes..." I tried to think of something clever to say, but like the Cavalry, it never came.

"Well, we'll peel your skin off until you're ready to say it."

They took Marmalade's horribly mutilated body off of the gibbet and put me in the manacles. Three of them held me to make sure I didn't get loose, but I was too numb to even resist. *Rabbit would have to come now*, I thought. *Please, Rabbit, my hero, come in the nick of time and save me.* The stink of Marmalade's corpse was worse than the piss that had dried all over me. *Please, Rabbit, come and take me away.*

"You know what?" Zack said.

"What?" Carcotti asked.

"I think we should cut her face off."

"That's an idea."

"You're not going to get away with this," I said stupidly.

Amused, he turned to Carcotti with a mocking tremor of doubt in his voice. He rolled his eyes as he spoke.

"Hey, you think we'll get away with this?"

The henchman pretended to think a moment, then shrugged.

"Yeah, probably."

The guy with the straight razor came forward, grinning wide. I stared into his eyes, trying to be tough, but when the blade touched my forehead the searing pain ripped a scream out of me. I could feel the sting and the warm, sticky flow of blood all down one side of my face. The guy dug his fingertips into my cheek and pulled. I

151

shrieked and wept and tried to shake him off, but there was no-where to go. There was nothing I could do.

He stopped.

"Where's your boyfriend hiding?" Scalisi asked.

"Fuck you!"

"Very impressive, but if you think he's still gonna fuck *you* after your face is peeled off, you're fucking stupid!"

"Eat shit!"

"Joey, you may continue."

More of the skin came away from the meat of my cheek and the bone of my forehead. Rabbit wasn't out there. I screamed until my throat was raw. The cut widened so slowly, the skin tore away millimeter by burning millimeter.

Please, stop, please please, don't do this to me! But the words wouldn't come. All I could do was cry. Please, God. Please, Jesus. I know I've been a whore and a stupid, stupid bitch, and I deserve to die, but please God, not like this.

"Tell me!"

I couldn't tell him even if I wanted to.

"I know you know, and I know he wouldn't go through even one second of this for you!"

Rabbit wasn't coming. If he was, he'd be here by now. He'd be—and suddenly it occurred to me. He was probably sitting just outside the room, waiting to see if I'd give in. To see if I'd chicken out, like at Cedric's house. Only it was stupid. I was grasping at stupid, stupid straws, and I was going to die here.

"You are a stubborn bitch, aren't you?"

"You're a pissant and you can't keep it up, you faggot! You suck dick and I'll never tell you anything!"

Then, like the Hammer of God, a deafening crack of thunder shook me, and the guy with the razor was against my blood-soaked body, sliding to the floor, fingers clawing desperately at my clothes.

His eyes were wide and startled, and I realized before he did that he'd been shot.

I watched dumbly as the men on the couch jumped to their feet and jerked sickeningly, a hail of bullets tearing chunks of meat and ropes of blood from them. A head whip-lashed back as a red mist flew from his dark hair, and then again, and half of his head was gone before he hit the floor. Another's trachea came out of his throat. Bodies flew this way and that, spraying blood on the couch and walls, as Rabbit's black-clad soldiers strafed into them with sub-machine guns. The last man fell, and the firing stopped. The ringing in my ears was just as deafening.

Rabbit took me down from the gibbet and I collapsed into his arms. I was bleeding all over him, but he didn't seem to care. I sobbed hysterically, and he held me, rocking me gently, shushing me and stroking my hair. My face was slimy with a mixture of blood and tears and snot, and half of it was just a flap of hanging skin.

"Be a good girl and swallow this," he said softly, putting a capsule in my mouth. I wasn't sure what it was, but at that point I didn't care. I swallowed it dry, and it felt stuck in my throat even though I knew that it wasn't. Two soldiers came and helped me up. I dimly saw Rabbit taking off his blood-soaked sweater and throwing it aside. His knotted muscles were shiny with sweat, and a little of my blood had stained his chest and shoulder.

Blue Tick handed him a wet towel, from the bathroom most likely, and he cleaned himself off with it while he issued instructions. He stepped over to Zack Scalisi, gasping blood on the floor, his chest torn apart. The smoking barrel of his gun mere inches from the man's nose, Rabbit smiled.

"Sorry about the shirt," he said, and fired, making a crimson pulp of his face.

Someone was bandaging my face back on, and then, somehow, I was outside in a car, watching flames flicker through the windows of the house. I felt numb all over, and strangely detached.

"Feeling better?" Rabbit asked, sympathetically.

"What did you give me?" It took forever to make the words.

"Painkiller. Can you feel anything?"

"No."

"Wow. That was quick."

"Huh?"

"My chemists made it. You swallowed it less than five minutes ago. I'll have to tell Bruce it's a success."

He leaned in and kissed my undamaged cheek.

"You are a very pretty guinea pig," he said.

I looked back out the window, and realized we'd been moving. I was vaguely aware that I'd started drooling on myself, but didn't feel interested in doing anything about it. I just stared out the window at the trees whizzing by, and the stars.

Dear Diary,

I awoke in a dingy apartment on a ratty mattress. The sound of television in another room and flies buzzing were all I could hear. I got up stiffly. There were nine other twin mattresses laid on the floor, with blankets folded and miscellaneous personal possessions. And guns. One sub-machine gun and one handgun per bed.

I got up unsteadily and stumbled to the bathroom. My face in the mirror was half-mummified. Déjà vu. I turned on the faucet, cupped my hands under the water, and drank greedily. Somebody heard my slurping and came in. I could feel his presence behind me.

"How do you feel?" he asked. I groaned at him.

"Yeah, I'll bet. We got Chinese if you're hungry."

I groaned again, this time in the negative.

"Okay." I felt his presence leave.

I drank my fill and then looked in the mirror. My face was pale and blotchy, aching numbly. At least I still had a face. Fucking sick-os. I took a small consolation in knowing they were nothing but ashes now. I was more than a little bitter about Rabbit arriving just *after* the nick of time, but I knew I'd proved myself to him. He could never doubt my loyalty after last night.

I went into the living room, where fifteen men sat watching TV or cleaning their guns. There were five more mattresses in there, drawn up and leaning against the walls to make floor space.

"Hey, Sleeping Beauty!" Blue Tick said. "Glad you could join us." I tried to smile at him. "Grab yourself an egg roll. We got pork fried lice, chung flung dung, and four-prong yang. Help yourself."

I was suddenly ravenous. My stomach rumbled loud enough for everyone to hear it. They laughed heartily. "Sounds like your belly button's rubbing a sore on your backbone," another soldier said.

"No surprise," I answered. "I haven't eaten anything since yesterday morning."

They all looked at each other.

"Uh, Red?"

"Yeah, Tick?"

"You've slept for three days."

I stared at him.

"Reuben doctored up your face and gave you shots to keep you quiet. It's Wednesday."

"...Oh."

"Now we get to go take care of your DEA friend and get the hell outta Dodge. We're moving the whole operation to South Beach."

"Really?"

"Yeah, so get your breakfast so we can get this show on the road." He called Rabbit on his cell phone while I dumped some lukewarm lo mein out of a carton onto a paper plate. It came out like wet sand from a child's sandcastle bucket, holding the shape of its container. There was a collection of plastic cutlery on the scarred kitchen counter.

"Mr. Haggerty?" Tick always called Rabbit Mr. Haggerty in front of the men. It was a respect thing. "She's awake."

He listened for a moment, then nodded. "Yes sir." Beep. "He'll be here in one hour."

I ate and took a cold shower in sulfurous water, realizing how badly I must've stunk before.

The bandages on my face got soggy, so I said Fuck it and peeled them off. When I touched what they'd concealed I felt my stomach fill with ice. There were nasty-feeling ridges and stitches of wire that felt like fishing line, starting on my forehead and going down my temple, past my cheek to my jaw line. Tearing the shower curtain aside, I stepped out and faced the mirror.

And screamed.

Rabbit's race was without emotion. He'd brought me a change of clothes and now we sat together outside the apartment, on the concrete stairs. The walls of the building had arched rust stains from the sprinkler system at regular intervals. A few hibiscus bushes here and there. Black children playing somewhere, out of sight but not earshot. The place had hot and cold running roaches. No one would ever have looked for Rabbit here, not in a million years.

When he saw my face, he didn't say a word. Didn't even bat an eye. He just came and held me, let me burst into tears and cry on his shoulder all over again. The rest of them sat in an embarrassed silence. Now, outside, he held me close to him with one arm around my shoulders and smoked one of Tick's cigarettes.

"So, what now?" I asked eventually.

"So, now we tie up the last loose end."

"Layla?"

He nodded. He got bitter when anybody mentioned that name.

155

I didn't want to hurt her, but if I didn't there were pictures that would send both Rabbit and me to the electric chair. Rabbit changed the subject, sort of.

"I worked in a slaughterhouse once. The first time I saw the sheep get killed just blew my mind. See, there's a ramp they walk up, single file, and they're real calm because they're led by a male who's been trained. They trust him, and when they get inside there's a fork. The male goes one way and the route is blocked off behind him. There's nowhere to go but the other way, so the rest of the sheep walk straight to their deaths. The male they use over and over again. He's called the Judas Goat. We give him a little treat for the special job he does. It's disturbing to watch the first few times, but it's a lot quicker and easier than the alternative. What I'm trying to say is—"

"I know what you're trying to say."

We sat in silence a while longer. Eventually I had to ask.

"Will you take me with you?"

He looked at me, and I covered my wound with one hand. Very gently, he took my hand away and looked deep into my eyes the way the movie star would. I've never felt more naked in my life, and I wanted to cry again. He held my face in his hands and kissed me tenderly.

"I don't want to be a stripper my whole life," I whispered. After Audrey was dead, I would have nothing without Rabbit. He had to take me. I'd given up everything for him.

"What do you want to be?" he whispered back.

"A wife. A mother. In Sicily."

I felt Rabbit's lips smile against mine.

"Ramada Inn, front desk."

"Good afternoon, could you please connect me with Miss Madeleine Vega in room 17D?"

"Certainly. One moment, please."

I motioned to a soldier near me that I wanted a cigarette. He nodded and put one in my mouth, lighting it for me while I listened to the phone.

"Hello?"

"Laney. Hi, it's me."

"Me who?"

"*Me* me. I want to see you. We have to talk."

"What about?"

I lowered my voice. "Catching rabbits."

Pause.

"Are you alone?"

"No. Can I meet you tonight?"

"Uh, sure. Hold on."

"Wait! I'm alone now, but I don't know for how long. Listen, I can lead you to him tonight. He has Zack Scalisi and he's going to torture him to death. You can catch him in the act, *and* pick up all his business at the same time. Everybody's going to be there."

"But I was holding out to find out who his suppliers were," she said. "All I have is…" She thought better of saying it.

"The lab? You know he had chemists of his own."

"They're not his. He works for someone else. ATF is in now, too, to get his gun supplier."

"You mean the Brazilian?" I was bluffing. I only knew what she knew, where the guy was from, and I'd only overheard it once. Rabbit's eyes widened, then narrowed.

"What Brazilian?" She pretended to be surprised.

"His rich Brazilian friend who's visiting. He came yesterday and they've spent a lot of time talking alone. He's got, like, ten bodyguards. He'll be there tonight, too."

"What's his name?" She seemed excited.

"I don't remember. Something Brazilian. He's got a big bushy mustache and he scares the shit out of me."

"Please, God, let that be him. My bosses made me eat shit after letting Rabbit get away last time. If I can catch his boss they'll give me a medal. Where is this place?"

"I don't know yet, but I can meet you at eight if you want to wire me up. Then you can follow us to the place where Blue Tick's got Scalisi, Rabbit's headquarters."

"You would do that?"

"You don't understand. Rabbit beats me. The fucker cut my face the other day and I've been waiting for my chance."

"He *cut* you?"

"With a razor. I've got these big-ass Frankenstein stitches in my face. I look terrible, Audrey."

"Oh, baby, I'm sorry. Yeah, we'll meet you at eight. Let me call you and tell you where."

"Good. Oh shit! I gotta go!"

"Okay—" I hung up, and everybody smiled at me.

"Very nice, honey," Blue Tick said.

"Brazilian friend?" Rabbit asked, strangely suspicious. I tried to remember when it was that I had overheard him mention his friend. Before I took over as my sister? Didn't matter.

"Yeah, I just picked it out of thin air. Why?"

"Just curious."

"Whatever. Look, she's going to call after she gets her people together. Then there's going to be a big sting operation with DEA *and* ATF."

"I'm flattered."

"We'll meet in a secluded place. Just like that time with Cedric. Everybody who's involved will be there so they can all coach me on what to do and say once I'm wired. They think they're going to track me to you and then follow us to wherever, some convenient place to bust us."

"But instead…" Blue Tick didn't have to say it.

Dr. Reuben Jiminez was tall and gaunt, and he always looked like he'd died yesterday. His hair was poofy, for lack of a better word, black and unruly and frosted with gray. His face was haggard and old, his eyes bloodhound sad, and he had a great big Stalin mustache. He was what I pictured when I invented the mysterious Brazilian.

I never asked how he had lost his license to practice medicine, but I made an assumption based on his whiskey breath. That might have had something to do with the erratic mess of black stitches in my face, guaranteeing I'd live with a big ugly scar for the rest of my life.

Now I stared into his bloodhound eyes and smelled his breath as he looked over his handiwork. I don't doubt for one second that the instruments he used he sterilized in his whiskey glass. He dabbed cotton balls soaked in alcohol on my wound, and I concentrated on not flinching.

"Well," he said. "It's gonna leave a mark. But it's a lot better than it was. I don't do my best work in the middle of the night, you know."

"Yeah, but your patients don't get hurt between nine and five, either." Rabbit sounded impatient with the man. He wasn't one to accept excuses, ever. "Just tell me if she'll play the piano again."

158

"Not if she keeps burning her hands with cigarettes."

Rabbit looked at my hands as if for the first time, and frowned. I could hear him thinking, and could do nothing about it. His wheels were turning.

"Is that what those are?" he asked finally. "Her sister had very similar marks on her, I remember. I used to wonder what they were."

"We both had a stupid habit when we drank too much. I don't know who started doing it first." I thought fast. "She had them everywhere, though. You've seen her naked, right?"

"No, not up close."

"Yeah, well, I only have them on the backs of my hands, while she made these stupid designs everywhere."

He frowned deeper, as if trying to remember, then shrugged and dismissed the matter with a wave of his hand. If he'd had time to realize I was me and not my sister I guess I wouldn't have to worry about the scar on my face anymore, because I wouldn't have a head.

"The stitches will come out in a few days. Lemme put a new bandage on you," Reuben said. I let him gauze and tape me so I could go out in public and not be everybody's finger-pointing side-show. Of course, the phone rang while he was doing this, so he had to stop while I answered it. It was Layla/Madeleine/Audrey.

"Hi, Simone?"

"Yeah, what's the story?"

"The story is, meet us at the top of that parking building by the library fountains downtown. Eight o'clock sharp. You know the one I mean?"

"At the end of Clematis, yeah. Just down from that old theatre." It was a lousy place for an ambush. If anything went wrong it would take forever to get out of the building. Then again, if everything went well, the pigs would be caught in a deathtrap.

"That's right. Not the one behind Liquid's."

"I'll be there."

"Hey! Simone…"

"Yeah?"

"Thank you."

My brain skipped like a scratchy CD, and for a moment, I lost my resolve. For a moment, I could not let this girl, my ex-lover, walk into my trap. But only for a moment. *Stay in character*, I reminded myself. *You're a ruthless, treacherous, scandalous bitch.*

"Sure, any time." I hung up.

At ten past eight, I turned off of Clematis Street and pulled into the eight-storey parking garage. A woman who did not look anything like a ticket-selling parking garage attendant handed me a ticket and raised the guardrail for me to pass. It was either the alert expression in her eyes or the bulge under her red vest that gave her away. I don't remember which.

I drove into the concrete bunker and slowly went up the first ramp. It was not surprising that the place was empty. I made an ascending spiral up the ramps, slowly, strangely calm. At the seventh storey I passed two vans and five nondescript sedans, with a bunch of guys talking and smoking, stopping to watch me pass.

I went by and up the next ramp onto the roof. There, two more vans and more people waited. I pulled up in front of them, sandwiching them between me and the roof of an office building next door. Madeleine wore black with the letters DEA on her chest, a matching cap, and combat boots. She had one of those CBs with a little thingy attached to her shoulder, a coiled wire running down to another thingy on her belt, and a fast food drive-thru voice telling her something or other she wasn't paying attention to.

"Miss Brennan," she said in her strictly professional voice.

"Agent Gray," I said, getting out and approaching.

They'd heard me pop the trunk when I killed my engine, and now two guys with their hands full of equipment were hurrying toward the rear of the car. I stood face to face with Audrey Gray and looked into her pale blue eyes, her expression also strictly professional.

"I want you to know we really appreciate this," she said.

Two sharp cracks rang out and everyone flinched, eyes darting to the two agents flying backwards, their equipment falling from their hands. A shape spilled out of my trunk as other shots thundered from beneath us. I reared back and slammed my forehead into Audrey's as I jerked my .38 from the waistband of my jeans. She staggered back, stunned, and I aimed over her shoulder and shot somebody in the face.

The agents' guns were drawn just as quickly, but I seized Audrey by her sweater and yanked her to me, firing from behind my human shield. Sniper fire from the office roof picked off agents who had scrambled for cover behind the vans, and the soldier who was crouching behind my Mustang sprayed machine gun fire into the rest of them.

I cursed as the hammer of my pistol fell on an empty chamber, then staggered as Audrey's elbow slammed into my temple. I swatted the gun out of her hand just as fast as she drew it, and decked her hard in the mouth. She staggered, but only for half an instant. Faking an overhand right, making me duck, she pivoted and threw a left cross that stunned me. I don't know where it came from, but her boot struck me upside the head.

My face hit the concrete. I could see Audrey's .45 several yards away. Her hand reached for it and *bam!* It flew spinning away.

She recoiled sharply, and there was that deer-in-the-headlights look again. All of her people were dead. Bullet-riddled corpses with drive-thru voices crackling from CBs. Rabbit's voice behind me, calm as always.

"Fancy meeting you here."

Then the night was alive with red and blue, and Audrey smiled.

"We have you surrounded!" a loudspeaker squawked. I was on my feet instantly. Rabbit's face was purple with rage, twisted hideously, a forked vein pulsing across his forehead. At that moment, I swear his eyes were glowing. Probably just a trick of the fluorescent street lights, but he looked like Satan's younger brother. He ran to the edge of the building, a .45 in each hand, and emptied them both at squad cards far below.

Our snipers on the office building roof took his cue and fired on those who took cover, and our soldiers on the roof—no more than ten, counting Blue Tick and the little guy who'd hidden in my trunk—also ran to the edges of the building. Over the din of gunfire I heard more sirens wailing.

There was nowhere to run.

It started raining.

We'd been idiots to assume the entire DEA/ATF expedition would be in the parking building, acting without the cooperation of the local police. When Rabbit had shot the agent posing as an attendant, making no more noise than a click, and led his men up the concrete steps, we were already dead.

Audrey made a break for the ramp and I tackled her. We hit the concrete hard and, grappling, started to roll down the incline,

161

and I felt her encourage the roll to shake me off. She managed to slip out of my grasp and tried to elbow me again, but I squirmed out of the way. Then she was loose and up and running. I got to my feet and pursued.   She ran halfway down the ramp and vaulted over the edge to the one below, vanished into the crack between them. I was there one second later, in time to see her get to one of the bodies strewn about the two parked vans. I desperately started toward her, hoping to get a gun before she did, but I was dead out in the open when she pulled a sidearm out of its holster and shot me.

I'd like to say that she hesitated first, that there was a dramatic pause, a meaningful and sentimental moment before she pulled the trigger. But there wasn't. That shot was deafening in the closeness, and it kicked me off my feet, knocking the wind out of me. I hit the ground like a sack of bricks, and was struggling for breath when she came forward quickly and shot me twice more in the chest to make sure.

Then she was gone, her rapid footfalls echoing in the distance and fading away.

Dear Diary,

I don't care what it looks like on all those cop shows, getting shot fucking hurts. When they get up and pull their shirts open to reveal a bulletproof vest, they grunt a little and then get up to chase the bad guy down and save the day. Well, it's bullshit. I dunno how long I lay there before I managed to get up.

Rabbit had given me Kevlar body armor and a padded bra to wear over it, but it still hurt like a bitch to get shot three times point blank. And no, I didn't pull my shirt off like they do on TV, so that when I caught up with Audrey she could see how I'd survived and shoot me somewhere else instead. I crawled as quickly as I could to another corpse and scavenged his gun and spare clip. Then it was all I could do to hurry after Audrey Gray.

Above, they were still firing on the besiegers, and below, I could hear the echoing sirens and shouts of distant men. If it came down to it, I had a bullet in my gun for myself. If I was lucky, I could shoot my way out of the building and run, counting on the vest to save me. Or I could just take the damned thing off and go out in a hail of bullets.

But as I mentioned before, that fucking hurts.

Before I was ready to be there, I got to the first floor. Ahead, I could see a barricade of squad cars. Men lay fallen across hoods and locked bumpers, spilling their blood onto the blacktop in the rain. I ran for the gaping entrance, with the ticket booth and the two mechanical guardrails.

I thought I heard a distant crash over the drumming of the rain and the thunder, like a truck hitting a wall, and frantic screams as people retreated. Then I froze as an unmarked van fell into view, crashing front-first and exploded just outside the entrance. They were driving the vans through the concrete parapet and off of the roof! The explosion touched off the car it landed on, and that blew up the one beside it.

Could they domino all the squad cars? I didn't know, and I didn't care. The cops outside had run to escape the falling van and now scattered in panic from the flames. They'd cleared a way for me. Another van crashed and exploded on the other side of the building, and I held my breath as I ran. I got to the ticket booth, glanced at the woman lying in a tangle of limbs with her brains splattered on the Plexiglas above her, and ducked under the guardrail. The searing heat from the roaring flames singed my face and arms, but I just gritted my teeth and edged between the bumpers of the two closest untouched cars. I could feel the chaos all around me, gawking bystanders, shouting cops, and all of them who weren't ducking bullets were pointing at the sky.

I put the pistol in my waistband, covered it with my shirt, and ran like fuck.

The news said they were all dead in the parking garage. Rabbit's snipers had been snuck upon and killed, and police snipers had gotten everyone on the roof. At a quarter to nine my 1970 Mustang Mach I, silver, with two white racing stripes and black leather interior, came screeching out of the building's exit and swerved between the wreckage of burning squad cars. It didn't get far.

Though taken momentarily by surprise, the cops opened fire and riddled the car with bullets, massacring it and the only occupant: a large bald man whose body could only be identified by the tattoo of a blue tick hound on his left shoulder.

The only survivor of the secret meeting with an organized crime informant was an unidentified woman who was taken immediately from the scene by officials who refused to comment. All that they would say is that a man and a woman, considered armed and extremely dangerous, were not found anywhere at the scene and are presumed to be still at large.

I had time to grab my nest egg, diary, and my dance bag before escaping my apartment. I was safely across the street in the pouring rain when the police arrived at my apartment and stormed in, guns drawn.

I walked for an hour or so, the night loud with thunder and the pelting rain, until I got to the marina, and I stood there like an idiot on the dock, staring at the empty slip the Capriole had occupied, watching the circles that spread from the rain as it dimpled the water.

Dear Diary,

I sat for a long time at the park bench where Layla and I had been photographed. I sleep there sometimes, when I can't find some kind stranger to go home with. The money I had didn't last long. A few changes of clothes and a motel, then some heroin to keep me company.

I'm not considered classy enough for Diabolique anymore. I now dance at a fifth-rate dive called Centerfolds, across the tracks. So what if I don't make the same money? I don't mind what I do. I'm happy enough. I like myself.

It's been raining a lot lately. It's cold and I'm aching for a hit. But it's Tuesday, and I didn't plan ahead for the week. I never do.

I got up and dragged my dance bag behind me in the wet grass toward the street. The night's going to be long and dark and lonely, just like yesterday. I got to the sidewalk and stooped to pick up a discarded cigarette butt. This one had almost an inch of tobacco in it. I was about to add it to my collection—I'm saving to make myself a whole one—when I caught sight of my reflection in the black mirror of a rain puddle.

Just another scar-faced whore peddling her ass for a spoon or a dime rock.

Have you ever seen a ghost?

I spend a lot more time in the cemetery these days. Salomé's grave is there, with my name carved in the headstone. I still have the .45, but I have too much hope to put it in my mouth. I know I won't be here forever. My Rabbit's still out there somewhere, and he'll come back for me.

I've proved myself to him, and I've lost everything for him. He had to come back for me.

He had to.

And I know he will.

BY THE SWORD

I

Tires squealed as Antwan's car peeled out in front of us, and Domingo screamed.

"What?" I asked.

"Stop them! Don't let them get out!"

I jerked the car into Drive and stomped on the gas before Domingo even got his door shut. His head whip-lashed back and the door swung into his leg, but he didn't seem to care. Pills were spilling all over the front seat of my Sunfire, and, even distracted, I could tell what was wrong. The Honda in front of us bounced up over a yellow speed bump and came down hard, screeching as it fishtailed around the corner of a line of parked cars. D'ingo cursed as he got the door shut and opened the glove compartment, getting his H&K USP 9mm.

We braced ourselves as we went over the speed bump. The whole car jolted upward, and then we were around the corner and right up on them as they made for the gate of our "pleasantville" type development. It was about eight-thirty, so most people were home in front of their prime time shows instead of on the road, but we still managed to miss three cars by a coat of paint coming out of the gate onto Seminole. They slammed on their brakes and honked furiously. My heart was in my throat as I held onto the steering wheel, but I tried to keep the fear out of my eyes with my friend watching. D'ingo was in a rage, screaming.

We were in the middle of making a buy, a thousand pills that Kendrick and Antwan had apparently switched at the last minute. If Domingo hadn't've checked the bag again just as he'd been getting in...

Somehow, I heard the click of the safety on the 9mm over D'ingo screaming in Portuguese. "*Maricão*" was the only word I caught. Weaving between the few cars on the road, we ran one red light, then another, then screeched our way through a long yellow, making a left onto Crescent with horns blaring all around us. The Honda wasn't holding up. I wasn't surprised—Antwan calling it Da Bomb didn't mean it wasn't an eleven-year-old piece of shit.

Crescent led into a residential area, and we skidded round one corner after another. When he thought it was safe, Domingo rolled his window down, climbed halfway out, and started squeezing off shots, peppering the white trunk of the Honda and crazing the glass of the rear window.

Antwan tried serpentining on the road, weaving all over both sides and nearly crashing head on with five or six pairs of headlights. The Honda started wobbling and I yanked D'ingo back in by his belt.

"What?"

"They're about to lose it," I shouted. The thrill of the chase was roaring through me, and I was surprised that the barrel of my own nine, a Browning Hi-power tucked into the waist of my jeans, was fighting an erection for dominion of my crotch. Damn, that's uncomfortable.

There! I could see it happen before it even started. The Honda came up too fast on a turn and lost control, fish-tailing all over the place and slamming into a royal palm growing out of the sidewalk. The rear tires lifted up off the pavement as the whole front end buckled, like a crumbled ball of paper, and the passenger door flew open the second they touched back down. We screeched to a halt as Kendrick's big dread-locked head appeared, and then he was gone, leaping fences and vanishing into the woods behind the neighborhood.

I was already out before I realized it, my gun drawn and aimed in that Weaver stance I'd seen on cop shows.

"Get out! Get out of the car, now!" I screamed.

The tree had bent sharply, raining two dead palm fronds onto the roof of the car and the street, and was looking ready to come all the way down. Domingo ran to the wrecked car and pulled the driver door open, yanking Antwan half out of his seat and pistol-whipping him over and over on the head until he was poured out onto the road.

When I got to his side, blood was swirling in the bright green antifreeze that pooled on the asphalt.

"Thought that was pretty funny, dintcha!"

D'ingo kicked him in the side of the head.

"Dintcha!"

Antwan was dreadlocked, like his brother. I grabbed one handful of the knotty hair and jerked his head around to look into his eyes, jamming my nine between them.

"You're a dead man, you piece of shit."

"Please!"

"You're about to be a headless corpse on the side of the road,

Antwan. I hope it was worth it."

"Please!"

Domingo tore through the car trying to find the money and the goods while I pressed the business end of the Browning into the fat black dude's forehead.

"I'm not seeing it!" D'ingo shouted.

"If he doesn't find our money," I said as calmly as I could, "your face is gonna be a grease spot."

"It ain't in here!"

"Where the fuck is it?"

"Shit, man! Kendrick took it!"

"Too bad for you, huh?"

"Please!"

"Do it," Domingo called from inside the car.

I held my hand up across the top of the gun to keep the splatter from getting on me. Antwan was crying.

"Do it!"

I squeezed the trigger halfway back.

One millimeter more.

"Oh God…" he whimpered beneath me.

All of a sudden, without seeing them, I knew there were a dozen faces pressed to their windows, squinting past their own reflections into the night, watching me.

Somewhere, a dog barked.

I listened to Antwan sobbing quietly, and let off the trigger, straightening and yanking him to his feet by his greasy dreads. Domingo clambered out of the Honda, and together we push-pulled him to my car and shoved him in the backseat. D'ingo got in behind him, pushing his head to the floor and sticking his gun hard in the seat of his pants.

"Get used to that feeling," he whispered to the bloody head as I got back behind the wheel.

Then, to me, "Where to?"

"Antwan," I called over my shoulder, peeling out. "You know you're an idiot pulling this shit when we knew where you live."

"We're going to his place?"

"Yep. And we'll get there before Kendrick does. If he doesn't show up, we'll see how much blood we can get to come out of his brother."

"Ha! You hear that?" I heard him kick our hostage.

169

Looking in the rearview, I watched him get out two cigarettes, light them, and hand me one. Our eyes met.

"This is bad," he said silently. I nodded.

Suddenly, he looked as young as he was. As we were.

Shit, and this was a school night, too.

Kendrick and Antwan dropped out of Jefferson Davis High School back in freshman year, got their own roach-infested apartment on The Hill, and have been cooking crack and crystal meth ever since. I made it until junior second semester, said hell with it, and got my GED. D'ingo was a senior, now. Varsity football and soccer. He lived with his sister Mariana, Mr. and Mrs. De Medieros, and Abuela in a three bedroom, two bath development house, and I rented space on their couch since I turned eighteen and Mom and Dad told me to go fuck myself. We were not the cast of the typical teenage movie. At all.

D'ingo and I had been best friends since getting in a fight in middle school when he'd caught me making out with Mariana under the bleachers. I'm not going to say who won, because to this day he says he did and I say I did.

History will decide.

Except for Domingo being a boy and Mariana being a girl, the two of them looked identical. The same black eyes and honey-colored skin, the same big smiles with the dimples, the same arched eyebrows that were sexy on her and arrogant on him, the same aristocratic nose. Well, there was one thing: her only imperfection was a small discolored blotch, kind of like what Gorbachev had on his forehead only not red like his, and hers was shaped like England. It was distracting, but not in a bad way.

The same temper. I'd never seen Mr. de Medieros blow his fuse, but I knew he had a short one. People still called him Grazi Mono, the name from Brazil where he, his wife, the kids, and Abuela were from until fifteen years ago. In São Paolo, as in Bogotá, the drug lords employ eight-, nine-, and ten-year-old boys to run around with machine guns and blow away whoever's on El Listo de Shit that week. In Colombia, they're called Los Something or other—Gamín, I think—in São Paolo, they're called Grazi Mono. That's Nestor de Medieros. He was one of those little orphans, trained to be killers.

The rumor is, he was taken in under a cartel's wing after *la bala perdita* had taken his mother and father on two separate occasions. I shit you not, that's a phenomenon down there, in places like Rio and São Paolo, it happens so often there's a term for it. It means "the lost bullet."

Whenever you see some asshole fire a gun in the air to celebrate something, or get people's attention, or when shots go wide in a gunfight, or somebody's trying to sell weapons to gangsters up atop one of the mountains outside the cities and lets them fire test shots out over the buildings hundreds of feet below—those bullets come down somewhere. But nobody ever seems to think about that. Nobody cares about the people walking their children to school, the little boys holding *Mamãe's* hand when suddenly her chest explodes, or a chunk of her head flies out of her hair, or her arm falls off and she collapses, screaming.

Little Nestor was holding the comforting hand of his *Mamãe* when she lurched sideways and fell. Her hand slipped from around his and he was left reaching out into the empty air, staring dumbfounded at her on the ground.

Struggling to rise. Choking horribly. This was not even a year since his father had been knocked against the peeling saffron-colored paint of a church he was passing by. Street urchins, such as he became, get picked up quickly by the brat-wranglers, and some of them catch on to what's expected of them quicker than others. Nestor caught on.

Having closed himself off inside, he had no feeling toward others and didn't fall into the trap the other children did. He never cared enough to start liking it too much.

He survived to adulthood and was given an underboss's niece to marry, sort of a trophy wife, but not *really*—something had to be done with the girl; she was pretty but a nuisance. A few years later he fled when the bosses wanted three-year-old Domingo to grow up under their wing also, following in his father's footsteps, and Mama's emphatic "No" wasn't the answer they were taking.

Whatever the truth of it was, Papa was a bad mothafucka.

His second favorite pastime was throwing buckets of blood and chum over the side of his yacht, then machine-gunning the sharks that came to get it. The first time he took D'ingo and me "fishing" we were twelve and I lost a Heckler & Koch MP-5 submachine pistol overboard.

I couldn't believe my eyes. A shark actually ate it.

They had a restaurant called Pecado, with exposed brick, mosaics, hanging plants, blond wood, brass railings, etched glass and ristras of red chiles like hanging firecracker strings. I thought the place would never be complete without a bunch of *mariachis*, with Pancho Villa-style bandoliers filled with little single-serving liquor bottles, pestering the diners and threatening to play their guitars at them, but Nestor wouldn't go for it.

Their best dish was veal with plantains, mango sauce and cayenne pepper, but their most popular was the cocaine they didn't list on the menu. I worked for them, but not as a bus boy.

Those six thousand dollars Kendrick was running around town with belonged to Grazi Mono. The thousand pills were *supposed* to belong to him twenty minutes ago. If we didn't get back home with either, or both, before D'ingo's curfew, I'd rather sleep in the street than face the old man.

We followed Blue Heron into the area we called Golgotha, where the streets were shattered canyons of cracked and blistered pavement, families lived twenty to a room in a shack with no door, the traffic lights didn't even work, and the Town Council couldn't give a rat's ass. We had a Third World nation right in our backyard. It wouldn't surprise me if people had leprosy out here. It's so hard to imagine this is South Florida; beach bunnies in thongs were stopping traffic on their Rollerblades not two miles from here, being ogled by fortyish "big shots" with tangerine Speedos and salt-and-pepper back hair, brain-bleached surfers, and old geezers in their walkers and wraparound sunglasses.

We watched people in the street as we passed, girls double-dutching, old folks sitting in plastic chairs on their yellow lawns, young men on the prowl—amid squalor and abject poverty—in suped-up rides with thousands of dollars' worth of paint and noise. Get a welfare check once a month, but be damned if you don't get a new set of rims this week.

Looking out the window, Varsity Domingo college hopeful muttered "Just think, Antwan: you chose to drop out of school and live here."

Our eyes met in the mirror again and his expression said Oh yeah, my bad. Forgot you dropped out, too. But then again, you live on someone else's couch.

We rolled into The Hill, which looked like project housing but was nowhere near that nice. The place was held up by its termites. The water out of the tap was brown and stank. We'd passed crack whores sway-backing down the street and thieves running from their healthier but somehow slower marks, and when they turned in for the night, those people came here, to The Hill, which wasn't even on a hill.

I'd been here once "to buy crack," but really to spy for Grazi Mono, find out exactly how this new super-crack was made. Instead of cooking the coke and baking soda, they were dropped dry into ammonia, strychnine, and other fun ingredients, where it clumped together and was fished out immediately, hardening without heat. It was exponentially more potent, more addictive, and more quickly fatal. Mr. de Medieros' idea was to supply this to his competitors, indirectly of course, and let them kill themselves. Just like giving roaches a slow poison that they take back to their nest and share.

But I digress.

We found the place, parked in front, and got out. Antwan was being very cooperative. I saw him glance away off towards the right where a little kid—six or seven, maybe —was doing that "I'm Bad" gangsta shuffle through the parking lot. He had on clothes fit for a kid twice his age and size, I noticed. He saw us, and Antwan flashed a sign at him, probably just a wave to the neighbor's kid. We went up the stairs to the second floor. As the fat guy, sweating with fear, fished his key out of his knee-deep pocket, I looked out over the parking lot again and saw that kid talking on a cell phone, watching us.

We went into the biggest pigsty I'd ever seen. While the furniture consisted of one ratty couch in the living room, the floor was still completely obscured by piles of clothes that rose sharply into Mount Laundry in one corner; cardboard boxes full of records—some fifteen to twenty, scattered without any rhyme or reason—various types of audio equipment plugged into overloaded power strips; plastic Super Big Gulp cups half-filled with orangey mildewed sludge; a TV stacked on a VCR on the burn-marred carpet, with tangled confusions of video game controller wires hanging about it from the precariously-perched Playstation on top; broken, stepped-on CDs; and a 'still that looked like it was assembled by monkeys.

"If I were you, I'd find us six grand worth of something quick, Antwan."

He looked at me with hate in his malevolent pig eyes.

"C'mon, *rápido,* motherfucker!" Domingo snapped.

We rummaged about in the living room and kitchenette, Antwan half-heartedly looking under things that obviously didn't conceal drugs, and we stumbled upon two gallon milk jugs full of GHB. It looked just like water, but we knew better, checking for the strong smell and salty soap taste that gave it away. One capful of the stuff would make you feel like you'd drunk a twelve-pack of long-necks, without all the spinning and puking. The two gallons weren't a fortune, but they were a start. It just didn't compare to the thousand tabs of AMT we'd had our hearts set on.

Athamethyltryptaline, a German-made designer drug, is a small capsule of brown powder, about the color of decent heroin. It's an amplifier, to be used along with any other drug, feeling like two parts Ecstasy and one part acid trip, and lasting twenty hours straight. One capsule sold for thirty-five dollars.

We waited for the phone to ring, either the cell or the house line, but neither ever did. Kendrick never called to see if his brother was alive or dead, so for an hour we contented ourselves with ransacking the apartment and making fatass Antwan carry all his audio shit down to my car. We got his turntables, a few good boxes of old-school vinyl, and his speakers, along with the G and half a pound of skunk weed when a station wagon came into the parking lot, creeping.

D'ingo froze, watching it, and I could feel all my short hairs prickling as it came slowly around the bend, like a prowling panther, and we watched with our breaths held as it approached an intersection of lanes. Passing under a lamp post, it looked exactly like what we didn't want to see. The gaudily-rimmed wheels were out-burned, jutting outside of the wheel wells. The chameleon paint job that would fade from yellow to green, turquoise, and metallic purple as it passed by. Front end lowered, rear jacked up. I could see orange dots glowing in the blackness of the opened windows, getting bright, then falling away. Three of them in the back seat, plus the shotgun and the driver who weren't smoking. The car came to the intersect, slowed…and swung our way.

Something, instinct maybe, made me turn and look the other way, and that little kid was still there, watching. Then I turned to Antwan, who was grinning a mouthful of gold teeth. He motioned us forward, walking out into the open toward the rear of the car.

174

"C'mon, let's see if we got evathang," he said, raising the trunk lid. When we didn't move, he grinned wider.
"C'mon, cracker! Make sure all the wires n' shit are in here. What's the matter? C'mere, Chico, *rápido,* mothafucka!"

The driver of the gunship punched the gas, surging forward as we broke and ran. The roar of the engine sounded like it was all around me as we raced for cover, and were brought screeching to a halt by the thunder of machine gun fire kicking chunks of concrete out of the wall just ahead of us. D'ingo broke left and I went right in a low running crouch across the lot, diving between two cars. In mid-air, I heard the rounds punch into a primer-gray Bonneville beside me, blowing the rear bumper apart and flattening both tires before I hit the ground. Then a piercing scream as the kid was knocked off his feet by a stray bullet.

I could see him from where I lay, looking under the other parked car, howling as he clutched the stump where his left arm used to be. More loud, flat bangs as Domingo returned fire from somewhere. I crawled to the front of the crippled Bonneville and peeked over the hood. Antwan was hunkered down behind my Sunfire, shouting advice and encouragement at the shooters. I couldn't get him from where I was.

With Domingo drawing their fire, I made my way to the screaming kid. He was gushing blood all over himself, tears and snot sliming his twisted face. I tore his oversized shirt open, pulling a large scrap of material away, wadding it up and stuffing it in his mouth. He bit down, hard, while I tore another piece into long strips.

"That's what you get for sicking them on us, you little shit!" I had no idea where his arm was, but I didn't care either. I tied a quick tourniquet and took the cell phone he had lying there next to him, pocketing it.

"Don't quit your day job, kid," I hissed, and ran. I got to the edge of the light, turned, and saw the station wagon stopped, the passenger side back seat gunner sitting up on his door, firing across the roof at something I couldn't see, while the guy on the other side fired out his window. The yellow strobe of the muzzle flashes lit their faces up so I could see their fierce glee, even from here.

I aimed and fired, crazing the windshield, but most of my shots going wild. Panicking, the driver put it in reverse and the wagon flew backwards, the gunner falling out of the window onto his head.

Apparently, someone caught his foot because he got dragged the whole way, screaming.

Domingo appeared in the corner of my eye, and I kept firing, moving sideways to keep the car in sight, cursing when the breech of my pistol locked open. D'ingo hauled ass across the lot toward me, and we vanished into the shadows.

"Fuck! Fuck fuck fuckfuckfuck!"

"Calm down, D'ingo!"

"How the fuck can I calm down? Shit!"

"I don't know, but just do it! We both gotta be cool."

We were down on the ground, hiding behind scraggly bushes that grew into the crisscrossing wires of a chain link fence. There was dog shit somewhere nearby. We could smell it, but this was the best place to hide for now, so we just had to put up with it. We couldn't see or hear the gunship anywhere.

"You got metal?" I asked.

"No, I'm empty."

"Me too."

"Shit."

"Uh-huh, you can say that again." I dug the kid's cell phone out of my pocket, turned it on, and hit redial.

"Who you calling?"

"We're about to find out." I listened to it ring twice, and an angry black voice came on.

"What up?"

"You missed us, motherfucker."

"Who dis is?"

"I'm the cat that's gonna splatter your ass, you piece of shit. Now put Antwan on the phone."

"The fuck! Nigga—"

"I'm a cracker, you monkey. You're going to find out the difference when you're sucking on the business end of my nine and I blow your pea-sized brain out the back of your doo-rag."

Domingo started laughing, and I hissed at him to keep it down. He clamped one hand over his mouth and shook violently. The guy on the phone was screaming at me but I could not make it out, so I hung up on him.

"What gang are Kendrick and Antwan in again?"

D'ingo was still vainly trying to stifle his laughter, so I punched him in the shoulder and repeated myself. He raised his free hand and made the sign of the Bacalous. I hit redial again.

"Hi, is Becky Lou there?" I asked.

Domingo gave up trying to hold it in, fell out howling. The dude started screaming again. Bacalous don't like being called Becky Lou, apparently.

"There's no reason to use that kind of language," I said. "Look, I just can't talk to you when you're like this. When you're ready to be civil I'll call you back." Click.

"Now what?"

Maya had been expecting my call for twenty minutes, but if she knew what was good for her she'd keep her smart-ass comments to herself this time. The last thing I needed was to be on the run, out of bullets, smelling dog shit *and* getting bitched at by my girlfriend. She picked up on the first ring.

"Evan?"

"Hey, Maya."

"Baby, are you okay? I heard something went wrong."

"Yeah, hon. Something went really wrong." Good. She knew. "I'm in a fix here, and I need you to come get me."

"Where are you?"

"Golgotha."

"What? What are you doing there?" Good. She sounded scared for me, just like she was supposed to. I told her everything.

"Oh God, baby, where's your car now?"

"Still in front of Antwan's place, probably stripped down to nothing by now." I made sure Domingo couldn't hear me; then said quietly, "Baby, I'm fucking scared. You know I'd never say that, so you gotta know it's true. We need to get the hell outta here."

"I'm going to call D'ingo's dad."

"No! Do *not* do that. No way. No no no no no no."

"Why?"

"I can't let him know about this, that I got his son into this fucked-up situation—"

"He *knows*, Evan. Who do you think told me?"

"Wha—huh?"

"Mariana called like, two hours ago, said if we heard from you to tell her immediately. Baby, you can't just go racing all around Ibis Estates and expect Grazi fuckin' Mono not to hear about it. He

177

wants you home *now.*"

"Don't call him, Maya. I'll get out of this somehow—"

"I'm calling him as soon as I hang up. Give me the number of the phone you're on."

"I don't know it, and no, you're not calling him."

"Then I'll star sixty-nine you. Don't waste any more of your minutes, okay?"

"No, God damn it!"

"I love you, baby."

"Maya!" Click. "Fuck!"

"What?" Domingo asked. I shook my head.

"We're dead. Either we're going to get shot tonight or your dad'll kill us when he picks us up. Either way, we're dead."

"Hsst!" his hand was over my mouth and he'd drawn his head, turtle-like, into his shoulders. I'd never seen his eyes so big. I strained my ears and heard it, the rustle of metal as someone climbed over a fence far away.

A couple of someones.

We lowered ourselves to the ground and stared out across what passed for park, a place in Golgotha not even the people who lived here ever came, and saw four figures emerge from the shadows. Each one carried something that wasn't a picnic basket.

"Oh shit," I whispered.

A bunch of noisy black birds scattered in the middle of the park, flapping frantically in every direction. Their harsh, guttural squawks seemed to scream, "they went thataway, over there by the bushes!" The four shadows were coming across the overgrown grass and scanning every inch of the park, fanning out twenty feet. Staring at them coming, all of a sudden I couldn't smell the dog shit anymore, or the grass, or the odor of the bushes. In my head was the stink of that first day, machine-gunning sharks on Grazi Mono's yacht. That salty, metallic reek of blood and seawater.

I could hear my heart pounding, covering the noise of the approaching footsteps. I tried holding my breath but that only made it louder, so I gave up. I tried to make my face look as mean as Domingo's. The figures spoke to one another, too quietly and too far away to be heard.

Then the fucking phone rang.

It was as loud as a thunderclap in the stillness, an obnoxious ringing like the noise of an ice cream truck, and D'ingo and I almost had a heart attack. All four of the shadows swung around in our direction, as startled as we were. The first ring stopped and I wound back and threw the phone as far as I could down one end of the fence, the second ring drawing their fire. They started spraying all over the area where it landed, and we ran the other way. Tearing out of the bushes, we just bolted in a blind panic, expecting at any second to feel a round from behind blowing our spines apart. Bullets came kicking dust spots out of the grass one step behind us. I hurdled a bench that appeared out of nowhere, and heard the firing stop abruptly. They were empty.

Somehow, I realized we were on pavement now instead of grass, and I saw my shadow grow long in front of me as I passed under a street light. Domingo, varsity hero and college hopeful, could haul ass, but somehow I was keeping pace with him every step of the way. A quick glance over my shoulder and I saw headlights. Not close, but still not far enough away.

Following Domingo's lead, we ran up on the stoop of a house and rammed our way through the door. Before I had any idea what we were doing we had both our guns drawn and in the faces of a skinny black dude and an even skinnier white girl with a harelip. Yeah, our clips were spent, but what these people didn't know wouldn't hurt them. They just stared at us bug-eyed, sitting cross-legged on the floor while Domingo put a finger to his lips.

Silence. A silence so complete you could hear a mouse farting behind a baseboard. Then the car. The eerie glow of its headlights shone in the only window that wasn't boarded with diagonal planks or taped up with a black garbage bag. The car passed, and the glow faded.

"We're not gonna hurt you," Domingo said softly.

They didn't move, didn't bat an eyelash.

That's when I smelled it, half a second before I saw it. There was that stale hospital stink of crack so thick you could feel it. They had a half-crushed beer can on the barren floor between them, the depression in the middle filled with ashes. I took my wallet out of my back pocket with my free hand and opened it in front of them, never moving the gun.

"We'll give you a dollar to let us sit here a minute."

Instantly, their expressions changed. "Five," the guy said. "Rent's five dollas."

"Ten." This from Harelip. "There are two of you. Two times

five is ten." She was very quick, this girl.

"Don't forget who has the gun, lady."

"Seven, then."

"Yeah, whatever."

She relaxed when I gave them the money.

"I'll suck your dicks for another five apiece," she said eagerly.

"No, you won't."

"Okay, two dollars." Jesus, she just didn't quit.

The guy introduced himself as Bundy, and she was apparently named Tunafish. We didn't ask. We just stood there and watched them smoke their dope with roaches skittering all around them. Flaked-off plaster hung in cobwebs, and the carpet crunched underfoot in the few places it actually covered the floor. I decided that if I'd had even one bullet I'd find a way to put them both out of their misery with it. Tunafish was a skeleton wrapped in pale, lesion-covered skin. She looked like if you sneezed on her, her canary bones would crumble into sawdust. Both of them had the eyes of a sleep-walker as they mechanically smoked and sat, smoked and sat.

Domingo stared out the corner of a garbage bag, diligently keeping watch, and I squashed roaches, trying to think.

Suddenly, Tunafish sat up straight, terrified.

"You hear that?" she whispered. We listened.

"Nope," Bundy answered, sucking on the mouth of the can as he moved the lighter in tight circles above it.

"Quiet!" We all listened some more. The only sounds were the roaches skittering about, and Bundy smoking the can, every toke a rasping hiss. Tunafish stared suspiciously at the wall out of the corner of her eye. Domingo signed to me that there was nothing outside. The girl tugged on Bundy's arm, rocking him as he tried to hit the nugget in the ashes.

"You hear it? You hear that?"

"No!"

"There it is again!"

"No, bitch, I don't hear it yet! Gimme a minute to smoke this and maybe I *will!*"

I had to laugh at that.

"There's somebody outside!" she insisted.

Domingo shook his head.

"Fish," Bundy said patiently, "Even if dey *was* somebody out

180

dere, whutchoo think dey goan do? Run up in here wit' guns? Dat already happened and we still okay."

Tunafish wasn't listening, she was just staring at the can. Bundy went to smoke again and she whined, "Hey, my turn!"

"Man, I ain't even hit it yet. You jus' gave it to me."

"No, I didn't!"

"Man, would I lie to you?"

"Give me the fuckin' can, Bundy!"

"Look, since you obviously disturbed inna head, I'll let you git it. But only cuz you my girl."

"Kiss my ass," she said, taking the can.

"Ha! What ass? You a straight line from the shoulder to the knees!" He looked over at us to see if we'd laugh, then sniffed when we didn't. D'ingo shook his head at me.

Five more minutes passed. No cars went by, and no people appeared, friendly or otherwise.

Tunafish was twitching and swatting invisible flies, still somehow oblivious to the roaches doing their food recon all around her. Then, suddenly, Bundy leaped to his feet and ran to the door, putting his ear against it, his eyes wide. I shot a questioning glance at D'ingo, who rolled his eyes.

The dude dropped to the floor and peered through the crack under the door. Tunafish hid the rocks under a loose floorboard beside her.

"What is it?" she asked.

"Shhhh!"

"C'mon, what is it?"

"Shut up, I'm trying to hear! I wanna find out what's out there!"

Domingo came over to the door, grabbed Bundy by his thick afro of kinky wool and jerked him to his feet.

"Ow! Hey! Whutchoo doing?"

With his other hand, my friend yanked the door open. Tunafish was up and backed into a corner, shocked. Then, D'ingo pushed Bundy onto the stoop and kicked him in the ass, sending him sprawling onto the sickly grass outside.

"You too!" he snapped at Tunafish, his gun aimed straight at her ugly lip. "Get out!"

"What're you doing?" she cried.

"Get the fuck out! Now!"

Following his lead, I seized her roughly by the arm and dragged her out of the house while D'ingo tore up the loose floorboard and got the money and the rest of the crack. In the road, under the orange glow of the streetlights, I told them to take a good look around. They nervously obeyed. The place was deserted, it seemed. "See?" I asked.

Domingo came out with the crack in one hand and his nine in the other. He strode angrily up to us and held out both hands to the crackheads. "Choose," he said.

"What?"

"Choose. Between your life and this pile of shit here."

"Fuck, man."

"You want me to decide for you?" He raised the gun.

"Man, we ain't done nothing to you!" Bundy screamed.

"Please!" Tunafish was shaking. "You can have your money back!"

"Listen to me very carefully. I'm taking this shit and I'm throwing it away, and I'll be back to check on you. You'll never know when. And if you try to hide from me, I'll find you. If, when I come back, you're still on this shit, I'll kneecap the both of you. Are we clear?" He put the gun right in Bundy's face.

"Yeah, man, sure! Whatever!"

"You agreed too quickly."

"I don't believe him, either," I said.

"I can't see any difference between you two and those roaches in there," Domingo said. "Now, you either quit cold turkey or I'll kill you right now. *Comprende?*"

The guy swallowed, sweat rolling down his gaunt face, and nodded.

"How 'bout you, *puta?*" He aimed at the harelip.

"I can't stop," she said. "Don't make me."

"You don't care, do you? You're dead soon, anyway."

It's hard to threaten the living dead.

"Please," she whimpered.

A sudden sharp crack, and Tunafish's chest exploded. She jumped against Domingo, covering him with her poisonous blood. It seemed to happen slowly, like trying to run away in a dream. Another crack. And another.

And suddenly, it occurred to me that it was three-round burst and the realization made the shots come faster. Another chattering

182

hail of bullets and Bundy spun around to look at me with half of his head gone. He stared at me with the one eye that remained and staggered a few steps before falling. Before I could see where the shots had come from, Domingo had pushed Tunafish off of him and bolted back up the steps and into the shack. I felt the hot wind of a bullet flashing by my face and ran after him.

We found the back door in the darkness and slammed into it, but it held. Damned thing was nailed shut to delay raiding cops. We scrambled to find another exit, but the only ways out were the window and the front door.

Then I remembered.

"D'ingo!" I pointed to the part of the floor with the loose plank. We ran to it, pulled it out, and tore up the ones around it. They were coming. We looked down into the hole and saw the darkness moving.

"Oh, hell no."

"Fuck it," I said, and dove in. I held my breath as I slid into the crawl space, but the stink was so bad I could taste it.
I rolled to one side and Domingo came in after me, choking and pulling the planks over us. I could feel the disgusting hairy legs and twitchy, feathery antennae of the cockroaches crawling all over us. Within two seconds, they were in our hair and inside our clothes, and there was nothing we could do. We crawled through cobwebs and reeking fungus, a few huge furry rats hissed at our intrusion, and then the tramp of feet brought us still. Angry voices and quick foot-falls heard overhead as they searched for us.

"*Ajudame, Deus*," Domingo whispered. "*Que aversão! Vôte!*"

Those disgusting things crawling all over us made my mind reel drunkenly, and twice I had to fight to keep my vomit in. The stench of the crawlspace made my eyes burn, no matter now tightly I scrunched them shut. The floor above us shook dust down every time the footsteps stomped by.
Before long, they noticed the floorboards and yanked them up, but decided instantly that we couldn't be down there.

"Fuck! They gone!" I heard Antwan say.
My lungs burned for air, but I didn't dare take a breath.
Perhaps it only lasted a minute, but in my entire life, the seconds never ticked by so slowly. Finally, they walked out, and all my unspoken prayers were answered. Even though we hated to do it, we held on another minute longer, just in case Antwan came back. The

curious rats and spiders and roaches never got bored with investigating us.

When we couldn't possibly stand it any longer, we drew our legs up underneath us, lowered our heads, and launched ourselves up through the rotting planks between the floor joists, bursting out of the nightmarish crawlspace. My first draught of air gathered inside of me, and brought out with it a flood of puke and bile. Beside me, Domingo rolled furiously, squashing bugs and swatting them off of him as I retched violently all over myself. The next few minutes were a blur, purging the horror. When I came to, D'ingo was wiping away the last of the bugs from my body and crushing them. He helped me up and together we cautiously left the crackhouse. What a fine pair we made, I thought. Me covered in vomit, and him in the blood of an infected whore. A long way to fall in two hours.

We stuck to the shadows, trying to avoid looking at the two corpses in the street. I couldn't help it, though. There were Bundy and Tunafish, lying where they'd fallen, dead because they met us. I tried to tell myself that it was just a matter of time for them anyway, but it was hard to shrug off.

Soon, the freaks would come out, only at home in the night. Like vampires. And Golgotha wasn't even safe during the daylight.

Shaitan was home alone when we burst into the apartment. She recoiled in horror at the sight of us, not recognizing her boyfriend for a moment. The stink of us hit her next, and she went green the second after she paled.

"D'ingo!" she gasped.

"We need showers," he said tersely. "And bleach."

"What happened?"

"Later, Shai. Wash our clothes for us, too. Or, hell with it. Burn 'em."

"But—"

"I said later, *manceba!*" He stormed off to the bathroom.

"Long story," I said.

Maya came over immediately, bringing me some of her thrift-store couture to wear. She always dressed like a hippie, but it suited her. Either that, or torn jeans and aloha shirts with half-laced combat boots and a concho belt.

Shaitan, on the other hand, took her appearance a little more seriously. An Iroquois of the Onandagas, she called her makeup "war paint" and had a pride I'd never seen in a woman. In her culture, the women were the heads of the households, and they acted like it. She had more dignity just sitting there smoking a cigarette than Mrs. de Medieros did welcoming guests at those fancy parties she loved to throw. If she hadn't been so shocked by our appearances, Shaitan would probably have thrown Domingo out for the way he spoke to her.

Iroquois means "terrifying man" in Algonquin. They deserved it. She was feisty, and would go toe to toe with the best of them. But now, after hearing our story, she and Maya just washed us, bleached us from head to toe, and washed us again.

To ward off evil, Shaitan prepared some medicine bags for each of us to wear. There was sage and cedar in them, and some other shit. Catnip, for all I knew. Then she burned something that smelled good, but that was probably because the apartment still stank from us being in it.

Maya and I left them alone, and she drove me to her place. Domingo would have to get home soon, but I wasn't about to face his father. Better let it wait until tomorrow. Or the next day. That would also give me more time to come up with some kind of a plan. Right now, the only thing on my mind was payback.

"What are you going to do about your car?" she asked.

"The only thing I can do. Report it stolen and get some insurance. That's the least of my worries right now."

"I know, baby. I'm sorry."

"Well, all I can do now is wait until Nestor cools off."

"Evan, I don't know why you're tripping over that. He's not mad at you, he's mad at *them*."

"I don't want to take that chance."

She fixed me a drink, an opium-based liquor from Greece called Ouzo, illegal now in the States. Her liquor shelf had all kinds of stuff like that. Absinthe from France, outlawed because of the hallucinogen thujone that gave it its own little kick. To me, it tasted like licorice. Licorice someone else had already eaten.

She also considered herself a oenophile, which apparently means "wine lover." Why she couldn't just say she liked wine was beyond me. Aside from the imported wines, which were stored in an old-fashioned wine locker, she kept everything from Ouzo to mescal in really crazy-looking weird shaped bottles that she got from some store that specialized in bizarre shit. She even had every different kind of Schnapps. I think there are more Schnappses than there are flavors at Baskin-Robbins.

Cheeseburger Schnapps.

Sweet Intimate Juices of a Young Woman Schnapps.

All of her furniture was Salvador Dali-esque twisted and surreal. I mean, she even had that melting clock on the wall. Beaded curtains, Aladdin's lamps, Oriental tapestries, Egyptian canopic jars, the whole nine yards. Bunch of Toulouse-Lautrec posters, the unimpressive advertisements that were considered *avant garde* back in the day. Some of her stuff was actually bona fide antique, though.

A gilt-bronze bodhisattva from the Asuka period, seventh century. A nineteenth century Persian rug. A translucent and variegated alabaster crouching-tiger-hidden-dragon sculpture, with a marble base and lace-like backdrop of intricately carven turquoise, with "Yingzhao" written underneath, whatever that means.

A lot of *feng shui* stuff, too. The ancient art of decorating your apartment to bring harmony and good fortune, she said, was a great way to avoid responsibility because if life didn't go your way you could blame the couch.

When I met her, she'd just heard that Hindu women have two kinds of dots on their foreheads—tilaks, I think they're called—and the red one meant Married. She wore a bright green one when she went out, meaning Go, until we hooked up. At least, I tell myself it's because of me she took it off, and not just coincidence that about that time she found out different-colored dots don't mean shit.

How I convinced her, at the club D'ingo and I had infiltrated, that I was twenty-one, is beyond me. Now that she knows it doesn't seem to bother her.

In the obscenely decorated bathroom mirror, I looked like death warmed over. Refried ass. My pale blue eyes were bloodshot, my curly black hair splitting at the ends from all the harsh cleaning it had undergone. My olive skin was a sickly pale.

The drink took all of the sting out of the night's adventure, and I went to bed and fell asleep in Maya's arms.

I'm not pretending to be a genius, but I damned sure ain't your run-of-the-mill, garden variety Thug. D'ingo and I aren't into *cholo* like most of our friends are. I don't wear my pants low so you can see my underwear, I don't have my hat on sideways, backwards, or pulled down so low I have to bend my head backwards to see under the brim. The only gold I have in my mouth is a filling.

Yes, I have tattoos, but they aren't stupid phrases like "Money Over Bitches," "Pain Before Pleasure," or "Thug For Life."

No barbed wire, no tribal, no obscure Oriental characters that may—or may not be—what I asked for. I don't speak Ebonics. I don't have shoes with lights in them.

But I watched my grandfather work hard every day of his life, and end up with nothing to show for it but triple bypass surgery. I watched my dad live out the cookie-cutter life all middle-class men seem to have mapped out for them, and he wasn't happy with it, so why should I be?

I chose a life less ordinary.

Fuck high school. Fuck college, nine to five, mortgages and insurance policies. My mother did all that crap, too, and whenever I looked into her eyes all I could see was boredom, like the distant light of a long dead star. The fire that once glowed in them had burnt out, and we just couldn't see it yet.

When I met Maya, she was in a white Acapulco shirt with huge red Paisleys on it, hand-batiked blue jeans, and platform sandals. Buddha-esque ear-weights. Not my typical girlfriend. But she walked to the beat of a different drum, had a quirky sense of humor, and could speak knowledgeably about the kinds of things my generation pays no attention to. Beautiful, of course, looking kind of like that chick in "Gone With The Wind," only not so stuck up.

Describing herself once, she'd quoted *Scaramouche,* saying she "was born with the gift of laughter, and a sense that the world was mad."

As hobbies, she made Ambient Trance music on her computer, and designed all the goofy shirts she wore under the name ATF. That's right, Alcohol, Tobacco, and Firearms. The first shirt she did was a collage of Martini glasses, grinning Zombie mugs with drink umbrellas, yards-o-beer, revolvers, automatics, loose bullets, and dirty stubbed-out cigarette butts. Another one had a bunch of hookahs, ornate and leaking tendrils of smoke. Another one of scattered autumn leaves. Very colorful, but certainly not your typical Ugly Print Shirt. Nary a Hibiscus or palm frond on any of them. Tarot cards. Christ, one of them even had huge iridescent insects and small flattened dead lizards.

187

She fascinated me.

"Never color inside someone else's lines," she said.

That motto became my philosophy after the first month with her. That was a year ago.

Let me nip an argument in the bud before it becomes a problem: I am not a racist. Not even close. I am like many middle-class white people of the early 21st century, not just an American, a South Floridian. I live in Coquina, on the East coast, in between Miami and Lauderdale, a melting pot of cultures. More on that later. I have learned from experience that there is a difference—and it's a huge difference, not just a fine line—between black people and *niggaz*. Black people are an admirable race of honest God-fearing, hardworking people, be they Caribbeans or Gullah, and niggaz, well, they're just niggaz. They'll make no distinction between white people and white trash, rednecks, Yanks, hicks, hillbillies, city slickers, and good ol' boys. No, they lump us all into one category: crackas. The blue-eyed devil.

Here's a prime example: I have not ever fought a black dude—not that I can think of anyway—but I have fought niggaz, and no small amount of them. Every single time, whenever someone asked why it had happened, I'd tell them the real reason, that either he was running his mouth or tried to put down on me in some way, trying me. But he won't say that. He won't tell the truth. He'll say the reason we fought was because I called him a nigga. And that's all. And people believe that. The fight was justified then, they decide, and I was in the wrong even though I didn't say that and wouldn't ever.

Well, now I'll call a spade a spade, goddammit. That very act of lying and putting up a false image of racial oppression, that is what makes him a nigga instead of a black dude. It isn't a fine line that separates them. It's a vast gulf of space.

In my circles, I deal with people of every color, but only one ilk. They all seem to have crawled out from under a rock. Wherever their race, they are all pretty much one kind of criminal or another; a sinner of some degree. Some are devout addicts, the chronically unemployed, some are just weekend users, and some can balance their pleasures so their recreation doesn't become their way of life.

When you get right down to it, though, there is no real distinction. A dime bag is a kilo, in God's eyes, and whether you're a sheep or a lamb, you're still mutton.

That said, I may continue to tell my tale honestly, without hiding behind politically correct euphemisms, half-truths, and outright lies. This is an exposé of niggaz, spicks, ragheads, wops, faggots, dykes, and blue-eyed devils. Bon appetit.

Maya gently woke me about ten in the morning, but it felt like I'd only been asleep two seconds. Bronze elephant-head earrings had stretched her earlobes down two inches, and through the holes I could see—

"Domingo's dad is here," she said softly.

"What!" I was instantly awake, and could feel his presence in the living room as if he were Darth Vader and I were Luke.

"Shhh. Put on a manly face and go talk to him." As soothing as her voice was, the words shamed me out of bed. Wiping the sleep out of my eyes, I took a deep breath and padded out. The mother-of-pearl beaded curtain clacked and parted, and there was Nestor de Medieros. He sat in one of the dinette chairs, motionless, like a coiled viper, and waited for me to come sit opposite him.

"Why didn't you come home?"

I stalled, fishing a cigarette out of the pack in my jeans.

He lit it for me with his gold lighter that screamed, "I cost three hundred dollars," and repeated himself.

"Sir, uh, I knew you'd be mad at me—"

"For what?"

"Well, uh…we lost the drugs. And the money. And… Domingo almost got killed. So, I thought—"

"Your problem was you *didn't* think, *moço*."

"Yes, sir."

"Don't say 'Yes, sir' when you dunno what I'm talking about."

"Yes, sir."

"From what my son says, you behaved admirably up until you refused to call me. Now it was manly to try to handle it yourself, and you were very brave. But stupid. You are not Charles Bronson."

"Yes, sir."

"Maybe you would still have your car if you had called me. Now we go into Golgotha, all we get is *vingança*, and maybe some drugs. Because you want to be the hero."

"Yes, sir."

"And you should have shot the son of a bitch. But you are soft-heart, like a woman, when it comes to such things. Probably a

189

phase you'll grow out of. If not, maybe you come to work for me at the restaurant instead." It was meant to be an insult, to shame me: the idea of a soldier serving other people food in an apron. But luckily, I'm not Brazilian, so that kind of thing doesn't work on me. I smoked my cigarette and blew smoke in every direction except his.

"Good. Now you take Esteban and Calibos to this place and kill those people. Then burn the place down."

"It's an apartment, like this. Other people live nearby," I said, regretting the words a second later.

"You've been there. You've seen them. They are not people."

I sat there, trying to think of something to say, and coming up with nothing. In the nick of time, Maya came in with her cordless phone, handing it to me.

"Don't forget to report your car stolen, baby."

"Thanks, Maya." I dialed the police.

"I always meant to ask," Nestor said. "Are you named after the Indians who lived in Yucatan before we came?"

"No, it's a Hindi word," she answered.

"Hindi?"

"The language of the Hindus. It means 'illusion'."

I listened to her give the explanation I'd heard a thousand times before while the phone rang. And rang. "But not just 'illusion'. The way a child goes to a movie theater and thinks what he sees is real, then only later can understand that it was a mirrored image projected from behind, spiritual growth enlightens us to the hidden truth that all the world is illusion as well."

Grazi Mono turned back to me, studying me for a moment. He rolled his eyes.

"Coquina County Sheriff's Office, how may I direct your call?"

"My car's been stolen," I said.

"One minute."

The hotline used to operate on a system of menus: "If this is an emergency, press one. If a crime has already been committed, press two. Blah blah blah, press three." But too many people had gotten murdered while waiting to talk to an actual person, so they went back to traditional operators.

"Officer Strickland."

"I'd like to report a stolen vehicle."

"Name?"

"Evan Lanthorne."

"Address?"

I gave him all my information, waited, and waited, while Maya brought Nestor his favorite drink—Cachaça, an amber-colored sugarcane rum. Eventually, Officer Strickland came back on the line and told me that my car had been found. I feigned surprise. "Really? Wow, that was quick."

"It was found this morning at the scene of a crime."

"Noooooo."

"Yessssss. A shootout last night. Gang-related. All that remained of your vehicle was the frame and the license plate. Oh, and your security alarm." He added that last part with a touch of amusement. "The tag was run, and one Detective Bancroft was planning to come around and see you. Now he will be accompanied by a Detective d'Argent. You are advised not to leave town, Mr. Lanthorne."

"How can I? I don't have a car."

"Smart-ass."

I filled Domingo's dad in on the news, and he was very pleased that I gave Maya's address instead of his. Grazi Mono was not fond of the police, and always happy to avoid them.

"Then we'll wait to visit The Hill," he said. "Get rid of these detectives and come home as quickly as you can. And either get more magazines for your weapon or learn to shoot better. At this rate, some nigger will eat your gun, and then where will you be?" He'd never forgotten that MP-5 I lost overboard, and he'd see that I never forgot it. He drained the last of his Cachaça and stood, looking around once more at the décor with obvious distaste. "Your mind has been touched by too many reefer," he said to Maya, who took the remark in stride. Then, showing himself to the door, Grazi Mono left. For a moment it felt like he was still in the room, and until that moment passed, neither of us spoke.

"Scrub your right hand real good," Maya warned. "The cops can put liquid paraffin on your skin so powder burns show up, see if you fired a gun."

"I washed last night."

"Do it again, just in case."

I listen to my girlfriend when it comes to stuff like this. Her father is a cop.

Detectives Bancroft and d'Argent showed up after lunch, looking like Good Cop/Bad Cop before they crossed the threshold. Bancroft was a salt-and-pepper goateed Joe Blow in jeans and a T-shirt, wearing his badge on his belt. D'Argent, on the other hand, was in a light gray suit with a lighter, marbleized gray shirt, open at the collar, a silver and abalone watch with matching cufflinks. His practiced-in-front-of-the-mirror smile may've been disarming if it wasn't so obvious. While he seemed just happy as a pig in shit to be wherever he was, Bancroft plainly resented having to be in public with his pretty-boy partner.

Introductions and sizing-ups out of the way, we sat around the table and smoked cigarettes, ashing in the gaping mouth of a ceramic drunken pig. The usual questions and answers were volleyed back and forth, and everything they said seemed routine until I noticed d'Argent watching Maya with a big bad wolf smile. Here it comes.

"So, Miss Macaulay, what do you do?"

She met his gaze squarely. "I'm a prostitute."

They actually flinched, and the smile vanished.

"Actually, I'm a network marketer, but it's essentially the same thing."

The detectives did not relax. They realized they were dealing with people who had very unconventional world-views and clean-cut people are never comfortable around anyone like Maya. I guess they feel threatened by what they don't understand. That's when Bancroft noticed the medicine bag around my neck. I'd forgotten I was wearing it.

"What is that?" he asked suspiciously.

"A medicine bag, to ward off evil."

The detectives exchanged a look, then d'Argent offered his patronizing smile to Maya. "Well, it must not be working, because I'm still here."

A pained look crossed Bancroft's face, as if he wished his partner were *anywhere* but here. I stifled a laugh. What a dipshit.

"You're on your way out, detective, so I'd say it works just fine. Any other questions before you go?"

"Yes, actually," Bancroft said, turning to me. "You claim to live here. At least that's what you told Officer Strickland. But your name isn't on the lease here and Miss Macaulay must list you as a roommate. Your legal address is 187 Barracuda Terrace, but your parents haven't seen or heard from you since you turned eighteen."

"I'm in between homes."

"You're also between probation meetings for possession of cocaine."

I said nothing.

"You're also between two shot-up neighborhoods, a little boy with one arm, two dead junkies, and a stolen police car."

Maya shot a surprised look at me. Oh yeah, I'd left that last part out. Bancroft wore the big bad wolf grin now, but he was no threat to me.

"What happens to my car or where it goes after someone steals it has nothing to do with me," I said.

"You'd be surprised how much it *does* have to do with you, Mr. Lanthorne. It was used in the commission of several crimes. It was described as matching one used in a high-speed car chase, culminating in one wrecked vehicle, a fair amount of property damage, and the kidnapping of one Samuel Purvis by one White and one Hispanic, both youths of about your height and build."

"There are a zillion youths of about my height and build. It's because I'm a youth. And the majority of Pontiac Sunfire drivers are either White or Hispanic. Youths. So there."

"And in the area known as Golgotha, all of the offenses reported last night were said to be committed by either two Whites, two Hispanics, or one of each."

"And what do you expect from an area full of nothing but blacks? Who else are they gonna blame? They'll be damned if they finger one of their own. Not unless you offered a reward—"

"Racism is not a—"

"Racism has nothing to do with it. It's common sense. They are drug addicts, criminals, and the poverty-stricken. If anyone shoots up the place, who are they gonna say did it? Someone from somewhere else. The same way a white guy in a white neighborhood sees his buddies doing wrong, he'll say it was a group of blacks. What did the people you talked to say when you asked them to describe the people? I got ten to one they said, 'I dunno, they was just white.' We all look the same to them and you know it."

"Nevertheless, we'd like to take you with us down to the station. Run a few tests," d'Argent said.

"Am I under arrest?"

"No, we just—"

"Then any tests you want can be done right here. After that, we'd appreciate it if you got the fuck out of our home and find the guys who stole my car."

They got irritated, but shrugged it off. Bancroft took a small vial out of his pocket and asked me to hold out my hands. Unscrewing the stopper, he used the medicine dropper it became to drip a reddish-brown liquid on the backs of my hands around the base of each thumb. Disappointed when my skin did not turn black, they asked if they could search the place.

"Do you have a warrant?"

"Not yet."

"Well, Maya? Do you mind?"

"Not at all," she said confidently.

So, I forgot to mention the stolen police car. Sue me. What happened was, we wandered in circles until, in a matter of hours, we ended up at the Hill again. By then, the night was alive with red and blue flashes. The neighbors had waited a respectable amount of time before calling the police, and the little kid had no parents to notice he was unconscious in the parking lot between two cars. Besides, Johnny Law always took his own sweet time coming to Golgotha. Lurking in the shadows, watching eight green uniforms investigate and count bullet holes, we edged closer and closer to the nearest squad car.

"What are we doing?" Domingo asked.

"Nothing, *meng*. Just follow me." After the night we had, I wanted the comfort of a twelve-gauge shotgun in my hands, and every police cruiser in Christendom has one in the front seat. I've been in the back seats of them enough times to know that cops, the most arrogant and careless people in the world, never take the keys with them, so a set of balls is all you need.

Opening the front doors and sliding in, I found the switch to shut off the rotating lights. Since there were seven others going, no one noticed the difference, as they surely would have if we'd left them on and driven away. The residents of the Hill were all intently watching the police, who were intently investigating and counting bullet casings and recounting them. I found the key that fit the little lock on the car's ceiling, releasing the twelve-gauge. Domingo lowered it gently, almost reverently, and I could see in his eyes how much power he knew he held. He looked like he wanted to shoot somebody with it, just to see what kind of damage he could do. I put the car key back into the ignition, and turned it gingerly. It was so quiet that no one nearby even seemed to notice. With huge, nervous grins, we shut the doors and backed out.

"I can't believe we're doing this."

"Me either," I giggled.

We turned through the maze of the Hill and came out onto the street. We took the long way out of Golgotha, skirting the park and the crack house, needing all of our self-control not to hit the siren and try out our zero-to-sixty. We drove in silence, except for our giggling, all the way out to State Road 357 and down to Forsythe. There, we parked behind a Git 'N Split and wiped down everything we may have touched. I took the shotgun, ran to a beige wall, and threw it over, knowing that there was a thick ficus hedge on the other side where it would be safe until I could come back and retrieve it. Going back to the squad car, I found Domingo on the radio, doing his best Cheech Marin impression.

"The request lines are now open!"

"Dude! What the fuck are you doing?"

"C'mon, Evan. When are we ever gonna have this chance again?"

I saw his point.

"Who the hell was that?" a voice crackled.

"This is Dunkin' Donuts with an early bird special—or would that be early pig?" Domingo answered.

"Identify yourself!" another voice shouted.

"This is the mayor," I said into the radio. "Mayor Dikfallov!" Domingo turned in the passenger seat, unzipped his pants, and sprayed all over the driver's side.

"Dispatch, run a tag on P-U fifty-five-Y,"

"Who IS this?"

"This is Officer Panties, I need an APB on Kendrick Purvis, brother of Antwan, son of Kong."

"Do you have any idea what kind of trouble you're in?"

"Urine? Why yes! I'm looking at some right now!"

"Stop! Stop!" D'ingo laughed. "You're killing me!"

"It's three a.m., Dispatch. Do you know where your car is?"

"Hey! Lemme talk to him," Domingo said. I put the radio next to his head and pressed the button. "When does a policeman smell the worst? When he's on duty! Get it? Doodee?"

"Ooh, clever, D'ingo," I said, laughing. Then our eyes went wide. Oh, *shit!* Domingo zipped himself back up and I wiped my fingerprints off the radio. Then, in a blind panic, we bolted, running all the way to Shaitan's apartment.

Okay, skip ahead, skip ahead, skip ahead. Detectives d'Argent and Bancroft found a grand total of nothing incriminating in the apartment. No surprise there, since we knew they were coming.

"So, what the hell do I do about my car?" I asked. "I can't drive around on a frame."

"We're working on it," Bancroft said.

"Working on it. Right. That's why you're over here searching the house of the victim. You think you're gonna find any hot leads in my girlfriend's bathroom? Don't you have any suspects other than me?"

"We're *working* on it," d'Argent said.

"At the rate you're going, you don't inspire much confidence. Meanwhile, I've called the insurance company and they don't want to give me squat for a frame and a license plate."

"And the security alarm," Maya pointed out.

"That's not funny."

"Yes, it is. Detectives, do you know Sergeant Neil Macaulay? I believe he works with you."

"Hum a few bars," d'Argent said.

"Curly brown hair, like me, only much shorter. Same brown eyes. And one of those mustaches only cops and principals have."

"Yeah," Bancroft said. "I see him around. Why?"

"He's my daddy. Tell him I said Hi."

They stared, obviously unable to believe that strait-laced, boring Neil could ever have spawned a weirdo like Maya Macaulay. Apparently they'd never met Brenda, the missus. They left, and instead of going straight to Grazi Mono's like I was supposed to, I dragged my sleepy ass back to bed where it belonged.

Maya and I used to play doctor with everything from scented oils, beads, chains, handcuffs, and Ben Wa balls to tantric metaphysics. Of course, the jaded get bored with even that, but she was a good friend and had a great body, so I stayed with her when other guys would have moved on. In this stupid world of petty wars and constantly watching one's back, a good friend like Maya is more valuable to me that any "fly ho" or whatever I'm supposed to call her these days. She may walk to the beat of a different drum, but

196

since I can't see the sense in much of the world anyway, I guess I do, too.

She also showed me that drinking pineapple juice and avoiding salt and garlic made your natural juices taste damned sweet. I don't know about myself, but Maya tastes so good down there that I can't get enough. Most girls are like eating sardines off a Brillo pad, but not mine.

She taught me from the writings of Kanchinatha, Vatsyayana, and Gedun Chopel. I read *The Alchemy of Ecstasy*, *The Perfumed Garden*, the *Kama Sutra*. I learned about karuna, churning, the eight different oral pleasures, and other techniques. Her favorite sex story that she likes to tell other people is the time I first bought a Tantra book. We were making love, and she watched me concentrate on going six shallow, six deep, six shallow, pull out and grind six, then repeat. She let this go on for a little while, then said "Evan, could you just fuck me, please?"

"Shut up, honey, I'm trying to count."

The girls have a good laugh at my expense, and even though I really don't remember this happening, I let her tell her little joke. The only friend of ours who wouldn't laugh was Shaitan. To her, sex was a sacred, untouchable subject. Even Domingo didn't speak of it in front of her, which made me wonder if they had ever done the deed at all. Like me—in fact, like most boys of our lifestyle—D'ingo had lost his virginity at the ripe old age of nine and had never looked back. But Shaitan, she was not one of us.

The American Indian of today seems to fit one of only three molds: bright and full of life, bitter and violent, or drunk and utterly hopeless. She had watched her father drink himself to death, and so refused to ever so much as smell alcohol. Her brothers had been those militant types who either die fighting, do time, get addicted, or just slip through the cracks into poverty and despair. They died fighting. So Shaitan hated violence as well, despite her temper. Gambling, too, because of how the Fed was trying to encroach upon the only territory her people had left, under the disguise of casinos. The Iroquois reservation was a sovereign state, but if the U.S. government could introduce their casinos, there would be palefaces everywhere. So no sex, no booze, no gambling.

What Domingo saw in her I couldn't imagine.

Maybe she was the only one he didn't have to be tough around. All that macho bullshit his people are so married to, it must be tough fighting and killing and dying over nothing all the time. Maya understood. I never had to play the hard-ass around her, like I did everyone else.

Oh. Right. Almost forgot something.

Coquina, another Floridian developer's wet dream from almost thirty years ago, somehow went the same way all the rest of these snowbird havens did. About halfway between Miami and Lauderdale, a large portion of "wasted" land stretching from the Glades to the beach was annexed and named after an indigenous rock (how quaint), then raped by bulldozers and steamrollers. The name was taken after another town—Coquina Beach, or whatever—was conveniently demolished in Hurricane Trishelle.

Palmettos, buttonwoods, mango trees, and sea grapes were nothing more than street names now. Poisonwood, pigeon plums, figs, and mahogany were now seen in landscapes and sold in oceanfront strip malls. Still vainly trying to maintain the brochure image of what this resort town was supposed to be, the town council imported conch, scorpion shells, starfish, and sand dollars from the Bahamas to scatter along the shore when nobody was looking. We would even have flamingoes from time to time, and as everybody who lives in Florida knows, the only time you'll see flamingoes is when somebody *puts* them there.

Drug money was laundered through "environmentally concerned" projects all over the Florida coast, but especially here. The beach was steadily washing out to sea, eroding us out of house and home, but barges would dredge it back up off the ocean floor and bring it back. The importing of exotic shells was more than just a maintaining of image. It was a new laundering detergent, just absurd enough to be convincing for the general public. That's Florida for you.

Apparently, the greed-driven developers and mindlessly optimistic politicians expected this zoning miscarriage to be different from the rest, to actually stay afloat. It was a success for almost three years. In the late summer of its third year, refugees from Miami crowded in, fleeing the devastation of Hurricane Shafiqua, bringing with them a plague of lowlifes. Invading one subdivision, the newcomers drove out the upper middle class and set up housekeeping like a pregnant fly in a fresh wound. When it was safe to return and rebuild their homes, the decent folks did, leaving the scum behind.

That area was jokingly dubbed "Golgotha" by a civil rights busybody at a civil rights busybody luncheon, and the name stuck.

Meanwhile, back at the ranch…

Shaitan was in the kitchen with Maya when I woke up. They were talking excitedly as they prepared some kind of complicated sauce for tonight's dinner. I brushed my teeth, washed my face, and joined them.

"Well, good morning, sleepyhead."

"Morning, Maya."

"Come to join the land of the living?" Shaitan asked.

"For as little time as I can get away with."

"Shai's come with some interesting news," Maya said. I sat down at the dinette and lit a cigarette, one of those minty herb things that Maya was so fond of, rolled in a dried maple leaf with a pink thread tied near the butt end. I tried to listen nonchalantly to what the dark and beautiful squaw had to say.

"Mr. de Medieros wants you to go back to school, posing as a kid who's new in town and planning to transfer. Since it's been years since you were there last, and time has not been kind to you, he doesn't expect the faculty to recognize you."

"Gee, thanks."

"Don't mention it. You will go everywhere that Domingo goes, and just watch his back. Jeff Davis is just silly with BLs, so he thinks they might try something. Now let me ask you something. Why in the hell would a school named after Jefferson Davis be full of black kids?"

"Why wouldn't it?"

"Don't you know anything about history?"

"Not particularly."

"Then you're doomed to repeat it."

"You like that word, don't you? Doomed."

"It's a good word. We don't have a word for it in Iroquois. Or oblivion. I like that one, too."

"Yeah, so anyway, I'm supposed to go undercover and be D'ing's bodyguard? For how long? And if this is a cover operation, what's my secret code name?"

"It's already been straightened out with the principal, phony records from your other school, Twin Lakes, and your perfect conduct and attendance record. Your name is something like Kevin Langdon."

"That's not very creative, is it?"

"No, but he thinks it'll be easier for you to remember."

"Well, he's not giving me much credit. If he told me to be Juan Jose de Vargas y Borsa, I could still handle it."

"Yeah? Say the name again."

"Why?"

"Just do it," she said with a sly grin.

"Uh, Juan Jose…this is stupid."

"C'mon, say it."

"No, this is dumb, and I'm not doing it."

"Ha! See? Maybe Kevin Langdon is too complicated. Perhaps it should have been John Smith instead."

"Fuck you."

The girls laughed, enjoying my defeat. "So, when is this supposed to happen?"

I waited, but they were still laughing. Girls. "Yeah, hardee-fucking-har."

"If my name was Don Jose de Vargas y Balsa," Maya said, mimicking me in this voice that sounded *nothing* like me, and they laughed like it was the funniest shit in history. I got up, found a glass, and poured myself some Ouzo. I drank sullenly while waiting for the comediennes to get tired of their little joke, and they kept me waiting.

Girls.

"So, you heard?" Domingo asked.

"About half of what I wanted to. Mind filling me in?"

We were seated in a booth at Pecado, eating from a huge pile of nachos and multicolored spicy goop that the menu called Cuitlahac, but I called Mount Bellyache. There were swirls of green, brown, orange, and yellow, with chunks of red, and specks of all of them, each ingredient completely unidentifiable to me, occasionally falling apart in tumbling food avalanches. Damned if I knew what it was, but it ate pretty good. We happily dug trenches in it with our nachos and discussed the brilliant plan Nestor had come up with.

While Domingo talked, he had one eye on every waitress that walked by. His father refused to hire any woman who didn't fit into this category: short, hot, dark, and heavily accented. Every girl with a Pecado uniform on was a swimsuit model underneath it. I couldn't fault him for looking; I was doing it too.

In the back, behind the kitchen, were several hundred pounds of uncut cocaine, heroin, marijuana, hashish, and every variety of worthwhile designer drug under the sun.

Whatever was ordered, the expo girl simply hid in the arrangement of food on a plate inside shrink-wrapped plastic baggies. The transfer was completely undetectable because it was all out in the open. Payments for orders not on the menu were simply left on the tables. Sure, they were three and four hundred dollar tips, but the busboys lost no time in collecting them.

The hostesses knew the faces of every cop and narc in the city, from a binder of mug shots and surveillance photographs they were required to study. Pop quizzes weren't uncommon, so the smiling young women knew instantly where a party should be seated if they recognized a face coming through that door. That way, no wandering eyes ever happened to fall on a customer pulling an eight-ball out of his rack of lamb with mint sauce.

The manager, Pedro Vizcaya, ran a tight ship. He was a Spaniard, a martial artist who'd gone through all but the final test for entrance into the French Foreign Legion. According to him, on top of all the physical, mental, and language requirements, recruits were compelled to perform certain acts of inhumanity to prove they were the hard, dyed-in-the-wool killers the Legion was looking for. These tests included swimming through a pool of cow's blood, which Vizcaya had no problem with. It was the very last test that kept him from making the cut. He could not bring himself to eat the barbequed flesh of an executed human being. Of all the horror stories he told of his adventures, that was my least favorite.

He was like an uncle to Domingo and me, having taught us *capoeira* from the age of fourteen, after we'd gotten our asses kicked by a rival gang one afternoon. He'd also gotten us that Marlboro pool table we played on all the time. Well, in a way, he did. He helped us hijack the cigarette truck one night, and we peeled off the Marlboro Miles of several thousand packs, sent them back to the company, and received a regulation pool table with a Philip Morris crest emblazoned on the felt about a month later. The horses, the crown, and the banner were all a darker green, leaving the "PM" and "veni, vidi, vici" normal green. That was when we were sixteen and a half, and he was more my father than the real one was.

In 1986, he fought under the ETA, an underground guerrilla group of Basque Nationalists, in San Sebastián against the police in several of the revolts that threatened the regime following Franco's.

Pedro rose quickly in Euzkadita Azkatasuna, living up to and even outdoing the reputation his people have held since the days of Rome. When own his father had been apprehended by the Falangists, he spared him the shame of capture with a sniper rifle. One shot to the head, and got a few of the badguys, too. His obligation to his duty bordered on fanatic, his daring and machismo exceeded legendary. He and his fellow terrorists financed their bombings through bank robberies until he was forced to flee across the Pyrenees into France, seeking a home among the mercenaries.

Uncomfortable with cannibalism, he instead rallied a band of desperate men together, using his knack for leadership to become their *condottiere*, selling their ferocity to the highest bidder. They found their way across the Atlantic to Colombia, fighting first on one side and then the other. A hideous man named Calibos Lugo fell in with them, and before long they ended up in Miami, Florida.

All of Grazi Mono's soldiers had been rejects of the French Foreign Legion, living from one struggle to another, with only two other exceptions: Esteban Ribeira, and Jeffrey Ashton—called Blue Tick by his brothers-in-arms.

Vizcaya's eyes would dance like a child's when he told me about his hometown. Pamplona was most famous for the Fiesta de San Fermín, when he ran wearing a red scarf across the river to the corral on Calle Santo Domingo, with six oxen and six enormous bulls pursuing in an explosion of thundering hooves.

On the next morning, he'd run from them again all the way to the Plaza de Hemingway, every July 14th, and riot with the rest of Pamplona until the bullfights. From the year he was fifteen, he proved his courage and his manhood again and again during the *encierro*, in those narrow cobblestones streets with death only one step behind him.

When Nestor, who never, ever danced, threw a fiesta in honor of Saint Fermín, and the black sky was alive with fireworks and music, Vizcaya would put on his gold matador jacket and dance the *paso doblé* with Teresa de Medieros, resplendent in her crimson dress that symbolized the bullfighter's cape. I never felt as exhilarated, anywhere, as I did at a party with Latin people. I don't think anyone loves life as much as they do, because nobody else celebrates with as much joyous abandon. And Pedro had the most contagious laughter of them all.

He schooled us in the proper ways to grow and harvest marijuana: how to "top it out"—prune it so it grew short and bushy, and after pulling the whole plant up by the roots, boil the root bulb in a pot of water and chase all the extra THC up into the leaves, then hang it upside down to resinate.

Besides what we grew ourselves, we also dealt in stuff like Lamb's Breath, a very soft and light variety, Colombian Gold, Colombian Red Tip, Maui Wowee, and had it shipped to us in crates full of apples so it took on their flavor and fragrance. And hash oil. God, hashish. Afghan hash, Blonde Lebanese, opium, tar so sticky you had to scrape it off the bag it came in. Diff'rent smokes for diff'rent folks. We kept a dime bag from every different variety we sold, labeled it with dates and specifics, in a categorized library. It was our own private humidor in the safehouse on Hibiscus Avenue, and the smell of it alone was enough to make your eyes glaze over. We were very proud of our collection. Pedro also taught us a quick way to make opium: double-boiling yohimbe. Hydronic heating, he called it. It wasn't the real thing, but it was an acceptable substitute. Stuff made you so high you'd cast no shadow.

It was he who laid all the mosaic tiles in the restaurant, displaying an affinity for the work that pleased Grazi Mono, who was a skilled carpenter himself. Machismo, I suppose, was what prompted these two capos to roll up their shirt-sleeves and do the manly work themselves. They made every table, from sawing the lumber to painting on the lacquer, and built the bar in less than two days out of oak and brass. Abuela took all the credit for the stained glass partitions, creating them with her gnarled brown hands that looked like tree roots.

Vizcaya was Grazi Mono's right hand man, and under him were Esteban and Calibos. All I have to say about Esteban was that he'd made a rosary out of gold-capped human teeth, pulled from the screaming mouths of drug rollers in rival gangs. Some open-faced crowns, but mostly solid gold caps, and just plain white molars in place of the large beads marking the decades. He actually prayed with it.

And Calibos, he was just an animal. A cruel, pockmarked face, pitted and cratered by horrible acne, and a huge Fu Manchu mustache made him scowl even when he was smiling. The two of them were the most brutal killers I'd ever heard of.

Esteban looked pretty clean-cut, but Calibos, Calibos had this long, shiny black hair that he cared for obsessively. I've never seen anyone—man or woman—as vain as he was, or as ugly. They sometimes talked about the white guy called Blue Tick they used to work with, who was supposed to be worse than the two of them put together, but that was hard to believe. Rumor had it that he'd gone to work for some crazy young drug lord and gotten himself deceased.

When they were drunk, they told some pretty tall tales, so I took most of what they said with a grain of salt. I realized Domingo was saying something to me.

"Huh?"

"Have you heard a word I've said?"

"No," I said to our waitress's ass as she walked by.

There's a story Domingo loves to tell, and others love him to tell it over and over again, especially in my presence. It's awfully convenient that in the story I'm stoned, because it's a great way to explain why I can't remember any of it happening, *ever*. It is the story of 'How The Burn Mark Got In Esteban's Probe,' and I'll tell it how D'ingo tells it.

"This was three years ago, when we both had our learner's permits but had been driving for a year already. Evan had snuck out of his parents' house and we were having a party at one of the Acreage safehouses. Most a ya'll been there—the one with the long driveway into the woods with the white fences on either side?"

"Uh-huh, with the orange trees," somebody usually says.

"Yeah, so we'd been drinking and mackin' on these cheerleaders from Cardinal Newman...well, at least *I* was. I don't know what Evan thought he was doing."

Pause for laughter. Ha ha. Funny funny.

For the record, I *did* get a handjob from Vanessa Townshend that night, who looked almost just like her sister, Veronica Townshend. That's *the* Veronica Townshend, the model, so you know her little sister was fine, only her tits weren't quite as big.

Yet, anyway.

"Well," D'ingo says, "I can hear tires squealing not too far away, and because we're back behind all these trees I know that whoever's car that is, if I can hear them, they got to be coming to see us in a *hurry*. So I go outside onto the porch to see these head-

204

lights coming up the lane fast, and when they screech to a halt in the light coming offa the porch where I'm standing, I can barely tell that it's Esteban's Probe. You know how it's that kind of red, in between Fire Engine and Candy Apple Red? Like kind of a Panic Button Red? And it has those pulsing neons on it like Knight Rider had in the hood, only under the car? Well, those neons were off and the car was splattered in mud and bird shit, it looked like, so it was kind of hard to tell it was Esteban until he opened the door and the interior lights came on.

"'*Ay cabron*!' I say, and he tells me, not Hello or *Oyé* or anything like that, he cuts straight to 'Take this to Billy's for me.' I ask him why, and he goes 'Just do it!' while another pair of headlights comes squealing into the lane up by the road and starts hauling ass toward us even faster than Esteban had. I knew right then it was Calibos because he always drives *way* too fast. Well, I tell him 'Dude, Billy's like, ten minutes up the road. Why don't you just keep going?' and he goes 'Cause I fucking can't, that's why. Now do it.' Calibos slides sideways in his pickup truck from the lane to almost crashing into the back of the Probe, slams on the brakes and his face appears in the passenger side window saying '*Well?* Get inna focking trock!' but Esteban says 'Can't. His Majesty here is too busy to take care of my car for me.'

"And Calibos looks at me." Here D'ingo usually pauses for emphasis. "You all seen Calibos. You know what he looks like when he's being friendly. Well, when he looks at me, he ain't Miss Congeniality, you know what I'm saying? Dude. You all *know* I'm no pussy. Never been. But God *damn* if my blood didn't freeze when he looked at me and started saying a buncha shit in Spanish I didn't understand."

Somebody usually asks 'Wait, I thought you spoke Spanish!' and the rest of us all just roll our eyes.

"Yeah, so, anyway," Domingo continues, as if nobody'd spoken. "I'm like, whoa, what the hell's going on? And I ask Esteban and he says to never mind about that, just drive the car to Billy's, and I ask why can't *he* drive his own car to Billy's and he says he *can't*, so I ask *why*? And he does this big sigh like he's talking to somebody stupid, and he says 'Because I got an alibi I have to get to.'

"Uhhhh. I'm like, *what*? He waves me over while he's edging between the rear of his car and Calibos' pickup, and popping open

205

the hatchback. I get there next to him just as he raises the hatch, and we're both bathed in this red light. It startles me, but then I'm even more startled to see the red light is coming from this red shit that's smeared on the trunk lights.

Then it takes a second to realize what I'm looking at all stuffed into the little compartment under this blue plastic tarp, because there's this dock shoe sticking out of one side of the tarp, and that red stuff on the trunk lights is *everywhere*, on the tarp, on the vinyl, on the glass, on the hatch raised right above my head, and Esteban next to me. Him and everything else is drenched in fuckin' *blood*.

"I look at Esteban and—you gotta remember, I'm just fifteen, okay?—and he says he needs to get somewhere ten minutes ago. I need you to get this car to Billy's *yesterday* while I get where I'm going.'"

And here's where D'ingo gets into his little comedy routine.

"Nope!" he says in a silly voice, walking away while everybody (except me) laughs. He walks around in circles whenever it's his turn to talk again. "Nope nope nope nope!"

Then, as Esteban, standing still and facing his audience: "C'mon, pull yourself together, kid!"

As himself, shaking his head, walking in a circle again: "Nope nope nope nope!"

Esteban, jabbing accusingly with his finger: "You better start acting like a man, you little sissy!"

Himself, shaking his head, walking in a circle, hands raised: "Not me! Find somebody else!"

As just the narrator again: "Then, here comes Evan, stoned like Saint Stephen out onto the porch."

Fresh from getting jerked off by Vanessa, I might add, but I don't.

He puts on this D'uhhh-which-way-did-he-go-George? voice that sounds *nothing* like me.

Stoned Evan: "Hey guys, what's going on?"

Pause for laughter. Ha ha. Funny funny.

"We ignore him. Esteban shuts the hatch and the red light goes out. He tells me one more time to take the car to Billy's. A light bulb goes on over my head—*ding!*—and I say to Esteban to gimme his phone so I can call my Dad. He rolls his eyes at me again, taking out his cell and pressing one of the speed dial buttons. It's going *doot-deet-dootdoot-deet doot-doot* while he hands it to me, and it must be the phone number for my Dad's red phone like Batman has and I don't know nothing about, because he's picked up before the ring tone even starts purring.

"I tell him in Portuguese everything there is to say in, like, a single breath, then wait for an answer. And he says, calm as can be, like this is no big deal, 'So why aren't you at Billy's yet?' I'm left standing there, listening to a click and a dial tone, with the three of them staring at me, and all of a sudden I'm completely sober.

I swear, it feels like the ground has disappeared out from under me. You know when Wile E. Coyote is chasing the Roadrunner and he runs right off a cliff, but doesn't fall right away? Takes fifteen, twenty steps across thin air before realizing, and then his nose and ears droop? That's what I'm feeling like.

"Fuck. Well, I shut the phone off and hand it to Esteban, trying not to look scared—"Aww, see his humility? He scores big points with the chicks in the audience while I still look like a dipshit—"And ask what I'm supposed to do when I get there. Dude tells me Just get the car there, that's all you gotta do.'"

Stoned Evan: "What's going on?"

Ha ha. Funny funny.

"I tell him to get in the car."

Stoned Evan: "What's going *on*?"

"I tell him 'Dude, shut up and get in the car.' There's no room to open the door to Calibos' truck, so Esteban just holds the window of the cab, one hand down on the door and the other up on the top part, steps on his own bumper and then jumps up and through the window, feet first, like he's some kind of superhero. I step out of the cut just in time for them to peel out away from next to me, tires smoking. Music's still pounding from inside the house; I look back up at Evan on the porch, the front door open and all the chicks and our boys in there having fun, and I'm still standing out there on thin air, just haven't fallen yet, and here comes Evan down off the porch with another 'Dude, what's going on?" I tell him to get in the car and we get in, me all scared and him all of a sudden like a puppy dog. 'Oh boyohboy ohboy! We going for a ride inna vroom-vroom!'"

Pause for laughter.

"Yeah, he hits the stereo while I'm driving and gets all—" He breaks off to do his rendition of a one-hit-wonder that everybody, including me, loved three years ago but, except me, hates now and pretends never to have liked at all, ever. D'ingo's audience laughs, "not at me, but with me," especially when he's doing the outdated and no-longer-cool dance moves that no one will admit they did even back when they *were* cool and they *were* the latest thing. Like Yaga.

"Bitch quit callin' me, callin' me, callin' me
Burnin' up mah minutes, bitch, dis shit ain't free
Write a letter, drop by, or jus' let me be
Quit callin' me, callin' me, callin' me..."

Of course, everyone takes this time to have a fuckin sing-along, looking at me with thinly-disguised contempt as if, 1) I'm the one who wrote the goddamned song in the first place, and 2) as if they themselves *don't* know the lyrics by heart because they studied the CD inlay card and memorized them back in the day, when every last one of them was "gaga 'bout Yaga." Like maybe they expect me to believe they picked up a rote memorization of those lines by fucking *osmosis*.

Cocksuckers.

"In the middle of that part where Yaga's telling her to whine about her problems to Rikki Lake instead of him, Evan suddenly turns the volume way down and asks me if I smell something. I keep my eyes on the road. Nope. I don't smell anything. He goes 'For real, meng, something stinks in here."

Again, everyone laughs, saying Meng over and over in Cuban accents. Finally, they're really laughing with me because I'm the one who started saying Meng like Scarface ever since I started hanging out with D'ingo, and it caught on. So we laugh and say *meng* over and over, sometimes drawing out the M to make it *mmmm*meng! and then saying shit like "Cockaroaches!" and "Say hallo to mah leetle freng!"

Hey, I never said we were mature people.

Anyway, eventually we get all the Tony Montana-isms out of our system and the story gets back on track. Domingo says "Evan keeps asking if I smell something and then describing what he smells as if that'll help me smell the dead body that's like, three feet away. I'm just like, nah, I don't smell nothing, and he's like 'Dude, tell me what's going on,' all the way to Billy's. We get there and it's this big ol' yard with the woods on three sides of it, and in the center there's this double-wide trailer with a wooden wraparound deck built and steps coming down from it. We pull up next to the steps and get out. Evan lights himself a cigarette and asks me what's going on. I go up the steps and knock on the door.

"There's kids making lots of noise inside, squealing and jumping around and I have to pound on the door for a while before somebody finally answers. Billy's this skinny guy with a bushy blond walrus mustache who works for my Dad in some way I know nothing about. He opens the door and he's wearing only a pair of blue jeans with white paint or grout or whatever smeared on them, and in the trailer behind him there's this gigantic obese woman wearing pajamas on the couch and like a dozen screaming kids bouncing around wearing little cartoon wifebeaters and tighty-whitey briefs. One of these Beyond Thunderdome feral children runs out the door past us, down the steps and around and around and around Evan, who's just standing there watching, smoking his cigarette.

"Billy steps out quick, shutting the door so none of the other little water-heads can get out, and he shouts at Evan, 'Catch 'im! Don't let 'im git away!' And Evan's over there watching the kid run around him in circles, doing donuts on his stubby little legs. Billy goes 'Ahh, fuck it. Who zat ya got witcha?' I tell him Evan's my brother, not to worry, he's got the kid under control."

Awww, see that? Throwing in a nod to me so he can win a few redeeming points with the butt of his jokes... which he does, I guess.

"He goes 'I dint know you hadda brother. Well, what kin I do ya fer?' And I say I've got something for him."

As Billy: "What?"

As Himself: "Uhhh, something Esteban and Calibos wanted you to have."

As Billy, staring: *"What?"*

"And, man, I just want to get out of there! I don't really know this guy, I have my fingerprints in a car with a goddamned dead body, I'm ready to just start walking with Evan back down the road, and he's asking me *What?* but I don't know what to say. So I say 'Look we need a ride back to the house we were just at, so if you could give us a lift—' and he goes 'You got a car right there!' And I say 'Shit, well, that's not my car, and I gotta leave it with you.'"

Billy: "The fuck you do."

Himself: "Why don't I?"

Billy: "Cuz I dunno what in the blue fuck you got in there, that's why."

Himself: "Look, my job is just to drive the car here and I did that, so now I'm leaving. But we need a lift if you—"

Billy: "You musta gone an' bumped yer head, boy. You ain't just gonna come along with someone else's problem and dump it on me. Do I look like a parkin' garage? Does my lawn look like Crazy Eddie's Stolen Car Lot?"

Himself: "Look, it's not the car. It's what's in it."

Billy: "What's in it?"

"And I turn and look at the car. Evan's still standing there, staring down at the kid, who's now dizzy and out of breath on the grass at his feet. All I can hear are the crickets for a second and then Evan's voice with a country twang, saying 'Yew gotta purdy mouth, boy.'

Billy: "What the hell'd he just say?"

Himself: "C'mere. I'll show you."

"And we go down the steps and over to the back of the Probe. Evan comes up just as I'm opening the hatch, and then the blood-red light comes on again. Evan puts his cigarette in his mouth, saying 'What's going on?' and takes a long drag. I hold my breath and reach down, grab the tarp and tug on it, but it snags, so I give it a yank and it holds for a split second then comes free, splattering us with blood or purge fluid or whatever that shit is, a nasty mist spraying out and freckling our faces, and with a loud *pthooo!* the cigarette goes shooting out of Evan's mouth, into the car, and all the way through it to ricochet off the air-conditioning vents in the dashboard, exploding in a shower of orange sparks, and land in the driver's seat."

Stoned Evan: "Holy Christ, that's a dead guy!"

"And Billy goes 'Well, shit, why dintcha say so?' He reaches in and grabs the dead guy by one ankle between his blood-drenched chinos hem and his dock shoe, pulls him out of the car with this sickening thud and farts of corpse-gas, and just strolls off around the car and toward the woods, dragging the dead guy behind him like it was nothing."

And that's the story.

How The Burn Mark Got In Esteban's Probe. The end.

I've heard D'ingo tell his goddamned story I dunno how many times, and with the exception of the one part he always neglected to tell—the part about me hooking up with Vanessa —I don't believe a damn word of it.

I realized the moment we parked behind Jefferson Davis High School just how much I didn't miss attending it. The place looked about as cheerful as a prison, with its gray walls and high fences. The little "Keep Off The Grass" signs were still in place, and the grass still had trails of dead brown runners from kids walking across it. All my old friends and enemies were seniors now, and a whole new crop of jitterbugs had taken up the places they'd left behind.

On our way to Home Room, my former arch-nemesis recognized me. Corey Walken. The fucker. He still looked like a ferret. He was the kid who carried his surfboard up and down the beach, but never went in. A bona fide poseur. He had the haircut and everything.

"I didn't think you'd ever show your face here again," he sneered.

"Corey, if I had a face like yours, I wouldn't show it anywhere."

I had a silenced little .22 in a shoulder holster under my jacket—"a little gun, for kids" Esteban had said—and I wanted to put a bullet right between Corey's running lights. But I decided that a left hook would have to do, if it came to that. It didn't, though, because he was still the same pussy he used to be. We made it to Mrs. Gibson's room and bull-shitted with the other kids for a while. No one bought that Kevin Langdon shit, except for Mrs. Gibson, who had a few screws loose anyway, and Principal Murphy. Fifteen minutes later, we were off to Algebra, and nineteen years after that (or an hour, real time) we went to History. Yadda yadda yadda, we went to English. Blah blah blah, Social Studies. And that's where I saw her.

Through the mind-numbing haze of school our eyes locked, and we both remembered Freshman year, when she'd been a skinny little thing with knobby knees and braces. The first thing I ever said to her was "Hey, I got a joke that will make you laugh so hard your tits fall off...oh, you've heard it already," and her face turned beet red. Asshole that I was, I followed it up with "So, are you the chairwoman for the Itty Bitty Titty Committee, or what?" and she burst into tears. I stood there feeling like I was about an inch tall. I didn't know what to do.

"Hey...shit, I didn't mean it."

I realized I hadn't been the first to make fun of her, and I felt so awkward and sorry for her that I had no idea what to do, so in a panic I hugged her close to me. She resisted, but I held her tightly

211

and stroked her long, curly blonde hair, shushing her gently. She was sobbing her shame out all over my chest. I hated myself at that moment.

"I'm sorry. Look, I was just making fun. I didn't mean it. I'm sorry, please don't cry."

She tried to choke the words out, stuttered and muffled by my shirt. I shushed her some more, ignoring the looks of kids walking by. Eventually, I understood what she was saying.

"You think I don't know what I look like? You think I *want* to look like this? You think I don't want to look like Britney fucking Spears and sit with Chrissy Martin and the cheerleaders in the cafeteria and get invited to all the parties you throw? Why can't you just leave me alone? What did I ever do to you?"

"I'm sorry."

"No, you're not!"

"Yes, I am. And there's nothing wrong with you. You're beautiful. I was just teasing you, that's all. I didn't really mean it. I just heard some other kid say it once and everybody laughed, so I said it. I didn't think it would hurt your feelings. Please stop crying." I started drying her tears and kissing her cheeks, telling her how pretty she was, and she argued with me quietly. She said she was a nerd; I told her she was intelligent. She said she was skinny; I said she was still growing, she'd fill out. She said she had braces; I told her when they came off she'd have a smile that lit up every room she walked in. She told me nobody liked her.

So I kissed her.

And now she was staring back at me, with the most beautiful smile, ripe Cupid's bow lips, and that curly blonde hair cascading past her shoulders, and high, firm, perfect breasts straining against the fabric of her shirt. Heather Roma had filled out.

I asked Domingo quietly for a piece of paper and a pencil, and he looked at me funny. "It's been a while, Evan. You sure you still know how to write?"

"What do you mean?"

"Here. Remember to use the pointy end."

"Thanks, *gêbo*." I scribbled out "You look great" on a sheet of loose leaf, folded it origami-style into a little envelope, wrote Heather's name on the back of it, and discreetly passed it to the guy next to me. I knew it wasn't a Cyrano de Bergerac letter, but it would have to do. She waited patiently for the note to find its way to her desk, and when she opened it, she beamed.

We could not keep our eyes off each other for the whole rest of the class. She was in an undersized pink shirt that said 97% Fat Free, and jeans so tight I could see exactly how un-knobby her knees had become. She was the only girl in the entire class without a single pimple. When she turned that beautiful smile back on me, I remembered us making out in secret, cutting classes, and the time we went to the Away dugout on the baseball diamond, and she showed her flat chest and bald pink to a boy for the very first time, and we made love violently and urgently when we were supposed to be in the cafeteria eating red bean casserole with rice pilaf.

"Y'ever fucked one of those skinny girls?" I asked Domingo afterwards. "The emaciated waifs that were so popular a few years back? That damn pussy bone'll rub off all your pubic hair. S'like fuckin a bag of chisels."

Then, I fell into the business, first as a runner for Nestor de Medieros, then as a roller, and wasting my time in school just didn't make any sense. I bought my own car with my own money, which pissed my dad off. I bought my own clothes and food when he gave me his bullshit lecture about his role as a parent, and after he realized I didn't need him anymore, he just bided his time. My eighteenth birthday cake read "Get Lost."

All during that time I was riding every girl I saw without a care in the world. I had more ass than any given chair did, and if there wasn't time for school, there certainly wasn't time for flat-chested mercy lay Heather Roma.

The bell rang, and I abandoned Domingo.

"Long time," Heather said.

"You look incredible."

"Thanks. You've grown a little, too." She was referring to the bulges under my own shirt. Pedro Vizcaya's tight ship had made me something of a Viking. I wasn't huge, not by any stretch, but there was no conceit in saying I looked damn good. As Jim Beam says, it ain't bragging if it's true.

"Flashier clothes, too," Heather noticed.

"Well, life has been good to me."

"Didn't you drop out?"

"Yeah, but…well, it's a long story."

"Tell me at lunch?"

"Sure."

"Good to see you."

"Good to see you, too."

We lingered, bodies hurriedly pushing past us, not saying more, but knowing there was more to be said. Both of us knowing it was there if we wanted it. So we just smiled, and enjoyed the looks on each other's faces. Domingo was waiting impatiently beside us, but we ignored him.

"Tick tock, tick tock, tick tock," he said.

"Well, I've got to go to Chemistry," Heather managed.

"You got plenty of that right here," Domingo observed.

"*Sossegado*! " I snapped playfully. "Ignore him."

"Bye."

"Bye."

And she was gone.

We went to D'ingo's Biology class, the last before lunch, which I eagerly looked forward to. I actually paid attention to what fat, bull-dyke Ms. Brandt was telling us about Gregor Mendel's early experiments with garden peas, and how he discovered hybrids. Then, she went on to further enrich us with overhead projections on the pull-down white sheet over her blackboard, showing how red snapdragons, fertilized by pollen from white ones, create pink snap-dragons. Yay. I decided that Gregor Mendel, being a monk with vows of celibacy and temperance, had way too much time on his hands. I drifted off a second, daydreaming about Heather, and Ms. Brandt gave the bottom of the sheet a sharp tug and sent it scamp-ering up into the metal cylinder. The sound startled the hell out of me, the way an old veteran must feel when you creep up behind him and yell "Incoming!"

No one in the class watched that clock more carefully than I did, and since my every sense was alert, waiting for the sound of that fire station bell, no one learned as much from that hour of class as me, except for, maybe, Juliet. Everybody knew a Juliet in school, I think. She's the black girl who wore a skirt and those barrettes and little bolo-looking things in her hair. She's humble, consistently makes straight A's in class, and gets a sad look on her face when someone tries to cheat off her paper during the math test. She doesn't sneer, doesn't put on airs; she just looks sad, and that'll make a kid feel guilty as hell for taking advantage of her...but he'll still copy her answers, because she's always right. She's the one that actually studies, goes to church, minds her parents, and is going somewhere in life, and the other black chirren hate her because when she gets there, she won't turn around and give them a free ride. They curse her because she sold out and turned White—which burns my ass because it's a bullshit label. Look at almost all the white kids in my school; they're all pretending to be black and failing because of it.

Because of busing, the integration of black kids who don't want to be with us, who intimidate us into being afraid to come to school, most white kids imitate their bullies in the hope of appearing kindred. They defy the teachers more than they did before, they show off their indifference to learning, and they don't dare excel in class because of the bell curve and the fear of getting their asses kicked—or shot, these days—if they raise the standards of the class so high that Rashawn or Kervince can't skate by with a forty percent. This wigger phenomenon caught on like wildfire until it had swept the nation, and A students relinquished their status in almost every public school we have, according to my Dad, with the weaker kids talking Ebonics and cakewalking through the halls with guns tucked in the low-hanging waists of their over-sized pants. Accepting minor injustices from the blacks every now and then rather than facing open conflict all the time. Of course, if you're white you can't say any of this, at least in South Florida. I don't know about the rest of the country. You get branded a racist and excommunicated, for lack of a better word, and that's only if you're lucky. Freedom of Speech? Oh, hell no. Not here.

No, Juliet did not become white. The whites became pussies...according to my Dad, but hey, what does he know?

But the irony of it is what I heard Antonio Jones saying to Mrs. Reynolds one day, years ago, when she threatened him with his permanent record keeping him from getting into a good college. He said "Bitch, check dis out. Ah'm a mino'ity. Ah ken git inna any school Ah want. Ah doan need *you*, ya feel me?" I don't know about Mrs. Reynolds, but I sure felt him. Straight up. Word. He'd get in any school he wanted (if he wanted) with a C average, but every white kid who'd given him daps in the hall and shared a blunt with him in the bathroom would be either dead or in Lancaster by then.

When the bell finally went off—two long minutes after it should've—I was a runner toeing his mark on the starting line.

"Relax, Kevin," D'ingo said patronizingly. "Her titties won't go away or nothing. They'll still be there."

"Naw, man, I'm just in a hurry to get some of that Salisbury steak."

"You're fooling yourself, sport. It's all soy now. Even the chicken."

We got to the cafeteria, and as I stood in line I looked everywhere for her. That beautiful blonde hair should've been a beacon, but I couldn't spot her. We got our tray of slop and our orange juice from concentrate, sat with our clique, and talked about whatever it was we were talking about. All the while I had my eye out for Heather when I should have had my eye out for BLs.

I was pissed off because I couldn't have a cigarette, being in school and all, feeling like a grown-up surrounded by children. Unable to relax. Where the hell was she? I hadn't sweated over a girl in years, but for some reason I had her smile and round, perky tits on the brain. And did she still shave the hair off her pink? Would she still taste the same as in that dugout, when I licked her fore and aft and told her how sweet it was?

There was a rock in my jeans that ached. God, I wanted to bury my face in those breasts that were just mosquito bites the last time. I remembered how her ribs stuck out under where her breasts should have been, and how my fingers fit right between them as I held her. I didn't know how many guys had had her since I'd been gone, but I'd been there first and I was coming home. But where was she?

Lunch ended too quickly, and the march to our next class was like the long walk to execution. Another mind-numbing hour, then the bell, then another long, grueling hour, and then suddenly school was over. We filed out and headed to the parking lot. The whole day was gone, and with almost twenty hours until the next watch started. Fuck.

"Evan!"

I turned to see her jogging toward me, disguised as a cheerleader, a crimson JD on her ample chest and a short, matching skirt below. Wow. Nice legs. She came to me around D'ingo's black Jeep and stopped, smiling. "Sorry, I forgot I had early lunch today. Are you coming back tomorrow?"

"Yeah, I'll be here."

"Good, I'll see you then. I have practice now, so…" She stepped in close, her warm cheek next to mine, her hot breath sweet, and whispered in my ear. "When I'm touching myself to-night, I'll be thinking of you." My breath froze in my throat.

And she was gone.

Domingo's voice came to me through a thick fog from a million light years away. I tried to blink away her words, the smell of her.

"Hey! Snap out of it!"

I looked at him through the open door, at the lit cigarette he was offering.

"Jedi mind trick, bro. That's all it was."

I climbed in, took the cigarette, and slammed my door. The second I heard it click, a rock bounced off the plastic zip-up window. I looked, and there was Corey Walken, laughing with his friends. I shoved the door back open and leaped out, like a train barreling down at a drunk stumbling on the tracks. Corey dropped his backpack and stepped to me, his arms out wide in the classic *What?* stance. When the gap closed and he expected me to throw a punch, I dropped and spun with my leg out, tripping him over backwards.

Then I was on him, my knee on the hollow of his solar plexus, and my fist smashing over and over into his face. His nose burst and splattered blood, then, as he screamed, two of his front teeth followed. Before a ring of shouting spectators could form around us, I was up and on my way back to the Jeep, leaving Corey to swell up and bleed on the blacktop. I didn't know whether I wanted Heather to be watching or not. If she was, she was, and if she wasn't, oh well. No harm, no foul. We drove away, and Domingo gave me another cigarette.

"Well?" Maya asked.

"Well, what?"

"How'd it go?"

"Nobody tried anything. Big waste of time."

"See any old friends?"

"A few."

"You going back tomorrow?"

"Yeah."

"Really talkative, aren't you?"

I looked at her, twirling a lock of her hair with one ringed

217

finger. Her expression was half suspicion, half concern. She knew something was up, and there was no use trying to hide it.

"Come here," I said. She sauntered over to the couch, climbing on top of me as I lay back. I brushed her long hair out of her face, kissed her, and toyed with the bronze kunukku ear weight that had stretched a two-inch hole in her lobe, Buddha-style.

"Seeing all those kids," I muttered. "I feel like a waste of life. Like I'm just some punk kid dealing drugs when I could be discovering something."

"Like what?"

"I dunno. But there are people out there making a difference in the world, and here I am chasing gangstas and getting shot at. If I tried to get a job tomorrow, who the hell would hire me? I've got no skills, I've got no talent, I don't know shit about shit." *And I'm about to cheat on you.*

"So what do you want to do?" She never gave advice. She always let me come to a solution myself.

"I don't know, but I know what I don't want to do anymore. I don't want to have to look over my shoulder all the time or have to watch my friend's back because someone wants to kill us."

"Okay, that's a start." Her face got serious. "Now, listen to me, Evan. Whether you want to sell dope for Domingo's dad, work in a button factory, or shovel elephant shit at the circus, you're my man. I love you, and I'm gonna go on loving you no matter what. So you decide where your place is in this world, and I'll be right there with you."

I felt like a piece of shit.

I *am* a piece of shit.

Because I'm going to cheat on her anyway.

She kissed me, tenderly at first, then deeply. Her tongue in my mouth became Heather's, the curly hair that got in our way was blonde, and the hand that snaked into my jeans and found me ready was the same one that at this moment was working feverishly at bald pink lips under a crimson cheerleader's skirt.

Mariana had decided at some point between making out with me under the wooden rollaway bleachers and going off to be a grown-up at college that I was her honorary little brother. Regardless, I looked at her with barely disguised lust in my eyes. She was short and dark and voluptuous, with the same heart-shaped face, big smile, and arrogant eyes as her brother, with long hair blacker than…I dunno, the night, I guess. Whatever. She was hot.

Maybe it was the fleeting taste I'd had of her that made her so desirable to me, and the fact that every other de Medieros would think of it was incest if we ever hooked up again.

She was down on one of her more and more frequent breaks from school, telling us all about her sorority and formals and events and freedoms, making me feel even more like a useless thug criminal. Maybe to her I was a loyal family member, but I felt more and more like a nothing while she was on her way to being a Somebody. If that makes any sense.

"You've got to promise me you'll never tell my brother this," she said.

"Cross my heart."

"Well, I was at this keg party in College Park, and I guess I'd had a little too much to drink, and a lot of us were in the hot tub down by where the pool was."

"Yeah…" This sounded interesting.

"Well, it was me, two other girls, and three guys, and we didn't have any bathing suits, so we were there in our underwear. And this one girl took her bra off."

"Right…"

"Well, she was rolling, right? And I couldn't help it, I kept staring at her breasts. And of course, one of the guys noticed and made a lesbian joke and the girl, she saw me staring, and she smiled. And she was hot, Evan. I would never say that a girl was good-looking, because, well, you know. But damn, she was fine, and she said, 'I want a kiss.' Well, of course, the three guys were falling all over themselves trying to kiss her, but she was looking at me. She goes, 'No, I want a kiss from a girl.'

"Well, the other girl, she got a little weirded out and the guys were like, whoa. And well, I kind of…I don't know how to say this."

"You kissed her."

"Yeah."

"Okay, so you kissed her."

"Well, not exactly."

"What, then?"

A pained look came over her face, and she put her head in her hands, letting out a groan. "Evan, I *kissed* her. I made out with her.

And I was groping all over her tits and sucking on her tongue and…and I liked it. I liked it a lot. I felt really sensual and free and happy, and she was so soft, nothing at all like a man. And I guess, something inside of me just clicked, like when you flip two magnets over and they snap together, and I was thinking all these strange thoughts like I wanted to drag her out of the hot tub and eat her pussy out right there in front of everybody."

She looked at me. I just stared back at her. Fuck, I didn't know what to say. Did she want me to high-five her? Give her daps? Comfort her? What? "So…"

"So?" she asked. "Does that make me a dyke, Evan? I can't be a dyke. I'm a girl."

I wasn't really following her logic. "So, you're worried that you're gay?"

"Evan, I've got to be gay, or else I never would've made out with her, you know? But I can't be gay. I'm…I'm fucking *Brazilian*."

"You're losing me."

"What am I going to do?" She looked miserable.

"Well, a lot of people think girls getting with girls isn't homosexuality because it's trendy, I guess. Like it doesn't really count. But it's no different from guys being, um, fags together. So, it's wrong. Now here's the part where I'm supposed to tell you that it's all okay as long as it feels good to you, but…"

"But that's a load of bullshit."

"Yeah, we'd have people running around raping each other all the time or, say, sleeping with their pet cat or whatever. I'd just say you were drunk and shouldn't worry about it."

"But I can't *not* worry about it. Now I'm all the time checking girls out and wondering if she'd go with me, and it's really fucking my head up. Plus, my roommate is a lesbian and she's all the time telling me that I should accept that I'm gay and—"

"Well, of course she's going to say that. She's fucking gay! She wants you on her team. She probably wants to get you greased up and nekkid in her pink clubhouse!"

"Yeah, I thought of that. But she's telling me about ancient Greece and this poet chick from the island of Lesbos named Sappho who started lesbianism and how superior she was, and now I'm just really confused."

I decided to spring this theory I'd come up with on her, and tried not to make it sound too rehearsed.

220

"Look, Mariana, this is how I see it. I think there are too many people on the planet, sandwiched in between a 10,000 degree core and the bitter cold of outer space, according to my girlfriend, the know-it-all. Only the surface can produce anything to feed us, and it can't sustain all of us now, as it is.

"The rate we use up our resources, and the rate we make advances in medical science to extend our life spans, we move faster and faster to eat our future out of house and home. Millions of people are starving now, but we're steadily multiplying and breeding more and more mouths to feed. So, God spread this disease that would kill you if you fucked around too much, hoping people would just stop breeding. But still, no one even cared, no matter how many people died, they just kept fucking and making babies.

"So, God took a bunch of people and made them want to suck each other's dicks and stuff, so that they didn't even *want* to reproduce any more. This is just a way to keep the population down. That's all. So there's no deep, hidden part of you that just wants to eat pussy, like your roommate says. It's not a *cool* thing to do, or a sophisticated thing, or whatever she calls it. You just saw a lot of population control up at college, people experimenting, and got a little drunk. If you want to make sure you still like guys, I just happen to have a penis and I'd be happy to—"

"Shut up."

"Hey, I'm just trying to help," I protested.

"I'm serious here. This is my life we're talking about. If I'm all of a sudden a rug-muncher, that would throw my entire world into upheaval. Do you have any idea what my dad would say? And Abuela, she'd have a heart attack! You promised you wouldn't say anything."

"What is there to say? That you got drunk at a party? Who hasn't? Especially at college, I mean, isn't that what college is for?"

"There's a little more to it than that."

"I think you'll live. Do you have any real problems you want help with?"

"You mean like, did I lose a bunch of drugs and money, and my car? No."

"Good, so put this little dyke thing into perspective."

"Thanks, Evan."

"Don't mention it. That's what I'm here for."

"So, how was your first day of school?"

My second day of school. This morning, Home Room was buzzing with how badly I'd whupped Corey Walken's ass. Kids who hadn't actually witnessed it made it out to be a lot more than it really was. To hear them say it, I took a bite out of his head and ate it. I have had worse reputations than what they were spreading, but fame and attention was the last thing I needed in this situation. People were looking, and talking, and that makes covert operations like this one a little tricky.

On our way to Algebra I saw him—how could I miss him? Both of his eyes were black and his face was swollen beneath the bandages. You'd think he would've stayed home, but from what I'd heard of his home life, his father probably made him come in, just to shame him. In the sea of bobbing heads, his miserable eyes found mine. Even from far away, I could see the hate burning in his swollen ferret head. The fucker.

Algebra passed. So did History and English, and I followed Domingo to Social Studies with my heart in my mouth. I felt a vague fear that I couldn't put my finger on, but it vanished the moment I stepped through the door and saw Heather watching for me. I broke away from D'ingo's side and went down her row toward her desk. She held out a note and I grabbed it, suddenly conscious of the .22 bulging under my leather jacket. I moved on, rounding the corner desk at the back of the room and went to Domingo's side.

I sat at the desk behind him and unfolded the origami complicated envelope she'd made out of her note. Her girlie handwriting was elegant, but the circles she made when she dotted her i's gave her away.

I could feel her eyes on me as I read, watching to see my reactions to her words.

"My dearest Evan," it started. Mmmm. "My favorite dreams of you are of the last time we kissed, on the last day you came to school three years ago. I was still a nobody, and you shocked all those people by kissing me out in the open. Deeply. Like I was somebody special.

"And then you walked out of my life forever. I always dreamed I'd see you again, but never once thought it would happen. After I blossomed last year, I would look sadly in the mirror, regretting that I could never share my body and what it had become with you. I wanted to reward you for the way you treated me when I was ugly by giving you something beautiful. Well, my long lost love, here I am. I want you to take me the way you did in the girls' bathroom so long ago, filling me so deeply and so hard, whispering my name. You took away all the hurt with your kisses and caresses, and you made me feel beautiful. I no longer feared coming to school, but looked forward to another precious moment I'd steal with you. I have always kept a special place in my heart, a place separate that no one else could ever touch. When you went away, you left a big Evan-shaped hole in me that no one could ever even hope to fill, and I want you to know that your place is still here if you want to come home to it."

There is no wonder on Earth as magnificent to a horny young man as the shameless baring of a woman's soul. I turned to look at her, saw her waiting apprehensively for my reaction. I could see a fear in her eyes as if she wished at the last minute she could take her words back. That fear of rejection. But I smiled and nodded slowly, mouthing the words to her that I knew she'd remember.

"Lunchtime? At our place."

And I saw relief and joy flood across her face. That old excitement of school romance came back to me, a feeling I thought was lost forever, buried underneath booty calls and one night stands. I re-read the note again and again, glancing up after each time to look at her and wait for our eyes to meet. Lunchtime was too far away.

The bell rang, startling me, and I rose with D'ingo, hurrying toward Heather for a few moments of stuttering conversation. She met us in the hall outside, amid the bustle of students chattering excitedly. We talked, about nothing I can remember, while Domingo waited with mild annoyance. We just stood lost in each other, the noise around us fading into one steady sound. I was so enchanted that I almost didn't him. Almost. It took a second too many to register in my brain, the black kid with the crocheted wool skullcap and the blue plaid flannel, cool-walking through the crowd in the corner of my eye. I glanced at him, then returned to my Heather's smile and worshipping eyes.

Domingo smiled, making a show of putting up with me. I can only remember what happened next in fragments. The sound of his heavy sigh. Heather rolling her eyes. The nagging image of the skullcap, the hard slices of his eyes in a brown face. I looked back at Heather, said something that made her laugh, while the wheels turned slowly in my head.

Then, suddenly, like two magnets flipping over and snapping together, the realization hit me with the panic of an ice-cold bucket of water in the face, and I wheeled about just in time to see the gun leveled at the back of Domingo's head.

The .22 was in my hand without me realizing I'd drawn it, my arm extending, putting the silenced barrel across my friend's shoulder, my finger tightening on the trigger, and a muffled *pop!* sending a bullet I could almost see into the suddenly wide left eye of the assassin.

Then the screaming.

All was chaos, kids scattering, the BL's gun going off and blowing a hole in the foam ceiling as the body fell to the blue-carpeted floor. Domingo's hand, clutching the collar of my jacket, trying to pull me away. But I'd turned back to Heather, and the horror on her face. Fear and revulsion, like I was some kind of monster. She took a step back from me.

"No, wait—" I took a step forward with the smoking gun in my hand.

And then she was gone.

Domingo stayed. I ran. Up the street toward One-Forty-Deuce where the strip mall was, and the pay phone. I dialed Esteban's cell phone, out of breath, and he picked up on the third ring.

"*Digame,*" he said.

"Este, it's Blanquito. They tried to get him today."

"Well?"

"I took care of it, but you need to pick me up."

"*Donde?*"

I told him where I'd be, at the head shop in the strip mall, and he hung up without wasting another word. I lit a cigarette and walked as casually as my racing heart would allow, replaying the scene in my head. Half a second later would have been too late. And Heather.

The look in her eyes.

Fuck! I kicked the side of a wall, again and again, then kept walking. The fact that I'd splattered a kid in front of many others was nothing compared to Heather seeing it. I'd had her. She was mine. And now I'd lost her because of this thug life bullshit. My eyes burned. My jaw clenched and my teeth ground.

224

Fuck! I could hear the distant wailing of sirens, and once again cursed the stupidity of my false name being Kevin Langdon.

I sat for a long time in front of Wonderland, the head shop, chain smoking and ignoring the potheads and freaks that came and went through the door, until Esteban came. He arrived in one of the nondescript, inconspicuous brown sedans that we used, and whistled to me to get my attention. He startled me, and when I got up and walked around to get in the passenger side I felt like the whole world was eyeing me suspiciously.

Esteban grinned at me as he started to drive, amused by how quiet I was. The rosary of teeth hung from the rearview mirror, and swayed with the turns. We got out onto 142nd and made our way to the restaurant.

"Did you kill him?"

"Yeah."

"Did you make sure?"

"He's dead, Esteban."

"*Bien*. I always knew you were a good kid."

I didn't answer. A good kid? Sure didn't feel like it today. I decided to tell Nestor this afternoon that I was out. I had no idea what I would do, how I would support myself, but whatever road I chose would be a step up. I would move off of the couch in the Ibis apartment and stay with Maya, and look for a job. Sure, Domingo would be pissed, and his old man would be furious and call me a gutless woman, but being a thug has got to be worse. It's got to be. Gutless women don't have to hide among spiders, rats and roaches under the floor of a crack house.

I felt it before I heard it, the vibration of bass rattling our car from somewhere nearby, the crap that some people call music. The thumps of a brain-dead beat, getting louder.

"Shit," Esteban muttered in annoyance. The whole car was shaking. We came to a red light and sat in the vibration. The car rolled up next to us and I turned to see four angry black faces, bobbing to the beat. In a station wagon. A hoopty station wagon. The driver's head glanced my way, drifted absently toward the cars going by in the intersection, then came sharply back. Our eyes locked. He knew me.

"Esteban!"

The gun appeared by the driver's head, and I had just time enough to jerk my head back before it fired. I pulled the .22 out of

225

the shoulder holster, squeezing off shots out the window as the wagon punched it, flying out into the intersection. We followed, but slowly. Esteban's foot was no longer on the brake pedal. A loud crash, then another, the gunship jumping one direction and the other as two cars plowed into it. I turned to look at Esteban as our sedan drifted into the road, at the red and brown chunks on the glass of his window, at the hole in the side of his head.

I jerked my door open and fell out of the car into the street. The gunship was on its side, mangled between two others. Stopped cars everywhere. People staring. A shape popped out of the window on the upside of the station wagon and bullets sprayed everywhere. People screamed as the BL strafed left and right in a panic, blowing out windshields and gunning down people who'd come to help.

I bolted for the sidewalk. Behind me, the shooter cleared a path and two others climbed out with him. One backward glance was all I needed. They pulled the dead driver out of a nearby car and hopped in. I ran. I could hear them coming after me. They must have known it was me who stopped their friend in the school, how, I didn't have time to imagine.

The car—a Lincoln—jumped the curb and screeched across the driveway of the oil change I ran to. I juked to the left, the silenced .22 still in my fist, useless against a car. An idea had leaped full-grown into my mind, and I raced away from the oil change, across the intersecting street. That gray Lincoln was on me like a fucking shark, bouncing over curbs and mowing down the short hedges that decorated them. If anything was going well for me today, it was this.

They chased me through parking lots and hedges all the way to the next corner. I led them around the square pillbox of a gas station building to a beige wall about ten feet high and leaped, catching the edge of the top and scrambling over. The car screeched to a halt as I dropped into the thick ficus hedge and searched for the shotgun I'd hidden there the other night. I found it almost immediately, nearby.

Seizing it, I racked the pump as a shadow fell across me from above. Wheeling around, I brought the barrel up and fired, blowing him off the wall.

Angry shouts from only two voices on the other side told me exactly where they were. I got a good foothold in the hedge and stood, bringing the twelve gauge around and racking the pump again. With one hand I reached out and grabbed a hold of a strong branch, then hauled myself up further. There they were! I aimed with the shotgun in my free hand and shot another one in the back as he turned to run. The third one got away from me.

Sirens again. Fuck!

I wiped the shotgun down with my shirt and dropped it back onto the leaf-carpeted ground. At least here there would be no prints. I clambered through the ficus to the face of it and leaped out, then ran for all I was worth.

I went in the side door of Pecado, the area reserved for takeout orders, zigzagging through the early lunch crowds, and went into the kitchen. The smiles in pretty brown faces faded when the waitresses saw my expression. I made my way through them to the back line where prep is done and the dishes are washed, and hurried to the office by dry storage.

"Pedro!"

Vizcaya's dark, unshaven face appeared. He was short and stocky, but there was obvious strength in him. He had a rounded widow's peak, a Roman nose that gave him an imperious look, and his dark eyes were eerily intelligent, like a baby's that never cried. He motioned me into the office where he handed me a cigarette, sensing my need.

"Tell me."

"Esteban's dead."

He didn't even bat an eyelash. His way when he saw bad news coming was to expect the very worst and work up from there. He nodded for me to continue. I told him everything from the moment I shot the BL to the present. He nodded with approval every time I told him I'd killed somebody.

"So, it's three to one, not counting the driver," he said.

"What?"

"We don't know if the driver is dead or not, so you can only put three notches on your belt. Do you still have the weapon Esteban gave you?"

"Here," I answered, pulling out the .22.

"Good. I'll get rid of it. Now, where were you today?"

"Right here, bussing tables. All day."

"That's right. We all saw you. You never left."

"What about Kevin Langdon?"

"Obviously some asshole trying to set you up. You'd never be

227

stupid enough to use a name that close to your own. Now, did you run into any kids that can positively identify you?"

"Of course. I used to go there."

"Did any of them see you shoot anyone? Or even see you with the gun?"

"Uh, yeah."

"Who?"

"This chick I used to mess around with."

Vizcaya stared at me for a long time.

"Is she going to be a problem?"

"What do you mean? No! Of course not!"

"What's her name?"

"Heather. Heather Roma. No, she won't say anything to the police. Never." I instantly regretted telling him. "No, she loves me. She worships the ground I walk on. She'd never say anything." Uh-oh. Lay it on thick and heavy.

"Would you stake your life on it?"

"Uh...sure."

He cocked his head, animal-like, to one side and raised an eyebrow at me. I shook my head and shrugged. Yeah, he didn't have to say, I know.

"Don't worry about her," he said.

"I'm not."

"Whatever. Go have yourself some nachos or somethin' while I call the big man."

I left the office and wandered out to the front, finding a seat in the smoking section. I waited, toying absently with the drinks menu. Eventually, Angelica came around with her perky smile and perkier tits to ask what she could get me.

"A lobotomy."

"Sorry, I can't serve you drinks. Pedro'll kill me."

"I know. Do you have any batidos lying around that you're looking to get rid of?"

"I'll rummage around and see what I can find."

"Gruchas macias."

She laughed. "De nada."

I didn't even watch her ass as she left.

Other restaurants usually keep ketchup and mustard, or maybe steak sauce, on all of the tables along with the salt and pepper shakers, but we have sour cream and yucateco.

The sour cream I'll get around to explaining some other time. The yucateco...*whew*, that's some rough shit. It looks so deceptively harmless in its little bottle, sitting there not bothering anybody, but god-*day*am it hurts. It's pale green, and looks like something dull and boring.

Now, I don't know when we started doing this, or why we would *continue* to do it after how much it hurt the first time. D'ingo and I play chicken, sort of, with the yook sauce. Both Maya and Shaitan hate it when we do this. They call us immature, they say we're embarrassing them, they tell us to act our age, and then remember that we're still in our teens, at which time they give each other that look. That look like they can't remember how they got hooked up with teenagers in the first place, and they wonder if they ought to excuse themselves from the table. Maybe run to the Ladies' Room for a conference.

What we do, Domingo and I, is we each put a small dab of yook on a fingertip, count down from three, and then wipe the stuff onto our tongues. Then, sit there. We try to hold still. We try to keep straight faces while sweat beads on our foreheads, our faces flame beet red and our heads catch fire, our eyes welling up with tears.

D'ingo always wins. I don't know how he can stand it that one whole second after it shriveled my tongue into a twig-thin cinder—he waits another entire One Mississippi second, just to make a point—but he says it's because he's Brazilian and I'm not. Oh.

Why I bring this up: because I'm sitting at my table out of the way, by the To Go section waiting on Angelica to bring me my Cuban milkshake. I'm just minding my own business, sitting there being all nervous and jittery, waiting, smoking a cigarette and feeling nothing from it, no relief, when I see the bottle of yook sitting in the corner of my eye.

I get this brilliant idea.

I'm going to practice.

Fuck, I'm such an idiot. But hey, nobody was looking, so I figured Why not? I hesitated. I don't know whether it was fear or common sense keeping me from reaching for that bottle, but the traitor inside me said it was fear, so this bullshit feeling of bravado came over me and I just had to do it. Just *had* to. Christ.

Well, I did it. And because there was nobody looking I didn't bother trying to keep a straight face. I squirmed and panted and let my knees piston under the table, and the tears rolled down my face as my guts collicked. It occurred to me that I hadn't bothered to time myself, so I tried to look at my watch; squinted at it, blinked, wiped my eyes and frowned at it, but I couldn't make out the hour and minute hands, much less the second. I heard a queer, high-pitched keening sound, like maybe the fire alarm had gone off, and it wasn't until Angelica's apron was beside me, her hand coming into view holding my glass, that I realized that noise was coming from me.

I was squealing like a little bitch, and yes, people were looking. Somehow, the searing pain was outshined by the shame, and I wanted to shrink away until I was so small I vanished. Angelica set the glass before me as I reached for the sour cream, and squatted down beside me.

"Lemme guess. Yucateco?" she asked.
I nodded, fumbling with the lid of the jar. She lowered her voice conspiratorially. "You know, one of the specials for lunch hour is fajitas with morphine. You look like you could use it."

Ha ha. Funny funny. Luckily, a car came to pick me up halfway through my batido and saved me. The driver was someone I'd never seen before, but that was not unusual. He drove me to one of our safehouses, where Nestor and Teresa de Medieros were overseeing the unloading of ten crates, each holding ten bags.

Four men were waiting to break down each five-kilo bag of uncut coke into eleven one-pound bags. From there, half of them would go to the dealers and rollers and the other half would go to the restaurant. Teresa had her hair up in a bun, strictly business. Her husband was constantly in motion, counting and inspecting, sharply changing direction like a shark in a tank until he noticed me.

"Evan," Nestor called, crooking his finger. I went to him and he put his arm around me.

"You're a good boy, Evan. My son is safe and I'm proud of you. In return, I will treat you to a new car of your choice, provided that car is a new Camaro."

My jaw dropped.

"I always suspected you might not have the heart for this business, but you've proven yourself worthy of the position I'm about to give you. You will take Esteban's apartment and begin training to replace him. You will never sleep on a couch again. Calibos will oversee your instruction. When it comes time for my son to take over where I leave off, I know this business will be in good hands. Your weekly salary will be one thousand dollars."

My eyes bulged. Now would not be good time to tell him I quit.

"The driver will take you to my house and you will gather your things, then he will take you to your new place. The car will be ready by five o'clock. Now close your mouth, Evan. You are not a fish."

A young black boy wandered into the house, dressed in clothes way too big and expensive for his age and size. A thick silver chain hung around his neck with "Moke" spelled out in ice at the end of it. He went to one of the couches and sat, digging wads of cash out of his pockets and setting them on the coffee table. A Glock followed. He counted all the bills and set them in denominational stacks.

"My own Grazi Mono," Nestor said proudly. "I have almost twenty children who are ready to kill and die for me. These blacks are easier to train than animals, and fiercely loyal. Maybe that's why they call each other dogs." He chuckled. "Moke there is the oldest. Good day at the office, Little Moke?"

"Like Ragu say," Moke answered. "S'all inna mothafuckin sauce."

"It would be easier for one of the children to go into Golgotha and kill those two who stole from me, but it's up to you to wipe the egg off your face. Tonight, without wasting any more time, you will bring me back the heads of Kendrick and Antwan."

"How old is that kid?" I asked.

"Who knows? Who cares? His mother was a crack whore. He had a hundred fathers. Life means nothing to a creature like that, so why should his birthday?"

Moke didn't react at all.

"Those detectives should be coming back to Maya's soon, asking questions. They have my fingerprints in a car with a dead man, and they suspect me of taking their police car the other night. There are two dead bodies where that car was found, and their forensics people will know that the missing shotgun fired those shots. What will I do?"

"Earn your pay and think of a solution yourself."

"Oh."

"You'd be surprised how simple these things are to handle.

231

You get all bogged down in worry, when all you have to do is think. Occam said that. The simplest solution is always the right one."

Moke looked up. "Word. Before you can roll the crap you gotta come off that six."

In my mind, I saw a thousand dollars a week, a new car, a pad of my own and before long, power and wealth like I wouldn't believe. Then I saw myself living with Maya, no car, no money, circling ads in the classifieds with a red pen. I made up my mind quickly, sold my soul to the devil and to Mammon, and knew immediately what to do.

The driver took me to Abbey Road apartments, which was nowhere near any place called Abbey Road. It wasn't bad for a one-bedroom, but the South American Catholic décor needed *immediate* improvement. Votive candles, a bigass Virgen de Guadalupe, wooden Jesuses, a couple of porcelain Marys, various saints, the whole nine yards. Its one redeeming feature was the elegant red felt pool table in the center of the living room, made of cherry wood and leather, with ball-and-claw feet and mirrors everywhere (I guess so you could see it from every angle). It was so much prettier than the Marlboro one that still sat in the de Medieros' house, the one D'ingo and I haven't used at all, lately. Aside from that, no TV. What he called his television was a torn out Playboy centerfold taped to the door of his microwave. Shitty stereo. Mirrors on the ceiling of the bedroom. I wondered if Maya would lend me some of her cool furniture. I went to the phone and called her.

"Gemini Sanitation Supplies," she said. "Can I interest you in a new septic facility?"

"No, dear. My shit goes straight to the moon."

"Evan?"

"Hi, baby. Star sixty-nine me and tell me what my new phone number is."

"What?"

Calibos lived in an apartment walking distance away. He supplied me with an AK-47 and five spare magazines, "since kids like you tend to keep that trigger warm." He told me he was driving me into Golgotha tonight.

"Don't want the same thing that happened to your last car to happen to your nice, new one, so we'll take my piece of shit." He smiled. God, he was ugly.

He showed me strategies for this kind of thing, stuff he learned while fighting with the guerillas in Columbia that he thought would be fun in the projects. Real stick n' move shit. I couldn't wait. We made our plans, and before too long, my beautiful brand new champagne-colored convertible Camaro was parked outside my new apartment, with all the papers fixed. The tag read "BGBDWLF".

Against Calibos's wishes, I burned herbs and incense that Shaitan gave me to ward off evil and make sure our spirit guardians were bright-eyed and bushy-tailed. There was no way of knowing if it would work, but it damned sure couldn't hurt. I wasn't about to put on a war paint death mask, but I figured I had all of the other bases covered.

When night fell, we drove out to Golgotha in Calibos's pickup truck. With him at the wheel and me in a hat, we looked like a couple of melon pickers on our way home from the fields. Paco and Cheech. The place was so depressing in the early evening, and terrifying in the wee hours, I wasn't comfortable there even with the AK.

We parked across the street from the entrance to The Hill, looked to see that no one was watching, and slipped out with the weapons semi-concealed in our jackets. It was a warm night, on its way to being muggy. We kept to the shadows and crept silently into The Hill. Occasionally, we had to skirt around moss-covered pools of sulphurous water that had leaked from somewhere and left rust stains on the buildings, and the stench of rotten eggs was nauseating. No, the world wouldn't miss the people who lived here.

We came upon a boy with one arm sitting sadly on a short wall jutting out from the tenements, waited for just the right moment, and grabbed him. Calibos's big meaty brown hand covered half of his face as we dragged him, kicking and thrashing wildly, into the darkness. We put him on the ground and I kneeled on his chest, pinning him. The business end of Calibos's AK was an inch from the boy's right eye.

"Hey, niglet," I hissed. "Remember me?"

His eyes bulged with fear.

"Betcha miss your arm, dontcha? You wanna try dialing a phone number with your toes when I blow off the other one? Well, that's exactly what's going to happen if you fuck with me now. Are your dogs in Antwan's apartment?"

He hesitated, then shook his head.

"I don't believe you. Here go your fingers."

He squealed from under Calibos's hand.

"What? I can't hear you. Speak up."

His muffled cries got louder and more insistent.

"Yes or no?"

He nodded.

"How many?"

Grunts, six of them.

"Good, and in any other apartment? Neighbors?"

Hesitation again, then a nod.

"What number? Use your fingers to tell me."

He did, and I smiled. "You're lucky I'm a nice guy—" A swift motion and a loud snap like a tree branch breaking startled me. I just gaped at the poor kid, then at Calibos's cold, inscrutable face. Just like that. I couldn't believe he'd broken the kid's neck, just like that. Oh fuck. I'm sorry, kid. Oh fuck, I'm sorry.

Calibos rose and motioned for me to follow, and I went, like a man in a dream. He explained to me swiftly that he would stand outside the door of the second apartment and kill everyone who came out when I started shooting up the first one. I ran softly to Antwan's, crept to the door, and listened to the persistent boom of rap and the loud voices within. Glancing up at Calibos across the way, I saw him nod.

With a short burst, I blew the knob and lock off the door and kicked it open, startling the fuck out of five guys in the living room. The lights were dim, but the apartment jumped into brightness as I strafed into them. Their bodies jerked as bullets tore them apart, splattering their guts and splinters of bone everywhere.

I ran as I fired, moving to the bedroom and kicking that door open as well. Antwan was on the bed, naked, with a fat black chick. I sprayed them both down, emptying the rest of the clip. Calibos was right. It did feel good to fire one of these.

Just then, the other bedroom door opened and Kendrick came out with two pistols blazing. In the flashing instant before I hit the floor, I saw he was in his boxer shorts and there were several others coming out behind him. All men. His shots were wild, fired in a blind panic. I rolled sideways further into Antwan's room, snapping the empty clip out and fishing a new one out of my jacket pocket. Bullets tore plaster dust out of the walls above me as I slammed the magazine home and racked the slide. I held up the machine gun and squeezed the trigger until it stopped kicking, rolled into the corner of the room, changed clips again.

I heard the hollow clicks of Kendrick's hammers dropping on empty chambers, and shouts of horrified men seeing their dead. I rose and hurried to the door, not giving them a chance to reload. They were all out in the open. There was no way I could miss. Flames spat from the barrel of my AK, the hard staccato bangs deafening over the music thumping from the stereo. The dark unholy joy of killing with only the touch of a finger intoxicated me, and I laughed as I splattered four more men.

Women screamed from the darkness of the back bedroom, and I ran in to shoot them, too. The acrid smell of gun smoke and the stench of blood and death made me dizzy, reeling, but somehow giddy. I felt like a god.

I left quickly, hearing distant gunfire. Once outside, I could see Calibos firing into an open doorway. Oh shit! I forgot to torch the place! I ran back in, yanked the old gas stove out of the wall, and hurried to the bathroom. There were a few aerosol cans of hairspray on the sink, like I knew there would be. I grabbed them all and took them to the microwave.

One minute on high. Beep beep beep! That oughta do it.
I left again, looking carefully to avoid getting gore on my shoes as I crossed the living room. Outside, I swapped magazines again, just in case. Standing on the stairs over-looking the parking lot, I blew out a dozen car windshields, just for the hell of it, and ran.

Calibos caught up with me in the darkness, and with a deafening roar, Kendrick and Antwan's place exploded behind us. I laughed all the way home, hopped in the Camaro, drove it to Maya's, and fucked the shit out of her on the living room floor.

Maya answered the door this morning with a sheet wrapped around her.

"Now's not really a good time, detectives."

"Why, you working?" Bancroft asked. "Oh, that's right. You said you were a telemarketer."

"Very funny. Get lost."

"We're here to talk to your boyfriend."

"Yeah, well, we're in the middle of something right now."

"A pressing matter?" d'Argent leered.

235

She slammed the door in their faces. They banged on it angrily, but it was locked firmly, and she was already back in bed, getting it done.

Maya has a wooden box, long, shallow, and rectangular, with iron hasps and a cute little lock. It's lined on the inside with red velvet, and filled with herbs and powders. Rhinoceros horn. Damiana leaf. Yohimbe. Ginseng. Pumpkin seed. Cocoa leaves. Saw Palmetto. Oyster extract. A dozen others. Chew the leaves, mix the powders in with a drink, and there's only one thing on your mind.

We used drugs to alter our states of mind and take sex to other dimensions, and often just to sharpen our conversation. She told me about existentialism, astral projection, and with the right combinations of drugs and herbs, our lovemaking could produce visions or even out-of-body experiences. We'd get high, then each suck down two chargers of nitrous oxide, then kiss. With our eyes shut and our tongues writhing together, we'd set every atom of our flesh tingling and every unit of whatever makes up our souls on fire. We would just sit and make out for hours.

We'd had sex for nine hours before Mariana knocked on the door. Since we were like family, she came in not minding that I was in my boxers and Maya wore only her lacy bra and panties. She laughed and slapped the erection that poked out of my shorts.

"Down, boy! You always were a snappy dresser."

"Want a drink?" Maya asked.

"Of course."

I went to the kitchen and fixed her a glass of absinthe. Glancing into the living room, I saw Mariana sitting on the couch next to Maya, and watching my girlfriend's breasts out of the corner of her eye. With my hormones still raging violently, I grinned at the evil thought that came to me. I went to the wooden treasure box and selected a powder. Emptying the packet into the green liquor, I stirred it with my finger, then sucked it clean, walking out and handing it to her.

"Merci," she said sweetly. I winked at Maya.

"I've come to congratulate you, Evan. My mom and dad haven't shut up about how proud they are. Evan this and Evan that. You've been like my brother for years, and now it's official. Maya, did he tell you?"

"Yeah, it's great. One minute he's worrying about where he's going, and the next, he's in the big time."

"What do you mean, 'where he's going'?" she asked, giving me a questioning look as she drank.

"Ah, nothing," I answered. "Midlife crisis."

"Yeah, I know what you mean. I recently had one of those, myself." She darted a glance at Maya's tits. I did, too, wanting them out again. I readjusted myself, tucking my insistent member back where it belonged. We talked about my exciting future, and Mariana seemed to grow increasingly aware of how little we were wearing. I lit some incense, a fragrance called Seduction, and the smell of the curling thread of smoke made my eyes glaze over.

"Whoo! That's a stinger," Mariana said after draining the last of her absinthe. "Mind if I have another?"

"Not at all," my girlfriend answered. I took the empty glass into the kitchen and refilled it, dropping in another powder, just to be mean. Already, Mariana was starting to squirm on the couch next to Maya. I chuckled to myself, an evil, devilish sound.

Mariana took a sip, then a gulp, then downed the rest of it in one go. Her eyes had taken on the same glazed look, and when they went to Maya's full, round breasts, they lingered a little longer. My girlfriend's eyes met mine, and I gestured subtly toward Mariana with a tilt of my head. She questioned me with a look, and I gestured again, as if saying 'go on, get it'.

Silence. The distant beeping of a truck backing up somewhere. Then, the sharp noise of an ice cube cracking in Mariana's glass, clinking against the others and settling.
"Um, where were we?" she asked.

Maya reached behind her back and undid the clasp of her bra; slid the lace off, and her perfect breasts were there in the open when Mariana's eyes came back to them.
Her lips parted. She stared, transfixed. With the delicate fingers of one hand, Maya gently stroked her chest and throat. "Is it hot in here?" she asked.

Mariana looked confused, but the drink and the drug were quick. Maya glanced up at me again, and this time I gestured only with my eyes. She looked into Mariana's eyes, at the mixture of nervousness, fear, and desire, and smiled reassuringly. She gently took a soft brown hand into both of her own, and laid it on her breast. Mariana swallowed hard as she hesitantly caressed the smooth swell of flesh and hard, erect nipple. Maya put her hand on Mariana's knee, tracing light circles with her fingers.

237

"Are you okay?"

She nodded slowly, staring at the pink nipple. Maya's other hand touched the heart-shaped face, guided it to her own. Their full lips touched with the sweetest sound, then again, and Maya's pink tongue peeked out to wet Mariana's smile. The brown hand on her breast tightened its grip. I could hear the breath sigh out from between Mariana's quivering lips, then they were pressed hard against Maya's. I strained my eyes, hoping to see two pink tongues sliding over one another, rewarded with an occasional glimpse. I knew this was a delicate process, and interrupting it might fuck up the mood and cause weirdness between Mariana and the two of us. I sat on the other couch and fired up a reefer, enjoying the show.

Maya lay back on the couch, pulling Mariana on top of her so she could move at her own pace. At first, they were content just to make out, but eventually Mariana's curious hands found their way south, softly gliding over the lace there.

Let's see, now, I thought. Once and for all, let's settle this. A tiny voice in my head, presumably my conscience, said this little experiment was cruel and *not* the kind of thing a friend would do. I told that voice to shut the fuck up. Something had definitely changed in me over the past few days, and everything except that little voice liked it. A lot.

The second dose of powder was taking hold, and Mariana practically tore her own shirt off. God her breasts had grown. I never really realized how much until I saw them fall out. She touched them to Maya's own, licking Maya's lips, trembling with passion. Maya took one of Mariana's hands and guided it between her legs, pressing it firmly to the mound beneath the lace.

"Are you okay?" she asked again.

"Yes," Mariana whispered back. "I want you. I want you so bad."

"Do you want Evan to join us?"

"No...not yet."

"Take your time, baby. This is for you, so take your time."

"Okay." Still trembling. Hand tentatively massaging the lace. Deep shuddering breaths. I watched, smoking my joint and grinding my teeth.

Two brown fingers hooked the lace and slid underneath it, exploring the warm lips and toying with them. I shifted in my seat, suddenly unable to get comfortable. I ached to watch and not join in. The fingers came out as Mariana was sucking on one hard nipple, and she brought them to her lips, still deciding how far she was willing to go.

I already knew Maya tasted wonderful, and she'd just washed before Mariana came, so the look on the curious girl's face was no surprise to me. Maya helped her slide the panties down her thighs, brought up her knees, and left her feet in the air after the lace came off. Mariana tossed the panties to me, put Maya's feet over her shoulders, and kissed a slow path to the raw and glistening lips. Maya caressed Mariana's hair as it approached.

Then, just as she was getting to her destination, she stopped and stared at what awaited in front of her. She glanced up into Maya's eyes, then back, swallowed, and made up her mind.

She bent her head and kissed the shaven labia, sighed as she smelled the sweet, intoxicating fragrance, and brushed her lips against them again, her tongue slipping out to taste them. Maya stirred and rolled her head to look at me with half-closed eyes, then shut them and moaned as Mariana's tongue found her erect clitoris. They stopped abruptly.

"I don't know how to do it," I heard Mariana whisper.

"It's okay," Maya said softly. "Whatever you do will be wonderful." Her fingers parted the black hair and moved it away, out of Mariana's face. "You're so beautiful, Mari."

Mariana made that sound all girls make when you touch their hearts just right, kind of a mewling "Ohhh," and she climbed up Maya's body to kiss her. Deeply. Maybe it was the weed, but the sights and sounds of two beautiful women in each other's arms made me feel blessed to see it. I seriously doubt it could ever be the same if the positions were reversed, but soft, feminine hands on soft, round breasts must be a sight God reserves for only a special few.

Maya reached for the front of Mariana's jeans, freed the button, and slid the zipper down. The Brazilian arched her back and wriggled her shapely hips, helping Maya push the denim over the soft swell of her ass as they kissed. The hands left her jeans where they were, slid up the smooth, round flesh and pulled her waist in, the pink-painted nails slipping under the thong she wore and caressing her.

Maybe five minutes or an eternity later, Mariana cried out, and my girlfriend held on as the Brazilian shook all over and finally went limp. I smiled at Maya, who smiled back, and Mariana just kissed her thighs weakly, whispering.

"Thank you. Oh God, thank you. Thank you."

Maya put her arms around Mariana's waist and hugged her upside down, face shining with her juices, and caught her breath. A peaceful moment passed, and eventually Mariana raised her voice. "Um...Maya?"

"Yes, baby?"

"Would...would it be okay...if..."

"It's okay, Mari. Whatever you want."

"Can I...would you mind if Evan fucked me?"

Both of their eyes rolled toward me.

"Sure, honey," Maya said. "But me first."

The sudden pounding on the door startled us.

"Police! Open the fucking door!"

We scrambled for our clothes, but with a thundering crash the door flew open, the frame splintering where the lock tore through the wood, and the apartment was alive with shouting men in green. I couldn't count how many there were, crowding in around us with shotguns and telling us either to get on the floor or stand where we were.

One of them knocked me down and bent my arms up around my back, cuffing me. I kept my mouth shut, but there were flames inside my head, a blind rage building like a storm about to break. Both the girls had tried to cover themselves, but were jerked roughly around and thrown back on the couch.

Naked except for my boxers, they dragged me out of the apartment, where detectives Bancroft and d'Argent stood smiling. They read my charges with the neighbors watching.

"Evan Christopher Lanthorne, you are under arrest for nineteen counts of first degree murder, grand theft of a police vehicle, drug trafficking, arson, attempt to—I stopped listening. The words and shouts all ran together in one incomprehensible din until d'Argent's voice cut through.

"Can't wait to tell Neil Macaulay what a dyke whore his little daughter is."

"I'll fucking kill you!" I screamed. Then the world went black.

I awoke in the backseat of a squad car, my head throbbing, the voices of laughing policemen somewhere outside. I struggled to sit up, already seeing the cold, smelly bullpen, crowded with other men making jokes about me in my boxers as we sit and endure the long post-arrest ceremony of booking.

"Yeah, they had some titties, all right. D'you see all those toys in there? I wonder how many they managed to fit up this boy's ass at one time."

"Shit, if he ever gets out, they'll be having to shove the whole coffee table up his ass, the way they'll rag him out in prison!"

More laughing. Yeah, that was pretty clever, asshole.

By now, the girls would have called Nestor. If they granted me a bond, maybe I could post bail before tomorrow. Oh, fuck! What if he doesn't bond me out? What if he refuses to get involved? Oh shit! What if he has me killed instead? Oh my God, that's only if I'm lucky. It's the fucking chair. Or ten years hard time, followed by the chair. Oh God. Oh shit. Oh, fuck! Fuck! Lord, I'm sorry. God, I fucked up. Please get me out of this. I swear, I'll never do anything bad again. I'll go straight, I'll get a job, I'll go to church, I'll give to the poor, just please, Lord, please get me out of this. I'm just a stupid kid, I didn't know what I was doing. God, please.

My bones felt limp as wet noodles.

I sat there for twenty minutes, praying, trying to ignore what the cops were saying. Eventually, a few of the cops said their good-byes and drove off, and the rest of us drove in a parade to the jailhouse. The hoosegow. The stony lonesome. I stared out the window at all the buildings I'd never see again, at all the cars going by, people who'd never go to jail because they'd somehow done it right.

Oh God, please, give me another chance.

I noticed absently that all the cars around us were black SUVs. *Wait a second.*

The windows in the passenger sides and back seats of the gauntlet trucks rolled down simultaneously and I ducked down to the floorboards. The sharp chatter of machine gun fire, and the car bucked and swerved sideways, the driver screaming, vertigo, a wave of dizziness, and the crash at the end that slammed me against the metal partition. I rose, shaken, and looked out the rear window at the bullet-riddled squad cards rolling along on slow collision courses. All of the SUVs vanished down side streets except one, which pulled alongside me. Calibos jumped out and backhanded the butt of his gun through the window of the cruiser, hauled me out, and I was free as suddenly as I'd been taken.

He hurried me into the truck, slammed the door, and we sped off to take a series of turns and disappear. "Looks like dey caw'choo wichoo pants down," Calibos said, grinning. I was still in shock.

"How...?"

"Sheet, kid. We cooden letchoo go to jail, and you sure as hell weren gonna get a bond. Not wichoo charges."

"But...?"

"Have a ceegarette."

"Uh...thanks."

We got to my apartment, where I showered and dressed. As much as I wanted to call the girls and let them know I was okay, Calibos had instructed me not to. Just in case, because you never know when the phone may be tapped. Mariana had been smart enough to call her dad on her cell phone instead of Maya's home line. I couldn't for the life of me remember what her cell number was, though.

So, I looked around at my new place and made some redecorating decisions. Getting a big garbage bag from under the sink, I went around and gathered all the saints, crucifixes, and God crap, dumping them in the bag. The walls were bare except for the mirrors, and I drove out to the mall for something more suitable. With the top down and the wind in my hair, I couldn't help but smile.

I sat with Teresa de Medieros at the dining room table of the house in Ibis. Next to us, working silently, Abuela sat cleaning three handguns, stoned on hash oil and happily engrossed in her task. The weapons lay on a stained towel, in many pieces, each greased and polished with great care. It was odd to see her smile. She only ever did it when she was working on something, and it was a strange little Zen-like smile that split her crinkled, brown, parchment skin. Her knuckles cracked often of their own accord.

Privately, Teresa had once joked to me that her mother was so old, the *u* in her name was written as a *v*. I had no idea what that meant, but I laughed anyway. I was fond of the old hag. She spoke rarely, but when she did, she revealed herself to me as an indisputably mature and sensible woman. But, because I am a teenager, and have been for almost six years, mature and sensible advice (more often than not) proved useless to me.

Teresa, however, was a proud, feisty spitfire who bowed to no authority but her husband, and held the world outside of his organization in contempt. She drove too fast, smoked too much wherever she pleased, and was ready to step toe to toe with anyone at any time. Damn, she was cool. And she had class. While many women in America today are oblivious of taste and decorum, she could've written a book on them.

To see her in peach moiré and tulle, diamonds flashing at her throat, and jealous anger emanating from her like smoke off of ice—as I had two Christmases ago when some young chippie flirted too closely with Nestor was a primally arousing sight. Naked aggression, stripping off a mask of civility, has always been a romantic sight to me. When hundreds of years of etiquette and sophistication just vanish to expose the depths a woman can sink to, to keep her mate, or protect her offspring; man, I just get a stiffy right then and there.

Having seen that glimpse of her inner savage, I found her captivating, and respected every word she spoke to me as we sat at the table and smoked too much.

"What you are, *moço*, at this time, is what we call a coal. A cheap, easily replaceable lump of black coal, useful only as fuel to burn *our* way to somewhere better. All our soldiers start out as coals."

"Uh-huh..." I didn't know where she was going with this, but enjoyed the insult in a strange, masochistic way.

"Since you show promise, finally, my husband has seen fit to train you. You will be forced to endure all kinds of pain, pressure, humiliation, and abuse. Why?"

"Um, to make me tough?"

"To make you tough. Is that the best you can do? What happens to coal when it's put through the kind of ordeal you have seen our soldiers face? What does it become?"

"It becomes a diamond."

"It becomes a diamond. The hardest substance on Earth."

"And the only thing that can cut a diamond..."

"Is another diamond," she was nodding slowly, pleased. "Now you know why a diamond is a girl's best friend. Because she knows it will always stand beside her. It will be with her all her life, never breaking, never fading in its beauty. Only the stupid women of the world, *mancebas*, think this means a rock instead of a real man. A real woman knows that men who can only give rocks instead of protection are not real men.

"When we are done with you, you will be a real man. A diamond. *Desverde.*" (I looked that last word up later. It means "no longer green." What, like a plant or something?)

"*Obrigado, Mamãe,*" I said, showing her my eagerness. She smiled.

"*Não ha de que.*"

I saw Abuela grin out of the corner of my eye.

"*Preparas tua endecha, moço!*" she cackled. I cast Teresa a questioning glance, and she shook her head.

"Prove her wrong," she said, not bothering to translate.

I had long ago mastered the use of glass ropes and nail bats, and Pedro had taught me how to make those childish weapons useless against my bare hands. I thought this made me hot shit, but my first day of training showed me how wrong I was.

The Spaniard had named his crew of mercenaries *Salon des Refusés*, French for "Art of the Refused." They may have not been good enough by the Legion's standards, but the self-deprecating phrase was way too modest. They were made of granite, steel, and whalebone, and making my softness hard was going to be blisters and pain, exhaustion and humiliation.

I'd rather not go into it. Long story, none of it funny.

But my aim improved in no time. My reaction time was cut in half, my hand/eye coordination sharpened until every kind of weapon I practiced with became an extension of my will, as light and comfortable as a dream gun.

They say some flowers only grow in the dark. I used to think it was a bunch of poetic bullshit, but now I knew better. What was in me now, this strange feeling, was me being pruned and topped out until I blossomed.

Now, I couldn't wait for the sharks to come.

This is as good a time as any to relate this crucial but apparently little-known bit of history. See, my Dad came here to sunny Florida in 1977 from Newburgh, New York. That statement alone ought to be full of such sinister foreboding that entire volumes could be spoken in it. I don't buy it, to be honest. I mean, if this really happened, why hadn't it been mentioned in any history class when I used to go to school? Why wasn't it in any documentaries on TV? I mean, if black people were *that* bad, there wouldn't be so much pro-black stuff in school....right?

I remember asking my History teacher, Mrs. McNally, about it the morning after my Dad told me over dinner, while everybody else had their books open and were studiously writing love notes and throwing shit at each other. Her eyes went wide and she hunched her shoulders, pulling her head in like a turtle.

"Shhhh!" she hissed between clenched teeth.

"What?"

"Why aren't you reading the chapter like everyone else?"

I almost laughed, but held it in, seeing how genuinely afraid she was. Christ. What're we, in a spy movie or something? Was this some kind of dangerous can of worms I wasn't allowed to open up?

"Go sit down," she ordered. "And I don't want to hear a *peep* outta you until the end of class."

But I didn't move. It was a defiance thing. Hey, I was fourteen, whaddaya want from me?

After a long moment, the stiffness went out of her shoulders and she sighed. "Come see me after class," she said quietly.

I did, but all she'd tell me was (and she even watched the stragglers carefully before speaking, as if they might over-hear—Jesus...such drama) that I could find the archives for Newburgh's *Evening Post* on the Internet, and that would tell me everything. Of course, I didn't do that because it sounded suspiciously like homework, so all I have to go on is the story I got from my Dad and grandparents. Since I wasn't paying that much attention at first, I don't know where exactly in Georgia in 1970 they saw this billboard when they were coming back up from vacation. They said it said "Go To Newburgh, New York, And Get On Welfare."

"Oh, come on!" I'd said, and they glared at me.

"Spare the rod, Dennis," Grandpa said to my Dad, like he was reminding him of something, and I saw the fossil of some long-ago but unforgotten argument. I never did find out what that meant.

Dad took over the story. "Our hometown, Newburgh, had been voted an All-American City," he said, and gave me a look that was his facial way of saying 'Get it?'

But I didn't. Gramma muttered something.

"What?" Mom asked as she reached for the pork chops.

"I said he doesn't appreciate what that means, what a great city we had, what it could've become if *they* hadn't come in and f—" here she cast a glance at me, sitting there at the dinner table with my innocent virgin ears. "If they hadn't loused everything up."

"Who's they?" I asked.

"The people who followed the billboard's advice," Dad said, taking the reins again. "See, Newburgh a place that everybody called Whitelandia back in those days. One of those safe places where you could go for a walk after dark, go down to the ice cream parlor with your sweetheart or—"

"Sneak out in the middle of the night," Grandpa interrupted, and Dad shot him a fierce look. "Go drink beers with your buddies down at the baseball field and puke in your mother's azaleas out on the front lawn."

"Wow! You did that, Dad?"

"Never," he said coldly, while Grandpa flashed me a grin, all teeth.

"It was a safe place to live," Mom said, smoothing over that little whatever-it-was. "Like Golgotha used to be, back when it was Coquina's west side, still. Are you going to eat those green beans tonight or do you want them for breakfast?"

"They're nasty," I said.

"That's because they're good for you."

"I don't like them."

"Christ, kid, eat the damn things!" Grandpa snapped.

"Now, now, Dad..." my Dad said.

"Spare the rod, Dennis. Spare the rod."

"Yeah, so, anyway, Newburgh was a really safe place, at least until I got to high school. I was going to Newburgh Free Academy on Fullerton Avenue when it happened. This was in '77, and my Freshman year was almost over.

What happened was there were these two Seniors, Milton Midogna and Joe San Filippo, both of them pot heads, and I don't know whether on this particular day they were buying or selling or what, but they were doing some kind of drug deal with these black dudes when they got into an argument. Now, I saw it. I was there. I didn't hear what it was about or who cheated who, or whatever, but I saw them start fighting.

"Now, keep in mind, this was in 1977, years after we'd seen that billboard in Georgia. My school was not Whitelandia High anymore. Seven years' worth of oppressed and resentful Southern blacks had immigrated into Newburgh to get money for sitting around doing nothing.

"These black kids overwhelming the white population were not the children of church-going, God-fearing people. They were *not* honor roll students. They were lazy, thieving, lying, drug-using hooligans, much like who you're going to school with right now, only they didn't have quite as much affirmative action bullshit to shout as their battle cry. Every one of them was just waiting for his chance to *get Whitey.*"

"Honey, your language," Mom said quietly.

"Huh? Right, sorry. So, anyway, all these other kids see a fight break out between whites and blacks, and you know how blacks are. Instantly they assume that it's over race and they want to join in and beat their oppressors down. It escalates right in front of my eyes to a full-blown race riot, all blacks attacking all whites. The police come, they try to restore order. I've got a bloody nose and my eyes are all puffy, and I didn't even *do* anything. I was just standing there when I get tackled from behind—"

"Take a deep breath, Dennis," Gramma said.

Dad's teeth were bared and he was holding his fork pointed at me, frozen in mid-gesture. He looked sideways at her and narrowed his eyes. She dipped a morsel of pork in her applesauce and put it in her mouth, started chewing in a very deliberate way that somehow pissed my Dad off.

He dropped his fork into his plate and it clattered loudly, ringing like a handful of change thrown down on the floor. He snatched up his glass of water and drank, his chin showing through it all distorted. The whole exchange had me lost but I didn't have time to wonder, because Grandpa picked up where Dad had left off.

"So your Dad gets escorted by the police, along with all the other white kids, onto the buses and back to New Windsor and Newburgh—that's the *town* of Newburgh, that lies just outside the *city* of Newburgh. I arrive there at about this time, because I've heard about it all the way down to where I work, and I drop everything to go get my boy, just like almost everyone else did. Because all these people are hurrying to the school to rescue their kids, the streets are a mess and I'm stuck bumper-to-bumper with the Joneses, so to speak, which is how I came to be there when the SWAT team stood armed at the front of the school, and from up the street came this tide of angry blacks. They came outta the woodwork, throwing rocks and bottles at the police, ganging up to flip the squad cars over—"

"You're kidding me!"

"I shit you not, sonny boy," Grandpa said gravely, and nobody bothered to admonish him. "Thank God your daddy was safe by that—"

"Time out," my Dad said quietly. We all looked at him. "It didn't happen quite like that."

We waited. He seemed like he had to get something off his chest, and it took him a moment to get his words ready. He took a deep breath.

"I was in the lobby there with all of those other kids, and we were packed in like sardines. It was just Milton against three or four blacks at first, and he was a brawler, so he was doing all right, until another black came at him from behind, and that's when Joe—who wasn't as tall, but just as bad—came flying past me like a bolt of lightning. Joe wore this big silver ring, and when he plowed his fist into that dude's head I saw his face pop like a zit...Then all hell broke and I got nailed from behind. The office was right there, so the Dean and all the faculty came swarming out—"

"Yeah," Grandpa said. "Like I said, the police got c—"

"No, it didn't happen quite like that."

We all stared at my Dad, his parents gaping at him in surprise, and he looked like he was ready to come clean about something he'd lied about for thirty-something years. The tension had suddenly become so thick that nobody saw me slip my green beans off of my plate and stuff them under my seat cushion.

Dad's head was bowed a little, and when his eyes came up to meet my grandfather's without his face raising with them, his voice was cold and hard.

"See, when it got broken up, we all went our separate ways. I went out to the front lawn with a lot of the other whites where we talked shit for a little while, went to open the trunks of our cars and get out our weapons."

"Weapons!" Grandpa exclaimed. "*What* weapons?"

"Oh, come on, Dad. We all had bats, switchblades, chains...but the black kids had guns."

"Dennis!" Gramma gasped.

"Well, I didn't have anything, not because I didn't want any-thing, but because I had nowhere to keep it. But when Nancy Johnson came out—you remember Nancy? She was a Senior? I wrote her name all over my folders? Right after we found out a whole bunch of jigs had jumped a kid on his way back from Toby's, beat the shit out of him with garbage cans for no reason...right after we heard about that, here comes Nancy, white as a sheet. She tells me—me! She didn't even know I existed! But I'm the one she tells this to."

I glanced at Mom, and she did not look happy to hear her husband talking like this.

"She asks me if I'd ever had the hair stand up on the back of my neck, and know, just *know*, to jump out of the way. I said yeah, even though I hadn't, and she nodded, kept talking, telling me she was at her locker when all of a sudden she felt it, and she spun around in the nick of time, just narrowly missing getting run through by a black girl with a knife. Nancy was trembling all over, then the dam burst and she fell into my arms, sobbing like a baby."

I stole another look at Mom. She had her lips pursed and was winding her napkin around her finger, tighter and tighter.

"I held her until her boyfriend, Billy Antonelli, came and pushed me away, taking over. But my shoulder was already soaked. You know how it is. I had to do something."

My Grandparents stiffened, bracing themselves. Mom's twisted rope of a napkin ripped.

"I went up to Kevin Kyle, who had the trunk of his car open, and I just reached in and seized the handle of a wooden Louisville Slugger. A short one, like you get for a kid who's in Little League. There were fights breaking out again in classrooms, in the halls, everywhere. People had been drinking beers, smoking a little reefer...I'd had a beer or two," he admitted. "And I went back inside before Kevin could stop me. The place was chaos. People were fighting here and there, the hallway lights were shattered, classroom windows got busted...I went into the closest girls' room.

"I don't know if she was the one who had tried to cut Nancy. But she had a knife. She was smoking a joint with four other girls when I walked in. They all jumped when they saw me. She pulled out the knife..."

We were all staring at him now, mouths open.

"And you know what I did?" he asked. "Dad?" He looked at me, then. "Evan? You know what your big brave father did?" His voice was dark and bitter, but his eyes were sad. "People will tell you they're just regular Joes, but nobody ever really is. Regular Joes're

249

what make up lynch mobs. Ordinary people are the ones who riot, who trample each other in crowded theaters."

"What'd you do, Dad?" I asked, a little too quickly.

He looked down at his plate. "Nothing."

I stared, feeling something drop out from under me.

"Didn't do anything," he said. "Dropped the bat and ran." Gramma and Grandpa breathed a sigh of relief, but I didn't.

"I ran back outside where they were putting all the white kids on buses, the cops and the faculty were. Where the cops had come from, I didn't know, but the place was crawling with them, herding us. Then we started pulling out, each bus with two cop cars, one in front, one behind. Our bus had to go down Fullerton toward South Street, and that's where all the blacks were gathered, flipping over the white students' cars, setting them on fire. They jumped in front of our bus, trying to stop us when we turned the corner. Bricks came flying, crashing through the windows. That's how my eye got swollen. A brick. Window exploded next to me..."

He said nothing for a long moment.

"I'd chickened out," he said quietly.

"No!" my grandparents both cried, rallying themselves. "Dennis, no! You didn't *chicken* out! You did nothing wrong! You didn't lower yourself to their level! You did the right thing! Why, you did what would've made us proud if only we'd known. You did what would be a good example for your son," they added when they remembered me, but it did no good. My respect could not be salvaged. I wanted to hear that he'd beaten up...God, it sounds so horrible when I say it now, but that's what went through my head. I wanted to hear how he'd gone berserk, just *lost* it, blown his top and clubbed someone (yes, even a girl) to death for trying to murder the girl of his dreams.

Looking into my father's eyes then, I think he knew it.

My Grandpa took up the story from there.

"So, right. Then they started rioting, looting, tearing the place apart. They set a building on fire. Shots were fired, more cops showed up, then when the firemen came to put out the fires *they* got shot at. All traffic going south into the city was stopped. The National Guard showed up, fixed bayonets and stood on Broadway. There were tanks, Jeeps with fifty calibers mounted on tripods in the backs of them. There was a shot of it on the front page of *The Evening News*.

"We decent white people, not the KKK, mind you, but decent ordinary white people, had gone back to our suburbs and neighboring towns for our own guns. We were hearing rumors about cars full of blacks rolling out of the city like gunboats, shooting up white houses, black houses, they didn't care what. We were ready to kill to protect our families. We were all sitting on our front lawns with our hunting rifles, many of us wanting to carry the fight into Newburgh to save our city.

"The blacks burned half the city overnight. *The city they lived in.*" He paused to let this sink in, for drama's sake.

"Our All-American City Council had to level the burnt buildings and replace them with low-income housing. Most of the businesses that were still intact pulled up their stakes and high-tailed it outta there. The buses stopped running downtown because they kept getting robbed and shot at. Of course, the drug trade skyrocketed, and the cause of all this trouble—the inappropriately named 'welfare' program—got worse. The greater the decay, the more our government paid the maggots. Crack whores became brood mares, shitting out babies as often as they could to bump that check up a few more dollars, swelling the population to get more benefits and create even more blight. Instead of giving money to those of us who were working two and three jobs just to stay afloat, slaving away like army ants for shit wages and paying it back in taxes to feed pimps, whores, and drug addicts.

"Since the Grand Union supermarket had to move away, following all of the other businesses, these maggots needed groceries and spread themselves farther out, closer to what stores there were in other towns, and it was this that threw open the door for Iranian carpetbaggers, swooping in to buy up foundering businesses and jack up prices—which nobody minded because they were paying with *food stamps* anyway!

"And then, completely by coincidence, the AIDS virus was released in Chicago the very next year. 1978."

Gramps sat there across the table from me with a strange little smile, and made a face like my father had.

Get it?

I met Maya and Mariana at the restaurant, finding them in a back booth, sitting close together. Domingo and Shaitan were on their way. I didn't doubt for one second that the girls had showered together and continued to experiment in my absence. The Brazilian couldn't keep her hands off of my girlfriend, but that's the way 'sexually awakened' girls are, I'm told. Always touching, caressing. She was the first of them to notice me.

"Out of the lion's den."

"Hey baby," Maya said.

"Yeah," I answered, sliding in opposite them. "It was like a movie, the way the cavalry arrived totally out of the blue, just in the nick of time. You shoulda seen it."

"Wish we could have," Mariana said. There was a silence, and the two girls looked at each other for a moment. Then, Mariana summoned the courage to speak, clearing her throat.

"Um, Evan?"

"Yes."

"Maya and I have been talking."

"Uh-oh."

"And we wanted to ask you if..."

Maya smiled her mischievous little smile at me.

"...If, well, of course, I'd ask you first," Mari said, toying with Maya's hand. "And if you say no, that'll be that. But what I'd like to do is...date Maya too."

"You want to date my girlfriend."

"Yes. Well, and you, too. We could all go out together, and well, all come home together, if you know what I mean."

I tried to keep the amused expression off my face. "I suppose, if it's all right with Maya—" I answered, which translates into "Hell yeah!" Of course, Maya already knew what I would say, what it would mean, but she enjoyed situations like this. She winked at me. Mariana was my gift to her, and she was giving her right back.

Life is beautiful.

Domingo and Shaitan found us and we all decided to move to a bigger table. They made me tell the story of my adventure with the police, and I was sure to omit the part about panicking and begging God to help me. It just wasn't manly. Plus, I should've had faith in Grazi Mono, not some imaginary super being.

"So, we are brothers now!" D'ingo laughed. "Dad won't shut up about the great job you did the other night, and I never did thank you for that day. You saved my life, Evan. I'm in your debt forever now."

"Talk Pedro into letting us all drink tonight, and I'll call it even."

"I'll see what I can do." He left.

Mariana looked at Maya again and smiled. Shaitan saw it.

"What's with you two?" she asked. "Is there some secret conspiracy going on? If so, I want in."

"I'm bisexual," Mariana said proudly. Another thing 'sexually awakened' girls are is 'demonstrative'.

Shaitan blinked in surprise. "Come again?"

"I just found out. Maya and Evan just helped me find out."

The Indian said nothing, but it was plain to see she was disgusted. Maya looked away.

"What is it?" Mariana asked.

"Sex is for men and women who love one another."

"Well, yeah, but see—"

"There are no buts about it. A vagina is for a penis and a penis is for a vagina. There is no other way." She was firm, but Mariana's newfound happiness made her argumentative.

"You don't understand—"

"No, I don't understand because it makes no sense. There *is* nothing to understand. You have succumbed to a sickness, that's all."

"There is nothing *sick* about what we do!" That feisty anger of her people came out in Mariana's voice and the flash of her exotic eyes. "It's beautiful, and it feels good, so it can't be wrong!"

"The heroin addict says the same thing about his foolishness, but that doesn't make him right. The only reason you think it's okay is because society today tells you it's okay. And the only reason today's society agrees with sexual perversion is because it is about to crumble."

"What the hell are you talking about?"

"It happened in Babylon, Egypt, Greece, Persia, Rome, and now it's happening here. An empire grows strong through courage and discipline, and then gets weak with laziness and depravity. It happens every time. The men get bored and start laying with men, and the women turn to each other. And then, the empire falls apart. You never see this disease among my people."

"Ha! That's because they've never been more than—"

Domingo hurried back to the table and interrupted.

"Hey! We got a problem."

Maya and I were grateful for the change of subject, but what

253

Mariana had been about to say stung Shaitan, even though she hadn't said it. It didn't matter. What Domingo said next shocked us all into a truce.

"We've got a snitch in the restaurant."

We looked with suspicion instead of lust at every waitress who walked by. When ours came with dinner, we all stared at her shirt, trying to make out the faint line of a wire. Well, I don't know about Mariana, but that's what the rest of us were looking for.

My roast duck with fried bananas didn't even taste anymore. It was just something I put in my mouth and chewed while I scrutinized everyone I saw. Of course, we saw nothing out of the ordinary. It's probably going to be someone I like, I thought. It's never the one bitch who gets on your nerves. Never.

I ordered a plate of some fried shrimp for the table, with a gram of coke. Lately, I'd been feeling that itch for it, that itch inside your head that only one thing can scratch. The plate came, and I pulled the little bag out from where it'd been sandwiched in between two crunchy tails. Everybody glanced around nervously—something you are *not* supposed to do—as I excused myself and went to the bathroom.

The men's was done in orange terra cotta, with totem poles and fake potted trees. I chose a stall, locked the door, and sat, opening the small bag. I wear a ring that Maya gave me, silver, a snake coiled three times with its tail in its mouth. The head and one coil pop off on a hinge and become a little spoon that you use to dip a bump with. I don't know where she finds this stuff, but she gives the coolest gifts. I remembered the gift tonight, Mariana, and had to smile.

The toilet next to me flushed, and the man got out, replaced by another who grunted. Men seem nervous in the bathroom and speak only in grunts. If they see a buddy, communication seems to be limited to an "I recognize you" nod. I dipped my little spoon into the bag, bent my head and brought it carefully to my nose. Sniff.

Zing!

Damn, this shit's good. We deal *only* in uncut cocaine, unlike the rest of the world who cut it with whatever's handy. Aspirin, whatever, but mostly baby laxative. Every time I get some crap like that, it gives me the runs, but this stuff—damn. Sometimes, bad coke affects my, well, makes me...unable to perform, if you know what I mean. Okay, impotent. It makes me impotent, and the finest woman in the world couldn't get me hard. And paranoia. But this stuff makes me want to fuck, or fight, or both, and I know in my balls and my bones that I will perform like a champion in either sport. We're talking Diamond-cutting Dick.

Sniff. Ahhh, hell, another two won't kill me.

Sniff. Sniff. Woooo! Somebody stop me! I noticed the stall next to me wasn't doing anything. No toilet sounds. I bent down and saw a pair of gray wingtips. Gray shoes? Who the fuck wears gray shoes? Whoever it was crumbled up a piece of paper and I heard it drop into the toilet. I stood, put my bag away, snapped my ring shut, and watched my door. Flush! Uh-huh, something's definitely rotten in Denmark. I opened the door and went out to confront the suspicious character. The powder in my head worked instantly, and strength surged through my arms all the way to my fingertips. I'm ten feet tall. Bulletproof.

The door opened, and I was staring into a pair of startled blue eyes. Detective d'Argent's startled blue eyes.

I wound back, stepped in, and decked him in the jaw as hard as I could. I was out the door before he hit the tiles. Rushing out toward the smoking section, I caught Shaitan's eye and made the sign. Her eyes went huge, and the rest of them turned to look. I mouthed the word "detective," and made for the door.

Rounding a corner, a tall stained glass Quetzalcoatl partition, I ran headlong into Bancroft. He was in the process of handing something off to a waitress, but all I could see of her was black hair and dark skin, which really didn't narrow it down. When we collided, he stumbled back, his hand clutching my shirt instinctively for balance, pulling me with him. I didn't give him a chance to see me. I reared my head back, grabbed his shoulders, and slammed my head right into his salt n' pepper goatee.

Shaking him loose, I shot straight for the kitchen, dodging tables, then rushing servers, shouting "one time, one time!" the code word for "police in the house." I passed through the front and skirted a dude with a load of dirty ramekins, jostling and almost tripping him on my way to the back line. The expo girl hurriedly began the two step concealment process for hiding drugs, and the guy with the ramekins backed up to delay any cops who might come running through.

"Pedro!" The dark unshaven face appeared out of the office. "I need a piece!"

He vanished, and reappeared an instant later as I fought my way across the slippery prep floor. He tossed me a nine, which I almost fell and busted ass in the process of catching. Behind me, I heard a commotion as Bancroft came tearing into the kitchen, accompanied by a chorus of helpful "he went thataway"'s, then the resounding crash as the ramekin guy stepped in his way and they went down. Picture perfect. I didn't even have to see it.

The back door, like most restaurants, has a green button you have to press to be released into the cage, a sally port, then a red button that unlocks the gate to the parking lot.
When Bancroft appeared by the dishwasher and shouted "Stop him!" Pedro made a show of grabbing at me, pretending to slip, and fell against the green button, at the same time slipping me a spare magazine. Keep that trigger warm. The door clicked the second before I threw myself against it and fell out into the cage, startling the employees on smoke break.

"One time," I said, turning around to see Pedro pretend to slip again and grab the wall mounted red button for support. Vizcaya wouldn't slip on ice. He was as sure-footed as a mountain goat, but you wouldn't know it to look at him now. The gate clicked, and I was out.

"Hold that door!" I heard Bancroft shout, answered by a chorus of innocent-sounding "Huh?"s, followed by the click of the gate relocking.

"Shit!"

I ran out past the dumpsters into a row of parked cars, switched off the safety on my pistol, racked the slide, and lay in wait. Earn your pay, I heard Nestor say. Yeah, I knew exactly what to do. I heard the door of the take-out side fly open, and in a moment, saw d'Argent coming out to head me off at the pass. As he came out into the ring of anti-theft lights, I rose and fired. I caught him three times, almost at once, just above the knee, once in the ribs, and in the armpit as he fell, screaming, his pistol bouncing away. Bancroft had just gotten out of the cage and turned back to catch the door, but a slim brown arm shot out, the fingers seizing the chain links, and yanked it shut. Click.

"Fuck!"

I turned on him and fired, barely missing with every shot as he bolted for the cover of the dumpster. The breech locked open, and I released the empty magazine, slamming in the fresh one before the first hit the ground. D'Argent was crawling awkwardly, as a bat crawls, after his gun. I aimed carefully, and blew the weapon out of his reach just as he got to it, laughing as he cried out in anger. I heard Bancroft calling me.

"Drop your weapon and come out with your hands where I can see them!"

"Okay!" I called back. Silence. I bet he felt stupid.

"Well?"

"I changed my mind!" Silence again. "Hey, d'Argent! I got a bead on your head right now! Tell me who wrote that note you were reading and I won't blow it clean off your shoulders!" No answer. "Do you think I'm fucking kidding you? I got a grand total of *nothing* to lose. Say the name and I promise I'll take off running right now!"

"You'll kill me anyway!" he cried.

"No, I won't! Cross my heart!" Still no answer. "Okay, let's try this: if you don't tell me, I'll shoot you everywhere *except* your head until you do tell me! I'm counting to ten. One!"

"He's bluffing!" Bancroft shouted.

"Five!"

"What happened to two?" d'Argent screamed.

"Oops, now it's seven!"

"Don't tell him shit!"

"Ten!" I fired, blowing off one gray wingtip. The man screamed again, and Bancroft started firing blindly from the side of the dumpster. I returned fire, enough to drive him back behind cover. "Now, I'm only going to count to three. Let's see how long it takes me to get there!"

"Angelica fucking Lopez!" the man shrieked.

"Thanks. Hey, sorry about the suit!"

I shot him in the head.

Bancroft started firing again, but I was already behind the line of cars, running for my Camaro. Stuffing the gun in the waist of my jeans, not bothering to engage the safety, I dug my keys out as I ran and hit the button to unlock the doors. Hopping in, I slipped the key in the ignition and started it, backing out and rolling as calmly as I could around the restaurant. Coming to the back side, the long way, I found Bancroft still crouching behind the dumpster in the shadows, his back to me. I rolled down the passenger window, pulled the gun out, and squeezed the trigger once. I saw him jump and gunned it, getting the fuck out of there.

Out on the road, I came to a stop light and looked in the rear-view mirror as I pressed the button to roll back my convertible top.

"You're a cop killer," I said to my reflection, and watched myself smile. I reached in my shirt pocket for my cigarettes and found only two left. Shit. On coke, and in my present situation, I'm going to need a hell of a lot more. I lit one up and drove to the nearest convenience store.

Parking along the side, out of the way, I started to get out, and stopped. No reason to take the piece with me, but you never know. Better to have a gun and not need it than to need a gun and not have it. I stuck it back in my waistband, untucked my shirt, and covered myself before getting out. My cigarette was only half-done, but I was about to get more, so I flicked it away and walked into the store.

Waving at the Asian guy behind the counter, I went to the fridge in the back, selected a high-fructose corn syrup carbonated beverage, and took it to the counter. "A pack of Marlboro Reds too, please."

The little yellow man nodded and sold me the pack without bothering to check my I.D. Glancing out the glass door, I saw a police cruiser roll by. Fuck. Keep going.

I smiled nervously at the cashier when he handed me my change, and left. The cigarettes were in one hand, the soda in the other as I walked to the corner of the store. The cop was parked in front of the Camaro, stepping out. My soda went *ffp!* as I opened it. He turned to me.

I looked away.

"You don't look old enough to buy cigarettes," he said.

"Thanks. I get that a lot."

"Let me see your I.D."

"I don't have it."

"You don't *have* it?"

"No. My wallet got stolen."

"So how'd you buy that stuff?"

"I only keep credit cards and condoms in my wallet."

"And your driver's license."

"Yeah..."

I saw Domingo's car go by, Shaitan noticing me.

"You driving this car?"

"No. You can't drive without a license."

"Doesn't matter," he said. "You're going to jail anyway."

"What? Why?"

"State of Florida, you have to have an I.D. at all times."

"You're kidding me."

"Nope. Put your hands on the car. You got any drugs or weapons on you?"

Yeah, both. I stepped off of the raised walk, moving away from the building and the cop. Needing a free hand, I put the pack of Reds in my pocket. He came after me.

"I said, put your hands on the car."

"You're not taking me to jail for no reason."

"Well, now I got a better reason: resisting an officer."

"What is this? Collars for dollars?" That's what they call it when a cop is about to go off duty and he makes an arrest for a bullshit reason, so he can get paid overtime for the hours he puts in booking the suspect. Yes, it's bullshit, but yes, they do it. Maya's dad told me all about it.

"Put your hands on the car!"

Domingo's car had doubled back and come around the gas station. Now they pulled up next to the air tank for filling flat tires.

"You're going to take me to fucking jail for not having an I.D.?" I asked, furious.

"That's another charge. Verbally abusing an officer. You want to try for any more?"

Domingo got out, and I lifted the hem of my shirt, yanking the pistol free. "Sure, motherfucker. Here's one."

Both Domingo and the cop took a startled step backward. The cop had his hands halfway up. "Whoa, hey, let's think about this."

"Time for thinking's over, pig."

You're a cop killer.

"What's going on, brother?" D'ingo asked nervously, coming closer.

"Cuff his hands behind his back," I told him. "Take his gun, and disconnect that CB."

"I don't know about this, *meng.*"

"I know you don't know, that's why I'm telling you. Now do it."

He heard the new voice I was speaking with, the new me that his father was so proud of, hesitated a moment, then obeyed. Shaitan got out of the car.

"What the fuck are you two doing?"

"Get back in the car, honey," Domingo said.

"Hell no." And she walked off into the darkness.

When TJ-fuckin'-Hooker was suitably trussed and disarmed, I motioned with the gun to put him in my trunk. Domingo walked him to the back of the Camaro and I pressed the button on my keys to pop the trunk. They looked in it doubtfully.

"I'll never fit in there," the cop said.

"You'll find a way to."

"Look, we can just forget all about this and walk away." He sounded like he was trying to stay calm.

"You had your chance earlier. But you wanted to arrest me for nothing. If only you knew what I'd just done, you'd have a decent reason. Now get in the fucking trunk."

He swallowed hard, and awkwardly climbed in. It took a minute for him to arrange himself. When he was comfortable, he looked up at me. Scared.

"You know, kidnapping a cop is a serious crime."

"I'm going to do a lot more than just kidnap you," I told him, slamming the trunk lid.

Domingo called Mariana's cell from the gas station pay phone, while I enjoyed one of the cigarettes I almost went to jail for. We learned that Pedro had called the police to report a shooting as soon as it was safe, and that—oops—one of the detectives was alive and well. But I'd shot them both. Or had I? Did I even hit Bancroft? Did I even bother to see if I'd hit him? Or did I just haul ass when I saw him jump?

We all decided to meet at my new place, and bring a bottle of something, because all Esteban had left me was beer. I completely forgot to mention what d'Argent had told me before his brain jumped out the side of his head. We left, Domingo following me to Abbey Road.

If you want to scare somebody, put him in the trunk of a car. The cop was banging around and shouting all kinds of threats and pleas, and I could still hear him over the bass coming out of my speakers, no matter how loud I raised it. What a little bitch. Please,

please let me go! You're in big fucking trouble, asshole! Oh please, I don't want to die!

"I'll get you for this, motherfucker!"

Oh, yeah. Danger city.

But talk while you can, because soon you'll have your own dick in your mouth, with your lips sewn shut around it. I couldn't help but smile.

Straight, no chaser, is the only way to drink tequila. That salt and lemon shit, which I call "training wheels," is for kids, and always seemed to me like taking an aspirin before shooting yourself in the head. You're not drinking this foul rotgut because you like it. You drink it to show other people how cool you are, and sucking on a lemon ranks right on down there with wearing condoms on my list of purpose-defeating wastes of time. What's next? You're standing at the bar all embarrassed because your girlfriend wants a frozen dead grasshopper in her drink with a twist of grapefruit peel?

No, the trick is learning to suppress your gag reflex and survival instinct. If you have to swallow a shot five times before it stays down, grit your teeth, set your jaw, and do it. Otherwise, don't even bother.

There are some that insist the only proper way to drink it is from the gas tank of a running chainsaw, and they are probably right, but we try to make do with what we have. Cuervo Eighteen-hundred Reposado may taste like dragon piss, but it's the best tequila in the history of the world and it comes in a really cool bottle.

Ahh, tequila. That foul rotgut that Tom Robbins called scorpion honey; O tequila, savage water of sorcery; Tequila, the buzzard god who copulates in midair with the ascending souls of dying virgins. After the second shot, you think you're handsome. Third shot, a great dancer. Fourth, bullet-proof. Fifth, invisible. Sixth, the President.

I was just working on developing super powers when the cop spoke up. We had him blindfolded and hog-tied on the floor while we decided what to do with him.

"Um, hello?"

"What?"

"If you let me go, I can be a real friend to you guys in the department," he said.

"Yeah, and I bet you've got a bridge in Manhattan you're willing to sell me, too."

"Look, I was just kidding around earlier. I wasn't really going to arrest you. I swear."

"Uh-huh. And I'm not really going to torture and kill you as soon as I get around to it."

"Please!"

"Shut the fuck up! The only things you can do right now are: beg for mercy, which you aren't going to get, and pray for a quick death. Which, again..."

Domingo looked at me strangely. Actually, everyone was looking at me strangely, as if they saw someone they weren't sure they recognized. Mariana's cell phone rang, and she did another shot before answering.

"Hello? Hey, Pedro. What's up? Nothing, I'll tell you later...yeah, but not over the phone."

Suddenly, I remembered. "Mari! Give me the phone!"

She questioned me with her eyes.

"I know who the snitch is! I'd forgotten."

Her eyes went wide, and she handed me the cell.

"Pedro, the waitress, Angelica, she's the one who's selling us out."

"Are you sure?" Vizcaya asked.

"One of the detectives told me, and I saw the other one handing something to her. You need to grab her before Bancroft lets on that d'Argent dropped her name."

"She's gone, *papi*. She disappeared during all that mess. You start looking immediately for her and I'll call the boss. Get Calibos to help you."

"Shit, this isn't a good time, *hermano*." I glanced at the cop on my floor. "Besides, I don't even know where to start looking for Angelica."

"It's never a good time. Now go." He hung up, and I called Calibos, filling him in.

"D'ingo, you got school tomorrow?" I asked.

"Yeah."

"Fuck. We gotta find that girl. Tonight."

"Angelica Lopez?" the cop asked.

We all turned and stared at him as he struggled to face us.

"What did you say?"

"Is that her last name?"

"Yeah."

"I know where she is."

We rigged him up to one of the toys I got at the mall earlier, a noose for what they call "autoerotic asphyxiation." I'd decided to furnish my place with as much of the cool stuff Maya had as I could find. Now we could do everything at my place that we could at hers, or better yet, I could do those things with somebody else. Another thing tequila does is make me ambitious; I want to fuck *everybody* in the whole wide world. Well, not guys, obviously, but you know what I mean. It's as if my dick has become a heat-seeking ballistic missile I just happen to be attached to. Ooh, look! There's a woman! Fire! There's another one!

The reason I mention this is, I have consumed a heroic amount of tequila, some outstanding cocaine, and was in the presence of two very fine women I was already licensed and authorized to fuck with impunity. So, full speed ahead, let's find this girl, kill her, kill the cop, and get to the good part. I'm a busy man. I don't have all night, you know.

Then a thought jumped, unbidden, into my head—the waitress Angelica is damned fine, too. Maybe we could tie her up and have our way with her. Mmm. No, that's rape, I think. Which is illegal, so never mind. Back to the matter at hand: the cop.

"How do you know Angelica Lopez?"

"I...can't...breathe," he managed.

"I know you can't breathe, dipstick. You've got a noose around your neck and everybody can see it, so you aren't telling us anything new."

"But...how can I talk...if...I...can't breathe?"

"If you can manage smart-assed comments like that," Maya said, "you can breathe just fine."

"So how do you know her?" Domingo asked.

"I...was...fucking her."

"Oh, you little stud, you. Until when?"

"Um...yesterday."

"So, you're going to lead us to a girl you're seeing," Mariana said, doubtfully. "Why don't I believe you?"

"We...just...broke up."

"Oh? Why?"

"She's...a...cheating...lying cunt."

263

"All right!" I said, clapping. "Now we're getting somewhere! I'll believe him if he wants her killed now."

"No, he's lying."

We all looked at Mariana for explanation.

"He's just saying that so we'll believe him."

"How do you know that?" D'ingo asked.

"I'm psychic."

We all blinked at her. Apparently, she'd had eight shots, and soon she'd be telling us she was a ninja. Man, I needed to fuck her, quick.

I took the little bag of coke out and found my Flying Nun. Fuck if I know why it's called that. I mean, it doesn't even *look* like a nun. It's a pill grinder with a screw-in lid that looks half wing nut and half spinning top. You put pills or rocks in the container and screw in the lid, and that triturates whatever you want triturated.

"Triturate" is one of those ten dollar words Maya taught me. You want to know what it means, get a dictionary and look it up. I'm not about to give a ten dollar word away for free. By the way, you can triturate shit quicker and easier with an electric peppermill, but you don't get to go through a ritual, and you don't get to call something a flying nun, both of which I kind of like doing.

Yeah, so, anyway, I triturated the rocks and crumbs and cut up a few lines on one of the mirrors I took down from the wall. Reveling in the very process of it, the sounds of plastic crunching granule, the cutting of lines with surgical care and precision. Domingo took over the interrogation and I stopped listening. Trying not to look at myself in the mirror even though it was hard not to. Extreme Close-Up of my face bent over the four snow-white lines, so close I could see my own pores. I can't help it. I look into my own eyes as I bend even closer, tooter in one nostril, the other pressed shut by a finger-tip. Sssss*niff.*

Zing!

My nose and brain burned and numbed at the same time.

"Did you bring enough for everybody?" Maya asked.

Unlike the rest of the world, I do not get selfish with my coke. I resent the way others will try to steal your line or pretend they didn't know it was yours or forget or whatever they want to call it, and I'm smart enough to know that it's the drug's fault, not theirs. So I make a concentrated effort not to be that way. I'm not an addict. I'm into it for the party, and it's not a party unless everybody's happy. Now, don't get me wrong. I *will* fuck with people, but it's all in fun.

A few times, when I've been out with the guys and one of them just gathered up all the stray grains and snorted a skinny line, the second he'd look away, rubbing his nose, I'd lean over the mirror and furiously rub my scalp. You can always get at least a mild sprinkling of dandruff. Then he looks back and sees what he wonders how he could have missed, and distracts you so he can sneak the tiny grains without you knowing. Serves 'em right. Why settle for just enough when you can shoot for too much, eh?

Ooh, you know what else is fun? When your buddies have been smoking crack and they're down on their hands and knees foraging vainly in the carpet for more, here's a great way to piss them off. A lot of apartments have popcorn ceilings these days. Grab a broom, wade out into the middle of them, and run that fucker across the ceiling a couple of times. When all of those little white pebbles hit the floor...chaos.

Hey, reminds me of a joke: Why do crackheads do it doggy-style? So one can look around on the floor while the other one peeks out the window.

Oh yeah, Maya was asking me for a line.

"Knock yourself out, lover." I handed her the fuselage of a ballpoint pen, snapped in half, that I was using as a tooter, and she bunched up her long hair with one hand to get it out of the way.

"Merci," she said sweetly, and she bent down. As her face came to the mirror, the reflection of her eyes met mine. She winked.

Moving her lips, she spoke to me in the secret language we have together. She and I can covertly communicate with the inflection of a single syllable, or by just a look sometimes, passing unspoken messages from across a crowded room. I nodded, almost imperceptibly.

Calibos came in and surveyed the room.

"Yunno, jew really cang leave the door unlock when jew doing thees shit."

"Damn. I'm usually good about locking the door."

"Yeah, well, cops doan *usually* come busting in. It's *usually* wheng jew doing shit you doan *usually* do. Jew feel me?" He went over to the cop and inspected him. "Da fock is thees all about?"

"He claims to know where Angelica is," D'ingo told him.

"Well, leave him to me ang we fine out for sure. After five

minute he tell me eef he wears lady underwear."

"Hey, look—" the cop began.

"Shutta fock up!" Calibos back-handed him hard across the face. "Jew not talking to keeds anymore. Jew speak when focking spoken to, and only answer my question! Eef I hear *wong* focking word come outchoo mout' dat ain't whatta wanna know, I'm gonna star' boiling a pot of oil. We ga *lotsa* oil, mudderfocker."

"But—"

"Are jew *deaf?*" Calibos roared, spit flying from his mouth, his face twisted into a purple mask of fury. For a second, this forked vein throbbed out of his forehead, then sank back in as his face turned brown again. Everyone else was startled, but for some reason, I could not stop laughing.

"He told us where she stays," Mariana said, eventually.

"Butchoo cang know for sure that he telling da troof unteel jew burned him enough. A smart meng will tell jew directions to a place where all hees buddies are waiting wit' gones. Besides, it ain't fun an' games unteel somebody get hurt."

"If you'll just—" the cop said. Calibos lost it, pounced on the man and beat him until he was coughing blood on my carpet. The ugly man didn't make a sound while he did it. I finally understood what "unreasonable" meant. Unhinged, uncontrollable. It's not when a dangerous man is screaming that you need to turn tail and run. It's when his lips curl in and his mouth becomes a tight, straight line that he's going to fucking kill you, and his eyes almost glow with rage. That's what Calibos looked like. Then, without a word, he dragged TJ-fuckin'-Hooker across the living room around the pool table to the front door. The noose had broken and was now just dragging behind the cop's bleeding head.

Flinging the door open, Calibos made a cursory glance outside into the night, and towed the pig away. We just stared after them until Maya closed the door. And locked it. Turning around, she dusted her hands theatrically off on each other. "Good riddance."

I set the mirror on a corner of the pool table and rose. In my fist I had gathered a few drinking straws and brightly colored plastic flamingo swizzle sticks, and I held them fanned out. "All right, let's get on the ball finding this girl. We'll draw straws to see who has to go looking first. Whoever draws the red straw loses."

"I'm not fit to drive," Mariana said.

"Then stay here and help Maya hold down the fort, C'mon

D'ing. We gotta move." I threw the straws over my shoulder and went for the door. Domingo followed. Outside, there was no sound except the crickets. The coke and tequila were roiling inside me, plastering a smile on my face that I could not have pried off. We went down to our cars and agreed to split up, checking in with the girls by phone if we came up with anything.

Coming out of Abbey Road, Domingo went left and I went right, circling the block, and going right back to my apartment. Inside, Maya and Mariana were already naked on the pool table. I shut the door, and locked it this time.

I awoke in bed, squinting in the harsh glare of the sun. Mariana lay with her back to me, sandwiched between me and Maya. I was instantly hard, pressing myself against her, and she stirred, moving with me until I was inside of her. She reached behind and squeezed my hand. I kissed her shoulder, and we made love very softly, very quietly, without waking Maya. My mind was years away, under the bleachers at school, and I realized that if you're patient, eventually everything you want comes around. I'd been looking forward to this moment since I first laid eyes on Mariana de Medieros, and here she was grinding her beautiful ass against my lap, her warmth enclosing my hardness.

Our hands clenched together and unclenched, fingertips caressing palms, feet gently stroking each other and muted breaths suppressing groans of pleasure.

Occasionally, Maya stirred or murmured in her sleep, but never awoke. When at last we came together, bodies trembling, holding each other tightly, it took all of our self-control to keep quiet. The feeling passed, and we sagged into that delicious languor, stroking each other idly.

"*Obrigado, papi*," she whispered.

Life is beautiful.

The whole world was looking for me, it seemed.

I'd become, almost overnight, the city's most notorious criminal, with a body count of thirty and rising—seven of them being police officers. Maybe I hadn't pulled the trigger on half of those people, really only killing, I dunno, seventeen *tops*, but I was taking the credit (or blame, depending on how you look at it) for all of them. The media was having a field day with this. Even though I was small potatoes compared to the people I worked for, they were all in the shadows. I had the notoriety of a public enemy. That would have terrified me last week. Now I swelled with pride. I was somebody. I was feared.

It felt like living a movie, where life and death was decided by the hammer dropping on a hollow point and the whole wide world was fair game.

A desperado, living moment to moment. The future is not even on the Top Forty list of concerns anymore.

I remembered praying for a second chance at life, and now that I've got it, I'll be damned if I ever waste one second of it being bored, or scared, or unsure of myself.

There was a poem I wrote in my English class, the last year that I attended school. I don't remember more than one stanza, but that's all that mattered: "How can we be so different if we fell from the same tree? If coolness has no substance, how can you have more than me?" I finally know the answer to that age-old riddle. It's all varying degrees of not giving a fuck. I couldn't care less about anything right now, and it's all going right for me. When I worried about every little thing, absolutely nothing worked out, and I felt like everyone else had the strange and hidden power but me.

I cannot explain the change that's come over me—no, wait a second. Yes, I can.

It's like two magnets flipping over.

I reflected on that as I went in to see Grazi Mono at the safehouse. He sat cross-legged on the floor, as still as death, staring at the bloody mess on his large wooden cutting board. A chicken's head was set aside with the two feet on one corner, and the rest of the body was a smear of blood and guts and feathers that he contemplated for several minutes. Three lit candles, "velas," stood in a triangle surrounding a bucket full of tarnished pennies, coconut husks, cat ribs, polished turtle shells, and chocolate chip cookies. His oricha apparently had a sweet tooth. All of this had been drenched in the chicken's blood.

I'd gotten used to the practice of Santería, and the fact that it would never be explained to me. As a gringo, certain things were taboo for me to learn. Fair enough. I was content to let Nestor play with his blood and act all spooky if he wanted to.

Voodoo, and other fun stuff, I'd learned a smattering of. How the Shuar people, the headhunting Jivaro in the forests of Ecuador shrunk their enemies' heads into Christmas tree ornaments. Great for breaking the ice at parties. And the houngons and bocors of Haiti. There's a lot more to voodoo than sticking pins in a doll. Tonton Macoutes, Cígouaves, Diablesse, Papa Doc's ghost still haunting the island. Real macabre stuff, but from here, those guys all looked like Scooby Doo villains. Now, Nestor de Medieros, on the other hand...

Eventually, the dark man looked up at me and said that I was walking that thin line between usefulness and liability.

"You are reckless, a loose cannon, but still very lucky. You attract the attention of the police, but manage to elude them and steer them away from me. And, in the process, obtain valuable information from them. I don't know whether to scold you, or..." He broke off and stared at me as I grinned. I knew in the back of my mind, that voice of caution, that I was supposed to listen to him somberly and with respect, but I was too impressed with myself lately for that kind of garbage. He must have realized this.

"...Valor pleases our gods," he continued, "and the blood you spill in their service brings me into their favor. It is not often that young men of your race are so fearless, especially regarding the police. But that barbaric foolishness you wear around your neck must be replaced." He indicated Shaitan's medicine bag. "My son came home the other night with that charm, and if I had not taken it from him, surely that monkey's bullet would have found him. Here," he said, extending his hand.

I pulled the necklace off, snapping the string, and gave it to him. He tossed it over his shoulder, picked up one of the chicken legs, and tied it to a rawhide thong, offering it to me. Without question I slipped it over my reverently bowed head. I felt ridiculous, but if it made the boss happy there couldn't be much harm in it. He turned his attention back to the mess on the cutting board. He might've been talking to the chicken, at this point.

"We have to find this girl who's bringing heat to my business. There's no telling how much the police already know, and we need to silence her before she tells any more. Your hostage sang like a bird before he died, but the waitress is still nowhere to be found."

"So, I have a better idea," I said.

"Tell me."

"We get rid of the police."

Nestor blinked at me. "What?"

269

"We kill the police. All of them."

"You can't do that."

"It's done in Sao Paulo. And all over Colombia, too."

"This is not Brazil, *moço*."

"Then, let's make it Brazil."

"So, you want to kill all the police."

"Everyone that knows anything about us, and destroy all of the evidence they have. When new people come in to replace the dead, they will have nothing. They will have to start from scratch."

"You are a damned fool." He started talking to the chicken again.

"I know. But they'll never see it coming."

"So, you want to just walk right in and do it?"

"No, I think we could cause some kind of a diversion, get a lot of cops out of the station to handle it. Keep them occupied. *Then* we walk right in, kill everyone, smash all their computers, and burn the fucking place down. The only people who'll be out on the streets will be the beat cops, the grunts. They don't know shit about shit, so they won't be a threat to us."

He was looking at me now and didn't notice the gizzards move slightly, stirred by his foot hitting the board.

"The alley cats could learn a lot from you," he said. "My crazy demon on a leash. So, go kill these police if you can. If I never see you again, it's no surprise."

He glanced down at the mutilated chicken and noticed something. Blinking a moment, he stared hard at whatever it was he thought he saw. Then he regarded me again, a bit more closely. When a man believes in augury, he can convince himself of anything, and it seemed that a random configuration of tissue and viscera was convincing an otherwise clever man of something.

"Well, the gods do not lie," he muttered. "But how do you know anything about the inside of a police station? Where evidence is kept? Where to go and what to expect?"

"I've got someone I can ask."

"Yeah, I told them we broke up a long time ago," Maya said. "They believed me, of course. You should have seen how relieved my dad was. Little princess dating a cop killer. He was sweating over it. Bullets."

"He never really liked me anyway," I replied.

"No, but he doesn't like anybody. Not even Mom."

"Now, your mom liked me."

"That's because she's a lousy judge of character."

"Very funny."

"I know. So, why do you ask?"

"I was wondering if you'd mind being kidnapped."

"What?"

We sat in the party room of Pecado, the isolated area reserved for special occasions and secret meetings. The table accommodated twenty, but only nine of us occupied it at the moment: Nestor, Vizcaya, Calibos, two other lieutenants, Domingo, Maya, and me. Yeah, I know that's only eight, but I'd never seen the ninth guy before, and I didn't know his name. He was an older white man with a pencil-thin mustache and beard, like the young Puerto Ricans wear.

He was red-faced and blond-gray, obviously a sailor because of the wide-legged rolling gait when he walked. He had a Dippity-Doo haircut preppie kids had in the Nineties and a Mickey Mouse watch along with his Polo-and-khakis outfit, to show (I guess) that beneath his gruff, weathered exterior, he was still a kid at heart. The weirdest thing about him was that the left side of his body was scarred and stunted, while the right was muscular.

"This is Jim Harding," Pedro said. "An associate of mine. He'll be helping us with the plan. What we have here is a layout of the police station. Of course, it's not entirely accurate, but it's made up of Maya's recollections and what she could piece together from listening to her father talk. It's not much, but it's better than nothing.

"We're going to call the police from a pay phone downtown, with Maya crying and saying 'Daddy, help me,' blah blah blah—"

"I've got the hyper-ventilating down to an art," she interrupted. "But some Bacardi Anejo would really get the tears flowing. You got any lying around?"

"No, *niña*. None for you. So, when the police trace the call, they will find this pay phone in a perfect ambush. They will most likely set up sharpshooters at the five vantage points I've selected. They are prime spots. The police will be overjoyed to have them. Jim, here, is ready to install some explosives armed with remote detonators in those five places, as well as underneath the phone. We will also have mines situated that will only become activated after the primary explosives have gone off." He seemed like he was really getting into this.

"We will wait until the area has been staked out. They will watch the phone for a second call to be made and see who makes it. We will keep them waiting. Then, after we are in place to storm the police station, we will call the pay phone. When it is answered, the six primary explosives will be detonated, and the entire area will become a minefield.

"Reinforcements and the Bomb Squad will be rapidly deployed, and the minute they leave the station, we invade. Maya's father will most likely be in the cordon downtown, out of range of the bomb blasts. Any questions?"

"Yeah," Domingo said. "Where do I fit in?"

"You get to watch," Nestor said. "That's the best part about being in charge. You get to sit back and enjoy the show."

"When will we do this?" I asked

"The first call will be placed at six o'clock. The area in town will not have so many people there, and this is right before shift change. The police will be looking forward to going home, instead of fresh and ready for action. It's twenty past three now, and our men are assembled at the safe house on Ponce de Leon, around the corner from the station."

"Can I have some Angel Dust?" I asked.

"I would advise against it," Pedro began.

"Sure," Nestor said.

Domingo and his father left, and Maya went with Calibos to the house on Ponce. Before he went, the hideous man leaned in to me and whispered, "Chool wear the foot of a chicken, but not a cross? The meng upstairs can see jew, *niño*."

"Let him see," I answered. "I have an extra clip on me, full of hollow points."

"Not even Esteban mocked God, and he was a thousang time more evil than me."

"And look where all his crosses got him."

He started to speak again, but I walked off to the kitchen and got a gram of PCP from the expo girl. While she was getting it, a waitress came in with an order and brought it to us, worried.

"This guy I've never seen before ordered four grams of heroin,

272

Katie. He was sitting with three other big guys and they looks suspicious."

"How do you mean, 'suspicious'? Like trench coats and fedoras and sunglasses?"

"No, like big jock types who stopped shaving on the same day and turned their hats around backwards. I mean, it's so obvious. They look like they dressed up as "slackers" for Halloween."

"And they wanted an eight-ball?" Katie asked.

"No, he said he wanted *four grams of heroin*. Enunciating. Loud."

"Damn. Okay, we're not selling anything else tonight. If they ask you again, just act all ditzy and play like they're kidding. I'll tell Pedro and he'll take care of it."

The waitress went away, filling drink orders, and Katie pressed a button that was cunningly disguised as a simple light switch. I don't know what it did, but somehow, Pedro was summoned. Appearing from the prep area, he raised his eyebrows in a facial "what?"

"Four undercovers in Section Eight," Katie said.

Vizcaya's lips curled into a snarl, and he was gone, heading for his office. He returned a moment later with an expensive-looking camera and a telescopic lens. Without a word to us, he exited the kitchen and went off to surveil the table. Katie called out to one of the cooks.

"Terry! I need a Montezuma on Christine's last order!"

The cooks laughed and made jokes among themselves that I couldn't understand. Restaurants all seem to have their own slang, and if you don't know it, you're left standing there, blinking stupidly. For example, we call a speedball, which is cocaine and heroin, "sugar n' spice." Liquid X is our "special sauce." You get the picture.

"Montezuma?" I asked.

"Laxatives. Prepare to evacuate bowels in ten, nine, eight…" Katie said, smiling. "Oh, we're going to make this *very* unpleasant for them."

"Damn. Spicy food usually does me in anyway."

"Well, for our more 'loosening' dishes, we usually mix powdered stool hardeners in, to be nice to our customers. It was Mrs. de Medieros' idea. But for unwelcome guests, we have stuff that'll make 'em shit fire in under a minute."

"Out*standing*."

"Ain't it though?"

She handed me the little baggie of Dust and I flipped the spoon out of my ring.

"Damn!" she said, her eyes lighting up. I dipped it into the powder and drew it out with a little mountain.

Sniff.

Zorch!

Move over, God.

"Whoa, easy, Evan," she said, when I dipped the little spoon back in. "That's the good stuff. Better make it last."

"I know what I'm doing." Sniff. That dark, unholy thrill roared through me. *You're a cop killer who can breathe fire and come lightning.* All of a sudden, I wanted to go out there to the table in Section Eight and kill those four cops with my bare hands. Maybe taking this stuff was a bad idea. You can *not* just sit around and do nothing on Dust, and here I was, trapped in the back of a restaurant with a couple of hours to kill. I waited until Pedro came back in with his camera and stopped him, grinding my teeth audibly.

"*Hermano,* I need something to do. Gimme a mission."

"Just stay here. Don't do anything."

"You know I hate sitting on my ass. I need to be busy. You got anything that needs doing, let me do it."

He let out a sigh and looked away.

A few seconds passed, each one of them taking an hour. Finally, he handed me the camera and told me to take it to the safehouse on Barracuda Terrace, which was only five houses down from where my parents live.

"Give the camera to Cristos so he can develop the film, get a new roll, and come straight back here with it. I can't have you running around all day."

Why he didn't get with the present and just buy a digital camera was beyond me. He was one of those people who would have to get dragged kicking and screaming into the future.

I went out the back door, getting one of the dishwashers to press the buttons for me, and found my car in the parking lot. The powder I was constantly sniffing back tasted like dissolved aspirin in my throat, and I wished I hadn't taken it. Actually, every time I take this stuff I wish I hadn't, but for some reason, that never stops me from doing it again. Maybe it's the feeling that all I have to do is push off with my feet to fly to the moon. Maybe it's the confidence of knowing you could put six shots in my chest but I'll still choke you to death before I fall.

I think it was Shaitan who told me that the reason Sam Colt invented the .45 was that American soldiers would empty their revolvers into charging Filipinos hopped up on PCP and the bastards kept coming. They'd tie tourniquets all over their bodies, eat a handful of Dust, and come howling out of the jungle like mad dogs, and no slug was heavy enough to knock them down. That's what scared those four cops so bad in LA, who beat Rodney King. The sonofabitch just got back up.

And that's how I felt now, like everyone was a challenge. I sized up everything I saw. Whatever it was, I wanted to break it just to show it that I could. With that desire, though, came the nervous fear that…maybe I would. Maybe I'd pounce on someone and fucking kill him before I knew I was even doing it. That's what I hated about this damned drug.

When I shut the door of my car and looked out the windshield, Shaitan stepped unsummoned into my mind's eye. Although she was a beautiful woman, I'd never been attracted to her. She had always seemed somehow separate from fleshly stuff. The only way I can explain it is to imagine Jesus or the Dalai Lama being Hollywood heart-throbs. No matter how good they might look, no girl would want to sleep with them, just…because. Forget it. You either understand me or you don't. Uppers do not a great orator make.

I saw her as I did the night I met her, in a black one-shoulder halter top, black hip-hugging bell bottoms, and those heels that turn me on for some bizarre reason I can't explain. She wore a bone choker around her neck that she'd made herself, and her hair was up in a sexily sloppy bun, with a few strands strategically loose and wayward. Domingo hadn't shut up about her, his new love, the leader of an up-and-coming band. Said they were like the next Rage Against The Machine, only they had a singer instead of a screamer. And *damn*, she could sing.

She was on the stage in a club called Swak, fronting the five other Onandagas that made up Warpath: two guitarists, one badass drummer, and two chicks; one on a flute, and the other fiddling fire from a violin. Who'da thought a violin and a flute could sound angry? But there they were, with the whole bar stomping their feet, as Shaitan howled.

A stolen stanza from Rage's "Wake Up", or an homage, whatever, brought a roar of approval from the crowd:

"I might give you a dose, but it could never come close to the rage built up inside of me!

Fist in the air, in the land of hypocrisy!"

Then her own words again:

"You bulldozed the woodlands, and left us with stones.

You took all the great elk and left us their bones.

Over the Black Hills where my ghost fathers walk,

Four huge white faces are carved in the rock.

Staring down at them so that they may see

That nothing has changed at all since Wounded Knee.

You say that we're conquered and it's just our bad luck, but you can shove your reservation—we don't give a fuck!"

The Irish Catholics had U2, the Gullah had War, the Jamaicans had Bob Marley, and the American Indian would have Shaitan Risingsun if she had her way. As the breakdown started, she went into her crowd-pleasing Indian dance. The lead guitar and bassist did their balls-to-the-wall instrumental, then backed off for the two squaws to duke it out for domination of the limelight. It was breathtaking to hear. Drunken fans were doing their crude imitation of Shaitan's dance, and taking up the chant her guitarists had begun.

"Paleface, go home, and leave us alone!"

It was as foolish as shouting "Kill Whitey", but the music had gotten into our souls and there was nothing we could do about it. See, Shaitan's realistic. She knows all of these people are hypocrites who masochistically wallow in guilt because the land they own had been stolen from her people—well, not *her* people, but people like her people, and that was close enough. They'd buy posters of Indians, souvenir medicine bags, dream-catchers, and tickets to her shows so they could sing along with her, but they weren't going to give up their spare bedroom or loan their car to Indian migrant workers. What they would do was feel a few hours' worth of Chinese food guilt, atone for their ancestors' sins with twenty, maybe thirty dollars, and go home feeling absolved until the next gig. It was a living, and it sure beat serving drinks in a reservation bingo hall.

"Paleface, go home, and leave us alone!"

As people must, we began clapping a steady beat to keep time, I guess just because an audience needs to join in sometimes.

Abruptly, the two chicks stopped playing and all there was were the drummer and the chant. His solo brought the chant to an exultant intensity, and there wasn't a single head in the house that didn't bob with the clap. Fists banged on tables, shrill whistles cut the din, and as the song built to a crescendo, the drummer rapped his snare once and left us hanging.

That one bang had the finality of a driven nail, and the club erupted in applause.

Shaitan explained to me later that the Black Hills are a sacred Indian burial ground, and the fact that the carved portraits of four U.S. presidents on Mount Rushmore overlooked them was an insult to her people and their heritage. I told her I'd never thought of it that way. She told me she knew.

It was the wise and understanding look in her eyes that moment that I was seeing in my head right now, behind the wheel of a champagne Camaro, with Angel Dust up my nose and a gun in my jacket. I imagined her lips form the words, but the voice that spoke them was my own.

It said, *Go.*

It's not too late. Just go away and leave this all behind you. Do it.

I blinked hard, shook my head to clear it.

Drive and drive and drive until you're someplace safe. Then keep going. Drive to the Pacific, trade the car for a boat, and just keep moving. Keep moving. Run away and never look back. It's not too late.

I forced the manic thought out of my head, but it was persistent. I made a mental note never to take PCP again, ever. Well, maybe I'd finish off the bag, but after that, no more. Except for the occasional bump or two. Fuck it. I took the bag out of my pocket, dipped my ring's ladle in and *Zorch!*

Woooooo!

Start the car. Vroom, vroom!

I left smoking black skid marks in the parking lot on the way out. I know that's not how to be incognito, but I just couldn't bring myself to drive responsibly. I cut the wheel hard coming out of the parking lot onto One-Forty-Deuce, fishtailing and cutting off a pickup truck. My tires screamed as I stomped on the gas, the Camaro taking off like a rocket. I weaved through traffic, jumping aside at the last minute and missing fenders by a cunt hair and a coat of paint, the dust in my head sharpening my reflexes and timing to a height that bordered on godlike. I expected the car to start talking to me any minute, calling me Michael in a snooty voice.

Screech! Whoa, shit, that was close. A chorus of angry horns blared at me, but I was a champagne bolt of lightning and was gone before anyone could even see me. The white lines in the road shot past me like stars in hyperspace, my shuttle blazing through the galaxy at warp-fucking-*ten*. The cops tend to frown on people who drive like this, but my splendid automobile was equipped with a radar jammer that made me invisible to their puny little speed guns. I made a mental note to install a smoke screen and oil slick just in case, though. Real "Spy Hunter" stuff. Little caltrops, too. Steel burrs to blow out pursuing tires. Maybe rotating blades on my hubcaps, too, like that hotrod in "Grease." I'll be unstoppable!

Whoa. Earth to Evan, better slow down a little.

I wrestled with the drug that roared through me, and managed to regain some semblance of sanity. Not a moment too soon, because the light up ahead was just turning red, and there was no way I could have stopped in time. I was already braking, but now I had to mash the pedal into the floor, the inertia pulling my guts and brain hard against the front of my ribcage and skull.

A bag from the Pornucopia adult novelty store slid out from under the passenger seat and slammed into the console. Oh yeah, I'd forgotten about that. The handcuffs and nipple clamps. For no good reason at all, I remembered the time Maya told me the difference between kinky and perverted. Kinky is using a feather, and perverts use the whole chicken. I chuckled and glanced sideways out my window at the same instant a pretty brunette glanced at me. We looked away, then did a mutual double-take. Her eyes went wide and mine narrowed.

Luck just doesn't get as good as this. I blew the girl a kiss and winked. With my superhuman eyesight I could see her knuckles turning white as she gripped the steering wheel.

The light turned green and our tires smoked, taking off the line, neck and neck, her the rabbit and me the fox. She tried to bob and weave, stick and move, but she was just a girl in a Volkswagen Beetle and I was the Big Bad Wolf. She juked down one road, then squealed onto another, but I'd done this before. And won. She was in a panic. Driving scared. I was in the zone and having a ball. It wasn't five minutes before she turned the wrong way on El Cid and into the cul-de-sac. She screeched to a halt and I had her. Trapped.

I licked my lips, not so much grinning as baring my fangs. The pistol came out. Without taking my eyes off the VW I grabbed the goodie bag and found the fuzzy pink handcuffs. They were cutesy, but they did their job.

Opening my door, I stepped half out, with my other foot holding the brake just in case she tried to do something brave/stupid. With the gun on her, I called out, mimicking the cops.

"Step out of the car, please."

Hesitation. Then, Angelica Lopez opened her door and got out with her hands in the air. Terrified. I beckoned her closer with the gun. She came slowly. I tossed the handcuffs to her and told her to cuff her ankles and be a good girl. When she had, I climbed back into the car and put it in park.

"Don't do this," she said as I approached her.

"Give me one good reason why I shouldn't."

"You're not like the rest of them."

"Not good enough."

"Then I'll give you a hundred better ones if you take me out to a house in the sticks."

"I don't have time for that. One. And two, you think I'm going to walk right into an ambush? I'm a white boy, not a green one."

I lifted her up easily and draped her over my shoulder, carried her back to my car. She did not resist, surprisingly.

"Don't you even want to know why I turned on Pedro and went to the cops? Aren't you even a little bit curious?"

"There are a thousand reasons you'd roll. Money, revenge, get out of a few charges…"

"Revenge! Listen to me—"

"I'm not interested."

"Goddammit!" she yelled, and then she told me.

What she said stopped me in my tracks, and I put her down on the blacktop to listen to her.

"How do you know all this?"

"I was dating a button man, a guy named Esteban Ribeira—"

"He's dead," I told her.

"It was just a matter of time. He told me all about it. Said he couldn't live with it."

"He never seemed like the type with a conscience," I said, helping her to her feet and into my car. I was still stunned by her secret.

"He wasn't all bad," she muttered, a little sadly.

"What's this about you going out with a cop named Douglas? He rolled on you and we hadn't even started torturing him yet."

279

"Douglas? You mean Degrass? A white guy with a sandy crew-cut?"

"Whatever."

"Did he say we were going out? That little prick. He kept hitting on me when I was talking to Detective Bancroft. The other guy too. D'Argent. They were like dogs, the way they kept trying me. I thought Degrass was going to hump my leg the last time I saw him. So, you believe me, right? You can't possibly take me back to Pedro knowing what he does."

"I have to see some proof. Take me to this house you were talking about."

"What about my car? I can't just leave it here with the door standing open."

I looked at her, not knowing what I was looking for, but trying to read her thoughts by the expression on her face. Angel Dust also makes me think I'm much smarter than I actually am, so at times when I should be thinking "No" I'm patting myself on the back for saying "Fuck it, why not?"

I took the cuffs off of her feet and told her to lead me to the house. Very confidently, with no doubt at all of my judgment, I watched her run to her own car. It hadn't even occurred to me this time that people in the houses up and down El Cid could be watching. Even if it had, I would not have cared.

I three-point-turned to get alongside the VW so I could get out of her way and still be prepared in case she tried something, but she just waved a *C'mon* and I followed her out. I had not forgotten the camera in the center compartment, but this new adventure took precedence over four new undercovers' mug shots. Angelica led me back onto Pine Hills Road and east into the Acreage—our local euphemism for cheap woodland outside of civilization. Someone had decided it sounded better than BFE, No-Man's-Land, the Middle of Nowhere, et cetera, and somehow it just stuck. Past the turnpike, there was nothing but casuarinas, sabal palms, sea grape and poisonwood, the smell of flora that grew only in sandy dried-out swamp, the real Florida. There were the occasional houses, inhabited by poor immigrants, recluses, and white trash, and they grew fewer the farther we pushed into the frontier. The drive was nine cigarettes long.

Eventually, we came to a dirt road and bumped along it for about ten minutes, occasionally taking turns I tried to keep track of, and finally arrived at a narrow trail with a gate. No Trespassing signs were posted on either side, and the ground underneath was a mohawk of tall grass between two dusty tire tracks.

We parked in front of it, got out, and climbed over. She said nothing, the expression on her face one of repressed dread, as if going with the police to confront a molesting uncle. There were none of the usual forest noises, just shadows and eerie stillness. We walked along the trail into the woods without a word. I couldn't sense any danger, only loneliness. If what Angelica said was true, there was nothing alive to fear here.

I took the pistol out of my jacket anyway.

We found the house, a dark and forbidding cabin with a circle drawn in the dirt around it. Within that circle, no grass grew. I spotted a lizard skittering along the ground and felt my short hairs prickle when it came to the circle, stopped, and seemed confused. It flared an orange membrane that stretched from its chin to where its chest would be. The dewlap collapsed, flared again, and it looked at us. Flare, fall, flare, fall, the hypnotic rhythm it used to mesmerize insects. Then it turned and scampered away from us along the circle.

I looked at Angelica just in time to see her make the sign of the cross, the shadows of leaves like moving bruises on her face, her eyes stained with some dark residue of emotion, and proceed into the ring. I sniffed disdainfully, but gripped the butt of my pistol tighter. Surprisingly, the front door was unlocked.

Inside, there was a smell I did not recognize but somehow still found hauntingly familiar. It was musky and dry, overpowering a more subtle bittersweet stink. It was the odor I always smelled in my head when I watched archaeologists in a movie enter a mummy's tomb. The way I imagined a moldering ancient corpse stuffed with flowers would smell.

The cabin was without modern convenience, containing little more than a long table, several chairs, a large trunk, and a charcoal brazier. There was a door to the left and one opposite us.

"Through there," Angelica murmured, gesturing toward the far door. I could make out a faint droning noise coming from beyond it, and did not like the look of the yellowed towel bunched up and crammed under the door crack.

I crossed the room, trying not to be unnerved by the creaking of the floorboards, trying not to wonder about the dark stains on the table. The door was locked. Setting my jaw, I took a step back, and kicked it open.

A foul stench billowed out like a cloud of smoke, and the drone became an angry buzzing of startled flies.

Millions of them.

I took one look and ran back to the front door with my hand over my mouth. Angelica was already outside, waiting.

There is a dark hole in my memory of that afternoon. I've banished the image of what I saw in that room, as I've tried to banish the unmanliness of how I reacted. I came to myself in Angelica's arms, on our knees outside in the dirt, her blouse soaked in what I realized were my tears. I had sobbed and choked and wailed like a little girl as she held me. Her eyes were as puffy and red as mine felt, but she was calm. I shook violently all over, unable to contain the horror of my whole world falling apart around me, of what I'd been a part of, and what I knew I had to end if it was the last thing I ever did.

I thought of that little kid Moke I'd met the other day. One day he would be old enough to think for himself, and that would be the last day of his life. As soon as he might pose even the slightest threat to Grazi Mono, the way he had twenty years ago become an enemy to his masters, the prepubescent assassin would be put to sleep like a mangy stray dog. Before he ever had a chance to bite the hand that fed him. Nestor de Medieros took no unnecessary risks. Ever.

But that wasn't the bad part.

The dark gods of the Amazon are hungry. I'd heard Abuela say that before, but never given a thought to what it meant. Just the insane ramblings of a senile old woman. The insane ramblings of a twisted people who poked around in the guts of dead things to divine the future. The freakish religion that sprang from African Orisha slave juju, along with voodoo and candomblé, all three of which were alive and well throughout the Caribbean and South America and now, apparently, in South Florida as well.

I worked for and had lived with a man who offered the mutilated corpses of children to his gods. He sacrificed them on a makeshift altar, burned their still-pulsing hearts on a barbeque grill, and left their twitching bodies for the flies.

I tore the chicken claw from around my neck and threw it into the bushes, I could smell the stench of maggots all over me, could hear them writhing on top of one another inside the rotting flesh of the little killers. I'd lived under his roof, eaten at his table, slept with his daughter, and killed for him. My life had gone this way, spiraled out of control into murder and fear because of *him*. Did he expect the last chapter of my life to be on his table in this house, too? As soon as I'd outgrown my usefulness?

As soon as I became a liability?

The shock of it came out of me in a flood of tears and racking sobs. What the fuck have I become? What the fuck do I do now?

What?

"Do you blame me for calling the cops, now?" Angelica asked me, rocking me gently.

"No...Jesus, no."

But that was not an option for me. I had no one to turn to now. My face was all over the news. I had to run. Run away and never look back.

No, not yet. Not until I kill that sick fuck and put an end to all this. My head cleared and I knew what to do.

Angelica led me back to civilization, and I drove to Barracuda Terrace with my heart in my mouth. I passed the safehouse and came to the stretch of road that used to be my playground. There was the spot where Bobby Sands broke his arm trying to olley over the fire hydrant, back when we all thought we were skateboard bad-asses. There's his house. There's the house where I kissed Allison Hall during Spin the Bottle one night, and thought my feet would never touch the ground again. There was the bush the gang and I hid behind to smoke our first stolen cigarette. And there's my driveway.

I pulled in and parked in front of the garage. My head was racing with fear. This was the house I'd been in such a hurry to escape, and now I was home. The front door opened. And there was Dad.

I swallowed hard and got out, walking up to the stern face that hadn't changed a bit, and tried to smile.

"Hi, Dad."

"Nice car," he said.

"You like it?"

"What happened to the last one?"

"Long story. Look, I've got a lot to say to you and Mom. I

want you to know that…that I'm sorry…and—"

"Save it," he said. His eyes appraised me and his lips curled into what could've been a smile, but stopped just short of it. "I've seen you on the news. So have the neighbors. So have all our friends."

"I know, Dad—"

"*Don't* call me that. You've made your mother cry. You've given my in-laws another excuse to hate me."

He looked me straight in the eye.

"If you ever come here again, I'm calling the police."

"What?"

"You're no son of mine. I don't know you. Now, get out of my sight, you piece of shit."

The door slammed in my face.

In a daze, I drove up the street to Cristos'. I felt the air grow close around me, like the pressure that builds before a thunderstorm. It was the world closing in on me, the intangible nameless terror that I should've been feeling these past few days, but was too stupid to. I began to feel the first pangs of what I would only begin to understand much later, that being on the run is not a romantic or glamorous thing, no matter what the movies say, and the novelty of spending the rest of your life as a fugitive and a vagabond wears off quick. Paranoia sets in. Satellites in the sky can see you, and hidden cameras watch your every move. After a while, every mirror you look into has a secret room on the other side where men sit and record your actions. The worst part is the way people look at you. Strangers. Even though you act completely normal, strangers stare at you out of the corners of their eyes, then quickly look away. They fall silent when you pass by.

The Bible wasn't kidding about that Mark of Cain stuff. Once it's on you…I pushed the thought out of my head as I parked in front of 187 Barracuda Terrace and dug the camera out of the center console. Cristos was waiting impatiently at the side door.

"Where the hell have you been?" Pedro demanded.

"I found Angelica Lopez."

The look on their faces was priceless. Jim Harding stuttered for a moment, but Vizcaya cut him off.

"Where?"

"I saw her on the road. She won't tell anybody anything else about us. When Cristos develops your film you'll see her body where I dumped it out in the Acreage." Her body lying in the bushes with ketchup, bits of hamburger, and a piece of a pickle slice on her face from her half-finished Extra Value Meal. Apparently, she'd just come out of a fast food drive-thru when I screeched to a halt beside her.

It didn't look *exactly* like blown-out brains, but I made do with what we had. If I wanted it to look like Esteban's head had, I would choose red Jell-O and spaghetti. That's about as close as you can get to a good exit wound without spending more than twenty minutes in the kitchen.

More stuttering, then congratulations, then instructions.

The hour was almost upon us, and I was supposed to be at the safehouse on Ponce de Leon. Harding's people had already rigged the area downtown, Maya's voice had been tape recorded, and everyone was in place but me.

Pedro told me to drink a milkshake, claiming that milk was the antidote to PCP and would yank my train to a halt instantly. It worked. I couldn't believe it.

Before I got into all this "life less ordinary" bullshit, my dad used to say I had a "packed head." He used to be proud of me, but those days were long gone.

Now, I haven't been accused of being smart for some time, but I could still handle a conversation with Pedro, who was a closet genius. Many thought him to be just another dumb immigrant because his English was heavily accented. The truth was, he spoke five languages *better* than English, and he had something to say worth listening to in each of them.

I remember a time he revealed his true character to me, something he tried very hard to hide, for some reason. He had escaped Spain and ended up here because he couldn't stand to see his people mistreated. Now he was the manager of a drug front? No, there was something hidden, but he managed to cover it back up before I caught more than a glimpse.

Ever since then, I'd watch him out of the corner of my eye, just as I watched him now, hoping he'd slip again. It had started as a short recollection, one he decided to share with me, and grew into an impassioned rail against the world today.

285

We were sanding down a few barstools, back when Pecado was still skeletal, and the place was cloudy with pine dust and cigarette smoke. I've loved that restaurant, only half because of its deep dark secret, more because I can look at anything in it and remember when it was just a 2x4, or an angle-iron. I guess that's why parents must be so disappointed in their kids when they turn out the way I did. They watched us grow from blueprints to…this.

We were sanding our barstools one more time before staining them, and Pedro was telling me about Spain. How much he'd loved it. How much he missed it.

"Few these days pay attention to it," he was saying. "But since 1879, one of the most extraordinary statues is in the Retiro Park. It's one of the most famous landmarks in Madrid, the only city in this Earth to dedicate a monument to the Devil himself."

He stopped sanding and looked off into space.

"You know, it doesn't look like that red guy with the horns and goatee that we've gotten so used to. That cartoon Satan you'd laugh at but never fear. He's an angel, falling from Heaven, trying to shield himself from the wrath of God. Cast in bronze, proud, a rebel like my people. Like we were supposed to feel sorry for him. Like we're supposed to cheer him on.

"Ricardo Bellver, the guy who sculpted it, defied tradition because he was bored with saints and righteous people, and erected this abomination that almost no one gives a second glance."

He sighed with disgust, turning back to me.

"This is how far we've fallen, *niño*. This is how, *como se dice?* Desensi—"

"Desensitized?"

"Yes, thank you. This is how desensitized we have become. We either glorify evil, or we ignore it. Little brother, tell no one I said this, but what we do, this drug shit, it's evil. It's wrong, but it's a step towards something better! All people who do drugs try to convert others to be like them. They think there is nothing wrong with it, like it's normal, natural. It's because they feel *shame!* They need company, because you see more with the sickness you have, and it doesn't look so bad. So they spread it, like fucking *smallpox!*" Hypocrisy, it sounded like.

I questioned him with a look, but he clammed up and went back to sanding. It took a few years, but I finally understand what he meant by that. I may not know what Good is, or Right, or Sane, but I know exactly what Evil is. It looks appetizing at first, when it's money and women and champagne convertibles, when it's all that bullshit you hear gangsta wannabes rapping about, but when you get to the heart of it, the stench that would make a maggot gag, there the confusion ends. When you kick the door open and see the swarm of flies scatter angrily off the corpses of mutilated children…you'll know what to do.

You stop patting yourself on the back for being a cop killer.

Pedro could not have known about the kids, the Grazi Mono, he could not have been in charge the way Angelica thought. Not the Pedro I know. Not the man who danced the *paso doble* with Teresa de Medieros. Not the man who took over where my father left off.

I still watched him out of the corner of my eye as he rushed about giving orders that had nothing to do with the serving of food.

"Whatever happened to those undercovers?" I asked Katie. She grinned, her mischievous eyes lighting up.

"You should've been here, Evan. When they left, they *still* had smoke coming out of their pants. Oh, how they suffered."

"So we don't expect to see them again."

"Not anytime soon."

I smiled in spite of myself. The restless paranoia started to dissolve, and I relaxed a bit. Leaning against the nacho bin, I sipped my milkshake and watched the orderly chaos.

I always loved being in the back of a restaurant, helping out. Of course, the only way I was helping now was by staying out of the way, but I loved the atmosphere. People were hurrying around, the air crackling with diligence like a beehive. Especially on a really busy night, when everyone's running to fill an order, I loved to pitch in. Roll up my sleeves and do some honorable work for a change. That's what I secretly saw as manliness: feeding people who were hungry, or building houses, doing something that actually mattered. Now, selling people drugs to take their minds off of life, while "exciting" and "lucrative," always seemed to me like one of the real bullshit ways to make a living.

Like marketing, and advertising, convincing people that they *had* to buy a bunch of shit they didn't need. By selling drugs, I was pulling the wool over people's eyes the same way Madison Avenue had pulled it over mine, blinding all of us to what was really important in life. But I always filed that away into the dark, shadowy, cobwebbed corner of my mind, because it meant I was a hypocrite.

Besides, it was *cool* to be a thug. It was cool to drop out of high school, to stop giving a shit, to live every day from one moment to the next. We bragged about getting arrested, who we slept with and what hearts we broke, how drunk or stoned we'd gotten the night before.

We bragged about how wrong we were.

As I watched waitresses and bus boys scurry about like chickens with their heads cut off, it occurred to me that turning to the right side would be just like that—always in a hurry to make ends meet, working hard to earn enough to pay the bills. I looked back at the past few years, at the money that had come to me, instead of the other way around. I looked at the enormity of the task before me; not just killing Nestor de Medieros and bringing his empire down in flames, but living an ordinary life after that.

For a moment, I wavered. A part of me clung to the dark side, feeling the "good life" about to be severed, but all I had to do was think of the kids. If somebody caught stray dogs and trained them to be killers, then killed them after a while, it wouldn't seem like a big deal to many people. PETA, maybe, but not John Q.

Children, on the other hand…

"One time!" a waitress screamed, but she was too late. The kitchen exploded with Sheriffs. They flooded the expo area, guns in the faces of petrified servers, slinging them to the floor, shouting and threatening so loud they couldn't be understood. I dove at the expo counter, scattering dishes as I slid between the aluminum shelves, and tumbled out the other side. The cooks were scrambling all over the line, trying to do everything they were supposed to do in an emergency like this, and many tripped over me as I hit the greasy tile floor.

I fought my way to the far end of the front line, in time to see many run out through the back door, opening the cage, and get knocked to the ground by more Sheriffs.

Before the cops could make it into the sally port, Pedro managed to yank the door shut. Whirling around to face the flood of people in the rear line, the prep area, he shocked me with the look on his face.

He was calm. There was no trace of panic or fear in his eerily intelligent eyes. He was in control, in his element.

"Hit that button!" he shouted, and I realized he was shouting at me. I looked around and saw no buttons. People were screaming bloody murder all around us, and I couldn't find the fucking button.

"The outlet! Behind the beans!"

Oh.

Another one of those secret buttons. It was disguised as a decrepit plug outlet, difficult to reach so it wouldn't be hit by accident, situated behind the steaming hot tureens where we heated queso, beans, and creamed corn. The back of my hand burned as I reached for the outlet, squeezing past the hot steel, but I didn't care. My scrambling fingers found the receptacle and pressed.

A strange grinding noise cut through the screams and the crashes of shattering plates. The fryers were overturning. The sharp squeal of metal on metal made everyone stiffen with fear, without knowing why.

Everyone except Pedro.

Splashing, and the rushing sound of the place being flooded. The sickeningly sweet smell of grease. I watched gallons of the brownish-black slop wash around the corners of the front line and cover the tiles, hearing cooks and cops alike shrieking as their feet were burned by it. Then, the sharp click of a Zippo made my brain seize, like a record skipping.

The lights went out, plunging the kitchen into darkness and terror. I felt a strong hand grab my arm and yank me into the cold storage walk-in, just as a spark burst into flame beside me. An unseen hand launched the small flicker of light and the heavy door swung shut.

The smells of many meats and vegetables engulfed us in the chilly air, and I was suddenly very glad to have been dragged in. A hissing roar and the screams of agony seemed very far away, as if crossing vast gulfs of space.

There couldn't be enough grease to wash into the front, since the floors all sloped downward toward drains, but everyone in the kitchen must be living torches, flailing about, shrieking, and blazing with light.

A dim glow flickered on at the back of the walk-in, and Pedro pulled me toward it, stopping at the rack where premade salad dressings and side dishes were stored in plastic tubs. He reached up and scattered a few pico de gallos aside, until he found one filled with green paste. Neon green, with chunks of crimson. He stuffed it into his shirt.

"What's that?" I asked, my voice sounding to me like it was

someone else's.

"What's it look like, bro?" he asked as we continued towards the light. There seemed to be a trace of amusement in his voice, but I couldn't be sure. Outside, the fire alarm was screeching and the sprinklers were spraying everything down. But grease fires *like* water. Oh, God. That was the whole idea.

"Guacamole?" I asked, trying not to think about it.

"Of course. We've got far to go."

The light was a small fluorescent in the liquor cage, the chain link section that only managers and bartenders had keys to. Pedro opened it and shoved a few crates aside. A secret panel slid open, revealing a treasure trove of cocaine, opiates and pills. And an exit. There are no basements in Florida, but this shallow adit brought us into a passage that met up with the city's storm drains. Pedro dragged the drugs into the passage and loosed them. Maybe they could be salvaged later.

"I thought it was another secret weapon," I stuttered.

"No," he replied, knowing I meant the avocado paste. "I take a tub of it home every night, but today we leave early."

Now I have to admit, we make some damned good guacamole, but eating was the furthest thing on my mind right now. But, monkey see, monkey do, especially in times of confusion. I grabbed a twelve-pack of the most expensive beer in the cage. I figured that as soon as the shock wore off and the stark reality hit me, a dozen bottles would really come in handy.

We slid into the passage after shutting the door firmly, and crawled through the wet darkness for I don't know how long.

The world was staring at Pecado, paying no attention to us. We had crawled out of a manhole cover, and now stood across the street, watching. All of the customers, or at least most of them, had made it outside and stood in a crowd with the cops who waited by all the exits to catch anyone trying to flee. There was no one among them in a Pecado uniform.

The restaurant was a roaring pillar of fire, twisting in the wind and blackening the sky. Fluttering ash floated by, scattered and still glowing with heat. I still felt nothing.

It took a minute to realize Pedro was on the phone, and had been. He'd wasted no time calling Nestor, and now the prerecorded call from Maya was being placed. I wondered if any of the Sheriffs who now watched Pecado burn would make it to the site in time to get blown up.

Katie was dead. Burned alive. So were Viviana, Terry the cook, and all the rest of that shift. Blackened skeletons by now, ashes in another minute, and nothing but memories after that. And I still felt nothing.

Taking the small baggie of Angel Dust out of my pocket, I looked at it for a second, then dropped it on the pavement and ground it with my foot like a cigarette butt. The powder drifted away in wisps along the ground, caught up in dancing swirls by the breeze. Katie had died for *this*.

Turning, I tossed my keys to Pedro, who frowned.

"My car is in the parking lot," I told him. He had a car, too, but he almost always left it at home. "I'll meet you there in a minute." He was still confused, but he wouldn't be for long.

I crossed the street.

In broad daylight.

I dodged a few passing cars, moving casually, and pulled my nine out of the waistband of my jeans. The silenced .22 rode in my cunningly designed shoulder holster, but I wasn't going to need it.

I was absently wondering why Colt Industries, after all these years, still hasn't come up with a snub-nosed bazooka.

I aimed at the head of the furthest cop. He turned, just in time to notice me, just in time for his face to register an "Oh shit" expression. Then I squeezed the trigger and a red mist jumped from the back of his head. The sharp crack startled the crowd, but not as much as the second one did.

Now I was running sideways, as Calibos had taught me, shooting cops down before they knew who to aim at, and Pedro was right behind me, cursing in Euskara and killing those I had missed. The crowd broke into a stampede of terrified animals. The cops were afraid to shoot and kill innocent civilians, but for us, it was much easier. Those green uniforms were so easy to spot. We killed them all. It got a little hairy, twice, when cops ran around the blaze and hid, but we got them.

Pedro cursed my stupidity all the way to the car, kept cursing as we drove away. But I loved that place, Pecado. When the daze melted away and I felt again, it wasn't Katie I was so angry about. It wasn't hate or vengeance for Terry, Viv, Noelle, or any of them. It was the building. It was the stained and etched glass that Abuela had made. It was the tables and chairs, and the tiles I helped lay. And the cops who laughed as it burned to the ground.

Nestor's couch wasn't my home. Neither was Esteban's apartment, or the house I grew up in, where I saw my father this afternoon. Pecado was. I can't explain it. The moment it finally clicked, I felt the last crutch I'd been leaning on shatter. Pedro could curse all he wanted, but I couldn't have just walked away.

I listened to him curse me in Euskara, French, Arabic, Russian, Portuguese, and English, all the way to Hibiscus Avenue.

And then, the first explosions went off.

By cell phone we were kept abreast of everything that could be seen from a sidewalk table in a trendy café. The hostage being a cop's daughter, the response was immediate. Like a swarm of black flies, they flooded the place. In a half hour, they had done exactly what we wanted them to do, and twenty seconds later, chaos reigned.

All five areas were detonated, the explosions rocking the nearby buildings and shattered masonry cascading into the street. Cars were crushed by falling rubble, a dust cloud mingling with the roiling black smoke to blind the shocked onlookers into a stampede that rivaled even the infamous 9/11 disaster. Citizens had gone from blissfully idyllic dates, enjoying their after dinner bullshit coffees, to being happy that they had front row seats to some kind of atrocity. Many were sipping their Maple Cheese Lattes or Blueberry Frappucinos, talking about how they might get to be on TV, when the telephone booth and the cop inside it erupted in a fury of shrapnel and shattered glass.

Jim Harding enjoyed recounting over the speakerphone the looks on his fellow diners' faces when the claymore slashed out of the booth into the cordon. Over the phone, he sounded like a little kid, and it wasn't hard to picture his lobster-red face go purple with laughter as he and his henchmen fled with the others.

"*Faux naïf*," Pedro muttered, turning away from the speakerphone, while Nestor shouted from the handset of another phone. I didn't know the name of that lieutenant, the one who was being yelled at. We all sat anxiously at another safehouse, on Bougainvillea.

"*Leve as crianças à—*" was all I caught. Something about bringing the children somewhere, then "*Tabaréu!*" which meant "lousy, stupid-ass soldier." I knew that last word well, having heard it enough in the past few days. Turning into a diamond is not a fun process.

In ten minutes, the proximity mines hidden everywhere would awaken, having given real people a chance to escape. The only ones we wanted to feel our wrath were the cops and the sickos we called "disaster voyeurs," and soon, the world would be several hundred assholes lighter. These would be the pieces of shit that slow down to get good looks at car accidents, or tune in every night to watch televised adultery and mayhem on sensationalist television, delighting in the misfortunes of others.

Pedro's phone rang then, and he rolled his eyes at the new interruption. Supposedly, Calibos and his men were storming the police station as we spoke, but if they called about anything, there had to be some kind of problem. And any kind of problem was inexcusable, because he and Nestor had a plan already for every contingency there was. That was one of the basic tenets of my training. Don't ever go in with one plan. Go in with ten.

His expression changed when he heard the guy identify himself. Now, he looked like he was simply annoyed with his time being wasted.

"*Cristos, que bola?*" he asked.

My blood ran cold.

I watched his eyes as he frowned the look of someone listening, then looking away in exasperation, then going blank, the face of digesting something unpleasant. Then, his eyes found mine, and I knew. I knew *he* knew.

"*Verdad?*" he asked, his tone somewhere in between disappointed and sad. My veins filled with ice. I considered trying to explain myself, then just gave up and bolted. Flinging the door wide, I ran for my car, feeling sharks on my tail. Gaining. Going to snatch me up if I dared one look back.

A pickle? Ketchup, ground beef, and a fucking pickle? I probably would've been better off with some of the guacamole Pedro's been eating with a spoon, straight from the tub as if it were ice cream. What the hell was I thinking?

Angelica and I had planned to meet up at a certain place after I'd killed Nestor, but that just wasn't going to happen. Luckily, but much to her annoyance, I had insisted that we agree on Plans B and C, just in case. Contingencies, yunno? Always be prepared. I raced off to our Plan B rendezvous and called her cell phone from the pay

293

booth, thanking God that everybody else in the world but me actually had cell phones. So what if I lived my life inaccessibly? As long as everyone else didn't mind ear cancer, I'd be fine.

She agreed on Plan C, meeting up on I-95, at this one exit. No problem. She hauled ass out of town, eager to lead me to L.A., where she had some family. I let her get a head start because there was still the second half of Plan A to attend to.

I parked kind of catty-cornered in the guest lot across from the building that Maya lived in, and hurried up to the door of her apartment. I startled the hell out of her when I came in, making her drop the phone she was reaching across the kitchen counter to hang up.

"Don't worry, babes. Only me." I picked up the handset and stuck it on the wall-mounted cradle, then pulled a bottle out of the wine locker and searched frantically for the corkscrew that should've been in plain view.

"I've been trying to call you," she said wistfully.

"*I've* been trying to call *you*. Phone's been busy."

"We really need to talk, Ev. You have a cigarette?"

She came out of the kitchen, around the corner and sat on one of the barstools, putting her feet up on another one. She was wearing only her bathrobe, the one she'd decorated with Chinese dragons, her hair pulled back into a ponytail. No ear weights. Her lobes just sagged for two inches, hanging limp. I got out two Reds and handed her one. When I noticed her ashtray next to the ornate and gilded hookah, I realized she must've smoked a pack and a half already.

"We have a situation here, honey," I told her as I lit hers and then mine. She handed me the corkscrew, which had materialized out of thin air. "A bad one."

"I know." She seemed impatient.

"No, you don't." I managed to get the corkscrew in the cork without shredding it.

"Actually, Evan, we have a situation so bad you wouldn't believe it. Listen—"

"No, you listen. We've got to get out of here. Now."

"What? I'm not going anywhere." She'd shifted her drawn up knees and hooked her toes on the edge of the other barstool, rocking it back and forth.

"Honey, let's pack your stuff and go. We have to get outta

Dodge before the fit really hits the shan." I was having a hell of a time trying to jimmy the cork loose.

"Evan—"

"Damn it, honey! We've got to go!" I shouted.

"I'm pregnant."

The loud pop of the cork punctuated her two horrible words, leaving an awkward silence in its wake.

I stared across the room at the bookshelves, at the gilded idol squatting on an ebony pedestal, flanked by a pair of smoking joss sticks.

I already knew there was no chance of talking her into an abortion. I remember her shouting at the TV once last year because these pro-choice people were whining about poor women getting raped and how they shouldn't have to carry some piece of shit's spawn to term. She said "C'mon, out of all the abortions, how many are had by rape victims? How many? You don't want abortion rights for rape victims, you want them for yourselves because you're too dumb or too lazy to be careful!"

What had sparked it was me seeing a commercial saying next Wednesday's Oprah would be about abortion survivors. Abortion survivors? Christ!

I came and told Maya that some of those babies apparently lived through that shit. She gave me a look as if she hoped I was kidding and knew I wasn't. Then, heaving a long-suffering sigh, explained that the women who've had abortions, not the babies themselves, were termed survivors as if they were victims, somehow.

Suffering the tragedy of having spread their legs one too many times, or not heeding the hundreds of condom commercials aired every day.

Oh. *That* kind of survivor.

People who survived taking the easy way out, survived not facing the music and being responsible. It's like saying "I survived getting laid."

Well, here we were with our money where her mouth was, and I knew she'd rather throw her life away than be a hypocrite.

"So, is it mine or Mari's?" I asked finally. She snorted a brief laugh and watched the thread of smoke that curled up from her cigarette, wavering in some unfelt draft. I stared at the smoky yellow bottle in my hand, its name sounding like someplace out of a Tolkien book, and let my cigarette go out. She cleared her throat, putting a tone of annoyance into it to recapture my attention.

Raising it quickly, I gulped down half of the bottle in one go, then sucked on my Red like a baby at its mother's breast. But that didn't change anything. I felt the floor shuddering beneath me.

"I found out after I got back," she said. "The plant's started growing." She'd taken a somewhat primitive test, but according to the books she'd read, it was infallible. She sowed two seeds in little soil-filled pots, watering one of them with her urine and the other with tap water. If it had sprouted after the tap water plant, we'd be in the clear. If it sprouted *first*...like it apparently had...

"Fuck," I said quietly. "Fuck, this is some bad timing."

"The fucking we get for the fucking we got."

"Yeah, well, that doesn't change the fact that we need to get out of this town. Shit, maybe the whole country!" I relit my cigarette and took another long pull off of the wine bottle. It wasn't my favorite, but after the day I've had, any port in a storm.

"I'm not going anywhere, I said." Her voice was very quiet and sad, making me choke on the wine. She'd stopped rocking the barstool and took another long drag. It had taken a long time, but I finally realized that music was playing, and her Aladdin's Lamp incense burner was spouting tendrils of fragrant smoke. She'd played one of those CDs she made herself, a "technopera," she called it. Delenda est Something.

"But you don't understand," I said when the choking had subsided.

"No, *you* don't understand. This is my home. When I raise our child, I want it to be around its grandparents. Not running from the law without knowing why."

"But that running away situation is a lot better for a kid than getting his mom and dad killed."

"No one will kill us! Move in here and grow a beard or something, I don't know. Nestor could get you a new identity, I hear. You can be Juan José de Whatever if you want to. Besides, the cops are all supposed to be dead, and whoever follows them won't know you from Adam, so chill the fuck out!"

"It ain't the cops I'm worried about right now."

"Then who?"

"*Nestor*, baby! He's sick! Plumb mad-dog crazy!"

"Oh, shit. What did you do now?"

"I'll tell you in the car!"

"No. Hell no."

"The restaurant's burned to the ground! And those kids! They're all—"

"What kids?"

"I'll tell you in the fucking car! Shit, I can't believe you picked now, of all times, to get knocked up!"

"Knocked up? What a great way to say I'm preggie."

"But we have to go, Maya! Now!"

"No, baby. I can't. I have a job here, and my parents, they'll think I escaped the kidnappers and you'll get yourself a new identity, and we'll all live happily ever after. Did you burn down the store? I mean, the restaurant? Did you betray Grazi Mono at all?"

"No, but—"

"Then everything's going to be okay. Just stay here and be our child's daddy. At least, help me come up with a name."

"I can't."

"Then get out of my sight." She got up, mashing her cigarette out in the pile of filters and ash, and went to the bathroom, slamming the door. The displaced air stirred the incense smoke into swirling eddies, waxed into prisms by the rattling beads in the bedroom doorway.

That was the second time I've been told to do that.

In one day.

I drained the last of the wine and poured a shot of Ouzo. It was swallowed before the shot glass hit the floor, shattering into a thousand pieces.

I ran three red lights on my way to Abbey Road, and screeched into one of the few empty spaces, denting a fender against my neighbor's Karmann Ghia. I grabbed only the necessary stuff out of my own place. Clothes, ammo, and money. My nest egg itself filled up the backpack I'd worn to Jeff Davis, that's how much I'd saved. I was just shutting the trunk lid of my car when Calibos appeared behind it, startling the hell out of me. He seemed to know everything, from the look in his eyes.

"Going away, *hermano*?"

"Just checking into a motel for a few days."

"Why? Jew no safe enough here?"

"Oh, sure I am," I said, thinking quickly. "But...hey, do you have any cigarettes in the house? I don't know where mine ran off to."

He looked at me for a long time.

"Choor," he said finally. "I got haffa carton insigh de house. Come ong up ang we sit an' tokka minute."

He'd seen the two pistols in the backseat of the car, and there was no way I could get at them without being really obvious about it.

"Yeah, sure. Hey, I'll meet you in there. I forgot something at my own place."

"What?"

"My lighter."

We looked at each other for another long moment, and both of us knew the other had lied.

"Be there in a second," I said, rushing up the stairs that led to my floor. Snatching the blue-striped ten-ball off of the pool table, I stuffed it into my pocket, crushing the cigarettes I'd pretended not to have. After making sure the bulge couldn't be seen under the hem of my shirt, I left.

Calibos was waiting at the door, in plain view, so I made a big show of locking the apartment up.

"Found it," I said as I approached.

He stepped aside to let me go in first, following me in, turning his head for one second as he reached back for the doorknob. In that brief second I pulled the ten-ball out and wheeled around, throwing it as hard as I could. We were close enough that the ball was only an inch away from my fingertips when it cracked into his forehead, just above one eyebrow. He stumbled back, but I caught him by the shirt and yanked him inside, closed the door.

He staggered a few steps, then fell against the end table by one of the couches. The cast iron vase-looking drum that sat on it bounced loudly away. I kicked him as hard as I could in the temple, then again just under the ear, right next to the curling tail of his scorpion tattoo that crawled across his throat.

He was out cold. I searched frantically for his own nest egg, knowing that all of his type were cash n' carry and didn't keep shit in the bank. He had a bunch of coconuts, decorated like jack-o-lanterns with the lips sewn shut, polished and hanging by long, flax-cn "hair" from shelves all around the place. Shrunken heads, they looked like. Cute.

The most morbid Art Deco in history, folks.

I found a couple grand under the bathroom sink, said good-bye to Calibos as he just started to wake up, kicked him again, and took a bow. One more kick put him back to sleep and I stepped over him, heading out the door into fugitiveness.

I tried Maya's place one more time, but she wouldn't answer the door. I tried every trick in the book, even the "I've finally come to my senses" speech, but she didn't fall for any of it. When I finally realized why, I just shambled away, hating myself. I'd failed her. And of all the ways I could have let her down, it had to be the one she teased me about the most.

I hadn't been manly enough.

Or maybe she wasn't home, I tried to tell myself.

Bullshit.

There are few things as boring as a road trip, living off of gas station junk food and watching the lines in the pavement flash by, listening to the same CDs over and over because the radio stations in that region only care about bass fishing. On the *radio*.

The few outposts of civilization reeked of diesel farts, enough to make my city slicker head reel, but we managed to find a few things to break the monotony of our trip.

A cyclops at one small town's only gas station filled up our tanks and squeegeed our windshields clean of splattered bugs while I was inside, paying the cross-eyed, hunch-backed cashier.

You could say of this small town, like Washington Irving wrote of Sleepy Hollow, that it was undisturbed by the rush of Progress. "Like those little nooks of still water which border a rapid stream; where we may see the straw and bubble riding quietly at anchor, or slowly revolving in their mimic harbor, undisturbed by the rush of the passing current."

Which would be horseshit, because it really was a hot and humid, muddy, hookwormy, banjo-plucking-albinoey, hillbillies-deranged-by-corn-squeezins-whose-li'l-sisters-are-their-druthersy dump in the panhandle of Florida, and its citizens were clearly more apt to chase me into the woods and rape me to death while chawing tabacker than give me accurate directions back to civilization. This due largely, I think, to the parasitic worm that came from outer

299

space to multiply and burrow its nest deep into their brains and befuddle them even further.

Sunshine State, my ass.

We made a detour to Memphis just for the hell of it. Graceland plays Elvis music constantly, and the people there never get tired of it. We saw the pink Cadillac with a headlight missing, bought a few T-shirts, decided not to go to Tupelo and see the King's birthplace, and heard something about Lisa Marie's plane making the best PB-n-Js in the world.

We decided just to take the guy's word for it.

After that, it was so damned boring there's no point in describing it. We would've been smarter to sell one of our cars and drive together, cutting our gas bills in half, but Angelica said we'd probably get on each other's nerves before too long and be unable to part ways. Besides, we'd be cramped as hell with both our luggage combined. So, we made do. We drove through the desert, seeing nothing but sagebrush, mesquite, and cactus. And sand. Lots of sand. The few cities we passed through were irrigated buttocks of prairie. Days passed.

I was about to go stir crazy when the Beetle in front of me turned on its blinker. *Oh,* I thought, *we finally got somewhere.* I must've been in a trance, turnpike hypnosis, whatever the experts call it.

I followed Angelica onto the Hollywood Boulevard exit, leaving Highway 101, thinking "Good riddance!" It was early evening, and the view of all the lights was breath-taking for someone who'd been staring at nothing for so long.

I saw smoke coming out from under the bridge and frowned at it, wondering if there was an accident. Turning back, I slammed on the brakes and jerked the wheel, just barely missing a sedan that had materialized in front of me and stopped.

Overcorrecting, I almost sideswiped another car, and then was panicked and weaving in and out of traffic, until the flow returned to normal. It was as if I'd suddenly forgotten how to drive, panic-stricken and surrounded by people who were even more clueless than me.

Angelica was nowhere to be seen. I was hopelessly lost in L.A. I stopped at a restaurant to rally myself, and twenty minutes later, my car was stolen. With all my stuff.

Except the gun.

And this is where the fun begins.

II

In the state of California these days, even being a bum requires a daily planner.

Fairmont Park, Riverside, wherever the fuck that is, is where I spent almost two weeks before I got bored and restless. I followed arbitrary directions while wandering until I finally stumbled upon the place, and in an odd way it was kind of fun living there. At least, until I got the schedule memorized, at which time it became boringly routine.

Monday—leftover donuts and pastries and shit from this town bus that comes by.

Tuesday—this is when the cops come through doing their parole sweeps, so everybody clears out and heads for the therapeutic center, where you get twenty-two dollars for your plasma.

Wednesday—the hot dog man comes. Yay.

Thursday—the Salvation Army brings stuff folks have donated. Mostly gloves, socks, and blankets.

Friday—some church bus comes by, bringing whatever they got.

Saturday—a different church, and we have this huge smorgasbord of great stuff, but they stamp your hand so you only get one turn. Gyp.

Sunday—the congregation of this Chinese church sets up two huge monster speakers, hands out tickets, and they preach this sermon we have to listen to before we can eat...but when it's over, good God *damn* do we eat.

The park is right next to this Greyhound city bus station, and it's got an armory, pavilions, bathrooms, a rose garden where the fags hang out, and sleeping bags all over the place. If you want to sleep inside the armory, you have to beat a mad rush when this horn blows to get in and secure a spot. Chivalry, of course, is not dead, so what you do is get an area and sign this list, writing down whatever chicks and hangers-on that comprise your own homeless entourage, and give them the spot to sleep in, then you squeeze in with them. Women and children first. Sometimes you manage, sometimes you sleep outside.

There was this old grizzled dude I'd talk to who said he preferred sleeping outdoors. Said that my hotel only had four stars, but his had a thousand. It might've been profound and inspiring if he

302

didn't say it fifteen times a night. Another place to sleep was the Santa Monica Pier, but I never made it there. They burn bonfires at night underneath it, I hear.

In this lifestyle, there are no real friendships. Bonds are formed quickly and dissolve even faster. This life is a whirlwind, and every day is measured by how many seconds you remain alive and not in jail. There is no trust, no honesty, but you can find a perverse, backward camaraderie among the other desperate liars and cut-throats you throw in with. A life less ordinary. Fuck.

My third week in L.A., I made my way to a place called Covenant House. I'd heard of it long ago, a chain of charity buildings started by a Jesuit in Manhattan who opened his door to runaways. Another one popped up in Fort Lauderdale, then Houston, New Orleans, Hollywood, and so on, giving showers to the dirty and cots to the tired. He was forced to quit when someone accused him of being a pedophile, but others happily took over for him. Right now, I needed a place like this. I still had some money, a few grand that I hadn't packed away, but it wouldn't be enough to last.

I was on Western, headed towards Sunset, when I saw a man on the sidewalk killing his dog. A little brown and gray terrier.

The guy wasn't very tall, but his shock of graying hair spiked up so high that he seemed like he was. Behind him, coming the opposite way, another guy about my age, tall with a mohawk and camouflage pants on, was staring just as angrily as I felt I was. The skinny freak was picking the dog up, and dropping it again, over and over.

My eyes locked with the other guy's, and he nodded. I quickened my pace to reach the dog-killer at the same time as the tall dude in the wife-beater and cammies, and as we came within range, we struck. My fist cracked the bastard in the jaw at the same time he was hit in the back of his head. The other guy's punch was so much stronger that the man we hit pitched forward, stumbling into me.

His crusty eyelids were scrunched into slits, pain twisting the crinkled gray parchment-like skin of his ugly face. I pushed him away, and the other guy pushed him back.

"What are you doing to my dog?" I asked. Shove.

"What are you doing to *my* dog?" Shove.

I bitch-slapped the asshole, and handed him to the guy with the cammies, who dragged him to the front door of the tenement we stood in front of.

"You live here? Answer me!"

The man nodded.

"You're giving me the AKC registry. Show me where your place is." With another shove, he rammed the man into the door and pushed him through. I stood outside, holding the terrier's leash and wondering where this situation was going.

The other dog-lover was tall and muscular, heavily tattooed, with a strange mohawk. His widow's peak was the point of an arrow, the shaft curving over his tanned pate and tapering to a point at the base of his skull. His goatee was also an arrow, what the French call an Imperial, the mustache being the barbs and point. I guess he wanted everyone to focus on his nose when they looked at him. Regardless of why, it was pretty cool-looking.

Tattoo-wise, besides a Reich Adler with a peace sign instead of a swastika, he wore three Latin inscriptions in Old English: *Veritas* on one shoulder blade, *Æquitas* on the other, and *In hoc signo vinces* in an intricate Celtic cross in between them.

I scratched the dog behind his ears and told him everything would be all right. His sad brown eyes stared up at me gratefully.

A minute later, the mohawk came back out and said we weren't cutting the dog in half, so we probably ought to flip for it. I laughed, and he held up a quarter.

"Evan," I said, shaking his hand.

"Seth. Heads or tails?"

"Tails never fails."

He flipped and caught it. I won.

"Now, what the hell am I going to do with him?"

"Give him a name and take him home."

"I don't have a home. I'm on my way to Covenant."

"Ha! You don't stink enough. You're not gay, are you?"

"No! Hell, no!"

"Good. C'mon, let's go."

I followed him to the corner of Hollywood and Western, where Gothic prison gates guarded the door of an arcade. I thought we were headed to the brown audio school across the highway when we got to the overpass, but he pulled me onto an exit ramp instead.

"Almost home," he said. This was the bridge I had crossed earlier, when I still had a car, and lost sight of Angelica. We got to an abutment, which Seth vaulted over. What in the...?

"Hold on, don't slip," he warned, reaching over and taking the dog from me. "I don't really live here so much as haunt the place."

Perplexed, I vaulted over and followed him. He pointed towards the wall.

"Remember the Three Billy Goats Gruff?"

Spray-painted in red on the side of the bridge was "The Trolls."

"Dammit, if we're trolls, we oughta have a toll booth."

I just stared at him, wondering what the hell he was talking about. Then, he showed me. In the gloom on the underside of the bridge were thirty-something mattresses, a bonfire pit surrounded by couches, and seven people. I couldn't believe it.

"Most of the beds are taken," Seth said. "But I'll find you one. Most of us are still out trying to panhandle, or working up at the labor pool."

The width of the bridge was four lanes, and a steep drop lengthwise went to the pavement, where cars were whining past at ungodly speeds.

"Is this…the Bridge?" I asked. Seth laughed.

"Sure is."

"The Bridge that the Chili Peppers sang about?"

"Yep. And you seem like a decent guy, so you can stay here, with us."

Oh my God. Hollywood Hardcore, and I'd walked right into it. I'd heard about it from drifters I sold to back home, read about it in books, and now, here I was.

Under the fucking Bridge. Damn.

"Who's that, Seth?" a girl asked. She was a late teen, clean-cut, well dressed, with a big nose and long black hair.

"My new best friend. Amanda, Evan. Evan, Amanda. We just saved this dog from a fucking psycho."

"Awwww, what a purdy doggie," she cooed. While she pattered it, Seth filled me in. Amanda was a Punk in spirit, but not appearance. She always came from her parents' house with supplies, and was passed around from one guy to the next. "On the house," she called it. She wore a perfume that didn't match her looks at all, but might've fit her self-estimate. And she kept grabbing my crotch as she talked to the dog.

"Over there, on the other side," Seth told me, pointing down the length of the bridge, across the road. "Live nothing but crack heads who trick and cop down the road. But don't worry about them. They know better than to come over here. Salvation Army feeds us, a few other people give us food, like the high school on weekends, but mostly we rob fags who turn tricks out on the strip. That's what I was coming back from when we ran into each other. Want a drink?"

We sat down on one of the couches and cracked a bottle of vodka. Getting comfortable, and also feeling that I should show I was dangerous, I pulled the nine out my jacket, setting it beside me. Seth didn't even glance at it.

We drank and talked, drank and talked and by the time people were starting to flood the place, Seth and I had become pretty good friends. He said nothing about his past, and I didn't push the issue. Vodka loosens my tongue a bit, and I found myself telling him everything he wanted to know. And quite a few things he didn't. Basically, giving me a bottle of Smirnoff is a huge mistake unless you happen to have a lot of spare time on your hands.

When the place was crawling with punk rockers, Seth told everyone about me and the dog, and I was warmly greeted by every freak there. Maybe it wasn't such a bad place after all. Covenant people came by to feed us at midnight.

We did home invasions at this hot pink apartment building near Capitol Records, got $550 apiece, then went off to some place called Tommy's on the corner of Hollywood and Wilcox, two blocks from the police station. It was a burger joint, run by an old Mexican and his spawn. There were many people there, just hanging out, but hardly anyone ate. Seth did a head count and bought everyone a Tommy Burger. God *damn*, they were good. The only thing better was an "Okie Dog."

The place was so loud that you couldn't hear at first, but when everyone realized Seth had the floor, they turned and gave him their undivided attention. Apparently, he was respected around here. He told everyone about me and the dog, said I was a stand-up guy and worthy of their friendship.

Whatever that was worth, I thought. Seth was cool, and he was strong, but it seemed like he was buying their friendship with his charity.

Giving money to beggars he didn't know. Or maybe he just did it because nobody else had.

It seemed like I'd have to totally reverse my opinions of the homeless, recalibrate my view of sanity, now that I was one of society's rejects. When Seth got off his soapbox, we ate more and talked in a corner booth. I asked him if this life's attraction was philosophical or desperation.

"Half and half," he said. "Many come out to the Bridge looking for shelter, trying to escape the world. It's comfortable enough on the fringes of society. Every day is an adventure, instead of a nine-to-five routine. Life never gets boring. See, the higher civilization climbs, with it rises the suicide rate. If you reduce yourself to barbarism, it's impossible to get bored."

"It's the easiest thing in the world to give up and die."

"Yeah. But when you separate yourself from all the complications we've inflicted upon ourselves *to make life simpler*, then you find a reason to keep going. It's almost like becoming a hermit, only we're all from LA, we couldn't possibly return to Nature because we don't know shit about it. I can build a fire. That's it."

"You don't talk the way I expected a Punk would."

"I'm smarter than the average bear," Seth conceded modestly. "Many of us are. And we were smart enough to see that the civilized world was suffocating us with its bullshit. I've been to college. Majored in business and was going to be one of those nine-to-five guys. You know, keeping up with the Joneses. But I got into this clique instead of a frat, and they got me reading Thoreau, Hiaasen, and Palahniuk. They taught me how to think for myself instead of becoming one of those automatons who just chant 'Think for yourself, question authority' while still mindlessly following some other guy's orders."

"Tyranny changing hands does not equal freedom." I said, trying to sound like I knew something.

"Exactly. And a lot of us here understand that. We'd been blindly abiding by customs and tradition even though they anchored us. Some guy, long ago, established a set of rules. Since we don't know who he was and never even think of him as a mortal, fallible man, just like us, we think of his establishment as 'Institutions' and 'Etiquette' and 'Sophistication.'"

"I'd been thinking about that, too," I said, awakening the cobwebbed corner of my mind. "I just never was able to put it into words. All my life, I've been questioning even the simplest things, seeing them as sheer stupidity and nonsense."

Seth grinned, seeming excited that he'd met someone who he

307

wouldn't need to preach to. "Such as?"

"Marriage. You need to do everything *properly*, which is just mimicking someone who did it a certain way before you. In the Bible, man, you just took the woman into your tent and made her your wife. Now, you need a fucking license!"

"I know, that pisses me off, too. It's so the government can tax it. They find ways to tax everything."

"I know! They make you pay them to do even the most natural things in the world. Like being born, for Christ's sake! You need a certificate to verify that you exist, and when you die, your family has to pay to dispose of you. You can't be buried under your favorite tree or—hey. There was a book my last girlfriend made me read, called *Shogun*, about the Japanese in the 17th century. And the woman who started Geisha wrote her death poem, and it was the coolest thing I'd ever heard. It was simple, and as generous as you could get, so unselfish. She said 'When I die, don't burn me, don't bury me, just throw my body on a field to fatten some empty-bellied dog.'"

"Damn," Seth said, grinning.

"Yep. You can't do that anymore. Instead, we waste millions of acres to store the dead, fertilizing land that we never use for agriculture. We line oak and bronze coffins with the finest satins and silks when the living go unclothed. We mark gravesites with monuments of marble when the living go unsheltered."

"And why?" he asked, eager to jump back into the role of lecturer. "Because those who established the establishment had family and friends in these businesses, and they made sure they could never go hungry by forcing us to use their goods. It's graft, but even though we know that, we still blindly obey them."

"You know what I want done with my body?" I said when I had a chance to. "I want to be stuffed. I want a taxidermist to do whatever it is that he does and have me posing in my kids' library or den. You ever seen a stuffed bear? He's usually standing up on his hind legs, the claws out on his forepaws as he's reaching for you, and he's got this really fierce snarl on his face. That's how I want to be when I go."

"That'll definitely be appropriate in my dad's study. He's got jaguar pelts, leopard and zebra skins, the stuffed heads of antelope looking at you outta the wall. All kinds of antelope, too. Eland, kudu, hartebeest, you name it. And skulls! There's this thing on the

308

Internet—Skulls Unlimited —that'll sell you the real skull of almost any animal, and museum-quality replicas of everything else. Like human skulls. You can't use a real human skull for a bookend for some reason, but you can get a pretty convincing fake one. My favorite skull in my old man's house: a babirusa. Ugliest motherfucker I've ever seen. It's a kind of boar."

"I've always wanted to make a bong out of an enemy's skull. There are people in Calcutta, the Aghori, who are allowed to live on cremation grounds, and the only thing they own is a burned-up skull that they turn into a bowl. But I'd love to smoke weed out of some asshole's skull, filling his brain cavity with smoke, stinking bong water where his thoughts used to be."

"What the fuck is an Aghori?"

"Worshippers of Shiva, the Destroyer. The most untouchable of the untouchables. They're like fucking roaches. They live in filth and feed off of nothing but the dead."

"That's disgusting. I thought we Punks were the untouchables here, but even we draw the line."

"You guys think you're untouchable because that's what you want to be. You're not outcasts, you cast yourselves out. You just like having mainstream, whitebread people be scared of you."

"No, Evan, those are Goths. The pathetic nerds who pretend to be evil so they'll stop being bullied. We Punks may dress this way, while they limit themselves to black but still try to be as weird as us, but we do it so that we can be ostracized (how's that for a word?) while they think they'll be feared. Vampire make-up and shitty music. *They're* the ones you're talking about. We aren't scared, like they are. We're mad as hell."

"So, this is why you're all moved under a bridge?"

"Sadly, no. Only a few of us. The rest are vagrants and drifters, who've found a home among good people. They get addicted to the life, to the camaraderie, but they never really understand the whole message behind it. Me, I had trouble reconciling my habits with my income."

"You were an addict."

"Still am."

"And you can see the bullshit everywhere else, but not in what you do?"

He looked down at the soda cup in his hand, as if stung by hearing someone else say what he'd known.

"You try heroin sometime," he said. "And see if you have any willpower over it."

"No thanks. I've sold it to many people, and I saw what it did to them." I thought of Bundy and Tunafish. God, that seemed so long ago.

"It wasn't just scag that made me throw it all away, though. Listen, I'm going to confess something." He paused to sip some of his Coke, grimaced when he tasted mostly water. "There are dozens of companies who make or break trends, who decide what's hot, what's not.

"One of them, three times every year, pick what it considers 'cool people' using a screening exam. Their agents recruit in high schools, video stores, coffee shops, et cetera. They find three hundred people who they think can set or spot trends, then give them the power to crush the work of hundreds of thousands of laborers with their opinions, banishing some product into obscurity just because they think its popularity should be ended, on a whim.

"Another one, they handpick kids based on peer-to-peer references and give them digital cameras, call them 'field correspondents' and turn them loose.

"They're uploading pictures they take all over the place of anything at all. See some little kid wearing those cheap sunglasses with the red plastic frames bent into hearts, think 'Ooh, that's so cute!' and *boom!* all of a sudden it has trend potential. But something that was all the rage yesterday, because a few of the other kids said 'Ooh!' and everyone scrambled to buy one for themselves and each of their kids, some other kid says 'Eww, that is so over' and just as quickly it's garbage. Wasted money, wasted effort. Great for the economy, sure, but shit for the parent trying to keep his kids from getting laughed at in school for having the wrong clothes on. Paycheck's gone and the young'uns are still whining.

"Take anything at all, pick something at random...this soda cup in my hand. So common, but if you think about it, imagine how much work was involved in this coming to be here filled with Coke. It's made of cardboard, which is made by pasting a bunch of sheets of paper together. Think about the guy doing the pasting, day in, day out. And who cut down and processed the tree to make the paper, and who made the equipment they did it with? And who made the glue that he's using? And after it's stiff enough, who put it in the printer to put this design on it? And who came up with the

310

design? And where'd the ink come from? And who packaged it and who drove it here to give it to the guy who filled it with Coke and handed it to me? And don't get me started on the *Coke*. I mean, *Christ*, that's a whole new ball a' wax.

"By the way, this particular company that has all these kids working for them? Says kids are the ages fourteen through thirty. One of the two founders, this Asian chick, said 'Thirty is different now. Thirty is really thirty-five." Like saying gray is the new black. The fuck does that mean? Left is the new Up! Toads are the new frogs! Boysenberry's the new watermelon! The fuck does that *mean?*"

"Hey, what about the starlets right here in Hollywood?" I asked. He took on a pained but long-suffering look, like he was being patient with a child to finish talking, but I said my piece. "Few years ago every one of them had to have a yappy Chihuahua, and then getting knocked up was the thing to do, and every one of them sported a big ol' belly. Now all those babies are born, so babies are the new Chihuahuas."

He nodded in a perfunctory gesture of appreciation, and continued as if I hadn't said anything at all.

"Okay, so, using the Net, these people send in their ideas of what's cool—not even their ideas, because somebody else did it and they just took a picture—and also, the company can email them all lists of product names and get them to vote instantaneously. These people get paid cash or free product samples, and—"

"Time out, dude. How do you know all this stuff?"

"Because I used to be one of them, those kids. A 'field correspondent.' This lady Irma, she's the one who started it, and she's the one who started that fad of women wearing diamond rings on their right hands. You've seen those ads?"

"Yeah?"

"That's her. She noticed that there were a lot of single women over thirty. Means people weren't getting married so much anymore. At least, *real* marriages weren't happening as much. Same-sex ones were, but I'll get back to that. She sees marriage on the decline, so she goes to the diamond people and tells them she knows engagement ring sales are going south. Pitches this idea of convincing women to buy diamonds rings to show their independence, and what do you know? They actually fall for it.

"Irma also told Time Magazine—when was it? This is im-

311

portant. September...shit. First week of September, back in `03. She predicted it would be strippers who'd start setting the trends. She said 'Strippers have become hugely important.' That's a quote. She said 'I think we'll see pole-dancing on ESPN in five years.' Do you remember what happened?"

"No, I don't keep up with stripper news."

"Well, that very same month, only a couple weeks later, city council here unanimously bans strippers getting within six feet of customers. This city council. LA. She said it from SoHo, but LA is the epicenter of the porn industry, a multi*billion*-dollar industry, and we've got a lap dance ban. A champagne room ban. A *tipping* ban. You can't walk up to the stage and slip a bill into some cooze's garter. You do that, you, she, and the proprietor all face up to six months' time and twenty-five hundred in fines.

"San Fernando Valley, owner of the Frisky Kitty got a quote in, asking if there were no lap dances, who's going to come in? Other cities and even some countries are following our lead, trying to cut down on prostitution. And don't tell me there's no prostitution in titty bars because I've seen strippers blow a guy for ten bucks right next to where I was sitting. Maybe not in Scores, but not in a dive, either. Ten fricking dollars, man. That's what a fix is worth to some people. But because of this ban, that came coincidentally right after Irma predicted the country getting even more depraved, the strippers have to get even more creative, finding ways to make money under the table when the table is much closer to the floor. And what do you know? The country gets more depraved.

"Now, consider how trendy homosexuality has become since the Nineties. Everywhere we look, we can see two chicks making out. Ooh, that's so hot, right? Poster sales every Wednesday, fall quarter on every college campus, you can't miss the two underage-looking girls making out. Bands fronted by two underage-looking girls who dyke-out onstage and in their videos. In PG-13 movies. On primetime network TV. In high school curricula, for Christ's sake."

"But dude, come on! Two chicks? How can you say that's not hot?"

"You're missing it, man. First it's the two girls, until we're so used to it we don't even pay attention anymore—"

"Ha! The day I don't notice two—"

"Will you shut up, already? You're the case in point here!

312

Gradually the bar's going to be raised until they can get away with selling posters of two naked guys together on campus."

"What? Never!"

"Mark my fucking words. The first one makes its appearance and there'll be an outcry, but all the queers have to do is shout Double Standard. We're being maneuvered into place right now. Already they have gay guys on primetime network TV, programming us to think they are cutesy and funny and have all the style. Same-sex marriages are popping up all over the place, here and in Canada. See how quickly public opinion has become not only accepting, but even supportive of deviance? These are symptoms of civilization's crumble, and they would have been unthinkable fifty years ago.

"So that's marriage down the tubes and taking the country down with it. Two guys can get married, while normal couples aren't anymore, both of which happening in rising numbers. Out of that comes the root of every major pathology, more significant than race or poverty—the lack of proper parenting." He started counting off his fingers. "We got truancy, drug addiction, violent crime, unmarried pregnancy, even suicide and wanton-indiscriminate-murder-then-suicide. The divorce rate is so high now that marriage means nothing. How do you think that relates to children? They need a mother and a father, and it has to be their own mother and father, not some trade-in for a different parent of equal or lesser value.

"That's why I abandoned civilization, like a rat swimming from a sinking ship. From here, I do everything I can to undermine the sickness that is rotting our foundation. In my works, hopefully, enough of a stink can be raised to call attention to how desperately our culture needs readjustment. How desperately we need to undo the damage that people deciding what was cool have brought about."

"You think these trendsetters are to blame?"

"Partially, the same way I believe the birth-control pill was responsible for all this bullshit in the first place. One supposedly harmless pebble that began a snowball that became an avalanche. These trendsetters are a cast-off that began a huge snowball of their own. That lady I mentioned? Irma? She was also a strong supporter of Hip-hop and cholo."

Ahhh. Cholo. Something Domingo and I saw much of but managed to stay away from, Hispanic subculture—or street subculture I should say—of lowriders, multiple sex partners, tattoos, and...yadda yadda yadda.

"But *you* have tattoos and—" I began.

"You forget, I'm undercover."

So there it is. My new friend was either a hypocrite, or insane. My diagnosis: insane. But probably right, all the same.

"I dunno about parenting being a major cause of crime," I told him. "Or really race or poverty either, because I had both my parents, who never hit me, we were not 'well-off,' but comfortable enough, and I'm white."

"Back up. You said your parents never hit you."

"Well, they spanked me a little when I was a tot, sure, but not when I grew up. They wouldn't dare touch me then."

"First of all, you never grew up."

"Seth, in my life I had to grow up quick."

"I've heard that so much it nauseates me. People who say it, they're always still kids. And your parents wouldn't dare hit you?"

"Yeah. That's right."

"You were brought up not having to face the main consequence of misbehaving. So what if your punishment is being made to stand in a corner for fifteen minutes, or go to your room? It doesn't hurt. It's not a punishment, it's an inconvenience. And that's how kids like you grow up: unafraid of consequences in the real world, irresponsible and blameless. You don't see any authority, not even God. Christ, you're all raised on video games and thinking that no matter how fucked up things get, even if you die, you can always press restart. God said spare the rod, spoil the—"

"*God* said! The Bible was written by men and you know it."

"Don't change the subject. You think you can distract me like that, I'll forget what I was saying so you can be off the hook?"

"Christ, with me, all you have to do is hold up your keys and jingle them. I'll stop in mid-sentence to look and admire the shiny noise makers."

"Fucking rodent, that's what you are. A *varmint*." He reached over the table and ruffled my hair, took a sip of his Coke. The liquid that came up the straw was completely clear now, and his face screwed up in revulsion. He gagged theatrically, clawing at his throat.

"Refill?" I asked.

"Nah, it's time to be heading back."

"What's the plan?"

"Take over the world."

"Really."

"Yep. Least, you drink enough whiskey, you can think the world belongs to you. Come on."

I'd changed the subject and managed to distract him. I didn't want to think about it right now, how I'd gone from a home to a couch to a pad of my own to a sleeping bag under a bridge, and tried to convince myself that it was a Life. I'll think about that later, but for now, I'm off the hook.

For now.

We went back to the Bridge and partied until dawn. There were several stereos, because apparently, whichever one that was playing inevitably got shot full of holes when the angry music went to somebody's head. There were drugs galore, and plenty of liquor. And even a little respect and consideration, because it was a rule that as soon as the first punk passed out, the music was turned down.

We had a few blacks among us who had tall mohawks. Being black must save them a fortune on hair gel, I thought. I spoke to one of them, and he told me that while Punks were against racism, the ones at least in this area couldn't help but hate niggers, like those that I'd seen earlier by Tommy's. He was rebelling against the way they tried to make him live and dress and act. Especially the ones who called themselves Africans as if they could pass for what their ancestors had been.

"African, huh? They dressing and *acting* African? Then lemme ax you this: why ain't they stretchin' they necks out wit rings? Like you can see in National Geographic? Puttin' another ring in once in a while til they got twenny of 'em? Or stretchin' they lips by fittin' plates 'tween 'em an' they gums, paintin' an' scarrin' they bodies, stickin' bones through they noses, an' wearin' grass? Try to imagine an au*thennick* African rapper, his words drowned out by the clackin' of his lip plates every time he shouts "party people!" or "pass the papaya, please!" Imagine a sistah doin' that chicken neck thing with her head when it's thirteen fuckin' inches from her shoulders. *That's* black style, untainted by the White Man, but why don't I see it on BET or in the projects?"

I had no idea what to tell him, so I shrugged and pretended to see someone I knew calling to me.

I talked to a girl who would've been gorgeous without all the makeup and liberty spikes, and told her so. But she didn't want to listen to reason. She told me that it was her way of showing everyone who she was inside. I argued that even though they dressed that way to be un-trendy, they were just following another trend. You can't show your nonconformity by conforming.

That's when she let me have it.

"Now check this out. I couldn't believe my fuckin' ears when I heard about this. Your foot has nineteen muscles in it, twenty-six bones, one hundred seven ligaments, and thirty-three joints, and every mile you walk will put more than one hundred thousand pounds of pressure on it. You need your feet and every part of them to work perfectly if you expect to go anywhere. You with me on this?"

I nodded, not knowing where she was going, but definitely with her.

"Good. Now, until a short while ago, the Chinese made their women bind their feet from childhood, the way a lot of savages make their little girls wear lip plugs, lip plates, rings around their necks, and weights in their ears so they grow up looking like some kind of freak in a Dr. Seuss book."

I winced, thinking about Maya, but let it slide. "I know what you mean. The Mayans used to bind their babies' skulls to reshape them."

She nodded. "So you see what I'm saying. Now, Chinamen wanted their women to hobble around on tiny feet, so they'd bind them to stunt their growth. We think that's fucking barbaric, but still we have *our* women wearing high heels, which can fuck up not only the foot, but also the knee, the pelvis, the back, even the shoulder and *jaw*, for Christ's sake! Back in `91 a study showed ninety percent of women will wear shoes two sizes too narrow, and another one in `93 showed that over eighty percent of all foot surgeries were done on women, mostly because they wore their shoes too tight. But this is just where it starts!

"These days, more and more women need surgery done to correct surgeries they've already had. Cosmetic surgery. Fake tits, face lifts, nose jobs, tummy tucks and liposuction weren't enough for them. Now they're having parts of their toes chopped off! That costs twenty-five hundred per toe, or they can get collagen injections at five hundred dollars, and God knows what else! The one in charge is Suzanne Levine from Institute Beauté in New York, who said she is, and I quote 'simply fulfilling a need, a need to wear stylish shoes.' A *need?*

"You see what fashion has done to us? Because shoes are now fucking icons of cultural status, women have surgeries that undermine the structure of their fucking feet and cause horrible pain! Did I miss the fucking boat here? Even trying to remove a bunion or inject collagen can seriously damage nerves so that you can't wear *any* shoes anymore except sneakers, and even that will hurt like a bitch. They cripple themselves in the long term for the honor of wearing this new season's Jimmy Choos or Manolo Blahniks. "Toe cleavage." Fuck.

"And the doctors that do this to them are encouraging them to do it because whyyyyy? Because it's not going to be covered by managed care anytime soon, that's why! They make a killing!

"What all of this 'fashion' amounts to is us telling our women they are not beautiful, and cannot be so unless they buy this or that bullshit product. They color their hair with dyes, color their faces with makeup, do their eyes with fake contacts, and their skin with bleaches or pigments. Get this! You know how we white people are so worried about being darker? Getting skin cancer from tanning beds and sun worshipping, spraying on Tan In A Can, or swallowing melanin pills?

"Trying desperately to be dark and look like we work outside in the sun, doing honest, honorable work instead of whatever bullshit job we *call* Work? Well, guess what? Just like we have ads in the back of our magazines advertizing the latest in skin-darkening products, the Central and South American magazines I've seen have skin-*bleaching* ads! I guess so they look like they don't *have to* work out in the sun like common, hard-working peasants. You believe that? The white people want to be brown and the brown people want to be white!"

"What color do the Asians want to be?"

"Dunno. I think they're above that, just happy being yellow."

"With scrunched-up feet?"

"Oh, no, they don't do that anymore. They abolished it."

"Well, how long do you think it'll be before the colors we already have won't be good enough for anybody and we end up with people who are candy-striped or tie-dyed? Or better yet, all neoned-out like their cars are, with implants under their skin? You brought up Dr. Seuss. How long before we have a real live bunch of Star-Bellied Sneetches?"

"You lost me on that one, buddy. But I see where you're going. I thought we'd already found all the ways to change ourselves in every way we could think of, until this shit with the feet started. I've heard they've got voice lifts, too, cosmetic surgery done on the vocal cords to make someone's voice sound younger, but I've only just *heard* about it. I don't have anything concrete on that yet. Changing the color of your hair, eyes, lips, cheeks, fingernails and complexion, and changing the shape of your head, face, ass, belly, tits if you're a woman, dick if you're a man, all this change wasn't enough. We had to go after the feet, too. I wondered what could possibly be next. Well, I found out."

"...And?"

"And I threw up my hands in disgust, turned away from society and came here, to the Bridge. I didn't want any part of it anymore, this bullshit world. You'll never guess what it was."

"...What?"

"I looked into the files of the US Patent Office. Since it opened it's issued more than six and a half *million* patents. The US Patent Commissioner all the way back in 1899 said that "Everything that can be invented has been invented." He thought. That was more than a hundred years ago, and I don't think they had a *radio* yet. Think of all the shit we've come up with since then! But even all this we're not satisfied with. We must invent more solutions for stupidass needs because we keep inventing stupidass needs, like the 'need' to wear stylish shoes. Well, I was astounded to find out that as soon as toe cleavage has become passé, when someone out there decides what the next dumb attribute must be, a certain fellow will become filthy fucking rich after his long, long wait."

"...Who?"

"The guy that—I swear I'm not making this up—"

"Tell me, God damn you!"

She laughed. "The guy who invented and patented a device that artificially produces dimples."

At that moment my brain seized up, and I froze for I don't know how long.

Finally, I managed "Dimples?"

318

"I shit you not."

"But...but why in the—?"

"Took the words right outta my mouth. And I'll tell you what'll be the next one after dimples, and may lightning strike me if I'm wrong. Take one guess. One guess, come on."

"Oh, Christ—"

"All right, I'll tell you. Look at all the pop stars and all their teeny-bopper disciples running around in their lowrider jeans and baby tees. All the girls have to show off their bellybutton, and the navel ring they got to accentuate it. Well, what if you don't have a good-looking navel? I can hear the stupid bitches whining now. 'Doctor, belly-button rings are out, now, but the tiny shirts are still in, *and outies are what's really in*. What am I going to do? Only the girls with outies are getting the boys!' And here's the good doctor. 'There, there, now, Tiffany, don't you cry. I'll inject your widdle belly-button with silicone and fix you right up!'"

I stared at her, speechless.

Every movement needed its foot soldiers, the cannon fodder that charged in the first wave to take all the bullets, and she was doomed to be one of them.

From observing Seth that night, I saw that he thought he was a bad guy, that he was evil in his head, but everyone else saw him as Robin Hood. He described himself as "Seth McHale, the scourge of...just about anywhere, really." The muscle head skater punk wanted to be considered a villain, but he just had too much heart.
Thank God he could never become a Nestor de Medieros. He was too thoughtful of others. He had no idea what real evil was like; just what California showed him. Good thing, too, because the last thing the world needs is a bunch of Darth Vaders.

The next morning, we got free bus passes from this guy Steve down at the Day Center. The place is an open bay dorm for the homeless, with donuts, coffee, a TV, and lockers next to the cots. Yeah, better than living under a bridge, but it just didn't have the atmosphere.

We took a Santa Monica bus to Venice Beach, about an hour and a half trip. Seth had a membership card for the weight pile, and I paid thirty-five dollars to join and work out with him and Hulk Hogan, who was a pretty cool guy. I missed Domingo's "Get Thick Program" but I tried not to think about it. We used to go to the gym almost every day, working hard, sweating like pigs, and admiring the girls on the Stairmasters.

I saw a lot of celebrities, and a lot of huge bastards whose necks were thicker than their heads. I have no intention of ever getting that big, being one of those guys who can't wear normal clothes. A bunch of them could bench six hundred pounds, but couldn't do twenty chin-ups. Maybe they could work down at the train station, lifting the cars and moving them from one track to another, but that's about it.

When we got back to Hollywood, we went to the biggest McDonald's I'd ever seen. *Damn*, it was huge. Three stories tall and just *packed*. Seth pointed out a bunch of Trolls I hadn't seen before. Apparently, Hollywood Hardcore was much bigger than I thought it was.

The sun was setting, and I still hadn't slept. Didn't matter. All the protein food and carbo drinks we had down at Venice Beach, plus the promise of another fun night of drunkenness and robbery, had me going strong. I wasn't running on fumes, the way I would sometimes on cocaine binges. This was a natural high of excitement. Let the sharks come.

We had stopped by a fag/dyke center that was right by the bus station, much to my embarrassment, where we acted gay and accepted friendly offerings of all kinds of free shit. Stuff like thrift store clothing vouchers, food coupons, all kinds of stuff. I guess it was part of their "We've got to stick together" campaign.

If Maya and Mariana had ever seen this, they'd laugh their asses off. That kind of thinking was dangerous, Maya had once told me. Those obsessed with sex, especially homosexuality and sadomasochism, allowed one small need of the body, one facet of their personalities, to become their entire identity.

But then, later on at Mickey D's, we encountered some people who'd let music take over their lives. The windows started to rattle. Just like the day Esteban Ribeira took the bullet I managed to dodge, we could all *feel* the "gangstas" coming, long before we heard them. Faces twisted in anger as the bass outside interrupted their good time. Apparently, this happened often.

Seth and I went outside, saw the assholes packed in their ridiculously "pimped-out whips," doing slow drive-bys just to annoy us. The crowd in the parking lot was watching them come around the block, again and again, until a few guys opened fire. Tires squealing, the hotrods screeched off, and Seth said it was time to go. Fast. They were 18th St. Crip cars.

We split to the liquor store, got ourselves a few bottles off the top shelf. Seth, as it turned out, was twenty-three. In the parking lot, around the back, we scored some liquid acid. At Tommy's, some heroin and a bit of skunk weed to take the edge off, and at the butcher's, food for the day. Then, home with the goodies. Seth called it the Cop n' Bop, because we copped the shit and then bopped on outta there. Following dinner he'd do the Plunge n' Purge, which he didn't explain. I'd find out all about that later.

I met two sisters from Zulfiqar, runaways, who called themselves Rat and Raven. They'd gladly cast off their *burkhas* for some punk gear, no longer having to hide their femininity under them. I had a soft spot for Muslim women, since they really got the shit end of the stick. Rat and Raven had gone a bit overboard with the makeup and the piercings, but who could blame them? Anything that was a way of giving their culture the Finger was all right by me.

Their piece of shit father, nouveau riche barbarian that he was, had tortured them the way they told me all devout Muslims hurt their daughters. Their clits had been sliced off, for starters. 'Nuff said.

They both had waaaay too many piercings. Eyebrow spike-bends, one in Rat's left eyebrow, one in Raven's right. Nipples and navels, hood and labia, septum, tongue, and lower lip, with dog collars—those choke chains they use in obedience school—looped in upon themselves around slim brown necks, the other end hanging free. They wore these bands of makeup that ran along eye level from one side to the other, kind of like Daryl Hannah in Blade Runner and Annie Lennox and Marilyn Manson. Scarlet, fading into the yellow-orange of a half-healed bruise. It made you think that they were wearing wraparound shades, but the whites of their eyes stood out so loudly that it just looked plain weird. Freaks. Fuh-*reeks*.

The adventure scheduled for tonight was to use me, since I was the "prettiest"—and man, that pissed me off, but I had to admit they did have a point—as a decoy on Santa Monica Boulevard. We went out there, a squadron of cheerfully violent psychopaths, Seth, and me. They told me that no matter who tried to pick me up, I must turn them down unless they were obviously rich, then lead them into a nice dark parking lot where the ambush would be set.

"Don't settle for the first dipstick in a pickup truck," Seth said, as if I didn't have a brain. "Remember, Mercedes, Beamers, and nothing less."

"Just for saying that, I'm gonna bring you some kid on a bicycle. See ya when I see ya."

I stood out there for about an hour, trying to look like the rest of the johns. I was a little uncomfortable. All right, I was a *lot* uncomfortable, but I did my best to look sexy and innocent, and most of all, harmless. Looking around me, I can see exactly what the real problem with homosexuality is. Fags try too hard to be women, and dykes try too hard to be men. Especially bull dykes—the hardcore feminists, the really militant ones—so eager to show how much they hate men that they end up mimicking men's worst traits. The same way queers mince about so daintily and fuss about uselessly superficial bullshit. I think it's this gross mimicry of those superficial things that mock what is deeper. Shaving legs, sitting down to piss, stuff like that. People not loving themselves and each other for what they are, but what they cannot be. If it were just women getting with each other because men are pigs and they can't get the tenderness they long for from them, maybe I could understand. Maybe I could understand men turning to each other because they were tired of women's bullshit.

But that's not what we have here. Mariana and Domingo told me about this friend of the family who'd come over for dinner the night before, and what he had said it was.

"Look at my dick, America! It's got shit on it! Let's go to court over the shit on my dick!"

And I think he's right.

It dawned on me finally why guys seem to find lesbianism so sexy. I can't believe this wasn't obvious before. It has nothing at all to do with it being unnatural, forbidden, taboo, or anything like that. It's not appreciated as a homosexual act. Lesbian pornography is nothing special because all guys want to see is a naked woman, aroused, in heat, doing what they wish could be done with *them*, but they can't get it to happen. Her masturbating would be okay for a while, if the guy pretends it was him she was thinking of, but it gets old. He wants to see her getting *pounded*, so he could pretend *that* was him.

But unless he's queer, the sight of another man giving it to his girl affects him on a deep, subconscious, animal level. He may not know it, but he's jealous. But he wants to see her. He wants to see other women, too. Ditch the man, the interloper, get his dick out of the picture. His bigger dick and better looks.

A man will deny this. I would've before I saw through the self-deception. Another man'll say that's just a bunch of bullshit. His masculinity isn't threatened, he just plain likes to see two women get it on. He wants to see lipstick smears on pussy folds. He justifies homosexuality, but only if it's girls, because he's lying to himself.

Or maybe I'm wrong.

Maybe modern men are just sick and perverted and so used to it, so desensitized that they don't even realize they are sick and perverted. Speaking for myself, though, I don't even want to see another girl spread her legs unless she's spreading them for me. Those guys who are still lying to themselves, they'll do what all men do when one of them stops lying. They'll call him a liar.

Or some kind of fag.

Or less of a man.

But I'd say that this makes me more of a man, stepping out of the herd and thinking for myself. Not giving voice to someone else's ideas and claiming them as my beliefs. Not being a parrot, prompted by other parrots.

But hey, maybe I'm wrong.

I have been before.

I'd been "cruised" five times, until one of the cars came around a second time and pulled up in front of me. A Jaguar. *Daaaayam*. A raspberry Jaguar, Vandenplas. The passenger side window rolled down, and an older, Jewish-looking man's face appeared behind it. A *rich* older, Jewish-looking man's face.

"Excuse me," he said. "How can I get to Dempsey's?"

"Practice."

He frowned and blinked at me a second, then laughed. "Oh, I get it. Funny."

I smiled. It didn't matter that I have no idea where Dempsey's is, because he didn't really want to know. I used to start up a conversation with girls by asking "Excuse me, you got a light?" when I had a Zippo in my pocket, so it was easy to spot his pick-up line. Plus, he was really obvious about it, and now, he seemed to have forgotten all about the restaurant.

"You sure are a witty fellow."

"I've been accused of that before."

"Ha! There you go again."

Groan. Man, he was laying it on thick and heavy, but I kept smiling.

"Say, have you ever considered modeling?"

"Yeah, every day. In fact, I'm thinking about doing some right now."

"Is that right?"

"Yeah. Your place or mine?"

"Ha ha! No, really, I'm a talent scout—"

Yeah, and I'm a chimney sweep.

"—And I'm looking for some new blood. Look, are you doing anything right now?"

"Nah, just holding the sidewalk down."

"Haaaaa ha ha ha, man, I tell ya…"

"You want to go somewhere and talk? Because you can't stay here, you'll get a ticket."

"Sure," he said, leaning over to open the door. "Hop in."

After he was covered in blood and out cold, we emptied his wallet, the car, and got his address off of his driver's license. We now had his house key, so whether he had an alarm or not, it wouldn't hurt to try. One of the punks, the most disguisable one, drove the Jag off to a chop shop they knew of. In this town, it wasn't so unusual to see a freak driving an expensive car, but too much was too much. The one who had a full head of hair put on the mark's sport coat and tucked his pony-tail down under the collar.

Stripping him off all his clothes, we left Marvin S. Baker naked in the parking lot, just for gits and shiggles. Calling it a night, we all smoked a blunt on the way home, and I showed Rat and Raven a few of the things Maya had taught me.

The next night, things didn't go so well.

"Hi, I'm Kyle," the man said. He wore a wedding ring.

"I'm Jasmine."

"That's a girl's name."

"Sure is."

"Hop in, Jazz." The guy was in his mid-fifties, dressed sharp, and driving a land yacht. As much as he tried, he couldn't hide the Texas twang in his voice. He didn't seem like the kind of man who'd go for boys, but in the lunatic fringe capital of the world, anything is possible.

It was when he ignored my directions and drove right past the alley that led to the ambush that I started to feel uneasy. I asked him where we were headed.

"Home," he said with a grin. For a minute, I thought he might be just like us, picking up queers under false pretenses and punishing them someplace where he could get away with it. But I had my nine, if it came to that, and I could *capoeira* the shit out of someone his size. The only problem with using a gun was how loud it would be. The last thing I wanted to do after shooting someone was to get chased through a town I didn't know.

But Kyle kept me at ease with what he must've considered witty banter. Real funny guy, Kyle was. Oh yeah, had me rolling.

"You realize that you'll be committing a crime when we get there," he said, glancing sideways at me over the rim of his sunglasses. Yep, sunglasses. Oakleys. At night. What a cool guy.

"What? Prostitution?" I asked innocently.

"Naw, Receiving Swollen Goods."

I pretended to laugh.

"You know, I've heard worse come on lines," he told me.

"You don't say."

"I *do* say. One guy in a bar asked if I needed my stool pushed in. Get it? See I was sitting on a barstool—"

"I get it."

"How 'bout this one? I got the F, the C, and the K—"

"All I need is U," I finished for him. "You know why the alphabet's all wrong? Because U and I belong together."

"That one's kind of cheesy. Try this one…"

And that's how it went, the whole way there. We ended up at a posh hotel in Beverly Hills, where I was startled by the opulence. A valet held his door for him, and he came around the hold the door for me. Kyle did, not the valet. The valet raised an eyebrow, but said nothing as he watched me slip and slide across the glassy floor.

In the elevator—really nice elevator—he didn't try anything at all, like I was afraid he would. What impressed me even more was that he used a keycard pass to go to the top floor. Penthouse. Oh, hell yeah.

We got to the door, where he winked at me. "Home sweet home, Jazz."

And he opened the door, letting me into a posh suite that out-shone even the de Medieros' house. There was some "I'm a fucking alcoholic and I'm getting shit-faced tonight" music on the stereo, and a beautiful blonde on the couch.

She didn't even look up at us, but glared straight ahead. Portishead. That's what she was listening to. Blue music, for when you're depressed and feel like wallowing in self-pity.

Wait a second. Yeah, she was blonde, but her roots were blacker than Alex Haley's.

She was either nineteen, twenty-five, or thirty-two. It's hard to tell with Beautiful People, especially these days. She was in blue jeans and a gray sweater, curled up barefoot on the ermine couch with a glass of red wine to keep her company. The bottle, almost empty, sat on the coffee table, and she looked ready for another. Pinot Noir, I could tell from even this far away. That's what comes with dating "oenophiles" like Maya.

"Honey, I'm home!" Kyle said happily. She flinched. I felt so bad for her at that moment, and when I cut my eyes at her husband, a tendril of red mist swam across them. I swallowed the rage before it got too strong, and tried to speak calmly and politely.

"Your wife doesn't seem too happy, Kyle."

"That's on her, Jazz." He led me towards the bedroom. "I told her the first time that she could join me if she wanted, but she'd rather drink up all the wine, instead."

"So this happens regularly?"

"Of course. One night out of the week is my Freak Night, and you're my Freak. C'mon, buddy."

The blonde just stared at the balcony doors, at her own reflection in the sliding glass. She couldn't be even thirty. She had to be a trophy wife or something. Regardless, she was the man's wife. First, I had panicked when I saw her, because I knew I couldn't beat the guy up without her hearing me. But now I knew I'd be doing her a favor.

"You'd better find some louder music, honey," her husband teased. She emptied the glass in one quick swallow and reached for the bottle. He laughed and crooked his finger at me. I went.

The second he shut the door behind us, I clothes-lined him, knocking him to the floor. He gasped and wheezed, clutching at his throat, trying to scream. I pulled the nine out and shoved its barrel into his gaping mouth, choking him even more.

"You want to suck on something, Kyle?"

His eyes bulged with terror.

"C'mon, boy. Let's git nekkid."

I wanted to squeeze the trigger so bad. It was pulled halfway back and all it needed was a millimeter to drop the hammer. One millimeter to splatter his spine out the back of his neck. I loosened the trigger a little bit.

Then he heaved his legs up, trying to kick me from behind, throwing me off-balance, and the gun went off.

The shot was so loud in that room, I thought the desk clerk could hear it. Fuck! I jumped up from where I'd fallen and opened the door, forgetting until later that my fingerprints were all over it. The blonde was on her feet, staring wide-eyed with shock and horror. I wanted to tell her it was an accident, I wanted to…come to think of it, I didn't know what I wanted to do besides get the fuck out of there.

I gave up and ran for the door, shoving the pistol back into my jacket. The place would be swarming with cops before I even made it to the lobby. Fuck! I ran for the stairs, then turned back around and ran to the suite. I didn't know where the fuck to go. I was in a full-blown panic, acting like a complete idiot.

Then, I saw the fire alarm. It just seemed like a good idea at the time, so I yanked the white bar down, setting off a whining squeal. Maybe the whole building would panic like I was and I could get lost in the crowd. But a better idea came to me. I went back to the suite and opened the door as quietly as I could. Blondie was screaming bloody murder in the bedroom. I slipped in, gently shutting the door, and went to the little kitchenette.

The cupboards under the sink were large enough and fairly empty, so I squeezed myself in. It seemed perfectly logical that, since she saw me run out the door, and no one in history had ever hidden at the scene of their crime (not under the sink, anyway) the police wouldn't bother to check.

So, I hid. Cramped as hell, sandwiched in among the u-bend drainpipe and various cleansers, listening to poor Blondie scream. I listened to the muffled voices of security goons, then the police, and told myself over and over that if someone opened the cupboards and saw me, I'd count the bullets. If I couldn't possibly shoot my way out, I'd do my best and save the last round for myself.

How do I keep getting myself in these stupid situations?

My legs fell asleep quickly, and I realized how poorly I'd do in battle, standing on rubbery, boneless legs that stung with the pins and needles of returning circulation. Didn't matter. I'd never be taken alive. Not again.

So, this is the life I made for myself. Far from ordinary. Goddamn. God *damn*.

What really shocked the hell out of me was the arrival of paramedics. From what I could hear, I had blown out Kyle's epiglottis—whatever the hell that is—but somehow missed his carotid artery and vertebrae. Miraculously, he would survive, if he got to the ER in time. Christ.

A noise of hurrying medics and the rattle of a collapsible gurney obliterated what little I could hear for a minute, and then, the drone of further questioning and the wife's hysterical drunken sobbing.

Then, they left. Silence. I waited.

It may have been an unpleasant position for me, but it beat the hell out of a crackhouse crawlspace.

That's when it dawned on me that I had fled from one side of the country to the other, and still, nothing had changed. I'd told myself that I'd start a new life, but I hadn't even bothered to try. I'm still a habitually criminal nimrod. All the anarchic philosophy in the world wouldn't change the fact that I'm a...what? There are criminal masterminds, the criminally insane, what does that leave me? A criminal idiot savant? Can there be such a thing?

These are the kinds of things I'm thinking about when I'm boxed in under a fucking *sink*.

Disgusted with myself, I pushed the cabinet doors open and dragged myself out. Hearing nothing, I lay spread-out on the vinyl tiles and let my legs grow back. It took a while, and I prayed constantly to whoever there was out there who still gave a shit about me not to let Blondie come by.

Finally, wondering where the hell she was, I got up and went to the bedroom. The bloodstains had been cleaned out of the carpet by the crime scene guys or whoever, and Blondie was passed out on the queen-sized bed. *Whew*. It was hard to tell whether her gazongas were Nature's Own or Plastic Fantastic, but good God, they were nice. Wow. I went to the closet and rifled through the hanging suits. Since Kyle had a bit of a paunch, most of his slacks and trousers wouldn't fit me, but the neck and shoulder were close enough. I took a charcoal blazer and a white French cuff shirt, and managed to fit into one of Blondie's black pairs of jeans. Finding some cufflinks—silver cow skulls, believe it or not—and Kyle's black Stetson. I checked the mirror, and decided to shave, too. I needed it.

Yep. A real dipshit cowboy. All I needed now was a big-ass belt buckle with my name on it. What was it Bruce Willis said in "Die Hard"? Oh yeah.

Yippie-kai-yay, motherfucker.

I felt horrible about abandoning my leather jacket, but I couldn't carry it out. The nine didn't bulge in the shoulder holster under Kyle's blazer, so it would have to do. I ransacked the place as quietly as I could, came up with three grand in traveler's checks that would get me nowhere. I thought for a second how funny it would be to try to pay for drugs in Tommy's parking lot with them, and left.

People outside were still chattering about what had happened, so I was able to get out of the hotel with nobody paying attention to me.

My heart jumped when I passed the valet at the entrance, but all he did was a double-take and frown, not entirely sure if I was me, or not. I felt his eyes on my back as I walked off into the darkness, probably wondering why a patron of this fine hotel didn't call a taxi or summon a rental car.

Whatever went through his mind, he didn't report it, because no squad cars pulled over to the curb to give me a heart attack. I had to ask a few whores and street urchins for directions (more than once because they couldn't make their minds which way was which), and I ended up talking to quite a few complete wackos. The fact that some of these people didn't drag their knuckles when they walked made me seriously doubt Darwin's theory.

"Hollywood and Wilcox? Shee-it, man, you can't get there from here," one of them told me, a whore who might've been a man.

"I can't, huh?"

"Noooooo. You new in town?" A look of pure game, like a beast spotting potential prey, came into the tramp's eyes.

"No, I was born here. Born and raised, and I'm fucking lost in my own hometown. What do you think?"

"You got a pretty slick mouth, kid."

329

"Look, does a mountain range cut through the city, and block the way? Or is there a cliff or something?"

"What? Man, you better watch what you say."

"And you better watch who you try to run game on."

"Game? I ain't playing no game!"

"Then don't try to give me any bullshit, talk me into walking into whatever trap you've got set."

"Trap?" Her look of indignant righteousness pushed me right over the edge, and the sarcasm became fury.

"Yeah, trap, you dumb bitch! I'm a white boy, not a green one!" I knew that line would come in handy again someday.

A big, burly wigger came out of the shadows, either her pimp or a wannabe knight-in-shining-armor. He was way too big for me to beat in a fair fight. Notorious for my shitty temper and poor judgment, I pulled out the nine and knee-capped him. He hit the sidewalk screaming.

"Swole!" the whore cried, and I pistol-whipped her backhand across her painted face. I hurried angrily away, thinking there was only so much of this city I could take.

I decided to make it a personal policy to cripple anyone I met who gave themselves a stupid nickname. I've met so many wiggers who worked out, "got swelled up," and called themselves "Swole". That's almost as bad as the jackasses who called themselves "Tupac", just because they liked his music—if you could call it that.

Unfortunately, once my head cleared, I realized I'd have to shoot more than half the people under the Bridge.

I heard more stupid slang and Ebonics on my way than I could stand. God, I had to find a way out of this city.

"Tighten up," I heard over and over. "You know what time it is."

"I know what the lick read," I was mercifully told only once. As soon as I heard one guy telling another that he was giving it to him "blood raw", I made up my mind.

The sooner I got out of this dump, the better. This city welcomed the greedy and unscrupulous with open arms, throwing its door wide for thieves and killers, conmen and whores. Oh yeah, and actors. Everyone thought he was in a movie, just because he lived here.

This wasn't the first time I took the Walk That Lasts All Night, but it was the first time I hated every step of it.

"What the fuck is San Andreas waiting on?"

Seth laughed and shrugged. I'd told him the whole story, and he made me tell it again and again to everyone who woke up or came home.

"So, what? You want to split?" he asked later. He was melting into the couch, having shot up his second spoon of heroin since I got back, but he still managed to hold a conversation.

"Damn right I do. But how can I?"

"Well, there's this Home Free scam. You go down to Greyhound and tell them you're a runaway who's had second thoughts. They'll take you anywhere in the Continental U.S. for free. Tell them that your home is Bumfuck, Nebraska, boom, you've got a free ticket to Bumfuck, Nebraska."

"No. With my yellow sheet, and my face tacked up in every post office, I'd rather travel more quietly."

"Stow away on trains. Shit, I've done it."

"I'll think of something."

"Well, while you're thinking, I say we get ourselves a change of scenery. You ever been to Haight?"

"Hate?"

"Haight-Ashbury. C'mon, we're going."

"What's a Haight-Ashbury?"

At the top of Haight Street, on a hill, is Haight-Ashbury Park, a San Francisco must-see if you're on the lam. Fourteen of us, including my dog, who I still hadn't named, drove up there in a stolen van—and eight got arrested a few minutes after we ditched it. There was a fag march heading up to the Park that day, and the police thought we might cause a few problems.

Luckily, the eight Punks' arsenal was in a duffel bag this cat Radcliffe was carrying, so they didn't catch any charges. They met up with us the next day, at the San Francisco Capitol Building. Apparently, that's the meeting place for everyone when they get separated.

The place is Tent City. The Sterno Hilton, some called it. I didn't ask why hundreds of people were camped out there, and no one bothered to tell me. Japanese tourists were constantly snapping pictures of all of the vagrants, and it made me uncomfortable.

That feeling vanished, however, as soon as we had regrouped

and made it to the Park. The place was Heaven for runaways. It was filled with hippies (nouveau hippies, since the original ones had given up on peace and love long ago). Hippies and Punks, even though on two opposite ends of the spectrum, get along surprisingly well. There were already scores of punk rockers there, mingling with the flower children. Seth explained to me that the Punk Rock movement was very similar to the hippies of the Sixties and Seventies, only they'd seen it needed more aggression to be taken seriously—and it still wasn't, no matter what they tried. They were very bluntly anti-war, racism, and hypocrisy, opting for anarchy over slimy politics.

He asked me if I'd ever tripped before. I said no, I'd never had the pleasure, but I'd been curious.

"Then be warned, little buddy. After you do it once, you'll never be the same again."

"Honestly, I don't like myself all that much as it it. Maybe some change'll do me good."

"You'll look at things differently. You might end up questioning reality to the point that you doubt yourself."

"Well? What're we waiting for?"

I followed Seth's example, spreading my arms, shutting my eyes, and yelling "Dose me! Dose me!" People were rather anxious to get newcomers on the same plane they were on. Eager to bring us up on their cloud. I remembered what Pedro had said so long ago about misery loving company, but this was different. This was *so* different.

A sugar cube was popped into my gaping mouth, and a lei of flowers slipped over my head. Opening my eyes, I saw a smiling girl with an expression of love and warmth. She was barefoot, as all the girls were, in a tie-dyed dashiki and a really long skirt, with a crown of daisies on her head. She reeked of patchouli and bong water, but her smile somehow made up for that.

"You're just in time," she said.

The acid on the sugar cube was quick. It hit me while I sat in this huge circle, one of many, waiting for one of the reefers or pipes to come back around. I was feeling the elusiveness of the first hints when a calumet was passed to me. A beautifully decorated Indian peace pipe with peacock feathers hanging from the bowl. It was somehow reassuring to smoke out of such a thing with a bunch of strangers. Catching TB didn't even cross my mind. Even though most of the people here didn't know each other, they all seemed to share this feeling of...connection is the best way I can think of to describe it. Anonymous unity.

About a dozen of the hippies in that circle, scattered at random, were playing bongo drums, picking up a rhythm and all of them running with it. A skinny, hairy guy even broke out a digiridoo. It was strange, but beautiful to be there.

After the trip began, I found myself wandering from one circle to another, listening to people's songs and poetry, watching the trees breathe and the clouds melt. The thing about LSD, wherever you are, you are certain that that is the place to be. That this event, whatever's going on, is a must-see and you feel sorry for anyone who misses it.

The Park took on an atmosphere of importance, and all my knowledge of the world beyond its perimeter vanished. I thought I'd always been there, and always would be. I met people I'd never seen before and we were certain we'd been good friends forever. A girl told me that was *Anam Cara*, soul recognition. We'd met in previous lives and were glad to see each other again. It made perfect sense. At the time.

I became convinced that everything, all matter around me, was energy condensed to slow vibrations. Water was slightly faster than solid matter, and gases faster than both. That's what a vibe is, when you tap into the vibration you have in common with someone else. I congratulated myself for realizing that, having no idea that such thoughts are simply the mindfuck effect of a drug.

You become "one" with everything, and you smoke whatever you can get your hands on. I applauded Seth's foresight in bringing two cartons of Reds along. Even if you *don't* smoke, you still feel the urge, and light your next cigarette with the last one.

Speaking of Seth, he appeared and told me he'd found out The Truth: that we are all part of a single consciousness that experiences itself subjectively. I didn't know what the fuck he was talking about, but it sounded pretty good, so I agreed.

Between recognizing complete strangers and mentally masturbating with philosophers, I enjoyed the view of a new world. There were patterns in the grass and on the bark of trees that seemed like a jumble of hieroglyphic alphabet soup. Many letters I recognized, but many others were foreign: Chinese symbols, Sanskrit, Druidic runes, and the flowing Arabic.

Across this alphabet soup scampered a gajillion and two brownish-gray squirrels. Many of them I realized didn't exist, they were merely replicas of the few real ones, but they were just as cute. For no reason at all, I remembered an old guy I used to sell to named Sal (he wasn't old, just old looking, because I sold to him a little too often) and I started giggling hysterically.

The dude had told me a story once about going squirrel hunting with his brother, long ago. His brother was laughing at him because the squirrel score was Eleven to Nothing, and Sal said the only reason he hadn't killed any was because they wouldn't find squirrels in any damn *forest*. His brother laughed and told him to go look on the beach or wherever else he thought squirrels lived. Sal disappeared, and wasn't seen again until dinnertime, when his brother and parents had started to worry. The goofy little bastard came into the house with a bag full of thirty-seven dead squirrels and his small rifle unfired.

"How the hell did you get all that?" his brother asked. "Where did you find them all?"

Sal grinned his goofy, buck-toothed grin.

"At the park. There were hundreds of 'em. You hold out peanuts and they come right up to you!"

His family just stared at him.

"I didn't fire a single shot," he continued, holding up the rifle. "Didn't want to scare off the rest of 'em. So I strangled them all instead. So, what's for dinner?"

That's what I was giggling about. I couldn't stop, not for about an hour or so, and my face hurt terribly by the time I could get up and walk again.

My dog had been wet-nosing people and letting them stroke him, eagerly running off when they were done to investigate somebody else. He was harassing some birds when I decided to name him Fredo, after the good-for-nothing brother in "The Godfather." I liked that dog, but he had no sense at all. Maybe that's why his previous owner tried to kill him. Damned dog couldn't even find his own tail. To be fair, though, at that moment, neither could I.

I wandered through the park, marveling at many things that seemed unfamiliar, all of them man made, and was astonished by how glaringly artificial whey were. I got to Haight's perimeter and stared at empty bottles, gum wrappers, and glittering cigarette pack cellophane. Runny ink on a rained-on newspaper, and crinkled plastic—the kind that turned white when you bent it—cart-wheeling along the pavement like autumn leaves. Tumbleweeds of garbage.

I didn't realize how late it was, and found myself mesmerized by the dappled sunset reflecting in bloodshot windows. I got the queasy impression that buildings were alive, that skyscrapers were monsters with a thousand eyes, and all this litter was the molt from their shedding. Exfoliating dust and flakes of dried paint. I turned and ran.

I fled civilization, running back into Nature's embrace, and crashed through a thicket into a sight that stopped me dead in my tracks. Cops. Zillions of them. They stood in a wide semicircle, squaring off with the Punks. A wog with the cruelest eyes I'd ever seen was arguing in another language with Rat and Raven.

I stood petrified, the Hippies all staring with the same horror that I must have shown, but the Punks...they stood their ground with angry defiance. The twelve Trolls that I came with had been backed up by every other punk-rocker in the Park.

It took a long time, but finally the cops left, leaving the girls' father standing there with a look of impotent rage. Then, after they seemed to agree on something, the wog stormed away from Rat and Raven. Everybody relaxed, and I went to Seth for an explanation.

"The girls are eighteen and nineteen," he told me. "The cops said their father had lied to them about that. By law, they can leave home and dress out if they want to."

"He tracked them down here?"

"Apparently, one of the guys who got arrested yesterday blabbed. We don't know who, yet." He was enraged at the betrayal.

"But the cops didn't arrest any of us just now."

"Florida must really be different," he said with wry amusement. "In this state, especially this city, there are too many politics. You'd never understand."

"No...I guess I wouldn't."

Rat and Raven told us what their father said, that their mother was dying and had begged to see them one last time. They needed a ride to someplace called Rosemeade, and all the Punks volunteered to be their escort. We said good-bye to the Hippies and left. The San Francisco Punks had a unity with Hollywood Hardcore, and more than enough trucks to carry everyone in the expedition. We looked like an army of freaks on our way to a siege. I've never seen anything like it.

My acid trip had taken on an entirely new tone. I now thought that the whole world was against people who just wanted to be left alone, and we were the last platoon of rebels left. We were making a stand, and, fueled by drugs, all Hell couldn't stop us. I couldn't count the trucks in our convoy, we were that many.

The sky and the road seemed to slide away from us, meeting at the horizon, and it took a lot of reasoning and logic to convince myself that we were not going to some ethereal cloud-city. The stubborn, persistent impression still worked in the back of my mind until we got there.

Rosemeade was a shithole.

We surrounded the hotel that the girls had been told to go into. Seth and I, because we each had a recent (ahem) *history* with the girls, accompanied them into the lobby, along with Roxanne and Piggy, two other chicks who didn't dress out.

The father met us inside and said only the girls could come up. Seth said we were there to make sure they were safe. The raghead got furious, but Rat agreed to cooperate, let us all meet in the middle. The boys could wait downstairs, and Roxanne and Piggy would escort them up. We all agreed.

Seth and I sat down, watching the floor tiles melt into one another and occasionally scaring the hotel people who stared at us too long. It was the first boring moment of the whole day, and we were at that edgy, teeth-grinding stage of our acid trip. The part when you just can't stop chewing, even though you have nothing in your mouth. Seth kept raking his tongue stud from side to side. It was loud and annoying, the noise of the steel post sliding between his clenched teeth, the sight of the stainless ball at the end going back and forth in his rictus grin. He'd told me it was a stress reliever, like those two Chinese silver balls you roll around in your hand. Ha! Stress relief for you, maybe, but not for anyone in earshot.

We heard the elevator arrive, announce itself with a loud *ding!* and spill two furious hellcats out of its automatic doors.

"Motherfucker pulled a gun on us!" Roxanne barked.

"Kidnapped our friends!" Piggy was shouting at the same time. "This whole thing was a trap!"

We were on our feet that instant, guns out. Seth went to the glass front doors, kicked them open, and theatrically racked the slide on his Glock. The waiting army erupted from their seat in or on the trucks and charged the hotel. Seth and I followed Piggy up the stairs to the top floor, not bothering with the slow elevator. Elevators are deathtraps, anyway. A strange whipping noise was vibrating the walls, but we paid it no attention.

Arriving at the door, I slammed my shoulder into it the way D'ingo had taught me, tackling it and splintering it open. It hadn't been locked. The place was empty. No dying mom, no girls, no piece of shit camel-fucker.

We outnumbered the Rosemeade cops, but we parlayed with them instead of cutting straight to the firefight.

"That man is the ambassador from Zulfiqar," the police spokesman told us. That's how he'd gotten a helicopter on the roof. We couldn't believe it, watching him give us the Muslim version of the Finger—open palm facing us with the middle finger crooking like it was waving good-bye to us—circling us over the parking lot, and carry his daughters away.

"He told us he was rescuing his poor kids from a bunch of Satanists."

"Satanists!" we roared, incredulous.

Fredo happily barked along with us.

"Calm down! Calm down! Look, there's nothing you can do about it now. Either you leave our town peacefully, or we all kill each other out here. Personally, I say we'd rather you left, because a lot of us have families to go to home to."

"You try to arrest any of us and you've got a fucking blood-bath on your hands!" I don't know who yelled that, but we all fiercely agreed.

"If you leave now, we have no reason to arrest anyone." He was trying so hard to be reasonable, but we were all eager for a fight. Acid and lots of cocaine tend to do that. I didn't find out until months later that the local SWAT team had been called elsewhere to deal with some other problem, leaving behind a small handful of cops who'd been told to assist an ambassador in any way, attracting as little attention as possible. Just a stream of coincidences, it would seem, but something I'd learned while becoming a diamond was echoing again in my mind's ear: "Terrorism is really just a diversion-ary tactic..."

"We don't want any trouble," the cops said. "We just want you to get the fuck outta Dodge so we can go home to our wives and kids. You scared the hell out of a lot of our citizens—shit, just by being here. You've got no bone to pick with us, and as long as you don't discharge your firearms, we don't care where you got them. Now, why don't you go back where you came from and pick on somebody your own size?"

We discussed this amongst ourselves for a while, and decided to mask our disappointment by calling them a bunch of cowards, questioning their ancestry, and advising them to run on home with their tails between their legs.

They took all this in stride and watched us drive off into the night. It was a bitter, bitter defeat.

The last time I tried to hook a john and bring him into our trap, no amount of arguing could convince him and his friends that I wasn't really queer. They just laughed. I was cornered, in *their* dark parking lot. They were doing the same thing Seth and the others used to do before I came along and became their bait.

When I pulled my piece, a few of them pulled theirs. A loud crack split the night, and I was punched backwards into the side of the decoy's car. I couldn't feel the pain yet, but my arm hung limply at my side. I tried to fight back when they rushed me, but I didn't have a chance. Every time a shoe field-goaled the side of my head, a white flash blinded me. It was the second fist that knocked me sprawling to the pavement, and after that, all I could do was curl up into a ball and shield my ribs and face. They hammered me into the ground. I was dizzy with pain, but there was nothing I could do.

My right arm screamed in agony, leaking blood all over me. Warm and sticky, it soaked me to the bone, creeping into the pores on my face and making my grip on consciousness even more slippery. The kicks kept coming, raining on me without mercy. I could barely hear the laughter, the taunts, the disgust, my heart was pounding so loud in my ears. I thought it would never stop.

When they were finally satisfied trying to kick me to sleep, I did what I could to get back to where Seth and the others waited. I ignored the people who stared at me, wishing I could stagger invisibly down the sidewalk and not leave a trail of blood to mark my passing, but instead, I tried to tune them out. They were the voyeurs of pain, those who must slow down and cause a traffic jam just to see a bad accident, those who crowded around disasters hoping for a souvenir. I tried not to feel shame, but even that was hard. I felt drunk, on the verge of passing out, but I was stone cold sober, moving as if I traveled in someone else's dream.

My head was throbbing, already swollen in places, knotted in others. I exhaled a mist of blood with every breath. I don't know how long I walked, but friendly hands and worried voices lifted the weight I'd been dragging, supporting me, so that I could just give up and let the black wave of oblivion wash over me.

A sharp, searing pain yanked me fully awake out of the depths of sleep. Strong hands held me down, keeping me from attacking Seth, who held a red-hot knife against the hole in my arm. The edges of the wound puckered, melted, and I felt my skin solder itself shut. The lancing agony of DIY cauterizing almost outshone the pain of being shot in the first place, but it was nothing compared to what followed.

Apparently, a light bulb had flashed over some idiot's diseased head. Whoever it was thought he was doing me a favor, his good deed for the day.

In the soft inner hollow of my other arm, a dull, reused needle strained its way through my skin and plunged into a vein. I almost didn't even feel it, but there was no mistaking it an instant later. A surge of pleasure filled me, an unholy pleasure, an unholy perversion that brought me relief and this sick joy I know I had to resist or become its slave. Just like I'd seen so many others sell their souls for just one more taste. But I felt some grinning traitor inside me shiver with delight, flinging open trap doors that led to my dark and secret places and letting this decadent ecstasy in to violate. I felt plundered, as if I'd been raped and found a way to enjoy it. The feeling made me shudder with fear.

"Heroin?" I asked, after everyone was calm.

"The only China I like is White," Radcliffe sang. Seth reached over me and slapped the shit out of him, while I drifted lazily away. Yep, heroin. China White, as opposed to Black Tar and Mexican Mud. Don't bother to keep your arms and legs inside the vehicle because we're going sooo sloooowwww.

It was at that moment, as the fingers of angels began to caress my soul, that I had my first smellucination.

"You smell that?" I mumbled to Seth.

"What?"

"I smell Maya."

"Who?"

"Maya, damn it. What are you, deaf?" I smelled the fragrance of her body. When you give your life to Shiva the Destroyer—if you're into that kind of thing—you must reject the coils of Maya. You must cast off all earthly and fleshly things, sever all ties to the world of illusion. Of course, my Maya sneered at such bullshit, happy instead to revel in all of life's illusions except the most blatant and obvious ones.

She wore no makeup, no war paint of any kind, nothing to disguise herself as everyone else did. She wore no perfume, allowing her natural scents of hair and skin to speak for themselves. She condemned men who were, to use her words, anointed with the essence of yaks or musk oxen dissolved in alcohol, and in the case of women, avocado raspberry grapefruit mint.

"Who would want to mate with someone who smells like a fucking fruit salad?" she asked me once. "Our natural odors are seductive enough without us spraying alcohol on our throats and armpits." And she convinced me to throw away the yellow shit in a bottle that I'd thought would get me laid. And her natural scent drove me into a frenzy whenever I smelled it.

And here it was again.

"You know when your mind plays tricks on you?"

"Yeah," Seth said, humoring me as I drooled on myself.

"You think you hear things, and sometimes you see things."

"Mm-hmmm. I was doing that all last night."

"Well, I'm smelling women," I told him. He laughed. His shirt was off, and every spot of ink making up his Reichadler tattoo stood out in striking detail. I never was a big fan of Hitler, but I had to admit, he came up with some pretty snazzy tattoo designs. The one on the back of Seth's neck was a gilded, teal Maltese cross with a crimson swastika behind it, its arms curling around to embrace it.

"You're smelling women, huh?" he asked.

"Yeah, Seth. They smell damned good."

"You're smellucinating."

"Wow. There's actually a term for it?"

Seth laughed again and put a couch cushion under my head. I stared at the graffiti all over the underside of the Bridge, mesmerized by a bright slash of cadmium yellow that sliced the tail of some arcane symbol through the blackness. A smoke blackened overpass, a honeycomb of freeways, and I couldn't stop singing to myself.

"I'm a fucking chimney sweep, yes I am...the only China I like is White...I didn't put up much of a fight..." I thought I was really clever to come up with that next line and make it all rhyme, but once my head cleared, I realized how stupid it was. So, I'll just keep the whole world in suspense about it, instead. Take my word for it, though. I was a blithering idiot for the next few hours, and I loved every minute of it.

Well, it did suck for a while, but those painkillers Seth would go and get for me made a big difference. What happened was this chick with liberty spikes was shooting me up and missed the vein, and instead of pulling out and trying again, the moron started *chasing* it around inside my arm with the goddamn needle. Jesus, that hurt. And *then*, Christ, the tip of the needle broke off inside, under my skin. We managed to dig it out with somebody's tweezers, and I forgot about it once I was high.

Next day, I had a small bump there. Hmm.

Day after that, it was bigger. Hard, too, like a rock.

I blinked, and somehow it was two weeks later, and I had a big ass lump an inch tall on my arm. The veins all up and down my arm, all the way up to my chest and snaking across under my collarbone, were red and standing out sharply under my skin. God, I was scared. The junkies who looked at it said it sure weren't no cotton fever, whatever the hell that meant.

Various people had been going up to whatever hospital to score me some painkillers—most of the time it was Seth—so I wasn't hurting at all. Whoever was looking after me would only ever check the bullet wound, never that other arm, and they'd started shooting me up in the leg anyway, so none of us looked at that arm at all.

Well, what they were doing at the hospital was pretending to have kidney stones, pissing in a little cup they'd dripped blood into. A lot of stupid people get busted doing shit like that, on account of the *kind* of blood they mix into the urine. When you prick a finger and try to say that blood came out of your kidneys, they can tell the difference. They call it prescription fraud, and the police come and you find another place to sleep for a while.

What you have to do is prick your gums, spit blood out of your mouth into the cup, and then piss on it. In that order. One drop of blood from your gums will pass for kidney blood because of the high white blood cell count. Do that, and you get morphine on diagnosis and prescriptions for Demerol, Percoset, Vicodin, Lortab, or whatever.

Well, when Seth went in after seeing what had happened to my other arm, he came back with this old guy, a gruff, no-nonsense type of old guy. He wasn't a doctor; I dunno what the hell he was, but I didn't care at that point. Maybe he was a doctor. Fuck it, I'll just say he was. See if he had been a doctor, he'd be required by law to report my gunshot wound to the police, but this guy didn't, so I'm just assuming. Whatever. Doc came and looked at me, gave us a lecture, all pissed off, and told us to go and get some bacon fat to put over the bump, wrap it in some gauze he gave us.

Bacon fat. Oh, gee, why didn't we think of that?

Bacon fat. Christ.

Well, somebody went off to get us some bacon, and we stripped the streaky fat off it, made a poultice or whatever those medieval things are called. Seth put on a British accent and said "I must hie me to the swamp, and fetch us a leech!" which some other dude laughed at and took up the routine.

"Pshaw, old bean! This isn't the *Dark* Ages; ye *must* know the poor chap 'as a dwarf or a gnome living in 'is buttocks! *That's* wot's got 'im ill!"

"Well, jolly good! That's just *bully!* Wot say ye we take turns trying to stab the little beastie?"

Medical science gives way to sodomy jokes. What's the world coming to?

Anyway, the next day there was all this putrid black shit oozing out from under the gauze. Stank like a mother. The lump had popped overnight, and the redness went down quickly, was completely gone after a few days. Seth had followed the rest of Doc's instructions, gotten plenty of raisins and made me eat them until I never wanted to see another raisin as long as I lived. Said it was to purify my blood. I dunno if it actually did that, but after those few days I was ready to hie me to a brothel, sink me John Thomas in some fair trollop's briny and, by thunder, shag it ta fock an' back.

When I finally sobered up, fully recovered, my shirt was Rorschached with bloodstains, and my body screamed to be back in the lazy state it had just left. I did what I could to ignore the urge.

I still had some money left over, miraculously, after getting my ass kicked and then lying delirious among a bunch of thieves. Seth led me to the train yard, Fredo following along and getting distracted by just about anything, running off to harass the birds every time he saw some. If nothing was around, he'd still be running ahead of us, sniffing and barking, looking back to make sure we still followed. Running over to urge us to pick up the pace, then running ahead again. If he saw anything out of the corner of his eye, he was determined to hunt it down and *pester* it. On what grounds, he never told me.

Seth filled me in on everything I'd need to know about being an official Hobo, including the proper dress code. "First off, you have to find some clothes like Jiminy Cricket wore. Get pants with buttoned ass flaps, a coat with patches on it, and a raggedy top hat. The top hat has to look like one of those old-fashioned work whistles. You know, where the lid flies up at quitting time? *Awoogah!* And some sad clown makeup. Oh! And the icing on the cake: all your belongings in a red-and-white-checkered handkerchief, or gingham even, gathered at the corners and tied into a pouch hanging from the end of a long stick. You can't be without one of those."

"All the belongings I have are on me right now."

"Well, no matter how cool it looks, that shoulder holster under your flannel is un-hobo. Totally."

Since I looked so conspicuous in Kyle's blood-soaked button-down and sport coat, and his wife's too tight Levi's, Seth had donated a red plaid flannel with a gray hood, some torn blue jeans (fashionably torn), and a gray knit t-shirt. I looked like the most boring youth in Christendom, especially with the two black eyes and fat lip. And track marks.

I'd gotten an eight-ball of smack from Tommy's last night, and already gotten good mileage out of it. A few new needles—rigs, or works, I was supposed to call them, like I gave a shit about slang.

Seth sat with me out in the train yard, talking, until my Eastbound started to chunk-chuck away. I shouted at Fredo, damn dog, until he decided, on a whim, to come running. The train hadn't picked up speed yet, but Seth still carried the squirming terrier as we ran, ready to pass him to me when I was safely on a car.

It took a minute to scramble into an opened door, but in good time I got my dog and we both waved good-bye to Seth McHale, the scourge of just about anywhere.

"So long, home skillet!" That was the stupid phrase he'd come up with when I railed against the even stupider crap that masqueraded as slang in his city. Home skillet. I don't know what the hell it was supposed to mean, but it sounded right and, before long, everyone in Hollywood Hardcore was using it. *Some scourge you are*, I thought as I shouted at his rapidly shrinking figure. So long.

Stowing away on trains is just as boring as it sounds. Sitting there either alone or trying not to stare at other bums who are trying not to stare at you. Fredo got sick in a corner, but afterwards went over to investigate my one…what? Car-mate, I guess he'd be called. The dog wet-nosed him and tried to make friends, hoping a snack might be available.

That was the highlight of my first day. Until I shot up a spoon, that is. The H that I got off of a dealer at Tommy's was soooo much better than Radcliffe's. I'd gotten a cheap Walkman to ease the boredom of hoboing, and it was on this small radio that I heard the Voice of God.

Bear with me on this, now.

Radio energy is racing around us all the time, at every second, everywhere we go, but we can't feel it. We can't have any way of knowing that all kinds of information and communication is passing through us, like light through glass, without this small device to make it hearable.

Audible. Whatever. Everything from cell phones, cordless phones, telephone satellites, walkie-talkies and CBs, AM and FM and UHF and VHF, faxes, pagers, and everything else they have out there that I don't know about. Uncountable individual bits of human discourse, filling an intangible medium that was unimagined a hundred years ago or so.

What was this medium originally intended for, by nature? What was its purpose before we came along to put it to work for us? This small device catches what was already there, not generating anything, but catching it as it passes by. Those transmissions supposedly do not stop anywhere once they've been transmitted, just keep on going forever, through our atmosphere and into the open space, speeding along forever, never stopping, not even if some alien being picks it up with a receiver of its own (and eventually, there has to be one—law of averages and everything) and it scratches its alien equivalent of a head with its alien equivalent of a finger, trying to make sense of "Gilligan's Island" as it passes by on its way.

As my brain swam lazily under the murk of heroin the radio stations passed in and out of clarity, or rather, I passed through *them*, and I was forced to endure static for long periods of time, helpless at their mercy. It was in the middle of one fury of static that a high-pitched whine shrieked into my head from the earphones, a steady *tweeeeeeeeeeee* that had to have some birth somewhere, some reason for being. It had me stumped for a long time, after the long time it took me to notice it was even there, but it came to me in a sudden realization—Eureka!—that's the Voice of God, speaking to the infinite particles making up me and everything around me, telling them what to do.

Either that, or I was really fucking stoned.

Either way.

That in turn got me thinking about other stuff, like oil. A non-renewable resource just hanging out in the earth until we came along and found out it could be fuel. That really threw me for a loop. *What the fuck was it doing there?* What other purpose could it possibly serve, besides helping us go somewhere? And if that's the only reason for it, what the fuck is the big deal about us using it like we're supposed to? I tried to ask my car-mate, but he kept shaking me off until I gave up, and the next time our train stopped, he grabbed his bag and hopped off into the night. Prick.

At some stop in Nevada, I managed to score a bunch of peyote from some Indians. They didn't ask for much in exchange for a small garbage bag full of desert magic cactus. Later on, sitting in the train yard cooking pork n' beans with my nameless hobo partner, I bought some more H off of another old Indian. Good stuff, too. Apparently, out in the middle of nowhere, they had plenty of supply and not enough demand. Fredo wolfed down his helping of beans and then got sick all over the place, from the other end this time. When he was finished, I took his face in both hands, looking deep into his eyes with my nose half an inch from his.

"I smell doggy shit," I told him. "I know it was you, Fredo. You broke my heart. *You broke my heart.*"

And that was the highlight of my second day.

The third day. That's when I met Windsong. She wasn't exceptionally pretty, but any port in a storm…

She told me she was Navajo, and there was no way I could've pronounced her real name, so I settled for the English version. I asked her if she'd ever heard of a band called Warpath, but she said her people didn't listen to the box-that-spoke. They lived out in the real world, where no rolling wheels left their tracks to mar the

Earth. She told me she rode on trains only so she could see if there was any diversity in the places they stopped.

There was none. Only overgrown crabgrass trying to smother decrepit, rusting skeletons of railway cars and the rusting, skeletal people who lived in them. People who lived in cardboard crates, plastic sheets, chewed-looking wooden pallets, and corrugated aluminum siding. People even the buzzards spit upon.

I decided we were going to take a vacation, somewhere out in her real world. At our next stop, we hopped off and bought some new clothes, with something to carry them in, a pretty decent tent and bedroll, plenty of food, and showers at a cheap motel. Then, armed with a huge sandwich and some high-fructose corn syrup carbonated beverages, we waited for our train to leave.

I told Windsong all about Shaitan and how she was patiently waiting for the revolution. I sang a few of her songs, and Windsong sang a few of her own. If anyone had stopped to listen, they would've been surprised to hear us sing songs that actually meant something, instead of the usual fare of people my age. We praised what had happened at Little Big Horn, and Windsong told me about her hero, Crazy Horse, who became one of my heroes when I heard the story. The only survivor of that battle with the Sioux was Comanche, a horse, who barely survived. Officially retired after his wounds had healed, Comanche became an alcoholic (no shit) and died at the ripe old age of twenty-eight. Horses do develop a fondness for beer and at the rate soldiers would oblige him it's a wonder he lasted as long as he did. He's stuffed in a museum somewhere.

Windsong laughed when I told her about Mount Rushmore, saying she'd heard of such a thing, but never seen it. In South Dakota, she was sure, a mountain had been carved into Crazy Horse as a response to the presidential monstrosity. We made a pact then to vandalize the monument, giving our trip a more definite purpose. We now had a goal in mind, instead of just the freakshow capital of the world. To deface everything artificial.

Just as the train was due to move out, we climbed aboard and sat, playing with Fredo the cheerfully oblivious dog and ignoring the scabious tramp sitting in a corner.

Windsong was about ten years older than me, about old enough to get herself a man, but her excuse was she hadn't seen enough yet. That's the biggest problem with being a drifter. No matter where you went, there was a horizon, and that made you

346

think there was something left to wonder about. As long as there were stones left unturned, there could be some ethereal cloud city floating around that nobody knew about.

I told Windsong about a guy who used to come to dinner at the de Medieros' house in Ibis. Domingo and Mariana told me he'd been a friend of the family's for years, and also, a "business associate." He'd come over every once in a while from wherever he'd been, and he was a really nice guy, considering. Considering he was a cold-blooded, ruthless evil fuck.

They called him Coelho, which I think means "rabbit." He had some business that he started, not a drug-front restaurant, but it had been inspired by Pecado. All I could pick up from eavesdropping was that it was doing well. But that wasn't what I told Windsong about.

I told her about the land where the sea meets the sky. The visitor had told me about this wondrous place in Sicily, the town growing out of the side of a mountain, rising tier upon tier from the beach to the summit, overlooking the Ionian Sea. According to him, the cloudless sky melted into the calm sea, and you couldn't tell where one ended and the other began. He had told us that that was the end of the world, the perfect place to settle because there was no place left to go.

"Did he ever say why it was like that?" she asked.

"He said the villagers just shrugged when he asked about it. Said it was the most beautiful thing he'd ever seen. He never noticed if this place had great sunsets because he was always out with the village girls at the time, and they outshone the sun so brightly that you'd forget about anything else."

"A bit of a poet, then?"

"Yeah, I guess so." I laughed. A cold-blooded, ruthless poet. Who'd a thunk it?

She taught me that wherever there are trees, there is water. Scoop out a handful of earth and sniff it. If it feels and smells damp, hunt around for some that's more so, then dig. About a foot down, water ought to start trickling, so you scoop out a round hole and pat the earth hard around the sides. She pressed the bottom hard with the heel and palm of her hand and threw all her weight against it, and a moment later, water was gathering around her fingers. She didn't let up until it was up around her wrist.

It was the best water I'd ever tasted. It wasn't mud, it wasn't dirty or...or *anything*. It was just water. It hadn't been treated with chlorine or fluoride or Paxil. I drank my fill of this freshly-squeezed dirt juice and I knew at that moment that I was far closer to being a real man out here in the wilderness than I could ever become in a city, with a car and a gun. Eventually, cars run out of gas and guns run out of bullets and the faucet stops running water, and if you don't know what to do then, it doesn't matter how many confirmed kills are notched in your belt or how many names are on your pussy scorecard. If you can't survive the way everybody did before you, because you've grown so dependent upon your indoor plumbing and your pimped-out whip and your microwave, you're just meat for someone who can.

I told her about how Shaitan once sat me and Domingo down to watch *Dances With Wolves*, the multi-Oscar-winning movie that she and Maya called subversive PC horseshit. The reason for this was that it condemned the white man while it praised the Lakota Sioux—the Indians' supposed Utopia cared for orphans and the handicapped, so it must be good. Except for Kevin Costner, every white man was an invader. They must be bad. We were supposed to forget that many of those invaders were oppressed farmers and craftsmen who'd fled to heroically forge a new life in unused land and carve out their territory among savages. Forget the Pawnee who inexplicably attack the Sioux. No context given. Hmmm. I wondered about that.

Shaitan gave us the historical context. The Pawnee, Crow, Shoshone, and Arapaho all hated the Lakota Sioux, hated their fucking guts, because—wait for it....because the Lakota Sioux were native to Minnesota. They'd fled west the century before, driven out of their land by the white man (escaping oppression) and carved out their new territory from the savages who lived there (sound familiar?) and they were still fighting to hold the ground they'd taken when Costner showed up. *Hmm.*

"Yes," Windsong said. "Everybody is an invader to everyone else. The world is like that. Always has been. If you are not strong enough to hold onto what you've got, or clever enough to take it back, you lose and that's all there is to it."

"Uh-huh. And before we came, the Sioux already had torture, kidnapping, exile, slavery...we didn't teach them anything new."

I remember asking Shaitan why she'd want us to see it this way. If pop culture was "brainwashing us with a politically correct history

348

curriculum hidden in our movies and TV" well, wasn't that good for her people?

"Hell no. The Sioux and the Iroquois weren't friends. We're not all one lump of noble barbarians, united against a common enemy. Besides, even if this bullshit here—" she indicated the screen. "Was meant to benefit *us*, no thanks. Lies do not become us."

Maya then pointed out how, back east, abolitionists were condemning the fetter and the lash but saying nothing while sweatshops in the north industrially exploited people of their own race.

Windsong gave me a curious look.

"What?" I asked.

"Maybe we are barbarians, and maybe that is bad somehow, but I don't have any stories like this to tell you."

"Like what?"

"About how people I don't know are telling me lies so I'll think differently about other people I don't know."

We abandoned ship somewhere in the Midwest, the middle of nowhere. If Rosemeade was the armpit of America, and Golgotha was the asshole, this place had to be the erect, pink nipple. God, it was beautiful. We explored a bit, kicking down rotting posts that were held up only by the barbed-wire they were supposed to support, and came to a lush valley, teeming with wildlife for Fredo to bark at.

We made camp in a place Windsong selected, since she knew a lot more about this stuff than a dumb city-slicker like me. The tent was a pain in the ass. Christ, it required an instruction manual, that's how complicated it was. Thank God they provided one.

"Trust you Palefaces to make something this hard."

"I got something much harder right here," I said, showing her my clenched fist. She laughed, and we finally got the damned thing set up. For few minutes I faced a serious dilemma. Shoot up a spoon, or eat some peyote? Windsong shook her head at me and made a face at the heroin, as if it stank.

Peyote it is, then.

Oh my God, it was better than acid. The mindfuck was so intense, all I could do for the first two hours was gape at the world around me. And the visuals...oh my God, the visuals. The bushes came to life and were dancing ballet. No shit. And not just bouncing around on their tippy-toes, but doing arabesques and pirouettes. Once, I was blessed by a bunch of butterflies fluttering out of the woods, swarming around me and raining gifts of forgiveness from Heaven. At least, that's what I felt it was.

Afterwards, I wasn't sure if they'd been real or not.

I heard everything I could see, and saw colors radiating from every sound. The shuddering drums of the breathing trees were thrown off-balance by a sneaky, counter-rhythm creeping into the mix from the sky, and the butterflies brought in a wailing trumpet glissando.

The pure song of the birds intensified the mix, bringing it all into a hectic and frustrating melody. Every time the climax started to unfold and soar towards a crescendo, something else would step in to distract it and take the music to a different level entirely. It was almost like sex with Maya. The completion was so close, only to be snatched away by another gradually building joy. Another bird. Crickets, now. I even heard a wild gray rabbit serenade me from the bushes. A tantric opera, I decided to call it, and I couldn't wait to go home and tell Maya all about it.

Even the ground I walked on had a pulse, swelling in time with my heartbeat, letting the alphabet soup hieroglyphics squirm and slide over each other. Some designs in the grass broke apart like the moon's reflection on the water, and always mended themselves again. I was fascinated by the grass, watching patterns break and flow back together like mercury.

Windsong's body, now mostly bared to me, became a moving statue of pliant, elastic bronze, glimmering in the sunlight. She found a fallen eagle's feather and planted it in her glossy black top-knot, then struck a pose. I laughed. I could not stop laughing.

Eventually, she gave in and ate one of the peyote buds, feeling lonely out in the realm of the Sane. I couldn't blame her. It was beautiful here, and I wanted her company. The cactuses, cacti, whatever, had taken on a kind of neon, phosphorescent glow that was their way of announcing how special they were. They almost demanded to be eaten. I obeyed.

"So this is the real world?" I asked. She shrugged.

"Yeah, part of it. A small part," she added quickly. Obviously, she didn't want me spending the whole time out here in chemical-induced idiocy. As I watched, these neon implants under her skin began to chase each other, slender tubes arranged in fetishistic tribal patterns, pulsing with colored light. In her eyes writhed holographs that I could've sworn hadn't been there before.

We talked about Navajo philosophy, a truly captivating topic, considering the circumstances. I don't remember very much of it, but it was revelation after resounding revelation, at the time. It changed my whole view of the world. Pity I've forgotten it all.

When night fell, the glorious sunset brought with it a timid hint of distant, joyfully malignant sound. Brazen and bloodstirring, it plunged out of deep, strange gulfs of space, the voiceless expression of pure, elemental defiance. It came across the sky in a slithering, iridescent blur, trembling in waves that made spiraling aureate wisps of nebulae shudder with joy. It sang to us and whirled in the crystal coils of star-spattered galaxies, and vanished into the sentient blackness. I was awestruck.

When it had left us, the stars hung like shimmering diamonds, swaying in the wake of the incredible song. The night sky out here was wonderful, untainted by the poisonous aura that hung over Civilization. The stars seemed alive with meaning. The constellations themselves had not changed, but now revealed an astonishing significance they had failed to make plain every other time I'd seen them.

Every glittering curve of sky around me became part of a vast and immeasurable design that was mocking in its magnificence. And I finally understood my place in it. Finally understood the role I was to play.

Unfortunately, these thoughts were merely the mind-fuck effects of another drug, and I forgot them as soon as they passed. Thus, I became an addict.

Just as those poor fools sucking on crack stems were only chasing a tantalizing, elusive high, I kept trying to catch up with the universal knowledge that was nothing more than an illusion in the first place. Heroin addicts, and sometimes crackheads, who can't agree on terminology, call it "chasing the dragon." There is no satisfaction in crack. There is no feeling of "Ahhh, that's it." Anyone who tells you that there is, and they've felt it, is a fucking liar. Every hit you take fuels the gnawing hunger for another one, and people give up everything they own to try and catch up to a feeling that doesn't exist. I became like them during those days on the pink nipple of America. Mindlessly chasing the wonder and unity with something I was not even a dust speck in comparison to.

Windsong tried to stop me in the next few days, then gave up and watched me sadly as my mind and soul withered away. I became a twice-a-day user, collapsing my veins one by one. Depending on which chemical inhabited my skull, I was either a zombie or a dervish.

In my few moments of clarity, I'd smellucinate things that were forever lost to me. Guava barbecue ribs, with garlic and hot pepper. Mamey sapote in batido milk-shakes. Mamey with strawberry Stoli and Cointreau, pineapple juice, and sugar-cane syrup. Guanabanas, the heart-shaped bananas, spiked with grappa. Christmas melon and Serrano ham. Mangoes. Cherimoya.

And Maya.

All of these intoxicating smells, and tastes you'd rather hold forever in your mouth than swallow and lose. It was the homesickness that Windsong used as the way to get me moving again. She'd pulled shame out of an adventure I told her about, telling me that I could get drunk and listen to Portishead while my love got fucked in the next room all I wanted to if I was a suicide blonde in a penthouse. But if I wanted to be a man—that old manliness ruse—I could not wallow in the pigsty. Though convoluted, her rail hit home. She told me I did not deserve these things because I didn't even want them enough. I could not want them, because I did nothing to chase them and earn them, to make them my own.

Instead, I talked to the bushes and cried out to the moon like a lonely wolf. I wasted myself on visions and laziness when there was a world to conquer.

"Your packed head is now a balloon," she said. "You waste away out here, blinded by what? Grass? A pretty bug you caught? Yes, this is the real world, but only if you *use* it. Fuck what those other Indians say, the ones with the dots between their eyes! Try chasing an illusion that will actually lead you somewhere!" Her words stung, but put iron in my blood. "But no! You'd rather let your ribs stand out until you can see your heart beating inside them. You let some drug crush out your life and you still try to kiss it with your dying breath! Don't you want to see a place with no horizon? That'll never happen if you don't get off your ass and catch the next train!"

I stood up, shamed into anger. Shamed into rage against the *loser* I'd become. I gathered up all of our stuff that lay strewn about for a week and piled it up beside the tent. She helped me dismantle the stupidly complicated thing, and we walked until we found the tracks again.

There was something born out of that shame that I didn't need Windsong to tell me, something that I felt on a deep, animal level. I had impregnated Maya. I had sown my seed, and it was growing inside her. Half of the baby she would bear was my responsibility, and a man who could not be a father to his child could never be a real man.

Being a man is not carrying a gun and using it on anyone you disagreed with. It's not sleeping around. It's not anything I'd deluded myself into thinking it was.

I will go to New York City and do whatever I have to, anything to rise up and become Someone, and then have the resources to return to Florida and finish what I've started. I will stamp out Nestor's disease like bugs beneath my heel, and earn the right to help Maya raise our child.

We walked along the railroad for some time, passing lean-tos and ramshackle housing, the crowded shantytowns where the poverty-stricken remained alive merely to spite themselves, the marrow of the concrete chutes under elevated freeways.

"This is what you wanted to be?" Windsong asked me. "Just one of these ghosts?" Her scorn and contempt were like bleach to me, stinging, but cleansing my wounds.

These people could not possibly have fit in with the tenebrous vibration of all energy, whose condensation to varying degrees became matter, gave form and substance to the Firmament. They couldn't be a part of the miracle I thought I'd been shown, and if there was anything outside the miracle, then there never really was one. There couldn't be. Even Tent City looked better.

The low, droning rumble announced the train coming finally, and we gave it a wide birth at a wind in the tracks. It was a religious experience in itself, standing there as a train blew by, but the wheels tried to suck us under them. The number one cause of death among hobos is getting run the fuck over by a train they were trying to catch. Gospel truth. A close second was hobos getting trampled by trains they were trying to jump off of.

We made it with only one casualty.

Fredo.

He panicked and got away from me as I tried to hand him up

to Windsong. My heart broke as I watched him get sucked under, and I felt myself start to stumble into the vacuum, but Windsong grabbed my gray flannel hood and managed to yank me back into reality. I clambered in and collapsed with her in my arms, sobbing uncontrollably.

I'd never thought I was that attached to the dog, but the loss of an animal comrade hurt me more than watching a friend die ever could. I don't know why.

My cheerfully oblivious dog.

Gone.

When we finally got to North Dakota we took a bus up to Keystone and, from there, caught a tour bus to Mount Rushmore. Great place. Really. We stood with the crowd of admirers and listened to the guide's spiel about what it represented, his jokes about who he hoped would be carved into it next, and how many people it took to clean it every year, making sure that the weather never eroded the artistry. Yeah, that's great. Keep up the good work.

Since spray paint was out of the question, considering all the ropes and pulleys and time we'd need to paint bright red goatees on the four faces, we opted instead for a quicker and easier vandalism. Back in town, we went to a hardware store and bought one large can of every color in the rainbow, and a few black ones thrown in for good measure.

"Whatcha paintin'?" the man behind the counter asked.

"The town," I said.

He laughed. That night, we snuck up to the very top and opened the cans, setting them along the summit. Then, giggling, we turned each one over, pissing color down the faces of Washington, Whatshisname, Lincoln, and Roosevelt.

Almost immediately, shouts and a siren screamed out of the darkness below.

Oops.

We hurriedly tipped over the rest of the cans and high-tailed it into the woods. Windsong ran confidently between the trees, while I crashed into every low-hanging limb that blocked my way. But I kept going. My drug-withered body wasn't up to this flight, but I gave it everything I had, and we made it out of there together, laughing as soon as we knew it was safe.

Somehow, I guess using the vibe antennae to zero in on other people like her, Windsong found some Cherokees. It had to be some kind of telepathy, the way queers use gaydar. In any case, she got us invited to a powwow. It wasn't Crow Fair, or the Oglala Sioux Sun Dance, but it was impressive enough, at least for me. I snuck only half a spoon that evening, so I'd still be able to function normally, and managed to hold friendly conversations with the people I met. When we told a few young braves about our vacation out on the Nipple, they seemed rather interested in getting some peyote of their own. I'd gotten the stuff for pennies on the dollar, and I sold it at a huge profit, but not enough to make anyone unhappy with the deal.

I still had a quarter of the original lot left, and it would be more than enough to put food on my table in New York. I was making out rather well. Of course, I knew how to do it—I could convince Straight Edgers to buy a few grams, for Christ's sake. But these guys had only heard about peyote and only ever done 'shrooms. As long as Chief Thumb-Up-His-Ass didn't see, they wouldn't have let me leave without having taken their money. College educated Indians return to their tribes in ignorance of traditions, eager to learn them but unable to shake off what they learned in the White Man's world. Drugs are not hard study.

That's how whiskey conquered the Red Man, and that's how I made a quick buck off of him. It did make me sad, though, in my oddly hypocritical way. Contributing to good people turning out just like me. I saw how my culture, with no spirit and no attachment to the land at all, respected those things about the Indians without bothering to adopt those ways.

Many people were decked out in Cherokee ceremonial costumes and dancing around a bonfire, some traditional dance to ensure good crops and ward off assholes like me. A few pretty squaws and the braves I sold to invited me to their circle on the outskirts of the crowd, just beyond the reach of the light. They lit up a calumet full of some good homegrown, and we smoked together. I was in the middle of telling what we'd done to Mount Rushmore for the third time (either others hadn't heard it yet, or everybody wanted an encore) when I realized that some damned good music was playing, and after shouting for silence I recognized the singer.

"Is this the Promised Land that King Jr. foresaw?

Is this what Rosa Parks stayed sitting down for?

355

Are you proud when ya gangstas make your mamas cry?

Was your gang bullshit worth it when you lay down and die?"

Then rage, full blown wrath, as only she could sing it. I jumped up and pushed my way into the light, where the band played up on a stage.

Shaitan! She wore a tunic with a fringed breechclout and a long tailpiece, the rest of it tight and sexy as hell. Feathers in her hair and silver ornaments with bone inlays completed the picture. No moccasins. She pranced about in her bare feet.

"You sang me that song," Windsong said, appearing at my side. I grinned and nodded in time with the beat. The guitarist's solo was balls to the wall, driving all the young bucks into a frenzy. I could see a few tribal elders watching, motionless, inscrutable, apparently not approving as much as the spirited braves did. But that's always the way with the old and the young.

"She sings it better," Windsong teased.

Then, "Dance with me."

"Huh?" was all the argument I could muster before she dragged me out into the open. A few people were angry to see a Paleface at their little shindig, but their more open-minded friends calmed them down. I felt like just by being there I was insulting them, but Windsong insisted that I dance. I mingled with men and women, sticking out like a sore thumb against their copper breastplates and Clydesdale-looking leggings of white horsehair. Faces were painted yellow with pollen and streaked with red ochre. They were riots of color, flashing pearls and polished shells at throat, wrist, and ankle. Some brandished long ceremonial knives with handles made of grizzly jaws.

I noticed some of the people I'd smoked with talking to them, the angry ones, no doubt vouching for me with what the news would probably call The Rushmore Incident. Dancing in a kind of prance around the bonfire, I noticed Shaitan noticing me, and waved as subtly as I could, a more friendly version of the "I recognize you" nod. Small world.

She cocked her head, animal-like, to one side, as if the record skipped inside her brain. Her eyes telegraphed a "What in the—?" expression, and I couldn't help laughing, but deep down, seeing her made me even more homesick. I missed Florida. I missed Pecado. I missed sneaking into the clubs with Domingo, getting plastered and dancing all night with Maya, Shaitan, and Mariana during her vaca-

356

tions from college. All three of them were over twenty-one, so without us, we always were afraid they'd go off on a Girls' Night Out and get swept off their feet by some Adonis, some Casanova. Some Evan Lanthorne.

I swallowed those memories and washed them down with a shot of firewater someone handed me as I passed. I needed a fix, another spoon to drown my sadness. Or maybe just a few more hits off of that calumet.

They played another song, this time a slow, bittersweet eulogy for all those who died on the Trail of Tears. One of those tearjerkers you don't really dance to, one of those where you just hold on tightly to your lover and shuffle a little bit. Windsong and I held each other loosely and swayed, wondering when the music would get quick and angry again.

Shaitan's soulfully resounding voice wailed, dragging out the words and showing us a few times how long she could hold a rich and vibrant note. The words rang out and stuck all of us—even the dour-looking elder—hitting that spot that makes us close our eyes and ride with it. It was beautiful, bloodstirringly poignant.

At the end, when the song rose to an emotional climax and Shaitan was drawing out a piercing final note, the whole band simply stopped at once, letting her carry it. She clutched the mic stand and parabolaed backwards, howling like a mournful wolf at the moon. Head tilted back, she arched so far that she seemed about to fall. She pulled that mic, pulling as if it could drag more breath out of her, until finally it quit. As suddenly as the power going out, leaving startling silence in its wake, the squaw cut it off with a gasp and fell to her knees.

An instant passed, and the rest of the band furiously brought back the signature notes in a sudden blast, slamming it down to punctuate her.

The crowd roared, screaming out obsolete battle cries and clapping until their hands stung. Shai got to her feet and winked at the audience, smiling as she tried to catch her breath. She hooked a finger into her bone choker and pulled, as she would a shirt collar to let off steam, theatrically fanning her face with the other hand.

"Anger is a gift," she said into the mic, making all the braves cheer even louder. Zack de la Rocha said it first, but she said it so much better.

"My throat's dry. Anybody want to make a donation to the

357

Shaitan Needs A Drink Fund?" A score of hands reached up to offer their cans and bottles, but she laughed and waved them off. "Nah. There's got to be some water lying around here somewhere. Hey, I know this twenty-four-hour diner, the Greasy Spoon, they call it, where after midnight they charge you two bucks for a lousy glass of tap water. You know, because only drunks ever order it that late, and they need it. You believe that shit?"

The especially drunk and rowdy ones shouted out their denunciation of that kind of racket, Capitalism taken to an absurd degree.

"I mean, water falls out of the sky! You can't get more free than that! Oh, thank you," she added to some guy who'd brought her a cold bottle of natural spring refreshment from the Alps or someplace like that. She twisted off the lid and emptied the bottle in three long gulps.

"Ahhh. Hit the spot. Do any of you mind if we take a short break?"

The refusals were many and loud. She laughed. "Let me re-phrase that. We are *going* to take a short break now. Try to stop us and we'll scalp your ass. Hey, our drummer is the only one who drinks, but he handles our share for us. Don't get between him and a cold beer. You can call his mother anything you want, but *do not* try to touch his beer. To be continued."

She stepped down off of the bandstand and came to find me. I met her halfway.

"You did great up there, Shai. Really great."

"Thank you, but what the hell are you doing here?"

"Oh, I was in the neighborhood, so I just decided to drop by. See how you were doing."

"Uh-huh. Right. So how long are you in town for?"

"Til I'm apprehended."

"Ha! Knowing you, that would be T-minus ten, nine…"

"I was just passing through, and my friend managed to get us invited. I had no idea you'd be here."

"Well, tell me you're just passing through to the reservation in Birmingham. That's where we're headed next."

"You know I don't plan as far ahead as tomorrow."

"Haven't you ever heard of stability?"

"No, routine isn't something I'm used to. Come on, in my line of work you don't even buy green bananas. So how are things back home? How's Domingo?"

Her face turned to stone. A moment passed.

"You mean you don't know?"

"Know what?" Pause.

"So who's that over there? Your new girlfriend?"

"Shai?"

"And where have you *been* all this time?"

"Shai."

The stone cracked, a fault line spreading open.

"Tell me."

"He's dead, Evan."

It's a real pain in the ass to try and get a needle into your vein when your hands shake as much as mine were, but finally, after concentrating, aiming, and holding my breath, I managed to stab myself quickly in just the right place. I'd put more in the spoon than I usually did, thinking I'd have to get wasted just to cope with this. Intoxiwasted, obliterated.

Shaitan wouldn't tell me how D'ingo had died. Just told me that she wouldn't cry. She knew how he lived his life, what to expect, knew it was just a matter of time. She finally told me what they were doing together in the first place, being so different and all. That he'd charmed her in the way that only he could, then confessed to her how scared he was, how this wasn't the life he wanted but didn't know anything else. Too scared to tell his father he wanted to go straight and follow the rules.

"Comes with the territory," she said quietly. "Live by the sword, die by the sword."

Just as I started to push down on the plunger, something made me stop. Motionless, I listened. Crickets trilled somewhere out in the darkness to one side, and tribal drums shuddered faintly to the other. I had stumbled out into the night, away from everyone, and now knelt in the grass with a rig plugged into the crook of my arm. Desperate and pathetic.

I looked out into the blackness, straining my eyes to see where the crickets could be. It was pitch dark out there. I looked the other way, towards the ring of light surrounding the powwow. Here I was, as usual, out in the darkness. Outside the circle.

I had the strangest thought at that moment, inventing a new stupid phrase that would no doubt catch on and be a cliché in no time. I realized exactly what I was. I was a moth. A social moth, always just outside the light, hovering around at the edge and trying to get in. Never managing to fit in. Not at school, not in my family, and not even in the business I gave the first two up for. Never found myself completely comfortable with anyone.

I sourly remembered how Maya and her friends used to laugh at me. Not in meanness, just poking fun. Cracking little jokes. Nothing but fun, Evan. What's the matter? Can't take a joke?

"Juan José de Vargas y Balsa!" Maya said in her I'm A Complete Idiot voice. "Shut up honey, I'm trying to count!"

"Some nigger will eat your gun, and then where will you be?" Nestor's eyes regarding me with contempt. I'd never hated anyone as much as I hated myself at that moment. Because I *took* it. I took it all. I let them laugh. I pretended it didn't bother me. I sat there and took all the teasing because I was too afraid of losing my niche. Afraid of taking a stand, just accepting all the little jokes because I thought it would get worse if I didn't. Submitting to insults and allowing people to underestimate me, just to maintain the peace.

Even with my girlfriend.

"You're not manly, Evan," I mumbled. "You're sad and crying like a little girl because your doggie died."

I bared my fangs and glared out into the darkness, putting scorn into the voice I talked to myself with.

"You crying just because you saw some dead children? You didn't even know them, crybaby! But boo-hoo-fuckin-hoo, some kids are dead. You're going to become a diamond? Little pussy, you're not even a worthless piece of coal. You're a fucking turd. You're pathetic. Just drink up some wine and try to think about something else, like what Blondie must do every Freak Night."

I yanked the needle out, throwing it into the night. Leaping to my feet, I ripped the peyote bag open and spilled the cactus all over the ground, stomping on them, mashing them into the ground. I burst the Ziploc my smack was in and threw it, watching it disappear into the gloom, scattering the powder like a cropduster. Good riddance.

My mother would've said I was being too hard on myself. My dad would say I was just giving myself a little pep talk. Honestly, I don't know which of them would be right, but whatever it was, it worked. The same fire I had in me before sprang back up inside me, fully grown. I felt again the confidence of a guy who takes cops hostage, who can get any girl he wants as long as he doesn't kill anyone in front of her. Someone as slippery as an eel when it came to the law closing in. Someone who'll steal a fucking cop car out from under their noses and get home without calling for help.

"Who you calling a pussy?" I asked the night around me, the whole world, as I walked back into the light.

I caught up with Shaitan by the stage, getting ready to go back on. She looked like she was trying to channel her grief and bitterness, make it into something she could use. I've seen the look before, but I was hopeful.

"How about Maya? She's pregnant, you know."

"No, she isn't."

"What? She told me she was, but—"

"Yes, she was, but not anymore."

"…What?"

She took a deep breath, held it.

"You should have been there with her, Evan. A woman can't rely on another woman to protect her. Women need men just as badly as men need women, and you don't know how badly you let her down when you ran off. She…she's been hurt, Evan."

"What are you talking about?" My voice was little more than a choking whisper. "She didn't…she didn't have an…you know."

"No. An abortion? Never. She didn't kill your child."

"Then," I licked my lips with a sandpaper tongue.

"Shaitan!" another girl called. The flautist. "Ready?"

She nodded, turned back to me. She looked very tired, and very sad. I'd never seen her this way.

"Whatever you do will be too little, too late."

She left me there, frozen, and walked up the steps onto the stage. She never looked back.

I guess that's where I went…how I ended up the way I did.

There's no right way to say this. Fuck. I'd been running on autopilot for a little while, with just a skeleton crew in charge of my sanity, and mutiny broke out inside my head. Mental chaos.

I lied a little back there, or said a half-truth. Whatever. The whole time since I left Florida, I was scared. Jumping at my own shadow. During my long walk out of Beverly Hills, before I lost it with that AC/DC prostitute, I was terrified. I'd tried to run away from my troubles, but there's just no place that far. I got myself into one stupid situation after another, and in 20/20 hindsight it looked like plain old self-destruction.

They don't make psychotropic drugs for kamikazes. People aren't interested in health anymore, just getting wasted. That's how America conquered its own people, by glorifying intoxication, making it chic. At least, that's what my old man told me, but what does he know? Self-ordained expert on everything under the sun, but couldn't raise a son worth a damn. If I ever needed anything, I needed him right now.

Yeah, he'd yell at me for a while, but that beats the hell out of running for the rest of your life. As much fun as I'd had on the dark side, I'd sell my soul to the Devil for another shot at life, college, nine-to-five, insurance policies, and fingertips unstained by black ink.

But I'd have nothing to offer the Devil if he showed up. My soul was already mortgaged to the hilt.

I left Windsong there, watching her from afar to make sure she was having a good time, and let the darkness swallow me.

If Los Angeles is supposed to be the pinnacle of Western civilization, with all the depravity and sin surrounded by glitter and neon, then New York is Hell's twelfth ring. I felt as if I were at the bottom of a well in the dark shadows of these gargantuan buildings, crowded close together, suffocatingly close. The City is a labyrinth, and I couldn't shake the feeling that it was the Trench, only a honeycomb instead of one line, miles long and only a few cubits thick. It was just paranoia, I suppose, but I remember the movies about the Western Front, somewhere in between St. Quentin and Ypres, all my thoughts drowned out by a storm of roaring guns.

The din of this city made me wish for something I'd never given a thought to—a glorious moment of *silence*. I'd heard it called the City That Never Sleeps, and that's gospel truth. The noise never lets up, not for one second, and if it weren't for the sky changing color every now and then, I wouldn't know whether it was day or night. And worse, I wasn't in a city. I was in an abyss, expecting to look up and see sharks float out of an alley, turn the corner, and swim off down the street to the bar.

I was already hopelessly lost the first day I was there, and every direction I chose just led me farther into its depths. In L.A., the city grid is warped with a sprawl of crosshatching diagonals that make up twenty different ways to get somewhere. It's illogical, confusing, and a pain in the ass for a boy from Coquina. New York, on the other hand, is terrifying in its maze of complexity. And the *subways*, fuck, they're a nightmare! This place wasn't Metropolis, it was Gotham, and no Seth McHales were going to show up and lead me to the Bridge. The few punks I met didn't give a shit about Hollywood Hardcore, were contemptuously unimpressed with everything Californian…come to think about it I think they were unimpressed with everything on Earth.

Everybody I met was. The ones that didn't seem like to me like predators probably were in one way or another.

I'd glimpsed starlets every now and then in Hollywood, but in the strange trench city I'd found my way into, the only movie stars I heard about were little girls in snuff films. The only work I could find was in a world born out of nightmare and lunacy, fighting death-matches in the basement of a porno circus. I didn't kill anyone, even though I was supposed to. Always showed mercy, just because I hoped someone would spare me if I'd lost. And against these animals, I barely squoke through myself.

In the ground floor, the day I stepped through the door, what I saw translated for me what the marker-scrawled sign said outside. *Lasciate ogni speranza, voi ch'entrate.* Italian, but not too far from Spanish and Portuguese, and the sleaze I laid my eyes on filled in the blank for me.

Abandon all hope, ye who enter here.

I did.

I slept wherever I could, usually on the floor of a different apartment every night. The few beds I found my way into left me feeling dirty the next morning, but that was probably all in my head.

Free after a few weeks of heroin's clutches, I tried to drown myself in tequila, but before too long, I seemed to still think in a straight line after draining a whole fifth. My tolerance had gotten so high that on some nights, trying to drink myself into oblivion, I'd greet the dawn with nothing to show for my efforts but an empty wallet.

The days melted into one another, and weeks would go by without my noticing. I still knew nothing about where I was. Hadn't bothered to study a map and learn what borough I was in. Sometimes, I'd go for a long walk, trying to stumble upon something better, but I usually ended up where I'd started. My most common

363

fantasy on these walks was turning into an alley where a drug deal had gone sour, both sides killing each other and leaving the brief-case in the open, for anyone to take.

It never happened.

I got mugged a few times, but I usually gained back the next day what I'd lost during the night. Except my dignity, but I'd given up the last of it anyway. I felt like an alien, trying to pass myself off as local on another planet, and that led me to lower my standards farther than I'd even thought possible. I learned to tolerate strange-ness around me until I was numb to it. Christ, this is *how* numb, how accepting:

I've seen die-hard rascists become fast friends with the people they hated yesterday, and it wasn't Jesus that made them change their tune. It was crack. White supremacists and black supremacists sat down together in front of my own eyes and smoked crack. Of course, it wasn't the first time they'd ever smoked, not even on that occasion. This was maybe the third or fourth session of their re-spective binges. And if one group had the rocks and the other didn't, all of a sudden those without discovered they had been long-time closet sympathizers with the other side, so deep in the closet they themselves didn't know about it. Like Peter denying Jesus, skinheads would say the swastikas tattooed on their scalps were a mean trick played on them once when they were drunk, and Nation of Islam fanatics in their Kill Whitey t-shirts and Malcolm X hats would reply that it was laundry day and this was their neighbors' shit they were wearing.

Seemed like a no-brainer to me: you want world peace, you cook up some crack. To hell with peace talks and cease-fires and summits and treaties. Parachute-drop a crack stem and a hundred slab into every camp in a war zone maybe five times over one week-end, and then drop pamphlets saying there's more stashed back towards home, the secret location's coordinates on sale now for the low, low price of: all the weapons and ammunition. Give them a day or so, and I guarantee they'd all give up everything down to their suicide pills for a single rock.

What I'm getting at is...well...

I...I smoked...um...I smoked crack a few times.

Hey, judge not, motherfucker, lest ye be judged. I'm an adult, I can do it if I want.

Besides, it's not like I'm hooked on it or anything. I just tried it. A few times. Like, I dunno, eleven or twelve.

Yeah, so, anyway...

Then, one afternoon, I found myself in the more upscale business areas. Not Fifth Avenue, of course, but someplace where Real People go to buy things, and I was leaning against a telephone pole, lighting a cigarette and envying all of the Ordinaries, when an unfamiliar sound startled me.

Laughter. The happy laughter of young lovers tussling in public and knowing that they shouldn't. I turned round and saw that I was in front of a lingerie shop, and a couple was coming out of the door a few yards to my right, hands full of shopping bags, filled with things they'd bought today that they'd use tonight. Their words were private, but it was obvious what they teased each other about. I stared at them, struck dumb, wondering if this were another of those dreams I confused with reality. It must have been.

Pedro Vizcaya caught sight of me from the corner of his eye, stopping in his tracks, and the beautiful woman who drew up beside him was Teresa de Medieros.

Neil Macaulay thought he must have been in one of those three-day blackouts left over from his college days, `cause there was no logical explanation for his waking up one day and finding himself married to Brenda Clower. He was a fairly dull guy with an abysmal lack of imagination, while she...*she* was clearly out of her cotton-picking mind. She was a geyser of blasphemy if someone got her started on religion. She was an avid midnight visitor of graveyards, and a painter of strange, disturbing pictures.

Her new father-in-law found many accurate words to describe her, but one of them stuck like glue.

Unhallowed.

She and her three sisters looked so much alike—petite, almost waifish, and ugly in a strangely pretty way—that it seemed like they hadn't been born (or hatched, as the mother-in-law so quaintly put it) in the traditional manner. They looked like they'd all come into the world on a cookie sheet. People would meet them and wait for the other halves of their bodies to show up, wondering if they were the setup to some joke.

They were known euphemistically as "general circulation girls" around the neighborhood. She turned out to be the looniest. She collected the brochures of every exotic religion she could find, trying to find one that best fit her level of weirdness. The only two creeds she didn't adopt were Jewry and Catholicism, just because she thought they looked like too much trouble. Her favorite pagan religion was Hindu, and no matter what else she tried to give a day in court, she always came back to it.

She kept trying to make her daughter join whatever the latest passing fad was, and expected her to jump at the chance to be mutilated in some new and trendy way.

Neil stood firm about the lip plugs, the tattoos, the shaved head, the neck rings, and the lip plates. Not happening. Uh-uh. The only thing he allowed Maya to get done to her was the ear weights, and that's only because she actually liked the idea. For once.

Then, there were the clothes. Burkhas, cheongsams, kimonos, sarongs, you name it. Maya would wear a sarong, sure, because it's just a cool-looking skirt. But as far as she was concerned, you could burn the rest of that stuff. She felt like she was her own mother's Barbie. Ooh, look! Hari Krishna Barbie! And here, try Vestial Virgin Barbie!

Yay.

And sex. Oh, gotta tell Maya 'bout the birds and the bees. First came the facts, then the techniques, then actually studying the Kama Sutra as if it were a text book. Then, history. Gotta know all about the Comte Donatien-Alphonse-François, a.k.a. the Marquis de Sade, who put beating the shit out of people for sexual pleasure on the map. Gotta know about Caligula, Vatsyayana, and Jenna Jameson.

Everybody thought Mrs. Macaulay was a nutcase, except Maya. She knew it.

She was just finishing a song on her computer, putting the last few touches on it, and lighting an Indian bidi, one of those minty herb things she was so fond of, rolled in a dried maple leaf with a pink thread tied near the butt end. Hitting the spacebar, she leaned back in her throne and listened to it from the beginning. The display that was scrolling along on the monitor looked like a polygraph test with lies registered all over the place, each mountain and valley, each wave and trough showing the song in black and white.

She smoked her bidi, knowing that she wouldn't be able to anymore, and feeling a little sad that the best gift she could ever receive had to come around like this. She looked down at her belly, slouching so it wouldn't look so flat and empty. Before long, it would be swollen, and she wished Evan could be around to hold it, hold her.

Coward.

She couldn't sleep anymore. The place was so empty to her; she thought she might as well move into a bare bulb warehouse. She looked around at all of her surreal furniture, wondering all of a sudden what the point of it was. She had a sort-of girlfriend, but that meant nothing in the long run. She needed a man. She needed *her* man back. All of this stuff in her apartment was a waste. Every sex toy, every powder and herb, every meal she cooked was all a waste because the man she enjoyed them with was gone.

Man? Hell no. *Boy.*

And then her beautiful face twisted into dry sobs and keening grief. Now what? Start all over again? Start all over from scratch with some new guy who'd probably run off, too? That's when the tears came, streaming down her reddening face, the sobs choking her and racking her body until she leaned forward to cradle her face in her hands. Shuddering and wailing like a child.

And that's how the Bacalous found her when they came through the door.

They found Domingo on their doorstep, passed out and naked as the day he was born. His mother gaped in horror at him, assuming him drunk and showing up like this, in the middle of the night. Then, she saw.

Nestor came barreling out of the bedroom when he heard her scream, a .357 Magnum in his fist making it impossible to tie the sash on his bathrobe. His wife stood hunched over in the doorway, shrieking at the top of her lungs. His first thought was *Damn, woman, don't just stand there.*

Shoving her to one side against the doorframe, he stabbed the gun out into the night, looking for someone to aim at. It was only an instant before he saw the shape lying across the stoop, and he didn't need to look to know whose it was.

His legs bending at impossible angles, Domingo slowly awoke. His eyelids cracked open and shut again, crusted together with dried blood. His pulped and swollen lips gaped wide under the stump of his nose, revealing only stalagmites of shattered teeth. The outside light was off, leaving only the glow through the doorway to see by, but what he saw made Nestor de Medieros go limp with shock.

367

His son had been castrated.

Pedro got the call seven minutes later, at 12:51. He was instantly awake and getting dressed with the phone resting between his
shoulder and ear. As soon as Abuela had hung up, he called every
soldier in Salon des Refusés, gave his orders swiftly and was obeyed
without question.

The women went to the house on Ponce de Leon, and the men
sped out to the house in BFE. Pedro had never been there, not
knowing what it was, but they all converged upon it with confidence. Ready for battle. The gate had been left open, and the black
SUVs filtered through and fanned out, parking in a wide semicircle
facing the house.

The only light besides their headlamps was from candles flickering inside, and what looked like a barbecue. Warily, taking in every
detail of their surroundings, the fifty-three mercenaries frowned at
the circle of death, exchanging glances of an unspoken "what the
fuck?" until the last truck engine silenced. Now, their eyes were
wide and fixed on the open door of the house, trying to see who the
strange singing voice belonged to. Inside the smell of cooking meat
was not unpleasant, but disturbingly familiar to the soldiers, whose
wide eyes narrowed into slits at what they saw on the makeshift altar
and at their employer's figure on both knees, arms outstretched
before him.

They stared at Nestor as he performed the rites of Santería,
calling upon every demon he prayed to, begging to be answered.
The sight was not scowled upon by only two men, strangers who
stood in the shadows. The flickering firelight reflected in one man's
spectacles, making him look like a beast whose eyes gleamed in the
light of an oncoming car. The other one was just a shadow, black
against the gray of darkness.

On the altar lay what Pedro supposed was the remains of Domingo de Medieros. But he couldn't really tell. Some might say the
boy had been put out of his misery, but not with this sort of enthu-
siasm for it. He had been turned inside out.

Salon des Refusés went outside to wait, disgusted.

They stood out in the night, smoking and grumbling amongst
themselves about how they wished they could work for someone
else. They used to joke about how ice water was so hot it would
melt Nestor's heart. But now, seeing this strange house and the ring

of barrenness surrounding it, they saw that there was much more to it than that, and none of it was anything they were comfortable with.

It had been an exciting past few days, storming the police station and blowing things up, and now they were ready to go to war with somebody else, but it didn't hold a candle to Colombia or Jerusalem. Change of venue was definitely on their Christmas lists.

Pedro came out, on the phone with Abuela, since her daughter was still hysterical. He had told the old woman that her grandson hadn't made it to the hospital, and she cackled at him like a witch. He was amazed that she found the boy's death so amusing, but when she explained to him what was done, he became speechless. Teresa didn't know, would never know, what Abuela and Nestor had decided to do. Her interest in Santería was only dutifully tolerant, because her mother and her husband adamantly believed.

Abuela told her son-in-law to offer the boy up to the gods, and they would grant him vengeance in return.

The Basque held the phone in front of his face and scowled at it, at the gravelly voice coming out of it, and wished it were possible to spit on someone through it. It was Nestor's phone. Pedro had answered it when it flashed its silent ring inside, since the Brazilian was still in his sorcery bullshit. That's why he reached in his pocket that moment to answer a loud ringing. His own cell.

"Buenas nachos, El Spickolo," an obviously black voice said merrily. Pedro's was the only phone number listed in the book, but how this caller had known his involvement with the family made no sense. Then, he knew. A sobbing girl came on the line, the phone being taken over to her and placed against her head. Another girl was screaming in the background.

Wheeling about, Pedro rushed back into the house, interrupting the "ceremony." His eyes were ablaze, and he didn't give a shit if the three men were disturbed. He jammed his phone on the side of his kneeling boss' face and held it there, the other cell clenched in his free hand, with Abuela's questions spilling out.

Nestor listened in the dimness, his eyes wide with a fear he hadn't felt in a very long time. He trembled, his lips quivering soundlessly, listening to his daughter being raped.

Outside, the soldiers crowded the door and windows, trying to see what was going on. The ones in the back kept asking what happened, and the ones in the front kept angrily waving them to si-

369

lence. All of them held their weapons as if the enemy would suddenly appear, ready to spray them down and take the rest of the city apart, so eager they were for battle.

Then, the most incredible thing happened. Nestor de Medieros began to cry. He crumpled to the floor and curled up, fetal with grief, and sobbed like a little girl. He shook violently, as if with fever, a high keening whine faintly mingling with the voices from the two phones. Both of his children, now...

Pedro lifted his own cell and told the speaker he would deal.

"How much is yo dottah's life wurt?"

"Neither of them are my daughter. Now, what do you want?"

"We wantcha boy. The white mothafucka, and whoever he went to da Hill wit."

"The boy is gone."

"Then these two dykes is gone, too."

"No! Give us some time to find him, and we'll bring them both to you. Where?"

"Out in the Acreage. S'about one-thirty, so best get steppin'."

Pedro did not need to write down the directions. The second the spokesgangsta told him, they were memorized. He was looking at Calibos, the Colombian's face bandaged and his head framed in a neck brace. The BL hung up, and Pedro told Abuela he'd call her back.

"They want you and Evan," he told Calibos.

"Then we say fock tha gorls and go to war!"

"No." He turned and watched Nestor shaking on the ground. "We give them exactly what they want."

He looked at the two strangers, who were talking quietly and looking with disgust at Nestor. The Spaniard calmly pulled out his pistol and shot them both.

"Go downtown," he said to his men. "Find a kid who looks like Evan, the boy who hung out with us. Remember what he looked like? Find someone who's close enough to him and bring him here. Rough him up a little so the differences in face cannot be seen. Go."

Calibos stared at Pedro as the soldiers went to their trucks, uncertain and worried. The Spaniard was standing over Nestor, regarding him with contempt. The boss's mind had clearly snapped.

"So that's the turncoat taken care of," Calibos said, his tone challenging. "Wha' bout me? I'm not going."

"The man who went to Golgotha was short and Latin," Pedro said. "So, we will give them a man who's short and Latin."

The two armies met and traded their hostages. There was a brief parlay, the BLs advising Pedro to get the fuck off their turf, and Pedro calmly promising that they'd never see him again. Surprisingly, almost all of the gangstas were white or Hispanic. It was the group of capos who were black. Pedro wondered which ones of them had done the raping, and whether they'd rape "Evan" and "Calibos" as well. To the victors go the spoils.

He carried Mariana to his car as if she were a child, placing her in the backseat, and a tall Dutchman named Klaus carried Maya. Nestor had been drugged, so he walked docilely as a lamb to the slaughterhouse. The white kid hadn't really looked like Evan, but after he'd been kicked to sleep, he could've passed for anyone. Salon des Refusés backed off and drove away.

Pedro frowned at Maya and Mariana holding each other with such familiarity, shook his head at the words they used to comfort and soothe. He sadly drove them to the hospital, back in civilization, wondering what the world had come to.

Behind him, each packed SUV slowed enough for everyone but the drivers to bail out, and continued on for appearance's sake. The drivers cursed their luck, but every one of them had drawn the short straw, and didn't get the pleasure of killing that night. The rest of them vanished into the woods on either side of the road. They hoped to either catch BLs on the road back to town, or surprise them at that house in the middle of nowhere, torturing their new playthings.

Pedro lied to Teresa about how brave her husband was, hiding the man's weakness and praising the sacrifice he'd made for his daughter. Then, he called Sgt. Neil Macaulay, waking him up with an anonymous, untraceable call, telling him his daughter had been released by the mysterious kidnappers and would be all right. They still believed the old story.

Neil and Brenda spend the rest of that night at the hospital, crying at the side of her bed.

Repeatedly raped and horribly beaten, the girls were tested for HIV infection, and the other trendy diseases. Mariana couldn't summon the strength to be relieved with her "negative", and Maya only mumbled "What else is new?" when she had been found guilty.

Her pregnancy was over after only a month and a half, the fetus dying within her along with her heart, her hope, and her faith in God.

Pedro kept his assumptions about them to himself, and just stayed in the background as long as it took for the girls to be well again. They left the hospital a week later.

A soldier was posted to discreetly keep an eye on Maya, and report any strange or erratic behavior. His watch was not uneventful. After going berserk and destroying half of her apartment, she sat down for a few quiet hours, then got up to empty all of her weirdly shaped, colored bottles of exotic liquors into the sink, wrote a short letter with her transfer paper so twelve copies were made the one time, and rolled them up, sticking one into each bottle. Got in her car and drove to the marina at Coquina's man-made harbor, where Nestor's boat was docked. Walked out to the inlet with a suitcase full of the bottles, and flung each one of them out into the ocean.

While she was gone, her shadowing soldier called another to break into the apartment and steal the page on the writing tablet that the indentions of the notes would have pressed through to. A pencil rubbing on that piece of paper showed everything she had written, what was floating away in those bottles.

The soldier burned the letter and shook his head when questioned, lying, saying it was illegible. He felt it was no one else's business. He then went to Saint Mark's Cathedral, lit a candle, and prayed for the soul of Maya Macaulay.

When he found out about Moke and the other children, Pedro sat down and had a long talk with them. The BL's house was emptied when the soldiers snuck up on it the previous night, so he came up with a better idea.

Disbanding the group of little assassins, he sent them out to look for work among other gangs, Bacalous, preferably. Moke, it seemed, was the cleverest. He had already "peeped the lick," and told Pedro he'd be up under the BLs before they knew what hit them. The Spaniard was pleased. He told them all to get comfortable working with the enemy until he reappeared with the Plan.

"Be patient, boys," he said. "I don't know how long we will be getting reorganized, but you'll know when we're ready. You just bury yourselves inside them like ticks. Do a good job and make them happy with you, so you'll get praised to the bigger fish, and maybe you will get to meet someone high enough on the totem pole that we can really do some damage."

One kid spoke up, a little "redbone" who looked so sweet and harmless that no one would've ever thought he was packing heat. Teresa had named him Shrike, after a vicious tiny songbird that acted like a hawk. As small as it was, it was a mean damned bird, nicknamed "the butcher-bird," and often impaled its larger prey on barbed wire, building up piles of dead things to impress the girls. It was always underestimated.

"You want us to find out where the big dogs live?"

"That's right. You get next to them and tell us where they are. Once you've done your jobs, we will have their business."

"Will we gets to go off on our own when we done? Like all the rest of 'em?"

"The rest of who?"

"Rashawn and the older jits," Moke said. "Uncle Nestor said when we turn ten we get to do what we want. If we want."

As long as what you want is to be lying on that table with your heart cut out, Pedro thought. He shook his head, unable to imagine killing a child.

"Yes. As soon as you turn ten."

"Why you sayin' yeah but shakin' your head no?"

"Because with Uncle Pedro, you'll get a retirement pension, instead of what you boys used to get."

"Straight up?" Shrike asked, impressed.

"Yeah. Straight up. Now, you boys want some ice cream?"

"Yeah!" Their eyes lit up and they fidgeted happily.

"Go see Cristos in the kitchen."

They all jumped up and raced around him, cheering, yelling out what the last one there would be. Pedro finally let his fatherly façade drop, and shook his head again, wide-eyed. *Killers?*

What's the world come to?

Teresa sat at her dining room table, smoking her fourteenth cigarette back to back. For the first time since they had met, Pedro saw her as a mortal woman. Her ethereal aura had faded like perfume at the end of the night, and lines of worry were finally creasing her handsome face.

She was on her third glass of cachaça, and Pedro decided to grab a glass for himself, just so she couldn't drink too much more.

He knew that pain must be faced head on and never filed away. He reached across the table and covered her delicate hand with his.

"Are you going to live?" he asked softly.

She nodded, staring at the surface of the table.

"So, what now, Your Highness?"

She laughed faintly. That had been his name for her since the first party they really enjoyed, when the Mariachis played a *sarabanda* and the Basque asked her to dance. He strode up to her where she stood trying to mask her boredom, tired of turning on her million-watt smile for her husband's "business associates." Pedro had toyed with the idea, trying to work up the nerve to breach etiquette, then finally said fuck it. Throwing caution to the wind and letting the chips fall where they chose, he went to her and stood stiffly at attention.

She had seen him coming and raised her eyebrows expectantly. He then spoke in his most solemn voice, offering his hand and making a big production out of it.

"May I have this dance, Your Highness?"

She regarded him with cool surprise, smiled faintly at his audacity, and felt the looks of other guests. Deciding not to look like a cold bitch in front of everyone, and also thinking it was about time *somebody* asked her, she played along with Pedro's act. Regally placing her hand in the Spaniard's, she strode out onto the dance floor under the stars. Nestor watched, half-jealously.

The lusty, ancient dance began; Teresa couldn't help but smile. She was good, as good as a gorgeous Latina was automatically, but Pedro was astounding. Her heart leaped as they moved together, the passionate music taking her away, and afterward…

Afterward…

She saw the man in a different light. No longer just a "business associate," but a man, a real man, whose very manliness made her tingle. Their clandestine love began that night, the flames fanned by the risk, and how slowly it rose in its level. The stolen, illicit kiss. The covert squeezing of hands. The longing gazes.

And now, they had the world all to themselves.

"Nestor was a fool," she said. "A fool with big dreams and self-importance. But I was the bigger fool for following him."

"No. You took a vow at the altar of Our Lord. Yes, we have sinned together, but you kept your vow. Now?"

"Altar of Our Lord! It was not our Lord's altar I married Nestor at. I don't know whose it was." Teresa's voice went quiet. "No, it wasn't any God I know we knelt in front of. My God wasn't in our house. We had a lot of saints, and a lot of candles, but no Bible."

She stared into her glass for a long time, then finally stubbed out her cigarette in the ashtray.

"Where do you stand?" she asked, her eyes meeting his.

He half smiled, squeezing the hand he held.

"Where I always will. Right at your side."

Her hand squirmed within his, and their fingers curled together. Her eyes warmed, but she remained serious.

"Do you have any problem working for a woman?"

"Not if she is Teresa Vizcaya."

"Then let's get to work."

Teresa and Pedro flew to Nassau on one of those tiny planes that look like they could be launched with a sling-shot. There, they went to Scotia Bank, the best organization for discreet investing in the Western Hemisphere. The young Bahamian ladies had the most bizarre filing system either of them had ever seen. The place was filled with tall stacks of folders, and the agents somehow knew exactly which one to go to. They were quick, efficient, friendly, and above all, confidential, all without benefit of computers of any kind.

Teresa wired almost two hundred thousand in hard currency to Pedro's account in Florida, and six million to her own. Now, there was plenty on hand for him and his men to move easily, without any hardship, and she was prepared for her new plans. Insurance was also claimed.

They dined at Iguana's, enjoyed a long walk on the beach at sunset, and went out drinking and dancing for the whole night. What they did on the beach in the middle of the long walk home is their own business.

Salon des Refusés was more than happy to be mobilizing and getting the hell out of Florida. The people were too strange here, and from what they'd heard, New York would be much more fun. Teresa kept the safehouses busy, but the dealers and rollers were cut off until further notice. Crates would be coming in, but nothing would be going out for some time. Loyalty would be tested.

Pedro then sat down with Mariana and Maya, who were only emotionally wrecked at this point. He promised that he would not expose them, and that they would not go unavenged. Since things would be unstable for a while, and they needed time to get their heads straight, he told them to pick a place—any place they wanted—and they would be flown there on hiatus.

Ibíza won by a landslide.

A therapist would lie and say that this was the wrong way, that expressing your grief aloud and whining about your feelings—and only to a qualified therapist for large amounts of money, not some family member or friend who actually gave a shit—was the only possible way to fully "survive" a "traumatic experience." Dwell on it. Wallow in pain and misery. Pity yourself. And do it for an hour, once a week, and bring your checkbook. For the rest of your life. Absolutely not, under any circumstances, should you move on. Get a hobby. Make new friends. Start over. The con men say Tell me about it, cry on my shoulder.

Some of them say Lie on this couch.

Some of them say Come into my church.

Some say Here, smoke this.

Okay, one out of three works, but we're digressing.

Teresa made a few calls, kissed her daughter good-bye, and made them both promise not to come back until they'd healed. She knew that some wounds take forever to close, and she would do anything to see Mariana smile again. If sending her to Ibíza with her friend would do the trick, she'd buy them a house there.

An old friend promised her that he'd take good care of them, and she knew if anyone could help them, he could. Mariana had shown a bit of little-girly crush on him ever since the man's first visit, and with good reason. Rabbit (he never told what the reason for his nickname was) had a magnetic personality, and made everyone within earshot pleased to be around him.

He was currently in some town in Sicily, but he told them not to worry about Ibíza. He claimed to have one or two friends on the island, and knowing him, that meant "hundred." Not that he was one of those superstar assholes everybody wanted to be around. Just that he was friendly, easy to get along with, and filthy rich. There were a few skeletons in his closet, but most of them belonged to law enforcement officials, so the de Medieros family couldn't frown on his past too much.

As soon as the nervous and paranoid girls were on the plane—first class, of course—Teresa turned her attention to Pecado, New

York. She tried not to think about how much the girls had looked like Chihuahuas, concentrating instead on arabesqued doors, mosaic floors, and stained glass Quetzalcoatls. And class-A narcotics. Can't forget those.

She and her mother discussed the new layout over a pack of Marlboros and a walnut coffee cake. Abuela preferred to be drunk rather than stoned on hash oil while planning, so she was thinking about her second glass before she'd finished her first. At her age, she liked the world a whole lot better seen through rose tinted glasses—or, more accurately, the amber goggles of *capirinha*. She was already planning a stained glass Tlaloc, the Aztec rain god, and Tezcatlipoca. The hostess's podium would be a totem pole, the famed Tsimshian "Hole In The Sky." She couldn't wait to get started.

The six million would be more than enough to purchase a lot in New York with a good location, location, location, and cover all the materials necessary to renovate it. Labor wouldn't be a problem; fifty-three mercenaries under one Basque were more than adequate.

Secretly, Teresa was grateful for the project requiring so much of her attention, and she would be sure to throw herself into actual production as much as possible. Anything that took her mind off the recent catastrophe was welcome. She would not be on her knees, spackling the nail holes in baseboards, but she would be constantly sweeping up, getting in the way, and being as much of a nuisance as she could.

There were no funerals, no ceremonies, and no wakes. Nothing. She firmly refused to spend any more time crying, and such things were useless anyway. Best to forget the dead and get on with her life. Her family had dissolved so quickly: her husband tortured, her son tortured, her daughter left alive but still tortured, and her adopted (in her eyes) second son running away, for what reason she could not guess. To stop and think about the futility of life after this would tempt her to give up, and she could not allow such thoughts.

She was Brazilian, after all.

"So, that is the news, little coal," she said. I had listened to them, sitting in a back booth of a coffee shop, alternating between one point of view and the other, me filling in the blanks myself. Pedro would tell me later what I suspected the truth about Nestor was, and until then, all I could do was gape in disbelief. The chaos

377

that had followed our bombings had been tremendous, much worse than I had supposed it would be.

The city's confusion, the looting, the blatantly-taken advantage over Order had been a horror they spoke nothing of, having seen much worse in their days. The repercussions hadn't made it into the circles I'd traveled, and I never was one to watch the news. But now, having been caught and raised back to a human level of existence, I was surrounded by people to whom such things mattered, so I found myself caring. If that doesn't make any sense, it doesn't surprise me. I've been on autopilot for so long that I find it hard to express myself. Basically, the way my mind re-awoke in Tommy's that night, my heart was stirring now.

We sat in a coffee house, and I still felt dazed by having two of the most important people in my life holding hands in front of me. I tried to look back and remember seeing any stolen moments shared by secret lovers, but their feelings for each other had always been invisible. Never had they given the public eye a chance to spot them, that's how careful they had been, how mindful of the danger. I had to admire them.

"So now, *niño*," Pedro said with a serious tone. "You will explain your desertion. I feel we have a right to know."

I took a deep breath, holding it in as an excuse for my hesitation.

"I found a house out in the woods," I told them finally.

"Ah, say no more."

Teresa and I were both surprised by Pedro, his look of understanding. The Brazilian questioned him with her eyes, but he shook his head, waving the matter aside until later.

"But you have had long enough vacation. Are you ready to come back to work?" His voice was stern, but not enough to hide the undercurrent of forgiveness. I could only nod.

"Good. Bring your things to our hotel, and—"

"I have nothing."

"—We will have...what did you say?"

"I have nothing. No car, no possessions, only what I'm wearing."

"...Oh. Well. That makes this easier. Finish your coffee and let's go home. We are bivouacked at the Ritz."

That's all there was to it.

They bought out a dive that had been doomed to low class customers, just on the outskirts of a higher class area, plus the bakery next door, combining them. Three point one million dollars. I'm told that's a paltry sum when it comes to business real estate, but just saying the amount, to me, is a religious experience. The rest of the money was spent on materials. Advertising was unnecessary.

Abuela went to work, etching and staining glass, with incredible results. Pedro, Klaus, Henri, and Oisin began gutting the place, getting the pleasure of destruction because they were the four top men in Salon des Refusés. Teresa, desperate to be busy, made sure that anything we needed was immediately made available, from the medium-sized crowbar to a bunch of ice cold sodas. She was thoughtful and efficient.

Another fine example of how packed my head is—or rather, *was*—is telling Pedro that I was sure that Quetzalcoatl had been real. He blinked at me, staring hard, before making a facial shrug. I pointed at the tall stained glass partition Abuela had just finished making.

"A feathered snake. Remind you of anything?"

He was obviously trying not to think I was stoned again.

"Pedro, I talked with Maya about a lot of things, and a few times I actually went into the library all by myself and looked more things up. Things I became curious about, and had to know. What Maya had told me was that many myths had been based on facts. True stuff that got embellished."

"Almost every religion in the world talks about a Great Flood."

Now I had his attention.

"If not only the Jews, but the Babylonians, Assyrians, Egyptians, Persians, Hindus, Greeks, Chinese, Phrygians, Figi Island people, the Esquimaux, American Indians from North and South America, Druids, and even the folks from Greenland all had a myth about a certain strange thing happening, it can't be a coincidence. It was probably just a bunch of glaciers from the end of an Ice Age melting, or something like that. But if you don't know about a shitload of ice being a ways north of you, when it melts and you get flooded, you're probably not going to say Hmmm, that was probably a big-ass glacier melting somewhere. If you're primitive, you're probably going to say Holy Shit! What'd we do to piss the gods off?"

Now he was blinking at me again, skeptically.

"But guess what else I found out?" I continued. "In 1997, in a place called Villa Angel Flores in Mexico, it rained frogs."

Pedro's eyes widened, maybe only a half a millimeter, but they did widen. I grinned. I had memorized everything, all the facts, before trying to tell him this. To impress him, restore his faith in me.

"A tornado picked them up out of a pond, carried them a ways, and then dumped them in this village. It happens. It happened a hundred-something years ago, *twice*, right here in the States. I read the microfiche of the newspaper articles. 1873 Scientific American, Kansas City, and 1883 Decatur Daily Republican. A plague of frogs fell out of the sky."

I waited for him to say something, but he didn't. Shit. I was trying to prove to him that I'd been *thinking* like he always told me to. "Confucius said 'think, think, think,'" he'd say.

So I kept on, telling Pedro what I'd learned. "It's not just frogs. We all know locusts come in plagues, too. All the time. So there's no real mystery there. When locusts come, there's a whole bunch, and we have a famine. No surprise. There's also a toxic alga that kills fish in the sea and makes people cough a whole mile inland when the wind blows across it over the water. It's called *Karenia brevis*, and it stinks like hell. It only sometimes happens near land, but it does happen, every year, and it blooms between a thousand to over a million individual algae per liter of ocean water... and it's blood red, Pedro."

He still said nothing. Those eyes were starting to give me a headache.

"A huge, stinky, red patch of water that kills fish and makes people choke...like the Nile turning to blood..."

I stopped trying to maintain eye contact, looked at his nose instead.

"So, what I'm thinking, this algae killed off the fish that had been living off the eggs of frogs. Those eggs hatched and became tons of baby frogs that went on land and died. Lying there, they attracted flies and lice and stuff. The lice carried this bluetongue virus, which killed off most of Egypt's livestock. The flies carried this bacterial infection that causes boils on people. I'm thinking after that, there was probably a sandstorm that lasted maybe three days, and in it the heat met an approaching cold front to make hail and thunder storms. The wind probably blew locusts out of Ethiopia and into Egypt. After the hail melted, locusts shit and water

380

made the grain poisonous. Egyptians, back in the day, gave their first-born sons the lion's share at dinner, so they ate more bad food than anyone else in the family, so they died. And that's that mystery solved.

"And while I'm at it, bread falling out the sky..." I couldn't resist the dramatic pause while I lit a Marlboro.

"There's this desert tree in the Middle East, northern Africa. It's dormant for a long time, until the conditions are just right, then it releases seeds. Since a lot of trees can't live close together in lousy soil, the seeds have to go a long, long way. That's why a lot of trees keep their seeds inside fruit. An animal eats the fruit and walks away somewhere, poops it out—"

"I know all that. Thank you, Johnny Appleseed. Now, get on with it."

I laughed. Took a long drag so I could pause again. "Well, this tree's seeds, they have to be pretty lightweight, so they can be carried on the wind to faraway places. A *lot* of them. On the wind. With this fruit that anybody who has eaten it always describes as 'bread-like.' In the north of Africa, in the middle of the desert, a whole mess of bread-like shit fell out of the sky."

Pedro looked away, suppressing a laugh.

"*Hmmmmm,*" I said, sarcasm dripping as I smoked.

"So how does this tie in to Quetzalcoatl over there?"

"That's what got me started on all this. Maya told me an archaeopteryx fossil was found in North America."

"A who?"

"The missing link between reptiles and birds, s'posedly. A step up from pterodactyls. A feathered lizard."

Pedro's eyebrows jumped, one of them almost arching off of his forehead, then he smiled.

"So what you think is—" he began, but I interrupted.

"It makes perfect sense! The Western Hemisphere had flying dinosaurs with feathers, so why wouldn't primitive people think the last, maybe, few of them, were gods? Shit, they thought *jaguars* were gods. The archaeopteryx died out, but enough people had seen at least one, so when they were gone, they decided it was probably a god coming down to do whatever gods to when they come down!"

"Eat people, probably."

"Sure! Why not? So, what do you think?"

"Honestly?"

"Honestly."

"I think you'll screw up the stain on that wood you were varnishing if you don't keep the wet line going."

I looked down at the task I'd forgotten about.

Shit.

He chuckled. "I missed you, little brother. It's good to have you back. Now get to work."

And we all lived happily ever after.

I wish that could be the end of this.

I wish it could be true, but no matter who says it, it never ever is.

We were visited by some "business associates" of a guy named Benny Califano, whoever the hell he is, and they tried to intimidate Pedro into also being his associate. We were on their ground, and if we told these guys to go fuck themselves the way Teresa's friend in Sicily had, there's no telling what would've happened.

Pedro asked what these men had in mind.

"This is supposed to be a classy restaurant, yeah?"

"No, just a restaurant. Nothing special."

"Well, if you wanna make it classy, you'll need to have some of our girls hanging around in it," the spokes-asshole said.

"What, as waitresses?"

The four Italians laughed.

"That's a joke, right?"

"No. I am confused. I don't know what you mean." Of course, Pedro wasn't confused at all. He never was. Ever.

"Okay, Einstein. There will be ten girls here, regulars, who will seduce your clientele, and charge them for it. Not only will you allow this, you will do everything you can to help them."

"Ahhhh. Prostitution. I see. You are pimps, then?"

"No, we're not pimps and this ain't prostitution, so you can cut out the legalese. Consider this as a partnership, because you will be working with us, and I'd advise you to consider it more as doing us a favor, because we could be much less friendly about it. *Capisce?*"

"*Si, capisco. Che cosa ottengo per esso?*" He surprised them by asking. "*Dai mi alcuni donne per piu tarde? Perché, allora?*"

"You don't sound Italian. Where you from?"

"Everywhere."

"Yeah, well, now you're here. So, unless you help us keep the citizens satisfied, you're not going to be under our insurance policy.

382

We can protect you from fires, robberies, guys coming in just to shoot the place up. You name it."

"Well, I'm interested. Tell Mr. Califano to drop by, and have all the papers ready for us to sign."

We were all surprised by Pedro's suddenly too-friendly attitude.

"Ha! Well, it doesn't really work that way."

"Look, if Mr. Califano doesn't want to do business face to face, like a man, then how do I know there really is a Mr. Califano?"

"What?"

"You could just be a bunch of people from some actors' guild."

"We're not acting. That's for damned sure."

"Then let us do business like men."

"We'll do business however we fucking want to."

"Fine. Then come in just to shoot the place up, and see what happens."

"You trying me, you fucking spick? Because—"

The room exploded with rage, Teresa's voice driving all of us back a step. She came in like a blast of wind from Hell, shrieking in barely intelligible Portuguese, her ferocity startling everyone. I've never seen such fury, not from men, women, or rabid dogs. She was a hurricane of flames.

What followed her made her words understandable, but somehow, they weren't as impressive. Forty some-odd men appeared out of nowhere, translating her words silently when they raised AR-15s, TEC-9s, Steyrs, and some the Mafiosi didn't even recognize. Her face twisted with rage, Teresa pushed Pedro aside and stepped up to the spokes-dick, still screaming, and spraying his face with spit from her foam flecked lips. She made a pistol out of her hand and jammed the tip of her index finger into the hollow of the man's cheek.

American women always disappointed me, not living up to what they're supposed to be. The female of every other species on this planet is more vicious than the male could ever be, but I'd seen too many women bow to the lie that they are the weaker sex. At that moment, Teresa de Medieros showed us all exactly how the lioness makes the king of the jungle seem tame.

As she roared, her mother smiling proudly in the shadows, Teresa pushed so hard that the man's head was forced back, his lip pulled away to show his tobacco stained teeth. He was shocked, more by her than by the cavalry that surrounded him.

Finally, she ran out of words and just glared at him, through him, her eyes blazing. He looked past her at the Spaniard, who looked even more proud than her mother did.

"She says she doesn't like the word 'spick,'" Pedro told them.

The other three goons couldn't make up their minds: go out in a hail of bullets, or chicken out and live to see another day. Their brains were cooking in turmoil. Go for their guns, or back down. Sometimes being smart and sensible feels like cowardice. If they slunk away with their tails between their legs, they could always come back, but...

"Here," Pedro said, offering his cell phone. "Call Mr. Califano for me. Let's do this properly, no?"

The spokesdick took the phone and thumbed in the numbers. Waiting for the phone to pick up, he looked into Teresa's eyes, promising himself that he'd kill her one day.

I heard the mumbling of someone answering, and the Mafioso asked for Benny. A moment passed, then:

"It's Luca. This guy wants to talk to you. Yeah, I know. Look, he wants—I *know*. Here." He tossed the phone over.

Pedro impressed me even more by speaking another language to the guy on the phone. The only people who understood him were the goons and a few of our mercs, and they never translated for me. It was Sicilian. Blah blah blah, pause, blah blah, pause, blah. Click.

"We have an agreement," Pedro said, smiling. He escorted the four wops to the door, as friendly as you please, even putting one muscular arm around Luca's shoulders as he told them how glad he was that they came by and how much he looked forward to doing business with them.

The blueprints changed that day.

Not only were we going all out with security, the walls were given five feet before another wall went up, so that the place had secret passages and walkways to every point with the upper part of the wainscoting being one-way mirrors. We could stand a foot away from someone and watch him covertly pick his nose at the table, and he'd never know.

We'd gone one better with the Mafia: our basement became a very classy, top-secret whorehouse, accessible by a secret door in the party room. Califano was pleased with this offer, especially with the concession that it was all his turf and we would have no profit from it, except for more customers. His protection for this little prostitution business would also cover our drug dealing, which he would not interfere with.

And if he did, we would always have the damning surveillance tapes that he'd know nothing about. The basement had more secret passageways than we thought necessary, but you never know when that extra mirror would come in handy. He claimed that senators, diplomats, and everyone short of kings would come downstairs for dessert. Perfect. If any of them ever tried to fuck with us, they would be guests at Riker's Island.

As soon as the restaurant was ready, Pedro went back down to Coquina with half of his men. Many of the dealers and rollers loyally came up to New York in the exodus, eager for a change from the ultra-strict new local government. The rest of them, those who rebelled and had kept doing business while we were gone, were executed.

Dozens of moving vans made their way north, carrying supplies that had been delivered from Colombia or made in an "associate's" laboratory. The associate came also, with all of his people, to set up shop in the City. A week later, we were ready, and Opening Night was tomorrow.

We had our fingers crossed.

Instead of ketchup and mustard, shit like that, our restaurant had sour cream on every table next to the Tabasco and yucateco sauce. Reason for this, not a lot of people seem to know, is that trying to put out the fire in your mouth from eating habanero, jalapeño, or chili peppers by drinking water only makes it worse. Capsaicin, which is what makes your eyes water and nose run, doesn't dissolve in water, so when you drink something it only spreads the chemical until the entire mouth burns.

About a year ago, Pedro had shown me and Domingo how to distill capsaicin from peppers—*pure* capsaicin—and then showed us what it was for. Even a single drop diluted in a half pint of water was enough to blister the tongue of one would-be blackmailer when it was funneled into his mouth. If that had been the only thing done to him, it would still have kept the dumb bastard from talking, that's for damned sure.

And now, the point of the sour cream. Like yogurt, it has this chemical inside it that somehow breaks down the bond between the capsaicin in the food and the nerves in the mouth. If you don't build up a resistance to high Scoville peppers and you try to gargle habanero sauce, sour cream (or yogurt, if you're into that kind of thing) really comes in handy. This is where we come around to the point of all this.

If you do not have sour cream handy, or if you've been taking your Krav Maga training a little too far, your brain will release endorphins to counteract the pain of eating blisteringly hot peppers. Endorphins are what the brain releases during orgasm. See where I'm going with this?

Eating scorching hot peppers has been known to produce mild euphoria, similar to what's called a runner's high, and there are actually folks out there who are addicted to peppers for that reason. Which brings us finally to the point.

Uh, hi. My name's Evan. And, um, I'm a pepper addict.

Hi, Evan.

Christ, this is what I've come to. Sneaking chilis in the kitchen to get what passes for a fix. And my tolerance has been climbing, from cascabels and jalapeños to Chile de Arbol, to cayennes, to chiltepins. I'll probably be hitting Red Savins by this time next year. Who'da thought that *vegetables* would be the thirteenth frickin' step?

The new place was just silly with skulls. Over the front door was a jaguar's, clutching a jade sphere between its jaws. Of course, the "jade" was just fiberglass, but the *balam* that imitated an afterlife-assuring relic in the Mayan Great Temple tourist attraction was authentic. The museum quality replicas all came from a website company I'd heard about, but the crocodiles had been hunted in the canals out in the Acreage. Over the men's room door was mounted a skull that had been bound during infancy to grow flat, elongated, and "beautiful" in the eyes of the ancient Mayans, who apparently had a few screws loose. Over the ladies' hung one that had the teeth filed into inverted T-shapes, to show devotion to the Sun God. The noses of both had been manipulated by binding and clay to grow long and ridged like dorsal fins up to the hairline. The teeth must've been a pain in the ass to floss.

The way so many franchise restaurants were decorated with meaningless clutter, as if the owners had gone to garage sales in search of ascetic, we had lots of Mesoamerican relics and culture.

The walls were adorned with Mayan "stone trees," bas-reliefs that told stories, predicted eclipses, and held the only worthwhile calendar ever devised by man. Pedro had insisted we pay homage to that in particular. *Insisted.*

"We, and I mean Europeans, have gone through so many calendars it's not even funny, but the one we finally settle on and use today is so screwy that all of the Western world celebrates New Year's in the middle of winter instead of March 25th. Why?"

I just looked blankly at him.

"The middle of *winter!* Instead of on the first day of spring!"

Uh…hmm. What the hell could I say?

"The Mayans followed Venus for 263 days, then it was gone for sixty, then it was back. No bullshit. No Leap Year. No Daylight Savings Time. Just dependability that made sense."

Jesus. I can't believe how mad he got about this shit. Cliff Claven, but with a temper.

Anyway, we had turquoise mosaics with bone inlays, running the chair-rail of a wainscoting all around the dining room. Weapons hanging on the wall at breaks in the mirror, imitation jaguar skins, conch shells that had been made into gilded ceremonial vessels, scorpion shells, starfish, feathers of peacocks, and a few Old World artifacts thrown in. The jawbone of an ass, for instance, to commemorate Whats-his-name. Samson.

No stupid odds and ends, like hockey sticks crossed under an old-fashioned leather aviator's helmet, you know, that skullcap with goggles. No dumb vintage signs, or old advertisements.

We had also imported huitlacoche from Mexico, a corn smut the Aztecs loved, and we use it in soup, crêpes, steak sauce, and stews. Tastes pretty good. For a smut.

And one of our best-selling desserts is something called Orizaba, named after a volcano so tall that it's rimmed with snow, holds a much more impressive ingredient than the four different kinds of chocolate and the ice cream inside the hard shell funnel.

An ounce of uncut coke, smack, or whatever your heart desired. To think that I could be stocking shelves at a supermarket. Or be forty years old and wearing a paper hat, taking orders from some PR kid who thinks I need to be told how many pickles go in a cheeseburger. No, this job'll do.

I monitor the basement, along with four other guys, moving about freely behind the walls of two-way mirrors. One-way, two-way, whatever these mirrors are called, you know what I mean. We are professional voyeurs, taking incriminating pictures of a mob capo's customers as they enjoy our subterranean champagne rooms. You never know when they might come in handy.

The bar down there is another marvel: a large Plexiglas aquarium full of colorful, exotic fish and bizarre, artificial rock formations made by dropping little multicolored pellets into the water and waiting. These things grew into a forest of spires, and in the long thin tank above the liquor shelves, piranhas. That tank is connected to the two that flank it by gates that briefly open every hour, on the hour.

Feeding time.

The stupid goldfish in the other tanks would swim through and be trapped, but the piranhas never caught on and sat at the doors, like Pavlov's dog, waiting. It was always a pleasant surprise: Oh! Look! A goldfish! Here, of all places! And they'd trip over one another trying to tear it apart.

That's the way I felt, like a clueless goldfish that just happened to swim in the wrong direction, but the piranhas weren't hungry yet. Sure, I was happy to be in a better situation, not hiding under a bridge with a bunch of lunatics, but the fear still lurked in the back of my mind that some kind of Santería sacrifices, or worse, might still be going on backstage. Shaitan had once told me that tyranny changing hands does not equal freedom. Maybe Nestor was feeding worms—or buzzards—out in the sticks somewhere, but that didn't mean Abuela had given up burning children and eating their hearts.

But at least I wasn't Evan Lanthorne anymore, running around with a price on my head. Teresa had talked to a friend, who talked to a friend, who talked to a friend who got me a new Social Security number. This guy did that for living. Made government wages assigning legitimate ones, and made *beaucoup* bucks selling phony ones to people like me. After that, all I had to do for a new driver's license and credit cards and passport, was apply.

Sure, I was stuck being called Jacob Marley, whoever the hell that is, but I guess it wasn't so bad. It was that guy Harding's idea, and he laughed at some secret joke when the name choice went through. He never explained it to me, but I've never asked. I don't really like the guy. Personally, I think he's a jerk-off.

"Hey, cheer up, it could be Boabdil," he said.

"Meaning?"

"Meaning, a lot more appropriate."

"Sit on it, Harding."

Apparently, getting a new identity is a breeze if you know the right people. Teresa said that another friend, the cat who was looking after her daughter and my ex, had five different names. I'd heard of this guy a lot from Domingo, but I took it with a grain of salt. It sounded too much like a movie to me.

As for Calibos, man, I didn't want to be caught alone with him. He had strict orders not to touch or even speak to me, and I had tried to apologize and explain my side, but he still had that look in his eyes. That look of a tiger saying Grace. There was something heartening, though. He wore Esteban Ribeira's gold-tooth rosary hanging off his belt. I guess whatever cop had kept it as a souvenir met him at the siege on the police station. It made me feel vaguely better, though I'm not sure why.

Aside from that, though, I'd have to say my biggest problem was looking at a calendar—a real one, not a stone tree—and seeing that I was only out of Coquina a month or so before I ran into Pedro and Teresa. How long was I in the City? It seemed like forever, in the Trench near Amiens, shooting up and wandering blindly, dreaming things that seemed so real. Thinking I had some kind of life, and constantly getting lost in a very uncomplicated city. How could I possibly have been so confused? First Avenue, Second Avenue, Third Avenue. Where was the confusion? I can't even remember. God, what fun drugs are.

I've been clean now for several weeks. How many? Shit, good question. The days just run together now, sober or not, but they're good days. I served only as a gofer while Pecado was being built. No carpentry or tile laying for me. No real responsibilities. Not like I was complaining about it, of course. After seeing the trainspots on my arm and looking at me sadly, Pedro had me put on some kind of meds and had my blood tested once a week.

A little unnecessary, I'd say, but he ignored me when I did say. I always knew I could quit whenever I wanted to, but he refused to believe that I had more willpower than those other schmucks I always heard about. Christ, give me a little credit, will you? But no. That's what they all say, but no one wanted to hear my side of it, see things my way. So now I'm sleepwalking through life, mentally gelded, so to speak. Oh well.

Could be worse.

I could still be making things up. Deliriously dreaming …what was it? Fighting death matches in the basement of a porno circus. Where in the blue fuck did I come up with that one? Hallucinating the sign from Dante's *Inferno*, hanging over the door to Hell. How the hell did I remember that in the first place? Another shred floating up from the long-distant past, I guess.

Many were coming, now. I felt as if my brain, long atrophied, was shaking off dust and cobwebs, and that even now it was a cocoon. Growing on its own. I thought of the long, drug-sharpened conversations with Seth McHale, his astute observations punctuated with gibberish.

But something had stirred inside me, regardless of the nonsense he occasionally spouted. I felt as if I'd been impotent all my life, and was now finally feeling an erection. A poor mental picture, but an accurate one. And the way some ex-eunuch would, I'm sure, I couldn't wait to use what had grown so suddenly.

My training resumed. I began to carry a piece as naturally as it should be carried: calmly, casually, without that unconscious swagger of someone who's packing heat and just can't wait to demonstrate what he can do with it. All men are like that, at first, their body language a flashing neon sign that screams, "I have a gun!"

With that calm comes the more relaxed aim, your weapon becoming just an extension of the hand, of the will. I didn't want to do the whole Tai Chi routine, I really didn't, but Pedro inflicted it on me. God, I felt like an idiot. No, I felt like I looked queer. Same thing.

Repulse the Monkey.

Christ, it's bad enough I had to go through the faggy motions. The *names* of them were like salt in the wound.

Tai Chi.

Zen.

Capoeira.

Hours at the shooting range.

And by night, photography. Mmm.

Yes, it could be a lot worse.

I had a look at the calendar again, determined to take more of an interest in time passing, and could barely believe that it was summertime. Early July. In another week, the *encierro* would begin in Pamplona, and a bunch of red scarf-wearing cretins would prove their manhood with bulls stampeding a step behind them. And I'd miss it. Shucks.

I didn't bother to count up the time that had passed. The night everything had begun to fall apart was back in March, sometime. Late April/early May, I was found on a sidewalk in Nueva York, as Pedro so quaintly put it. Half of the space in between was a blur, but it didn't matter. Everything was going to be all right. Especially when I heard about our Coquina project.

All in good time.

We have someone else working with us, now. A cat only nine years older than me, an associate from near home. Apparently, he was floating around in the Miami area for a while with half of a transient business in tow, the other half mysteriously disappearing in West Palm after an epic gunfight. Quite a story.

Some other time.

This drug lord, in over his head without his estranged partner, had jumped at the chance to join us after being told Teresa was "the Brazilian" his partner had dealt with. He had a troop of disavowed doctors and scientists with him, who came with a mobile lab they made goodies in. No bathtub meth, this was, but highest quality designer drugs, combined with extracts of stuff like Nightshade, Angel Trumpets, Devil Trumpets, Morning Glories, and a few others I've never even heard of, plants that were poisonous in small doses, but magnificently hallucinogenic in tiny ones.

When I tipped him off to a great source of dirt-cheap but excellent peyote, he tried to hide his excitement. Failing miserably, of course, but he did try to appear nonchalant about it, to maintain some image or other. He sent people off to Nevada with the instructions I gave them, and within a week, they returned with enough to keep the entire City's population tripping until the *encierro* was due to end. I keep mentioning this event because we watch it on TV at the apartment Pedro and Teresa share. Fascinating. Really. But back to Todd, the entrepreneur.

Unlike his last business, the lab was not located on the front's premises. A warehouse somewhere I'd never heard of, and wasn't that curious about, was the site of drug production that greatly enhanced our menu. When Benito Califano saw the windfall these designers brought about in the third week of operation, he tried to drastically raise his percentage.

"Are you getting greedy?" Teresa asked mildly.

"Hey, you holding out on me and have the balls to call *me*

greedy? You never said nothing about these pills."

"You didn't ask."

"That supposed to be funny?" he asked, arching his Thufir Hawat eyebrows.

"No. This is."

A manila envelope appeared in the hand of one of her henchmen, and was tossed across the tabletop. Fixing her with a cold, withering look, Califano tore the packet open and slid the contents out, only glancing down.

That glance became a frown, and then a long stare.

I didn't get to see who the pictures were of, but a few were candid, close-up shots of children. Their eyes had been poked out with a hole-puncher. The rest were pics of adults. Who? I didn't ever find out, but it didn't matter.

"Where the fuck did you get these?" he snarled finally.

"Can't you tell from the backgrounds? The surroundings?"

"Where. The. *Fuck*. Did you get these?"

"We have many more that would make great portraits. A few you might even like to have framed, give to your wife when your anniversary comes around."

"You have no idea who you're fucking with."

"Sure I do. I am fucking with an over-the-hill wop who thinks *way* too highly of himself and his has-been organization. The Mafia is a joke now, Benny. Can I call you Benny? This isn't Prohibition, Benny. Your time has passed. I don't care what city this is."

"Listen, you spick bitch—"

"Want to see some more pictures?"

Another envelope appeared out of nowhere, landing on the table with a slap and sliding toward the capo.

"You're dead! Dead!" he screamed, rising.

There was a chorus of muffled *pings*, and all the Mafioso's soldiers dropped. Our people hadn't even moved. Califano stood frozen. We were all in *his* place. *His* bar. But we had the upper hand. All his men in the back had been dead for about ten minutes, put to sleep silently by a squad of our soldiers coming through the back door.

They took up their positions and waited.

"No, Benny," Teresa said, lighting a cigarette. "I'm just getting started."

We brought Benito Califano to one of our new safe-houses, outside the City, where a stranger awaited. Teresa gave the young man a kiss on the cheek, introduced him to the old man, and we all went down to the basement.

"Have you ever salted a slug, Mr. Califano?" the well-dressed, good-looking young guy with movie-star hair asked. He looked strangely familiar, but I had no idea where from… and of course, Benito Califano couldn't answer, on account of the duct tape wound around and around his liver-spotted old head. The man continued anyway, gesturing to the two goons holding the old man to bring him over to the tub he'd set up.

"My grandmother had a specific chore for me when I was a boy. See, she had quite a bit of trouble with slugs in her garden, and she appointed me Lord High Executioner. Every time we visited, she handed me the salt-shaker and sent me out to play. I loved my job. My little mission. It was just to get me out of her hair, but what did I know?"

There were four posts welded to the tub's frame, with handcuffs mounted on them. Califano was stripped naked, struggling futilely, and forced down into the tub. Spread-eagled, he was cuffed to each of the posts, his shriveled body embarrassingly exposed.

"For a kid, though, even a job like that can get boring. So, of course, I dragged it out a little, to make it more fun. One little grain at a time. One by one, getting absorbed into that spongy black skin. I always wondered what it would be like to do that to a human being."

He paused to drag over two buckets. One was fastened with a lid, and the other was filled with water. I had no idea where he was going with this.

"We're about to find out," he said, and upended the water bucket, splashing Benito Califano from head to wrinkled toe.

"And what is your salt, Rabbit?" Teresa asked.

"Lye. You're welcome to leave if you want."

"Lye? As in soap?"

"No, lye soap is lye soap. I mean pure lye, as in caustic as fuck when combined with water, and will spread, like a grease fire, if more water is used to wash it off. I know. I once forgot to neutralize a lye hair relaxer once with vinegar before washing it out. Fried my whole scalp."

Califano was thrashing about wildly as he heard this, trying in a blind panic to tear the handcuffs loose. The guy called Rabbit merely smiled at him.

"Trust me, Mr. Califano. This will hurt you a lot more than it will hurt me."

Muffled screams of terror, soon to be shrieks of pain.

"Oh, right. I almost forgot. The whole point of this is to get you to rat out all of your associates. Cocksucking pieces of shit, if you ask me. I'm half Italian, myself, on my dad's side. Neapolitan. Can't stand the way you give us all a bad name with your somehow-glamorized extortion, blackmail, usury, and false dignity. The cowardice you call security, meting out responsibility so the fat and lazy bosses never get their hands dirty. Taking protection money from people just trying to live, people who wouldn't need protection if you didn't fuck with them in the first place.

"So, we're going to ask you a few questions, but let's get this out of the way first, shall we? I want to make sure you're really getting into the spirit of the occasion. We certainly don't want to waste any of our time with you lying, or threatening, or any other kind of rudeness. Okay. Comfy?"

I was really beginning to like this guy.

Califano tried to shout something from under his gag, his rheumy eyes bulging with fear. Rabbit arched his eyebrows in a facial "What?" and leaned forward, bending one ear as if to hear better.

"What was that?"

"Mmph mmm-mmph!"

"Speak up, Mr. Califano."

Another scream, louder, more insistent.

"You want me to start on your genitals? Why, that's a good idea, Mr. Califano. I think I just might do that. Hold still, now."

The pictures we'd taken of made men and politicians, crooks of equal degree but with different collars, were supposed to be a deterrent, a card we would use to keep the Califano family at arm's length. Sadly, we had to switch to Plan B, so early in the game. By dawn, we had detailed instructions about the businesses and homes of Califano's enemies and allies alike. Plan B looked more fun, anyway.

Rabbit had promised the old man that he would not only stop with the lye sprinkling if he told us what we wanted to know, but give Benito enough painkillers to make him actually glad to be here with us. Of course, it was a lie.

But we did learn an awful lot about human anatomy.

Rabbit gave us a crash course with plenty of visual aids, flaying the old man's skin very carefully and showing us which organs he could live the longest without—removing them to prove it. He also pointed out, rather clinically, that people being tortured begin to feel a perverse relationship with the one inflicting the pain. This had been documented as far back as ancient China, in books he didn't find in the library. Then, he told us a linguistic pet peeve of his, people who weren't in the Mob calling the Mob "Cosa Nostra." This thing of ours. No, he thought it should be Cosa Vostra, "that thing of their's," but nobody ever asked him. Califano choked horribly halfway through it and gave up the ghost.

"And that, sports fans, was a homicide!" Rabbit said.

Christ. Thank God this guy's on our side.

He was just a small asset, though. Salon des Refusés was just too small to take on the Mob, so Pedro set about finding recruits. He wanted to find desperate men with good, red blood, and I knew just the place.

Before we set off for L.A., Rabbit introduced himself to me, saying he'd heard a lot about me. He had something in his eyes I couldn't quite define, when he handed me a CD jewel case with a little red bow taped on it. It was somebody I'd never heard of.

"Shrike?"

The image on the front was a gibbet in a marshland, chains dangling with manacles opened, wreathed in gloomy mist with the sky a yellowish bruise behind it. Below, the album title in old-fashioned typewriter font. *Ex Oblivione.* I raised an eyebrow at Rabbit.

"Maya wanted you to have this."

"What?! Maya?! You know her? How is she?"

"She'll live."

"But where is she now? I have so much to tell her!"

"She doesn't want to hear it, Evan. She's gone. But she doesn't hold a grudge anymore, and she wanted you to know that."

"But," I said, his face wavering as my eyes filled with tears. "But I have to tell her—how sorry—"

"It's enough that you are. She doesn't need to hear it. She's moved on, Evan."

The look in his eyes wasn't contempt or pity—neither. It was very calm and understanding, the look of someone who knew everything and didn't feel one way or another about it.

"But I failed her. I...I'm not a man."

"Don't cry like a woman, and you can start making up for what you've done. Whatever you saw that freaked you out enough to drive you away, it's nothing compared to what she went through. And she doesn't cry. Not anymore. Dust yourself off and move on, like her."

"I just wish—"

"There are no wishes. This isn't a fairy tale, there aren't any genies or leprechauns and life doesn't have a rewind button. Regret accomplishes nothing, except maybe an ulcer. Now, learn from your mistakes, stand up straight, and be a man. Bring us the Trolls."

I stared up the ramp at the Bridge, thinking about how fickle fate can be. Lighting a cigarette, just so I wouldn't look awkward I trudged up the pavement to the concrete abutment, vaulted over, and left the twilight, entering the darkness.

Only a handful of shapes were huddled around the fire pit, but one of them was familiar.

"Amanda," I called. She looked up miserably. Damn, she had changed in only two—no, three, now—months. Fallen far. Not hit bottom, yet, like the company she kept, but it was only a matter of time. There was a sore on her lip that was not a pimple. Also only a matter of time.

"Hey, Ev. Welcome home."

"Where's Seth?"

"County. Facing Armed Robbery and Assault. Been a few weeks now."

"Shit. Bail?"

"High. Astro-fucking-nomical."

"No problem. I'll be back. I need you to tell everyone that there's something big about to happen, and Seth'll be in tomorrow to tell about it."

"What? What's going on?"

"A surprise."

Fuck. Complicated already.

As Pedro and I sat in our little rental car outside the jail, waiting for the bondsman to bring out the Scourge, I listened to Maya's CD again for the third time. I didn't need to tell her about tantric music, like I'd heard—or rather, felt —during my vacation on the Nipple. She was way ahead of me.

It wasn't really anything I'd dance to. It was more of something you'd see on stage, pay a bunch of money to dress up and go to the opera house to watch, except for a few tracks that I couldn't believe had come out of her. It was like, hmm, if Madonna and White Zombie had a child. Loud, angry, but *good.* It sounded so…I can't explain it.

I wished her luck.

Seth came out with the bondsman who, if everything went according to plan, was going to get really screwed out of the deal.

"That's him?" Pedro asked. I nodded. "Why's there an arrow on his head?"

"You got me there."

We stepped out of the car to greet the two of them, shake hands, talk about the case and little formalities. Seth kept his mouth shut the whole time until we left, when he finally cracked a smile.

"Jacob fucking Marley! Damn, that's a good one!"

"Yeah? Glad you think so. Seth, this is Pedro."

"Pedro, eh? That's a far cry from George, what the bondsman called you."

"Why?" Pedro asked. "Jorge is a common name."

"Well, hey, I never really thought much of names, anyway. Sure, they come in handy sometimes, when you're trying to find somebody, or you're gossiping. But otherwise, they're just examples of your parents' imagination.

"Or lack of it."

"Or lack of it. That's right. So, tell me, what good wind brings you here, to release me from that fun home away from home?"

"A business opportunity," I said. "Right up your alley."

"You're kidding," he said finally.

"Nope. Sounds like a movie, I know, but it's the kind I know you'd want to see."

"And you're the head of it?" he asked Pedro. The Basque nodded solemnly, leaning back on the hotel pillow with his hands behind his head. We'd finished a damn good room-service dinner while I told Seth our story, and he already looked bribed enough to believe anything I had to say.

"It's a miracle. Housing, a steady job, adventure. I don't know how many of us would go for it, though."

"Why not? I thought they'd jump at the chance."

"You'd be surprised. A lot of them are too in love with their situation, too content with being bums. You could give them a mansion, on the house—no pun intended—and they'd burn it down within a week."

"Not after a week with us," Pedro said.

"You think you can beat them into shape?"

"I know I can. They'll go from coals to diamonds in no time, if they are what Evan tells me. Hard men only get harder, when training begins. Even the softest of them must want something better."

"Well, I'm in. I'm not stupid enough to think prison would be a vacation, and that's where I'm going if I stay here. The last thing I need is a home like that."

"Better to be a skinny wolf than a fat slave dog."

"You said it, amigo."

"So, you will talk to your people?" I asked.

"And how."

We could not have found a better spokesman. With his natural charm and flair for the dramatic, he took the soapbox and seized the Trolls' attention, somewhere in between Shakespeare's Mark Antony and that "Give me liberty or give me death" guy. From where we were standing, Pedro and I missed the opening part because the people around us hadn't shut up yet.

"—We've lost sight of the point, here. Gotten too familiar with the lifestyle to remember why it began. We're here because we hate the world, and we've done what we can to escape it. Christ! We live under a fucking *bridge*, for God's sake! And we fight the Establishment in our little skirmishes, eking out a living by doing the same damned things our enemies do. Crimes. Beatings and robberies that don't even make headlines. At this rate, we're no better than those we hate! Are we just a gang of bums? Are we misfits who dress bizarrely just to get attention? Or are we Hollywood fucking Hardcore? If the opportunity to wage war against all that we hate was dropped in our laps, would we charge into it like rabid dogs? Or would we listen to what our allies had to say, nod as if we agreed, and then go off to the shadows with a bottle? Let our lives and our rage waste away?

"We don't live under this damned overpass because we want to. Many of us think we do, but be honest with yourselves for a moment. When you were a kid, did you say to yourself, "Hmm, when I grow up, I want to be a homeless addict, hanging out with other homeless addicts?" Did you ever walk past a group of Punks and say, "Shit, I admire those guys"? Don't lie to yourselves and say you did, because I'll bet you green fucking money you wanted to grow up to be Robin Hood. Or Batman. Or Wyatt Earp. You wanted to be a hero, standing up for what you believe in and destroying everything in your way. You wanted to make the world into what you know it should be, and you would give anything for a chance to do it. Am I warm? I have to be, because I know that not a single damned one of you was hanging out with the "cool" kids and dreaming up new ways to torment the nerds. No, you were spending your time angry, hating the world around you because it lied about what it wanted and punished you for trying to fit in. When I look at you, I don't see a bunch of Goths, a bunch of skirt-wearing nancy boys with vampire makeup, hanging out in cemeteries and trying to look spooky. No, I see an army ready to grab this world by the throat and make some noise!

"This is the part where you all either look at the ground and mumble your excuses, or shake your heads and say I'm too damned drunk. This isn't the first time someone's tried to light a fire under our asses, but I want to be around the first time it actually works. Right now, there is a group of revolutionaries—shit, there are many, but these fuckers are actually serious. They're not talking. They're doing.

"Remember a few months ago, when all that shit went down in Florida? An entire police station was burned down, the department massacred. Slaughtered. That was them, and maybe, us. This isn't a group of kids on a high school shooting spree. This is an army of mercenaries. Dyed-in-the-wool killers, and this isn't Che Guevara I'm talking about, either. Their plan isn't a hostile takeover, to replace our bullshit government with Communism—tyranny changing hands. It's total anarchy. It's nationwide panic, riots. Open rebellion. If we join them, we'll make Tiananmen Square look like a playground sandbox. I'm not talking about bombing the FBI building, or crashing planes, or sending anthrax through the mail. This is guerilla warfare.

"Organized attacks on all the right places, so that when the news shows the world what we are doing, the viewers at home will go for their guns in outrage. We will turn neighbors against one another, simply by battles in states they've never been to, killing people they've never met. The bloodlust will spread like wildfire, and Nature will take its course. You think Rodney King was a good excuse for the yawms to go crazy? That's nothing compared to what men of all races will see on prime time.

"We have been offered money, homes, training, and most importantly, a chance. A chance to make this into *our* world. A place where *we* are on top, and those who bullied us before we found each other will kneel before us. No, *grovel*. I've been waiting for this all my life, and I won't miss it. Not for all the smack in the world. Not for all the booze, the music, and the lonely mornings when everyone else has passed out. Not even for a Tommy Burger. Why? Because if I do miss it, that's all I'll ever have. I don't want to be an old man with a long purple beard and what's left of my hair gelled up like beach grass, living under a bridge. Traitor to the lifestyle? Shit, if you want to call me that, go right ahead. But at least I'll try. It may not happen, but at least I'll have tried to live up to what I've said I was. A rebel. An angry motherfucker who's sick and tired of being sick and tired and ready to do something about it. Yeah, Ah have seen da promised land, and I'm headed there with a torch."

"You said something about homes, and money," someone asked.

"That's right. A real roof over our heads, and a steady paycheck, weapons, training, and not having to walk to Covenant House to take a shower."

"Here?" someone else asked.

"No, New York. Our first enemy is the Mob. Then, we take down all those gangsta wannabes in Miami. We're not fighting their soldiers; we're assassinating the bosses, the kingpins. These people have a spy network that makes Satan's look like a bunch of bungling Keystone Kops. These are the people that are hired to overthrow governments. Black ops."

"So, what the fuck do they need us for?"

"They don't," Seth lied. "But I want in. Do you?"

"Who are they?"

"The brass is standing over there with Evan. Remember Evan?"

Everyone turned and found us, looking skeptically.

"What? *Him?*" some heckler laughed.

"Give us room," Pedro said to everyone else. "And I will show you what I can do. What I can teach all of you."

"Ha! You think those fancy kicks they do in the movies stand a chance against one of us?"

"There's only one way to find out," Pedro answered, smiling.

"Give them room!" Seth shouted. "It's your funeral, Radcliffe."

Radcliffe? Oh, yeah.

The crowd parted, and the fuchsia-mohawked punk stood like a fool, regretting his big mouth. He was a bit of a brawler, though, and stepped forward to back his words up. Pedro took out the pistol no one else knew he'd even had, and gave it to me, walking out into the circle. The light was dim under the bridge, jumping shadows from the fire pit and the 55-gallon drums, but it was enough for him to judge his terrain.

Before he was ready, Radcliffe was startled and overwhelmed by a blur of savage kicks that showed Pedro was just toying with him. The "fancy kicks" were dazzling, gunshot swift, and could obviously break his bones if only they weren't purposely misdirected. There was nothing Radcliffe could do but draw himself in like a turtle and retreat, stunned. Abruptly, the Basque stopped and stepped back.

"You are not my enemy. We do not need to prove anything more than what I just have."

Someone stepped forward and aimed a lightning-fast punch at the side of Pedro's head. I blinked, and didn't get to see how exactly the Punk's arm got broken, but everyone else was astounded. The sucker-puncher was on his knees, screaming.

"I wasn't ready!" Radcliffe said, belatedly.

"You have to be ready always. I will show you how."

"You'll teach us karate?" a liberty-spiked chick asked. Pedro snorted contemptuously.

"Karate is for children. I will teach you *ninjitsu*. I will teach you to kill a man with one finger, five different ways." An exaggeration, of course, but it impressed the audience. "No one will see you coming—except if you keep that orange hair—and your mark will be dead in a heartbeat. I will teach the weakest among you how to kill the largest. I will teach you to kill with every kind of firearm, as well as your bare hands."

"How much will you pay us?"

"Only one hundred dollars a week, but that's only until you finish training without giving up, taking a little bit of cash and running off to get high. Your room and board is free, so just consider what you would have paid as already deducted."

"But how much after we're ready?"

"It doesn't matter!" Seth shouted, cutting the Basque off. "Why do we worry about wages when we have to much to look forward to? Look a gift horse in the mouth? I'll get paid what I earn, and that's good enough for me. What? If you feel you're getting gypped later on, after learning all this, after being fed and clothed and housed, you have the nerve to complain? Then stay here, a homeless thief. Me, even if I quit after I'm trained, I'll have something to show for the time I spent. A little money, and lots of skill."

"Fine then," Radcliffe said, looking down at the guy who cradled his broken arm and rocked from side to side. "Where do we sign up?"

"What the fuck is that?" I asked, putting on my I'm-in-charge-of-something voice. The punk frowned, the smut magazine he was shoving in his bag arrested halfway. I could see the bright words etched against the gloom, standing out sharply across the naked bodies of surgically-altered white trash whores.

"What's it look like?" he asked, indignant.

I snatched the smut away from him and read it aloud.

"Pussy Rabid Bondage Cunts!" That got everybody's attention. "'We fuck your asshole, stick our spurs in your side, and ride you like a dog!'" I paused to raise an eyebrow at him. "'Ride you like a dog'?"

Before he could reply, I shouted the next blurb.

"'Lick My Shoe You Whore! Get down on your hands and knees and hang on, 'cuz I'm gonna shove this spike heel right up your ass!' Is this garbage supposed to arouse you? Listen, all of you! If you waste any room in your luggage carrying shit like this, then you might as well stay here. *We have no time for masturbators!*"

I made that speech because I (correctly) assumed it would please Pedro. I knew that kind of sex was twisted, but had learned to tolerate many things in my career. It was necessary, though, to put everyone in the right frame of mind, and anything I could do to help, I would. Distractions like this were dead weight. Period.

Something snagged my attention, just as I was winding up backhanded to hurl the magazine from me. Another ad, diagonally down to the left of Raunchy Grannies. A beautiful redhead with a telephone pressed to the side of her face, mouth open, the receiver pressed so hard out of either passion or—more realistically—revulsion, that her upper lip was lifted into an Elvis sneer. A beautiful redhead, with a beautiful blonde bending over her, sticking her finger down her throat.

A beautiful redhead I used to know.

$5.99 for the first minute, $2.99 each additional minute, Visa/MasterCard accepted, call now.

Vomit Sluts Are Waiting For You!

I can't think of who the redhead is, but I know I'd met her. It'll come to me eventually. No time to think about this shit right now. I've got bigger fish to fry.

Part of my training, and part of the training these Punks would go through, was to be taught not only what the rules were, but *why* the rules were, and that makes them all the easier to learn.

We will become a coed army without any of the problems that come with it, because we will understand those problems. I'd found out that gays and women weren't kept out of the military because of discrimination against them... well, at least not for discrimination's sake. It was because a bond forms between people who share hardship, and if that bond can turn into something sexual the soldier's first loyalty will not be to the Cause; in a pitched battle they will desert their posts to protect their lovers instead. It is not that an army is no place for women and queers. An army is no place for affection.

Ditto for pussy-ass sensitivity training. Ever since the beginning of organized warfare, soldiers raped and pillaged. It was their nature. To the victors go the spoils. That is the one place a society *needs* their bullies, their thugs, their motherfucking assholes. With them removed from society they cannot prey upon their own people, and instead, can serve and protect and defend them, doing so with the savage cruelty they need so badly to express. We need sick, wild, evil fucks on the front lines where they belong. Not caring, sensitive, and love-distracted wimps who've already glutted their urges with each other, or on the pages of some sex magazine.

That is why our soldiers will train together, sleep and eat to-

403

gether, shower and shit together until all consciousness of flesh is washed away and they become, not men and women, but soldiers. Soldiers only conscious of their rage against what cast them out and their loyalty to what took them in.

We left California with almost four hundred recruits, male, female, some only teenagers, and not at all what Pedro was hoping for, but after seeing them all come together for the sake of two Afghanipakiranistanians they didn't even know, I knew they had what it took. Besides, the way we were going to get the bad guys, it wasn't the traditional way you see in the movies. We're going to the park, to hold out peanuts, and get 'em to come right up to us. Like Sal going squirrel hunting, we'll get our enemies easily, because we are crafty and ruthless and we hold nothing sacred. I personally had to turn away several people from under the Bridge, like Amanda, that I knew were only camp followers at heart, only along for the ride. It was sad to leave them behind, but this isn't charity.

It is war.

THE KETTLE BLACK

I

"We are digging the pit of Babel."
—Franz Kafka

Maya entered her apartment like a stranger to the place, as if someone else had moved in. The surrealist furniture was still the same, except for the upset coffee table and the broken chair in front of her computer. Oops, the screen saver was still running—of course it was, nobody had ever come in to shut the damned thing off.

Incredibly, nothing had been stolen while she was in the hospital.

No, wait. Everything was stolen. This was all just *stuff*, now.

It was all tainted. Violated. Her inner sanctum was invaded by those monsters, and now it could never be her home again. She stared silently at the carpet, at the crusty smears of dry blood she didn't remember shedding. Was it hers? Or was it what the doctors had scraped out from under her fingernails?

As one who looks on the ground and sees an ant, then sees ten thousand, the enormity of the wreckage hit her. Next to the brown bloodstains was a stubbed-out reefer roach, and beside that, a cigarette butt in a windrow of ash. And beside that, scores of them. No, hundreds, mingling with shards of broken glass where she'd been thrown into the TV.

Her ashtray, an S-shaped, waist-high, black iron stem set on a splayed pedestal, with the scallop tray perched on the crest, lay in the middle of the floor, among her trampled first editions. The human skull bookend, with candle wax frozen in dripping trails down the forehead where she'd set a Santería candle, was now minus its mandible and the *vela*.

Silence.

The refrigerator clicked and began to hum.

Somewhere, a dog barked.

Moving as one in a dream, she gingerly stepped through her belongings, and came across a rectangular wooden box. Its contents were spilled across the floor, some bags stepped-on and ground open, bleeding powder into the carpet. Aphrodisiacs, worthless now.

With a choked scream, she kicked the box into the wall, whirled, and snatched up the artsy-fartsy ashtray by its stem. Reversing her grip as she stumbled, she backhanded the monitor, smashing the glass and the dancing colors. Blue sparks jumped, hissing, but she didn't notice, battering the CPU and bringing the entire console crashing to the floor. When there was nothing left of her computer to destroy, she turned on the wine locker, every blow jarring her arm from wrist to spine. Bottles exploded in bursts of froth and glass.

It was a long time until she came to herself again, until she realized she was sitting in the middle of the floor, noticing absently that it had started to rain.

There was a book beside her, written by someone her girlfriend knew, someone her girlfriend's mother said they were going to be staying with for a while.

She hadn't liked the book at all, finding it grotesque and immature, but she picked it up and began to read it again anyway. Wondering who the hell her host was going to be, what he was like. Would he be another of those sickos she had tolerated all her life? Would he really be the sweetheart her friend said he was? How could he be, and write books like these?

And what kind of a name was "Rabbit," anyway?

Prologue

I had that dream again, the same one I've had since I was little. I remember being a small child and seeing myself as I am now, all grown-up, rather than as a buck-toothed, bug-eyed five-year-old, standing at this same crossroads as I do now. Knowing without wondering that this good-looking man would someday be me. I somehow knew back then that the roads were symbolic of life's journey and all the possible choices. I couldn't make up my mind which path to follow, so I turned around and went back the way I'd come.

The pavement stopped immediately, and I made my way through barbed agavé plants, treacherous Spanish bayonets, and massive thorn thickets to a place where it was suddenly warm early morning, close and humid. Dew sparkled on spider webs woven between the branches of gnarled and twisted trees, their shrivelled leaves rattling in the sullen air. There was an odd, stale-smelling fungus growing everywhere, and I was eager to press on. I passed fragments of other dreams I'd had or would have, but didn't stop to visit them. I passed empty fields with tumbledown stone walls; bleak, windswept moors; gates hang-

ing half-off of their hinges; a scarecrow with his rags blowing in the hot wind; a gallows with a meaty skeleton swinging from its arm; a man crucified upon a wheel, desperately begging me to release him; neglected gardens; the ruins of Gothic vaultings couched in the lee of a fallen pendentive, decorated with lichen and garlands of moss and ivy. An open grave. A spear driven into the mud, a long-haired skull impaled upon it.

I came to a gate that only I could open, morning glory creepers and blossoms twined about its Gothic black iron bars, and I entered a secret garden. A chill came into the breeze, and I was more comfortable. I used to wonder, when I was awake, what exactly it was that I did there, but it was always a blur. I was alone, but not lonely. There were fountains of cracked and algaed stone in the hubs of converging cobblestone paths. Marble monuments of gods and demons I did not know lounged in the sun or menaced from the shadows of gigantic banyan trees. Legions of bougainvillea threatened to overthrow anything man-made, their feverish color dancing in the pleasantly biting wind. Cardinals, blue jays, and yellow jackets went about on hectic errands, dodging hibiscus, and I was content just to watch them for many years, wandering in my garden doing whatever else.

Once, at about age thirteen, I visited my garden again and noticed the wall.

How I'd missed it before, I had no idea, but I was swinging Tarzan-like through the branches of banyans, ficus, and poinciana trees, leaped to the ground and there it was, its gray stone blocks stretching forever upwards.

Enraged that someone had invaded my private place and built this monstrosity, I howled and beat against it with my fists, throwing myself against the rough-hewn stone and bloodying my knuckles, shoulders, and face.

Tonight, when I found this wall again, I tried to scale it. Consumed by the desperate need to know what lay on the other side. Digging into finger and toeholds easily found, I hauled myself up. I climbed for hours. Once, I looked back and saw my garden, so small and far away, the lands surrounding shrouded in mist. I cursed and climbed higher. I came to and passed through a layer of clouds.

I looked over my shoulder and saw the deep blue of the sky fading off into inky blackness, and the gray cyclopean wall stretched on forever to all sides. My mind reeled at the sheer enormity of that horrible thing, my nerveless fingers slipped out of the cracks and I plummeted down, the garden rushing up at such abominable speed that I vomited myself awake.

I sat up in bed, sweat-soaked and sticky, chunks and slime on my chin and throat. I peeled myself away and took my sheets with me to the shower. The sense of insignificance still over-powered me; the flesh-crawling horror took a long time to wash away. As the mirror fogged, the word HELP *appeared in childish scrawl across it, written there God knows when. I never bothered to wipe it off.*

When my sheets and I were clean, I went to my computer and sat down, turning it on and lighting a cigarette. I had a stack of disks full of high school creative writing assignments, short stories, poetry, abandoned attempts at novels, and drug-induced ramblings. I opened the word processor and started a new file.

I stared at the blank page until the screen saver came on, the same as I did yesterday.

My creative juices are as stagnant as a corpse-clogged river.

I haven't been able to write in two years.

I have nothing to say.

Chapter I

I would like to seize this opportunity to introduce my girlfriend, the stupidest girl in the world. She is a fucking retard. Danielle, that's her name, is a redhead, and the fact that she isn't blonde astounds me. Anyway, this is how the whole mess started, and you can see it really isn't my fault at all. She was naked on the floor of my kitchen, stoned out of her skull and toying with me about this Xanax bar, which she'd offer to me and pretend to forget about, to see how pissed off or frustrated I'd get. Truth is, I really couldn't care less.

It was one of those yellow ones, but she had no idea I'd already taken three of them out of her bottle and stuffed them under the line of carpet where it met the linoleum while we were rutting. That's one of the reasons why I won't buy a bed. We always have to shag somewhere different. On the floor or coffee table or kitchen counter, a position from which all manner of things can be done. Once, I did my dishes while she gave me a blowjob.

So anyway, she's on the kitchen floor with her tattoos and piercings and Xanax bottle, smoking my last clove without asking, and I'm slicing mozzarella, tomatoes, bell peppers and some other shit with my only clean knife, my huge Rambo butcher knife which was a free gift for buying something or other I saw on TV that I couldn't possibly live without.

So I straddled her there with the knife in my hand, lightly dragging it over her brown limbs and enormous breasts. She giggled, then pretended to sigh like I was really turning her on. This is the prologue for her whining begging session for me to Oh put it in her, oh baby, stick it in me now and fuck me God I love how you fuck me so hard with your big enormous dick. Sounds like she's reciting this garbage, like she memorized it from a porn flick or trashy novel. Seriously, it's insulting that she thinks I believe her, that she thinks I'm falling for it.

Now, this is the part where my memory of it takes on that murky haze that all of my drunken or drugged memories have. The tenebrous shadows of nightmarish shapes crowd the edges, always creeping in closer and shrinking away.

I twisted one of her nipple rings and the "begging" commenced. With her eyes closed she couldn't see me mouthing the words right along with her, knowing every word she was going to say. She's done this routine that often, verbatim, that I've memorized it too.

This bitch who calls me up just to put me on hold.

"Hello? Jared? Oh, shit, could you hold on a sec?" and five minutes would pass before it would register in my stupid, gullible mind that she was on the other end just seeing how long I'd wait. See how much talking to her mattered to me. See what a sucker I was. She calls up her ex-boyfriends when she thinks I'm asleep. On my phone, even.

"Oh, gee, I must have dialled your number by mistake. So, what's up?"

She will sandbag every single beer in my fridge. Open one, drink a few sips, then leave it somewhere to go flat while she opens up a fresh one. I'd wake up the afternoon after she'd visit and find an entire twelve-pack opened and gone to waste, stinking up my home.

In the midst of her praise I stuck the point of the knife at the base of her throat and, breath held, plunged the blade as hard as I could into her trachea and spine and back out into the linoleum beneath. It startled me, the way her body jerked violently up beneath me, her eyes suddenly wide and crying, her mouth gaping in a silent scream.

She only struggled for a few moments, but Christ, it seemed like an eternity. When she was done, I put a garbage bag over her head to catch all the blood leaking out on the floor and finished smoking the clove. Then, staring down at her lying still and naked with her tattoos and piercings and death, I realized that I probably should have shagged her again first.

After only a moment's hesitation, I dismissed the idea of necrophilia and got dressed, so I could go outside and somehow dispose of the body. I checked outside the door and saw no one. I hadn't realized night had fallen. We'd been drinking, smoking weed, popping pills, and fucking all day with the shades drawn, and my how time does fly. Turns out it was early yet□ eightish, so I shut the door, lit a joint, and swallowed the pill I'd been offered seven times.

I have a TV, but I almost never watch it. Sometimes I plop down on the couch and flip from MTV to that twenty-four-hour cartoon channel, and if there's nothing on either of them, I'll reread a book from the shelf, lying in my hammock with a stiff drink. Tonight, however, I have some pay channel free as a preview, so I spend the evening smoking three packs of cigarettes and watching Apocalypse Now.

410

I hadn't seen it in ages. About the time What's-his-name goes in there to meet Marlon Brando and it's all dark except for Brando's bald shining head, I noticed something. There, in the corner, where the screen was really dark, the glass reflected a bare woman's foot with the toenails painted red.

I had to think for a minute.

Oh yeah! Shit, Danielle, right. The dead girl in my kitchen with her head in a garbage bag. Jesus, I'd forget my own head if it wasn't screwed on tight. Reminds me of my father's joke: I'm suicidal, but I procrastinate. I'm a murderer, but I'm absent-minded. Saturday Night Live would milk that idea to death.

Oddly, I wasn't having any other kind of problem with the situation. I was relaxed. I felt almost relieved, like I'd accomplished something I'd been putting aside forever and just gone ahead and done it. I even had time to realize and appreciate having a purse full of cash and a bottle of Xanax. The yellow ones. Maybe it just hadn't sunk in yet. Maybe I was stoned.

I got up, reluctantly, and pushed Danielle's foot farther into the kitchen where I couldn't see it, then sat back down to watch Brando tell What's-his-name he was an errand boy for grocery clerks.

I found Danielle again when I went to the cupboard for some chips and thought "Oh dear, someone must have killed my girlfriend. What a tragedy." It wasn't until really late that the TV switched to a test pattern and woke me up that I remembered the corpse on my floor had to be removed quick, fast, and in a hurry. I found myself doing my Ned Flanders impression, going "I'm a mur-diddly-urd-ler!" over and over while cleaned up the evidence.

I should've stabbed her somewhere else, so it would've taken her longer to die, the bitch.

The late Danielle Morgan was what you would call petite, so she managed to fit with some difficulty into this large blue duffel bag I had in the closet. With one hand juggling my keys, a lighter, and a cigarette, and the other supporting my murdered lover on my shoulder, I left my apartment and went for a walk. It was hot and muggy out, and the air stank because it had been raining all day. It had been nice, the rain falling on us in the lounge chair on the balcony while we made love or fucked or whatever. Lying exhausted, her on top of me in the rain, holding each other. We went inside to smoke a joint and did it again, and that was our morning.

Now she was in a bag on my shoulder and I was whistling "She'll Be Coming Round The Mountain."

Out of the shadows, a figure strode into the circle of light. More than a dozen stray cats loitered and glared accusingly at the silent back door of the salumeria, until the intruder startled them. His approach, through casual, was silent, and a few of the more paranoid strays bolted. A few had remembered the man and were not alarmed, but the rest tensed with arched backs and eyed him warily.

From the inner pocket of his sharkskin jacket, he pulled out a bundle wrapped in cellophane and wax paper. The night that had been alive with mewling pleas for the long-shut door to open was now quiet except for the crinkle of the bundle opening. At the first hint of the contents' smell, the cats' demeanor changed. Eagerly, they pressed forward, low purring growls of anticipation rumbling among them. The air was filled with the fragrance now.

Mindful of who got what in the scramble for meat, the man scattered scraps of prosciutto into the crowd. Those who were bullied out of a portion and were left disappointed got a larger scrap thrown straight to them, and the glowing eyes that watched uncertainly from the darkness got a large clump to fight over.

The man couldn't stand to see the ribs standing out under their fur, and hated to see the villagers' disdain for them. No one had any qualms about throwing bread to pigeons, but the stray cats were spat upon like the gypsies who drifted through now and then.

When all the ham was gone, the man wadded up the packaging and tossed it across the alley, rebounding it perfectly off of the wall and into the crescent of space left by an ajar trash can lid. It was one of the many useless skills he'd perfected over the years, for appearance's sake, never missing a shot in wastepaper basketball. The cats looked up at him with imploring eyes, hoping there might be more coming, but he shrugged at them and pulled a cigarette out of the pack in his shirt's breast pocket. As a few of the more appreciative cats rubbed their flanks along his shins, he lit the cigarette and showed off another of his often-practiced useless skills. Six perfect smoke rings drifted out of the light to dissipate in the darkness of the alley. He'd tried to quit smoking, but every time he started again it was out of guilt; without smoke coming out of his mouth, he couldn't blow smoke rings. All of that effort to learn gone to waste.

He waited until the cats were through showing their gratitude, scrubbing their loose hairs off onto the gray trousers he wore, and bid them good night. Back out on the town's main street, the commercial center of a village that rose almost vertically up the side of a mountain, he took a long pull off his hip flask. The fiery liquid burned its way down his throat and into his belly, chasing away the feelings that tried to invade him, the alien sense of Not Belonging.

Screwing the top back on and tucking it into the waist of his trousers where it hugged his hipbone, he took another long, calming drag off of his cigarette and flicked it away, half-smoked, into the night. He smiled his crooked half-grin and strode down the street as if he owned it, pleased with himself and his "good deed for the day" and ready to balance it out with depravity.

In the light of the cobblestone street, his movie star styled hair glinted with the sticky residue of gel, and the cat hairs that decorated his trousers stood out like dandruff under a blacklight. Neither would matter where he was headed, especially with the warm reassurance of tequila, so he didn't bother wasting his time with vanity. He'd had enough of it in front of the mirror before he'd left, making sure his appearance was impressive enough to not give a shit about maintaining. He had succeeded.

His sharkskin jacket, gray, with lapels like a suit coat, practically screamed "I cost two grand" and the stingray belt and shoes echoed it. Everything he wore was a shade of gray, complimented by silver. Cuban link necklace, two Greek fretted rings, the belt buckle an interlocking Gucci double G, a spike bend eyebrow piercing adorning his Jack Nicholson scowl, two more in his left earlobe, and one spike horseshoe in his left nipple, occasionally appearing when the wind blew his half-buttoned, marbleized shirt open.

His appearance was so meticulously planned to disguise him as the kind of person who, well, liked himself. The kind of man who didn't drink to drown the rage that boiled in his guts, who didn't feel hate, contempt, or revulsion for the world around him. Somehow, people would occasionally sense something amiss about him, unable to put their finger on it, but still by instinct felt disturbed. After "rationally" considered, those feelings were discarded, because the man's face seemed so innocent and harmless.

Only close inspection would show that his nose had been broken a few times, skewing his contagious smile into a charming crookedness, but his face was redeemed by a strong chin and mischievous eyes. A passing glance, of which there were few, typecast him as some kind of movie star.

The same way he used to be pigeon-holed as a nerd, and wouldn't ever be seen clearly as a cold-blooded killer.

Bianca, the Florentine guide for her two foreign exchange student friends, staggered out of the front door with them where they stumbled, holding each other for support, and collapsed, giggling onto the curb. She'd led the two American girls, Jennifer and Andrea, on a Tour de Bar through Italy, making a pilgrimage first to Rimini's Sant'Archangelo—about two hours south of Venice—and then staying a week so that they could sample Via Covignano's Paradiso on Friday and Saturday, then Byblos on Via Pozzo Castello on Sunday. It was truly a religious experience.

From there, they backpacked south, all the way to the Calabrian toe of the Boot, then took a small plane to Palermo, the capital of what's being kicked. The trek across Sicily ended in the eastern corner, halfway up a mountain in a charming town called Taormina in the Peloritani Mountains, not too far from Mount Etna.

Andrea was convinced that in Sicily, even the ugly people were beautiful in a way. Bianca, the polyglot, told her the French called them *jolie laide*, but Andrea put it down to being simply Sicilian. She was pleased to see elderly couples walking hand in hand down the street, both of them square-bodied, both of them bald, and neither of them giving a shit.

She also loved seeing Moorish features on a pale, white face, and Caucasian features wrapped in chocolate skin. The diversity was lovely.

For this reason, none of them thought twice about the handsome figure who swaggered out of the shadows, dark-skinned and smiling at them with piercing green eyes and looking like a young Paul Newman with a Caesar cut. He stooped and picked up Jen's wayward high heel that had slipped off and tumbled away as they laughed on the sidewalk. Trying to hold a straight face, Jennifer stuck out her shapely leg at him and wiggled her toes, offering her foot as a woman would present her hand to be kissed.

The man knelt down with the shoe and gently took hold of the foot, fixing a faint, crooked half smile on her.

"*Ecco*, Cinderella."

Slipping the shoe on and rising, stepping around them to enter the bar. They stared after him, music tumbling out of the door as it slowly closed. Looking at each other, they burst out laughing again, revelling in the happiness that only red wine can bring.

"Cinderella!" Jennifer gasped, and they convulsed even harder.

It seemed forever until they could get to their feet and make their way, giggling and holding onto each other for balance, back to their hotel.

Inside, the short, young man was happily greeted by dapper old men and buxom maidens, the men of his own age viewing him as unwanted competition, but tolerating him because he was just too nice to be resented. He was grabbed and kissed by Lucrezia the barmaid, who wished so badly that he'd sleep with her, and Silvana, the waitress he *had* slept with last weekend. It was nothing more than bragging rights they were after, and the one lorded it relentlessly over the other.

Valentina, an apprentice bartender, hurried over to him with his usual, a stout Cuba Libre—Coke for color—and presented it to him, eager for his favor. He was well-known to be an irrationally big tipper, a reputation he was happy to cultivate, and proved to this young girl.

"*Grazie, squisita,*" he told her with mock solemnity, then raised his glass to drain it all in one go and hand it back. Here, a Cuba Libre, as any other drink, was made properly for a change. Once, in America, he'd ordered one and gotten a blank look from the barmaid. "Uh…we're all out of that. Sorry," she said, and all the real drinkers at the bar fell out laughing.

"What?" she asked.

"A Cuba Libre is Bacardi and Coke," the bouncer said. Red faced, the girl began mixing the drink, muttering.

"Then why didn't you just ask for Bacardi and Coke?"

Hearing her, Rabbit made everyone laugh even harder at her. "Lady, if I wanted a Long Island Iced Tea, would I ask for a Long Island Iced Tea or list all the ingredients?"

But all over Europe, with the exception of Spain (for obvious reasons, unless you listed the ingredients instead of calling it by its name) the oldest cocktail in the world was made with real work ethic. Some places here even squeezed in half an orange before pouring the rum, dropping in a wedge of lime and a cherry, like Val would. It did the trick, and tasted damn good.

Cesare, who had welcomed him as the new singer for his swing band, companionably punched him in the shoulder, staggering him back a few steps to get his attention. He could get away with it, since he played good saxophone and could match the blow-in shot for shot, all night long. Hands were shaken, hair was ruffled, and the newcomer was dragged by the lapel to where the band was set up and had been playing, singerless, for an hour and a half.

Handed an old-fashioned microphone, the kind whose head was an oval bulb with silver ribs, the man wet his throat again with someone else's rum, crooned a short intro to get his audience to pay attention, and the band launched into an Italian version of "You And Me And The Bottle Makes Three" that Rabbit had translated and insisted upon, officially starting a party that would last all night.

Chapter II

I would like to take this opportunity to introduce myself.

I was born small, myopic, buck-toothed, and sickly, wondering what I'd done in a past life to deserve coming back as a runt. Thanks to civilization, technology, and modern medicine I am now strong and handsome, with a perfect smile and contact lenses and allergy pills and shots and inhalants and operations.

Thanks for nothing.

In the world I see, the weak die early, yielding to the strong. In the world I see, the blind catch no game and fall easy prey to wild beasts and wilder men. In the world I long for, those who sneeze and cough in the great outdoors don't last one night.

A runt wouldn't suffer too long. A runt wouldn't have any illusions about what he can become with a little pluck and heart. A runt won't be too disappointed when he discovers he's been lied to.

Ungrateful?

Hell yes.

Unappreciative of all I have?

You ain't just whistling Dixie.

Contacts dry up and fall out, glasses break. Pills don't last forever. But where I should embrace my saviors and weep tears of joy that mine is a better life because of them, I instead choke on bile and resentment. I wore braces for two years, and then a retainer. Every time I got punched in a fight after school with everyone watching, my lip snagged and bled and it had nothing to do with other guy's strength or prowess. But they cheered his empty accomplishment as if he'd knocked my eyes out of their sockets. This perfect smile that I wore braces and bled to get is nothing but enamelled bone exposed by flesh to grind my food into a digestible pulp. That's all.

You have a lovely smile.

416

All the better to eat you with.

My beautiful eyes are football-shaped and diseased, and worthless unless I stick little pieces of plastic directly onto their surfaces. My muscles would never have grown without the aid of chemicals and scientifically tested and guaranteed supplements the US RDA hasn't approved yet.

I'm not a liar or a poseur, but I will always be a fraud.

In the wild, nothing grows old. When an animal becomes too weak to fight, something stronger will kill it. In Nature, there are no senior citizen's discounts. There are no walkers or wheelchairs or huge wraparound black visors because there just isn't any time for the weak. People like me exist so much more now than ever before because somebody decided we all had the right to live.

Misfits thrive, our species suffers; somebody has to do something. Quick. It won't happen overnight, but I'm getting started now.

Something that really pisses me off: my generation is all about being different, but you have to be different in the same way everybody else is, or there's something wrong with you. Sober, this confuses me. Drunk? I take it personally.

Every condescending or unimpressed look I get in a club for doing exactly what everybody else is doing makes me see red. I'm not a bad person. In fact, I can be a really nice guy. But I seem to be the only one. The worst are the couples that are there together, looking at me with their triumphant disdain. Their even being there makes me wonder. You go to a club searching for possible intimacy, find it, and then what? Back to the club. I guess because maybe the searching is all we know these days, and we're clueless about the having.

Like Jane Goodall with her chimps I have been making a study of the morons I share this planet with. Something I've noticed is that there seems to be a wide variety of wallflowers these days. A hierarchy of cowardice, if you will.

There are those who make continuous circuits of the club so they look like they have people to catch up with somewhere, others who ring the balconies and ignore one another while they watch braver people dance, and the ones who refuse to be seen anywhere other than the dance floor, but they still stand around doing nothing. All they do is get in other people's way and sneer at you.

I love the dancers too. These assholes who breakdance but can only do one move. They make everyone else clear the way while they do their one move, then they bolt to their feet, walk in a circle looking at where they just were as if they're trying to negotiate some tricky terrain. Hmmm, how should I go about this? Which is the best part of this perfectly flat surface for me to try my move again?

Maybe they'll wipe their noses in a way that shows they have Attitude, whatever the hell that is. Oh, yeah, I respect you. Really. Pull up your fucking pants.

And I must have been on another planet when they decided I couldn't

417

handle going to the bathroom by myself.

    Here's your soap, sir.

    What?

    Your soap. I've got your soap, right here.

    Good. Thanks. Look, I can reach the fucking faucet by myself, buddy. No, I don't want any cologne. I don't want a haircut or a manicure either, now get lost. What are we, fuckin' infants? Have we gotten that lazy, we need to pay someone else to hand us our fucking towels and soap? I can't believe I have to get mad about this shit. I can't believe I'm the asshole because I'm potty trained and I can prove it.

    I leave the bathroom, ignoring the looks I get on the way out for not tipping the bathroom attendant and making inane small talk with him. Colored people have been free from slavery for over a century and they still take jobs like that.

    Oh, and another thing. If you want to charge me eight bucks for a lowball drink when the full bottle you made it from costs ten, you're not getting a fucking tip. Period.

    I smile and step aside to let two drunk girls pass, who roll their eyes at me in return. I do not smile or step aside for the herds of extra-Y chromosome Neanderthals in their frat-boy uniforms: untucked polo shirts, khakis, and white caps. And, Christ, flip-flops.

    The rest of them seem to be Hilfiger ads, only with the Kangol caps on backwards the way Samuel L. Jackson wears his. Mimicking an actor, oh yeah, that's different. Cutting edge. Avant garde. Pull up your fucking pants.

    I get three more drinks at the bar and throw two of them down right there. I ignore the frown for not tipping the guy and go off to find my friends, sipping the third.

    The only thing science couldn't cure was my height. I'm still five-seven and there's nothing I can do about it. My friends, however, must have been fed something that just wasn't on my mom's shopping list. There's not one of them under six-two, and I feel like I'm at the bottom of a fucking well.

    There they are, crowded around Mark, my best friend, like they're his disciples. I try to keep my distance from them for two reasons. One: I can't hear anything they say anyway, and two: I get a crick in my neck trying to include myself in their conversation. Besides, if this were a movie, I'd only be one of those minor recurring characters, Short Guy #2, an unbilled member of an entourage with no lines…but I try not to think about it.

    "Oh, there's Jared." That was easy to lip read.

    "Jared, where the fuck have you been?" That too.

    My response, however, is not so easy to lip read, so I am blinked at and then ignored. My friends.

The only one who's actually my friend is Mark, the Viking. He's tall, blond, handsome, and strong, the kind of fellow who'd have been Hitler's wet dream. He gives no thought to culture, the pursuit of knowledge, or the future. A strict hedonist. He knows everything about designer clothes, the latest trend, the newest breakthrough in technology; provided it has some entertainment value. He's got a great stereo. Huge TV. All leather, oak, neon, and chrome. His nipple-, ear-, and eyebrow-piercings are solid gold. He has a girl for every day of the week, and two for Sunday.

Deep inside, I hate him because I cannot be him.

The girls made their way through the bustling crowd of tourists in the staggeringly bright mid-afternoon, passing outdoor cafes and bougainvillea-rioted side streets, the feverish colors tumbling off of the latticed sides of restaurants and clothing stores. A little hair of the dog was brought to them at breakfast by a waiter who understood perfectly how they must've felt, and as soon as their heads were quieted, they had marvelled at the buffet of San Domenico Palace.

It wasn't so much that the food was damned good, but that everything was covered with nets to keep out marauding wasps.

Wasps?

Sorties of large, dangerous looking wasps on food recon were squirming under the nets and flying away with chunks of scrambled eggs and bits of ham that seemed way too big for them to lift. And no one else seemed bothered by it. Other guests would passively swat them away without any fear of being stung, or just ignore them entirely, as if they were all merely sharing their breakfast with a different kind of people, scooping out eggs or tonging bacon strips that the evil-looking insects had just walked across.

Jennifer and Andrea were amazed. In America, everyone was so concerned with their paranoid fear of germs that if two trips to the buffet were made with the same plate, the second helping would be contaminated with God knows what. But in Italy, unless the trespasser was a cockroach, the food was untainted and perfectly fine. If flies had walked across fruit in the outdoor market, big deal! That's what water was for. Nowhere in sight were the typical American cosmeticized foods, either—apples waxed and dyed red or green, oranges dyed orange, using chemicals meant to beautify but not be digested. Nowhere in sight was an attractively orange and tasteless package of "processed cheese food," a sacrifice of worth in exchange for shelf-life. Nowhere in the country that the girls'd been had they encountered the obsession they'd grown up with, the need to shade the unpleasant and the entirely natural, promote the ordinary into fancy, and air-brush the inevitable. Italians are a hardy people who take no stock in unnecessary worry, and Sicilians, they will build their homes on the rims of active volcanoes.

But *wasps?* These things were *huge!* And they were making off with scraps of food three times their size, carrying them away onto the balcony that overlooked the Ionian and vanishing over the rail. Unconcerned, the waiters acted as if they'd done their part by setting up the nets, and if the raiding wasps could still make off with bacon, melon, and Eggs Benedict, more power to them.

Now, cured of their hangovers by a hearty breakfast and a few girlie cocktails, the adventurers went shopping. Laden with bags full of things they'd ship back to Florence, they made their way among the sharply-dressed natives and all the stupidly-dressed tourists. The latter, wherever they'd come from, all wore the same ugly sandals, the same shorts that displayed laughably pale legs, white as a fish belly, hats they wouldn't be caught dead wearing at home, and fanny packs.

Jennifer pointed out that when she was old, there would be time enough to wear a bag on her hip.

Andrea laughed. Bianca didn't get it.

They came to the plaza where artists were camped out with their easels erected and wares displayed, and were either painting quaint cityscapes or drawing caricatures for the passersby. Stopping to admire them, they came upon the man they'd seen last night.

"Ah, Cinderella!" the man teased, setting down the Corona with lime he'd paused to refresh himself with. He had no stack of price tagged paintings or an easel, just a large watercolor pad with one page propped open to dry. It was of a woman playing with her child, and the background was identical to the mouth of an alley across the street. The same garments were swaying in the breeze, hanging from clotheslines stretched across the top of the painting.

The girls paused, then remembered the half forgotten incident.

"It's your Prince Charming, Jen!" Andrea laughed.   Jennifer blushed.

The man stood and stepped away from his seat, gesturing toward it.

420

"Seduti per me, bella." Sit for me.

She shook her head, but the other two teased her and made her sit reluctantly, despite all of her protests about a "bad hair day." The artist picked up the pad, making sure his painting had dried, found a pencil, and sat down cross-legged across from her.

After turning to a blank page, he peered up at her over the rim of his way-too-expensive sunglasses.

"Come ti chiami?" he asked. Again, reluctantly, she answered. He wrote the name in pencil in the bottom right hand corner, then studied her carefully for a long moment.

She felt uncomfortable sitting there, but knew if she didn't pose for him her friends would never let her hear the end of it. With them hunkered over and watching, glancing up now and then to check on details, they spectated as he began, occasionally commenting in English about how cute he was or how good he smelled. When Jennifer relaxed, she made a subtle face in co-appreciation of his looks. He was too busy drawing to notice. He didn't get far before he looked up for another moment, memorizing her, and smiled.

"Bene. Ritornate piu tardi."

"What? Come back later?" Andrea asked, surprised. "He's not even half-done!"

Jennifer frowned, standing up. He waved them away and rose to reclaim his seat, draining the last of the bottle. Bianca shrugged and started to lead them away when Jennifer stopped her.

"Wait a sec. How much is he charging for this?"

Bianca asked him, and he told her he wasn't charging anything.

"So, this is free?"

"Questo faccio per me, non per lei." This is for myself, not for you.

"Che?"

"Ritornate piu tardi." And he went back to work.

Confused, they left, and went off for coffee. In between wondering why this weirdo would draw a stranger just for himself, they remarked on his good looks and tried to figure out who he was. He made no sense at all, and they found themselves more than a little curious.

Bianca mentioned that he wasn't speaking Sicilian or any other dialect commonly spoken, but academically pure Italian. It was obvious that he had learned it from a course and not his parents. He didn't even speak in Americanized Italian. Maybe he was an expatriate who'd returned to the land of his forefathers. There was no trace of any accent when he spoke, though. He'd learned well.

Changing the subject, they outlined their plans. This was the final stop in their journey, and they had just enough money to get back to Florence in time for classes to start again. There were many cities and small villages that the American girls had wanted to go broke and be stranded in, but they resisted and went on to the next place they'd never want to leave.

Their heads cleared by strong coffee, they left the café and made their way back to the plaza. The artist was busily swizzling a brush in his coffee mug full of brown water, holding two others like mandibles sticking out of his mouth, the pad balanced on his knees. From what they could see as they approached, he had colored the portrait in completely, adding a background of the buildings and flowers and mountain.

Damn, that was quick.

He looked up as they came near, and smiled, the paintbrushes in his mouth spreading like open arms.

"Wow," Andrea remarked when he held up the portrait. Bianca raised her eyebrows at it, but Jennifer was uncomfortable. Something about the accuracy of it, considering how little he'd started with, made her vaguely uneasy, especially since he had captured her look of uneasiness that she'd tried to pass off as a bad hair day. It wasn't her hair that had been a problem. It was the last of her hangover; the pasty skin, the slightly bruised bags under her cloudy blue eyes, the dark residue of a long night and the nervous smile she'd tried to hold.

It wasn't flattering. It was brutally honest. Every other artist was doing either comical caricatures with exaggerated features or forgiving watercolors done to a romantic ideal. This guy made her look human.

"Quanto costa?" Bianca asked, offering to buy it and ignoring what he'd told her before.

"Pranziamoci." Let's all have lunch. She turned to them for their verdict, trying to hide her own amusement and surprise.

"Did he say what I think he said?" Andrea asked.

"Sure did." Now, they both turned to Jennifer, eyebrows raised. There was an awkward lull, which the artist seemed to enjoy.

"Yeah, you talked me into it," she said finally.

"Good," the man sighed, rising. "I could eat a horse if you put enough ketchup on it." He folded up his chair and held it under one arm with the pad, the three girls staring at him. Dumbstruck.

"You, uh…speak English?" Jennifer stammered. He smiled.

"Fluently. Come on, the best restaurant in town's around the corner."

"So, you got a name?" Andrea asked, walking beside him.

"Nick," Rabbit said. "Nick Coniglio."

"That means 'rabbit', doesn't it? But you're not supposed to pronounce the 'G'." She looked back at Bianca for agreement.

"Mm-hmmm. But everybody in the States says it wrong and my family's gotten used to it."

The truth was, he picked a name that matched his nickname just for sentimental reasons, and he liked the way it sounded with the G. It had a ring to it.

"So, what do you do here? You work here?"

"Ahh, I'm sort of on vacation."

"That right?"

"Yeah. A word of warning about this place we're going to. The eggplant's really good, but it'll give you wind, something terrible."

"Wind, huh?" She cast a look backward at her two friends who followed, raising one eyebrow at them. They were both still too embarrassed to be amused.

"But the veal, ohhh the *veal*…hey, none of you are vegetarians, are you? I don't want to be eating some poor little calf in front of girls who only eat salad."

"No, no, veal's fine," Andrea assured him. "It's already dead, so we might as well eat it, you know? Now, if I had to kill it…"

"I know. I probably couldn't kill a cute baby cow, either. One of the big, ugly, grown-up ones, sure. But a calf? Now, my folks took me on a trip to Alaska when I was a kid, so we could club baby seals, but that's different. That was more fun than Whack-A-Mole."

"What!" Andrea stared at him incredulously.

"Otters, too. I got to shoot otters with a twelve-gauge."

"No!" She couldn't' tell if he was kidding or not.

"Yeah, then we fried them up at the lodge. Made damn good fritters."

"Okay, check please!" But she kept walking next to him.

"Only messing. I've never killed anything in my life," he lied. "Here we are." He led them into Amici, kissed a middle-aged wait-

423

ress, and got them a table. When they were seated, and the bread had arrived, Bianca found her voice and decided to break the ice.

"You say you are 'sort of' on vacation. Is this a sabbatical then? Or...*come si dice?*" she asked Andrea. The American thought a moment.

"Hiatus?"

"You could say that," Rabbit answered. He wasn't sure what it was.

"Where are you from?"

"South Florida, last time."

"Before that?"

"Oh, all over, really. I get bored easily and need a change of scenery every now and then."

It wasn't really any of their business that Interpol needed to be thrown off his scent from time to time.

"So now you paint strangers in Taormina?"

"Only if I don't want them to be strangers anymore." He didn't wink at Jennifer, but she felt like he had. She wasn't a big fan of eyebrow piercings, but they were so common these days that she couldn't hold Rabbit's against him. It was something about how cold and sharp the spikes looked, though, shiny as surgical steel. And yeah, he was handsome, sure, but something about him gave her the creeps.

He asked them about Florence, the classes they were taking, and whether Il Duomo still looked like it was made out of *spumoni*. They joked about the huge statue of a boar and the numbskull tourists who came and rubbed money on its snout for luck, then let the coins slide off into a donation grate. Bianca, laughing, told Rabbit that once she'd seen a British woman try it with a thousand lire note, holding up a line because the bill kept fluttering down and wouldn't slip into the grate. She just kept doing it over and over, like a bird flying into a window.

"Stupid tourists," Rabbit agreed. "The boar has nicely faded with corrosion, the way Il Duomo had before the city decided to scrub it clean and remove that patina of antiquity—same with the Sistine Chapel, remember?—but the damned snout is polished clean by all the jackoff tourists rubbing it every day. It's like what hundreds of years' worth of assholes have done to that statue of Saint Peter in Rome. They reach out to rub his big toe, and it's crumbling away into nothing."

"The boar at the New Market, and the Dome, and Giotto's Tower, yeah, they look stupid," Bianca conceded. "But my uncle was one of the ones who cleaned the Chapel's ceiling back in the '80s, and he got Persegati to let me and my brother and my cousins sit and watch some of it. That wasn't a—what do you call it? Patina of antiquity? That was five hundred years of soot from altar candles, torches lighting it at night, and open fires keeping it warm inside during the winter. It *had* to be cleaned off. You couldn't see it."

"They could've left at least a little on."

"It'll come soon enough. But I do have to say, I was up there on the scaffolding with Persegati when the hands were wiped clean. The hands of Adam and God that are almost touching? We were overcome. It was a beautiful moment. And the old man, he measured the space between the two fingers, just because, and I think about it every now and then, when I feel close to God. Three quarters of an inch," she held up one hand, her thumb and forefinger that distance apart. "That's the farthest I'll ever be away from Him."

Rabbit started to patronize her with his smile, but caught himself. "I feel sad that no sealant can be put on the frescoes to protect them, like the animal glue that attracted even more dirt and made them darken faster than they would have without it. Every way of preserving them seems to destroy them just as quickly."

"You talk as if you really care about it."

"It's strange. I'm passionate about things that most people don't give a second thought, and the things that mean so much to them, you can burn for all I care. *Chianti, per favore,*" he added to the waitress.

"You sound like Jen," Andrea said, alarming her friend. "She's that way. She'll pay more attention to whatever's going on in the background when we're watching the news than what the reporter's saying. There could be a twenty car pileup on the freeway, dead bodies everywhere, and she's laughing at some wreck's bumper sticker."

Rabbit turned to the silent girl, seeing her in a new light. She stared accusingly at Andrea, wishing she hadn't been put in the spotlight. She didn't know why, but she wanted to go back to the hotel, crawl into bed, and hide under the covers. Maybe it had something to do with Nick Coniglio glancing every now and then at the restaurant's front door, as if out of habit. She never trusted anyone who couldn't sit with his back to a door. Maybe it was the way

425

he kept directing the conversation away from himself.

Maybe it was because she'd watched too damn many spy movies.

As he often did while being thoughtful, Rabbit absently cracked the knuckles of one hand, one at a time, by folding the fingers under his thumb and pressing. The other hand toyed with a cigarette he'd brought out but never lit. He could smell her fear the way a dog could, and couldn't make up his mind about it. It half worried him, half turned him on.

"So, what do you do when you're not bouncing all over the place?" Bianca asked. She was determined to find out *something* about this guy.

"I'm a writer." That was safe. He had been one a while ago.

"Yeah? Anything we've heard of?"

"Maybe. It's pretty dark stuff, usually. My first novel was called *Heresy*, but the one that did the best was *A Mind Diseased*."

Andrea's ears perked up. She stared at him hard for a moment.

"I read a book called that," she said. "The author was Will Danaher, though."

"A pseudonym." The only pseudonym he used legally.

"*You're* Will Danaher?" The bottle of wine arrived with four glasses.

"Yeah. That was the name of the bad guy in *The Quiet Man*. Victor McLaglen's character."

"Holy shit." He wasn't kidding, she thought. That *is* dark stuff. It's psychotic filth.

"Did you like it?"

"My boyfriend did. He quoted from it constantly. He gave it to me to read, and I had to totally rethink him after that. I mean, the diary of a fucking *serial killer*? And especially the cannibalism part."

"It's fiction, that's all." Again, a lie.

"Yeah, but *still*. It had to take a sick, twisted mind to come up with that, and an even sicker one to think it was funny."

"It was just a different way to package *Heresy*. It was easier to get people to listen to what I had to say if I disguised it as a story. And it should say something about America that such a book did as well as it did."

"You did have a lot to say about America in that."

"Well it's a shitty system based on an intricate and delicately balanced bunch of lies. Look at all the brain dead cretins it produces, all centering their lives around Jerry Springer and MTV."

"Yep. You're Danaher, all right."

Now, Jennifer looked at him with interest, as girls do when they meet a man with his pet python coiled around him. She'd found an acceptable category in which to pigeon-hole him, and once she'd had him pegged, he was fine. A dark, mysterious, sexy artist who thought a little off-color and wouldn't ever get boring. Not at all a closet paranoid who secretly hated the modern world.

Like her.

It was safe for Rabbit to admit to that one small part of his past because William Danaher only existed on paper, and not the same papers Nicholas Coniglio had—a Social Security card, several well-maintained charge cards, a driver's license, passport, and a justifiable income verified with honest records from shrewd investments—all of which were capable of holding up under any kind of search. Danaher could only ever be found on a bookshelf, so he had no problem with sharing him.

"What I want to know," Andrea was saying, "is how did you come up with all of that other stuff you hid your messages in if you didn't feel it already? The anger that kid was feeling?"

"You really want to know? Time out." The waitress had come back with another bottle of wine, ready to take orders. She knew from experience that bottles didn't last long when Sr. Coniglio was dining with only one girl, and three? If they continued at this rate, Jesus would have to show up to replenish the wine cellar.

He thanked her and allowed the three girls to order before playfully "demanding" some veal scallopine. The waitress pretended to take him seriously, asking him not to shoot the messenger, and going overboard with apologies when she reminded him that he'd eaten up the last of their veal yesterday. He looked shocked.

"*Infamita!*" he gasped, making her giggle. Heaving a sigh, he shrugged and told her to surprise him. She nodded solemnly.

"*E prosciutto e melone,*" he added, gathering up the menus for her.

"Aye, aye, captain," she answered, leaving. Those were the only English words she knew; one of the cooks told her to say that when Sr. Coniglio demanded something, and it had become a ritual.

"Yes, we really want to know," Andrea prompted.

"Okay, this was back in the old days when I used to do drugs. I was like Jekyll and Hyde, then. Take the right pills and mix them

427

with the right liquor, and I'd become a totally different person. I never remembered the next day what had happened the night before, and I'd be surprised as hell to get turned away from some bouncer at a club, saying I was barred for life. I always thought they had me confused with some other guy, you know? An impostor.

"But I decided that this Evil Nick, my doppelganger, could probably get me out of this rut I'd been in, this writer's block. So, I'd pop a handful of Xanax, smoke a fattie, and drink whiskey all night in front of the computer, just to see what would happen. I'd black out, then wake up the next afternoon, still in the chair, ashtray full of a mountain of butts, the stereo blaring, and seventy new pages on the word processor."

"And you never remembered writing them?"

"No. As far as I knew, someone could've come in when I was passed out, typed up a few chapters, rearranged my furniture, and split."

"So, Evil Nick wrote all that, then."

"He must've, because I sure as hell didn't. It was weird, reading something I'd come up with not even twelve hours before, and it being totally new to me. I even laughed out loud at my own jokes."

"Do you still do this?" Bianca asked, dipping her bread in olive oil.

"God, no. I don't take any drugs at all anymore," (which was true) "and the last thing I need to have happen is get myself barred from some place in *Sicily*. Bouncers have no sense of humor here."

"Yeah, you'd wake up with fish staring at you."

"If I'm lucky."

"What have you written lately?"

"Nothing."

"Why not?"

"Well, these days, it seems so few people are into subtlety, wit, irony, unless it's something so easy to catch on to that it defeats the purpose. Nobody reads Oscar Wilde anymore, or Shaw, or Shakespeare. The people today want violence, suspense, explosions, what *they* consider drama. If not helicopters, speeding cars, and rocket launchers, they'll settle for nail bats and piano wire. At the very least, a frayed elevator cable and a dozen trapped people who can't get along. Not some drunken doctor's blunder, not some discarded lover's broken heart, not some prodigal son.

"No one wants to read a romance unless there is steamy sex.

They are voyeurs, drooling over the private moments of imaginary people, while I prefer to write something old-fashioned and poignant that no one will read."

That was not the whole truth. The truth was that he had nothing to say anymore, and wouldn't know of a way to say it even if he did. Everything he was angry about, he'd already said, and had never gotten any less angry.

"Plus," he added. "I guess I'd written the same stuff every angry radical does. Emphasis on the bad, ignoring the good, down with the system, up with us. Only there was no Us. I had no solutions then. I have one now, but it can't really be written down and sold in stores." The suspicions that arose from that cryptic comment were distracted by their waitress arriving with their antipasto: prosciutto-wrapped chunks of melon, salted and peppered. They dug into it. Only stray cats like prosciutto better than they did.

"So, you can write," Jennifer said, surprising the rest of them after her long silence. "And you're a good artist, and you can speak Italian. What can't you do?"

"Plenty," Rabbit said, after waiting to swallow. He minds his manners, too, all the girls noticed, approving. "I can't play a musical instrument, except maybe the kazoo. I'm clueless when it comes to machinery. I can't dance at all unless I've had some tequila, and after a few shots of that, I'm convinced I can do anything. Which, I guess, is all that really matters. The confidence. I can't bench more than two hundred ten pounds, can't do math in my head, and I can't juggle."

"Can you tie a cherry stem in a knot with your tongue?"

"Of course! I thought you wanted to know about actual challenges."

"How many shots can you do in a row?"

"All of them."

"How about a back flip?"

"Child's play."

"Prove it."

"Right here?" He started to get up.

"No! Later."

"How much later?"

She regarded him for a moment, a faint smile curving her lips.

"Tonight. After you match me shot for shot, and we go dancing."

Silence. All three girls looked at him with amused expectation.

"Want to make this more interesting?" he asked.

"Oh, it's interesting enough."

"No, we're all grown-ups. We don't take dares. We place bets."

Another silence, the two girls turning to face Jennifer now. She held his gaze, trying to outstare him. A no-blinking contest is a stupid way to compete, but nobody ever wants to be the first to look away. Rabbit didn't understand the whole point of it, but he suspected it was left over from cavemen staring down bears the way people today did with their pets.

Regardless, it was another useless skill that people put stock in, so he'd practiced. Knowing it was stupid, he practiced anyway.

It didn't last long. Pretending she was bored with such childish things, Jennifer quit and reached for her wine glass.

"We'll jump off that bridge when we come to it."

Chapter III

Danielle and I met a year ago, at work. She called herself an actress, but I refused to hide behind any euphemisms. I knew what I was and that's what I called myself. Janitors who call themselves "custodial engineers" make me sick. Ditto the "holistic massage therapists" who give you blow jobs in a spa for thirty bucks. Danielle Morgan wasn't an "actress," or an "adult entertainer," or even a "copulation demonstrator." She was a whore. And so am I.

I answered an ad in the paper. It was a weekly rag that ran classifieds for things like pornographic talent searches, right next to personal ads in the following categories: MEN SEEKING WOMEN, WOMEN SEEKING MEN, MEN SEEKING MEN, WOMEN SEEKING WOMEN, and MISCELLANEOUS. Miscellaneous? I thought all bases were covered.

I couldn't resist. I placed an ad in the Miscellaneous section: "BURT, ASPARAGUS, tall, slender, wishes to meet single, sincere broccoli for dinner, dancing, and Miracle-Gro." I also placed one in the MEN SEEKING WOMEN category, half as a joke and half because I—well, never mind. Mine was the only completely honest ad there. I advertised myself as a NEUROTIC SWM, 23, ATHLETIC, HIGH MORAL FLEXIBILITY, IN SEARCH OF INSECURE, ATTRACTIVE WF WITH DRINKING PROBLEM. I actually got a few replies, which I ignored.

Regardless, this ad I answered wanted adults for locally made films, paying up to $1000 for one shoot. I called them up and described myself. James Dean with a six-pack. Medium endowment. They asked me to stop by. The two *people in the office were in their forties, a man named Perry who was flaming gay and a woman named Leibchen who, frankly, scared me.*

I'd taken a few pulls out of my hip flask before getting out of my car, to get my nerve up, and was glad I did.

"Well well well, you must be James Dean," Perry said. "You weren't kidding. Ooh, I like your eyebrows. Very arrogant-looking. Determined chin. Arrogant-looking, wouldn't you say, Leibchen?"

"He's baby-faced. How old are you, boy? Twelve?"

I swallowed. "Twenty-three."

"Tattoos? Piercings?"

"Tongue stud. That's about it."

"Everybody's got one. Okay, show us what you got."

"Excuse me?"

"Give us a little strip show. Don't be shy. I want to see what you consider medium." I took a deep breath and got it over with. Naked. I was limp. Of course. Perry inspected my entire body. Leibchen only saw one part.

"Can you do something about that, please?" she asked.

Embarrassed, I closed my eyes and thought about an old lover, this chick Katy from when I was a teenager.

"Ahh, there we go. Not a monster, but it'll do. Turn around...nice ass."

The door opened and Danielle walked in, stopping short, taking off her sunglasses and looking me up and down, smiling.

"Is this furniture or just a conversation piece?"

"My dear," Perry said graciously. "This is Jared. We just hired him."

"Charmed," she said.

I asked Danielle if we should go out to dinner or something first and she laughed. We were to shoot the next day, my first time, her third. They thought we would be a perfect match; she with her tattoos and piercings, her fiery red hair, and me with my clean-cut golden boy innocence. She played a wild woman, a temptress, a force to be reckoned with, and I was the good kid she corrupted. She lured me away from my straight A's and wholesome white-bread nuclear family, and showed me the power of the dark side. At least, that's what was supposed to happen.

The set was made up to look like a high-school classroom, and I was her tutor. I pretended to explain cosigns, which I didn't even understand, and she stared at me, chewing on her pencil suggestively. Our eyes met. The pencil slid in and back out, slowly.

I was supposed to start trembling, but I forgot. I leaned forward, my eyes holding hers, and kissed her. She kissed me back. We came slowly out of our

431

desks, into each other's arms, and onto the floor. It was real. We weren't acting. We made it real. They said later that there was chemistry there on the screen.

Unfortunately, that chemistry ended up on the cutting-room floor.

"Cut! What are you doing?" the director yelled. "That looks like you like her!"

I looked into her big blue eyes and whispered.

"I do."

She smiled.

"Get back in the desks. Jared, be shy, and Dani, rape him."

And she did.

Danielle and I never dated each other per se. But we didn't date anyone else either. We'd sleep with different people on the set, but only with one another afterwards. It was odd. She wasn't good with people; neither am I, really, and her friends disapproved of me, and vice versa. We never spoke on the phone except for "Come over," and when she or I arrived we'd drink, smoke a joint, make love, eat pills, smoke more, fuck, and I'd fix dinner. We never took in a movie, went dancing, met for drinks, or hung out with others after the first few times—which were disastrous.

My friends didn't say anything about her, which said it all, and I overheard her friends say "He's an asshole," or "He gives me the creeps." We mutually agreed to keep our relationship on a fuck-only basis, and told our friends we'd broken up so they'd leave us alone.

Sometimes we'd go months without seeing each other, sometimes we'd live together for a week. She could be fun sometimes. Sometimes she was intolerable, and I loathed her and myself. And after a while, both our minds would wander during sex. It became perfunctory, an act to be completed out of habit, just something to do and get through. I don't know why we bothered.

It was always a pleasure to work together on set, though. We each knew what the other wanted, what we needed to make the moans genuine, and that looked better on the screen. They called it chemistry.

Since nobody I knew watched the news and I didn't watch TV, I heard about the murders by way of rumors, and I pretended to dismiss them as such. Bodies were supposedly turning up in dumpsters, drainage ditches, bushes by the side of the road, and water traps on golf courses. I was just getting started.

"Really? Who?" I would ask, feigning interest.

"Jodi, you know, that girl who sold pills at Diamonds."

"Brad, that one dude, you know, with the hair."

"This candy-raver, I don't know her name, but you used to see her every-

where. You know the type. Lives for clubbing, does nothing during the day, has to take serotonin by the handful to undo the damage she does to her head every night, you know, just to feel good about herself. I'm pretty sure you fucked her once in the hot tub."

"Oh, yeah, her. Oh well."

"Yeah, what a tragedy, huh? Got her neck broken."

It was always on a Sunday morning, the body was discovered. Never stopped anyone from going out next Saturday, though. No one cared. It was as if my entire generation was just waiting around to be killed or OD, and they were determined to be fucked up when they met their maker. Someone actually said "Well, that's not gonna happen to me."

"What's serotonin?" I asked, more concerned with the chemicals than with a dead girl I slept with once.

"You know when you're rolling and you feel all, I dunno, good or whatever? That's serotonin. It flows regularly through your brain to make you feel happy or in love, and goes in, like, a door and out, like, another door. But what X does is it shuts the exit door."

"Uh-huh." Listening to these people feel like having my brain pushed through oatmeal.

"Yeah, so it builds up and it builds up and you feel great, you're rolling, and when it's over the exit opens back up and it all drains out, leaving you, I dunno, all ate up or whatever."

I swear to God, that's how people talk. My friends.

"So this girl had to take extra serotonin to keep herself up?"

"Yeah, lots of them do it, so they don't get all depressed."

"About things like having no real lives and being killed off every week?"

"Something like that."

I don't want to be a part of this bullshit lifestyle, this subculture, this scene, this whatever you want to call it. But I'm so scared of being a nerd again, of being alone, or considered uncool by people I'm superior to in almost every way.

Scratch the "almost."

I want to be popular. I'm desperate to be popular. And I hate myself because of it. If someone looks up to you, you must look up to me. That's what I want. That's what's on my mind every day, all the time.

Can you blame me for what I did?

Of course not.

Jared Layton, until his senior year of high school, felt that Fate had played a lousy trick on him at the moment of his birth. It had

433

allowed him to survive. His mother, who had continued to smoke and drink throughout her pregnancy, didn't have the common courtesy to miscarry. The various maladies that afflicted him up until puberty never had the ambition to finish what they'd started and put him out of his misery. Instead, they were replaced with some award-winning acne and an unexpected growth spurt that made him look even more gangly and awkward that he already was.

Once, and only once, he asked the jock piece-of-shit bullies what he'd ever done to them, right before they knocked out three of his teeth. He never got an answer, nothing more than laughs.

He blossomed at seventeen. His father finally let him trade his glasses in for contacts, his braces came off, and his skin cleared up almost overnight, as if by magic. Now, the only pockmarks on his face were his eyes. His weak and whiny voice was the rumbling of a fault line. And in the tiny black raisin that passed for his heart, bitter fury raged.

As soon as his parents died their too-early deaths and his unexpected inheritance opened the world for him, he set about changing the hand that had been dealt him. He took classes in kung fu, jujitsu, and jeet kun do. Then, he got his eyes lasered and his penis enlarged. Good eating plus a grueling routine at the gym filled him out. He was still not huge, but he could have passed for an underwear model. There were a few misadventures here and there, a few false starts. A few botched attempts at a college education, but his real higher learning began shortly afterward.

Not too long after that, he started killing people more methodically, and his wyrd was set.

Now, he would sometimes sit among the flowers that garlanded the mountain and stare out at the haze over the Mediterranean, the strange blending of sky and sea that obscured the horizon, and wonder why he was still incomplete, over ten years later, with more money scattered in hidden accounts than he could possibly spend. He was still a misfit. An outcast.

The only times he ever felt comfortable, really comfortable, was at the house of his friend, Nestor de Medieros. The Brazilian was as twisted by the world as he was, as full of hate for the whole mess of it and as eager to exterminate all the garbage that infected it. When they were together, they each felt whole. The family that welcomed him to dinner adored him, especially for the way he made the taciturn king of the family smile.

Nestor was not a tyrant; he doted on his children and worshipped his wife, but only on the inside. He kept those feelings hidden.

Only when Rabbit came did he show any emotion. Only when his apprentice returned from his latest adventure did Nestor allow himself to open up and show that he was human. He was crippled inside, and he found a strange feeling of camaraderie when he knew another like him existed.

He had allowed the young, aspiring drug lord to control the rope when they dangled a screaming traitor from his yacht's outriggers, dunking him playfully into chum-filled waters as triangular dorsal fins cut through them. He allowed him the pleasure of teasing the victim, dropping him perilously close, pulling him a short way back up, and then letting him splash back down. This was the only therapy for people like them: the cries of terror, the pleas for mercy.

When he looked back on those moments, sometimes, Rabbit felt himself starting to cry. But he never did. He would force himself to grind out any remorse, thinking instead of how he'd been the world's piñata for so long and how he deserved a little vengeance.

He thrived on other people's attention. He had no friends, but he had all the disciples money could buy. He was admired for all of the wrong reasons: material possessions, irresponsible generosity, fighting prowess and cunning, and the bloodthirsty will to do what his enemies would not.

He tried to see himself as the good guy, but knew he was only fooling himself. He was a monumental fraud, one of three that he knew of, their true mentor being a man who called himself Jim Crowe. This man encouraged Jared's "growth," teaching him the skills necessary to be whomever he wanted, wherever he wanted. Independent wealth, disillusionment, and the will to change the world were what Crowe required for his tutelage. An avid believer that history is made by individuals and not the masses, he was eager to give Antichrist lessons to anyone who showed enough promise, and of his three best candidates, young Jared Layton was the cream of the cream of the crop.

They made it their business to exterminate anyone they considered a waste of good air: thieves, whores, rapists, pedophiles, crooked businessmen, liars, litterbugs, and drug addicts. They were drug lords because that was the easiest way to kill off their customers, to enslave them and slowly poison them with what they wanted in the first place. They were pimps so they could spread plague. They had a plan, the men and women at the top. Their protégés knew only the idealistic objectives, and *their* servants knew nothing.

Men like Rabbit knew nothing of the mentors behind their mentors.

"You know what I want to see?" Jennifer asked. "I really want to see some self-pitying, emaciated, California cunt explain her bulimia to an Ethiopian. Really, in the same country where folks are digging in dumpsters for table scraps, some bitch eats a decent meal and then sticks her finger down her throat. I want to see these bitches try to cry on the shoulders of starving people and see what happens."

"I know," Rabbit agreed, disgusted. "And yunno what tickles me fucking pink? They have the nerve to call it *purging!*"

Jennifer made a face and nodded, snorting, and downed her third shot of whiskey. Andrea and Bianca had left the two of them alone and gone off to another table with Cesare and Tomassino, the drummer, so that they could rail against societal evils in peace.

Lucrezia and Silvana weren't pleased, but Rabbit didn't care.

"I saw a few of those talk shows a while ago, the ones that everyone in Audienceland are so obsessed with, and saw people who made a big deal out of secretly being queer, as if everyone watching daytime television should give a shit. People out there are starving, and this guy's biggest tragedy is that he'd rather be a girl? Is this some kind of joke?"

"Worse!" she snapped, banging her fist down on the table and making the meniscus of her one remaining shot jump up and spill over the rim of its glass. "Worse! These fuckers drag their girlfriends out to this show to confess what should be private in front of a bunch of cheering strangers so that the people who love them can be humiliated on national TV!"

"And vice-versa. Girls do it to their boyfriends, adultery is celebrated, mothers put to shame—" She thumped the table again, hard, this time bringing her clenched fist down on the rim of the ashtray. Rabbit pretended not to notice the cigarette butts that were launched over her shoulder onto the floor. Apparently, she hadn't noticed at all.

"Let's not talk about this crap anymore. This filth gets me in the kind of mood I don't want to be in on a perfect night in Sicily with Prince Charming buying me drinks."

"Deal. May I have this dance, Cinderella?"

"Thought you'd never ask."

They clinked shot glasses and downed the last of the eight they'd ordered for Round One. Her friends were surprised at how well they were getting along, and Cesare couldn't believe he'd seen "Nick" actually lose his cool in front of a lady. From what he knew, his front man hadn't had even close to enough drink yet to be able to dance well, but lo and behold, the tirades had given him a natural rhythm. It must've been his mood, Cesare decided. The girl had gotten him started and a fire had crept into his eyes. Maybe he really was Italian.

Lucrezia was disturbed to see Nick's *ghignata,* the "evil grin of a man thinking ugly thoughts." *Ghignare* was something only fiends did, not good-hearted, rich pretty boys like Nickie. It made her reconsider him. No, this man was not the *farfanicchio* the other men put him down as.

Feeling himself with another of his kind, Rabbit relaxed, didn't feel like he had to pretend anything.

The music was in his soul and he didn't need his mind numbed to run with it. He and Jenny—she had been promoted to a Jenny, in his opinion—moved together comfortably without any of the self-conscious stiffness he was used to, and he was elated. It was the same happiness that comes with finally mastering some useless skill, like whistling.

Jennifer, too, felt a strange release and new power from finally giving voice to her anger and having it agreed with. Now, she wore her own *ghignata*, devouring Prince Charming with her eyes and thinking *Ha! Vegetarian? No, I'm not a vegetarian, I'm a fucking man-eater.*

Grabbing a fistful of his sueded shirt, she yanked him to her, locking her lips to his and forcing her hot tongue down his throat, tasting cigarette and whiskey breath. Pressing against him, grinding against the surprisingly large bulge that she'd found, the animal inside her took over. God, he could kiss! And the size of him! And his smell, the natural, uncologned scent of his skin and hair made her drunk with lust.

Her toes curled, the peach fuzz on her forearms stood up on end.

Lucrezia scowled.

Round Two.

"Damn," Jennifer said. "That felt just like a record skipping."

"Yeah, me too, but there's a reason." A reason for breaking everything off in mid-kiss and dragging her by her white-knuckled hand back to the table. Passing Silvana, he'd asked her for eight more shots of whiskey, and Jennifer tried to swallow her frustration. She asked him to explain.

"One, I don't like an audience. Not anymore. It's bad form. And, two, the night is young and I love the sound of your voice." Neither of his reasons were true.

The fact was that once he knew getting laid at the end of the night was written in stone, he enjoyed the hell out of waiting for it. Making it into a long, drawn-out state of mutual horniness with groping and teasing was much more intimate to him that just cutting to the chase. He left immediate gratification to the sexually illiterate, and ended up having much more fun.

They joined Cesare, Tommasino, Bianca, and Andrea at their table in the semidarkness. The girls had to give up the interrogation they'd started, trying to find out everything they could about the mystery man. All they'd learned was that he kissed all the girls but only slept with a few—his choice, not theirs, proving he had a few screws loose—and he sang with a voice no one saw coming. He had this weird talent of being able to mimic almost anyone he met, could duplicate their handwriting, and had an unbroken record of perfectly drawing a portrait in seven minutes flat.

Andrea was relieved to hear nothing that matched up with the narrator of the horrible book she'd read. Maybe this Evil Nick had written a lot of it, but he hadn't based it on himself. Regardless, she began a thinly disguised interrogation of him face to face, trying to pass it off as small talk.

"So, where in Florida did you say you lived?"

"I didn't. But I spent time almost everywhere."

"What'd you do while you were there?"

"Oh, all kinds of things. Drinking, mostly. Speaking of that, is anyone thirsty?"

Cesare cut his eyes at Andrea, silently advising her to cool it. She was drunk and uninhibited enough to theatrically roll her eyes, having no clue that tact might be a good idea. The sax player had already told her that Nick was a private guy, letting people's imaginations run wild about him they way they do in small towns, but noooo, she wanted the goods and she was going to get them.

Rabbit found it easy to ignore her, pretending he couldn't hear all that well over the pounding drums and bass, the ethereal spheres and layers, and needling tweaks of the techno that so many shadows were jerking about to in the strobe light. When Silvana arrived with the tray of shots, he offered them around to make sure no one would resent him downing them all with Jen. They politely declined, and all eight disappeared quickly.

"Now," Rabbit said with authority. "I demand to know...*why* ...in the fuck...are you wearing a dog whistle around your neck?"

Jennifer grinned. "Oh, the jewelry store was all out of diamonds."

Rabbit made a loud annoying noise like the buzzer on a game show.

"Well, it hums in candy—ahem. Comes in handy. You never know when you might need to piss a dog off, yunno? Girl Scouts taught me to be prepared."

Rabbit did the sharp buzz again. "*Ehhngh!*"

"Okay, because nobody else would wear one."

"Ooh, an innovator, not an imitator."

"Don't make fun."

"Honey, it's a dog whistle."

"Could be a dog collar. Or a choke chain that those slutty girls wear to demean themselves."

"Honey, it's a dog whistle."

"All right, I'll explain. Back in the day, back before the war, I used to wear this really cool Maltese Cross, right? No, wait. It was a formée, but everyone called it a Maltese Cross because nobody knows what a formée is, and how different the two of them are. Anyway. But so many people kept accusing me of being a racist. Idiots. And I ask how a *cross* makes me a racist. They say it's an Iron Cross, and that I'm a Nazi. So I have to point out that the Maltese Cross and the formée were adopted by the Germans for World War *One*, and the Nazis weren't around until the 1930s. *And* the symbol *they* used, they stole, too. The swastika was taken from the *Hindus*. Just like Christians took the cross symbol from the Egyptians, when we should have been wearing a fish or something. The *Maltese* Cross was the sign of the Knights of Malta, some crusaders who ran about doing stuff in the name of just plain do-gooderism."

439

"Honey, it's still a dog whistle."

"Yeah, well. I looked and looked for a symbol no one else had already adulterated—wow, I could just *barely* pronounce that word, adulterated. I'm started to get a little tipsy. Adulterated. Better...shit, what was I talking about?"

"Adultery."

"The hell I was. Oh yeah! A symbol! But I realized how stupid it was for me to be looking for someone else's sign to identify myself. You notice how we all do that? Try to express our individuality by using someone else's ideas? Try to do this: try to invent a new letter for the alphabet. A b that isn't a backwards d or upside-down p, or q, or something. A new symbol that doesn't look *anything* like one we already have, that isn't a variation of another or an amalgamation of a couple. Ooh, d'you hear that? *Amalgamation.* I said that rather well."

"You're rambling."

"Sue me."

"Are you going anywhere with this?"

"I *was.* Damned if I know *where*, though."

"You talk in italics when you're drunk."

"I do *not!*"

"See? Did it again."

She clammed up, then.

She felt herself floating in the "in between" feeling she loved so much. She secretly thought that drink elevated her to another plane, another dimension, where the rules were different. That was her way of justifying the way she behaved. Right now, she was stuck in that overly romantic transitional period, where she could still think in a straight line while floating in that blissful phase that characterizes either religious transcendence or the onset of alcohol poisoning. Her gaze was burning a hole through Rabbit's clothes, trying to imagine the muscles she'd felt through them, and one in particular. Yeah, the night is young, she was thinking. That means we can get a damn head start.

"When do you have to go back?" Rabbit asked.

"Back where? Oh, to Florence?" He nodded. "God, don't remind me. I've been trying not to think that this will have to end."

"Having that good a time, Jen?"

"Nickie, this is the best vacation I've ever had. No responsibilities, nothing to worry about, nights like this...can you come to

Florence with us? Look, let's just dispense with the bullshit, okay? I like you. I don't want anything really serious right now, so don't get scared off, but the last thing I want is to leave in a few days and always be comparing guys to you. With my luck, we'd probably go together a couple months, then break up for some reason, but at least I'll have gotten some good mileage out of you, instead of spending the rest of my life with some guy I settled for and wondering What if? What if Nickie and I worked out? You know what I mean?"

He looked at her for a long moment. She was the type he usually went for: slim and shapely, small-breasted but blessed with a perfect ass and really great legs, handsome-faced with a few flaws that he tended to appreciate more than absolute beauty. She had a slight overbite, but a great smile. Her nose was a bit pixie like, but her dark blue eyes more than made up for it. Her hair was long and golden brown, high-lighted convincingly (or maybe naturally) and her skin had the few small scars that showed a spirited childhood.

Bitten nails, though.

She regretted being honest with him, expecting rejection, and it showed in her eyes that she was trying to hide her embarrassment. When he lowered his gaze, she thought he was looking away, buying some time. Only Andrea noticed that he was actually looking at her well-shaped foot, encased in its patent leather t-strap. Her mind flashed back to the book she'd read, the serial killer having a foot fetish and trying to explain why. Hmmm, she thought triumphantly.

"I'll go up there on one condition," Rabbit finally said, looking up.

Her lips parted.

"We stop by Venice together."

Flooded with relief, she seized his face in her hands and kissed him tenderly. They put their arms around each other and held on tightly.

Jennifer's eyes squeezed shut. Rabbit saw Lucrezia watching and he smiled at her. At least, he thought it was a smile. She saw a *ghignata*.

"Jenny?" he whispered into her ear, just loud enough to be heard.

"Uh-huh?"

"Do you like tequila?"

Chapter IV

I ended up going with Mark to Chrome after all. We got separated, which was more my doing than by chance. I was looking for something else tonight. And I found it.

He was well dressed, his skin, teeth and hair immaculately cared for. If it weren't for his hands I'd think he was a pretty girl in reverse drag. He asked me a question, the answer to which was No, but I told him Yes.

I felt like a snake, but not in a bad way. I was a predator, a monster, a fiend that seized and crushed out the life of anything that came too close. Like a boa constrictor. Or a python, yeah, I liked that better.

This must be what vampires feel like.

"My name's Paige," he said, even though I had seen him IDed by a bartender and his card said Frederick Something.

"Charmed," I replied, and shook his hand.

Twenty minutes later, I had both hands around his throat and his green eyes bulged, his face turned a ghastly blue, his tongue lolled out and he died in my living room. The look of surprise on his face, Christ, you shoulda been there.

Something occurred to me then. Here was a person, a living breathing human being with hopes and dreams and secrets just like me. He'd had a childhood, an adolescence, confusion, happiness, curiosity and disappointment, and it all came screeching to a halt because one night he met me. What occurred to me was that death is the most intimate moment you can ever share with another living thing.

Look into the rheumy eyes of an old man who has lived a rich, full life and is satisfied that he'd spent his time wisely, then look into the crying eyes of a strangled faggot who realizes he's never going to find Mr. Right or see Paris or become a famous concert whatever. It was touching to see Paige/Frederick die so unfulfilled at the age of, according to his fake ID, twenty-one.

What a waste, I thought, how marvelously tragic.

I put the corpse in my bathtub and ruined a perfectly good handsaw cutting him up into, well, you know. Pieces.

I took a time out after getting all the limbs off and halved at the elbows and knees, and tried to smoke a cigarette with my blood-slippery fingers, dropping it twice. I looked down at this guy who thought I'd sleep with him, this guy who thought he'd have a fun night sodomizing me.

I went and fixed myself another drink, realizing dimly that my dinner was only a distant memory, and I needed desperately to soak up all that alcohol that was boiling away in my guts. There were no leftovers to speak of. And then...hmmm.

"You thinking what I'm thinking?" I asked my reflection in the mirror. What exactly does human flesh taste like?

"Chicken. Ha!" No, seriously. I'd read about wild beasts that, upon tasting Man, would settle for nothing less, and there were still cannibals in the world. The Asmat, for example, in Papua New Guinea, I think it is, recognize only two races of men: themselves, who they call "the people," and everyone else, who they refer to as Manowe, "the edible."

There are roughly twenty thousand of them, and they can't all be wrong, can they? Who would blame me for being a little curious? What if I could improve on my recipe for veal scaloppini by changing only one ingredient?

I skinned one thigh, cut it into strips, breaded them with a beaten egg and parmesan-basil bread crumbs, then fried them in vermouth and olive oil. It was pretty basic, but I was impressed with the result. Not bad at all with noodles and a garlic-butter-olive oil-lemon juice sauce and some grated parmesan.

One day, I realized, the population problem would get so out of hand that governments would be forced to legalize cannibalism. Think of the restaurants. I giggled like a schoolboy for a good twenty minutes or so when I imagined the ad campaigns and commercials on TV. "What's eating you?" would be a great slogan.

I resolved to grill a few steaks, then roast the ass before tackling scaloppini. Maybe I should invite Avril and Alistair over for a barbecue. Or better yet, they'll walk in, ask what that divine smell is and I'll open the oven door, slip on my oven mitts and drag out a limbless Paige/Frederick, stewing in his own juices with an apple in his mouth.

I'd have to test the waters first, though. Be certain of the extent of their moral flexibility before springing something like this on them. I finished my meal, rather pleased, and wrapped the rest of a tragically unfulfilled young man in aluminum foil, sticking him in the freezer.

The Asmat are not the only ones in the world today. People seem to think that because they have running water and salad shooters and video rentals that all the world does. They refuse to believe that there might be savages in their very own backyards. They'll come to see it before too long.

I'm not the only one, and I'm just getting started.

Either people don't know or don't believe—or don't care—that only twenty-eight percent of the entire continent of Africa is wilderness. Only twenty-eight percent. North America is roughly thirty-eight.

Check an atlas. Do the math.

And to be honest, there are more wild things in metropolitan areas than in the Great Outdoors. Stalking their prey. Reveling in the joy of victory and devouring their victims back in the privacy and comfort of their own homes.

Wild things like, say, me.
And I'm not the only one.
And I'm just getting started.
I made a mental note to see about turning the skull into a bong or some-
thing. Take the necessary steps to clean it out and properly bleach it, that kind
of thing. It could wait until tomorrow, I thought, yawning. I had to be at church
in the morning.

She plopped down on his couch while he fixed them both another drink, vodkas and Red Bull. There was no television, just a small and dignified stereo on an end table, and a bookshelf crammed with leather-bound first editions, a few recent bestsellers, and even fewer paperbacks. A few odd but beautiful original paintings hung about the house, and one stunning nude portrait of some dark-skinned hot blonde chick. Jennifer scowled at it, then decided it came with the wall when Rabbit bought the place. No sentimental attachment whatsoever.

The stereo's digital display suddenly flashed to life and the CD inside began to spin. The remote control seemed to have materialized in his hand out of thin air. What came on was a classical something-or-other that she didn't know, but found pleasant.

Rabbit brought the two glasses over, handing one to her and sitting down. She smiled at him and drank, her eyes gazing at him over the rim in her best attempt at Seductively. He decided it would do.

"Feet hurt," she said, grimacing. "Dancing in these heels."

Rabbit couldn't resist. He took a quick drink and set his glass on the end table beside him, holding out his hand expectantly, beckoning.

"You would?" she asked.

"Give 'em here, Cinderella."

She smiled, bent down to unfasten the straps, and slipped the shoes off. Leaned back and put her feet in his lap.

He began by rubbing gently along the outer edge, deliberately avoiding the arch, and grinding his thumb in a circle at the ball of her foot with one hand, the other kneading her heel. She shifted, getting comfortable, and closed her eyes, a slight frown creasing her brow. He massaged each of her toes then, and ran one fingertip along the top of her foot between two bones where he knew a cluster of nerves to be. She smiled, and he went back to the pinkish underside, getting gradually closer to the arch with a slowness he knew she'd find frustrating.

Her feet were perfect. No protruding veins, no calluses, just slender and elegant and well cared-for, the toenails painted burgundy. He finally came close to the sensitive arch and felt her body tense with anticipation, so he backed off, just to tease her. He allowed her a second to be disappointed before doing what she'd expected, one long stroke, firmly, and he grinned as she tensed again.

The toes of her other foot felt him harden where they rested against him. He closed his eyes and felt his heart quicken. Rubbing the arch in long, slow caresses with three fingers, each varying in pressure, he bent his head and kissed the pad of her big toe, lips parting and the warm tip of his tongue coming out for just an instant. He didn't know how she'd react. He opened his eyes to look up at her and smiled. Her eyes were shut tightly, her mouth open.

She'd set the half-finished drink on the floor beside her heels. She wouldn't mind, he decided.

He slipped her toe between his lips, closing them at the base, and sucked, pulling back slowly and hearing her gasp. He took her into his mouth again, this time grinding it against his teeth before passing it through them, and gently gnawing the underside on the way back out, still caressing her instep with his fingers. She squirmed, letting out a short moan of surprise, and he did the same to each of her toes, passing his tongue around and between them, then running it back from the smallest to the largest along the underside, at the bases.

She was writhing and breathing heavily, and so he went back to sucking and raking his teeth against her smooth, padded flesh. He turned gently, positioning himself, and took hold of her other foot, bringing it to his lips. She ground the one he'd just released against the now-pulsing hardness. He saw her hand snake down her stomach slowly, uncertainly, and come to rest on her belt buckle. She hesitated, and all of a sudden he could not remember being more turned on. He reached and took that hand. Her fingers curled into his, tightened, and he pulled it closer to him. Placed it between her legs, and let go. She started to move it away, but he grabbed it firmly and brought it back. She sighed again, feeling decadent but comfortable, and touched herself while he kissed her in places she'd never been kissed before. She was tingling at her cheeks and scalp

445

and the back of her neck.

When he looked again, her hand was under the waist of her skirt and the fabric rose and swelled, like the crest of a wave rolling forward. And like a wave, it broke and receded, returned, and rose and fell, her breath a long shuddering sigh.

He reached to the belt buckle, unfastened it and loosened the skirt. Taking the hem of it, he tugged gently. She arched her back to help him, raising herself and pushing it down with her free hand. They slid her skirt over the soft swell of her ass, and pulled it off as she drew her knees up to her chest until her shapely legs were fully bared, and brought them down draped over his shoulders.

He crept forward slowly to watch her hand work underneath the cotton of her underwear. Opening her eyes to lock gazes with him, she drew her hand back out of her panties, hooked a finger under them near the widening stain of her juices, and drew the fabric aside. He stared down at the glossy sheen of her shaven lips, smelling their perfume, and she parted them with her ring- and index finger, slipping the middle inside.

Her other hand fumbled feverishly at the straps of her shirt. One snapped and she bared her teeth in irritation, like an animal, ripping the shirt open in one savage wrench. Her finger came out and she touched his face, slipping it into his mouth. She tasted sweet, and he sucked it dry, the taste of her driving him into a frenzy.

He glanced into her eyes and saw them glazed over, framed between her pale, pink-nippled breasts. She put her hand in his hair and he dove, lapping her madly in front and behind, her warm thighs squeezed tight against his ears, the sound of her racing heartbeat trapped in his head by them. Her back was off of the couch, her legs in the air, trembling. One hand in his hair, tugging fiercely, the other hand squeezing his.

Then suddenly, he bolted to his feet, seizing her with startling strength and throwing her over one shoulder. Marched her off to the bedroom like a cave-man.

At first she was scared, but it didn't last long.

I'm not a "shrimper," and fuck anyone who says I am. I don't have a foot fetish. Those people are sickos. I have no idea how you'd classify me and I don't see why I have to be classified anyway. First of all, a fetishist has a narrow range of interest that never changes. Some kind of sacred scenario that brings comfort

446

through repetition. Ritual creates order and order relieves anxiety, yadda yadda yadda. Fuck all that. I like to suck on girls' toes sometimes, provided they have pretty feet. No second toes that are longer than the big toes, none of that shit. They have to shrink in size diagonally from the big toe, in line with each other, and the littlest toe can't be so small that its nail is just a little shard scrunched in on itself. And they have to be clean and healthy; no crusty heels and blue spiderwebbing at the ankle, and thick yellow toenails. And I want to see a nice S-curve. No flat feet, and for God's sake, leave your fucking flip-flops at home unless you're going to the beach. That slapping noise on your heels is trashy. Christ.

When I found out that people like me are so prevalent I looked them up on the Net and found out just how like me these fucks are not. They're podophiliacs. Eww. Not me. Submissives like getting stepped on by chicks in high heels. Dominators like to tickle torture girls until they're laughing hysterically. Cops enjoy cuffing feet. Some get off on ballerinas in tutus and toes shoes being bitchy. Gimpers are subs who put on leg casts so they can't move while shit's being done to them. Pedal pumpers download videos of bare feet revving engines, making that loud mechanical roar. Bug crushers will jerk off while watching girls squash bugs, getting graphic close-ups of mangled wing cases and wriggling little legs smooshing up between pretty little toes. Transference of killing power, blah blah blah.

Perverts ruining a good thing by talking about it.

I, personally, think about the evolutionary process. A foot's movable parts have been reduced to maybe a third of its length. While the big toe used to be opposable, the equivalent of another thumb, now all it does is keep balance when the transference of weight ends in a completed step. Do I sound like I thought about this a lot? That littlest toe? The one that goes "Wee wee wee all the way home" is on its way out. Like the appendix and the tail-bone, it's shrinking away until, in a few generations, we'll only have eight toes in all. We don't need it because we don't climb trees, and we're spending more and more time indoors. We're evolving, or degenerating, depending on how you look at it.

I say pretty feet are a symbol of evolutionary status, rank on the Ladder.

Aside from that, I don't know why I like to do it. And I don't really care why, so leave me alone.

Much, much later, as they lay in each other's arms, Rabbit waited until Jennifer's breathing became deep and regular. He whispered her name a few times to see if she was awake, then gently disentangled himself. He'd asked her earlier if she minded him playing a CD to help him sleep, and she exhaustedly shook her head. It was white noise, an hour and a half's worth of rainstorm, wind, and occasional thunder. Now, that CD masked the sounds of him quietly slipping out of bed and getting dressed.

Long ago, in a two story luxury apartment with a high ceiling and indoor balcony, he'd ended a long acid trip with his friends in college, sitting together and talking with the storm raging, the darkness split by the sporadic flashes of two intermittently-set strobe lights upstairs. It had been peaceful and pleasant, until they forgot it was all artificial and got a wild hair to run around outside and play in the rain.

Throwing open the door, they raced out onto the porch and came up short, bewildered. The night was silent, cloudless, with only the twittering of birds to break the lonely stillness. After laughing hysterically at their own stupidity, they went back inside and talked at length about the chaotic night they'd reveled in, all the crazy stuff they'd seen and done.

Every time he listened to the storm, he remembered that night. He and his few real friends had partied and then gone out into the woods to wander inquisitively, investigating perfectly normal and common things with childlike wonder and delight.

He trusted the rain to put Jenny to sleep, but now she lay wide awake, suspiciously watching him get dressed from under her slightly open eyelids. Where the hell was he going at this hour?

As soon as he padded out of the bedroom into the small villa's kitchen, she quickly put on her underwear, skirt, and his suede shirt, then quietly snuck out to spy on him as he rummaged through the refrigerator. In the fridge's light, he found the remains of a pound of shrimp, leftover sausage, and some carpaccio. Dumping them all into a paper bag then grabbing a quart of milk, he shut the door and plunged the small house into darkness.

She waited a moment before following him outside, slightly off guard from how calm and quiet the night was when she still half-expected rain. She could barely see him walking downhill in the starlight until he stopped and fired up a cigarette. Now, she carefully tiptoed after him, barefoot on the pavement, as he made his way down the mountain toward the commercial center.

Oblivious, he whistled a catchy tune and led her to the strip of shops and restaurants. She cursed under her breath for not having shoes, knowing her high heels were lousy footwear for sneaking around in the middle of the night. She was still pleasantly sticky from their lovemaking, enjoying the breeze as it cooled her bare skin through the unbuttoned shirt, but the thought of Nick running off to see someone else enveloped her in jealousy.

Occasionally, he opened the bag and threw a scrap to a moving shadow she hadn't even noticed, and one by one, a handful of cats came out of the darkness to parade behind him. He looked like the Pied Piper with an entourage of tabbies, and the feelings of suspicion gradually dissolved.

No longer worried, she turned back uphill and stared at the steep clutter of cottages, realizing she could never tell them apart and find her way back to his villa before he caught up with her. Shit. Turning back, she hurried after him. They came to the town center after turning a few corners, hopping fences, crossing lawns, and descending short flights of stone stairways. An alley opened up into the wide plaza where a beautiful fountain served as a quick drink of water for the natives. There, a herd of stray cats excitedly greeted him. She hid in the shadows and watched as he happily scattered bits of meat into the crowd.

"Sorry I'm late, chirren," he said affectionately.

She couldn't help but smile, hugging herself and leaning against one wall of the alley. When he was out of food, he knelt and played with the cats, allowing some of them to crawl on top of him and nuzzle. The night was alive with their grateful meows, until the tone changed into eagerness as he opened the jug of milk. They crowded forward as he poured it onto the ground, then scrambled backwards when it ran in rivulets through the creases between the cobblestones.

The street around them became a honeycomb of spreading little white rivers, and they purred happily, lapping it up.

When the jug was emptied, he stood and gingerly made his way through them to the fountain. Cupping his hand under one of the spouts, he quenched his own thirst and turned around to see Jen smiling in the alley's mouth. Trying not to appear startled, he smiled back, took his bag and jug to a nearby trashcan, and met her in the shadows.

"I'm sorry I followed you," she murmured.

"Don't be." He took her hand and led her back up the mountain. "I'm flattered that you did."

"Do you do this every night?"

"Mm-hmm. I'm practicing to be an angel."

She sighed and leaned against him as they walked. "You already are one, Nickie."

After they'd showered together, each taking turns washing the other and her being more surprised by his gentle thoroughness, they went outside in bathrobes to sit with coffee and watch the sunrise. Jen had never been happier. She'd finally found Mr. Right, a man she could never be good enough for but who seemed like he felt the same way about her. He was someone she wanted for keeps.

The shrill ringing of the phone inside shattered the peaceful moment. He had a look of startled shock in his eyes, not the irritated scowl she would have expected. That was not a house line, but the distinctive whine of a satellite phone. Very few people had that number, and they were all scattered around the world, far from Taormina, Sicily. It was one of those ridiculously expensive marvels of sophisticated technology, one that bounced a crystal clear signal off of a satellite and could not be listened in on, even though both ends of the conversation were on opposite sides of the planet. To him, it was the phone Commissioner Gordon called Batman on.

He hurried inside, followed by Jennifer who, although knowing it was none of her business, was too overcome with curiosity. He answered, frowning, listened, and then his eyes lit up.

"Ahh, Teresa! *Tudo bem, obrigado. E tu?*"

Then, he frowned again. A second later, his eyes went wide with anger and he had to sit down. He was silent for a long time, then nodded and spoke quickly, unintelligibly, but with a reassuring tone. The conversation lasted a long while, and Jennifer could understand none of it. When it finally ended, Rabbit tossed the phone onto the couch and stared at the wall with haunted eyes. Coming over to sit beside him, she put one arm across his shoulders.

"What's wrong, baby?"

He sighed, leaning against her.

"You ever been to Ibiza?"

"But we have to be back at school," Bianca said.

"He told me he'd cover all expenses, and he'd take care of school, said he could pull a few strings."

"Pull a few strings with whom? Has he ever even been to Firenze?"

"I don't know, but he was all broken up over this phone call

450

and he said he needed company to go to Ibiza."

"Where's that?" Andrea asked.

"A Balearic island," Bianca said. "It's one big rave, a mecca for jet-setters and European technoheads."

"It's like Pleasure Island. Damned expensive, and we can go for free."

"You don't want a party," Andrea teased. "You just want to follow Nickie like a little puppy dog."

"Shut up."

"Oh, Jen, I'm going to Antarctica. Wanna come? *Ooh, can I?*"

"I said shut up."

"Ha! You are so *whipped*, Jen! Admit it, you'd follow him to Rwanda."

"Look! You try fucking him and then go about your business. You can't! It's impossible! And it's not just that…he's perfect."

"Really? Is he that good?" Bianca asked, meaning sexually.

"*Amica*, he's all that and then some."

"Mamma mia."

Jennifer sighed heavily, putting her head in her hands. "I think I'm in love with him."

"Oh, Christ! Jen, you just met the guy!" Andrea laughed.

"I know, I know."

Bianca thought for moment, sipping her coffee.

"What's he have to do in Ibiza?"

"You're never gonna believe this. He says one of his best friends, out in the States, he got murdered, his son got murdered, and his daughter was gang-raped. She's alive, but pretty messed up by it, so Mom is sending her on vacation to get her head straight." Her friends just sat there, stunned. Jennifer nodded sadly. "Yeah, this girl and her friend need to spend some time drunk and on good drugs so they can get over the whole thing. The mother asked Nick if he'd take care of them, and he says he's no psychiatrist. He says what they need is other girls, so he asked us to help."

"Well, shit." Andrea muttered. "I'm no psychiatrist, either."

"He said we wouldn't be there for support, just company. According to him, you don't get over shit like that by talking about it in therapy support groups. You have to have a good time and forget about it."

They sat in silence, drinking their coffee just to be doing something.

"Well, if you think about it," Bianca finally said, "it *is* a worthy cause…" The others cut their eyes at her. "We could stand a free trip to the best party in the world, I guess. Hell, it's our duty."

"Yeah, us girls have to stick together."

"So we'll go?" Jennifer asked. Andrea laughed.

"Yeah. You talked us into it."

A few hours' drive brought them to the marina at Mondello, where Nick's boat was docked. Actually, it was Harold Layton's boat, which his son had inherited, sold to Michael Lapine, and re-sold to Warren Haggerty before it finally came under the ownership of Nicholas Coniglio, but if anyone ever saw photos of the four most recent owners, they'd think it remarkable how much they looked alike. Slightly different, of course, but not enough.

A '63 Rybovich, one of the last ones built, it was a modest fifty-one feet, just big enough to be called a yacht. Not caring about fishing and not planning on dangling anyone from the outriggers, Rabbit had removed and sold them, along with the tuna tower and the cockpit fighting chair. The Capriole became just a sleek and beautiful cruiser.

Rabbit had insisted that the girls take a few Dramamine, regardless of how much they protested, and the two American girls were secretly glad to save face and still get the pills because Bianca would've teased them mercilessly about being seasick babies. They strutted across the desk after dockhands helped them cast off, and Captain Nick, thrilled, couldn't make up his mind which of them looked best in their neon bikinis. It was the kind of day poems were written about.

The Mediterranean was only slightly choppy, the sky staggeringly bright and clear. Music blared from the sound system, the girls stripped off their tops, and Rabbit could not remember being happier.

Sadly, after only an hour or so the sea got choppy and the girls retreated to the safety of the chairs in the cockpit where they would not get splashed. Jen eventually came up to the bridge to keep Rabbit company, but had put on a t-shirt and a cap. Oh well. A wise man once said that all glory is fleeting.

Finally, after a few days of cruising comfortably, they docked at the Marina Bota Foch, on the edge of Livissa. Rabbit turned his guests loose to explore while he washed the salt off his beloved boat, flatly refusing their dutifully-made offers to help. He'd be done in no time, and needed to speak to a few people privately afterwards, so he was eager to be alone.

They spent the afternoon in the dignified serenity of Dalt Vila, the oldest part of Eivissa. Enclosed by a ring of walls, the hill was crowned by the Catedral, built on the ruins of a mosque, a Roman temple of the god Mercury, a Palaeo-Christian church, and a Carthaginian temple. A little something for everybody. In Plaça Catedral was the Museu Arqueologic which, for history buffs like Jen and Bianca, was the world's best collection of Punic artifacts and relics.

On Via Romana at the foot of the hill, they wandered through Puig des Molins, a necropolis with over four hundred Carthaginian tombs. It put even New Orleans' City of the Dead to shame. There, they were told by an over-enthusiastic tour guide that the street plan was almost unchanged since the Carthaginians founded Eivissa in the 7th century BC, naming it Ibosim. The girls pretended to be interested, smiling and nodding with "Is that so?"s every once in a while. The middle-aged Ibizan went on to inform them that five thousand of the sixty thousand residents were foreigners. More nodding, only now with looks of feigned surprise. Wow, that's fascinating. You don't say.

Finally able to make their escape, they went back to the strip mall that surrounded the marina. For the first time in years, Bianca heard people talking and couldn't eavesdrop.

The natives spoke Eivessenc, a dialect of Catalan, which isn't too different from Provençal, but Bianca knew none of those. Luckily, so many spoke English that there was no other problem. The island was such a melting pot that every voice was colored by a different accent. People from all over the world mingled freely and got along.

The girls had never seen anything like it. Unlike Gibraltar, where tour guides boasted that you could see Muslims and Christians having a drink together, which is horseshit, in this place no one bothered with prejudice; men in *kufis* partied with chicks wearing crosses, and everyone was brought together by the music, the party. Nothing created unity like hedonism.

Ibiza was club culture at its best. A forum for electronica, it was one of the places where acid jazz began, and careers were made or broken there. It was a haven for those in search of the world's most sophisticated nightlife, and an evening that began at fashionable bars near the port usually ended at dawn in some of the planet's most exotic discotheques. The Beautiful People of Los Angeles had nothing on even the ugliest people on Ibiza, it was said, and Rabbit believed it.

His hatred towards some of the Eurotrash vacationers was curbed by his love for the island. Often, he was prepared to deep-six some British wanker or German swine, but he could not bring himself to spill blood on Ibizan soil and give the place a bad name. It was only the fact that ex-nerds had a chance to win popularity and even stardom there that kept his wrath in check, allowing litterbugs and nude beach gawkers to leave unharmed, and con men to remain, working their trade.

As the girls sat waiting for him at one of the many restaurants' outdoor tables, listening to the Babel of passersby and the windy snapping of the blue awning overhead, they tried to get used to their situation.

Here they were in a place that made adults feel like children at Disneyland, a prize that had just been handed to them out of nowhere.

"Oh my God," Bianca said suddenly, her brown eyes widening.

"What?" the other two asked in unison.

"Something just occurred to me. Look around."

They did, as if they expected to find Waldo in the crowd.

"All these people are different. Different cultures, different races, all of whom used to be confined to their own worlds, but now all congregate here, interbreed, and will eventually become one. The way every different color of light will come together and become white, or every color of paint will mix to form...kind of a nasty brown, I suppose, these people will gradually meld into one race. Like Europe is slowly becoming, Ibiza is at a much quicker rate. A unified—"

"Where the hell are you going with this?" Andrea asked.

"It's kind of half-baked, but cut me a little slack, here. I only just thought of it. Now, listen. Marco Polo traveled all the way to China in A.D. 1270-something. Took a long damn time, plenty of time for him to be gradually exposed to many different things. He came back, with the good intentions of establishing trade routes, but he brought back everything he'd been exposed to as well, introducing it all at once."

454

"You're rambling, Bianca," Jennifer said.

"*Ascoltami*! Polo returned when? Late thirteenth century? When did the Bubonic Plague sweep across Europe?"

The two Americans stared at her. She continued.

"Then we go to the New World and spread smallpox and yellow fever, killing off millions of Indians. What people have that they've become used to, what is now a part of them, will massacre another people just by coming near them. Maybe God does not want us to mix. We should stay apart and remain different, not be the same. Now, this place, all of these different people coming together. Think about it. Remind you of anything?"

Andrea blinked, but Jennifer understood, nodded.

"The Tower of Babel."

"And God destroyed it, scattered the people all over the world..."

"You think we're history repeating itself?"

"Okay," Rabbit said, startling them. "It's all been straightened out. We can go home now." He plopped down in an empty chair and signaled the waitress. The girls stared at him with startled horror.

"Wh...(ahem) what?" Jennifer stammered.

"Our work here is done. Hope you all enjoyed your trip."

The waitress, an attractive blonde, came over smiling. "*Caro!* So good to see you again!" Her accent was impossible to place.

"I know—I mean, thanks."

She laughed as one used to his mock conceit.

"How long do you plan to stay?"

"Oh, about half an hour. Gotta hit the road."

"No! You cannot!" *Cannot*, not *can't*. Has to be her second language, Bianca thought absently, still staring wide-eyed at Rabbit.

"Hey, I'm a busy man. Got people to do, things to see," he said.

"You *must* stay. Cyrano is here, at Quarantine!"

"Cyrano? The big-nosed guy?"

"Yes! DJs only play his two big hits, *Throw Down* and *Candy-striped*, but he spins all of his music, and it's wonderful!"

"Is it? Hmmm." His straight face finally cracked a little. "Well, I suppose we could stay a few days."

"Fucker," Jennifer breathed. "That wasn't funny!"

"What?" he asked, a model of hurt innocence.

455

The girls chose to stay in one of the city-center hotels instead of one of those out of town that promised peace and quiet. The noise and activity outside would be high, but they would much rather stagger a few blocks home than suffer a cab ride to the outskirts, the latter being somewhat anticlimactic. Rabbit chose to sleep on the boat, giving each of the girls an allowance to spend around town, and arranging their access to drugs of their choice. Not avid users, they only got a few tabs of the highest quality Ecstasy, thinking it was better to have, just in case, than get a wild hair and be forced to do without. Better safe than sorry.

They all went to an early dinner at Sausalito in the Plaza Sa Riba, where the owner greeted Monsieur Coniglio and they exchanged pleasantries in French. All Bianca had to translate in whispers was that the owner recommended either the swordfish or the lamb, which the place was renowned for anyway, but the fact that Nick seemed the man about town here as well as in Taormina was enough to wonder about.

"So, where are the girls we're supposed to meet?" Andrea asked.

"They're laid over in Madrid. They'll be here in a few hours."

"They're not supposed to know that we know about them, I assume?"

"No. Absolutely not. And the only reason you do know is so that you'll cut them a little slack for acting the way I expect them to. After what they have been through, they must be treated...you know."

They knew. But Nick found he couldn't talk about it. The very thought of Mariana beaten and raped, her father killed, her brother tortured...the very thought made blood gather behind his eyes. He felt the weight of the two asps that hung in Velcro sheaths under his jacket, the presence of which he'd grown so used to, until times like this when the maddening urge to beat someone to death with them made his muscles twitch.

The extendable batons were a step up from those that American policemen wore. Instead of lengthening them with a flick of the wrist, the asps would spring like switchblades into two feet of steel at the touch of a button, with enough force to shatter bones if used correctly.

Rabbit now wondered how he would resist the temptation.

456

Teresa must have some kind of a plan for revenge, and he wanted desperately to be a part of it. Wading ankle deep in a lake of blood—he saw through a fog the wide-eyed faces and shook his head as if to clear it, realizing he must've had that look in his eyes again. The three girls were disturbed by what they'd seen as he stared off into space, and were now not at all fooled by his cheerful smile.

"So, hey, I hear the swordfish here is fantastic."

With plenty of time on their hands, Mariana and Maya went out to find Retiro Park and the only public statue of Satan in the world. The screaming angel was bent over backward, cowering, a great serpent coiled about his feet, one arm raised to protect himself from the wrath of God. It raised no eyebrows. It was of fine workmanship, but unimpressive to anyone who'd looked true evil in the face.

Maya couldn't help but investigate one detail in particular, and it was disappointing. You'd think the Prince of Darkness would have a more impressive pingle-wingle than that, she mused. Oh well.

A few hours later, after getting a connecting flight in Valencia, they touched down on Ibiza and were greeted by Rabbit. Mariana hugged him, but Maya only shook his hand when he introduced himself. It was a limp and unfriendly gesture. Her bitter eyes seemed to size him and everyone around them up with contempt. Aside from that, they were empty, as if her fire had long gone out.

Rabbit was surprised for a moment. Here, the girl he cared about was making an effort to appear brave and strong, and he should have been pleased, but this other one he didn't even know made him grow cold. She was beautiful, or had been, and little things about her—like the bronze elephant ear weights—showed a person who looked at the world a different way. But now, she was just a timid little girl who tried to hide behind hate.

She glared at him when she saw the pity in his eyes, and was about to speak when Mariana intervened, putting an arm around her and babbling to him in Portuguese. He listened silently, trying not to glance at her and make her feel even more self-conscious. What Mariana had to say about her made his teeth grind.

"I'm sorry," he said finally. "I know that it won't change what's happened, but you will be avenged."

Maya regarded him coolly, looking him up and down in a manner that she meant to be insulting, but Rabbit ignored her. Instead, he asked if her name was an allusion to Hinduism, which startled her.

"Yes…it's what you are supposed to reject."

"Only if you buy into that bullshit. This island is a monument to Maya."

"That's why we're here, I guess."

"Well, whatever you choose to indulge in is at your disposal. Your hotel is right next to the marina I stay at, so I will always be easy to find if I'm not with you already. We'll be going to the Quarantine tonight if you're up to it."

"Rabbit…or Nick, whatever I'm supposed to call you, what I'm up for right now is absinthe. Is it legal here?"

"Maya, legal or not, everything worth having is accessible. If you want endangered species kabob for dinner, let me know, and you will have it."

Mariana saw her girlfriend smile faintly, and was relieved. Maybe she'd get to see a bigger smile soon.

Andrea knew right off the bat that Maya and Mariana were, um, *more* than friends, but Bianca wouldn't believe it and Jennifer didn't care. They were going to enjoy the night and that's all there was to it. They had all met up at Quarantine, gone through the formalities, and were trying the neon green liqueur that Maya had ordered. Mariana frowned after her first sip.

"It doesn't really taste like your stuff," she said to Maya, who didn't bother to explain the presence of another ingredient in the doses that Evan, her recent ex-boyfriend, had once served. Instead, she just shrugged and drank.

The discotheque had impressed them with a revolutionary new light, or system of lights, that somehow made all the colors it shined on run backwards. It was an eerie effect, like seeing a movie made with the film of photo negatives. Everyone glowed with a bright opposite: flesh tones became bluish, dark hair became white, positive gleamed negative. The flashes of strobe and blurring spears of laser were even more disorienting, giving the club a more dreamlike quality and the promise of more memorable hallucinations if the girls decided to swallow the pills they'd gotten.

Dramatic bursts of flame spewed from decorative jets every

now and then, and glitters that looked like tracer fire in a pitched gun-battle illuminated the jerking, colored shadows of ravers. The music, if it could be called that, was a frenzy of sound that made those who were obviously rolling have seizures out on the floor, leaping about with wild abandon.

Everyone was very well-dressed; even the designer clothes that imitated ghetto and gutta fashion were finely-tailored and expensive —completely contradicting the concept. There were a few similarities to American nightclubs though; the vacant expressions of the candy-ravers, people whose weekend recreation had become their way of life, and the cowardly and uncertain wallflowers with their posturing.

An aspiring young British DJ who had opened for Cyrano tried to impress Mariana at the bar, putting on airs, and the rest of the girls watched with barely concealed amusement, except for Maya, who appeared ready to pounce at any moment. Mariana toyed with him, though.

"So, that was you spinning earlier? Not bad."

"If you liked that," he replied with an overdone Cockney accent. "You oughta hear some of the new stuff I been working on. It's bustin', if I do say so myself. I'm droppin' it, man. Heavy."

"Oh yeah?"

As he did his best attempt at Suave and Debonair, he helped himself to Mariana's drink, and with practiced sleight of hand, dropped something into it as he placed it back on the bar, misdirecting their attention with a flamboyant gesture of his other hand. One spectator, Rabbit, watching them from a distance, wasn't sure whether he'd seen it or not.

"I tell you what, love," the Cockney said, trying to sound as if he were letting Mariana in on something. "If you want, you can come by the crib wimme tonight and I'll let you hear some more."
It was all the Brazilian could do not to roll her eyes and walk away.

"Sounds tempting. What's your name again?"

"DJ Igneous."

All the girls stifled their laughter. Except Maya.

"No, I mean your *name*."

"That *is* my name. That's my identity, who I am."

"You don't say. Why Igneous?"

"Because I'm hard, a rock, and volcanic in origin."

Now, there was no holding their laughter in, and, chagrined by their mockery, the fellow tried to walk away, but Mariana called him back so they could catch their breath and humiliate him properly.

His embarrassment became rage, and he cursed them all roundly, calling Mariana in particular everything he could think of. Calmly, Maya asked the bartender for five fingers of bourbon, neat.

As soon as the glass arrived, she snatched it and splashed DJ Igneous in the face. Recoiling, the liquor stinging his eyes, he shook like a beach dog, clawing at himself and accidentally knocking Mariana's drugged glass out of her hand. When he could see again, his eyes were scarlet, matching his face and temper, and he took a step toward his attacker. The other girls, the bartender, and a few people near enough to see it all now gaped at Maya, who held her flaming Zippo up in front of her.

"I dare ya," she said.

Igneous stared at her in murderous rage.

"Cunt, you're a dead woman!" he hissed.

"Prove it."

Even Rabbit was amazed. He stood a little way off, frozen in midstep just like the Brit, but with one hand behind his back, underneath the jacket. The hate that seemed to shimmer in the air between them was repellent to everyone who looked on. The DJ's eyes blazed horribly, but were matched and held squarely and steadily by Maya's, as cold-blooded as a viper's.

"Your flame won't last forever, you whore."

Turning, Igneous stormed off to the Gent's to wash himself off, get a bit less flammable so he could return and avenge himself. No one noticed Rabbit follow him through the door, "just for a friendly chat."

The man was persuaded to bury the hatchet at the bathroom sink.

"Oh, how much was that, before I forget?" Maya asked the bartender, as if it had just slipped her mind. The tall Swede stared at her a moment, then smiled, shaking his head.

"How much was what?"

"That drink."

"What drink? All you've asked for was absinthe, and it's paid for."

"Don't I owe you for a bourbon?"

"I never saw you with any," he said, laughing and filling another order.

460

The rest of the girls stared at her, astonished. She took a bidi out of her handbag and lit it with her intricately decorated bronze Zippo, took a long, satisfying drag, and noticed the other four still gaping.

"What?"

After a few more shots of absinthe, one of them washing down a tab of X, Mariana announced that she wanted to dance. Maya told her she'd probably join her in a few, sparking one of those girlie arguments about dancing *now*, which eradicated any doubts the others had about their, um, "friendship." Maya won, though, insisting that someone had to stay behind and hold down the fort.

"But gimme some sugar before you leave," she ordered, and was given a tender kiss. Bianca frowned, but said nothing. When they'd gone, Rabbit appeared and asked the bartender for an absinthe.

"I had to blow dust off the bottle," the Swede told him. "Nobody drank that stuff until tonight."

"We're all American. It's illegal there, so we rarely see any of it."

"Ha! Murder's illegal there, too, but I hear there's no shortage of that."

Rabbit shrugged, glancing down at Maya's hand resting on the bar, her bidi burned down to the pink thread near the base. Rabbit's drink was set down on a coaster beside it, and as he raised it to his lips to drink, he frowned a moment, staring at the ring on her middle finger.

"Ouroborus," he said finally, and drank.

"What'd you say?" Maya asked suspiciously.

"I'd forgotten what your ring was called for a moment. The snake that's swallowing itself. It's an Ouroborus, a Greek design."

Maya stared at him for a moment, surprised.

"Not even I knew that," she said, meaning it as a compliment.

"Do not be fooled by my devilishly attractive façade, Miss Macaulay. I'm a nerd in disguise."

"I know."

"Do you?" It was Rabbit's turn to be surprised. "Is it that obvious? Maybe I need more practice at being cool."

"No, I've read all your books. Mariana's brother gave them to me."

A moment of sad silence passed, Rabbit remembering the kid whose hair he used to ruffle. He raised his glass in a short toast to the thin air, and drained it, calling for another one.

"The real stuff is so much better than that legal crap they tried to market across the Pond. Absi-whatever they called it."

"I was disappointed in it, too," Maya agreed. "But lemme ask you something. And I already know about you, so be honest."

"Shoot."

"Are you really a serial killer, or just a murderer?"

She must not have known much. Rabbit stared at her, inscrutably, for a long moment. If she was the girlfriend of his little sister, considering the lifestyle she already knew about and had accepted—and apparently, even approved of—what harm could there be in telling her? Hell, she might even be impressed. He smiled.

"Does a one-legged duck swim in a circle?"

"So you are. Hm." She looked down at her stub of dried leaf and tossed it into an ashtray, her free hand fishing out another bidi.

"Serial killer, no. Knight errant, if anything. Mind if I try one of those?" he asked. She gave him one, and he lit both of theirs with a kitchen match sparked off his thumbnail. Looked pretty cool, she thought.

"When I read your books, I couldn't agree with you. Well, except *Heresy*, but the rest of them I didn't understand because I'd never felt hate before. Now…"

"…Now?"

"Now I wonder what it would feel like to make things right."

Rabbit sat down on the stool next to hers and sighed heavily.

"I can't really describe it, you know, how wonderful it is. Such power that you never thought you could have, when you look into the eyes of someone who underestimated you and see what's going on behind them. Watching them realize how wrong they were."

"I want to see that. I want to see the pieces of shit that made me cry…my God, I want to see it. I want to watch them suffer."

"They will."

"No, they won't! Nestor's dead, his whole empire is over!"

"They will suffer, Maya."

"How? And don't give me any shit about Judgment Day—"

"There isn't any Judgment Day. All that is just the coward's way of reassuring himself that his revenge is not necessary. There isn't any Heaven or Hell. There is only life, and it is what we make

462

of it. I promise, those who hurt you'll spend the rest of their lives in agony."

"Bullshit. It's never going to happen. No one can find them."

"Teresa has a plan. She also has many friends."

"Enough to kill every gang member in Coquina?"

"We won't kill them."

"What?"

"When you kill somebody, their suffering ends. Theirs will not end."

"Explain."

"If I know Teresa as well as I think I do, these people will be captured, crippled, raped, blinded, then set free, with their tongues cut out so they can tell no one about it."

"I want their dicks cut off, too."

"No. They will be burned off. It'll be their children we castrate, so their seed dies and they live to know it, live with the blame of their kids' ruined lives. Their women will be made ugly, and their houses burned down. Their parents will drown in lakes of blood. The people who did this will suffer, Maya. We won't kill them, we will rape their souls."

"You're just saying this to cheer me up."

"Ha! Listen to yourself."

"It's working."

"Good. Let's have some tequila and blaspheme for a while."

Mariana's dose kicked in, abolishing all the misery she hid so well. This was pure methylenedioxymethamphetamine, the real Ecstasy that far outshone all the diluted designer drugs that passed for rolls in the States nowadays. For someone who had only ever gone joy-popping with bubblegummers, this was an incredible, mind-blowing high. It was impossible for someone to hold a grudge on *second-rate* X. This…Heaven paled in comparison to this feeling.

She made her way to the bar where her lover sat, talking to Rabbit. The two of them seemed so beautiful they put angels to shame, and she wanted so badly for them to join her. Arriving between them in a gust of wind, she snatched Maya by the hair and pulled her head around, planting her lips on hers. Not embarrassed by the feverish passion of their kiss, or annoyed by the interruption, Rabbit simply slipped another bidi out of Maya's pack, lit it with the useless-skill flourish of a Zippo snap trick, and turned his back to them for privacy.

Even though lesbianism to him was nothing more than a deviant perversion that somehow had became trendy, he knew that the girls had many issues to work through, and it would be many a moon before they turned their attention back to men. If they were to heal, Nature had to take its course.

Many stared at the two girls as they made out shamelessly, either in appreciation or horror, cheering or shouting for them to get a room, but Rabbit ignored them all. Raising his shot glass to Jennifer in salute, he had to smile at the look on her face. He told himself as he downed the shot and drew on the bidi that he'd give the ladies thirty more seconds of PDA before he'd give up on them and dance with his own woman.

They stopped for breath at twenty-seven.

"Take one of these pills, baby. That chick Andrea's holding them. You have to have one, Maya. I'm rolling my ass off."

"I noticed."

"Come on, you need to get where I am."

"I'll be there in a minute."

"You'll drop one?"

"Sure. Go get it from Whatshername for me? I'm in the middle of something with Nicholas here."

"Nicholas? Ha! Rabbit, I forgot your new name! Nickie! What was your last name again?"

"Coniglio."

"No, I mean the one *before* this one. Your *last* name."

"Oh yeah. Haggerty."

"That's right! Warren Haggerty. *Warren!*"

"If I coulda stuck with my real name, I woulda."

"Layton? What's so good about Layton?"

"My dad had it legally changed to Layton a long time ago, he thought it would be better for business than his Italian name: Lattante. Means 'breast-fed.' We—"

"Breast-fed!"

"Go get that pill, honey," Maya told her.

"Oh yeah! Right. Back in a sec."

Mariana zoomed off on drug recon, leaving them staring after her. Both were pleased at how happy she was, but he thought the price of it, the obliteration of sense, seemed a bit too high. Rabbit could, and would, drink an army under the table, but never to the

464

point that he couldn't think in a straight line. The minute he lost the ability to react like a steel-spring mousetrap, that's when some enemy would happen to walk into the room. There were just too many snakes out there to not be a mongoose.

"Where were we?" Maya asked.

"Every religion there is, is a pile of dogshit."

"Right. I should know, I was subjected to all of them by my mother, who's got rocks in her head."

"An opiate for the masses, that's all religion is. A way to get the stupid, primitive people to follow your rules; simply tell them that they're God's law."

"And burn them at the stake if they question you. Now, *this* is what heresy is. You didn't even touch on religion in your first book."

"No, because that was against all of the new substitutes for religion that we've pulled over our eyes. Every obsession that blinds us to what really matters in life, the bullshit we devote our lives to."

"You mean Culture?" she asked sardonically.

"If you call being a lemming or a sheep 'culture,' then sure."

Mariana came back, her smile unnaturally wide.

"Go on," Rabbit said to Maya before her girlfriend arrived. "Indulge yourself. It'll do you some good."

"But what about you?"

"I'll be with Jen, but don't worry. I'll always have an eye on you two, just in case DJ Igneous shows up." He said the last with a grin, letting Maya know that, for reasons he would not divulge, the Limey would never come back for revenge. Funny how persuasive a few calm words and the casual toying with an asp could be.

"Open wide," Mariana said happily. Tilting her head back, eyes shut and mouth open, Maya let her slip the pill between her lips. The Brazilian's eyes would jiggle sometimes and she'd sway as if the floor rocked beneath her feet. She shivered with delight, and even with her eyes locked on her girlfriend, she seemed to be staring off into the distance.

"It only took about twenty, thirty minutes to kick in," she said. "You won't have long to wait."

"Don't drop another one," Rabbit warned. "One's plenty, trust me."

"Nickie, if I rolled even harder, I couldn't even spell MDMA."

"Need a lollipop?" he asked, pulling out a red one.

465

"Trust you to carry one around with you! No, I don't need a lolly, I got one right here." She touched a finger to Maya's lips.

"Careful how far you two go," he started to say, instantly regretting it. Maya flinched. He was sure she knew he'd meant they shouldn't be too public here, but it still reminded them that Maya was...sick.

"Buzz-kill," she muttered, gulping down her last shot.

"I meant, don't get too carried away. Bad form."

"I know what you meant."

Mariana blinked. "What? I missed it."

Rabbit went up the stairs that led to the roof—called the Sky Room—and stepped out into the warm night air. A bunch of little cliques were already up there, but he found a private spot in the corner of the wall. Punching in a number on his cell phone, he kept mumbling to himself. He was far from legless, but he was a bit past tipsy. The hallucinogen in the absinthe was reacting rather well with the five shots of tequila he'd followed it with.

"Pick up pick up pick up," he chanted under his breath. He was six or seven hours ahead of Florida, where Jim Crowe usually was, but there really was no telling where he might be right now.

Probably conquering some country. Wherever he was, he answered.

"Dan's Pleasure Playhouse," the Woolagaroo said. "Dan speaking."

"Hey, Chief. Me here."

"Ahh, long time no talk. What can I foo ya dor?"

"Tiny favor. I need to get my hands on a red pill."

The antidote for HIV. The small group that created it had, of course, made sure the splendidly mutating virus had a cure before they unleashed it upon the world as part of their Kill Off The Swine Campaign.

"Did you get some bad pussy, little brother?" The voice on the other end sounded disappointed.

"Long story. I'll tell you some other time, but can you help me?"

"I'll have to talk to some people. Where are you?"

"Ibosim." They were confident that no one could be listening in, but it never hurt to be careful. All their calls were like this.

"Keep your eyes peeled then. Gotta run, I'm in the middle of someone."

Rabbit laughed and hung up. He wasn't sure why he'd decided to go to such expense to heal Maya. Maybe so he could lord it over her and become a god in her eyes. Maybe just because she was a starving stray cat with her ribs showing.

His mentor was truly unique; one of the few, if not the only, Australian Aborigines who'd traveled over the entire "mutant" world and decided to do something about what he'd seen.

In the Dreamtime mythology, the Woolagaroo, the devil-devil man, was a *golem* carved of wood with crocodile teeth and stones for eyes. The Never-Never version of Pygmalion had tried to breathe life into his creation, just like Victor Frankenstein had, and he'd unleashed a demon among the Sons of Man. Crowe, or whatever his real name was, said that it was mutant men who'd made him into what he was now, so he was the Woolagaroo. The whole world was fair game.

Unlike most of his people, Crowe felt the unholy lust for blood, even more than Rabbit did. The atrocities he'd seen in the flesh, evidence of the stories he'd heard from his elders and read about in history books, sparked in him the urge to make things right and hasten the return of the Dreamtime. More than thirty years before, he left Australia on a walk-about, and was still going.

While Rabbit knew very little about Crowe's other friends, with few exceptions, he did know that they ranked among the world's most powerful captains of industry. One, whose business was bio-chemistry, had made a team of experimenters available to Rabbit the previous year, to help along a new business venture. One of these chemists, a disillusioned young woman who had studied hard with the dream of going on to win Nobel prizes and curing cancer, had let slip to him one morning that some of her colleagues had been involved in the creation of AIDS, the synthesizing of anthrax for a Muslim terrorist group, and a few germ-warfare projects for the US military. Having spent a long night drunk and then in bed with the notorious Warren Haggerty, she found herself telling him quite a few things it wasn't his business to know.

When she assured him that vaccines and antidotes existed and were available to a select few, he just filed that away in his mind for a rainy day. That rainy day had finally come.

Downstairs, he found Jennifer, checked up on the other girls with a quick, silent headcount, and slipped back into the role of a caring boyfriend. She pulled him off to one side.

"Personal question," she said.

"Fire away."

"When was the last time you were in love?"

"About ten...fifteen minutes ago."

"I'm serious!"

"So am I. That one girl Maya has these really great cigarettes, and when I caught sight of my reflection across the bar, smoking one and looking so cool—"

"Knock it off. I wanna know what I'm up against."

"Sorry, that information's classified."

"Look! I'm kind of nervous right now, so please work with me, okay? I want to take one of those pills, but I don't want to get all lovey-dovey like M&M over there if it'll spook you."

"Honey, stop worrying about what I might think. Just be yourself. I swear, this paranoia will spook me more than any cuddling will."

"Oh, shit. I'm spooking you now, aren't I?"

Rabbit dropped all pretense and looked her in the eye. "Jen, it is stupid of me to say this, but I've been drinking a little and that justifies my irresponsibility. If you could see me as I am, if you ignored all of my material possessions and just saw me as a mortal man with no giltwork, *you* would be the spooked one."

"No, I don't believe it."

"Believe it. Realize that I have faults just like you, maybe a few personality flaws, a quirk or two, and some issues."

"Shit, we all do."

"That's right. Now, come back down to Earth, give me a kiss, and take one of those tabs if you want to."

"...I'm so worried, sometimes."

"Have another drink. That usually cures it."

"I mean, you know how Ecstasy is. I might say I loved you or something and you'd think I'm some kind of codependent—"

"Jen, if you fall in love with me, don't sweat it. You're only human."

"What if I told you I think I love you already?"

"It will assure me that you're perfectly sane."

"Nick, you're perfect." Damn, she was drunk.

"I've worked hard to become so."

"And some of those things you did to me, nobody had ever

done that before. I couldn't believe anybody *would* do those things."

"Did they feel good?"

"Oh God, yes! Where did you learn all that?"

"Instruction manual. All guys get one when they hit puberty."

"If I take a roll, would you...would you do some of those things for me again? Please?"

"Ha! Jenny, I'm planning on doing them to you until you get bored with them. That ought to be, hmm, about a week or so."

"I will never get bored with you!"

"You'd be surprised."

"I think I'm drunk."

"I know you are."

"If I tell you I love you tonight, just shrug it off, okay?"

"I can't promise anything."

"I just want to say it, okay?"

"Well, try it and see what happens."

"I love you, Nickie."

"Nah, you're not good enough for me. Get lost."

"Nick!"

"Tell you what. Drop some X, we'll dance a while, sneak off somewhere, and I'll do that one thing with your...um...you know."

"The...my...um, you mean my...?"

"Yeah. Then we'll dance some more, and I'll do the other one. Then, we'll go to another club, and I'll do something else you wouldn't even believe, right in front of everybody on one of those couches. It's not sexual, but, you know, sensual. And I love doing it."

"The suspense is killing me."

"Hang on." He left her standing by the dance floor, striding off toward the bar where a Greek chick he knew was stationed.

"Hey, sweetie. I need a favor."

"Nick! I thought that was you, but I wasn't sure."

"In the flesh. Does your boyfriend still drive for those limo people?"

"No, we broke up."

"But he still chauffeurs, right?"

"Sure."

"Do me a favor," he said, laying a bribe on the drink-ringed bar. "Call his work and get a car to wait on us. It needs to be stocked with top-shelf, the works. And a masseur, too."

"A masseur? Not a masseuse?"

"No, a guy. There will be two girls riding with us and they're not that way, so they'd just be sitting there feeling left out while the rest of us are going to town. We can't have that. They'll be rolling, and some guy— good looking, too, has to be good looking—some guy who knows what he's doing will really keep them occupied. I can't have anybody being a third wheel."

"Are you serious?"

"Trust me, it's a matter of life and death."

Rabbit had made up his mind, so it was. He had gotten it into his head that he wanted to roll too, and nothing short of a crowbar could get that off the brain. He was sick of being careful. He owed it to himself to get *wasted*, once in a while.

The bartender looked at the banknotes, a couple thousand *pesetas*, and met his eyes again.

"Why don't you ever invite me on these orgies?"

"I'm saving the best for last."

"Oh, get bent. Yeah, I'll see what I can do."

"You're a doll. I'll remember you in my prayers."

"Fuck your prayers. Remember me in your will."

"Done." He went off to find Andrea and confiscate a tab of Ecstasy.

They were sky-high, all six of them rolling so hard they could barely stand when Rabbit announced they were leaving. Next stop, Feuer-Trunken. When they breezed out of the Quarantine's front entrance, Declan the Irish chauffeur was leaning against the side of a stretched white limousine, chatting with Eusebio the Ibizan masseur.

"Damn, who's that for?" Andrea asked loudly.

"Us." Rabbit swaggered straight up to Declan, shaking his hand, and they opened the doors for the astonished ladies. The rear door that Rabbit held was a suicide, so the gaping entrance between him and Declan exposed a wide vista of blasphemous luxury.

"You're kidding!" Jennifer gasped.

"I shit you not. Climb in."

Hesitantly, they all came forward and slid inside, arranging themselves as Rabbit and Declan shared a grin, the Irishman raising his eyebrows in a leer of co-appreciation.

"One of those nights," Rabbit said, winking, and climbed in

after them.

The girls were gaping in wonder, still not quite believing what they saw, even more surprised when Eusebio found a seat and was introduced around. They stared at Rabbit, who shrugged.

"All the taxis were booked."

Feuer-Trunken was not very far away, but Declan did a few laps around Eivissa to give his passengers time to get into the swing of things. By the time he finally pulled up in front of the disco-theque, Mariana was topless, Andrea and Bianca groaning as Eusebio caressed them with each hand, and Jennifer squirmed in her seat, clawing at the white leather as Rabbit sucked and gently gnawed on each of her toes. With two of the middle ones in his mouth, and his tongue sliding up to part them, he opened his eyes and drew his head back, releasing them with a wet smack.

"We're here. Everybody out!" He was answered by a chorus of protesting moans, but he put his foot down—and Jennifer's also, slipping each of her heels back on. Maya put her gasping lover's top back on for her, licking her fingers with a grin. The doors swung open and they staggered out into the night, alive with neon and trance, stunned by the beauty of a world that the sober take for granted.

It was only midnight.

Strange figures paraded through the crowd in the pulsing mag-ic of Feuer-Trunken. Stalking around on six-foot stilts hidden by long grass skirts, local strippers—women and men both—made extra money by simply looking odd in their devilish wooden masks, palm frond plumage, and flower leis. There were a few erotic faeries in outlandish costume perched on pedestals here and there, taking the concept of go-go dancing to a bizarre new level.

The girls all made their way to the floor while Rabbit got them bottles of cold water at the bar. They were lost in the liquid dream of flashing lights and beautiful music when he joined them. They sucked the bottles empty like infants at their mothers' breasts, and their host dutifully collected them to be thrown away properly. Jen-nifer followed him, and after he had handed them across the bar, she grabbed his wrist and dragged him into the thicket of bubble-posts, seven-foot water-filled cylinders with rising flows of bubbles and colored light, that decorated one wall. Pushing him against the plaster mural, she plunged her hand between his belt and washboard abs, seizing a hold of him. As she dropped to her knees, he did another quick headcount out of habit before he tensed and sagged against the wall, his eyes rolling up.

Bianca and Andrea searched for the handsomest men who didn't seem to have girls spot-welded to them, and when they found who would do, they made perfunctory small talk and then dragged them out to dance. The insistent pounding beats took hold of them, the layers seeming to well up waves of emotion inside them, and the tweaking loops made them shudder from tailbone to brainstem.

Aureate wisps of nebulae followed their every movement, gleaming contrails of orange light streaked and floated in midair behind every cigarette, in mimicry of the lagging slashes of light the glowstick artists wove for ravers, helping them "blow up."

And, shivering with delight, Maya smiled, from the heart this time.

For the first time since That Night, who she was and what she'd become was washed away. A lingering sadness that it would drift back ashore tomorrow still haunted her, and the image of a life without sex kept trying to surface in her mind, but the beauty and drug-induced joy of the night blanketed it like a snowstorm over a city dump. Whatever happiness she could get, she seized, and would not let go. She clung to these moments desperately.

Mariana, however…

No matter how sorry she was for Maya, no matter how scarred by the night they had shared together, and even though she berated herself harshly for even briefly thinking this, a pragmatic little voice inside her whispered *Better her than me.*

She would kiss her passionately, hold her tight with their young breasts mashed together, and caress her fondly, but couldn't even bring herself to look at the poisonous…*thing* that waited like a spider between Maya's shapely legs. She chalked their whole relationship up to her simply going through a phase, knowing in her heart that what her friend Shaitan had told her was right all along, and this experimental stage of hers was coming to an end. It had been nice, but…

And Maya saw it coming a mile away. Someone else to be abandoned by.

Soon, all she would have would be her folks, and considering who *they* were, she might as well go off and be a hermit somewhere. Reject the coils of Maya, and wait around to die.

472

All of these thoughts were filed away for tomorrow, when they'd be chased off again some other way. She wondered now and then why she'd catch Rabbit looking at her curiously, now that he'd stopped his girlfriend and dragged her back out on the floor. He had this look in his eyes, one she never expected, like some developer staring out over a plot of virgin land. Like her teachers back in grammar school when they saw potential, as if they knew she'd grow up to be Somebody. Or the way her mother had the day Maya sprouted breasts. *Sorry*, she thought. *You were all wrong.*

And Rabbit, Rabbit couldn't help but gloat. He pictured himself at his high school reunion, talking to all the ex-cheerleaders who were now soccer moms and the jocks-turned-car salesmen, watching them all turn green with envy. All those who'd laughed at him and beaten him, their idea of being bad was coming home early and fucking the baby sitter. Those whose idea of "wild behavior" was a new position, or maybe the living room couch instead of the bedroom. Oh, you're president of the PTA, huh?

I'm the fucking Antichrist.

He ordered everybody back to the limo, telling them he wanted to stop by this other place where his buddy Caulfield was MC. A surreptitious wink to Declan instructed him to take the scenic route, which was the whole coast of a two-hundred-twenty square mile island. None of his passengers really minded that they never made it to this other nightclub.

When the sun finally rose and everyone was dropped off, the chauffeur and masseur went off to have coffee and count their money. Eusebio had much to talk about.

I stopped a guy in the mall today, coming out of Spencer Gifts, and asked him if he played for the Chicago Bulls. He narrowed his eyes and turned his head to look at me sideways. I asked him if he was on his way to a game right now. It wasn't any of my business, of course. I just wanted to know why the fuck he was down at the mall buying black light posters and novelty whatever in a basketball uniform. You don't see anyone running around in a baseball outfit, do you? With those socks that you pull up, and loop thing that stretches into the shoe? Or better yet, you pretend to be a swimmer, run around in an elastic skullcap, goggles, and a fuckin' Speedo. So why the basketball getup?

T-Bone, or whatever his name was, didn't appreciate my curiosity.

"Da fuck you tryin' me fo', comin' all slick out da mouf?"

"Hmmm? Sorry. No speako El Spanishio."

"Say what?"

"Oh, that's English? My bad, yo sponge dub diggy dog."

"What?"

"Is my grammar off? I'm just learning Ebonics."

"Man, you trippin'. You got me fucked up."

"Word. Damn skippy. I'm off the chain with that hoe-assed fuckshit. Blood raw, and tha's real."

"Bitch, you lookin' fo' a fade? Bes' be flexin' cuh I'm fi'na cap yo punk-ass!"

"Uh...what?"

"I ain't down wit' all dat kee-kee. I'll put dat thaaaang on yo ass. Head-up. Cracka."

"Oh yeah, I was just about to say that. So look, what I'm trying to figure out, is if you get the right to impersonate the players of some sport, just because you like to watch it or play it, does that mean I can wear a goddamned sumo wrestler diaper to the grocery store? Honestly. Can I?"

T-bone, or whatever, was a white guy. In case you were wondering. With gold teeth. I could've sworn gold teeth were a sign of shitty hygiene, bad habits finally taking their toll. What happened? And what's next? Are these dumb fucks going to start wearing eye patches?

Yo, mah nigga, check out mah fly-ass hearing aid.

Bling-blingin' wit' da peg-leg.

I don't run around town in a sumo wrestling diaper 'cause I'm not a sumo wrestler. Same reason I don't dress up in drag. What the fuck is it about this day and age, we have to always pretend to be whatever we are not? Are we that disappointed in ourselves?

Are we?

Two days later, for variety's sake, they all met at El Shogun on Paradis for lunch, passing around sushi, sashimi, sukiyaki, and other Japanese delicacies with hangover names. Rabbit preferred places like these the morning after because his speech was slurred anyway, so no matter how much trouble he had with consonants, he still spoke well. An Ecstasy hangover usually leaves a raver incapacitated for the whole next day, so for Rabbit and the girls, this *was* the next day. Seemed like it, anyway. On top of that, he'd not exercised since the day he'd met the girls, and the most he'd done that morning was calisthenics. He felt sluggish already, bloated and poisoned by only a few days' laziness. He cursed himself for giving in to temptation, but there was nothing for him to do but live with it.

474

Knowing that his guests were low on funds, he felt it proper to take them to the more expensive restaurants, and knew it was bad form to allow girls to see bustling trendy commerce when they couldn't have any part of it. So, he took them shopping. Perhaps it was a residual belief left over from the old days, when he had to have all the friends money could buy, but the way he saw it, shit, he had a few things to pick up for himself anyway. Might as well.

The first stop was a party clothing store called Carpe Noctem, with the signature symbol of some insane designer displayed proudly over the door under the laughably boastful inscription: *In Hoc Signo Vinces*.

"By this sign, you will conquer," Bianca muttered when Andrea shot her a questioning look. When they went through the door, they saw why she rolled her eyes. On any other island or continent, anybody wearing these clothes except on Halloween would be crucified, unless they carried the fashion license only pop stars were given, at which time they were more respectable than vestments.

Holograms on clothing? Handprints where your mother doesn't want you touched? Once these jeans had been sewn, a model had slipped them on so a man with colored ink all over his hands could grope her. One pair after another: okay, next, grope, fondle, next! And whoever the guy was, he had some big fucking hands. Right over where the Mons Venus would be located, partially marred by a black fingerprint, the symbol from the sign blazed with reflected holographic light.

These were the raiment of sluts and "womanous men." And pop stars.

It did, however, have a really cool jewelry department, with rings of every imaginable style for every conceivable body part. It even had ear weights for Maya to browse through. Some of the piercings, namely the tongue studs and vaginal rings, were glow-in-the-dark. A few were stained with iridescent patterns like oil on water. Most of them, however, instead of steel, were solid gold or ivory.

A middle-aged, plain-looking woman ran the place, appearing completely incongruous but acting as if she were perfectly at home. She sold Rabbit the ivory equivalents of his silver piercings and told him Sorry, no, we don't even know what an Ouroborus is. Hearing this, Maya came over to the two of them and took Rabbit's hand, slipping her own silver Ouroborus with the secret bump ladle onto his ring finger. He was going to protest, until she looked into his eyes.

The woman that ran the store looked from one to the other and back again, sensing what was passing unspoken between them. When Maya walked away to look at some shoes, the saleslady flashed a knowing grin, but Rabbit didn't even see it. He just stared into space.

Mariana was pretending to examine an ivory stud carved into the shape of a chess bishop, the piece she always secretly thought looked like a hoo-hoo-dilly. Instead of admiring the creativity and the workmanship, she was watching Maya out of the corner of her eye. Her girlfriend had been even more withdrawn than usual this afternoon. Distant, as if the joy of last night had been a taste of the life she could never have again.

The Brazilian felt herself drifting farther and farther away, seeing the girl who'd awakened so much passion and liberation in her now as just another girl. The magic just dissipated, like a fog that had clouded her vision finally lifting. As soon as Maya's sex toys, powders, and technique became useless, the novelty just wore off.

As she'd lain back into her seat the night before last, letting her lover kiss her body, she stared instead at Rabbit and wished she could be Jennifer. She caught herself wanting to shove Maya aside and crawl to the corner of the seat, pushing Jennifer as well, and take what she had wanted for years. As much as she'd loathed men since That Night, the drug was strong, and her father's friend looked like a steak at the end of fasting. She couldn't tear her eyes away from the pole of flesh that seemed too ridiculously large for him. It was even bigger than what those gorillas had, but she saw nothing threatening about it.

Once, Rabbit's eyes met hers, startling her, and he scooted away, moving Jennifer in between them to block the view. Still shy about some things, she supposed. Now, she watched Maya looking at a collection of strange belts with only half-interest while she folded in upon herself. A slowly imploding star.

"Can you imagine what kind of people would wear this?" she heard Andrea ask Bianca, holding up a pair of zebra jeans. Bianca snorted.

"People who don't care what other people think," Mariana answered.

"Ha!" Jennifer said, butting in. "People who try to tell you that they don't care what people think are usually desperate to have those people think they don't care what they think!"

Everyone in the store (who spoke English) frowned. Many also smiled, nodding faintly in agreement. But it was Rabbit who turned and stared at her, as if he suddenly realized how right she was, and that the finger she was pointing was aimed straight at him. The game was up. Now, he went outside to smoke a cigarette, just to be doing something while he saw himself in this new light.

Maya came out to join him, a bidi already smoking between her lips.

"Touched a nerve, didn't she, Jared?"

Rabbit didn't answer.

"Sometimes I feel that way. I heard someone say 'if you can't beat 'em, join 'em', and I tried to join 'em so I could beat 'em from the inside. Made an effort to be so different, but enviably different, that I invented an entire new personality for myself."

She paused for a long, thoughtful drag on her bidi.

"Look where it got me."

"I need to talk to you," Rabbit said quietly. "But now isn't the time."

"Why? Need to build your image back up?"

He glared at her with the alarm of a co-conspirator about to be exposed. She nodded, her lips smiling but her eyes not.

"I'd rather listen to you right now. Don't pretend anything, just talk."

"I'm not *pretending,"* he snapped. "I—"

"Look, you want to blaspheme? Call yourself out. I want to see some heresy at your own bullshit image and role-playing. I've got nothing to lose now, so I'm finally being brutally honest. With you, with myself, with everybody."

"What do you mean, you've got nothing to lose? Are you just giving up? At least I'm trying."

"Look, Rabbit," she said, sighing heavily. "I don't know if you knew about this, but my life is pretty much over. Those pieces of shit gave me the hiv, and there's nothing on this Earth that'll fix that."

"What? You think the world revolves around sex? Is one small facet of your personality so important to you that as soon as it's gone, you throw in the towel? Isn't there more to you than that?"

She stared, hearing him say the same thing she'd said to her last boyfriend once. Coincidence? Or do great minds really think alike? She had meant it as an attack on others, never thinking it applied to herself.

"But…"

"No buts, Macaulay. Just because you can't get laid anymore is no reason to give up, unless you're nothing more than a walking pussy."

"But all my life was wasted, to make myself a great lover."

"Isn't there more to you than that?" he repeated.

Silence.

"I thought you made music."

She looked down at the sidewalk and shrugged. Noticing her bidi had gone out, she relit it and stared at her lighter, remembering how she'd had it custom-made so that it would stand out from everyone else's.

"Aren't you trying to make electronica into an art form that will be recognized by more than just ravers? From what I hear, you're a composer who ranks up there with Dvorak, just using a computer instead of an orchestra. Are you going to let that dream fall apart too? This isn't a Yeats poem. This is life."

"Yeats?" she asked quietly.

"'The years to come seemed waste of breath, a waste of breath the years behind.' It's the lament of a soldier, a celebration of self-pity."

Now, she looked up, staring off into the distance.

"If all you cared about was getting off, then go on ahead and kill yourself. Or, if you want it to last a bit longer, I'll buy you all the X and absinthe you can stomach, and take you back with us to Florence. It shouldn't take long for you to waste away and die.

"Or, you can keep on fighting. Don't even settle for being the next Dvorak or Grieg. Be the first Maya Macaulay. I'll help you, give you my patronage. We're in Ibiza, hon. Take advantage of everything life has given you, instead of crying over what it's taken."

"I can never compete with these guys. Not even DJ Igneous."

"Then I had you pegged wrong," he said, flicking his cigarette away.

"I can't think about anything, now that I know I'm going to die."

"Shit, you're going to die no matter what. We all live under a death sentence, but most of us keep going anyway. My advice: go ahead and kill yourself. God forbid you spend what little time you have left doing something you can be proud of. Just go ahead and OD. I'll get you a few spoons of heroin, you can go out on the beach late at night, get naked under the stars, and shoot up. Maybe you'll have long enough to masturbate one last time. Might as well, that's all you seem to care about."

She glared at him, her teeth grinding, eyes ablaze.

"Or we can go over to my friend's house, play on the computers, make some music that really is *music*. Get famous, simply by getting him to play it down at his house club. This *is* Ibiza, yunno. If something new and good comes on over the system, *someone* will hear it. Deals will be made, hands shaken, records cut, and your name will be in lights all over the world before you know it. The way I see it, a heap of blessings surround you.

"Or, there's a third option. You can go back home, let your pathetic life dwindle away into nothing, and die a Nobody. Just an eighty-pound stick figure who's good for nothing besides taking up space." He had seen the anger start to fade, so he kept it alive. Gotta feed it to keep it hungry, he thought. "John Wayne once said it perfectly. He said that real courage was knowing you were beaten and saddling up anyway."   Silence. Moments passed.

"...How did you have me pegged?" she asked finally. "You said you had me pegged wrong."

"One bad bitch with a real set of balls. Steel balls. And the rest of you, carved out of kryptonite."

She met his eyes, her own wide. He turned away from her and opened the door, ready to go back in.

"Don't prove me wrong," he said, glancing back over his shoulder.

Apparently there was something different about me tonight. Maybe it was the way I carried myself, I don't know, but people I've spoken to every time I've come to this place, Nessun Dorma, have been reintroducing themselves to me.

"Hi, I'm Heather. You come here often?"

"Uh...no, first time."

"I didn't think so. I'm sure I would've seen you."

"Hi, I'm Stacy. How long have you known Mark?"

"Hey, I'm Dawn. Who are you here with?"

We got into a VIP thing, up the stairs and on this dais with velvet ropes and leather couches. Mark whispered something in the VIP guy's ear and the guy nodded. There was a flock of blondes gathered at the foot of the stairs, waiting for some moneyed drunk fellow to invite them up. Mark pointed at four of them and the VIP guy opened the red velvet rope to let them through.

I threw in two fifties on a bottle of Dom Perignon, and some girl tried to put strawberries in my flute, which I took and fed to her instead. She pretended that it was erotic in some way and said something about getting some whipped cream to go with it. I rolled my eyes, drained my glass, and stuck it out to be refilled by a tall Amazon woman named Veronica.

That Heather girl I was talking to earlier murmured something to me that I couldn't make out, and put something in my mouth, letting a finger slip briefly in after it. I swallowed the whatever-it-was with a gulp of champagne and kissed her. Murdering Brendan Aguillard was suddenly at the bottom of my list of things to do that night.

I bought another bottle of Dom just for the two of us and let her work her money-grubbing, gold-digging charms on me. The whatever-it-was turned out to be some great X. When it hit me the world shook. All the lights in the club were for me. I was the guest of honor at a party thrown by God. On my dais, looking down on hordes of painted, ornamented savages, while drinking champagne surrounded by gorgeous women, Mark raised his glass to me in salute.

I toasted with him, kissed Heather again, watched her kiss another girl, and then I kissed her too. Mark was rolling as well; his smile never left his face.

Over his shoulder I saw something I knew wasn't real, but I stared anyway. A black flock of ravens erupted from somewhere and filled the club, flapping and squawking, until all was blackness and that's the last thing I remember.

I awoke, blinked, and had no idea where I was. It was obviously a girl's bedroom, satin sheets on a king-sized bed, tasteful art adorned the walls. I was naked.

I rolled over and felt a warm body next to me. Correction: three warm bodies. Heather, Mark, and some other girl were sleeping next to me. It must have been fun. Pity it was just a black hole in my memory.

I touched Heather's shoulder, she stirred, and opened her eyes. She turned away from me, moved against me, and I moved with her until I was inside. Mark and the other girl woke up and chuckled, said "Good morning," and then it started. After a while we swapped partners and I wondered if this was what they called risky behavior. A part of me that was obviously not my friend said it was, but I ignored it.

When it was over the girls went to the bathroom together and we put our *pants on and smoked cigarettes, saying nothing.*

We went to Denny's for breakfast. I found out the other girl's name was Chastity, which I laughed at but she didn't. It didn't matter. That morning felt like the beginning of some new era of my life, one that could someday be called my best years if it lasted that long.

When we finally got home I slept until early evening. I awoke to the phone ringing and answered it tiredly. Alistair said he and his sister were coming over with steaks for me to cook and I didn't argue. The shower I took felt so good I just sat under the water until it ran cold, and it came back to me in flashes. The men's room. Brendan Aguillard telling me some joke. The bathroom attendant with his hand out. Both of them dead in a locked stall, sitting on the toilet with their throats torn out.

Blood on my hands.

See? I can wash my hands all by myself.

I remember taking a mint from the tray and walking out into bright lights, loud music, and pink champagne with strawberries.

Two days after that, Mark got me a job.

For many, the first time doesn't count. It's over too quickly, leaves one shaking all over with a flood of adrenaline, and the best parts can't be remembered. Just a blur of pleasure, almost like the first time having sex, Jared thought.

It wasn't planned or expected. All he wanted to do was talk to the guy. Coming up behind him, he grabbed him by the scruff of his neck and forced his head around. His face was only inches from the other guy's when he started talking, calmly, he thought. He didn't realize until later that his thumb must've pinched the carotid artery on one side of Brendan's neck, the tips of his other fingers just happening to squeeze the one on the other side. His stomach muscles were clenched, just in case the son of a bitch tried to elbow him in the gut, which is what *he* would've done.

While he was hissing his warning at Brendan, telling him he'd had enough, the bully rolled his eyes. Jared squeezed harder, trying to let the dickless piece of shit know he was serious, not noticing that Brendan's face was bright red, and the look on his blushing face was *not* a mocking grin. He'd been struggling, but Jared somehow held him easily. The guy just kept on pissing.

Now the fucker wasn't even looking at him. His eyes were still rolled up. Look at me when I'm talking to you, cocksucker! But then, surprise of all surprises, Brendan stuck his tongue out at him.

481

Oh yeah? Can't take me seriously, can you? Still calmly, Jared wrapped his other hand around the cowardly piece of shit's throat, the dick-licker who didn't have the balls to fuck with anyone without his posse to help him.

While he tried to keep his temper under control, his voice quiet so that no one else might hear, Jared tried to tell Brendan that if he wasn't left alone forever, he'd kill everyone. I said, *kill*, motherfucker! You think this is some kind of joke? Quit making faces at me! Look at me! *Look at me!*

He shook him the way he'd been shaken so many times, then let him go. Brendan just fell, making no effort at all to catch himself, and his head cracked— *boom!*—against the tile floor with a horrible noise that echoed, and kept on echoing, over and over and over as Jared stared down at him in shock.

The bastard's eyes didn't even blink. Blue eyes, open so wide they looked like they'd roll out of their sockets, bulging, swollen.

His mouth was open, his tongue sticking out. Not all of it, just the tip, peeking out between his teeth.

His face was ashen. No, *purple*. Almost black.

He didn't move.

Jared's knees were knocking together.

He shivered, even though he felt intense heat, and was suddenly aware that anybody could come in at any time. His surroundings snapped abruptly into such sharp detail that he found himself weirdly appreciative of them. The smell of disinfectant clinging to the shiny white tiles, so unlike most public restrooms where he felt like he needed a dose of penicillin just from breathing the piss-rank air. The dully gleaming metal box set into the wall, holding the coarse brown paper towels that smelled funny when they got wet. The air dryer with the same words scratched out of the directions as in every other restroom across the nation. The air vents with gray fur growing on each metal slat. In one crashing instant, the adrenaline rushing to his brain sharpened his senses such that in one panicked glance, he memorized the phone number of Rachel, the world's best fellator—fellatress?—saw the jump in progress of a glory hole in a stall's side wall someone had started five months ago, and heard the footsteps of a woman in high heels click-click-clicking past the door outside. The clack of a toilet seat coming down in the ladies' room.

Brendan farting slowly, the first gases escaping his dead body.

Jared reached over and flushed the urinal that the late Brendan had been standing in front of. Quickly, he dragged the body into one of the stalls, sat it on the toilet, locked the door, and slid under the wall.

Looking at himself in the mirror, he saw a pale, terrified face. He shook horribly and moved as he did in his dreams. Splashing some cold water on his face, again and again, he tried to stop hyperventilating. Fuck it, just go. He toweled off and left, trying to walk calmly through the mall, back to where his girlfriend waited in the food court.

Thinking, *so this is what they mean by Assault-whoops-Homicide.*

Strangely, he found himself craving meat. Sarah didn't even notice him as he walked past her. She was reading the lyrics printed on the inlay card of one of the CDs she'd just bought. He went by and stood in line in front of the Chinese place, grateful for some time to get his thoughts in order. Even more grateful that the woman behind the counter barely spoke English and didn't notice him slurring his words.

He got one of everything. Taking it over to the table where Sarah was still engrossed in what Jerry Cantrell had to say these days, he grunted a greeting at her, which she returned, and he dug into the mound of bourbon chicken that had been generously heaped between the lemon chicken, honey chicken, teriyaki, steak and peppers, pork fried lice, egg rolls, and handful of fortune cookies.

Somehow, nothing had ever tasted so good.

As he wolfed down one nugget after the other, pausing only for sips of the best Pepsi ever, he felt some hidden part of him, the voice that lurked behind the voice that told him what to do at all the wrong times. The dark shadow bust a gut laughing.

Since then, all of Brendan's pack but one had followed him to Hell, all but one of his little posse, his troop of bullies. Peter Gattoni was still out there somewhere, hiding with his tail between his legs. Even a fucking idiot like him could apparently see a pattern in the murders of all his old high school friends. One by one, over the years, they were found dead for no discernable reason. Girlfriends were questioned, a few times arrested, and even twice convicted on trumped-up charges because, damn it, in Florida, cases needed to be closed.

Now, ten long years after poor, misunderstood Brendan Aguillard's tragic unsolved murder, for the first time since his memory began, Jared was finally passing a whole day without fantasies of killing someone. Not once did he even take a moment alone to scribble a threat on a cocktail napkin and crumble it up. No ghosts of bullies or hecklers taunted him from beyond the grave, making him wish he'd drawn out their suffering before he finished with them. He didn't even re-enact a moment of sweet vengeance. It never even crossed his mind.

Nobody needed to die today.

They shopped some more, buying clothes and CDs, sculptures by demented artists, decorated their bodies with elaborate henna tattoos that would fade in a few months, and marveled at the city in general.

Though still feeling removed, detached, Rabbit always watched the world around him with one eye, and more than once saw a familiar face lurking in the shadows. Watching.

A leftover hallucination?

He wasn't sure. When drug addled, no one can ever be too sure, and he was enough of a pessimist to never doubt his senses. Excusing himself while they browsed a sculpture exhibit, he melted away into the crowd of tourists. And was followed.

As casual as he could pretend to be, he felt awkward in the suffocating closeness of his still-present hangover, and was certain that in everything he did, every overly self-conscious movement or expression, he looked like a bad actor in a B-movie. Whether his shadow noticed it or not, the bastard was always in the corner of his eye when Rabbit checked.

Leaning against a store front, pretending to feed the birds. Checking his watch, looking around as if waiting for somebody.

Pathetic.

Definitely not a professional.

Relieved, but still furious at himself for stupidly taking a drug that impaired him, Rabbit found a pub that he knew had a one-at-a-time restroom. There, no one could barge in on him. He stumbled a bit trying to make his way through the afternoon crowd, waited impatiently for an elderly Ibizan to finish his business, and locked the door behind him.

It was a tiny little closet with a toilet in it, no sink, and a mirror. Hurriedly, he slipped off the detachable heel of one of his shoes, and dug out the hidden rig. It was a hypodermic needle broken up into tiny pieces like a briefcase 30.06, which he snapped together as quickly as he could. From within the heel of his other shoe, he selected a tiny vial from his arsenal.

Adrenaline. Pure adrenal gland extract.

Filling the syringe, he tugged the sock down one foot using the toes of the other, exposing a vein on his ankle he would much rather have a trackmark on than any other, if haste might not allow a clean shot.

What? This? Oh, an ant bite.

DJ Igneous was still waiting outside the pub when Rabbit emerged, too nervous to see the difference in his quarry's confident swagger. The designer shades Rabbit wore hid the hungry burn in his eyes and the dark cloud that gathered behind them. The Cockney followed, grinning smugly, when the apparently oblivious American turned and sauntered down the street and, as luck would have it, wandered into the most convenient alley for an assault and battery. Igneous couldn't believe his luck, and felt his spirits soar.

Perfect.

Turning into the alley, he saw the cocky American looking for a place to piss. Wait, didn't he *just* go to the Men's Room? Damn. He must have a pretty weak bladder. No surprise. These yellow-bellied Yanks—oh, *perfect*.

Rabbit had wandered all the way down to a skip, a dumpster they called it here, looked pleased, shrugged, unzipped his fly and stepped behind it.

Igneous approached quietly, working a blackjack out of the waistline of his jeans. Hard going, considering his paunch getting in the way, and his shirt being a little too tight. He had to hurry, though, because there was no better time to catch someone unaware than when he was taking a leak. As soon as the rubber-sleeved steel was free, Igneous held it at the ready and tiptoed as fast as he could up to the skip. The far corner hove into view, and he lunged forward, swinging his body around to get the best angle and—

And Rabbit's blade flicked out and unzipped the Limey's belly from left hip to right, spilling obscene sponges of yellow fat out of the shiny rayon shirt that bulged over his belt buckle. A flash, and Igneous felt his arm go limp, the crook of his elbow sliced clean, severing the tendons that connected his hand to his brain. Before the blackjack even hit the pavement, Rabbit jabbed the knife up into the jowls under the angle of the jaw with a rooting, troweling motion.

Blood sprayed from Igneous' lips and nostrils, darkening his blond goatee as he kicked frantically, one leg still instinctively trying to run. A quick glance down at the mouth of the alley, and Rabbit seized his victim by collar and belt, leaving the knife embedded, and with a tremendous heave, lifted the body up over the lip of the dumpster.

Igneous was vaulted into the trash, crashing down among table scraps, coffee grounds, and algae.

He tried to scream, but the knife pinned his jaw shut, cleaving all the way up through the roof of his mouth into his sinuses. Clambering over and dropping down on top of the DJ, Rabbit seized the handle and jerked it back and forth, mostly to work it free, but partly just to be mean. Igneous squirmed and whimpered piteously.

"I told you once," Rabbit hissed through clenched teeth, yanking the knife free. "Didn't I?" With another quick glance at the alley's mouth over the rim of the dumpster, he climbed out and dropped back to the pavement, ducking into the shadows.

Quickly cleaning off the knife and his hands with an elegantly monogrammed handkerchief—with someone else's embroidered initials, of course—he could faintly hear his prey kicking in the garbage.

As soon as the knife was back in its hiding place and he was sure he looked presentable, Rabbit tossed the blood-soaked rag and hauled himself back up to peer at DJ Igneous. The Brit was feebly clawing at his face and belly, looking up at him with bleary eyes. Rabbit winked, put his finger to his lips, and yanked the lid of the skip down to plunge the man into darkness.

It took a long time for him to die.

Jennifer went to stand casually next to Bianca in front of a large plaster Pietá, so casually that her friend knew it was anything but. Girls just know that stuff.

"Hey," she said.

"Hey yourself. What's up?"

"Is there an Italian word, *farfanicchio*?"

"Yes. Why?"

"What's it mean?"

"Um...I don't know if there's an English word for it to translate into. There should be, but I don't know it. It's a little man who puts

486

on airs. Why?"

"…Nick said it in his sleep."

They stared down at the Pietá, at a grieving Mary holding her son's dead body in her lap, saying nothing for a moment.

Then: "He has nightmares."

Bianca frowned.

Jennifer walked away.

The girls greeted their host when he returned, and showed him what they'd bought. Bianca was the only one to notice the bloodstain on his cuff, which, on a regular day, he would never have missed, but she said nothing. No one bothered to roll that night, still feeling what was left from two nights before. There was no limousine, just drinking and dancing at one discotheque, mingling at a strip club afterwards, and then going out to dance again somewhere else. The night passed in a warm, liquid blur, bleeding into morning and another staggeringly brilliant day.

By contrived coincidence, they all just happened to be having a snack at El Brasero, passing around plates of duck and salmon, the six of them sitting at a large table with two empty chairs, when two of Rabbit's friends just happened to walk in and see them.

With exclamations of sufficiently plausible surprise, the three men greeted each other warmly, and the two Brits were invited to sit and eat.

"Everybody, this is Caulfield," Rabbit said, introducing a heavy-set man. "And Treble," indicating the thinner of the two. "These guys have the corniest stage names in Christendom. Jolly Roger and Union Jack."

The one named Treble scoffed. "And if we let you join the gang, Nick, you can be Lucky Pierre." They went through the manly ritual of punching each other companionably in the shoulder a few times before sitting.

They looked like a couple of ordinary Englishmen, labor class, not dapper or debonair at all. There was a bit of the obligatory small talk, a few references to adventures since the last time they'd spoken, a little gossip, and a lot of toast-drinking when the cute waitress brought a round of pints.

"What this place really needs, though," Treble said eventually. "Is a new sound. It's all new versions of the old scene, and it's getting tiresome." It sounded rehearsed to Rabbit, but not at all to the girls.

"Aye," Caulfield growled. "I'm still riding the laurels of last year."

"So do something new. How hard can it be?"

"Humpf! Nickie, my boy, it is unpossible. I swear I've milked it for all it's worth." A lie. "All we can do is root around in Classical for inspiration and rip off the dead fellas."

Maya's ears perked up, just like Rabbit knew they would.

"What does everybody else do when they get desperate for a new gimmick, instead of trying to grow artistically, they go 'retro' and just plagiarize somebody else's sound," Treble said disgustedly. "They branch out into hip-hop, steal the signature from some old, famous song, and just repeat it over and over. It's pathetic. Or just blatant rewrites."

"So what will you do?" Rabbit asked

"Ach, whatever everyone else does, just do a cover of some Eighties song. There has to be at least *one* that nobody's stolen yet."

"Eighties have been plundered," sneered Caulfield. "Everything, back to the fecking Forties. I won't be surprised to stop by Pacha and see the crowd jiving to *Who Threw The Whiskey In The Well?* by this time next week. In fact, I've got ten to one. Any takers?"

"Nah, I hear in America they're revamping *Yankee Doodle Dandy*."

"Gee, what a shock. No offense, ladies."

"So, you have no ideas?" Rabbit prompted.

"Oh, sure. I hear that new guy, Puff-something, is going to rip samples from Middlebrook Primary doing *Ca' The Yows*. We could head him off at the pass."

"Shit, at this rate, go all the way back to cavemen banging rocks together. I've heard the theme songs of Seventies shows, the credits from B movies, the whole works. What's next? That midget Tattoo from Fantasy Island doing *Rapper's Delight*?"

"The world's coming to an end, Coniglio."

"Hey, Maya," Mariana said. Rabbit almost rolled his eyes, thinking *Christ, it took you long enough*. Maya was still looking at Caulfield, but arched her eyes in a facial "hmm?"

"You brought some of your CDs from home, didn't you? I think you were listening to them on the plane."

Maya only nodded.

"What CDs?" Treble asked with feigned curiosity. Rabbit thought he looked just like a shill in the crowd. Which, in a way, he was.

"Maya makes her own music, too," Mariana told them. "Good stuff, none of that minimalist shit that the so-called geniuses are putting out. She makes some music you stop and listen to." She tried not to sound like she was bragging, but it was a bit too obvious. She was tired of these *men* who came along and hogged the spotlight, and wanted some focus brought over to her end of the table for a change. "To be honest, I don't really care for techno, except when I'm dancing, but whenever I play one of the copies she burned for me, I have to listen to the whole thing. What did you call that one long one, baby?"

"Aria Fifty-One," Maya said quietly. "It's a technopera."

"That's right, Aria 51. Like Area 51, because that's where the real freaks are. That's my favorite one."

"And what're your songs about?" Caulfield asked. Maya glanced at Rabbit, then back, and smiled faintly.

"Heresy."

"Ach!" Treble said, approvingly. He and Caulfield leaned forward.

"A pleasant change from all the love and euphoria, no doubt."

"Let us hear a few?"

Again, Maya glanced at Rabbit. He gestured with a tilt of his head and an expression in his eyes that read "What are you waiting for?"

"I happen to have my Discman on me," she said.

"Does it happen to have a disc in it by chance?" Caulfield asked.

"Yeah. 'Delenda Est Rap'. It's a—"

"Rap must be destroyed," Rabbit said, suddenly more interested. "A play on Cato the Elder."

"Uh...yes."

"Might be appropriate here, especially since this was a Carthaginian city." Only Jen and Bianca, the history buffs, understood the reference to Roman propaganda. Maya dug the CD player out of her handbag and handed it to Treble, who was the closer of the two. Slipping on the headphones, he leaned back in his chair in comfortable Listening Mode. When he pressed Play, there was an uncomfortable lull in the conversation, everyone watching him expectantly

489

even thought they knew they wouldn't hear anything.

Maya fidgeted uneasily. Knowing this would happen, Rabbit had come prepared. Another Discman appeared out of nowhere. "Luckily, *I* just happen to have my own with me. You got any others in your bag for Caulfield to hear?"

Now, Maya's eyes flickered with understanding. She cast a quick look at her host, letting him know she saw through all of this lucky coincidence, and had to smile. She appreciated his underhanded way of choreographing good fortune.

"You know, luckily, I just *happen* to have a *few* of them."

It started out as polite listening, but before long, both DJ's eyes flared with interest. Occasionally, they glanced at Maya and nodded their approval at certain parts. They didn't bob their heads or twitch dramatically, the way some would, but they couldn't hold still either. It wasn't just a basic melody repeated over and over with a thundering beat. It followed all the rules of Classical music, and when she sang, she actually had something to say.

It wasn't what anyone would get drunk and dance to, most of it, but it was *music.* It was art.

"A lot of your samples are easily recognizable," Caulfield said, "but that makes an audience automatically give you credit. They don't listen to the whole thing with a critical ear, you know? They just assume Remix and go along with it."

"I didn't have much to work with," Maya said.

"Problem not. If you want, you can come by our studio and play with the toys. Free of charge, so don't give me that look. Have fun and see what happens."

Treble had taken off the headphones by this time. "You won't need any samples. We have every kind of instrument that exists and quite a few that don't, all at the touch of a button. You can make a beat with everything from a gong to a timpani to a bodhran. Strings? We've got sitars, kyotos, ukeleles, you name it. Everything you can imagine, all on MIDI or computer program. Knock yourself out."

Maya looked from one to the other, then at Rabbit, then at Mariana, and back again to Treble. She cleared her throat.

"Really?"

"No, we just made that all up. Of *course*, really!"

"When can we do this?"

"Whenever you're ready, love."

She looked uncertainly at everyone else again.

"Go," Mariana told her quietly. In a daze, she got up and left the restaurant with them. The others sat back and smiled at each other, hoping they'd just seen a star born.

"One down," Rabbit said with a grin, signaling the waitress.

"You set all that up, didn't you?" Bianca asked. They could almost see a halo floating over his head as he feigned innocence.

"Why, I don't know what you mean."

II

"Can it be done?" Rabbit asked. The deep voice on the other end of the line chuckled.

"It already has been," the Woolagaroo answered. "Now, I hope you've learned your lesson. You know what they say about sleeping with the dogs, little brother."

"It's not for me. It's for...this girl."

"Ha! Listen to yourself! Darwin is vindicated, and you take pity on some slut when she has to face the music!"

"It's not that. She got sick from being raped."

"That's what they all say."

"Got it on good authority. She doesn't deserve it."

"No, be honest. With me and yourself. You want her cured so you can get a piece of her, that's all."

"That's part of it."

"Ha! I need a crystal ball and a turban; I'm good at this shit." Crowe cackled like a madman, which, in a way, he was.

"I think she's one of us."

"You always think she's one of us! No matter who she is!"

"Har-dee-fucking-har. I mean it this time."

"Ah well, there's only one way to find out."

"You think?"

"Where is she from? You pick her up in a bar?"

"No, she's from Coquina. Your own backyard."

"All the world is my backyard, son. I'm in Port-au-Prince right now."

"That so? You getting some more of that...?"

"Yes. I finally ran out. But the church in Florida is busy."

"Have you been there in a while?"

"I just left. I won't be back for some time, though. But the congregation caught on rather quickly, so they are proceeding on their own. If the next ones I start do as well, at this rate I'll be setting up franchises all over the world."

"How many parishes are there so far?"

"One in every major American city, at least. Bible Belt's tough, but the Lunatic Fringe, piece a' cake. It was amazing how quickly those people will grasp at what you offer them if you just tell them what they want to hear."

"Funny, I think Hitler said the same thing."

"Hitler was a fool."

"A good orator. Almost as good as Jesus."

"But nothing more than that." Crowe's voice was stern; Rabbit would get an idea sometimes and run with it, and his mentor didn't want someone like Hitler's name in the kid's mouth, just in case.

"I'm glad your church project is working out."

"It's not *my* project. I am just one of many. But I am happy too. It won't be long now."

"Good. Maybe I should send this girl to you."

"No, you keep her yourself. When your interest begins to flag, then you will know. Tell her nothing while your infatuation blinds you."

"It's not like that—"

"Tell her *nothing*. Nothing at all. Remember: no loose talk, no second thoughts."

"...Sorry."

"Good. Your package will be at Whatshername's any day now."

"Thank you."

"You know where to send the check to?"

"That one friend of yours, the Canadian fellow."

"Right. Oh, and Rabbit?"

"Yeah?"

"She'd better be worth it."

The barrel and slide recoiled, the barrel arrested about halfway, the slide continuing backward, cocking the hammer and slamming against the receiver as the empty casing was ejected. Springing forward again, the slide peeling off the next cartridge from the double-rowed magazine and, shoving it into the chamber on its way, it re-locked the barrel and surged back into place.

At the same instant, spiraling at over one thousand feet per second, the bullet scattered off particles of molten metal into the brain as it shattered the left zygomatic arch. Ricocheting off of the occipital bone, a mashed and fragmented chunk of hot, copper-jacketed lead came to rest in the right temporalis muscle, only to be blasted out of the way a nanosecond later by a second round.

It was beautiful.

The ejected shell, spinning away with fresh extractor and ejector marks along it, tried to aim for a hard-to-reach spot to come in for a landing, but Rabbit kept one eye on it for later retrieval. The barrel's spiral rifling had carved a clockwise set of grooves and lands, as unique as fingerprints, into the slug that could identify the pistol to a ballistics division if he wasn't careful. He tried not to think about that right now, though.

Worries of that sort tended to spoil the moment, like stopping to put on a condom, or taking out a toothbrush while he was still chewing some chocolate cake. Instead, he reveled in the purely elemental joy of reducing what was once Joel Sadler to a heap of bloody, useless flesh.

The part of a brain that had once enabled hands to clench into fists was now honey-combed and pulped, a mush of singed gray matter, all from the twitching of a single finger. With the deafening cracks of escaping gases and the oddly-pleasant stench of cordite, two more bullets plowed into the bloody face and tore their way through the brain pan, just to deny his family and friends an open-casket funeral, just to make his mother cry more.

Just to be mean.

It was beautiful.

The moment came back to him as he leaned sideways in his chair, one leg hooked over the armrest, a nice, cold Cuba Libre in his hand. Unburnt powder had peppered that hand seven years ago as he pulled the trigger, sending Joel Sadler's black soul howling down to Hell.

Call someone a fag in your next life, you fat fuck.

Beat some little kid up now.

It had been a little over four years since Rabbit had last been sucker-punched in the school hallway when he turned a street corner and collided with Sadler. For once, the fat fuck was alone. Probably on his way to the bar Rabbit had just left to meet the friends that had infested the place. Sometimes swallowing your pride and leaving a potentially bad situation pays off.

Like now.

"Watch where you're going!"

"Sadler?"

"Huh? Well, I'll be damned. Skittle dick! You're all grown up! Hey, remember that time I broke your fu—"

"There's something I've always wanted to say to you, Sadler."

"Oh yeah?"

Bang.

494

Rabbit sighed heavily and rattled the ice cubes in his drink, smiling.

"Okay, you ready?" Maya asked.

"Let's hear it."

She hit the spacebar and sat back while Treble and Caulfield leaned forward. Like Grieg, the melody began faint and ominous, grabbing their attention and making nape hairs prickle in anticipation. Out of nowhere, the signature notes sparked briefly to give a taste of what was to come, and all present could see how the club lights would shatter the darkness for a teasing moment in time with it. The melody swelled somewhat, macabre, but with the promise of blood-stirring intensity.

Again, louder, the bright notes. The three men smiled and closed their eyes, slipping into daydreams set to the exotically haunting—whoa, shit! The third blast carried it into a fully grown riot, the creepy melody now vibrant and accusing, the beat a thunder of arrogant percussion. As all music touches a different nerve and calls up the appropriate emotion, this made the three men grin evilly and want to move—dance, run, whatever, just *move*. It was not the kind of angry sound that would interfere with Ecstasy. Ravers wouldn't find it repellent at all; it was a different kind of anger, one that inspired confidence, making those who heard it feel they were capable of anything.

Maya had created the song silently, with the exception of several sounds that she played a few times just to make sure of them, and designed the whole thing visually. The computer screen just looked like a polygraph test, one taken by a pathological liar, with sharp peaks and deeps troughs of the sound line gone haywire. The fact that she made it all come together by sight alone...

She hit the spacebar again, stopping it abruptly.

"So, what do you think?"

"It'll do," Rabbit said carelessly.

"I'd already had it running through my head, trying to set notes to this poem I wrote. I can't come up with a chorus that isn't a blatant rip-off of this rap I heard from the Eighties. You know, the one that goes "Move, sucka, *move sucka*, now groove, sucka, *groove sucka.*" I mean, that's not how the rap goes, but everyone will know that's what I took it from. So I've been tinkering around with something and all I need now is someone to sing it."

"Sing it yourself, "Treble said, pointing to a microphone.

"No, this is an angry song."

"Love, when a woman sings, especially angry... man, you wouldn't believe how sexy it is to hear a woman howl."

"What I need is an angry man with a good voice. Not to *rap* it, but shout with a decent voice and sing... what I need is Maynard."

"Maynard?" Treble and Caulfield looked at each other in confusion, but Rabbit's faint smile became a grin. Maynard James Keenan.

"Reverend Maynard?" he asked.

"Mm-hmm. Tell me you know him."

"Never had that honor," Rabbit said. "But now what we do have is an idea of what you want. I think the program can alter a decent voice and make it a great voice. Can't it?" he asked Treble.

"We can cheat up to a point, yes."

"Here," Caulfield said, leaning past Maya to move the mouse, click it a few times, and bring up a specific voice program. "Just go. We'll go back and smooth the edges, put in echoes where you want them after you finish. Then, we can chop it up and put it into the tune later. Just go."

She went. She knew it by heart and did her best. She didn't have a trained voice, but she had anger, and sometimes that's enough. Shaitan had always said that. Anger is a gift. Her tone was harsh and accusing, aimed not at the Beautiful People blowing up on the dance floor, but at the timid little 'fraidycats that stood nervously along the edge. The moths.

"Wallflower!
You think you lack some hidden power
So you piss away those hours
When you should be living life,
And meanwhile your future wife is waiting for you—make your move!
Now where's your groove?
It's at the bottom of your drink,
You can't be smooth—you're just a coward!
Libido soured,
Well, by this song be thee empowered..." Then she broke off, shaking her head. "I can't do the chorus by myself. Yunno, the 'bust a move' part."

"Then cut to verse two," Caulfield said. She took a deep breath.

"Why'd you bother to come out tonight?
If not to find your own Miss Right?
Don't resist the beat of every song
Hide in the shadows all night long,
And end up going home alone, to an empty bed and silent phone, when all you had to do was…
"Um, there's another chorus here."
"Keep going!"
"Okay…Instead you hide in a bottle of booze!
You act hesitant and confused
But what the fuck have you got to lose?
Now's your chance
Get up and dance!
Pretend there's manhood in your pants
Or you'll regret it! Now go out and get it!
You gotta stand up and be proud, and while the music is still loud
Fill your every waking minute
Put sixty sexy seconds in it
Get your ass out on the floor and…!" she tapped the space bar.
Silence.
"That'll do," Rabbit said.
"Um, I wasn't ready."
"It'll do. Write down the chorus and I'll find somebody."
"Not just anybody!"
"Of course not. I'll call Maynard right away."
"Funny."
"Tell you what. Let's go outside, have a cigarette."
She got up and stepped through the semicircle of chairs behind hers. As Rabbit arose to follow her, he winked at the other two, who winked back.

The studio wasn't so much a studio as an apartment dedicated to cutting records. It was Spartan except for the clutter of instruments and equipment and towering speakers. On the balcony, there were only two chaise lounges and a coffee can for cigarette butts. They plopped down on the lawn chairs and Maya dug out two bidis, tossing one to Rabbit.

"Much obliged." He offered her a gulp of his drink, hers being long gone, but she shook her head.

497

"So, what do you think?" she asked timidly.

"What do you want me to think?"

"Am I good enough?"

"You already know you are. You just want to hear me say it?"

"I mean, should I give it a shot? Be honest."

"Anyone who doesn't give their dreams a shot doesn't get any sympathy from me. If you want to settle for a nine-to-five, be my guest, but if you want anything worth having out of life, you've got to give it everything you got. *Make* it yours."

"Shit, that song is about getting off your ass. Putting the possibility of embarrassment aside. Makes me look like a hypocrite."

"Segue," he declared, changing the subject. "Mariana told me you make some of your own clothes."

"As a hobby, yes."

"Like what?"

"Well, besides tie-dyes and batiks, a lot of Aloha-type shirts with really unusual designs."

"No hibiscus and Woody station wagons?"

"Nope, not a one."

"Surfboards? Palm fronds? Parakeets?"

"Uh-uh."

"Okay, what then?"

"Well, alcohol, tobacco, and firearms. One has all kinds of pipes: calumets, chibouks, hookahs, all kinds. The wisps of smoke form silly designs over the glowing bowls. Dead lizards. Different flattened small animals run over by cars—"

"Roadkill?" he laughed.

"Yeah, with brightly colored flies buzzing around them."

"I'll be damned."

"Well, those are the shirts I make. I draw all the designs out on transfer sheets, iron them onto short-sleeved button-downs, then color them in with fabric pens. Everybody laughs, but no one would ever wear them but me."

"Don't bet on it. So, you can draw?"

"I'm all right. I get the job done."

"If you had a silk screen, would you try to sell your stuff?"

"Who'd buy it?"

"This is Ibiza," he reminded her. "Start a new trend."

"Gosh. I'd never thought of it before. I wonder…"

"There's only one way to find out. Yes or no?"

"Why are you doing all this for me?"

He stared at her, wondering that himself. He bluffed his way out. "I try to show people who they are. If you're a bad person, I punish you. If you are the kind of person I agree with, well, I do what I can to encourage you. Give you the incentive to keep it up. I like you, Maya. I don't want to see you give up."

"But—"

"No buts. There is such a thing as brotherly love with no strings attached. You got way too much going for you to just quit."

"What? What do I have going for me? I'm—"

"You can dance and sing and draw and make music. You've got a brain between your ears, you're drop-dead gorgeous when you're not frowning, and you think for yourself."

"I was born with a gift of laughter, and a sense that the world is mad," she muttered to herself.

"Sabatini wrote that. Damn, you read too?"

"*Scaramouche* is one of my favorite books."

"How about *Prince of Foxes*? You read that one?"

"No, what's it about?"

"Cesare Borgia's right-hand man. Andrea Orsini."

"I thought that was Machiavelli."

"No, Machiavelli was Borgia's *left*-hand man."

"Did you say 'Andrea'? That's a girl's name."

"No, it only sounds like one. It's the Italian Andrew, like Pietro is Peter and Mateo is Matthew. Now, Andrea Orsini finally got it through his thick head that working for Borgia was worse than selling his soul to the devil, and he switches sides. Great book."

"You know, I was reading *The Portable Machiavelli* out in the park, and people kept coming up to me and asking if it was about Tupac. Can you believe it? I mean, the name was spelled correctly and there was a portrait on the cover of *a white guy*! Tupac?"

"That's the world we live in. Now, what you have to decide is, are you just going to complain, or are you willing to do something about it? History is made by individuals, not the masses. Borgia, Hitler, Christ, all of them made a dent in the world, but went about it wrong to get the job finished. Christ was too far on one end, Hitler too far on the other, and Borgia too much of an asshole. I say, if we learn from their mistakes…"

"Delusions of grandeur, Nick?"

"Call it 'vision'. I like that better."

"How about 'paranoid schizophrenia'?"

"Nah, if you have that, you also wet the bed and shoplift. I never stole anything."

"Ha! Bed wetter!"

"Joke."

"Bed-wet-terrrrr!" she sang like a child.

"Say it again and I'll kill you."

"Did you actually wet the bed? Tell me."

"Oh, sure, up until I was three."

"Promise? Cross your heart?"

"Take Jennifer's place tonight and find out."

She made a face at him. "Have you forgotten?"

"What? That you have tuna pox? Big deal."

"Tuna *what?*"

"Tuna pox. Hell, chicken pox smells nothing like chicken, but tuna..."

"Shut up."

"Well, you gotta admit—"

"I admit nothing. I drink my pineapple juice like a good girl."

"Huh? You lost me."

She started to explain, but the glass doors started to vibrate with the earthquake shudder of music playing way too loud. The first blast of the signature notes startled her, and then she could make out the rising, ominous melody. She could've sworn she heard a stir of echoes swirling about like wind-blown leaves, her own voice. Her eyes widened, but Rabbit only smiled, enjoying her surprise.

Then the intro leaped into the galvanizing riot, and in the middle of it, Maya's voice rang out like a clarion call, demanding the world's undivided attention. The music settled a little, giving her space, and a rich, vibrant, faintly echoing version of her voice cried out from inside. It sounded to her like someone else. Someone *good.*

"Ain't technology somethin'?" Rabbit asked.

She was speechless.

"Now, all you have to do is come up with a catchy name."

Still silent, eyes wide.

"Oh, and you forgot about the chorus," he noticed.

I have become one of them. It has begun.

After it was all explained to me and I was inducted into a secret society as

fabled and sought-after as the Illuminati, I saw the pompous and idiotic hierar-
chy of Coolness for what it really was—pompous and idiotic. I couldn't believe
my ears. And the coveted wealth of information that best friends would stab each
other in the back to hear even the echo of a whisper of, I rolled my eyes and
sneered at.

Christ, I thought, gimme a fuckin' break.

The divas and demigods who stride past the long lines to a nightclub's
entrance, make kissy-kissy with the bouncer, who enrages all of those standing in
line by opening the velvet rope for them and them alone; those who waltz through
the doors with a little wave to the girl who charges everyone else twenty bucks; the
upper-echelon fops and dandies and chippies and twats; what the hell is it that
makes them so special? Who bestowed upon them the right to look with con-
tempt and condescension upon people superior to them in all the ways that mat-
ter?

My buddy Mark, that's who.

At the bottom tier are the doormen. Those snooty fuckers. They judge who
gets to come in. They choose. It's not the next people in line, the people waiting
their turn. There are actually meetings during the day to discuss who the door-
men ought to look out for, and it's based on shit debated in these meetings
whether you and birds of your feather are worthy of admission. They use fancier
language, though. They say they "select patrons" who they feel "will most en-
hance the ambience within." They are trained in feeling out vibes from people
trying to get in, who'll cause trouble and who'll bring in money.

On the second tier, as of this afternoon, is me. The promoter. I am the
false sense of acceptance into this society that convinces rabble that they are wel-
come to come in and spend money. Moneyed rabble. People like, well, me. I can
comp you a ticket, introduce you to the doorman who will promptly forget you
but pretend to look out for you on a crowded night. Introduce you to the cover
charge cashier, who'll pretend to put your name down on The List. Introduce you
to Tony the bartender, who'll give the two of us a free shot as long as you don't
tell anybody else. Make you feel special. Introduce you to a Heather or a Lisa
who'll encourage you to buy her drinks all night. Motivate you to spend even
more money. I can get you a table on the VIP dais, convince you to throw in two
fifties on a bottle of Dom.

The Lisas and the Heathers and I are paid cuts from the entrance take
and the bar tabs, and we hand out passes to people we "feel will bring in good
energy" and "personality" and "cash flow." Then, when their passes are rejected
by the cover charge girl for being expired, they'll call my cell phone and get a busy
signal for an hour or so, hoping I'll come out and rescue them, set the cover
charge girl straight, make sure their name is on the list, until they give up and

501

just pay the twenty bucks to get in. Then they'll spend a fortune just to drink away the wrinkle in their mood and catch up with the rest of the party.

To appease them, I will admit them into the tentative sub-VIP clique, an arena of treacherous, conniving backstabbers who will form temporary alliances to conspire against one another, try to thin the herd and make themselves look better by comparison so they can gain entrance to the real VIP.

Aaaaaaand spend more money.

That's what I do. And on the tier above me, I have learned, is Mark.

Fuck if I know what he does.

Aside from sit in at meetings and discuss favoritism, then sit back and smile at the Lisas and the Heathers and the Sergios and Brads, the divas and the demigods, the upper-echelon fops and dandies and chippies and twats, as they boast and pose and sympathize with each other for being an endangered species. Then he catches me watching him watch, and he winks. And I'm In, man, like Flynn.

An endangered species?

I beg to differ.

You are not endangered. You are fucking doomed.

And I wink back, smiling.

"And all I need now is a name," she told the girls.

"How about Straycat?" Jennifer suggested, smiling at some secret joke.

"What's Portuguese for vagabond?" she asked Mariana.

"Doesn't matter. You're not Brazilian."

"Or Portuguese," Bianca helpfully pointed out.

"No, I'm Irish, Cherokee, and French. That doesn't give me much to work with. I want a pretty name."

"The Italian word for 'gypsy girl' is *zingara*," the polyglot said.

"I *like* Zingara!" Andrea chimed in. "For short, you can be Zing! Like, that's how fast you are. Zing!"

"Uh, no. *Innominata?* That means you don't have a name."

"What's wrong with Maya?" Mariana asked.

"There are about twelve girls out there called Maya, already."

"It beats the shit out of Igneous."

They laughed, remembering and mimicking the Cockney accent.

"I'm hard as a rock!"

"Volcanic in origin!"

"Yer flame won't last feriver, you hoo-er!"

502

The other patrons of the coffee shop stared at the laughing girls, most of them vapid tourists who didn't remember real laughter.

"What's the other one? Sedimentary? Fricken metamorphic rock?"

"I'm DJ Sedimentary!"

"Or wait, I've heard of guys called DJ Lethal and DJ Homicide. Why not some other crimes, like Shoplifting? Why does it have to be murder? I'm DJ Malfeasance of Office!"

"I'm MC Insider Trading."

"No, that's all false advertising. I can't be something I'm not. I'll just settle for Verbal Abuse or something."

Thank God all of them had the presence of mind not to say Rape.

"This is not an easy process, naming yourself."

"Fuck it. Steal somebody else's name, like Makaveli."

Maya considered this for a moment, thinking about a little kid she had known that worked for Grazi Mono. In what capacity, she was uncertain, but he was a helluva kid.

"How about Shrike?"

"What's that?" Andrea asked.

Mariana smiled broadly.

"The Butcher-bird. A psychotic little songbird that thinks it's a hawk."

"Butcher-bird?"

"Yeah. It kills bigger animals, field mice, and other birds, by impaling them on thorns or barbed wire; make these big heaps of dead things to attract females with. Rapacious little fucker."

"And you want to be this?"

"It's a songbird," Maya said, as if that explained everything.

"A songbird," Jennifer agreed, smiling. "With a shot of bourbon and a Zippo. That's you."

And Shrike it was.

Rabbit never asked where his milk came from, though he did wonder when the favor he'd requested arrived with his newest order. The viriphage was stored in the large package he got regularly wherever he was, always within a few days of it being frozen.

After defrosting, it was as close as he could come to drinking a quart freshly squeezed from mothers' breasts. Whose, he also won-

503

dered, but never asked.

Had he known, a man named Han Fei-Tzu would surely have died. Army of bodyguards or not.

As far as the Chinaman was concerned, those women weren't people anyway. They were brood mares, impregnated by the finest specimens. Incredible advances had been made in genetic engineering, but to some old-fashioned businessmen such as Han Fei-Tzu, low-tech always won out over high. His hobby was the breeding of human thoroughbreds, of champions, and his goal was not the winning of blue ribbons and trophies.

Han Fei-Tzu was building an army.

But Rabbit, oblivious, defrosted a pint's worth of his milk to drink after his morning exercises, and wondered how best to slip the cannibal virus into Maya's system.

That night, while the other girls were dancing, Maya sat with Treble, Caulfield, and Rabbit at a corner table of the Quarantine, and Ouroborus Records was born. The four of them, after a few shots of absinthe, Ouzo, some caipirinhas, and a locally-spawned liquor named Bleach, formed an alliance and vowed to shake up the music industry. Caught up in the passion of drink and ambition, they found themselves philosophizing and railing against the modern world, the two Brits trying to keep up with Rabbit and Maya. The young lady, who Rabbit finally decided was a cross between Vivien Leigh and Hedy Lamarr, was angrily denouncing golf courses as being the last green places in America and off-limits to everyone except political hyenas and locusts. Treble and Caulfield weren't sure what she was talking about, but telepathically agreed with each other that she looked great saying it.

Rabbit then took up the standard against court-ordered anger management courses, anger being a perfectly natural emotion, especially considering the lack of greed and selfishness courses. America was then symbolized by a gold-capped tooth in a "gangsta thug's" mouth, which are famous for collecting food particles that fester and rot without the "flossing baller" noticing. A gleaming golden shell encasing nothing but decay. And Florida, especially. Sinkholes and sunscreen. Maya applauded his metaphor, and the Brits just smiled and nodded.

"At the rate we're going," she declared, "in another twenty years we'll see a commercial announcing Soylent Green now available with Retsyn flavor crystals. Mark my fucking words."

"No doubt," Caulfield grunted with a sidelong glance at Treble. Thinking, "Um, what?"

Luckily for them, the conversation steered itself toward religion, something they had opinions on.

"Notice many Christians never bothered to become Christianized?" Treble asked, happy to include his own opinions, finally. "In their hearts, they're still pagans. They love war and worship false gods, give themselves over to greed and hate, and still manage to convince themselves they're righteous. Where else do you see such hypocrisy?"

"In the States," Rabbit snarled. "In the land of the free." His harsh tone was automatic, the fossil of an old and continuing argument.

"Aye, your people blind themselves with their dumb shows and phony wrestling, the same way we mindlessly bow to Original Sin."

"Not me!" Caulfield said. "I'm Pelagian."

"Who?"

"Pelagius. Fifth century monk. The Irish say he was Irish, and we say he was a Brit, but personally, I don't give a feck who he was because all that matters is that he had the right idea. He said that it's no fault of ours what some imaginary punter ate a billion years ago. You go to Hell if you're an asshole, and Heaven if you're straight. Period."

"But no. We force-feed guilt to our kids, so they don't know how to feel about this and that, and we end up with the warped lives of blameless children!" Treble was really starting to get into it. Rabbit had known already their views on religion and where they stood on their country's Irish situation: any creed that could be split into sects that murdered each other was a pile of hogshit. The Orangemen and the IRA could all go to hell as far as they were concerned, because none of them abided by their causes' tenets. Of course, they were both mistaken about the two factions' motives, but so was a lot of the world. It was about the end of segregation, not too far different from 1960s' America, more than whether prayers should be said in Latin or English. But the two Brits felt strongly about it, that an eight-hundred-year-old feud was fine until you lied about the reasons for it, hiding behind a façade of hypocritical holiness.

Knowing that they felt this way, the manipulative Rabbit had steered the rants onto the subject so that Maya would feel something in common with her new business partners, feel as if they shared more than just an interest in music. It worked. She wasn't alone, and she didn't have to think she was. She could speak her mind and be agreed with, and that made her smile more often.

Hedy Lamarr playing Delilah with curly hair, Rabbit decided. And two-inch ear lobes. And a death sentence that only he could lift, making her his Damsel In Distress, and he her Knight In Shining Armor. His current lover, who watched him with one eye from the dance floor and wondered when he would start paying attention to her, was already fading from his mind. Maya—Shrike—was more his type, and from her occasional laments about all the wasted sex education she'd endured, she was certainly more promising than the I'll-just-lie-here-and-let-you-do-all-the-work Jennifer.

Patience.

Reminded of her, and feeling her eyes on him, he turned and winked at her. A perfunctory effort, but a dutiful one. He had to keep up at least a pretense, for appearance's sake. Maybe, if his conscience plagued him, he would have to fulfill his promise and go with the students back to Florence, just for a little while, because he remembered from the old days what a broken heart felt like. Hurting girls' feelings no longer gave him that sense of superiority, that satisfaction.

Besides, the gelattarias in Firenze had some damn good ice cream. And no shortage of stupid tourists to hunt in the labyrinthine streets.

"Meeting adjourned," he said, thumping the table with his fist. "We cannot neglect our women."

Maya nodded happily. "I'll drink to that." And she did.

The nega-color lights had lost a little bit of their novelty once they had been enjoyed under the influence of Ecstasy, but the music was good enough for Rabbit to dance easily and without that awkward self-consciousness. Also, since he felt no need to impress these people anymore, his contempt gave him natural rhythm. It was all he could do not to stare at Maya, though.

Now, *she* could move.

She had discarded her hippie thrift store couture and now wore the ATF clothes Rabbit had asked about. The pistols shirt, with martini glasses and zombie mugs, was unbuttoned to her cleavage and then tied underneath, exposing her flat midriff, and a pair of tight jeans she had bleached and batiked stood out sharply in the lights. On her feet, unlaced and sloppy-looking combat boots, artistically scuffed by a belt sander and then stamped with red lipstick kisses. Her belt was a beautiful silken Hermés scarf, tied where a buckle would be.

She had said something about contrast; dressing up like a weirdo had to be contradicted by one classy item, not to redeem your outfit but rather to mock that one addition. It was a stupid idea, Rabbit thought, and he made no attempt to hide it, but she didn't care either way. She didn't care what anybody else thought, and really didn't care whether they knew that she didn't care, which was refreshing. He didn't know how she was before, but now, knowing that her days were numbered, she was making the most of them. She almost glowed with an intense vitality that had nothing to do with the Quarantine's cool lights.

Quite calmly, and without a shred of doubt, Rabbit decided he was in love with her, and began considering the best possible ring to propose with. A diamond, as big as an ice cube? No, not a conventional, boring, unimaginative diamond. An emerald, maybe surrounded by diamonds, would probably go well with her complexion. Actually, an amethyst would look the best, but who the hell would settle for one of those? Jennifer might, but she seemed so easily impressed that driveway gravel set in plastic might do the trick. But for Maya? Nothing short of kryptonite.

He glanced down at his clothes: napa, baby alligator, kangaroo leather, and rayon. Maybe he wasn't what Maya was looking for. Shit. Maybe he needed to buy himself a dashiki and some damn Birkenstocks, he thought, then caught himself, realizing what he'd been thinking. That he would change himself to suit what *someone else thought*. Like he always had. Impostor. Fraud. Poseur.

Nerd.

His whole life flashed before his eyes, a series of pathetic attempts to impress people. The clothes. The cars. Everything. The primal scream welled up inside him, threatening to tear his body apart if he didn't let it out. He shook feverishly, trying to hold it in, his face burning with the heat of shame. Where the lights made his face glow a light blue, the rush of blood made it seem green, his eyes a blazing pink with white flecks that made Jen shudder away.

Desperate to drown out his self-loathing, Rabbit stalked toward the bar, still trying to maintain dignity while he hurried. All five girls noticed and Treble tried to pretend he didn't. When they all looked questioningly at Jennifer, she could only shrug. Caulfield sat at the bar with a pint of bitter, about to take his first drink of it when Rabbit jerked it out of his hand, slopping head-foam on the bar.

"Make that two," Nick Coniglio growled to the Greek behind the bar, and drained the glass in one long go.

"Oy, wanker!" Caulfield snapped, but Rabbit just silenced him with a baleful glare and an I'll-fucking-kill-you look of psychotic rage. Twitching fingers trying to dig like claws into the drink-ringed surface of the bar. There wasn't even a challenge in Rabbit's eyes —just mindless hate.

The Greek chick pulled two more pints and set them in front of the American, who pushed one toward the Brit.

"Three shots of tequila," he managed to choke out as he raised his glass, then, "Sorry," to Caulfield before he drank.

"I think you might—" the bartender said, but Caulfield cut her off, saying something Rabbit didn't hear.

Nerd. He swallowed with sick desperation. All the friends money can buy. He clung to the anger, hoping it would outshine the self-pity and the misery, the pathetic sorrow. You're nothing, Jared. You're a joke. Skittle-dick. Pussy. Faggot. Nerd.

Kill yourself.

Put an end to it, you waste of life.

No, kill someone else.

Fuck no! Just drink until sweet oblivion comes and everything will be okay. Hide in the darkness, just like the old days.

His tolerance was so high from years of drowning the truth that his liver would probably give out before the hate did. Plan A was to drink so much the room spun, and see who held his forehead while he puked, and who stood off to one side and laughed. But what if it was everyone who laughed? Like last time?

He felt a gentle hand on his shoulder, and almost smiled. Please be Maya. Please be Maya. He turned, and it was Mariana.

"*Como vai você, irmao?*" she asked, her eyes wide with concern.

"*Tudo bem.*" How am I? Great. Top of the world.

"Liar."

"I'm leaving." He stared accusingly at his almost-empty glass.

"Where to?"

"I'm going out on the boat. See you tomorrow."

"You need adult supervision, Rabbit. We're coming, too."

508

"We?" He turned to see Maya standing on his right side, squeezing in between him and Caulfield. She didn't have any worry on her face at all, just a calm look of these-things-happen.

"Do you remember what my father used to do on his little pleasure cruises?" Mariana asked.

"Of course. I've got gallons of chum in the freezer." He reached out with his elbow to lean on the bar, and missed. Mariana stifled a laugh.

"Then maybe it's just what the doctor ordered."

"We gonna play with the big toys?" Maya asked.

"If you want," he muttered, trying to regain his composure.

"I want."

Rabbit looked for Jennifer, just for the sake of looking, and saw her only making a few glances in his direction. Fuck her, then. He reached for one of the three shots, but Maya snatched it before he could. Mariana grabbed the second one, leaving only the third.

"You're among friends, Nick," Maya said. "You don't need any more."

He just stared at her, wondering if he should be mad, but when she scooted the last shot glass over to Caulfield and laid a wad of pesetas on the bar to pay with, she winked at him.

Mariana and Maya cast off the lines and the Capriole rumbled out of her slip. The night was clear, the sea calm, and the girls came up to join their host on the bridge immediately. Trolling out into the Mediterranean, where the only light was the gibbous moon in the star-spattered sky, they sat in silence. It was a beautiful night, far away from the neon distractions, the only music coming from the wind and the lapping of the waves. After smoking a few bidis in peace, Rabbit weighed anchor and went below to get what, after a few quick phone calls, had once been DJ Igneous.

"How often does he get like this?" Maya asked.

"My dad said every now and then. Rabbit's just one of those guys. He gets sad once in a while."

"Doesn't surprise me. That happens to everyone who tries to buy happiness. His clothes, this boat, all this great stuff..."

"He and my dad used to be really good friends. So alike."

An uncomfortable silence settled over them, and they remembered what may have not been the good ol' days, but would definitely be missed. What would the world be like when they returned to it? The whole city would be different for Maya, and Mariana would find a sad home with just Mama and Abuela—in New York, of all places. No more D'ingo, no more Papa, no more Evan.

Then the anger clicked back on, like another line that had been put on hold, and they both saw the sheer stupidity of what had happened, all that pain and death, all because two pieces of shit tried to rip off Evan and Domingo. Kendrick and fucking Antwan, may they rot in hell. All this, because of them.

Rabbit came out onto the cockpit with two large buckets, pried the lids off, and up-ended them over the port and starboard sides. The blood and entrails were frozen, but they still stank, making the girls wrinkle their noses as they came down the ladder. The warm water would thaw out the splashing gore before too long.

"That jacket you had on last night," Maya asked. "Was that something you killed yourself?"

"Yep. Why, you want one?"

"Sure, a girlie jacket."

"Then let's go fishing and get you one."

Rabbit let them choose from a selection of handguns, since they didn't want to lose anything heavier overboard like *somebody* they used to know had. Maya got a strange look in her eyes as she hefted the .357 Magnum—the look of a little wounded girl who just realized that she was dangerous. In her hand, she held enough power to take a rapist's head off, with one finger. With this, she could make anyone back down and get the fuck out of her apartment, so she could cry in peace.

She must've been staring for some time before Mariana shouted "There's one!" Rabbit shined his ridiculously strong flashlight at the triangular fin, illuminating the shark's whole body. Thumbing the safety off, Mariana took aim and unloaded at the shark, the bullets kicking splashes all around it. She even hit it a few times, but it wriggled away and swam off.

"Shit, I scared him away!"

"His friends'll eat him," Rabbit assured her. These weren't stray cats to him. They were bullies. They deserved to die. Maya gasped.

"Ohhh shit. And here they come now."

The night was alive with gunfire, the echoes rolling back and bright purple after-images hanging before their eyes in triple exposures. As their frenzied prey thrashed about in the water with bullets tearing through them, they saw even more come to feast on the spilt blood. Instead of stopping to reload, the girls just switched guns. The joy of killing took hold of them, and it wasn't long before they said Fuck it, and grabbed the AR-15s.

Emptying entire magazines within seconds, they sprayed the sharks mercilessly, Maya on the port side, Mariana starboard, with Rabbit shooting stragglers off the stern. Every kick of their weapons shot jolts of obscene pleasure up their arms, every round that tore its way through those thrashing engines of destruction a nail hammered into their private Walls. Mariana had done this before, but Maya was screaming with childlike delight. The stench of death somehow became a fragrance she breathed in deeply, finally understanding what Will Danaher had tried to explain. The purely elemental joy of slaughter.

It was better than sex.

So much better.

When the last sharp crack rang out and its echo faded away into nothing, her knuckles were still white, the trigger still tight against the handle. Her face was split by a Cheshire Cat grin when Rabbit pried the AR-15 out of her hands. Mariana was already cleaning up, gathering all the spent casings off of the teak.

"Go fix yourself a drink," Rabbit said, his face also flushed with excitement, his own fangs bared like hers were. She couldn't speak, could only nod quietly and strut into the salon while Mariana put the guns in their cases and Rabbit brought out his gaff. Together, they hauled the best shark up out of the water and dragged it into the cockpit, where Rabbit started to skin and clean it with his huge Rambo knife.

Oblivious, Maya sat on the couch inside, scribbling furiously on a yellow writing pad she'd found. Writing songs.

They sat up and talked all night. In the morning, after taking all of Maya's measurements, Rabbit had gone to a leather tailor with bundles of sharkskin, and then to an artist with jaws and teeth to make a necklace and the coolest-looking dreamcatcher ever conceived. The necklace would not be the typical shark tooth on a string, but actual jewelry with more meaning than just pretty stones could have, and the skins… there was enough for much more than a jacket. The tailor would make the finest leather jeans out of them and several of those halter tops that looked so damned hot on the right girl.

When Mariana had mentioned going home soon, Maya had looked sadly at Rabbit, and he knew that Coquina had nothing for her anymore. He told her she could stay if she wanted, have an apartment, and take the earlier conversation seriously. That drunken alliance formed with Treble and Caulfield.

"I don't owe you any lies," he said. "I don't just go around shooting my mouth off to make people happy for a moment, then pretend to forget about it. Ouroborus Records can be real."

"That wasn't all talk?"

"Hell, no! We'll have a studio and you can start ATF, or whatever you want to call your clothing line."

"It sounds too good to be true."

"Well, that's what I do for a living. You don't have to settle for an ordinary life, and no, I'm not trying to buy your friendship."

"You're really a great guy, Jared. Don't ever tell yourself that you're not. You've been really great to us, and I don't mean just money-wise. I mean…"

"Doing my job, Maya. That's all."

They talked about everything. Life, where they'd been, what they'd done, and what they thought about it. They were, all three of them, truly honest about themselves for the first time. No group therapy, no hugging, just honesty and friendship. Rabbit admitted who he was inside, and Maya convinced him that there was no better type of person than a nerd at heart.

According to her, the original caste system they'd come up with in India had only four separate categories for people to fit into, and back then it worked out fairly well. After they came up with a fifth class, the untouchables, and changed the segregation to being hereditary, they went hogwild until they ended up with the three thousand-something they have today. But for a while there were only the manual laborers, the producers who told them what to do, the administrators who told *them* what to do, and finally the seers. None of these people would mingle because their very nature made it impossible for them to understand each other. Workers couldn't grasp what administrators said, and administrators couldn't believe that workers were so stupid. At the top were the seers, who, well, saw. They were the enlightened ones who had that illusive gift of understanding, who lived apart and pursued the arts, and studies, and philosophy.

"In Western society, our castes are less clearly defined, but observed with every bit as much scrutiny. God forbid someone from one caste try to hang out with someone from another. Just look at high school, for Christ's sake. Or read Eckhard Tolle. He said something about the realization that you're different from everybody else forces disidentification from your socially-conditioned thought and behavior patterns, automatically raising your level of consciousness above that of the unconscious majority. I think being an outsider makes life hard, but also places you at an advantage where enlightenment is concerned.

"I like to think that I, a nerd at heart, might be a seer," Maya said. "Because I see things as they really are. Long ago, in my speech class, the teacher told me to picture the audience naked to overcome my own shyness. So I did. I saw them as thirty skeletons sitting at desks, wrapped in meat, all slowly ticking towards their expiration dates. Under their skin, that is all they were. Behind their sneering lips and contemptuous eyes were just bone, nerves, and tissue. Oh sure, they were all unique, but that loses its novelty when it's *everybody* being unique. I started seeing everybody as just an organism who moves around, eats and sleeps, eventually dies, and in dying is forgotten. Just like me. Once you put that into perspective, what one of them calls you doesn't matter at all.

"But with that comes fatalism, if you're not careful. The futility of it all can swallow you whole. It is the enlightenment that leads to madness. Sunsets may be pretty, but that's only because cloud moisture and carbon and hydrogen molecules block out the blues and greens of the spectrum, and beach sunsets are only prettier because salt particles kicked up by crashing waves block everything except red. Remember when you were young enough to still believe that that scimitar of a moon was following you as you peered at it out the backseat window of your parents' car...like a book you've read before, you know the ending but you keep reading as if you don't. Just like knowing that one day you'll die, but you keep on living as if you never will. You don't think of the moon as some scarred derelict rock in our orbit, pimpled and pockmarked, and romantic only at the *vast* distance we see it from. You think of it as something mystical, and you live as if you actually matter in the Grand Scheme of Things.

"History speaks of many people who some called god-spoken

and others called insane, because they rejected what they finally saw as transparent. Instead of either, use this to your advantage. See all others as warm skeletons and you will not be blinded by what they cover themselves with. Never allow yourself to be put down by some temporary voice from a temporary body. And know that your own death is coming, sooner or later, but inevitably, and nothing you do will stop it, or grant you any continuation afterwards. You cannot get credit in Heaven by showing Saint Peter your pussy scorecard, or your high school trophy collection, or your Oscar or Grammy. All you *can* do is make sure, before you die, that you weren't the same pointless skeleton as everyone else.

"I forgot all this when..." Her voice trailed off and she exchanged glances with Mariana. "Well, somehow my perspective got screwed up and I forgot all this for a little while, but what you said the other day..."

"Yeah, whatever," he said, dismissing the uncomfortable subject with a careless wave of his hand. To keep her from continuing in that vein he reminded her that she had never explained the pineapple juice reference, and the suspense was killing him, so she told him that every food ingested affects the taste of your "sweet nectar." Salty food makes ejaculations, both male and female, especially salty. A lot of garlic makes you downright nasty. Pineapple juice will counteract just about everything, but certain cures work better in some instances. After drinking lots of beer, following it with lots of citrus won't sit well, but a chocolate bar will, and the improvement it makes in your "personal intimate flavor" is dramatic.

Also, the people who commonly eat seafood or dishes with lots of garlic, vinegar, et cetera, and have for many centuries—namely, the French, Italians, and Greeks—were not just the pioneers of great food and wine, but also lovemaking. If anyone would notice the difference in their lovers' personal, intimate flavors after eating certain foods, it would be them. So, trial and error established the rules of what to drink along with what meals, not *just* because they were pleasant to the palate at the time, but *afterward* as well.

"Who told you this?" Rabbit asked.

"No one. I thought of it myself."

"You made this all up?"

"No, I realized it. There's a difference. And if you don't believe me that I've conducted exhaustive research to come to this conclusion, both with men and women, you can try experimenting yourself."

"What, with you two? Okay, let's each open up a different bottle right now. I'll take the Pepsi challenge between the both of you in the name of science, and you can fight over who gets to sample me."

They both burst out laughing.

"No, come on! It's for a worthy cause."

"Keep your shirt on, Rab," Maya said, still laughing. "The best way, I've found, is to sample your own after different meals. That way, you always know the conditions and have an unbiased opinion."

"What do you mean, sample your own?"

"Well, masturbate. Duh."

"I don't do that."

"Oh, right. You don't. Everybody says that, you know, that everybody else does, but not *them*. Oh, no, not *me*. I thought we were being honest, here."

"I am. I have never done that. Not once."

"And I'm supposed to believe that?"

"Well, it wasn't easy growing up that way, my hormones going crazy without release, but I worried that if I satisfied myself I would stop producing the pheromones and excess testosterone I'd need to attract all the girls I never managed to get anyway. And also, I was afraid I'd like it too much, and get addicted to the rush of endorphins I could have at any time. On top of that, masturbators miss out on very entertaining dreams. So, I abstained. And as a consequence, I ran around consumed with lust for every girl I laid eyes on, always falling in and out of love, so testosterone-charged that I was the most temperamental little bastard, getting into fights with every motherfucker who called me—" He caught himself, realized he'd gone too far, and changed the subject. The sudden new direction was not lost on them.

He never told Maya about the cure for HIV, which he had already administered earlier that night with one of his tiny syringes, distracting her with an artfully executed pickpocket stumble against her. After the antidote, a rival virus that fed on the HIV, had killed off the plague inside her and then died itself with nothing left to feed upon, he would suggest that she take another test, just to be sure. It would take some convincing, but the look on her face when

515

she unfolded the results and saw the 'negative' stamped on it would be more than priceless. She would insist on a battery of tests, and once she was sure, he'd simply tell her that the hospital must've mixed up the blood samples.

These things happen.

Gross negligence, malpractice, and needless cruelty, but an accident. The relief on her face, he wouldn't miss it for the world.

And maybe she'd marry him.

Maybe.

He looked forward eagerly to a long and drawn-out courtship, something old fashioned. In this vulgar, uninhibited age, it would take their inability to touch to give them real romance: the façade of decorum with hidden exchanges; the longing, wistful gazes; the illicit kiss. A sad resistance that would make sexual fulfillment, when it finally came, so much more appreciated.

"There was a book I read—" Maya began. Rabbit remembered that they'd been talking, and shook his head to clear it, scolding himself to pay attention.

"Bless my stars! Imagine that! Maya read a book," Mariana teased.

"Fine, one of the zillion books I read, the hero is this poor kid that gets bullied a lot, and he realized that (and I quote) the power to cause pain is the only power that matters, the power to kill and destroy, because if you can't kill then you are always subject to those who can, and nothing and no one will ever save you. Unquote. I didn't believe it, though, because I always thought there was something called basic human decency. I used to think logic and respect meant something."

"Sadly, no," Rabbit had said. "When it comes right down to it, you have to be able to kill those sharks somehow. There's no reasoning with them. But in *Ender's Game*—I read that book too, by the way—it shows you that if you aren't strong enough to fight the bullies off, you can still survive. You've got to use your brain, though. Put your mind to it, and you can find a way to fight back, even without violence. I don't want you to think the only way is to get a gun, because that opens you up for even more trouble. Prison..."

"So, what then?"

"Disciples. You can get so many people to support and defend you that they become an army, and they don't even know that's what they are. Look at men like Bismarck, Lenin, Thomas Paine,

Hitler, all of those great demagogues. They managed to stir up nations, making those people want what they wanted them to want, just by saying it the right way at the right time."

"But what forum is there to accomplish any of this? The only way to speak out is on a political soapbox, and the lemming-brained masses don't pay attention to politics."

"But they *do* listen to music. You remember those monsters you had your little misadventure with? They don't read, they don't watch CNN, and they sure as hell don't discuss any civil issues, but they have *hate* for everyone who isn't just like them. That is because they have been programmed to hate who the rappers they listen to want them to hate. Ever notice how even the most ignorant dumbfucks you see all feel strongly about a few things that they know very little about? Guess why."

"But you can barely understand the words!"

"You don't have to. All you have to do is like the music. Once this guy has your attention, then he can appear on MTV or in some magazine interview and say whatever he wants, and you will listen."

"Shit. I've noticed that."

"And not just in the music industry, I'll bet. In Hollywood, and all it represents: movies, fashion, culture. In church, too."

"Definitely."

"So you can see where I'm going with this?"

"I think I can."

"Good. So, win over everyone in Audienceland. You can't do it overnight, but you *can* start now. Speak out, raise an army of followers, and before you know it, a random spark will ignite rage between them and your enemies. Just stand back, and let what happens happen. Let Nature take its course."

"That's a little too optimistic, don't you think?"

"Machiavelli said that sometimes you must be like the prudent archer. If your enemy is too far away, aim much higher than you think you should, and you'll get the bastard."

"Aim high."

"Don't worry. You will be one of many. There are so many of us out there, stirring up our different vats of shit and raising a stink that soon cannot be ignored. But we don't have anyone in music yet, that I know of. We need a good rabble-rouser for those who don't pay any attention to anything but music."

"But you *can* have one!" Mariana said, leaning forward suddenly, her eyes wide and bright. "We have a friend, this girl that my brother was going with, who fronted a band. She was so full of rage at the world, and it came out so well in her songs that even her enemies had to stop and reconsider what they did!"

"Who is she?"

"Shaitan Risingsun. Her band is called Warpath, and right now they're doing a circuit of Indian reservations. They don't have enough money to cut any records, but they play live in bars and at powwows all the time. They are hugely popular, they just haven't found an A&R man."

"They have now. If you say they're good, I trust you."

"You mean you could do it?"

"If it will stir up the people, and do something to help the friend of my friend, you're damn right I can. And will."

He turned to Maya and winked happily.

"Ouroborus Records just got bigger."

"So hey, where'd you go, psycho boy?"

Rabbit stifled a laugh, an unpleasant one.

"Fishing."

"Oh, in the middle of the night?" Jennifer didn't believe him.

"I guess I needed some time off."

"Those roses for me?"

"What, these? No, I didn't get these for anyone. I'm just holding them for a friend."

"What's going on, Nickie?"

"I can't tell you, it's a big secret."

"You're with someone else, aren't you?"

"Not yet."

"Jesus!"

"Hey, I'm kidding. Look, they're for Maya. She's been working for two days at the studio and she's just cut her first record. These are celebration slash congratulations roses."

"Long-stemmed red ones?"

"They were all out of yellow."

"A dozen of them?"

"No, thirteen. It's a lucky number for me."

"Thirteen."

"Yep."

"And in the parcels?"

"A few things I had made for her."

"Hmm. You haven't had anything made for *me*."

"I must've something in my ear. Could you repeat that?" The ice in his tone was almost as startling as the sudden blaze in his eyes. He'd already put her on a rear burner, but now she was officially off and out of the picture. Maybe even shark bait.

"Um…I was just…no, look, all I meant was—"

"You're fired."

"What?"

"Apparently, I was dead fuckin' wrong about you. I thought you were different." She flinched, and, feeding off it, his voice grew sharper. "Here you are, having what you told me was the time of your life, not because you had any reason to deserve it, but because two friends of mine were gang-banged, *raped*, and as I try to reward them for making progress, you want to be selfish and ungrateful. Maya has finally snapped out of the rut she was in—fuck, she's got *AIDS*, goddammit—and you think I'm trying to get in her pants? No wonder no one loves you, Jen!"

Ooh, touched a nerve there.

"I haven't seen anyone this self-centered in a long, goddamned time! Shit, since the last time I turned on a TV!"

She looked up at him, her eyes questioning.

"Some bitch on a talk show, whining about her *feelings*. But her complaining doesn't even hold a candle to this audacity of yours. Haven't I given you enough? All I can give her are party favors, material things, but you! Shit, don't get me started on what I've wasted on you!"

She was hurt, on the verge of tears, her face twisted by the pain of her insides knotting up. It felt so good to see.

"What a fucking hypocrite! You go on about bulimics, but you are no better than the most pathetic of them, that you can accuse me of paying more attention to people with real problems than I do to my own girlfriend. Ooh, the ultimate crime! Real compassion! But you're right, what was I thinking?"

So he was fudging the truth a little bit. A little license taken during emotional abuse was permissible in his eyes. Sometimes he had to stretch the truth a little to push the right buttons and put someone in their place.

Many girlfriends would have split immediately after the first time Bipolar Jared surfaced, but all had hung on, thinking this was a once-only venting of pent-up frustrations. Infatuated with the Happy Rabbit, they stuck around after the second and third times also, stubbornly trying to nurture and to soothe whatever haunted him, each one hoping to be the one who could catch him as he fell.

He could never explain to himself later why he had taken so much pleasure in hurting people that way. Why he had exposed them, the little personal imperfections, quirks, and fears that they tried to hide from everyone else, and even themselves. It was as if he just sat back and let his mouth take over, marveling at how well he could squash someone like a bug with nothing more than words. Of course, he felt terrible afterwards. Always. When he replayed the looks of horror and misery, he could never understand why he had caused them.

But it was a sport, and he always triumphed.

Now, leaving Jennifer on the sidewalk where she had stopped him, he strode away with his spirits soaring. The wickedness in his eyes was gone in only a few moments, replaced by the minor annoyance of what his French teacher had called *esprit d'escalier*. Thinking, shit, I forgot to point out how lousy she is in bed. Oh well. I'll try to remember next time.

Clingy, needy, paranoid…Christ, where do I find these girls?

Damn, she's crying.

Don't turn around. Don't look.

Fuck, what the hell did I do that for?

Man, I'm an asshole.

When he finally got to the studio, he surprised Maya out on the balcony. Her smile washed away all the feelings of guilt.

"Roses! For me?"

"Mm-hmm. I picked them myself."

"Oh, Rabbit. You are such a sweetie." She kissed him on the cheek.

"And here, put on a little fashion show for me."

"What?"

It was like Christmas, watching her open the parcels and gush over what she'd found. He wished so badly that there could be a ring for her to find, but it was just too early. God, how long had it been? A week? That's it? But much can happen…

The sharkskin was lined with satin on the inside, so comfortable, so perfectly fitting as she did her little catwalk sashay and stop/drop shoulder/turn for Rabbit that she didn't even want to take them off and try on something else. The gray jeans revealed the most arousing curves he'd ever seen, the one shoulder halter-top hiding something he ached to even glimpse. The necklace and earrings of silver-bound fangs had come out well, and the shoes…

The shoes.

God, those heels. The elegant ankle, the finely-sculpted arch, the perfectly-shaped toes. Her muscular legs, the supple rear end, firm, the flat stomach with just a subtle and sexy hint of ribs. Her breasts peppered with a faint sprinkle of freckles. A beautiful throat. Oh, God, her face.

Oh shit, she's staring.

Oh *shit*, whoops, *I* was staring.

"You okay, Jared?" A faint smile. "See something you like?"

He swallowed, hard, his mouth suddenly dry.

Pause. One of those long silences that revealed much more than words can. She frowned.

"Um, I'm sorry, Jared."

He could only stare up at her, shy and embarrassed by having nothing clever to say, and she just stood there with her hip cocked.

"Please don't look at me that way." Her voice was quiet, and sad.

"I can't help it," he mumbled.

"Don't do this. I'm damaged goods. You can't have me. *Nobody* can have me, and this'll only make it worse."

"There is medication you can take…"

"It won't cure me. It'll only hold it at bay, and trust me, you don't want to anchor yourself to me. I can't allow you to do that, just give up every other possible mate for a doomed mercy relationship. I can't let you do that. I won't."

"It won't be like that." This wasn't even close to the way he'd planned it.

"It will. You're a great guy. Don't settle for me."

"You're not someone people can settle for. People *pray* for women like you. If you'll have me, I won't let something so small I can't even see it get in my way. If you'll have me."

"Oh God, please don't do this."

"Do what? Be crazy about you? Can't help it."

"Get my hopes up. You could never stay with me, and why would you? You'd end up going somewhere else to get your rocks off, we both know it, and that would just break my heart."

The phone rang, startling them both. It was the bat phone. Rabbit let it ring, just looking up at her from the couch, until she turned and went to the fridge.

"Speak."

She got herself a bottle of Nepenthe, which she'd become addicted to in the past few days, and wasn't trying to eavesdrop, but he snagged her attention with "—I'm with her friend right now."

Tense silence while she listened to him listening.

"Oh, really? I'm not sure whether she wants to know that or not...no, they're both doing real well, I think."

Teresa? Who else would it be? And what didn't "she" want to know? Was he even talking about her?

"No, I don't know much about him. Mariana said something in passing about this guy, but...oh, I see. Oh."

She twisted the cap off the bottle and the little kitchenette filled with a smell like carbonated cheap perfume. Drinking deeply, she felt it glow inside her.

"Do you want to talk to her? Okay. What was his name again?" Pause. "Evan? Right—"

The bottle slipped from nerveless fingers and shattered on the tiles.

"New York?" Mariana gasped. "The blue fuck was he doing *there?"*

"I don't know, but he's with your mom again," Maya said, chain-smoking. She took him back, and she wanted us to know."

"Oh, yeah. I really care. That traitor..."

"Rabbit said your mom didn't even know why he split, but Pedro understood immediately and vouches for him. Won't tell, though."

"So, what? Everything's supposed to be all better now? Just like that?"

"I don't know. I don't even know where he's been for the past month, or whether I even care or not."

"Well, what's going on there?"

"A new restaurant. I don't have details."

"In New York, though? Jesus."

"And Rabbit said he was supposed to go there and help put something together. I don't know what, but he's going when we're ready, he said."

"And when is that gonna be, you think? We came here for a vacation, and we've only been here, what? A week? Not even."

"Well…I don't think I'm going back."

Mariana just looked at her, waiting for an explanation and not bothering to ask for it. They both felt it then; newly dumped people feel phantom lovers the way new amputees feel phantom limbs. The awkward pause was long until Maya broke it.

"Rabbit was apparently serious about getting me a place here, and…"

"Beats the shit out of the Apple, I suppose."

"Well…wait a minute. Don't make me feel guilty here."

"I know, I know. It's just…"

"We're girls, Mari. Both of us. We can't try to use the same tricks on each other that we use on guys. You know the situation, *I* know the situation, do we really have to beat around the damn bush?"

"What do you mean?"

"You know exactly what I mean. I'm not going home to Coquina, since it's just not home anymore, and I'm certainly not going to that godforsaken city. We can keep in touch, but I don't owe you any lies. It's that time, Mari."

"Hon, you're even starting to *talk* like Rabbit."

"Shit. I am, aren't I?"

"Okay, so I guess we've got the obligatory bush-beating out of the way. Now, we can be honest. Of course you should stay here! My God, Maya, you're just being handed a chance at stardom, and if you throw it away, you're out of your mind! It'll cost a few bucks to have all your stuff shipped here, but I think I can convince my mom to cover it for you. Don't even bother telling your folks, because they'll just try to talk you out of it."

"I know. They were even against me coming here with you. If they had their way, I'd be locked up in the closet where no big bad wolves can ever find me."

"If Rabbit wants to get you started with your music, your own clothing line, and a place to live, I don't see anything to argue about. Jump on it. Luck like that doesn't come around every day."

"No…" she muttered, thinking about what she hadn't mentioned. The words exchanged, before and after the phone call. After she'd been told that Evan was back, and she filled Rabbit in on what that meant.

"I met him about a year ago at a nightclub called Swak. That band Mari told you about? Warpath? I had gone to see them play, and the lead singer had been dating Evan's best friend. Well, I was sitting at the bar with my bottle of wine—"

"What flavor?" Rabbit asked, wondering what food she'd recently eaten and was trying to counteract the "sweet nectar" effect of.

"Pinot Noir," she told him.

"What were you wearing?"

"Ha! You're kidding me, right?"

"Do I look like I'm kidding? I demand to know."

"Um, okay. Well, one of the shirts I'd made, I think. Some jeans I had batiked. Pair of platforms."

"Have I seen this shirt?"

"Yes, it's the one with the gigantic fractal paisleys on it. I remember now."

"Damn, that one's tight on you."

"Yeah, I bought it small and then shrunk it, so it would only button in the middle but still cover my boobs. Cleavage and midriff exposed, and it didn't look slutty—at least, not as slutty as all those Britney wannabes look in their super tight lowrider jeans that show off the other kind of cleavage. You know what I mean. Intentional plumber's cracks? They think that's sexy, looking like they're on their way to fix a U-bend somewhere."

Rabbit laughed. "I know *exactly* what you mean. And I've seen a few aping that "gangsta" style with the baggy pants hanging so low you can see their underwear, only these little chippies had them riding so low that the top button must've been rubbing against their clits when they walked, and their panic button red thong underwear was hiked up to arch over their hip bones, flossing their asses. They weren't T-backs, they were *y's*."

"Oh God, I've seen it. They call them side moons, for whatever reason. Can't they have any dignity?"

"Apparently not. They've got "whore" written all over their faces. And "stupid" stamped on their foreheads."

"It's probably just to piss off their parents."

"You don't think it's to show off to anyone looking how little they think of themselves, how far they're willing to go in their pathetic need for attention?"

"Did you change your mind about wanting to hear the story?"

"I'm sorry, please continue."

Evan came out of the crowd in front of the stage, a young guy, good looking, dressed well. She didn't find out until much later that he was only seventeen with a fake ID, a high school dropout working for his best friend's dad, a Brazilian drug dealer. By then, she'd already fallen for him, a charmer six years younger than her.

He stopped short when he saw her, as most guys did. Usually, they looked with startled disapproval at her elongated earlobes, but he didn't see any difference between Ethiopian, Mesoamerican, or Asian fetishistic decoration and modern piercings. Same thing, as far as he was concerned. What he was openly startled by was appreciation of her beauty.

He recovered himself and came to sit on the barstool next to hers. She ignored him, knowing he would try to hit on her in a minute. It was *how* he did it that made the difference.

After ordering a beer, getting carded, and still getting the longneck, he sat there scraping the label off with his thumbnail, fidgeting, feigning nervousness. She continued to ignore him, watching the band play. Finally, he reached into his jacket pocket and fished out a small book, flipped through it. His prop.

She didn't mean to glance over, and she knew she shouldn't, but she did anyway. The title on the book's spine was "1,001 Best Pickup Lines." She rolled her eyes and looked away again. After a short while, he put the book down, assumed a Suave expression and demeanor, turned to her and spoke in an exaggeratedly "cool" voice.

"Excuse me, I seem to have injured my penis."

A moment passed, Maya staring straight ahead. Then, the awful implications of that statement hit her, and also the doubt that she had heard him correctly. She frowned, opened her eyes wide, and blinked slowly, shaking her head as if to clear it. Evan checked the book again, nodded, and resumed.

"Would you mind massaging it until the swelling goes down?"

She scrunched her eyes tight and looked away, not wanting him to see her crack a smile. Evan pretended disappointment.

"Shit, it didn't work? Hold on." He looked up another. "Okay, here's one: Honey, you must be wearing space panties."

She looked back at him, eyebrows raised questioningly.

525

"Because your ass is *out of this world*." He dropped the book and snapped the fingers of both hands, making little guns out of them and shooting at her with a big, goofy grin.

She snorted a brief chuckle, and he put on a Forlorn look.

"No, huh? Hang on." He memorized another one, took a swig of his beer, and stood up. "I'll start over."

He walked back over to the crowd, leaving her shaking her head, watching him go. Turning around, he put a predatory Slick face on and, with people watching in curiosity/contempt, he walked back with the kind of swagger that wannabe cool dudes practice. It was a slow motion runway model strut, only with lots of swaying and shoulder action. He struck a pose when he got to her, dramatically lit a cigarette, and took a drag as if he enjoyed it way too much, held it a moment, and Exhaled. She almost laughed, but contained herself. Barely. He deepened his voice and laid it on thick.

"Do you believe in love at first sight...or do I have to walk by again?"

She fell out, laughing in a giggly high falsetto.

"Let me see that book," she gasped as soon as she could, and they took turns reading to each other. She had a good time, and he joked with her about this and that until it was time to go. He invited her to the band party afterwards, of which she was skeptical, but he turned out to really be the singer's boyfriend's buddy, and he was fun to be with the whole time without actually putting the moves on her. He kept it friendly, and it worked.

She did not sleep with him for the first month, only ever letting him get to second base. Even though she was a sex fiend, she had really only ever slept with six people. Four guys and two girls. He had fifty-one notches on his belt even with the age difference.

His work took a nasty turn, though, almost a year later, and he brought it home with him. Gangsters came looking for him, the night she told him she was pregnant and wouldn't run away with him, and he abandoned her. When they came for him, they found her instead.

She and the Brazilian kid's sister, Mariana, whom she and Evan had been sharing, were each raped by over thirty men in a house far out of town. She lost the baby, and contracted HIV. And there you have it.

She fell silent, her story ending abruptly. The studio became heavy with grief, and Jared took her in his arms. She resisted a mo-

526

ment, just long enough to realize his intent was not romantic, realize this was a Hug, and she hugged him back.

Then, the tears came.

He held her tightly and stroked her hair as sobs racked her whole body, letting her crumple against him and let out all the pain she'd bottled up inside her. She didn't know how long it lasted, but it was quite a while. Long enough for someone, either Treble or Caulfield, to open the door, stop short, and quietly leave. She never knew how good it would feel to just be held, and cry until the misery was gone.

When she was finally finished, she stepped back and looked at the mess she'd made of his shirt, looked up to apologize, and was startled to see his eyes, though dry, as puffy and red as hers.

"How does that song go?" he asked quietly. "You and me against the world?"

She shook her head, then hesitated, and nodded.

"I just want to be with you, Maya. I don't care if I never make love again, so you'd never need to worry about me running around on you. There aren't very many of our kind out there. I can't just give up the best one there is to go looking for another."

"But you'll regret it, someday. I know you will."

He shook his head. "No. Never. I could never settle for anyone else."

"But I won't live very long—" she muttered.

"All the more reason for me to get you now."

"But what about later, though? When I'm a stick figure? What then?"

"We'll jump off that bridge when we come to it."

They had a few drinks together, him gradually becoming conscious again of how good she looked in her new outfit, the other parcels still sitting in the bathroom where she had changed. What she was wearing now was only the beginning of the fashion show. She noticed the bulge beginning to swell underneath his trousers, and tried to ignore it. The memory of what she'd seen in the limo ride flashed in her head, but she shut the mental trapdoor it had sprung from. Instead, she tried to diffuse his want.

"Have you ever been in love?" she asked.

He looked away, swallowing hard, uncomfortable, which was exactly what she'd wanted him to do. They sat on the couch, facing each other, she with one knee pulled up and the ankle tucked underneath her. She waited.

"I've, um...I've thought I was. I always wanted to be, and I guess I was looking too hard."

"When was the last time?"

Ooh, touchy subject, judging from the shadow that passed briefly across his face. But he collected himself.

"A couple years ago," he said. "It still seems like yesterday, though."

"What was her name?"

"Hm," he grunted at the fossil of unforgotten hurt. "Well, I don't really know."

"You don't *know*? How could you think you love some—"

"She lied to me," he said coldly.

"Oh."

"She was an undercover agent. She seduced me to bring me in. It's a long story."

Pause. As long a pause as followed Maya's story.

"I have a portrait of her hanging in my house, in Taormina. For a while, I stared at it every day."

He thought for a moment, then killed the rest of his drink, got up to mix himself another.

Oops, Maya thought. Wrong topic to choose. She watched him while he messed around in the kitchenette, just to be doing something, and stared at his hands. It took a moment, but suddenly, something dawned on her. She stood, walked softly across the room to him.

She touched him, he froze. She gently took the bottle from his hand and set it down, taking that hand then into both of hers. They both stared at it, him feeling on fire by the warmth of her fingers.

"Your hands are small," she said softly.

He swallowed again, looked up at her face still down turned, and looked back at her hands on his.

"It's not that they're small...they're proportionate to the rest of your body...*most* of the rest—"

He jerked his hand away and turned his back on her. She reached around his waist, touched his thigh.

He stiffened, felt a stirring down within him.

"I just noticed that," she continued. "Why did you do it? What was it you didn't like about yourself?"

528

He gritted his teeth. Hissed through them.

"Don't make me say it. Drop it, Maya."

"No. Tell me. Be honest with me."

His teeth ground audibly.

"It was too small."

"Who said so?" Her voice so soft, so gentle.

"Everybody."

"Who?"

"Girlfriends."

"They would actually say that? They would?"

'No...'

"Then what did they say?"

"They didn't," he sighed.

"What, then?"

"It was the way they looked at it. The way they held it so carefully like they thought it would break off or something."

"Did they ever say anything?"

"They said...they said it was a good size."

Which all girls knew was a nice way of saying it was small. Maya turned him around slowly.

"Tell me how big it was."

His teeth grated again. He would not look at her.

"It can only get so much bigger with surgery. Two workable inches, the last I heard. And last I saw, you look plenty workable. So you can't have been small. Now tell me what your good size was. And look me in the eye when you say it."

It took a moment, but he did finally meet her eyes. He took a deep breath, feeling his face grow hot.

"Five inches," he said quickly, before he could stop himself. He expected a look of understanding, sympathy, maybe even pity, but was surprised when she frowned.

"*What?*"

"...You heard me."

"You had five inches and you thought that was *small?*"

"Um, it is, isn't it?"

"Oh, Christ, Jared, that's the average size for a white—"

"No, that's just what girls say so we'll feel better."

"The hell it is. Look, five inches is just fine."

"Then why did they act like it wasn't? And why did all those guys in school call me Skittledick? Why?"

"Those guys were all pretending that average was small so no one would suspect *theirs* were small. It's like when closet queers gay-bash. And any girl that can't be satisfied by five inches has obviously worn her own equipment out. Being a slut makes a girl lose her elasticity. So a normal sized guy feels inadequate inside of her because *she* is inadequate. You didn't need a new rooster, Jared, you needed a better class of girlfriend. One who at least did her Kegel exercises. Besides, if two people are meant to be together, why would all the pieces fit except for one?"

She stepped back and looked down at his pants, appraisingly. She looked for a long time, and Rabbit began to feel uncomfortable again. He felt as if she might affix a jeweler's loupe to her eye to better examine him. When she spoke, still looking down, her voice had gotten soft once more.

"You know, I always felt it was handier for a guy to have three, maybe four inches. It's less than that to reach the G-spot, and it's nice not to gag when I'm going down on it. Imagine something as big as you've got plunging down your gullet. Ewww, right?"

She looked back up at him, took his hand again.

"Come with me."

Leading him into the bathroom, she gently kicked the parcels and blossoms of tissue paper aside, clearing the way for him to stand in front of the full length mirror on the other side of the door. Standing behind him, she reached around with both hands and began to unbutton his shirt.

"What are you doing?" he asked, eyes wide.

"Shut up and don't move."

It looked to Rabbit like he'd grown another pair of arms that were handling his shirt while the normal arms hung at his sides. When the last button came undone, she pulled the shirt back off his shoulders. He unconsciously flexed his six-pack, the way all guys will. She pretended not to notice, the way all girls will. When her hands found his belt buckle, started working the other end toward it to make some slack, he was instantly hard. When his trousers finally dropped to the floor, he just stood there feeling stupid. She peered over his shoulder.

"You know what I see? Jared, look at your reflection. You know what I see? Not a hotshot playboy in flashy clothes, with a humongous rooster—a rooster that looks a bit more than two workable inches over five—I see a man. An organism, flesh and tissue and organs and bone, just like everyone else. Different sizes and shapes, some more visually appealing than others, but all essentially the same thing. What's different about you, Jared, is your soul. That is who you are. Not *this*. This is just clothing, the same as what's laying on the floor right now. This all is just my namesake, what the Hindus mean by illusion. When this shell grows old, grows soft and wrinkled and ready to be discarded, you will still be you. No matter what you may look like, you will always be the most beautiful man I have ever met."

She stepped away from him, kept backing up until she reached the shower. He turned to face her.

Shrugging off the jacket, folding it carefully, she draped it over the toilet tank. Sat down on the edge of the bathtub. Slid a finger inside each slingback of her sharkskin heels to ease her shapely, delicate feet out of them, and stood.

"This is all just the clothing we wear so we can recognize each other." She unfastened the button of her leather jeans, slowly slid the zipper down, put both hands into the waist to pry them down and away from her skin. Slipped them down her perfect legs to her knees. She was naked underneath them, as he had been. Smiling faintly, she grasped the hem of the left leg between the big and second toe of the right foot, tugged and stepped out of the sharkskin, repeating it with the other foot until she wore only her one shoulder halter top. She kicked the jeans away. Grabbing the top with both hands, she lifted it up over her head and set it on the jacket.

Rabbit stared, cotton-mouthed, at her magnificent body. He longed so desperately for her that he was willing to take his chances, put blind faith in the viriphage and hope that it had worked its magic already, but he knew she would never allow it.

"What you see is nothing," she told him. "It's temporary. You helped me to understand that, and now you must come to understand it. When we both shed our skins and change into new ones, hopefully we will be able to recognize each other in the next life. Until then, we have to make do with what we have.

"Have you injured your penis?" she asked, startling him. He frowned, standing there feeling stupid again with his pants around his ankles and his shoes still on.

"What?" he asked.

"Your penis. Does it hurt? Because it looks like it aches a bit. All red and pulsing."

He shifted his weight from one leg to the other.

"It, uh...(ahem) it does ache a bit, yes."

"Then maybe you should massage it a bit until the swelling goes down."

Rabbit gaped at her. She lightly touched her flat stomach with the fingertips of both hands, ran them slowly up to her breasts and over them, up along both sides of her throat and into her hair. Combing them through the long, dark curls, raising her mane up over her head with her eyes closed and pivoting slowly on the ball of one foot, turning around to show him her beautiful ass that looked so much like a peach ready to be bitten into.

"Touch yourself for me?" she asked, turning further to look at him through the triangle of space between her bent arm and her hair. He hesitated. Turning fully to face him again, she dropped her hair back down over her shoulders and ran her fingers back the way they had come, over her breasts, her flat stomach, her hips, to the dark triangle between her legs. Her fingers parted the lips and toyed with them, sliding over one another until they glistened, and she slipped the middle finger of one hand inside her. Two knuckles deep and curling back to touch her anterior wall.

"Please, Jared," she breathed. "Make me feel beautiful."

And he did.

Later, when they had showered together and he washed her shell as tenderly and thoroughly as he had Jennifer's, they dressed silently, then stared at each other for a long time. It was strange and awkward, and he hadn't yet decided how to feel about it. He'd been deflowered. This was a different kind of lost virginity, and the beginning of the strangest affair in his life, one where almost every tryst would be conducted over a telephone.

Abruptly, without a word, he took her face in his hands and kissed her once, then turned and left.

The door closing with a soft click leaving an oppressive emptiness behind him.

Silence.

The refrigerator clicked on and began to hum.

Somewhere, a dog barked.

And Maya began to cry.

Jolly Roger and Union Jack were happy to look after Maya

532

while Rabbit was gone, assuring her that he only had to tie up loose ends after he took the girls back to Florence, and would be back in less than no time. Meanwhile, she could stay with them until she found her own flat, and have an extra key made for the studio. She felt a little nervous, standing there on the edge of something new, but she lied about it when anyone asked.

It was a mystery to her why that Jennifer girl had so suddenly gotten all desperate and pathetic around Rabbit, but it was also none of her business. When she shot a questioning glance at him, Jared/Nick/Whatever just shrugged, but let slip a faint smile at some secret joke.

Dump her softly, she said to him silently, and from only seeing her eyes, he seemed to understand. He nodded.

"Terminal," he said, looking around the airport concourse. "What a reassuring name for a building."

Jennifer's sycophantic burst of laughter made all of them cringe with embarrassment for her. Mariana rolled her eyes and kissed Rabbit on the cheek.

"I'll see you at my new home," she murmured, and then loudly ordered him to take good care of Maya for her when he got back from Italy.

"But he'll be staying in Florence," Jennifer interrupted.

"She means months from now," Rabbit assured her. "When I come back just to check up on her." His tone was only subtly patronizing. He'd changed his mind about her; there was a lot of work to be done, but a little cultivation of her angst would definitely make her into someone useful.

Maybe even dangerous. But only time would tell.

Bianca was staring curiously at Rabbit, wondering about the changes that had come over him, not just in his attitude but in his appearance. He had stopped shaving a few days ago, and looked a bit scraggly. He had on faded blue jeans, a gray t-shirt, and a wrinkled button-down that looked like it was thrown on as an afterthought. Unimpressive sneakers. A worn baseball cap with a Quiksilver logo on it, the wave crashing over the mountain, reminiscent of Japanese art.

The luggage he'd brought from the Capriole was mismatched, not at all what she had expected a man of extravagance to have. He even had some of his things in a backpack, hanging by one strap from his shoulder. He looked completely unassuming. He looked...like a typical foreign exchange student returning to school in Florence.

Flying with them, back in Coach instead of First. Like someone who didn't want to stand out.

The weird girl with HIV and deformed ears took a colorfully gift-wrapped package out of a hemp sack on a string that served as her purse, and held it uncertainly. Rabbit frowned.

"A little something I had made for you," she said.

He looked at her shy smile and returned it, the both of them feeling like actors in a Hugh Grant movie. He took the present and put it under his arm. Leaned in and kissed her on the forehead. Turned around and walked off toward the duty-free, just to be doing something.

It had been seventeen minutes since Rabbit had gone to the lavatory up in First Class, fourteen since Jennifer had followed him. A few of the flight's more affluent passengers had stood impatiently outside the door for a little while until it became obvious what the holdup was, and swallowed their pride, condescending to relieve themselves in Business and Coach.

Bianca left her seat and went to the ones Rabbit and Jen had left, reached over the sleeping middle-aged doughboy in the aisle seat to grab the book in the middle one. A crumpled up ball of gift wrap lay on top of it, and when it rolled off as she lifted it, she saw a symbol stamped into the gray leather cover, an image of Cerberus, the three-headed dog that guards the gates of Hell in Greek mythology.

Maya had said something to Rabbit once about how she always thought that this dog, though scary to many, would still make a great pet for someone else, and if you treated him right, he'd lick your face with all three tongues. She'd said something cryptic then about that being like everybody, in a way, and then left him to wonder about it until he saw it stamped on the cover of this book.

534

The doughboy stirred underneath her and opened his eyes, found himself staring up at her and grinned lecherously. Gritting her teeth and baring them, she hissed *"Scusi,"* straightened, and carried the strange book back to her seat. The man craned his neck around to watch her go.

The book's covers were of a very rough leather, light gray mostly, but darkening toward the bottom, and on the back, a round hole with singed edges exposed the board underneath the thick skin. A high caliber bullet hole. She opened the book to the title page, the paper made to look time-yellowed and stained here and there. In Old English style lettering, crimson ink, was "Mayanomicon." A lipstick kiss underneath it, as red as blood.

She started flipping the pages.

The flight was half over. The skin of Jennifer's face was mashed against her reflection, a mist of breath fogging the mirror and starting to fade but immediately renewed. Her lips writhed back and her teeth clicked against the glass, again, and again. Her insides clenched in a sloppy rhythm of unfamiliarity, but she was learning.

The book had called them her constrictor vaginae muscles, what she clamped down on him with, flexing them as he pulled out, relaxing as he plunged back in. Its cold and clinically-dehumanizing name was the pubococcygeus, and the anterior wall of the vagina, the urethral sponge that he hammered brutally, that was the Gräfenberg Spot. The book was Maya's *grimiore*, everything she knew, what she'd learned from Kanchinatha, Vatsyayana, and Gedun Chopel, what she'd figured out for herself, everything. Printed out at a shop in Plaza Sa Riba from a data CD she had in one of her zip-up cases with all her music. He'd need it more than she would.

When Rabbit had unwrapped the present after takeoff and sat there staring at it, smiling faintly, Jennifer leaned in and peered over his shoulder. Asked him what it was.

"It's everything you don't do."

Snatching the book away, she picked a lesson at random and read it, eager to change for him.

"Are you in the Mile-High Club?" she asked when she was done. He lied and told her No. She bit her lip.

"I'll need to practice this."

It's usually the lavatory way in the back of the plane that new members use to join the Club, behind all the other passengers so that there is at least an attempt at discretion. And people wanting to pass unnoticed don't normally rub everybody's nose in their getting laid while the rest of them are strapped into uncomfortable seats and watching crappy movies, eating prefab meals and drinking shotglass-sized beverages. But sometimes, you just gotta.

Bianca shut the book, her thumb running over the bullet hole and tracing a circle around its edge wonderingly, like Doubting Thomas. She climbed back into the aisle and made her way forward to return it, hoping that old doughboy was asleep again, just as the red Occupied sign slid over to a green Vacant in the lavatory door. An old woman stepped back to make room and sneered disdainfully at Jen peeking out.

Jen swallowed, pretended she didn't care, and stepped out on legs that trembled light a newborn foal's. Rabbit followed, gazing down at the old woman with sleepwalker's eyes, smiled with only half of his mouth. Chuckled at her expression.

"Hey, we didn't miss the movie, did we?"

On their way to the New Market, the bazaar over which the Florentine Boar stood guard and got his snout rubbed in thanks, Rabbit and Jennifer stopped into a tabacchiao for cigarettes. They stood at the end of a line of tourists, students, and a few locals buying stamps, postcards, and newspapers, and Rabbit browsed absently among street maps and shit like that while Jen put on her headphones and listened to Depeche Mode sing something about her own personal Jesus. A few thumb twiddling moments passed.

Eventually, Rabbit lost interest and glanced around the small shop.

And froze.

Zero to sixty for him had slowed down to almost a full second since he grew up and chilled out a bit, but fury engulfed him instantaneously now. Blood rushing to his head stained his face crimson and made his eyes flame horribly, his fingers suddenly claws that dug into the air at his sides as if it was the man at the counter's neck. A shred of rational thought remained, and Rabbit knew he must not be seen, especially like this, so before anyone saw him he seized Jennifer by the belt and yanked her to him, planting his lips firmly on hers.

For an instant she resisted, but the surprise wore off quickly and her arms went about him. The Florentines in the tabacchaio grinned at each other, but the students and tourists either grunted in annoyance or muttered for them to get a room.

When Pete Gattoni took his change and turned around, saw what the grumbling was about, he rolled his eyes and walked out past the couple, unconcerned.

Rabbit watched him go, and smiled.

Feeling his lips spread against hers, Jennifer opened her eyes, saw him staring over her shoulder, and shuddered at the hate that boiled off of him. Shuddered half in fear and half in arousal. His blazing eyes slid over to meet hers, and he whispered brief instructions. She nodded, almost imperceptibly.

He left, followed Gattoni through the crowds, wondering how the bastard could be here, what he was doing. A visitor? A student enrolled? He doubted that, as the ugly fuck wasn't much of a student back in high school, so why be in college over ten years after? He could be here getting in touch with his roots, maybe. Fuck, no telling. But Rabbit had to know before he acted. Motive was everything to him. Investigators couldn't just shrug away a lack of evidence at the scene. They looked deeply, and Rabbit obsessed over leading them on wild goose chases away from him. It seemed, to him, the proper way.

Keeping a respectable distance behind Gattoni, Rabbit followed him to Il Duomo, watched him window shop at all the Piazza stores with their ridiculously marked up prices that prey upon tourists too lazy to explore and find realistic rates. At one gelateria, Gattoni stared a little too long at a beautiful girl stacking triple scoops of ice cream onto waffle cones and handing them over the counter to eager hands. The girl must have felt his eyes on hers, glanced up at him through the plate glass and her smile faded.

Gattoni looked away guiltily and marched off to a table outside a nearby cafe, sat down and lit a cigarette. Rabbit wandered into the gelateria, glanced at the selections' names printed across the transparent sneeze cover, and saw a bucket of ice cream he'd never heard of before. *Bacio*, with several shades of brown, chunks of black and swirls of white, meant "kiss" and looked like a popular flavor, so he waited in line for it. Memorizing everything the girl said and every way she said it, every cadence.

When he was next, she looked at him expectantly, eyes questioning.

"Un bacio, per favore," he said. The instant her eyes widened and smile froze, Rabbit realized how stupid he'd been. It was like the commercials where the wife of a cereal-eating man asked what was for breakfast and he said "Nut 'n Honey." Preoccupied with her stalker, the girl—Letizia, according to her name tag— had easily misunderstood, and now his face would be stuck in her mind. Shit.

"Il sapore," he said belatedly. The flavor. *"Il sapore del gelato. Il Bacio."*

She closed her eyes and laughed silently. Worse, a few others who'd overheard laughed as well. More who'd remember. Letizia turned to the other girl behind the counter and chattered in rapid-fire Italian, and they both laughed. Great. Perfect. Just what he wanted them to do.

Eventually, Letizia got around to scooping the ice cream into a waffle cone and selling it to Rabbit. He left, expecting Gattoni to have left by now, but he was still sitting outside the cafe, smoking his cigarette and feeling sorry for himself. Rabbit slowly window-shopped his way toward him, stopping only when he took the first lick of his ice cream.

He actually did a double-take, as if this were an advertisement for that gelateria, staring in amazement at the cone.

Holy Christ, it was good. There was hazelnut...the swirls of white turned out to be marshmallow. It was better than pussy, for God's sake. The black chunks may or may not have been dark chocolate.

Struggling with every ounce of his will to maintain inconspicuousness, he devoured the cone with barely-disguised relish, even licking his hand clean and examining the napkin he'd held it with for hidden reserves that might have escaped his notice. He debated going back to get another one, but good judgment eventually won out.

Remembering his quarry, who was now nursing a drink and staring off into space, he made his way across the square to a small store called *D'altronde*, which sold knick-knacks, and from which he could keep an eye on the lovelorn Gattoni.

Rather than just browse with one eye and then leave, which tends to arouse a storekeeper's suspicion that someone is, say, following someone else, Rabbit bought a few things. When he saw Gattoni ask the waitress for another drink, Rabbit asked for whatever he had bought to be gift-wrapped. About the time that he was ready to leave, so was Pete Gattoni.

The ex-bully made his way along via Calzaioli to a forest of sculptures, an exhibit of some insane artist's work, and beyond to the square by the water where Michelangelo's David and Cellini's Perseus stood guard outside the Uffizzi Gallery. Rabbit made a mental note to stop by and get a better look at them.

At every corner there was a black man with a blanket spread out on the pavement, his merchandise on display. Stolen handbags, stolen art prints, stolen whatevers, all marked down to "Asda prices" by the "lookie-lookie men." While they were passing through on via de' Neri, Rabbit and Gattoni both stepped aside for another black hissing a warning to each hustler he passed in some African language. The lookie-lookie men all snatched up the four corners of their blankets and brought them together, making them into sacks which they slung over their shoulders and hurried away with.

Those tourists unfamiliar with this phenomenon paused and glanced questioningly at each other until two policewomen in snappy uniforms came strolling down the street. Behind them, a black face peered around the corner, and disappeared again. The policewomen took their own sweet time, knowing the blacks were nearby, and were taking pleasure in their frustration, but not particularly interested in catching them. When they were finally gone, the Africans came back and resumed their posts, laying out their wares and tidying the display.

Not too far on, Pete Gattoni turned into his hotel, the Palazzo Vecchio, and Rabbit returned to La Piazza Del Duomo to stalk Letizia as well.

That night, creeping along the rooftops, Rabbit came upon the hotel, which he'd known had an open air restaurant and bar at the top with a great view of the city's skyscape. Sure enough, there was Gattoni, sitting alone and drinking what appeared to be Campari. From his coat pocket, Rabbit took out what looked like a black magic marker, but was actually a small telescope. Taking off the cap, which contained its own lens, he pulled out the extendable tube and slid the cap along it to adjust the focus.

He watched Gattoni with the patience of a viper, for almost an hour and a half, until his prey called for the check and signed it to his room. Rabbit froze the image of the signature in his mind.

He'd practiced Letizia's voice again and again, experimenting with different words, and was certain he could pass for her when he called the hotel the next day with a furious message for the man at the desk to take down while Gattoni was out. He scribbled out "Peter A. Gattoni" in his pocket notebook before the accuracy of his memory might fade and blur at the edges.

The signature would go on a short note under "*Mi dispiace*," tied to a long-stemmed red rose that Letizia would find outside her door the next morning, and that afternoon, Pete Gattoni would be dead.

Fingerprints can only be a pain in the ass if you don't know what you're doing. The police have gotten very clever at discovering the perpetrator of a crime, and if the crime is severe enough, forensics technicians will stop at absolutely nothing to find the guilty.

Before killing someone, Rabbit would use an exfoliator pad to scrape off all the loose skin that might flake off at the scene of his crime, should anything go wrong. He would brush his hair vigorously to remove any hair that might not be rooted firmly in his scalp. He carried a small spray bottle, what once had been the department store test sample of a cologne, now filled with ammonia to spray on any of his blood that might be spilt. The only way he could be linked to a homicide was if he came in second against his victim and his dead body lay at the scene.

The problem with fingerprints, which are left by the skin's secretions on almost any surface and can be seen, if latent, with iodine vapor, ninhydrin solution, electrostasis, or fluorescent lighting, and even X-ray photography if left on human skin, was that even gloves don't help as much as people think. Hands sweat in latex gloves, and the prints will come through before long even if the wearer does *not* sweat. Especially if he's nervous, or has eaten fruit or a salad that day. Leather gloves are as unique as the prints that they cover, being that they came from animals, and have wrinkles and scars, pores and stretch marks that are unlike any other, and a visible print from one is as damning as a found bullet or its cartridge.

The only thing on Earth that can baffle the police and steer them away is a set of latent prints made with someone else's hand. The trouble with that is rather obvious. If that hand had belonged to someone known to be dead, detectives' eyebrows would jump and the investigation would be dramatically intensified. The forensics people —who have nothing else to do with their time—would

540

search even more feverishly, knowing that the criminal they were after was no typical perp. They would find him. Even if there was no way for them to get their man, they would invent a way to get him.

Besides, carrying around a severed human hand, even if the original owner's body would never be found, wasn't that easy.

Instead, Rabbit had used a koala.

Koala bears have prints on their paws so similar to the prints of humans that they have actually been found to confuse forensics investigators. A thin glove made of their paws, or a patchwork of different paws, could allow the killer's hand's natural secretions to come through and set the whorls down on a murder weapon and mislead the police. The prints would be run through NCIC or Interpol's computers, but no match could ever be found, except maybe in the evidence of some other unsolved case if the killer had gotten careless, cocky, or lazy.

Confident that his plan would work, he went out to the clubbing area deep in the maze of Firenze, to celebrate. Free of all self doubts now, the voices in his head finally stilled, he danced happily in many different bars and discos, pausing only to call Maya every once in a while to talk dirty to her. The strangest affair of his life.

Eventually, he found himself in a chill-out bar, a laid-back place called *Dormiglioni,* or "Sleepy-heads." The lights were low and the mood sedated. Soft glows of light and quiet ambient trance music pandered to those who shied away from bright colors and pounding fury, preferring conversations that were liquor-dulled or drug-sharpened. The seats and tables were all soft, yet stable, and could support patrons if they wanted to dance, sit, or make love on them.

It was a lounge for higher class, mellowed-out depravity and voyeurism. Rabbit loved it immediately. First thing first, though, he made his way to the Men's Room. Well known drinker's fact: drink a pint, piss a quart.

He still had not noticed Bianca following from one place to another, her outfit always changing, at least one article of clothing swapped with what she carried in her little candy-raver backpack. Never the same in one bar as the last, hair always altered by glitter pomades. She took up a spot in a dark corner and pretended to implode drunkenly, watching Rabbit vanish into the Men's.

The bathroom had a dimly-lit antechamber with pay phones

541

that kept the bright lights beyond from intruding on the calm of the lounge outside. Passing through it to the bright sterile whiteness, Rabbit came up short.

Peter Gattoni stood at a urinal, the only man in the room.

Peter Gattoni turned and looked at him, his eyes dull from a long night, but flickered with recognition.

"I'll be damned. Layton, is that you?"

Fuck.

So much for Plan A.

Plan B is looking like an Assault-whoops-Homicide, the body locked up in a stall, propped on the toilet seat. Rabbit smiled. "In the flesh, Gattoni."

"Christ, I never thought I'd see you here."

"I've heard that before."

"You know, Layton—" he shook himself off, zipped himself up, and flushed the john. "There's something I've always wanted to say to you."

"Is that right?"

"Yep." Gattoni was slurring a little, and he staggered a bit on his way to the sink. Washing his hands, he looked at Rabbit in the mirror as he talked. "It's about when we went to high school. Christ, that seems so long ago. Wait, it *was* long ago, wasn't it? Shit, what have I done with my life? Shit. Look—" He paused to rip out handfuls of paper towels, way more than he needed, to dry his hands.

Rabbit locked the restroom door and moved slowly toward him.

Gattoni turned to look him in the eye, suddenly sober.

"I can't tell you how sorry I am, Layton."

Like a record skipping, Jared stopped.

"Look, I know it's way too late for it now, but I mean it. I want you to know that...look, it was you or me. Brendan, he had us all beating up nerds and people he just didn't like. And I know this sounds like Nuremberg or something, but I really was just going along with it. To be honest, I kind of felt sorry for you, but what could I do? If I didn't do it, I'd be next."

Rabbit stared at him.

The hate began to drain out of him, and he didn't know what to do. The look in Gattoni's eyes was of genuine remorse.

"When I saw those school killings on the news," he continued.

"You know, in Arkansas, Washington, Alaska, and Mississippi? Then Columbine? And then all those copycats, more and more kids doing it because the news kept showing it? Next thing you know, if it hadn't happened in a whole year they'd show the last one again to keep it fresh in everyone's minds so the next pissed-off kid would consider it a solution. When I saw what happened to all those kids, because they pushed those other kids too far, it got me thinking. I decided if I ever saw you again, I'd tell you I was sorry."

Rabbit swallowed.

Gattoni offered his hand.

"Well, I'm sorry."

Rabbit stared at him for a long moment.

Then struck in a blur of speed, jabbing Gattoni in the eyeball with his middle finger. Reflexively, Gattoni bent his head forward and put his face in his hands, crying out, and exposed the back of his neck. Rabbit stepped sideways and pushed his victim's head a little bit to make room, and judo-chopped the neck under and behind the left ear with the heel of his hand.

When the motherfucking cocksucker hit the cold tiles, Rabbit grabbed him by one ankle and dragged him across the floor to a toilet stall where he bent down, grabbed the other ankle, and hoisted him up to dunk his head in the toilet water. Gattoni thrashed wildly, but Rabbit held him steady, lifted a leg to kick the toilet lever and flush, lift and drop him face first.

Gattoni fell, collapsing loudly onto the wet floor and lying sprawled as Rabbit walked out, happy, calling over his shoulder.

"Sure, I forgive you. So long!"

Cruised out past Bianca, walking on air, and went back to his hotel.

Jennifer Crawford used to be a Goth chick. A self-pitying, nocturnal, all-black-wearing "graphic novel" reader, who composed morbid poetry and epitaphs for herself, drinking too much and staying up all night trying to work up the nerve to commit suicide. She never pretended she was a vampire, never sat around with Dungeon geeks arguing over life points in role-playing games, and never actually picked up a gun, noose, or razor blade. But she did stalk young men she'd become temporarily infatuated with, read comic books without heroes, and practice Wicca. She cast spells which accomplished nothing, and dabbled in everything that was cutely or romantically "evil."

Rabbit found all the evidence of this in her college dorm room at Florence U of A while she studied in the library. In her photo album, he also saw her reinvention as a Pentecostal, running around barefooted and long-skirted, legs unshaven and face unpainted, a not uncommon college girl empowerment cult that also leads nowhere.

Now she had tried to become one of those trendy suburban chicks who somehow remained teenagers until they reached fifty—at which time they became uppity yacht club cunts with servants and poodles. She hadn't gone all the way yet, to worshipping magazines and trading in God for Revlon. She hadn't gone as far as capri pants, glitter makeup, and ridiculously tiny backpacks. There was still hope.

What she was, according to her diary, was secretly terrified she'd grow old alone and die a cat lady, one of those sad women that all the neighborhood children deemed a witch and dared each other to spy on.

A fraud.

A poseur.

A nerd.

Holy shit, he thought, as his perspective sharply shifted, as real context became apparent. An echo of Crowe's voice rang in his head, something about the greatest sin one can commit is to masturbate, and on a grander scale, to masturbate one's way through life. To be a wallflower watching others dance, to be a voyeur watching others make love, to stagnate while others live. Not taking any action, letting things slide, becoming complacent, getting bored and still not doing anything. And here he was jerking off over the phone to some girl while there was a bona fide psycho to be cultivated right under his nose the whole time. Maya isn't one of us at all, he decided. Never was. But Jenny can, and will be.

Satisfied, Rabbit left the dorm room as he'd found it, with one exception: unscrewing the nozzle of the shower head, he stuffed a small bouillon cube inside and replaced it, smirking at the screams he wouldn't get to hear. It was a harmless prank. Either Jen or Andrea would take a shower and find herself sprayed with chicken soup until the cube dissolved fully.

Slipping back out the window and into the night, closing the window behind him to exactly the level he'd found it when he scaled the building, he made his way slowly to the roof, ran lightly to the far side, and was about to climb down the easy way, when a voice made him wheel about, his knife drawn.

"Fancy meeting you here, Nick." Bianca stood and came out of the shadow of an air-conditioning turret.

Rabbit said nothing, just waited, standing poised in his black cat burglar ensemble.

"I know who you are," the Florentine said. "Not exactly *who*, of course, but I know you are not who you pretend to be."

Rabbit took a menacing step forward, Bianca taking one back, her hands raised placatingly.

"Don't misunderstand. I mean you no harm."

"Then what do you want?"

Her mind flashed on the Mayanomicon, lessons entitled "Pieces of Cloud," "Lotus Petal," and "Karuna." Her thoughts turned to exotic vacations, to yachts and limousines, and people disappearing after threatening Rabbit's friends.

"You are teaching Jen some things?" she asked.

"...What do you want?" he asked again.

She hesitated, then: "I want you to teach me, too."

Epilogue

I came again to my secret garden, the iron gate squealing open on rusted hinges, its black paint bubbled and flaking off. I came to the fountains, dry now in the weed-choked cobblestones, verdigrised pennies in the basin that I hadn't known about, tossed in over the years on vain wishes. The hibiscus were dead. The bougainvillea dry and shriveled. The ground was carpeted with brown leaves that crunched underfoot, the statues overrun by fungus and lichen.

I came again to the wall, looming huge and terrible, and leaned heavily against it. There was a crack in it by my feet; I saw light streaming through in the corner of my eye. I knelt and ran my finger down it, the stone and mortar crumbling easily away. With my fingernail I scraped a trench, and then another.

Kneeling, I tore into it feverishly, pulling the dry, dusty masonry away, the light growing brighter and brighter, bathing my face with its brilliance until a hole gaped large enough to crawl through.

I sat back on my knees a moment, reflecting. It was not too late to turn back, leave the garden, fight through the thorns and Spanish bayonets to the crossroads. It was not too late to choose a path.

Yes it was. It was way too late.

I put my hands into the hole, pulling my head and shoulders through. Inch by inch, I wriggled into the gray stone, and came out in a sterile whiteness. It was with enormous relief that I dissolved into that comforting warmth, absorbed by oblivion, but feeling like I was eclipsing the sun. For an instant I was happy, and then I was gone.

"Jared? Jared."

The voice was intruding, unwelcome.

"Jared!"

I shook myself out of my reverie.

I stood naked in my kitchen with a butcher knife in my hand. Looked on the floor and saw Danielle, propped up on her elbows, staring at me. Her blue eyes were filled with bewildered concern, her long red hair sexily tousled.

"Maybe you don't need another Xanax, baby. Are you okay?"

"Fine, Dani. Hey, do me a favor?"

"Sure."

"Turn on my computer, while I heat this up."

She nodded, frowning, and pushed herself up from the floor, her tatooed body suddenly beautiful again, and disappeared into the bedroom. I put the sliced tomatoes, mozzarella, pepperoni, and bell peppers into a bowl, sprinkled some more olive oil and basil, covered it, and put it in the microwave for a mi-

nute on HIGH. I heard the computer beep and whir in the other room.

"You sure you're okay?" she called. "You were staring off into space for a long time."

"Just high, baby, that's all."

"You want me to fix you a drink?"

"Nah."

She came into the kitchen again, as the microwave beeped.

I took out the bowl and handed it to her with a fork.

I took her face in my hands, kissing her tenderly, surprising her.

I went into the bedroom, sat down at my computer, opened the word processor, and began typing at the speed of light.

AFTER THE FLESH

"I am not convinced that faith can move mountains,
but I have seen what it can do to skyscrapers."
—William H. Gascoyne

*On the last day of August, Inmate 03-35386 Geiger,
Dark W/M—and the last part meant "White Male" even if he
was Asian, Hispanic, or Eskimo—was found dead by Corrections Officer Cornelius Williams in cellblock M3B of the
Coquina County Jail. There were no visible wounds, no sign
of struggle, but the body lay still on its ratty green mattress,
with no breath or pulse. Thirty-six other men in orange coveralls watched from the windows of their cells, their breath
fogging the plate glass, as the body was carried out and laid
on the cold terrazzo floor to be examined by a nurse, who
pronounced Geiger officially dead.*

*At nine-forty that morning, the corpse was transported
to Sacred Heart Hospital's morgue, rolled down track lit
halls on a wobbly-wheeled gurney to a table awaiting au-
topsy and storage in a metal drawer.*

*At five minutes past ten, that corpse rose from the table,
beat an intern unconscious, stole his clothing, and then
calmly walked out of the hospital with a tag still on its toe.*

If I ever strike it rich, I'm going to fund charities that'll actually put a
dent in the world's pain: Prisoners Abroad, Delinquent Bar Tabs, and Free
Porn for Hungry Orphans. I also think people who can't afford health
insurance should be eligible for faith healing vouchers.

Hey, at least my heart's in the right place.

When I stood in the morning sun, breathing clean, fresh air for the
first time in over seven months, I came up with another one: Cigarettes for
the Walking Dead. Zombies like me ought to at least get *one* free pack.

I went to the nearest gas station, checking the contents of my new
wallet. Nineteen dollars, a student ID, one maxed-out credit card, and an
expired condom, had belonged, according to the driver's license, to one
Charles L. Porter of 1533 Primrose Avenue until about ten minutes ago.

Oh, the look on Charles L. Porter's face.

I replayed the scene in my head for the fourth time since it had happened, congratulating myself again.

I had awakened in a cold and indifferent white room that I had, at
first, assumed to be empty. Carefully rolling my eyes without turning my

head, I realized the room was full of the dead. There was a locker room stench of many naked bodies, and the faint humming of a man not far away. The elastic slap of latex gloves being tugged on. The clink of surgical instruments rattling together. When the maker of those noises came close enough, I began to twitch. I heard his footsteps stop, so I jerked violently, then again, and a third time. Then, trying not to smile, I sat up and looked Charles L. Porter straight in the eye. Because, come on, wouldn't *you?*

His tray of instruments fell to the floor.

When he turned to run, I leaped off my table and tackled him to the cold tiles, beating him to a bloody pulp.

If that doesn't grab headlines, I don't know what will.

Still trying to keep a straight face, I walked to the Speedway where a gum-chewing black girl at the cash register sold me a pack of Marlboro Reds, a lighter (pink, but who gives a shit?) and a cheap pair of sunglasses while police sirens wailed past on their way to the hospital. It was unnerving, that shriek wracking my frayed nerves, but Vondella the Cashier didn't seem to notice. Or if she did, she didn't seem to care.

Outside, I lit the first cigarette in more than half a year, sighing a cloud of smoke into the salty air. I could smell the Intracoastal Waterway on the wind even surrounded by gasoline fumes and diesel farts, reveling in the recognition of it.

The police lights were turning in front of the hospital entrance, far away, but still way too close for me to be comfortable. I went to the pay phone by the sidewalk and, with change from the purchase, called Misery.

My little sister, Misery Elizabeth Geiger, lived with her boyfriend, whose name I can't remember. I don't care to, either, because such an epic dipshit doesn't deserve the space in my brain it would take to store such useless information. Man, I hate him, the prick. But to his credit, his name wasn't on any list the police would have of people I might try to contact. If I remembered correctly, the apartment was leased to him but she paid the rent every month, in cash, so it was really hers.

"Yeah?" he asked on the seventh ring.

"Let me talk to Missy."

"Who's this?"

"Publisher's Clearinghouse."

"Get bent."

"It's her brother."

"Oh. Wait a second, aren't all your calls collect?"

"Just get her."

I was trembling all over, impatient and struggling to hide my excitement. I'd done it. I wasn't out of the woods yet, but I'd done it, and all I needed now was a ticket out of Dodge.

550

"Hello?"

"Missy!"

"Dark."

"How the hell are you?"

"I'll live. How's jail?"

"I wouldn't know, I'm not there anymore."

"What?"

"I escaped. Just now. And I need you to pick me up."

"You escaped."

"Yes, dammit, I *escaped* and I need you to meet me somewhere."

"How'd you escape?"

"That's not important right now, sis. What *is* important is that I will be re-apprehended if I am on foot, and I won't be if I'm sitting in your apartment with a nice, cold beer, watching TV."

"Where you going to be?" she asked, finally believing me.

"In the playground behind our old school."

"I'm already there," she said excitedly, hanging up.

Trying not to appear hurried, I walked a block, cut across a few lawns, taking my time, savoring every step, until I came to a side street with no cars. Looking around first to make sure no one could see, I danced a jig. Laughing like an idiot and smoking my cigarette with undisguised relish. Crossing the street, I danced my way along the sidewalk until I got to the corner, and skipped—skipped, yes, but I couldn't resist—to the patch of trees at the dead end. I had taken my time.

On the other side of the high chain link fence, behind the little cluster of casuarina, was an enormous expanse of dewy grass, a combination baseball, football, and soccer field. And beyond that, the black Karmann Ghia I wanted to see. Damn, she'd come quickly.

I flicked the cigarette away and scampered up the rustling mesh of the fence, vaulted over the top, and fell stupidly on the carpet of dead pine needles. I couldn't bring myself to care. Giddily, I got up and ran, trying to dodge the rotating arms of the sprinklers and getting sprayed anyway. Half-atrophied by the inactivity of county time, I got winded quickly. My throat closed as I ran, my heartbeat thundering in my ears. I could see her leaning against the car, smoking, checking her watch. I got a stitch in my side before I was halfway to her, so I had to settle for walking instead. Another stream of sprinkler water came around faster than I could avoid, but I didn't really care.

When I finally got to the parking lot by the playground, I was soaking wet and wheezing. Not the grand entrance I'd wanted to make, but considering the grand *exit* I already made that morning, I figured I could cut myself a little slack.

"Dark!"

"Hi, Missy."

She ran to me and jumped into my arms. I held her tightly, not realizing how much I'd missed her until now. My sister was adorable—to me, not in the eyes of the rest of this world. Petite, her long brown hair falling in waves down the back of her sundress, her eyes hidden behind oversized sunglasses.

"I thought it was some kind of joke," she said into my chest.

"No joke."

She squeezed me tightly. "How'd you do it?"

I had to laugh. "I played possum," I told her.

We went to her apartment where Whatshisname was carving a tiki statue in the living room. He had four feet worth of a palm tree's trunk, upside-down with the roots meant to be the idol's wild afro hair. He was holding it steady with one hand and had made a mess of little wedges and chips on the carpet with the hatchet in the other. A snarling face had half-taken shape when we startled him coming through the door.

"Fucking hell!" he snapped. "You almost made me chop my thumb off!" He wasn't even swinging the stupid hatchet.

"You're making a mess all over the floor," Missy said.

"Well, where else am I supposed to make it?"

"Try outside."

"Yeah, you put me outside. That'll be the day."

She sighed. "Excuse me a second, Dark."

She walked to the bathroom and slammed the door.

"She's been bitching at me for two days," he said, as if he expected me to sympathize. "She's always like this when she gets the gouge." He turned and shouted at the bathroom door. "Yeah, keep it up, I'll give you something to bleed about!"

I would've killed him on any other day.

Well, shit, I couldn't've killed him because he was a member of my church. I couldn't really have done anything to him, actually. But if it had been anyone else, I'd split his skull to the teeth with that ax.

"Fuckin' squaws," he muttered. "So, you got out, huh?"

"No, I didn't. I'm still in jail right now." I lit a cigarette.

"I hear you. I hear you. So, how'd you do it?"

"Prayer."

"I hear you."

I sat down on one of the barstools by the kitchen counter, next to an ashtray made to look like a Catholic baptismal font. I remembered the day my other sister, Ana, brought it home from ceramics class and gave it to our mother. It was painted red, beige, and light blue with golden fleur-de-lis and *In Nomine Patris, Et Filii, Et Spiritu Sancti*" around the lip.

Mom had hated, among other things, Catholics. Having grown up one, bullied by hypocrites, she had every reason to.

She also hated all the stupid names the other girls had: Faith, Hope, Prudence, Charity, Joy, et cetera, none of which they lived up to. She preferred Despair, Rage, Grief, Fury, and Hate. And for the stupid flower names like Daisy and Rose, she liked Thorn and Weed. She said the last straw had been that Eighties rock star, Bob Geldof, naming his daughters Little Pixie, Fifi Trixibelle, and Peaches Honeyblossom. Something had to be done, a statement made.

When my older sister was born, Heresy was already taken so Anathema was the next best choice. Misery was one of a set of twins, but the other died and Missy's still just hanging on. Mom and Dad quit trying after that. Enough said.

Now, staring at wood chips on the carpet, I decided this dipshit didn't deserve to hear my story, or anything, for that matter.

Misery came back out of the bathroom and told me to shower while she found me some clothes. Dipshit was about my size, muscular—we all are at our church—and he had decent taste in raiment. I was eager to get under a shower that didn't reek of chlorine, and wasted no time. Jails recycle their water, and that smell gets inside of you until even your soul stinks. Drink it, and I swear it gives you instant heartburn.

I stayed in the shower much longer than I needed to, savoring it, washing the jail off me. When I got out, I spritzed some of Dipshit's cologne on, that blue bottle shaped like a man's torso, that stood by the sink in His & Hers fashion next to the perfume equivalent, a pink woman's torso wearing a Madonna-esque pointy-titted bustier.

My reflection in the mirror was disappointing. Vampire pale, skinny from refusing to eat the slop they serve in County. My build, once impressive, was now half of what it had been. My face looked drawn and haggard, my goatee resembling sickly beach grass. If anything, I'd say I was redeemed from ugliness only by my honey-colored eyes.

Honey? All right, yellow.

Strange features run in my family. We all have really low amounts of melanin in our skin and eyes, so we sunburn easily and our irises are translucent to light. Ana has an extra pinkie finger on her left hand, and the twins were born albino. Missy's eyes are as red as blood, her skin and hair milk-white when she doesn't dye them. On top of all that, I have a forked tongue, but that was no accident of birth. I cut it from an inch and a half back to the tip, down the middle, with a red hot scalpel I'd heated on the stove. The heat cauterized it instantly, and it was only swollen for three days. Hurt like a mother, even though I'd swallowed a handful of painkillers beforehand. It took a month to train the two tips to move independently of each other, to slide in opposite directions while…cunnilinging, I guess the word would be.

My sister, on the other hand, did not bring her deformities upon herself, like I did. The poor girl's been through more operations than I could count. Her eyes were lasered to correct near blindness, and she's been through bone marrow transplants, kidney donations, and heart surgeries. Her sister died very early, and our parents refused to lose her too. They said they could see the future when they named her Misery. They couldn't have been more wrong.

She was the sweetest girl on Earth; gentle, kind, and generous, even though she'd been teased in school about her appearance by everybody. I did not know children could be so cruel. When I found out her nickname was Lab Rat, I came home bloody, every day.

In time, I was taught *jeet kun do*, Bruce Lee's fighting style, and no one ever made Missy cry again. When she was old enough, as close as she would come to being fully developed, we were able to either correct or disguise her deformities. If it weren't for the church, though, she could never have been healed on the inside. She would still think that her shortcomings were her own fault, instead of a cruel prank by the twisted god who made her.

A knock, and the door opened. Missy handed me a pair of chinos, a wifebeater, and a button-down. Charles L. Porter's shoes were too big, but that wasn't nearly as big of an emergency as his clothes were. His wardrobe might be a contributing factor to the condom in his wallet never being used. I dressed, styled my hair with Dipshit's gel, and went out to the living room where the two of them were "loving each other in a noisy way."

"Because he's my brother, that's why!"

"Well, he's not *my* brother! Why don't you lend him *your* clothes?"

"I can't believe you're being such an asshole."

"Oh, so *I'm* the asshole now? I guess you never do *anything* wrong!"

"Actually, yes I do," she said, her voice getting suddenly calm. "Every time I take you back. Now, get out."

"Yeah, sure. You'll call me back in like you always do!"

"Not this time! I don't ever want to see you again!"

"I've heard that before! Besides, *my* name's on the lease, so you *can't* kick me out."

I lit a cigarette and leaned against the wall, watching.

"All you ever think about is yourself," she snapped.

"Well, gee, I don't see anyone else thinking about me!"

"What's that supposed to mean?"

"You know exactly what it means."

"If you're talking about what I *think* you're talking ab—"

"You bet your ass, I am!"

"*Hello!* I'm on my period! I can't have sex right now!"

"You're *always* on your damn period."

"Well, once every month, yeah!"

I cleared my throat.

They both stopped and turned, startled. I made a face of 'Oh, excuse me,' and held up my hand.

"Don't mind me. I didn't mean to interrupt."

"This is a private conversation," Dipshit told me. Oh.

"Hey, Missy. This outfit isn't really me. Mind if I borrow one of your sundresses, instead?"

"Listen—" Dipshit started to say, but I flicked my cigarette straight at his face, a shower of orange sparks erupting from his forehead the instant before I crashed into him. Caught off balance, he fell backwards and slammed into the kitchen counter, parabolaed by the lip of it catching him in the small of the back. Misery was screaming, but I could barely hear her. All I could see was Dipshit's face swimming in a scarlet haze, his mouth gaping as my hands found his throat. I felt the old joy again as I put every scared and frustrated day I spent in jail into my hands and squeezed them.

Dipshit's face turned red, then blue, then gray, and I dimly felt something tapping me on the back. Misery, beating me with her fists. I was laughing. Dipshit's eyes bulged from terror and the pressure in his head. I could see myself reflected in them, in blue eclipsed by the black of dilating pupils.

I saw the face of ugly, blind, mindless rage.

I let him go, and the world got very quiet.

I don't know how long I sat there, watching the color drain from his face, the eyes sink back into their sockets. Slowly, I became aware of sounds. The hum of the refrigerator. The whisper of the air conditioning. Misery crying softly.

And, eventually, Dipshit breathing.

I sighed, got to my feet and picked up the cigarette that had been burning a black hole in the carpet. Plopping down on the couch, I let the smoke fill and relax me, and it wasn't until the fourth drag that I realized I'd been shaking.

"Missy," I said. She looked up at me, tears running down her cheeks, making trails through the tan-in-a-can that she wore and exposing the alabaster skin beneath. She sniffled.

"Missy, I think we all have to go to church. Right now."

She nodded.

We went to see a man named Jim Crowe, the pastor of our church. The man who had taught me *samadhi* yoga. He was black-skinned, but not a Negro; a big man with a blunt nose that had been broken more than a few times, but otherwise rather handsome features. He had a tendency to wear three-piece suits, usually linen, in the heat of South Florida and not even break a sweat. Of course, being an Aborigine from the Australian Outback, where I hear it gets a little hotter than this, he might be comfortable dressed to the nines. Three-piece suits and Panama hats, and usually the chain of a pocket watch hanging across his vest, the timepiece sitting all old-fashioned in a waistcoat pocket. He looked like one of those pimps who dress up with actual taste instead of the zoot suit hepcats in the black area of town. Or the gangsta rap assholes in Golgotha, whose stables are filled with crack whores. That's what people often mistook Crowe for—a classy black pimp.

He could pass for a Haitian if he wanted to, which he proved by infiltrating a voodoo cult outside of Port-au-Prince. Learning the black arts from an old *bocor*, he returned to the States and passed them on to a disciple I do not yet have the honor of knowing. Then, stripping some of the pigment from his skin and shaving his head, disguising himself as a Hindu, he journeyed to India. Falling in with a group of fakirs in Calcutta, he learned *Samadhi yoga*, the finer points of dervishism, and fire-walking-type illusions. In his travels, he had learned so many other wonderful things that he only hinted at, so I know little else.

And now, Brother James Crowe tutored promising young men and women at the church we attended. According to him, I am one of his star pupils, but I suspect that he says that to each of us. I had learned, among other things, the Indian art of meditating until I could reach a state of total control and manipulate my own metabolism. I can lower my heartbeat to one pulse a minute. A human being can live for over a month that way, appearing freshly dead to all but the most thorough examination. Hair and fingernails stop growing. The digestive system calls a time out. No breath, no pulse, no warmth, no sign to betray me.

Just last night, on my bunk after the evening count, I closed my eyes and relaxed until I reached a place beneath the subconscious. I set my inner alarm clock for eight hours, and slept a dreamless sleep.

And they just carried me out of jail.

I don't know what the statutes are for death and resurrection in this state, but they probably still want me tried for kidnapping, assault, and attempted murder.

When Crowe commended me for my escape, he did ask me why I'd waited so long. A few months of biding my time, sure, but seven? For the first time in my life, I lied to him.

"I had a few people to convert in there," I told him.

He beamed proudly at me and ruffled my hair. Today's suit was off-white, the watch chain gold. He wore no tie—he never did—and rubies gleamed in a ring on his right hand and in his left earlobe. No vow of poverty here, but no overstatement, either.

He put on a stern face and turned to Misery and Dipshit, whose name turned out to be Blake, but I decided to call him Dipshit anyway.

"You two are supposed to be lovers," Crowe said. "What are you doing speaking to each other that way?"

They looked at their hands and said nothing.

"It's supposed to be both of you against the world, and all that romantic drivel, not 'I'll give you something to bleed about.' Now, if you can't love each other when you're supposed to *be* lovers, who else can you expect to be loved by?"

They fidgeted and looked at each other's hands instead.

"You know why most marriages fail? It's because couples stop doing the things that they did to get each other in the first place. Where are the flowers and the little love notes and cute surprises? You made sure you were polite and complimentary in the beginning. Why? So you could trick each other into liking you? So you could fool one another? That sounds like the World to me. You're acting just like the world you hate, the world that rejects and condemns you. I thought you were smarter than that. You should be finding a way to hide our brother Dark from the police. You should be cooking up false identification and finding living quarters. Have you even bothered?"

"We wanted to talk to you first," I told him.

"No! Never depend on anyone else. Of course, I'll help you, but always try to do it on your own. Always think for yourself. Never submit to authority. That is the way of sheep, the way your enemy wants you to behave. Psalm 23 even comes right out and says it."

"Yes Brother," we said in unison, out of habit.

"No! You see that? You're still doing it! Don't even consider *me* your superior. I'm your teacher, that's all."

"Yes—" we all said again, and caught ourselves.

"Now, since I plan ahead for situations like this, I have several identities just floating around right now, some Social Security numbers and names of imaginary people who've just been hanging out and amassing good credit. I borrow under their names just to pay back on time. Dark, you will go down to the DMV with your new Social Security card and apply for a driver's license. Go through all the legal channels, and that way, everything will check out. You can be, hmmm, Dwight Saffron. That's a good one."

We all made the same face.

"What? It's a good name."

"It sucks, Jim."

"Of *course* it sucks. That's why it's good. No one would ever *choose* to be named that. It's like Murray, or Herb."

"Or Warren."

"Or Warren, yes. Now, dye your hair brown. Everybody dyes their hair from brown to something else, anything else, so it's the most mundane and inconspicuous. Shave the goatee, also. Can't have any kind of individuality, Dwight." He went to his desk and opened a few drawers, rummaging through them. "Do you have money?"

"Yeah, my older sister emptied my apartment out when I got arrested, because Sutton Place was going to evict me. Something about bad publicity. So, she's got all my stuff, including my piggy bank. I could just move in with her."

"No. Absolutely not. Find another place, cheap and out of the way."

He found what he was looking for and brought it over.

"Ahh, here we are: Dwight Saffron's social and his credit cards. Be responsible with them, Dwight. You've an image to uphold."

"Thank you, Jim."

"Hey, it's the least I could do. After all, I'm the one that got you in this mess in the first place."

We stared at him, startled.

I'd never thought of it that way, but once I did...

The Wiccans sacrifice vegetables in their rituals and certain ceremonies, offering up some asparagus or cauliflower to their gods and demons as an incentive for their prayers to be answered. Just like Cain did. That's how stupid they are. Remember what happened to Cain?

God royally screwed him over.

> "Abide by Wiccan law we must,
> In perfect love and perfect trust,
> In all we do, our hearts be real,
> Harming none, do what ye will,
> Let this message flow in your heart,
> Merry we meet, and merry we part."

Just what you'd expect from a bunch of broccoli-wielding douchebags. No wonder their stupid spells don't work. If you want to get anything done, you have to ask the right people.

And the right people like blood.

Seven months ago, it was my turn to get it.

The guy's name was Joshua Buckland, and he went to a different church. He had one of those little mustaches like you try to grow when you turn thirteen and all you can manage is darker peach fuzz. He'd never had a pimple in his Bible-thumping life, and he hadn't so much as copped a feel while making out with his goody-two-shoes girlfriend the night I sprang on him and knocked his ass out. They'd gone to a movie, rated G, of all things, and gone for ice cream afterwards. *Ice cream,* for fuck's sake. He had vanilla. Boring old non-risk-taking vanilla. They walked together, holding hands and licking ice cream cones all the way to her father's house, where they sat on the porch swing.

They sang in the choir together, and she wore his name on a little chain around her neck.

They were in love.

They were so wholesome and whitebread they deserved to die. I considered them one step below that stale and homogenized cookie cutter life I abhor. One step below, because they actually believed they were above. They never strayed from the straight and narrow, never smelled the roses, never ate of the fruit. They constantly whined on their knees to their god to do this, do that, and never shut up about how it didn't matter when He ignored them.

It was just like that Santa Claus bullshit. Be good, because he's watching you, boys and girls. If you're good he'll bring you lots of presents. If you act deaf and blind and dumb in life you'll get raptured to Heaven. Stupid people paranoid over their invisible authority figure.

Well, apparently, Joshua Buckland's god was with him that night long ago.

He walked back from his sweetheart's house with a little spring in his step, enjoying the evening. My car was parked along the curb ahead of him, across the sidewalk from the tall ficus hedge in which I hid. The street was empty.

Through the mask of the leaves I saw him approach, like an incautious deer in the forest wandering into the jaws of a lion. I waited, tense and impatient, my heart racing. Closer, closer. I knew there were easier, more sensible ways to do this. But this tactic just appealed to me. Closer.

As he passed, I reached swiftly through the leaves and seized him by the collar of his shirt, jerking him to me. Yanked off balance, he struck the small branches with his cheek and yelped, and in the next instant I sprang, erupting from the hedge and slamming him to the sidewalk. Straddling him, I drove my fist again and again into his face, spattering blood with every blow. From my back pocket I pulled a set of handcuffs and bound his wrists behind his back. A quick look left and right, and I dragged him to my car, opened the back seat door, and stuffed him in.

A car was coming.

I calmly shut the door, walked around to the driver's side and let myself in. The excitement of the act felt like standing too close as a train blasted by, but I contained it, maintaining an air of normalcy. I slid the key into the ignition, watching the car approach from behind in the rearview, and turned it.

For the first time in history, my car refused to start. It cranked, loud and obnoxious, but refused to turn over. I tried again. Loud coughing, sputtering, accompanied by my irritated urging to 'Come on, *start* you piece of shit.' Black smoke drifted in tendrils from under the hood, and the car behind me slowed down.

I couldn't believe it.

I tried again, on the edge of panic, and now the smoke poured out of the creases in-between hood, fenders, and grille. The approaching car pulled alongside me, and a nice-looking family smiled at me sympathetically. I smiled weakly back.

They passed me and pulled up to the curb in front of me, the Dad getting out and coming toward my badly smoking deathtrap. I tried the key again in desperation. Scrape, cough cough cough, sputter, cough, clank. Fuck!

And then the good Samaritan's face was smiling good-naturedly into my window and asking stupidly:

"Car trouble?" Then he just happened to glance into the back seat and say, just as stupidly: "Oh dear."

III

All of the details of my apprehension and the whole post-arrest ceremony with the fingerprints and photographing and hours of holding cell storytelling are unimportant. As tedious in the retelling as in the experiencing. Suffice to say, it sucked.

By the way, if you go 'up the road,' beware of anyone who tells you that he isn't an inmate, he's a convict. It's just semantics, really, but there is an underlying message that he isn't just a guy that made a mistake, and is currently locked up for it. He's telling you right away that he will cheat you, and that you shouldn't believe a word he says. I don't know why they admit it so readily, but they do. The "convict code" is "might makes right," and "You mah bitch, white boy."

And I don't give a god *damn* what all the affirmative action people try to tell you. I honestly don't. Poor Tyrone in the cell with you is not an honor student who got falsely arrested in a case of mistaken identity by racist cops, and Julius caught red-handed with his heel pressed on the night watchman's throat was not acting out a desperate cry for help.

Take a moment to look up "Chris Rock civil war" because he can get away with saying it, while I can't.

Sure, there are black honor students, but they're not in jail. Yeah, every once in a while, there is a false accusation or some poor guy gets framed, but *he's* not the one I'm talking about.

Hector and Miguel are not products of their environment. Even Sean with the surfer haircut and the tan and the capped teeth is not an innocent Presbyterian who got steered wrong by a bad crowd—but as bad as he is, he's not as bad as them. If he's sitting in here with a red armband around his wrist, feel free to judge him; prejudice is survival.

And sure, there are a few guys in jail, black, brown, white, whichever—you can tell them by their eyes when they look at you—who are not pond scum. Get to know them, and you'll find out they just made a mistake in life, and are now paying for it. Some are even good people who got framed or railroaded or whatever.

But admit it, they don't have dreadlocks and gold teeth.

Not all of the blacks, but most of them, see you with your white skin and ignore those orange coveralls you're wearing. They don't even see the orange. You are not a fellow criminal, another sad and desperate soul whose life is on hold in this horrible four-walled world. You a cracka. You are the root of all their troubles. You put them here.

Now, don't get me wrong. There were some pretty stupid white guys in there, too, and some real scum. That's why they were in jail. They *belong* there. And I suppose I belonged there, too. It's what you do when you get out that matters. They call it the Department of Corrections in the hope that you will get corrected. The people I am talking about are the ones that are in there frequently, and openly *brag* about it. They call it Thug Life. Your number of times being In is a badge of honor.

Yunno how so many Muslims hate the West, because they see Miley Cyrus and Kim Kardashian on TV, and think *all* of us are like that? I have talked to racist whites to find out why they feel the way they do, and they assume all black people are like the ones they see in gangsta rap videos and movies. If that is what people are shown all the time, that's what they believe. In my experience, most Southern men are Andy Griffith, and most black men are TD Jakes. I'm not talking about them. I'm talking about Tyrone and Julius, Wang-Wang and B-Money.

Tyrone and Julius will beat the living shit out of you because your skin is white. They'll call it revenge for what happened to their ancestors, even though more British, Scottish, Irish, and Germans were slaves in the New World long before Kunta Kinte showed up. Dat doan mean shit. It doesn't matter if you're a white trash deadbeat either—you da rich white mothafucka who's keepin' da black man down. They will rob you and beat you and sodomize you until you either strike back or tell a guard, at which time they will kill you.

If you shake your head at this and try to say I have it all wrong or that I'm a bigot, you are either a liar or an imbecile. You weren't there to contradict me. Or, Tyrone's your cousin.

Tyrone has a shank hidden up his ass. It's the handle of a toothbrush, the plastic of one end melted to hold a single-edged razor blade. He melted it by shoving the point of a pencil into the day room electrical socket where the dorm's TV used to be plugged in—this was before he and Wang-Wang threw it off the upper tier walkway because the crackas got together and tried to hold a vote over what we'd all watch that night—and when sparks jumped out, he caught them in a wad of toilet paper. A small bloom of fire leaped up out of his hand to lick at the air, and he hurried back to his cell with it before a guard might see.

Every two days, the guards brought around disposable razors that we'd cut our faces up with for twenty minutes, then came around again to collect them. The weak and feeble, or white and scared, usually had only splintered plastic to turn in since the blade had been confiscated by the guys with "Thug 4 Life" tattooed in an arch over their navels or across their traps and shoulder blades. Uh-oh, cracka. Shakedown time. And you know better than to point out who took the blade from you, so you'll accept the blame and wear the charge, because going to the box beats getting killed.

Oh, and those tattoos? A lot of them had been done right here, using the most primitive method I've ever seen. They'd burn dominoes or chess pieces that get donated by well-meaning people for us to pass the time, burn them underneath the metal writing desks in our cells, then scrape the soot off the undersides, mixing it with the shampoo or some other shit we can buy out of the commissary once a week, and then pick-'n-poke the design into their skin with a staple. Real high quality art we're talking, for people with standards.

These fine specimens are the people who are staring at you when you're led into the dorm, a dungeon with four cells (two upstairs and two down, enclosed with a common space where we eat and congregate three times a day) each of which is meant to house four men but contain eight or nine, and sometimes as many as twelve. They watch you carry in your fireproof ratty green mattress and bedroll, scuffing your feet in the orange shower slides you must wear if you don't want to get warts all over the soles of your feet. They watch you while the shackles are taken off of you. Then, after you've already been strip-searched, photographed, fingerprinted, bullied, pushed around, and strip-searched again, now you get *tried*. Tyrone wants to charge you rent to sleep on the floor. Julius wants you to suck his dick. All Hector wants is to beat your ass, because hey, it's fun. And every last one of them is going to try and get your tray at chow time, that tray of brown mud and cold soggy noodles with snot sauce, nothing edible on it except (sometimes) the dessert, which every now and then is a tiny little raisin cake, oatmeal cake, whatever, with the cream filling in it, or a dinky red apple.

They put a red armband on me that meant I was somewhere on the criminal hierarchy above Monster, and I spent one night in Population before doing the only smart thing I could do. I picked a fight.

Without books to read, "solitary" confinement is nothing but masturbation, pushups, and sleep. The isolation cellblock is comprised of forty two-man cells, almost all of which contain dreadlocked assholes who pound on the doors and rap all day and all night. It is, for a civilized man, almost as maddening as being chained to a dripping faucet, surrounded by people rapping.

Because the guards were all black, and the three inmates I beat within an inch of their lives were black, I got sentenced by the DR board to one month, and spent a mind-numbing week of it alone.

Until Day Eight, when a strange-eyed skinny black man named Roosevelt came in.

Man, that dude was out of his fucking mind.

We stared at each other for hours in silence before he startled me with his impassioned views on sheep.

"You better not feed me no fucken sheep, man. A female sheep has a vagina just like a human woman, so I'd never eat no fucken sheep. I don't like the Devil."

I stared at him in startled amazement.

"A corrupted angel is a fucked-up situation, man," he continued. "Rivers of blood and bodies of women hanging by their tongues from meat-hooks, man. Corrupted angels'll eat eggs and fucking bacon sittin' there surrounded by *cat* shit, man. Fire, Devil, evil, horror, blood. I'd shoot the Devil, and I don't care if he *does* have a size thirteen foot."

I could think of no adequate response. He'd spoken with such conviction and I had no idea what he was talking about. He paused, then continued almost as an afterthought:

"That's it, man. Don't feed me no fucken sheep. Life is just too short, man. Life is too precious."

Wind screamed along the outside of the jail, rustling the barbed helixes of razor wire.

"What the fuck are you talking about?"

He must not have heard, because he kept talking. "I wonder what she-devil pussy smells like."

I felt something pop inside my brain. It was as if I got stupider just listening to him. He had broken-off comb teeth stuck in his earlobes, eyebrows, and nostril, to keep the holes from his confiscated piercings open. It pissed me off that a complete wacko like him could think of this while I did not. The holes in various parts of my body where I'd worn rings and studs had already closed.

"Would you fuck a female ghost? You'd have to cuz if you didn't it'll kill you so you don't tell no one she axed you. You know a female?"

It took a second to realize he was asking me a question, and even then I didn't understand it.

"A female?" I asked.

"Yeah, like, no dick or nothin'. A woman."

"Uh…yeah?"

"Well, you dunno what the fuck she could be. She could eat you, man. You be fucking a girl and her eyes start glowing, you get the fuck up out of there, man. That's real."

I stared at him.

And that was my life, day and night, hour after hour, for three weeks. Twenty-one days, five-hundred-one slow dragging hours in a tiny bathroom with two bunks, a tiny window, and a foul stench.

"My uncle killed his wife and buried her body in the backyard, then dug her back up three days later and fucked her, man. They didn't send him to no prison, man…they sent him to the nutty house."

"Yeah, I'll bet."

"My soul's in danger for all time."

"That's great, buddy."

"Do you think if bunny rabbits could talk, you'd still eat 'em? You'd go to jail for it, I promise you."

"Is that right?"

"Yeah, they could tell you all about maaaath and what they did yesterday."

"And carrots?"

"Yeah, man. Yeah."

I wanted to kill him. I really did. The only thing that saved his life was that I would be the obvious culprit. Duh. So, instead, I stared out the window, watching clouds creep slowly across the sky. Counting birds perched on the swaying razor wire. Replaying memorable moments in my life, revisiting them. Vines snaked through fence links and across brick walls green with moss and brown with stains from rusty water.

And that was just the first month.

IV

I could sit and listen to James Crowe preach all day. Which was handy, since he missed no opportunity to do so. One of his favorite openers was a paraphrased quote from Christopher Hitchens, his deep voice dripping with sarcasm.

"I am responsible for the horrific torture and death of a man eons ago, whom I never could've known about had I not been told? And it compensated for an earlier crime with no victim and the consequence being self-awareness and mortality? And if I, who am free to choose, decline the vicarious redemption through this awful thing, completely ignoring the needs of those I personally *have* sinned against, I'll suffer a fate far more terrible, forever? Well, that makes perfect sense."

He'd produced a four-hosed hookah and we smoked some fine opium he grew himself. Now we reclined and listened to our teacher's wisdom.

"Regardless of our Creator's intentions, we have become what we are. Blame Eve and the serpent if you will, but the facts are, quite simply, we are what we are, and our governors have laid down rules for the supposed salvation of our souls that are *wrong*. They defy reason.

"The Bible commands us to be sober, to be vigilant, hold your natural tendencies in check, ignore all things that benefit your flesh, forgive others who do you harm. These efforts lead inevitably to failure and bitterness in those who attempt them. They become confused, and their tense and determined attitude toward these self-destructive pursuits become an intolerable burden, a fever and a torment. Love, compassion, loyalty, humility, honesty—these are the plate-glass windows that we small birds repeatedly crash into, stupidly bashing ourselves to pieces against the unattainable. We foolishly struggle to go where we cannot, to be what we simply are not wired to be. And who is to blame?"

"Jesus!" we answered eagerly.

"Good. The advocate of cowardice. And who else?"

"America!"

"Why?" He pointed to me.

"Because our bullshit country and its bullshit politicians have pussified us, twisting actual passion and good old-fashion courage into personality disorders."

"I couldn't have said it better myself. I've decided to hold a Mass tonight, Dark, to celebrate your return. We'll give you a dose of everything you've missed in the past eight months."

"Can't wait," I said.

In the year of their lord 2001, a company called Intel announced the development of transistors only twenty nanometers in size, exactly one-billionth of a meter. These transistors could turn on and off over one trillion times in one second, completing roughly a billion computations in the time it takes a speeding bullet to travel an inch. These transistors spawned microscopic memory chips capable of storing up to four hundred billion bits of data.

Forty years prior, the only computers were calculators and filing systems, and anything more complicated was the size of the room that contained it. One hundred years before that, there weren't even radios. In the time of Christ, the most complicated weapon was the bow and arrow, and the most common was a rock. Modern man can kill his neighbor's entire nation, half a world away, with the push of a button and a few minutes' wait. In Old Testament times, Aristotle decided that everything was made up of one tiny building block called an atom. Now we can destroy our entire planet, eradicating all life and every sign that we had existed, by splitting that atom.

We're even going so far as to prevent tornadoes by firing microwave beams from satellites at cold downdrafts, trying to keep them from reacting with warm updrafts. We're experimenting with oil spritzed over seawater to keep it from evaporating, to weaken hurricanes. In 2003, it was revealed that an Israeli scientist named Goldstein was implanting human genes into chicken eggs, and South Koreans had been fusing our DNA into the blastocysts of mice. The US turned out to have been doing this with monkeys for two years already.

Playing God.

And all because a serpent supposedly gave a woman an apple. No wonder God hates us. We have become capable of things He never even dreamed of. We can create life in a petri dish and journey to other planets.

The crux of our religion is: what the fuck do we need Him for?

Dark Geiger's mother, Connie Bristol, met his father at a summer camp. Her friend Donna talked her into going after her first period year, when she became "awkward." Apparently, she got instant acne, and not just the regular horrible stuff. She oozed. No one would speak to her unless they were making fun of her. On top of that, she got braces.

She ate alone at lunch, she sat alone on the bus, and she stayed home from school dances. She bought every kind of miracle cream, concealer, or antibiotic there was, and was disappointed in every last one. Then, for what seemed like no good reason whatsoever, one of the most popular girls in school decided to be her friend.

Donna Kavanaugh invited her places with her family—the zoo, Busch Gardens, horseback riding—and told her never to listen to what her classmates called her. This was all towards the end of that school year, and when school was out, Donna asked if Connie could come to summer camp with her. A special spiritual retreat, she called it.

"Why have you been so nice to me?" Mom finally asked.

"Are you complaining?"

"No, but it doesn't make any sense."

Donna told her it was because Connie wasn't like other kids their age. She knew that everything their Catholic school force-fed them was a load of crap, and that no kind and loving god would allow young girls to endure the pain and humiliation my mother had to. They'd already seen eye to eye on the hypocrisy of the Church and stupidity of memorized repetitious prayers. A religion that could invent indulgences—redemption from sin by paying a fine beforehand—was surely just a huge scam.

They discussed the Crusades, the Holy Inquisition, the auto-da-fe. Burnings at the stake for those who only wanted to read the Bible for themselves. Genocide. The sheep of the flock dying of plague and starvation while the shepherds lived in ease and luxury.

It was not hard for Mom to agree with her new friend. At the camp they met many young kids who felt as they did, and many fascinating counselors who actually cared for each of their charges. They did all kinds of fun things, and everyone treated Mom as if she were someone truly special. She was somebody again. She mattered.

And they cured her acne.

A doctor there gave her pills to take and a rinse to wash her face with, and in one week her face was as smooth and beautiful as she'd only dreamed it could be.

At the end of the summer, after many classes where free thought and discussion were encouraged, Connie Bristol knelt in front of an altar and gave her life to Satan. Naked in front of the entire camp, she was washed in blood and made her vows, holding her left foot in her right hand and placing her left hand on her forehead, pledging all she held between her hands to the Church of Adam.

Three hundred other adolescents also swore allegiance to the Devil that day, and received their baptism in blood. The Church of Adam gave praise to the serpent for giving Eve the Apple of Knowledge and liberating Adam's will. He gave them freedom from mental slavery, and the precious gift of being able to think for themselves.

Donna's family was of good standing in the cult, and she'd been made a recruiter. Dark's Mom could never have known that her "friend" put a little something in her food at lunch the year before and caused a severe epidermal reaction. Her body began producing oils much more quickly than normal, and with her hormones already raging, her face and body became a hideous aberration overnight.

The camp doctor, having created the disease, naturally knew the cure. He administered it in her food upon arrival, secretly, and the miraculous week was the last stage of healing. The pills were psychotropic, making her feel unnaturally elated, and the rinses were boric acid to burn away the damaged skin. Her skin was already clear and healthy underneath. All it needed was the cleansing.

And Mom fell for it hook, line, and sinker.

Ana opened her door and screamed, throwing her arms around me. Missy laughed at our sister's unexpected reaction.

"Surprise," I said.

"Where did you come from?" She squeezed me so tightly I could barely respond. I didn't know she'd missed me so much. She stepped back and we got a good look at each other. She was dressed simply in jeans and a tight white tee shirt that said Fuck the Whales. Another hug, and then she dragged me into her lair, and Misery followed.

Over Ana's shoulder I saw many of my things adorning her apartment. My gigantic American flag was tacked, upside-down, to the living room wall, reaching from the sliding glass doors to the arch that led to the other rooms. My oak and chrome bar set with three stools, took up a large wedge of space in the corner of the room. My Wurlitzer CD jukebox with the neon and the bubbles, and a host of other odds and ends.

"I love what you've done with the place," I told her.

Adamistic Satanism foretells the coming of the Antichrist in a somewhat different way than the world is used to. We await the return of God in human form as the redeemer of all men, and we are prepared to welcome him. As He made a bride for Adam, we will likewise offer him a fitting consort in return. The Antichrist will be God himself, tempted away from his mission by a slightly different Fruit of Knowledge.

This bride, the Temptress, has to be perfect in every way as far as flesh and mind are concerned. She must have the power over all men that only a special type of woman can. Every generation has its ambitious vixens who train themselves according to the teachings of our lord Satan, who should know better than any what the task demands. These hopefuls are

569

measured against the highest possible standards.

The mission of our offering is to seduce the Christ, become His consort, and act as ambassador of Hell, petitioning for Satan to be reconciled with God. It is the dearest wish of our lord to return to Heaven, and the vixens of our church vie bitterly for the honor. Once a high priestess turns thirty-six the parishes all over the nation choose a delegate and send her to New Orleans for a sort of Satanic Miss America. The departing priestess presides as judge, then retires into obscurity.

And the rest of us do what we can to facilitate the Second Coming by making sure that the world is depraved, degenerate, and desperate enough to warrant it. While other criminals and miscreants range from selfish and greedy to wicked, we specialize in excessively ghastly and horrendous crimes against nature.

We make the seven deadly sins look like the equivalent of spray cheese in a can.

My sister Ana is one of our two most likely candidates for the priesthood. Her hair is long and many shades of blonde, her skin artificially bronzed and flawless. Her eyes, mostly yellow but streaked and haloed with scarlet and peppered with flecks of gold, can hold men mesmerized like a snake toying with a bird. Her body is the perfection that only discipline can achieve. The piercings in her ears, nipples, navel, and labia are all solid gold. On top of that, she has the cunning and craftiness that so pleases our Lord.

The only people in this world that she trusts are Crowe, Misery, and me.

In a corner, her "relentless watchdog," a long-in-the-tooth Bassett hound named Enoch, cracked open one bleary eye to see what all the fuss was about, wagged his tail half-heartedly as if he really couldn't be bothered with it, and went back to sleep. He wore a leather collar studded with spikes like you'd expect to see on a Rott or a Doberman, the kind punk rockers and leather-fags wear. If any burglar had ever tried to climb in a window, or a gang of home invaders kicked the door in, they'd probably piss themselves in terror at the fearsome sight of Enoch the Bassett hound dutifully asleep on his blanket in the corner, snoring deeply and harrumphing his jowls.

He watched us for maybe three seconds, tops, before deciding he wasn't missing anything, and relentlessly went back to his doggy dreams while we laughed and wrestled, slinging each other around the room, still locked in embrace.

Missy followed us in and shut the door, going to her favorite armchair and plopping down, content to watch Anathema and I try to lift and throw each other. Losing our balance, we stumbled and fell to the floor, giggling like little children.

I told her everything while she fixed us all drinks at the bar —Disarrono and Bacardi Limon with cranberry, which wasn't bad, and we munched on communion wafers from a Catholic supply warehouse, dipping them in salsa. At the best part of my escape story, she cheered and applauded. After I was finished, she asked what my plans were.

"Hell if I know," I said. "I'm getting a new identity, but aside from that, it's all up in the air."

"So, nothing's set in stone?"

"It's not even written in ink."

"Move in here."

"I can't, Crowe says it's a bad idea."

"I mean, into this apartment complex. We need to all be neighbors." Missy's place was only a short walk from hers, in a place called Abbey Road.

"Or I could travel. I always wanted to hitch-hike around the country…with a sawed-off shotgun."

"That could be fun."

"Yeah, I'd live from car to car."

"You know, it's hard to believe you beat out one million other sperm," she said. I laughed. She turned to Missy.

"Remember how he used to mumble gibberish and gnaw on Dad's tires when he got excited?"

"What? I never!"

"Dark, if you'd been any stupider I'd've had to water you."

"Funny."

"Want another drink?"

"Of course."

"Help yourself, then."

I told them about my lunatic cellmate Roosevelt while I fixed another Whatchamacallit, and had them in stitches.

"There's no way he said that!"

"I promise he did, on my eyes. His belt didn't go through all the loops, if you know what I mean."

"What was he in for?"

"You know, I never asked. But I'll tell you what his ambition was. He said the next time I saw him on the street, he'd have platted hair down to his ass with pink and yellow barrettes in it, he'd be dealing with the Mob, and riding around on a fly-ass bicycle."

They screamed with laughter, throwing their heads back and clutching their bellies, feet stomping on the floor.

"I'm serious. He said he wanted to get so rich, he could do coke and stay up watching cartoons all day and all night. Oh, and he could take all the showers he wanted."

"Showers?" Missy gasped, her eyes shining with tears.

571

"Yep. All he wanted was to be clean and watch them cartoons, yo. He even listed all the best cartoons of all time, the ones he'd watch at least once every day. *Secret of Nimh, All Dogs Go to Heaven, Watership Down, Charlotte's Web...*"

"Stop! Stop! You're killing me!"

"No, wait, he then says *Animal Farm*, so I decide to launch into a lengthy tangent about how that cartoon had influenced Charles Manson."

"What?!"

"I made it up. I just started talking, giving him a taste of his own medicine, hoping he'd shut up."

"What'd you say?"

"That since the pigs in *Animal Farm* were the ones who took over and started a totalitarian regime, Pig became the derogatory word for the establishment. 'Establishment' was the term imported along with the Beatles and miniskirts from Britain in the '60s, and over there it had some validity, meaning the solid block of quiet, continuing power, of permanent civil servants who were non-political and non-partisan and so could outlast all changes in government. But here, where any change in the administration brings an overabundance of new aides, advisers, image-makers, lawyers, fixers, and yes-men, where the only objective is the opportunistic lining of pockets in a brief window of power, you can't really say anything is established but greed. So, anti-government Americans called them Pigs, after *Animal Farm*, and that's what the Manson Family meant when they wrote it on the walls in Sharon Tate's blood."

"Okay," Misery asked. "Did it work? Did he shut up?"

"He looked at me for a long moment, then blinked a couple times and said 'Yuh, I was jussa bout ta say dat.'"

They shrieked and leaned heavily against each other, shaking. I couldn't help but chuckle myself.

"He's out of his goddamned mind!" Ana managed to say.

"You don't know the half of it."

"How'd you ever survive being locked up with him?"

"Long story."

V

"Sometimes this place is like a zoo, the way pimply adolescents are paraded by our cellblock to observe us like we're monsters in captivity. These promising young honor roll students destined for some civic career where they'll fester and commit more obscenities in government, perpetuating the cycle that keeps producing delinquents like us that the next generation of young nerds will gawk at through plate glass walls smeared with saliva, hair grease, and sperm."

"Huh?" said the guy I thought I was talking to.

He, like the rest of the dorm, was oblivious of the high school field trip that had been watching us with vague repulsion. I gave up and tried to ignore the idiots around me, all staring slack-jawed and wide-eyed at their "reality show." On the screen, one boy stood with a camcorder while two others poked a sleeping bear with a stick.

I would find out later that the purpose of the field trip was to show juvenile delinquents what lay ahead of they continued on the path they had chosen. It's a program called Scared Straight, and it's as effective as nailing jelly to the wall. Used to work, though, back when prisoners were allowed to yell and throw shit at them, but the politicians had gotten ahold of it and made it *this*, shooting themselves in the foot. Now, all the inmates do if they see some exceptionally pretty young girls out there is gather along the glass and openly start gunning. Up to five of them will stand there, side by side, jerking off without even a shred of shame. They'll blow their load all over the glass and walk away, letting another take his place.

So I was wrong about who the kids were. I'm still dead on about where they were headed.

Outside, through our little windows, the same sickly yellow grass climbed into the diamonds of the chain link fence, and grew between the cracks of the discolored concrete paths. Nothing ever changed outside that window. The same little heaps of unidentifiable plastic things, mashed cans, and half-decomposed anonymous garbage. Same as yesterday, same as the day before. Same as tomorrow.

"The fuck you looking at?" I screamed at the plate glass wall, startling the sightseers. Their escort—tour guide, whatever—ushered them away to the Reptile Exhibit.

I closed my eyes and tried to picture sunbeams spearing through silver-lined clouds. Distant mountains, a deep wide valley, a rambling wood creeping raggedly into the hills, its roots spreading into the rock. The twinkle and glittering light of a sun dappled river. Low, twisted branches of trees and dancing gusts of color—flowers tossed in the wind. A place where the stars were never dimmed by the pink aurora of city lights. The world Crowe told us about. The world that needed to be brought back.

I tried to picture that, but was conspired against by that stupid TV

573

show and the idiots shouting at it.

"Haw! Git 'im, bear! Git that li'l waterhead!"

"Ooooo-whee! Snap, yo!"

Their shouting startled the cockroaches and sent them scurrying for cover, out of sight.

I may not be in Hell, but I can see it from here.

At about ten or so, we all go back to our cells, to our ratty, flame retardant green mattresses and mind-bogglingly stupid conversations.

There are four cells in a dorm, with four bunks in each fastened to the walls, and two double bunk racks made of angle iron welded together, plus a couple of mattresses on the floor. Between ten and twelve men sleep in each four man cell.

"Nigga, I peeped da lick, right off rip. I *know* whut da lick read, mah nigga."

"Word. But dem shits be off da *chain*."

Linguistics enthusiast that I am, that all of Crowe's disciples are encouraged to be, I have been struggling to interpret what these guys are saying. Sometimes I don't think *they* know what they're trying to express, judging from how often they ask "know whut I'm sayin'?" I've managed to figure out that "off da chain" is a reference to slave days, and being off the chain means to be wild, or free. I'm thinking if I publish this I might win a Nobel Prize, or in the very least a Pulitzer.

A point cannot be gotten across unless stated *ad nauseum*, the louder the better. That's how little faith they have in each other's comprehensive skills. We whites and the Hispanics (not the chicos, mind, but the Hispanics, and there is a difference) have a little joke amongst ourselves: "Ah'm gonna repeat mahsef, yunno whut Ah'm sayin'? Ah'm gonna repeat mahsef. Ah'm gonna repeat mahsef, yunno whut Ah'm sayin'? Ah'm gonna repeat mahsef."

Their repetition will continue until acknowledged. They need what they say to be acknowledged, or they can't seem to continue, hence the inevitable question: "You heard me?" When they ask me if I heard them, especially if I'm sitting two, three feet away, I love to just stare off into space, waiting. They fidget. The awkward pause lengthens, until they have to ask again. "You *heard?*" I finally look over, say "hm?" with my eyebrows raised, and they suck their teeth in irritation— *"stck!"*

I love it. Hey, entertainment is scarce in here. You have to make do with what you've got, and the longer one lowers his standards...well, strange horizons.

And "assed" is a suffix. At least, I think it's in past tense. Maybe it's just "ass." We have only two phones in each dorm, and fights are frequent over the use of them, on account of "dem in-love-ass niggas be hoggin' da phone *all* mothafuckin' day." Oh, and my new favorite insult is "Dick-suckin-ass fuck-bitch," as in "You see dat one cracka over there? Well, I knew him up da road, and he a dick-suckin-ass fuck-bitch." Them're no uncertain terms, right dere.

Those are *quotes,* verbatim. So are these other examples of one dog ejamacatin' anotha: "Escape? Yeah, dog, dat's da shit now, escape. *All* dem niggas be escapin' dese days, know whut I'm sayin'? Yeah, dog. Escape. Dat's real." Like it's a new fad, something prisoners have only just started doing.

"Dat nigga's one mothafuckin'-ass mothafucka, mah nigga. Ya feel me, cuz? Know whut I'm sayin'?"

On my mother's eyes, I am not making this up. And some use the N-word in one breath so many times it doesn't even sound bad to me anymore, first addressing the guy they're speaking to with it, calling themselves it, and concluding with it.

"Nigga, you betta not be runnin' up on a nigga, mah nigga. Puss'ass shit. Fuck wrong wichoo, mah nigga?""

"Nigga, I'm tellin' ya, she doan *want* a nigga to be takin' no blood test, mah nigga, cuz den they's *proof* it ain't mah baby, mah nigga. Tha's real."

I have a list of pejoratives and catachreses going, a list of things I've heard them say when they were trying to use big words and sound intelligent. It's become a hobby of mine.

"I fear the uninvitable has occurred," is one.

Another, if the speaker takes no interest in something: "Dat doan even fit mah quaiteria."

"Yuh, dat'll be sufficious."

"I'm glad we in agree-ence."

Another guy who'd smuggled a couple of joints in when he'd gotten arrested had them hidden under his foreskin, because his "dick is uncircumstantial.'"

Another was worried about maintaining his street cred because he "had a repudiation to uphold,' and it was 'incumbent upon' him 'to persevere.'" Okay, so the second part was grammatically correct, but that first part wernt and, on the whole, it was a mouthful of self-inflating, pompous language.

I have been asked to help some of my cell mates with their spelling when they write to their baby-mamas on da street, cuz I be all about dem words an' shit. I can only remember part of one sentence, the rest of the letter fading into a blur in my mind's eye.

"...menchoning mabe are relashunship be threw cuz weer buisy wit odder shit, mabe need som woop-creem and shit 2 spice up da flava."

Woop-creem?

I shit you not.

But, to be fair, Pee Whiskey (that was his name) did manage to spell "spice" correctly. I boosted his self-esteem by telling him his spelling was tight, yo, straight. To thank me, Pee Whiskey told me to bet dat up.

Whenever a homosexual was brought into the dorm, all the inmates gave him a hard time, puffing out their chests and acting manly. When they were making fun of the bitch later during lockdown, they continued to voice their disgust, until Pee Whiskey said "Yeah, but up da road—" meaning, if they got convicted and were sent to prison.

"Oh yeah, up the *road*," responded all the others.

"Yeah, dog, dat be different."

"But we be *here*, and dat punkass shit be *whack*."

"Up da road, now, you ain't got no choice!"

"You *gotta* be hittin' dat ass, cuz dat all you got."

"Damn skippy."

"Word, know whut I'm sayin'?"

"Word. Gotta *work* dat shit. Skeet-skeet-skeet-skeet!"

They all laughed and gave each other "daps."

And if they're not talking, they're rapping. Beating on the stainless steel sink and toilet and writing desks, rapping about crack and firearms, and the solace found in the arms of fallen women, and how them crackas got them down and won't let them go, won't let them be free. This is *not* "Swing Low, Sweet Chariot," I am forced to listen to. This is "Kill Whitey" and "Cash Dat Welfare Check So's We Can Git Mo' Crack Rock," but none of them seem to understand that if they kill Whitey there won't be anyone to *write* the welfare check.

Now I'm going to say something that needs to be said. It's on everybody's mind, but no one has the balls to say it, because they all know they are going to get publically destroyed for it, but I'm at the end of my rope and don't give a shit.

I heard several of them talking about how dey hate to wear condoms, ain't never goan do it, and ain't never goan pull out neither, like dem crackas be tellin' dem to, cuz it don't feel no good. And each a dem had several kids. One twenty-one-year-old thug boasted that he had *ten* kids. And there he was in jail.

Every last one of these asshats is a bastard. Think about it. Black community illegitimacy went up from 24% in the early 1960s to over 90% in what's called the urban core, and 70% nationwide. Sure, there are white, hispanic, and Asian bastards, but damn, not as many, and not for the same horrific reason. The willingness of "economically disadvantaged" girls to start having babies at the tender age of sixteen, with 'bad boys' who neither can, nor will, be able to support them, induces a *massive* burden on society. Said bad boys are seen to be appealing due to their overtly macho and combative behavior, including gang membership and criminal violence. Now, for women in general, all is forgivable, because it's sexy.

Sexiness is seen as all-important, to the detriment of Western society, and here's how:

Sexy bad boys don't produce the nice things women want, such as a safe and secure environment, don't work toward an expanding economy, and they don't do anything to advance technology or medical practices. Instead, they produce a rapid descent into poverty and violence by not committing to the raising of their illegitimate offspring.

No, screw that flowery language.

They don't raise their bastards.

They are, therefore, poverty factories. Their bastard kids grow up to beget *more* bastard children, requiring exponentially more tax dollars to feed their kids, who will, in turn, raise the taxes once again. A social welfare system under huge pressure from this already unwieldy and exponentially multiplying underclass is unsustainable.

Statistically, white and Asian parents, more often than not, have children they can afford to have. They're *responsible*. They are then forced to pay for the subsidization of people with no interest in responsibility. Not just that, the subsidization of people who will knowingly beget *more* bastards for the express purpose of bumping up their welfare check, with no interest in providing for those children, who'll grow up as easy prey for gang recruiters and drug dealers who will act as their surrogate fathers, and urge them to commit even *more* crimes and acts of violence, and beget their own bastard kids, to make everything even worse.

So, what it all comes down to, these guys in the dorm with me, excluding the comparatively few people of other ancestry who were just plain bad or stupid, owe their very existence to white people for paying their mothers to have them, and here they were, talking about how the white man is keeping them down. And they wouldn't even be here if they weren't violent or stupid—or just plain evil—and had committed crimes.

Now, here's where I, no doubt, look like a hypocrite, because here I was in jail too, but for trying to do what I thought was "right." Here was genuine evil, the desire to hurt someone else without even the motives of greed or lust or selfishness, for no reason whatsoever, and I am far from it. And I have begun to hate the people who effectively created these people around me, by creating welfare and then writing higher checks to the crack-whore broodmares and knowingly increasing the strain on our economy until its inevitable collapse, to hasten the day that people will say Enough.

Now, I have reason to believe that this isn't some mistake that the government made and is now stuck with. I think that it is a way to continue slavery by putting it out in the open.

A few years ago, a much-contested anonymous open letter claimed that top music industry executives promoted gangsta rap, to encourage people to more actively pursue the glorious life of crime, ultimately to fill private prisons they had a sizable financial interest in. Because of poor grammar in the letter, some felt it was a hoax and was unfairly painting a bad picture of black youth—even though the letter never once included the word "black."

The gist of it can be summed up in this excerpt: "We were told that these prisons were built by privately owned companies who received funding from the government based on the number of inmates. The more inmates, the more money the government would pay these prisons. It was also made clear to us that since these prisons are privately owned, as they become publicly traded, we'd be able to buy shares. Most of us were taken back by this. Again, a couple of people asked what this had to do with us. At this point, my industry colleague who had first opened the meeting took the floor again and answered our questions. He told us that since our employers had become silent investors in this prison business, it was now in their interest to make sure that these prisons remained filled. Our job would be to help make this happen by marketing music which promotes criminal behavior, rap being the music of choice. He assured us that this would be a great situation for us because rap music was becoming an increasingly profitable market for our companies, and as employees, we'd also be able to buy personal stocks in these prisons."

Critics of the letter said that it was preposterous, because nobody goes to prison just for listening to music.

Sigh.

Of course, people don't get arrested, much less convicted, for *listening* to music. They do, however, go up da road following the example set by those rappers. Glorification of violence, drug use, and misogyny isn't something people just enjoy for its artistic merit and then go on about their day. It is a lifestyle that people adopt. They imitate what they see and hear, and it leads inevitably to the commission of crimes, and the subsequent three meals a day, roof over their heads, and laundry done, all at the expense of the state, of which they are proud.

I was asking Sherfonki Robinson one day if he understood this, that if he kept up the way he was acting when he got out, he'd be right back in again. His reply?

"Dere ain't no question! Dere ain't no *question!* Dere ain't no question, dog. Dat's real!"

Ah'm gonna repeat mahsef, I thought. I wonder if I ought to look him up on the FL DOC offender search, and see how many times he's been in since. One day, if I'm not too busy.

There are two kinds of prisons you can go to: work camps and psyche camps. You go to the psyche camp, to avoid work, and are made into a guinea pig. You'll still have to do manual labor every weekday, but it is significantly less. Instead, you'll take whatever pill they give you, every day, and report how it makes you feel to a caseworker once a month. Then, they take you off it and put you on something else, to see what happens.

This is what they mean when they say Clinical Trials.

578

The other camp is slavery, but afterwards it turns out to be less horrific, which makes you twice the sucker.

So, the point? I believe that welfare creates the people that will do either free clinical trials for Big Pharma, which I'll explain later, or free labor for the state, perpetuating slavery that people will enter more or less of their own free will.

And brag about it.

And dat's da troof!

There are two thousand three hundred and four bricks in the day room of my cell block. Some have Puerto Rican flags colored on them, some have the Folk Nation trident scratched in the paint by overgrown fingernails. Some say "Bloods," "Crips," or "las Ñetas," and many of them simply say, "Fuck." That's the best these people can do. Here and there, a vague gang related insult like "Becky Lou," but nothing creative or original. Just a bunch of two-bit hoods expressing their individuality by drawing someone else's signs on someone else's bricks.

I laughed at a chico who wrote "Vanpire Mexican Raza," spelling "vampire" wrong, and he turned to me, thrusting his hands defiantly into his shorts. They all stand that way.

"What you say, dog? Bitch, don't be disrespeckin' me."

"You think your dick's going to fall off if you let go?"

"What? *What?*"

"That means, don't step to someone with your hands in your pants. If you can't defend yourself—" I jump-snap-kicked him in the chin, catapulting him back into the wall, "—this might happen. *Comprendes?*"

"*Mira! Mira!*" I heard above me. Four other chicos came hurrying along the upper tier toward the stairs to defend their comrade. I waited calmly for them all to run down to the day room in a group, while a crowd gathered around to watch. When the five gangstas were all at the foot of the stairs, I ran at the halfway point and leaped, catching the rail and running up the rest of the way, vaulting nimbly over the banister. Now, I held the higher ground on the staircase.

Imbeciles, they all came running back up the steps, not even thinking they'd be hampered by their numbers. Grabbing the rails on either side, I swung my legs up and kicked the two forerunners in the teeth, and they all rolled down the concrete stairs in a tangle. I dove after them, landing with one knee on an exposed flank, staving in three ribs with a sickening crunch. My other knee hit the guy everybody called Flaco in the gut, and he retched violently all over the guy lying next to him.

Then, I knelt on the pile and beat them all savagely until the guards came and dragged me off of them, cuffing me, and sent me back to the hole.

Every time you fight in jail, after you serve your time in confinement, they move you to a new cellblock to prevent future revenge attempts, and there are only so many dorms on one floor. If you can't play well with others, eventually you'll wind up in the Chaplain's cell. That's where all the wimpier criminals go, who want to hide from the bullies. Or maybe those words are too strong. Let me rephrase that: all the guys who want to use the phone and eat their food like civilized people, without getting beaten or raped. Oh, one or two of them actually believe all that Bible-thumping garbage and want to change their lives, but most of them have what's called Jailhouse Religion. They'll pray and sing and put on a big show, even snitching on others who don't edify their Lord enough, right up until their god sets them free, and they toss their Bibles in the trash on the way out the door. All of them had to put in requests and wait in line to get moved into the dorm.

Except me.

VI

We had three church services a day with volunteer speakers coming in for an hour's worth of spiritual masturbation apiece. The funniest were Reverend Barnes, Harrison, and the dynamic duo I called The George and Everett Show. Barnes was this enormous ex-boxer/ex-drunkard with no nose, a bullet-shaped head, and a serious underbite that made him look like a cartoon character. He had that Negro Pentecostal way of screaming fire n' brimstone while spraying spit all over everyone. Harrison—great guy, Harrison, I really miss him—he was the stereotypical snake-oil salesman who was always anointing people, laying on hands, speaking in tongues, and then pushing them over. If you didn't just let yourself fall, if you tried to catch yourself, you were full of demons and in desperate need of an exorcism. It was The Emperor's New Clothes all over again. I loved it.

The George and Everett Show, now there was a real piece of work. Picture an old man with a pompadour who plays these archaic gospel tapes and sings along with all his might in a voice that sounds like he's been gargling glass, while his poor partner stands next to him with his comb-over and Coke-bottle bifocals, looking embarrassed.

Those three acts were the real stars, the life of the party. The rest of the preachers just read aloud out of the Bible and told you what it meant. Yay. Remedial discussions and over-analyzation of simple parables to make sure the message gets across to the slowest minds.

Every Friday our homework assignment was to choose a scripture out of the Bible and read it aloud, one at a time, in the day room at church time. Rather than refusing, I followed the Letter of the Law to a T. When my turn came around, I'd stand slowly and, with great ceremony, open my book of lies. With all the pomp and circumstance I could muster, I would clear my throat and address the congregation, voice booming.

"The Book of the Prophet Isaiah...Chapter 3...Verse 21," —and here I would clear my throat again—"'The rings and nose jewels.'"

Wait a beat for the echo of my voice to fade...then snap the book shut and plop back down into my plastic chair.

Hey, look, they said to read a scripture. *A* scripture. Well, that's *a* scripture. So is John 11:35.

"Jesus wept."

Period.

I followed your little rule. You want me to waste my time? Here, then.

Isaiah 28:8.

"For all tables are full of vomit." Take a bow.

The Second Book of Kings.

Chapter 9.

Verse 35.

"And they went to bury her: but they found no more than the skull, and the feet, and the palms of her hands."

Imperious glare at every face looking up at me, my bearing as sanctimonious as I can manage, wasting *their* time.

Contemplate *that*.

I do this because the only alternative is to go back to the box, and I just can't take that any more. I couldn't take it the last two times I was there, but those were unavoidable. I *had* to fight those guys. The first one took an old man's false teeth while he was asleep, shat in an empty milk carton saved from breakfast, stuck the teeth in it, and sneaked it back under his mattress at the corner of his bunk.

Why? Because Pop wouldn't give his milk to a bully that morning. The old man said No. When Pop woke for dinner and found his teeth, he didn't even say anything. Didn't stomp his feet and holler, didn't go to the guards and complain, he didn't tell anybody.

He just flushed the carton, teeth and all down the super-powered toilet, and did without.

Supposedly, he was in jail because he was rich, and he had an evil deadbeat daughter who'd done the prodigal routine too many times. She wasn't getting another cent out of him, so she and her boyfriend cooked up this story about how he molested her when she was a child and she's finally coming forward. He didn't have to get convicted of it. A lot of child molesters get shanked or beaten to death in jail by other inmates taking revenge for them having been molested by *their* fathers, or uncles, or whoever. If he died in jail, she'd get all of his money because he hadn't drawn up a will yet.

I don't know if he did it or not. He might've, and told us the story so we wouldn't kill him, so he'd be just an innocent man wrongly accused who we should stick up for. It didn't matter. I'd talked to him, played cards with him, and chess, and he seemed like a good man, so when I found out about his teeth I went to the guy who did it, cornered him in the cell he shared with nine other guys, and beat him until every tooth in *his* head was on the floor in a puddle of blood. His homeboys tried to hit me from behind, but I barely felt it. They tried to drag me off of him, but I'd locked my legs around him and wherever I went, he was coming with me.

I stopped when I was finished, and no sooner. All energy drained out of me and left me weak and shaking, like it always does, and I went to the guards who'd just come running in and calmly let them cuff me, lead me away without having to get maced again like last time.

The time after that, the son of a bitch just wouldn't leave me alone. Usually, a guy will just try you once and get the hint when you flash your eyespots, or maybe you have to rough him up a little to get your point across, and that's it. But this guy, though, he just couldn't let me be. The final straw was when I was working out with my cellmates in our room

582

upstairs. I was underneath a rack we'd pulled out from the wall and cleared the mattresses from. A couple of the smaller guys had climbed on for extra weight and I was benching them from the floor at one end, when that fuckhead came in and hopped up onto the rack, bringing it crashing down. If I hadn't been lucky, if I hadn't moved quickly enough, or if this or if that or any number of things, my neck might've been broken. My hands, in the very least. Somehow, though, I was scrambling to my feet hearing him laugh and the others shouting at him, and I caught hold of him between the two guys blocking us. Those two guys stopped yelling and got the hell out of the way.

That time I had to get maced again before I'd let go.

In the course of my studies outside of these walls, I have infiltrated many cults. It's not hard. Modern public opinion is that you should just shop around until you find a religion that best suits your tastes. Browse, as if there were some kind of Great Spiritual Truth flea market.

Ooh, this sect of Christianity makes me feel good about myself, promises salvation, *and* sanctifies my biweekly habit of throwing group masturbation parties, watching my dog fuck my cat!

Where do I sign up?

The inconvenience of righteousness has spawned so many different creeds, each condemning all Evil *except* for (fill in the blank), until every scatophageous gastropodophiliac can comfortably share his perversion in support groups under the guise of blessed Christianity.

And to this, I say Hallelujah. The more these wackjobs spread within the horde of my enemies, the easier my job becomes. They preach the consequences of their own actions, threatening themselves and each other with Judgment, then go home and continue helping *my* Lord.

The beginning of this beautiful disease was brought about by a man I consider one of my personal heroes: Henry VIII. In 1534, when the Pope refused to grant him a divorce, the King of England told him to go screw himself, and started his own church. It caught on because it was more convenient.

Now, that church has degenerated to the extent that it has homosexual bishops. Openly homosexual. *Bishops.*

Not just closet pedophile priests, but higher ranking demonstrators of a perversion my church helped to make accepted. My church, not me. I confess that I do not agree with all of my church's doctrines, but the ends do justify the means.

The controversy generated by this helps to spread further dissension among those so-called "flocks." We study Scripture only so that we can denounce it more thoroughly. We debated these issues in M3B, and I did what I could to feign Christianity because more would listen to me if they thought me one of them. To openly oppose is to automatically be disbelieved, but to sneak about as I did and plant my seeds of doubt is a time-tested method. I guarantee that more than half of the Christian churches in this country have parishioners of *mine* in their midst. We're not wolves in sheep's clothing. We're grains of sand in the oysters of other beliefs. We irritate until they conform to suit us, wrap us up in their own protection to make us less troublesome, and we emerge as pearls do. Prized and coveted such by outsiders that they go searching for more, even planting their own irritants where they don't belong.

An example:

Standing in front of us, Willy Barnes opened up his Bible, licking a fingertip to turn a few translucent pages, tilting back his head and raising his eyebrows to see through the lenses of his reading glasses perched on the tip of his flattened nose. With his forehead wrinkled up toward the fluorescent lights and his page-turning finger running down the text searching for the right line to start with, the word that came to mind was "supercilious." Like one of those guys who steepled his fingertips when he wanted to appear thoughtful. He even went so far as to clear his throat before reading.

Reminds me of, hmm...me?

"Chaptuh Fo' of da Gospel Accodin' ta Maffyew," and he paused to clear his throat again. "Then was Jesus led up of the Spirit into the wilderness to be tempted of the Devil and when he had fasted *forty days and forty nights*—think about that, men! Think about it! Forty days and forty nights! Amen! I betcha he was hungry! Do you think you'd be hungry?" he asked, bending down to peer over the rim of his glasses at one of the prisoners. The startled guy managed to shrink his head back on his neck a few inches, but Reverend Barnes was still uncomfortably close to him. *"Do* you?"

Almost all of us had seen the small white fleck of spit that had shot from one man's lips to the other's. I squinted at it, staring in fascination. The guy was too scared to say anything! I couldn't believe it.

"How 'bout choo?" Barnes shouted at Flaco sitting in the next seat over. The Puerto Rican winced, wiping at his eye, and said "Yeah, I guess so."

"You *guess* so?" Barnes asked incredulously, shooting back upright and bouncing a little. "Uh-*unh,* brotha, you wouldn't be hungry. You'd be dead!"

Nervous and embarrassed laughter broke the tension. I was still watching the spit.

"An' that's what the Devil figgered when he showed up in the wilderness, that if Jesus wasn't dead by now, well, he must be the Son of God. But he knew, if the Son of God was even bothering to fast, he musta bin hungry by now, mighty hungry, else what was the point of fastin' in the fust place? So he went to temp' him! Say, you really in human form, ain'tcha? 'Cause if you wasn't, you wouldn't care 'bout food, but that doan re-ally mean you the Son of *God,* now does it? If you was the Son of *God,* you could take these *stones* and make 'em bread!

"And Jesus said back to him—lissen to this, lissen!—'Man shall not live by bread alone but by e'ry word that proceedeth out of the mouth of God.' Do ya *hear* that? Do ya *hear* that, brefren?" he shouted, bouncing on the balls of his feet and strutting about the day room like a rooster. Holding his Bible shut in one hand with a finger inserted to mark his place, he started gesturing at people with it to emphasize what he was shouting. "You doan *need* them drugs! You doan *need* dat likka! You doan need them fancy cars or them fancy clothes!"

"Amen!" the spiritual yes-men of the dorm said. "Amen! Yes, Lord! Preach it!"

Barnes wiped his foam-flecked lips and mopped his face with his handkerchief.

"So then the Devil try this," he said, opening up his Bible again and reading more calmly. "'Then the Devil taketh Jesus up unto the holy city and set him on top of the highest temple. And he said unto him if thou be the Son of God, cast thyself down, for it is said that the angels watch over thee, and in their hands they shall bear thee up, lest thou dash a foot upon a stone.' And Jesus—lissen to what he said, men! Lissen! —'And Jesus said unto him it is written, thou shalt not temp' the Lord thy God!' But the Devil, he still ain't givin' up, what he do nex' he took Jesus up to the *highest* mountain this time and showed him all the kingdoms of the world. And he say lookit the way I taken us all over the place so easy. Lookit all the things I can do. You can't do diddly squat 'cuz if you coulda, you *woulda* by now! See the great things I can do?" And here Barnes shut the Bible again, started using it for enunciation once more. "I can do more than that! See all them fine houses and fancy cars and fancy clothes, in all these kingdoms of the world? Well, if you fall down an' worship me, all them things will I give unto thee! But Jesus—what Jesus do?—Jesus said 'Get thee *hence,* Satan!'"

Several people winced in the front row.

"Get thee hence!" Barnes shouted, throwing his arms out, spit flying every whicha way.

"Amen!" the yes-men cried. "Amen! Thank you, Jesus!"

"Get thee *hence,* Satan!" Barnes screamed again, jumping up and down. "For it is written! Thou shalt worship the Lord thy God, and only *him* shalt thou serve! He shook off the Devil!" Barnes went down on his knees so fast, with his fist and Bible shaking above his head, that until I got up for a better view I thought he'd done a James Brown split. "Jesus shook off the Devil! Jeeee-zuss!"

"Amen!"

"Amen-amen!"

"Yes, Lord!"

"And you men can do it too!" he shouted, getting back up. "Who's ready to do it wi' me? Who's ready? Who's comin' to Heaven wi' me? How 'bout choo?"

The man he'd rounded on sharply jerked back, swallowed, and nodded. There was applause as Reverend Barnes shouted '*Hallellujah!*' and laid his hands on the poor man's bowed head, chanting 'Oh, rashumba dudda darosha! Rashumba dudda da-rosha! Amen, Lord! Oh, rashumba dudda da—"

"What's he doing?" one of the chicos asked no one in particular.

"Speaking in tongues," a half-believer said out of the side of his mouth.

"Speaking in the language of the angels!" Barnes hollered.

"But I can't understand none a that. In Corinthians 14:5 it says—"

"Then you ain't got Jesus in your heart! You still gots the *Devil* lodged in you!"

"I got plenty a Jesus," the chico said indignantly.

"No, you don't, not if you can't unnerstan' God speaking through me. Maybe you *think* you got Jesus, but dat's the devil telling ya you do when you *don't,* leadin' you furder astray!"

"Now, waitaminute—" he started, but the others seated near him started shushing him urgently.

"Anybody *else* not unnerstan' the tongues I'm speakin' in?" Barnes asked us all.

"Oh, no! Nope! Uh-unh!" everybody but me answered.

Yep. They were reading him loud and clear.

"Good. Oh, rashumba dudda da rosha! Rashumba dud—"

And that was the chink in his armor that I burrowed into. Talking to the chico later, I told him all about how Maryknolls converting pagans to their bullshit religion would integrate any of the indigenous practices they had to in order to make it stick. If the locals insisted on saying Rashumba diddly whatever, while clutching people's heads and rolling their eyes up, well, let them. But they'd give them a different reason to do it. Say, oh you're right to be doing what you're doing, but you are doing it for the wrong reason. *This* is what Rashumba-doodle-doo *really* means. Now, aren't you glad we came into your godforsaken land to tell you that? Good. So, amen-amen, salvation all around. Now you can tell all these other servants of the Lord we brought with us where the gold and ivory is.

"The Holy Trinity, for example," I said. "Is not anywhere at all in the Bible. No implications, even. The idea of a Triune God didn't find its way into the Church formally until the fourth century, under Constantine in Rome. It was adopted into Christianity because of politics. Mesopotamians had Anu, Ea, and Enlil. Egypt had Horus, Isis, and Osiris. Babylon had Ishtar, Sin, and Shamash. India had Brahma, Shiva, and Vishnu. So, we had to have them all, too, if we wanted a hold over those people. That's why we changed the Sabbath to Sunday. The day of the *sun* god. We took the sun disks from Egypt and turned them into haloes. We took the Goddess and called her the Virgin Mary. Where do you think the miter, the altar, doxology, and Communion came from? Pagans! Yunno, in India, when Krishna was born? Their book is a lot older than ours, and they say that baby Krishna was visited by three kings who brought him gold, frankincense, and myrrh! Then Constantine brought all this shit under his roof because that's the quickest way to get people's loyalty—through their gods."

I told the chico that this was the root of it, how we ended up with all of this false religious dogma he had to pretend he believed in or be cast back into the den of wolves. I told him that's all "churchianity" and there was no real dogma to believe in, no Hell to be sent to, and no good reason why he should stop tasting of the fruit. But go on pretending like everyone else does, I told him, or else they'll know you know, and they'll find a way to silence you before you can open anyone else's eyes—just like the Spanish Inquisition did, calling people like *you* who ask questions blasphemers and heretics and burning them alive in public so everyone else could see what happens when you *think*.

And his eyes narrowed, his jaw set in determination, and he said—like so many have before him and so many will after—"*Guero*, I tell my family wha jew tell me. I call them now. I tell them an' I make them stop geeving money to tha church."

"Good. Tell them to spend that money on getting you set free instead."

Ooh, I bet the lawyers in my church appreciated that.

And, maggot that I am, I grew fat inside the Christian dorm. I had a great time being a heretic, pointing out contradictions and discrepancies, spreading dissension and causing unrest, until a man named Gallegher came in and changed my life.

VII

The girls took me down to the DMV, got Dwight Saffron a driver's license, then we swung by the mall and got Dwight Saffron some clothes, and eventually found ourselves in a classic car lot called Ragtops, buying Dwight Saffron a 1959 Chevy Impala. I figured a walking dead man was entitled to a little indulgence. Yeah, I know, it's irresponsible. Sue me.

There's something about living in a cage for a long time that makes you realize what's really important. It's not your hamster wheel nine-to-five or the stupid shows you're in such a hurry to get home and watch. The shame of it is, it definitely takes doing time to figure your real priorities out.

I looked at myself in the side mirror of my new convertible, almost not recognizing myself. My Satanesque goatee was gone, my blond hair conservatively cut and dyed by Ana, and my pale skin bronzed by Missy's Tan-in-a-can. My new ID recorded me looking totally different from any photograph or memory a cop could have of me. But what was truly alien was the look of pure puppy-dog bliss in my eyes.

It was also pleasant, since it was a *used* car lot, not to be offered bullshit alternatives such as taupe or ecru interiors instead of beige and gray, by a merchandising associate instead of a salesman. I paid in credit all at once, instead of initiating a payment plan to assist in eliminating any potential nonperformance of financial resources. It was all straightforward. I lied to a salesman and effectively stole an old car. It's a beautiful thing to walk into a car lot and buy a red and white shark with imaginary money, drive to the finest steak house in the city in it to buy dinner with more imaginary money, and have the witnesses to laugh about it with.

So, then we traveled to a gourmet dining establishment to delight in an incomparable dining experience, assisted by a server who'd introduce herself as if we gave a shit, then introduce the chef if we wished to enjoy a pyrotechnic performance in tableside preparation of any sensational flambé dish of our choosing. When we got to the restaurant, I ordered a thick, juicy red steak smothered in a garlic-whiskey sauce, surrounded by shelled shrimp and fried potatoes, all seasoned with an award-winning blend of eleven herbs and spices, as described in the padded imitation leather-bound menu with decorative tassels, along with a delectable domestic burgundy presented ostentatiously by a sommelier. God *damn*, it was good. I'd lived so long on cold brown slop with watch-springs floating in it, and cold macaroni, that I wanted to cry when I tasted this.

The restaurant was very successful, not only because its food and service were excellent, but because its owner was a member of our church and his longtime feud with the prior top-ranking steak house owner ended as soon as this place opened. The other owner had a couple of food critics in his pocket, and was planning to bribe them into a smear campaign, our spy network warned us.

Not a problem. Crowe's reach is long, and his projects are many and diverse. He didn't just raise livestock out in the Everglades, but pathogenic microparasites as well.

Taenia saginata and *Taenia solium*, respectively beef and pork tapeworms, are two of the three most disgusting yet intriguing parasites that infect only humans, and can grow to over fifty feet long.

What we do is feed the embryos to certain pigs and cattle, and the larvae emerge in their digestive tracts, boring through the intestinal walls into blood vessels. They are then carried into muscle tissue, where they encyst—form a protective capsule around themselves—and develop further. If they are eaten alive in raw or undercooked meat, or a visceral organ like, say, liver, they attach to their final host's intestine and mature into their adult stage. From there, the victim becomes an unwitting participant in a diet program. Whatever they eat from then on is stolen by the parasite, who takes all of the nutrients, and the food completely bypasses the digestive system. A fat person can eat and eat and eat and will still shed pounds at an alarming rate. It beats even a crack stem and a hundred-slab. Jenny Craig has nothing on a tapeworm.

It is an obvious fact, but somehow not well known, that in many situations it is the peon who has more power than the CEO. In the justice system, a judge may sentence a criminal to Life Plus Ten, but it is whomever types the sentence into the computer who matters. One "accidental" tap of a finger can change a convict's prison time to just a year and a day. Twenty years to twenty months. Oopsie. Who but the criminal's family is going to check up on it afterwards? Certainly not the judge or the prosecutor; they have a docket full of new cases waiting. At the end of the day, it's that nobody with the dead-end job who wields the real power. So it is in the food industry. Meat may be inspected thoroughly ten times before leaving to be distributed, but all the truck driver has to do is make one quick detour.

And Crowe's reach is long, his disciples many.

The rival steak house did not last long.

But that's all in the past, water under the bridge. And there was no need to worry about medium rare meat at the place we dined, because only the choicest cuts came here. The drivers, loyal parishioners, saw to that.

During that dinner, I smiled and laughed more than I ever have in my entire life. There's no way to aptly describe the deep happiness of learning to love the little things.

I was reflecting on that when, all at once, I felt it. Something dark inside me opened its eyes. The dormant, hibernating voice awoke, and the satisfaction of a wonderful evening wasn't enough anymore.

Not even close.

Our waitress reappeared and leaned across the table to fill our water glasses with a pitcher, and there were her breasts in front of me. Straining against the fabric of her shirt. I smelled her scent, the natural fragrance of her body, and breathed it deeply. She set my head buzzing. I thought for moment that if I weren't careful, I'd seize her by the arm and yank her into the booth with me, or maybe lunge, bite her breast and shake it as a rat is shaken by a dog.

And then she was gone and Missy was staring at me. Ana's face split into a devilish grin.

"Did you see something you like?"

"Not her, but somebody. And quick."

"Well, keep your shirt on, Hedgehog. We're all going to church as soon as we leave here."

"What time's Mass?"

"Same as always."

"That's too far away."

My fingernails were gouging furrows across the curliqued grain of the table wood. The blind, stupid need came over me like a sickness. A hungry look like a horny dog's made my sisters laugh hysterically at me.

The Church of Adam looked like any other church, and to any passing glance, it was. It didn't lurk, the way it might have been expected to. Instead, it was nestled comfortably in the shade among banana trees and royal palms, its hedges decorated with red and purple bougainvillea. We pulled my two-toned shark into the manicured driveway and followed it around to the parking lot in the back.

We were early, but that was fine. Crowe had taped all of the news stories about me and invited us to laugh at them with him in the rectory before Mass. I had never seen the inside of his modest little house before, having only ever visited his office in the sacristy. We parked and went up to the door, which was perched atop three wooden plank stairs, and knocked Shave and a Haircut.

As we waited, Missy noticed a snail on the step she stood on, next to her foot, a thin trail of slime glistening on the wood behind it. Daintily, she crushed it under the toe of her sandal. It crunched noisily as she ground the shell into slimy shards. I frowned. Ana wasn't paying attention.

A few muffled noises came and went behind the door, then footsteps. Then, the door swung inward and the massive Woolagaroo smiled down at us, winking at Missy as she scraped the snail off her sandal.

"Well, you look different enough, Dwight. And Ana, a pleasure to see you as always. And what is that miscarriage behind you?" he asked, indicating the Impala, parked strategically under a lamppost for better viewing. I swelled with pride.

"It's my new car."

"I'm underwhelmed. Misery," he assumed a tone of mock disapproval. She smiled sweetly up at him. "Have you killed another of God's little creatures?"

She nodded innocently.

"Good. Try not to track its sacred and holy guts into my house." He stepped aside to make room for us and put on a deep and ominous voice. "*Enter.*"

We filed in past him, inspecting the house. His was the most unaustere rectory in Christendom. Artifacts and graven idols from all over the world guarded his walls and corners: Zulu shields with crossed spears; Chinese lions; statues of Vishnu, Ganesh, and Kali; bonsai trees; shrunken heads made of coconuts and hemp; and tiki statues, much like Dipshit makes. There were weapons hung here and there—halberds, katanas, nunchaku, sai, battle-axes—relics of ancient war-glory.

In the center of his living room was the most ornate coffee table I'd ever seen, glass supported by sculpted bronze almost Celtic in its intricacy. Surrounding it were four couches facing each other in a broken square. An ancient Persian rug covered the hardwood floor beneath them, garish in its peach, ruby, and teal.

One of those flat TVs was set into the far wall, and the VCR, though present, was nowhere in sight. The screen was paused on the face of a middle-aged news anchoress, Marcia something, her lips pursed as though ready to receive a kiss.

We sat on the opposing couch and accepted some Ecstasy. It would hit us just in time for the Mass to begin. Crowe un-paused the show, and Marcia told us all about the incredible events at Sacred Heart Hospital.

"There is simply no explanation for what happened, aside from gross incompetence at the county jail. The nurse and guards who pronounced twenty-seven-year-old Dark Geiger dead are facing inquiry pending their termination and possible charges of criminal negligence."

They showed my mug shot—a hilarious shot of a man with long blond hair, pierced eyebrows and lower lip, and a tattoo climbing out of my collar and up the side of my throat. My grin in the picture was from ear to ear. The tattoo was henna— long-term temporary—and had faded after a few months of incarceration. I'd gotten it to see if I'd like to keep the design for the rest of my life without making the commitment. Lucky I did, because now there was plenty of confusion about my appearance.

"Police records describe Geiger as five-foot-nine, with an unmistakable tattoo of a geisha girl turning into an albino tiger on his side, chest, and throat. The intern that Geiger beat after his astonishing resurrection describes him as having *no* tattoo."

There was a review of my heinous crime, followed by urgings to contact the authorities immediately if we see this man. We were gravely warned not to try and apprehend him ourselves as he was extremely dangerous, but call the number on our screen."

Crowe winked at me. "I've already spoken to a friend who owns a bar in the next county. They will say that that man, only with shorter hair and no piercings, got drunk in their bar tonight and bragged to a girl there that he had escaped from jail. They will describe the imaginary girl and the car they drove away in together."

"Thank you, brother," I said.

"Don't mention it."

How could I not mention the momentous relief of being out of that dungeon? Every moment under the naked sky was a treasure, as every moment spent rotting in that cement block tomb under perpetually glowing fluorescent tubes was a torture. Only two things saved me from a swan-dive descent into madness: 1) the futility of a suicide attempt, and 2) the stubborn determination that characterizes all in my family, the perverse refusal to accept defeat under any circumstance. Well, all right, three, but the third I don't want to think about right now.

We watched Marcia invite commentary from some street reporter sticking a microphone in the face of—of all people— Joshua Buckland. Once again, he'd gotten an unasked-for fifteen minutes of fame on the evening news. Predictably, he had not changed at all in his appearance. Except maybe for the paranoid nervous way he kept glancing over his shoulder, as if some lunatic was going to jump out of the bushes from the corner of his eye and take a bite out of his face. Aside from that, he was still plain old him.

"How do you feel about the escape of the man who attacked you seven months ago?" the reporter asked stupidly.

"Well, obviously, it worries me," Joshua Buckland said.

"And could you tell us why?"

"Uh, hmmm. Because he attacked me and handcuffed me and brutally beat me for no reason whatsoever?"

"Please share your feelings about what happened." Pause.

"Well, I guess I'm sick of being asked stupid questions by mongoloid reporters like you."

We roared with laughter at the look on the reporter's face, at the stricken silence that must've fallen over the crew at the news station. The camera swiveled to a headshot of the sheepish-looking reporter.

"Er, back to you, Marcia."

"Thank you, Ken."

592

VIII

Midnight stole upon us, and with it, the sweet distortion of Ecstasy. Everyone rolled during Mass. How better to feel the spirit of our lord of the flesh than in indulgence? We left the cottage and entered the vestry, where our black robes and cowls hung waiting. Crowe himself wore white robes with an intricately-worked black scapular. We were naked underneath.

We entered the dark basilica and lit all the tall black candles with long strands of uncooked spaghetti, the glow of the small tongues of flame giving an eerie unreality to the hall. It seemed that somehow even morning sunlight would be diluted into gloom once it entered our place of worship.

As we were lighting the candles behind the altar, under the inverted crucifix, our congregation glided silently in behind us. Dark shapes, like shadows melting out of the blackness, like soot on tar. We liked to joke that we were only wearing black until we thought of something darker.

My eyes trembled, shaking all the pinpoints of candlelight, little REM jiggles. Lightning bolts of euphoria shot up through me as I made my way to the front pew to stand by (I assumed) my sisters.

Our shadows jumped in the firelight as Crowe took center stage before the altar and raised his arms, fully extended, and brought them together. We sat, making a simultaneous creaking of wooden benches that echoed in the gloom.

"We have gathered tonight…" Crowe intoned in his rumbling stentorian voice. "To welcome our brother back from the abyss. Dark has been missed. Tonight…" He let his voice echo until it trailed off. Silence, like our breaths, held.

"Let's show him how much."

A lone figure made its way up the aisle, bare feet making no sound upon the flagstones, and ascended the steps to the altar, carrying a peach in two reverent hands. With a flourish, the robes came off and Enolah Gaye Taylor faced me, her perfect body shimmering in the flickering candlelight. Her hair fell about her shoulders in a black cascade, her full bow-shaped lips parted, her breasts—I didn't waste my time enjoying the sight.

I leaped onto the dais, tearing my robes off, and Crowe stepped ceremoniously aside. Enolah had taken a step backward, rising up on her toes and setting her perfect ass on the altar, scooting back. I seized her by the shoulders and planted my lips on hers. She pulled me up onto the altar with her, lying back as her hot winterfresh tongue slipped into my mouth. There was no time for foreplay.

I felt her grab my hardness and guide it over her pierced hood to the hot, wet lips, and I was inside her. The burning spread in shudders all over my body, tingling my cheeks and the back of my neck, standing all my small hairs at attention.

Her hips rocked savagely forward, taking me entirely in, and I was only dimly aware of Crowe chanting behind me. I felt, rather than heard, the congregation take up the haunting, hypnotic chant. I looked deep into Enolah's blue eyes and she smiled as I thrust into her like a crazed dog. The warm, tender muscles inside of her clamped down on me like a little mouth, and tried to hold me there.

"Welcome home," she gasped.

At first, the chant was nothing but whispers, the sounds of smoke curling away into nothing. Enolah's face came to mine and our lips met, holding on through our moans and gasps for breath. My eyes closed, and I could feel light rising beneath her. The din of voices rose as well and fast grew deafening, until it was one horrific noise of swelling song and howl.

Her lips broke away from mine and she pressed the peach into my mouth. I felt the dry, fuzzy skin against my teeth and bit into it, the sweet juices flowing down my chin. She bit into the other side, and we held it between us as we rutted on the altar in front of Jesus' sad, upside-down wooden eyes.

The light I felt grew immense and obliterated everything, and it was so beautiful that I lost all sense of myself and the world, until all I knew was Wonderful.

In the entire history of this church as I know it, never once has Crowe stood aside and given his place in the orgy to another. By now everyone had found a partner behind me, and not one soul under that roof could imagine a heaven more complete. Tonight, all the world belonged to us.

In the dead of the night, when even the crickets slept, we drove out into the civilized world, having made our decision. Our supremacy over the Dead God and all his followers had been demonstrated, and celebrated, and now in a moment of reckless spirit, we decided to remind the world of our presence. We would do something to make everyone forget that I was a wanted man.

Brother Crowe distributed the plastic sandwich bags filled with white dust; an ounce and a half of chlorine powder and a certain brand of fertilizer. Along with these were the addresses of Joshua Buckland's fellow church members. To avoid confusion, we each chose one, marking them on a list, and prayed together. Then we dressed, hugged one another, and said good night. I, of course, got the honor of visiting the Buckland residence myself.

I kissed Enolah one last time and left with my sisters.

"Well, that was lovely," Ana said. We were all still rolling hard, and as we approached my car I decided I'd never owned anything quite so cool. We walked with our arms around each other's shoulders.

Now, driving slowly down Magnolia Avenue, we found 581 sleeping soundly. It was a two-story brick perversion of architecture, with a Volvo parked in front of the garage. I parked along the curb a block away, killing the lights, and jogged back to 581. The stars each glowed a different color, and danced as if dangling by strings from a black ceiling, swaying in the soughing breeze.

Silently, I crept up the driveway to the Volvo and found its gas tank. Pulling the little door open, I unscrewed the black lid and slipped my rolled-up baggie into the well. Replacing the lid and freezing at a dog's sudden barking, I cursed and waited for it to stop.

It didn't. It came from the gate to the Buckland backyard, and its vicious warning got louder and more insistent. A light came on in a second-floor window. My heart was pounding so hard my vision pulsed, dimming at the edges with each beat, my throat crimped tight with fear. The window slid upward and a head came out.

"Quiet!"

The dog, loyally doing its job and angered by his master's response, barked louder. The pajama man shushed desperately. There was no way Rex would stop until I'd left his domain, and I didn't dare step out from behind the car until Mr. Buckland put his aureoled head back inside. But there was only so long I could wait. The plastic bag would dissolve any second.

Looking around desperately, my eyes came to rest on a small rock, about the size of a hen's egg. With as little sudden movement as possible, I crouched and reached and took it from the dew-wet grass.

"Quiet! Hush!"

"*No*, damn you!" the dog shouted back. "There's someone in the driveway fucking with your car! *Look!*"

But Mr. Buckland didn't speak Dog, so he just shushed Rex more angrily. When I had mustered enough confidence, I threw the rock as hard as I could at a different window. The shattering glass drew the man's head back in, and I could hear him running to investigate.

Without a look back, I ran like a bat out of hell to my own car. We'd turned around and gotten just past the house when the Volvo exploded, hurling jets of flame into the night. Comets of metal arched into the yard and street, followed by showers of angry orange sparks. The bang and the flash were so sudden we nearly jumped out of our skins, and before the first eyes came to a window, we were gone.

I dropped Missy off at her place, Ana off at hers, and just before dawn I knocked on Enolah's door. She opened, looked at me a moment, and took my hand to drag me in.

Enolah was named after the B-29 that dropped Fat Man on Hiroshima. Physically, she was my sister Ana's equal, and in all ways she was her rival. Her high, beautiful breasts were pierced with spike-tipped horseshoe rings, as were her navel and hood, and left eyebrow. Where Ana was a deep burnished bronze, Enolah was a flawless white.

When she sang at Strega, her soulful voice could move you to tears or lust. Ana's band, her namesake, was more Perfect Circle than Alicia Keyes, and could not be compared to Enolah's because of the difference. They weren't just in different leagues; when the two of them put their everything into a song it wasn't even the same sport. Enolah sang in a dim smoky nightclub with eight black men in suits and fedoras behind her. Ana slung her hair and howled with four scantily-clad, heavily tattooed lunatics.

Almond-eyed, graceful, cunning and manipulative, Enolah vied with wild and uncouth Ana for world domination, and it was close between them.

I awoke in a tangle of lavender silk sheets, surrounded by orchids, white candles half-melted over the furniture, and fake autumn indoor trees, their rose and gold silk leaves scattered on the carpet beneath them here and there. A stag's skull was mounted on the wall facing me with a stuffed blue jay perched on a prong of its antlers, held there by wire wrapped around its taloned feet.

And on the nightstand—the *nightstand*, of all places—her black stiletto Manolo Blahniks, a classier version of a dominatrix heel that had grommets in them, that she wore just about everywhere in jeans, lingerie, or like last night, just by themselves.

I could hear her in another room, making clank-scrape-hissing noises, and I rolled out of bed. Slipping into a terry-cloth hotel bathrobe, I went out to the kitchen where she was fussing about over a skillet full of blackened cinders. She was wearing one of those sexy satin robes that shimmered and just barely concealed her perfect ass. I slipped my arms around her waist, hugged her from behind, and she leaned against me as I kissed her neck.

"Good morning," I whispered.

Toast popped up with a *chunk!*

"How do you like your eggs?"

I looked over her shoulder at the charred mess.

"Burnt," I lied, and kissed her on the cheek.

We ate what she called her "post-apocalyptic omelet," and she told me about how she'd have visited me in jail but Crowe told her not to. Her seeing me would lead investigators to pry into her life, then our connection with the church could be uncovered, and the whole thing would snowball and—

"I understand, baby. That's why I never tried to call."

"I missed you."

"I know, and I don't blame you."

"Dick." She threw her balled up napkin at me, bouncing it off of my

596

forehead, so I jumped up and seized her by the arm, jerking her out of her chair. She tried to resist but I twisted her arm around her back, tore her robe open, and pushed her down over the breakfast table. She cried out, struggling, as I opened my own robe, kicked her legs apart, and savagely thrust into her from behind. Our glasses of OJ spilled over.

"Ow! Damn it, Dark! I'm not ready!"

"You're not supposed to be ready, this is rape."

"You could at least brush your teeth!"

"Oh, you're right. I hadn't thought of that."

I backed out of her and walked off to the bathroom, leaving her where she was. When I came back, she'd retied the sash around her waist and was cleaning up the table. I grabbed her again and pulled her toward the balcony door, composed of two huge sliding glass doors.

"Did I give you permission to move?" I snarled.

"What the hell do you think you're doing?" Enolah asked, incredulous. I ignored her and yanked on the drawstring that bunched all of the blinds over to one side, exposing us to the afternoon parking lot.

"Are you wet yet?" I pushed her hard against the glass.

She gasped. "What are you doing? Anyone can see me."

"I know."

I felt a shiver go through her and grinned. Without warning, I tore her robe open and mashed her breasts into the glass. The horseshoes in her nipples clicked loudly.

"Someone is going to see," she hissed. "Let me go!"

I said nothing, put my hand between her legs and pinched her lips, hearing her moan. I felt the wetness come.

"Please, Dark…shut the blinds and we'll go to bed."

I ignored her and teased her lips with my fingers, pulling on her small thatch of hair, occasionally brushing her clit. She was moaning, writhing against the glass. Over her shoulder, I saw a car pull into the parking lot. She placed her hands on the glass and leaned into me, not aware that the car was drifting by us.

"Do it now," she choked, moaning and thrusting her hips to capture my fingers.

"No, Enolah," I whispered smugly. "*I'm* not ready."

The car hesitated, then pulled into an empty spot directly below us. Whoever was in it was not getting out. Inside my robe, my cock was painfully pushing against the fabric and her firm, beautiful ass. She groaned again and bucked her hips faster, trying to get my fingers inside her.

"Someone is watching you, Enolah," I said softly into her ear.

"Oh no," she moaned, but didn't stop. With my other hand I pulled her robe back, then ripped it off of her. "Noooo!" she cried. The tatters of satin slipped off of her to the floor, and I pressed her pussy against the glass door. Carefully, I spread her lips so that her swollen clit came into

contact with the door. Shamelessly, she rubbed herself on it, making breathy animal noises. Another car pulled into the lot.

"Good girl," I whispered into her ear as she ground her pussy into the glass. It was giving her no relief, which was what I liked the most. I played with the rim of her anus, enjoying her little cries of pleasure and pain. Her clit and nipples were pressed firmly to the door and neither of the two cars' passengers were getting out. I toyed with her ass as I spoke.

"Don't move. Stay here and I'll be right back."

At that, her eyes opened and she turned her head to the side.

"You're *leaving* me?" she wailed. She turned around immediately. Angry, I pushed her ass up against the glass and spread her cheeks. I wasn't about to risk losing my spectators. Taking her hand, I led it down to my hardness, still inside the robe. She caressed it. I could see how red and swollen her pussy was, how the wetness had given it an erotic sheen. Her breasts were red and irritated. I took her hand away and roughly rubbed her tortured pussy with the head of my cock, which had peeked out from between the folds of my robe.

"I won't be gone long," I said.

She was grinding against me and couldn't have cared less.

"I have to get something, Enolah. Turn back around."

She groaned in the negative, and my voice got hard and cruel.

"Disobey me and I'll make this much worse for you."

I had to turn her around myself, and squashed her breasts against the glass. I looked out at the parking lot once more to make sure my audience was still there. Both cars were parked, front row seating. I practically ran to the utility closet.

I quickly found what I was looking for, and when I returned, wasn't surprised to see Enolah on the floor away from the window. Her fingers worked feverishly between her legs.

"You little bitch!" I snarled, grabbing her long blue-black hair, yanking her to her feet by it. She cried out and I shoved her back onto the glass and held her there with my body. I couldn't tell if the cars were still occupied.

I spread her legs roughly with my knee and put her hands high above her head. Tearing strips of the duct tape that I'd gotten from the utility closet, I taped all four of her limbs securely to the glass. She growled in frustration and I laughed, slapping her ass. She started rubbing her hips against the glass, her ass moving in tight little circles. She couldn't move very much, but I decided that wasn't good enough. I had to bind her waist as well. Taking four long strips of tape, I pressed her belly to the glass and secured it there. She squirmed but could not get loose.

I opened her lips again and pressed her clit to the glass. Her juices were smeared all over the door and her thighs. Over her shoulder, I saw definite movement in the first car.

"I want you to do something for me," I said quietly, teasing the inside of her pussy with my fingertips.

"What?" she practically sobbed.

"Accept Jesus Christ as your Lord and Savior."

She stiffened. I smiled, knowing I'd startled the fuck out of her. I could hear her brain spinning inside her skull.

"You're kidding," she said softly. I pushed my finger into her tight little anus and she cried out.

"Then you can stay here all day, and all night."

"You'd never do that to me," she gasped.

"Dare me."

There was silence. Regardless of what was going on in her mind, her body demanded release. My finger was moving in her ass and her clit was still grinding at the door.

"I'll be right back," I said. "Don't go anywhere."

I left again, going to the half-cleared breakfast table. The butter in the butter dish was still warm. No good. I went to the kitchen instead, and Enolah was whimpering when I returned.

Gently, I spread her cheeks and unwrapped the cold stick of butter halfway, smearing it on her. She squealed. Amused, I spread her cheeks further and began teasing her anus with it. The butter pressed into her for a brief second and then I was rubbing it in slow circles again. The hot, melted butter began to drip down her thighs. She moaned and writhed against the glass. When the butter was dripping on the floor, I threw the wrapper away. She was slick and oily, her gorgeous ass glistening. I slid my index finger easily into her again.

"Dark…" she groaned. "You're not…you're not going up my…down staircase, are you?"

"Honey, I'll stick my whole arm up your ass and use you as a hand puppet if I feel like it. Now confess."

She banged her hips against the glass and clenched her cheeks around my hand as I gently thrust in and out.

"Confess your sins, Enolah."

"I've been a very bad girl," she gasped.

"How bad?" I gently licked her ear, taking the ridges of the helix between the two tips of my tongue, and slowly traced it until it met the antitragus, followed that up into her concha —and set her tingling. Tasting the firm edge of the hood and sliding under it to trace back underneath, channeled by the smooth contours, the coil that spiraled into the skull.

"Very," she moaned.

"Renounce Satan, and give your life to Jesus."

Car number three was just pulling up and the man in the first car had his face pressed into the windshield. I could just picture how she must've looked. Her tits were firmly crushed against the glass, smears of saliva on the door by her mouth and a mess of butter and girl-come around her raw and aching pussy.

"Let Christ fill your life. Let Him fill the hole that Satan left."

"*Never!*"

The guy in the first car finally stepped out, making no more effort to hide the fact that he was watching. He folded his arms and leaned against the hood of his car.

I slid my middle finger up into her pussy and thrust slowly with both as she moved her clit vainly against the door.

A woman walked by with her dog and looked up briefly, and just as quickly looked away. The man and the woman in the second car had gotten out as well.

"Do you think you'll ever be a useful servant of the Devil if you could let anyone do this to you? You think you can beguile the Messiah if a mere mortal can torture you this way?"

"Please, Dark!"

"Satan will use you just like I am now, only when *he's* done he won't hold you tenderly and tell you that he loves you. He won't take you into the shower and clean your body. He'll throw you into flames and forget you!"

"No," she hissed, her whole body slick with sweat. Her arms strained against the duct tape. I sighed.

Regretting it, but unable to deny myself any longer, I took my fingers out of her and ripped the tape off of her waist. She screamed, but as I parted her lips from behind with my cock, she was begging and thanking me.

I watched the spectators when I slid inside her. The little group was bigger now. They could see me entering her from behind, thrusting deep into her slippery heat, so wet I nearly slipped out every time I pulled back. With my eyes on the people in the parking lot, the excitement of them watching, I came with only six or seven thrusts and then spurted all over the glass. The audience applauded.

She still had not come at all and I took as much pleasure in her wail of horror as I did in orgasm. I left her there, going back to the table and lighting a cigarette. Her pelvis moved in wider circles on the glass, smearing it with large streaks, her piercings clicking and scraping. The people were still watching, but I'd lost interest. I blew smoke at my girlfriend and sighed.

Converting Enolah was going to be harder than I thought.

The most amazing thing about Gallegher was that he was not a preacher, and never pretended to be one. He was an inmate, just like me. I don't know how old he was, either fifty-five, or seventy-two, or a hundred and eight, I couldn't tell. The only way to describe him is...think Gandalf. Or a skinny Santa Claus.

I can't recall much of anything he said to me the day we met. It's all kind of a blur, but I listened to him for some reason and felt a great weight of sorrow and guilt press down on me. I was suddenly aware of how everything I had done in my life had affected other people, and I wished I could make it up to them. It may have been hypnotism or brainwashing, or an evil spell, but it worked. Somehow, I let him talk me into praying with him.

It had to have been some kind of an illusion, the power of suggestion planting thoughts into my head that my imagination just ran with. That's what it *obviously* was, now that I look at it from out here in the World, but in there, it seemed so real. The imaginary weight that had grown and grown until it was suffocatingly immense, was suddenly lifted the instant I asked Christ to come into my life. I collapsed onto the cold terrazzo floor and cried like a baby.

Some people clapped and laid their hands on me, and I didn't mind so much. They tried to congratulate the old man, but he would have none of it.

"Leave the boy alone!" he growled. "Poor kid has enough trouble without all of you making him claustrophobic!"

"But we're praying over him," one of the guys protested.

"Go somewhere else and pray for yourself."

When they had gone and I'd dried my face, I felt strangely happy. I felt more at peace than I ever had before. There was a light-headedness and a warmth in my belly, just like I was told was the way being in love felt, but had never known for myself. I felt like no matter what somebody said or did to me, I could let it slide.

By and by, I started asking Gallegher questions about the many parts of the Bible that made no sense. He nodded knowingly and spoke. I noticed that although his eyes were kindly, gleaming underneath his bushy eyebrows, and that the set of his mouth, half-hidden under his long white beard, was always pleasant or sympathetic, his face was creased by many more squint and frown lines than smile wrinkles, showing a man who hadn't always been an amiable fellow.

"All that stuff takes a while to understand," he said. "You see, the Bible was written by men. Then it was translated by other men, over and over and over until you get the version we have now. And you see, it's a bit...well, flawed."

"You're goddamned right it is," I muttered.

"That's because it was written for idiots. For those of us who think, and question, all we need to know are the basic tenets. The rest of it, all that gibberish, that's just gravy. The first problem is our conceit in claiming God created us in His image. No! We created "God" in *our* image. The real god is everything and everywhere. God is not He or She because It can and will never be limited by either. God never came down to Earth because that very act proves It wasn't there already. That presupposes opposition, and there can be none.

"*Satan?* What's *that?* An opposing viewpoint to God? Then something larger than those two must exist to have created them. It is utter stupidity to worship a creation and not the creator. To say our God is a jealous god, and attribute human weakness to It, is a blatant effrontery, openly opposing Romans 1: 'Professing themselves to be wise, they became fools, and changed the glory of the uncorruptible God into an image made like to corruptible man.'

"What is the Old Testament, but mythology? Propaganda to sanitize and justify David's rule and dynasty. What better validation for a king than a mandate from heaven? And the rest of it? Sanctification of Jewish policy. And the phrase that should set the alarm bells ringing, the very slogan of brainwashing: 'accept this on blind faith, or face the eternal fires of Hell.' How better to pacify the mindless masses than threaten them with such an outlandish punishment? Tell the herd man that an invisible authority figure, who's always watching him, demands that he lead a strict, joyless life. Or else.

"Then, Christ came. No matter who you believe he was, you must agree that he had the right idea. He told the world that they could all get along and be happy if they just tried to be nice to one another. And if they slipped up once in a while, that was okay. All they had to do was apologize and try not to do it again.

"All very reasonable.

"And when he was murdered, and his followers lost heart, someone said 'Don't worry, he'll be back.' There's nothing like prophecy to give people hope. As long as there is something vague but worthwhile to look forward to, people will be optimistic. They will be comforted.

"But nowadays, mankind is governed by his own selfishness, his own petty and cowardly greed for peace and ease, that anyone who renounces the neon distractions of modern civilization is declared insane. For one to give up the worthless and confining hindrances he calls his life is considered lunacy, when before it was enlightenment. When Siddhartha Gautama walked away from greed, selfishness, and confusion, he walked away from the "World" and returned to the Earth, where he found contentment.

"Those who follow in his footsteps in the East are called Buddhists. Those in the West are called vagrants. I found *God.* I believed the words of Christ. I gave my house to a family that was starving in the street. I gave my car to a man who had somewhere to go, and told him that once he got there, he should give it to somebody else. I gave money to people who played music in the streets and filled passing ears with joyful sounds. I gave my money to the Salvation Army, and to young people who looked too thin. And I was content.

"Then, I tried to explain myself to a police officer who'd stopped me, and he told me I needed a place to call home. So he brought me here. I'm in jail for being a vagrant, a nuisance, and a pest, somehow. In truth, I am here because I followed Christ, and you are here for being against him."

He sat back against the peeled paint and let me absorb his testimony. For the first time, I could find no flaw in the reasoning. It all made perfect sense, except one part.

"So how do you punish those who take advantage of you? How about the cop? How do you get back at him?"

"I don't," he said. "I don't waste my time with hatred because he doesn't deserve to dominate my thoughts. Gandhi'd said something about not letting people run all through your mind with their dirty feet."

"So, you just let anybody who wants to hurt you get away with it?" I couldn't believe my ears.

"No, I just pray that his conscience will convict him, and I can be the instrument by which he changes."

"…Oh."

"Not as much fun as revenge, is it?"

I shook my head.

"But if I take my vengeance in any worthwhile manner, I will have broken one commandment or another, either God's or the state of Florida's. On the other hand, I can respond with love, temperance, meekness, and long-suffering, against which there is no law."

"Aha!" I said, eagerly. I had him now. "But you're in jail anyway."

He shrugged. "I'm not staying."

So simple, yet so convinced.

"I'll be the governor's guest for a while. I'll eat his food and sleep on his itchy mattress until he lets me go, and he eventually will because he has to. In the meantime, I don't have any particular place to be right now."

"You could be here for years!"

"But the second I walk out of here, those years will be nothing but a memory. And memories are lighter than air."

"No wonder they say you're crazy."

"*Hmph!* If all the world's wrong, and only one man is right, why should he change his mind? If nine million people do a stupid thing, it's still a stupid thing. And if all the world is insane and only I rebel, they will point their fingers and call me a madman, but they are still insane."

"You can't fight them all, though."

"That's why I don't."

I made a face and sniffed, but he was still right.

"Romans 8 says those who seek after the spirit will attain eternal life, but those who are carnally and physically minded, who seek after the flesh, will find only death."

"Doesn't mean you can just—"

"I've heard about you, you know," he interrupted, changing the subject. "You raise a lot of good points, getting people to think. Think about this: people often wonder why the Bible doesn't mention anything about Jesus between age twelve and thirty. Know why? Because he wasn't around. The Hindus in their book talk about a mysterious young holy man who came out of the west to perform miracles and teach, and *be* taught, and he went away having learned a lot from them that he wanted to spread to his own people. Matthew even hints of it. Makes you wonder."

"Yeah, I know what. When Krishna was born—"

"Gold, frankincense, and myrrh. I know. Tell you something else, about Christmas."

"Oh, I know *all about* Christmas! People talking about how we should put the Christ back in Christmas, how it's become too commercialized, all that shit. Truth is, Christ wasn't really ever there!"

"Do you know when it became this way? Commercially, I mean?"

"Er, no."

"Merchants started promoting it in the 1870s, that's when. And now what was really Yuletide pumps $37 billion into our economy. Hell, FDR even moved Thanksgiving—the authentic American holiday!—back a whole week so there could be more time for Christmas shopping."

"Yeah, it's tragic."

"No, it isn't."

I stared at him, blinked a couple times. "What?"

"Commercialized Christmas, with the Coca-Cola red Santa Claus and the jingle bells and all the mistletoe is great, because people are happier, and actually care about each other for a whole *month* instead of grousing and bitching about how much life sucks. You know, any merry-making at Christmas time was banned in America for a long time because Cotton Mather called it 'an affront unto the grace of God.' Actually *banned*. But we knew Cotton Mather was a prick, so to hell with him. Decent people *had* to bring back Christmas cheer with all this commercialism because life without it, this 'affront to God,' well, sucks, especially in the wintertime.

"Do you know about Easter? Christ, do you know about Spring Break, even? What an interesting phenomenon, all these college kids coming to Florida to get drunk and fuck strangers once a year, to just go wild. Hmmm. Sounds suspiciously like the same fertility festival that every pagan culture had since forever.

"Now check *this* out. Persecution of the Jews started up because of revolts against the Romans, 64 to 70 and 132 to 135 AD. Up until 70

AD the Christians were considered just another branch of Jews, so they got suppressed along with them, so what they did was start celebrating Easter instead of Passover, to distance themselves. They made up this Easter thing, assimilating pagan festivals that just happened to be around that time anyway. Tammuz and Ishtar. Attis and Cybele. Adonis and Aphrodite. Death and resurrection celebrated by fasting and then feasting.

"Here's a perfect example of how obvious it is: dead on Friday, risen on Sunday? *Hello!* How did three days and three nights turn into one and a half days and two nights? Any kind of rationalizing it for Sunday undermines Jesus' prediction. He had said three days. Period."

Late one night, after a long talk with Gallegher—of which there were many—I stared out the narrow plate window at the rain pelting the rooves of the jail below, the wind rustling the wire and tossing the fronds of neighboring palm trees. I asked whoever was really in charge out there, the guy who was making that rain fall, to set me straight. I couldn't just go against everything I'd grown up with, right off the bat, but I had to know which side to be on. We've got frameworks in our mind, formed from childhood, that all our perceptions are based on. At least, that's what psychology books say. Those frameworks are hard to rearrange.

The moment my memory began was in a Mass, moving in the darkness slowly, not knowing where I was. Tall, black-robed figures all around me took slow steps forward. I felt like a little lamb or calf, following without knowing why, moving across the cold stone floor because that's what those around me were doing. The memory of my first thought was panic, then confusion, then the wondering if any of us knew where we were going. Or were they all confused and following the guy in front of him just because he looked like he knew where he was going?

My next conscious thought was déjà vu, a flashback to a past life as a lemming, moving mindlessly in a swarm toward the cliffs and the sea and our death. I remember trying to steer away out of the line, but a firm hand ushered me back to my place. From then on, in all things, I've obeyed. The dreamlike eeriness of "Where am I? How did I get here?" I would come to feel again after drink- and drug-induced blackouts as a teenager, and the haunting familiarity of it left me with a vague fear. Nightmarish paranoia.

The chant began, and it seemed everyone knew it but me. I was lost, with no way to catch up, and I have been faking it ever since. Sometimes I feel like I've been faking my whole life, terrified that someone might find me out.

Lightning crashed, splitting the sky, thunder chasing it. A storm is a beautiful thing when you're in jail. Gallegher and I would stare out of our window every time it rained, and wish aloud that we could be out in it. There's almost nothing like a walk in the rain. You see all the movies where a guy escapes from prison and comes out into the rain, raises his arms, and the camera rises up from his smiling face. The music swells and everyone wants to cry, and they do it in every damn movie you see. Well, you spend time in jail and you'll be daydreaming crap like that, too.

Of course, no voices came booming out of the sky and no angels appeared to tell me Satan was a liar. There was no Old Testament-style revelation or anything like that at all. All of a sudden, I just knew.

I knew I was a pawn, and the butt of some huge cosmic joke, and that all of that Hollywood Good vs. Evil stuff was a bunch of horseshit. I cannot describe the relief I felt, suddenly knowing that I'd been worrying over allegiance to figments of my imagination. No red guy with horns and a tail was going to appear out of the ground and pop my head like a zit because I had been disloyal.

What I'd really been hesitant to let go of was the rage that had burned in me all my life. The rage against people who hurt the weak and kicked them when they were down. The bitter, unthinking hatred of liars and thieves and manipulators who put on coat hanger halos and Amen Brothered or Hallelujahed when their very own habits were condemned.

It seemed sometimes the staunchest supporters of Christianity were the most satanic.

Until I realized it was the Satan inside them that made me grind my teeth until they bled. It was the Satan in them that I wanted to torture and rape and kill. And it was the Satan in me that I fed by not letting it go.

I couldn't blame God for the evil men do, especially not when I was doing the same as them. Or worse.

That's what I realized in the space of one lightning crash.

And, of course, that all went out the window the minute I stepped out of Sacred Heart Hospital, resurrected.

X

With Crowe's help, my father and I built two break-barrel shotgun pistols in our garage when I was a kid. They were like flare guns, almost. Pop the barrel and insert one twelve-gauge shell, snap it shut, and it's like a glorified Derringer, but since there was almost no barrel length to keep the shot straight, accuracy was shit past fifteen feet. Put a slug in there and you could get about forty feet, but the whole point of them was point-blank collateral damage.

The handles were black walnut, and the rest nickel-plated. Goddamn, they were pretty. When they were finished, we gave them as gifts to my sisters, and I admit I was the teeniest bit jealous. Not that I was selfish. It's just that I, kind of, got the impression they were going to be mine.

We mixed up a collection of different shells to load them with, so every time another shell was fired it was kind of a surprise. There were bolo shells, with two or more metal balls connected with wire that would come out spinning. Flechettes, a couple of fin-stabilized solid metal wire pieces. Steel core and truncated cone that pierced armor. Then there was Dragon's Breath, my favorite, a shell containing exothermic pyrophoric misch metal that blew a fucking fireball.

Along one side of each barrel, where the name and caliber usually were, was the embossed word "dagger."

My sisters loved them, and carried them in their purses or handbags or little clubbing backpacks for a little while, until the novelty wore off. Man, I was green about that.

That is, until my eighteenth birthday that December, when Dad presented me with Switchblade.

It was, hands down, the coolest gun ever. Did you ever see in the movies where the bad guy has a suppressed barrel pop out of his sleeve with a loud *shunk!* and he squeezes a trigger that wasn't there a second ago, and blows some guy's brains out who's about to shoot him? It's not a little Derringer that jumps into his hand, but a spring-loaded weapon harnessed to his forearm?

Mine had a silencer, and fired ten .45 caliber slugs, making no more noise than cracking a knuckle.

With practice, I got so good with handguns that I could juggle three of them, firing sporadically, and hit a target reasonably well every time. I don't know when that would ever come in handy, aside from bragging rights, but Dad wanted me to do it, so I did.

The minx Enolah went off to work and left me to my own devices. She blew me a kiss in the parking lot as she drove away, and I vaulted over the side of my Impala into the driver's seat. My first mission was the obtaining of a newspaper for a) gloating over anticipated headlines and b) circling little job opportunities in the classifieds. I am qualified to do a lot more than professionally juggle firearms and fake a convincing death, but unfortunately, my boredom threshold is too low for me to tolerate most occupations.

I will not work in a cubicle, having spent too much time recently in small, stuffy surroundings. I will not sell chewing gum, breakfast cereals, or tampons. I will not clean toilets, floors, or automobiles. I've already been fired for irresponsibly answering phones at a crisis hotline, spiking restaurant entrées with laxatives, and sabotaging cars at an auto service garage.

I'd work at the post office, reading mail and altering it to screw with people's lives, but the act would be too impersonal. It wouldn't give me the satisfaction. No passionate arsonist can set a building on fire and not watch at least part of it from a safe distance.

I used to use my police scanner in nearby college dorms to eavesdrop on students' conversations. With information easily obtainable from the lobby, I could find out who was who, and from my spying tell what room the resident drug dealer lived in. Then, impersonating the police with a few of my friends, we would raid the place at their most vulnerable moment. We'd confiscate everything—drugs, money, computers that "may have been used in the organization of drug traffic," and anything we saw that just happened to look cool. College students invariably possess assorted cool stuff.

Locking them up in our van, we'd scare the shit out of the kids to get them to work out a deal. They'd give us the names and addresses of their suppliers, we'd go raid *them* too, and then dump all of them together out in the middle of nowhere. Who would they complain to? The real police? I think not.

Of course, that doesn't constitute gainful employment.

Maybe we could use the scanner idea again to spy on people who use psychic hotlines. Once we know their deepest desires or concerns and have the inside scoop on them, there's no telling what we could do. But in the meantime, what did Dwight Saffron, law-abiding citizen, do for a living?

Things had gotten pretty hairy the months I was in County, and our town and the lands adjacent still hadn't gotten back to normal. Apparently, our police station had been blown up. The only cops left alive were those cordoning off an area downtown where *more* bombs were taking out more than three-score people. Martial law was declared shortly afterward, while the populace was rioting and looting left and right. Curfews enforced at gunpoint, all kinds of fun stuff.

The chaos swiftly abated, and a new police station was being built, the replacement cops bivouacking at the fire department. The news promised that everything would soon be back to normal, and my congregation was determined to make liars out of them.

The President's speeches about "The War on Terror" had long since gotten stale, considering what had happened on what was cutely dubbed "9/11," the Oklahoma City bombings, the "Rahowa Crisis" of this past year, and everything going on in Jerusalem. Everyone had grown so desensitized that no disaster, no atrocity, could hold anyone's attention longer than the next commercial for the impending summer blockbuster. Insectine attention spans.

Problem not. Soon, we will grab the nation by the balls and not let go.

Brother Crowe had promised it, so it must be true.

The US Mint has been making some of my occupations slightly more difficult, especially while I was away. I had been required to study everything on this country's paper currency to prevent some of the fuckups that Joe Counterfeiter Schmoe commits on a regular basis.

A bill's serial number begins and ends with letters; the first one identifies the Federal bank that issued it, and the last one tells how many times the number between them has been run. Five other parts of the bill repeat the first letter in the serial number in different ways. Any discrepancy in those automatically ring alarm bells when you know what to look for. Say the letter in the big circle off the right of Washington's head is a B. The first letter of the serial number must be a B, and the four digits in a long rectangle across the front of the bill must all be 2s. The short letter-number immediately to the left of the upper left hand 2 tells the position of that particular bill on a 32-note printing plate. The one above the lower right hand 2 tells which plate was used.

"Novus Ordo Seclorum," which is Latin for "New Secular Order," is contradictingly near "In God We Trust." "E Pluribus Unum" was protested originally by Ben Franklin, who wanted to slogan to be "Rebellion to Tyrants is Obedience to God." Shame he didn't get his wish. The motto on the very first US coin, though, was "Mind Your Own Business." I had to learn all that.

But these days, there's not only a clear polyester thread embedded vertically in all but Ones, but a watermark portrait, a microprinting lining the central portrait's rim, and color shifting ink.

You'd think this would pose a problem.

But the symbol in the middle of the Great Seal, the *trinacria*, inspired me. The pyramid with the shining eye floating above it, that's a Freemason symbol. It means, in a nutshell, "change."

So, I did.

With all the advancements to thwart counterfeiting, I decided instead to try a different tack.

As Dwight Saffron, I look like a clean cut, respectable citizen. Dressed properly, I could pass for a Fed, so on this, my second day of freedom, I did.

Sitting with several members of the next parish, we copied down the serial numbers of one hundred twenty-dollar bills. Real bills. Nothing counterfeit about them. We typed all the numbers and printed them out using shitty ink on low-grade paper, because using anything better would look home-made, and this had to look like something efficient the cops would use. That shitty ink that fades pretty quickly, and you end up with a bunch of blank paper where you used to have receipts.

It looked official. The accomplices, they all looked suspicious. They looked like what they were: wild, fun-loving kids from another town. And I looked...well, the way you'd expect a Dwight Saffron to look.

The accomplices, they were from the Palm Beach County parish, so we drove south, all the way to Miami. I stayed out of sight while they spent money all over the place, buying up this and that, whatever they wanted. Tons of top-shelf liquor.

That night, we partied much like last night, only it wasn't blessed and unholy. Just a party.

Bright and early the next day, in a nondescript brown sedan we too-easily stole, I went to every establishment they'd purchased goods from the previous day, marched in with grave confidence, flashed my badge that Crowe had somehow supplied, and informed the managers that there was reason to believe counterfeit bank notes were circulating in the area.

"Oh no," most of them tried to reassure me. "We check every bill, twenties and up, for watermarks, micro—"

'Yes, and I'm glad you do," I interrupted. "But the gang we're chasing are very clever. What I have here is a list of serial numbers. If any twenty dollar bills have been passed here, you have been fooled into accepting counterfeit money. If we find any, I will write you a receipt, and see that my superiors reimburse you for any money lost."

And whaddaya know? I wrote a lot of receipts.

And that was my third day of freedom.

These days, the security guard in a bank is paid to stand around and do jack shit if the place gets robbed. He is not to interfere whatsoever. That is the job of the local law enforcement. The reason for this is "customer peace of mind." The presence of a security guard is a reassurance, nothing more. If a gang of shotgun-brandishing lunatics in balaclavas burst through the front doors, screaming and shoving people to the floor, they will be caught within a mile of the bank and that bank's patrons will breathe deep sighs of relief and continue to keep their money there.

If Dudley fucking Do-Right plays the hero and there is a bloodbath down at First National Bank of Wherever, no one will want to go in there ever again. So, halfway intelligent bank robbers know to just walk leisurely in, not causing a scene, and calmly rob the bank.

Mostly intelligent bank robbers know about things like bait money and dye packs. The last section of the drawer has a small bar that ostensibly holds the stack down in place, but really activates a silent alarm whenever it's raised. Dye packs are more fun. Just try blending into a crowd with a huge red splotch on you. Try spending bright red money. I have owned a few dye packs in my day. They're great for breaking the ice at parties...well, as long as it's someone else's party.

Very intelligent bank robbers know about the many other different ways to be apprehended, or at least thwarted. It takes quite a bit of studying to make a completely successful bank robbery. Quite a bit more to make a career out of it.

Surely you can guess how I spent my fourth day of freedom.

XI

But back to Enolah.

I've been leaving Enolah since Day Two, but I never seem to get out the door. The explanation must come in a roundabout way. In the Church of Adam, we all receive our "fruit of knowledge" as soon as we are old enough to. There's none of the longing or the fantasizing about what it must be like, because as soon as we become curious, it's available. All things are sanctioned, so we miss out on all the sneaking kisses and illicit, backseat steamy fumbling and heavy breathing and exhilaration of adolescent conquest. It's no lie that you appreciate more what is difficult to obtain.

Since the novelty inevitably wears off, we go the way of all the Jaded. We degenerate and deviate, we split for new ways to achieve the old feeling, and the quest for something fresh has strange horizons. After years of twisted debauchery, I'm sorry to say, you'll end up with the sex drive of a panda.

I got out of sado-masochism when I graduated from high school, spurning it as "kid stuff." Hurting and being hurt is only fun when your mind is confined by the flesh it lives in. The way I've always seen it, since I was a child, your body is only something you wear so others can recognize you. There is nothing you can do to it, without maiming, that will not be forgotten sooner or later. Physical pain and pleasure are fleeting, and as I've said before, my boredom threshold is low. Besides, with the popularity of piercing and self-mutilation these days, it is way too frustrating to be a sadist.

Graduating to D&S—Domination and Submission—I was able to touch minds and emotions, touching people in places and ways that could leave a dent in them only intense therapy could hammer out. There are fools who indulge in the bullshit they call "tradition," but it's just some crap a guy made up a few years ago and said "This is how we're going to do it." I take no stock in "collaring" someone in a ceremony with their "leather family." All that is Scene, and Scene is when you stop doing something so you can talk about it instead. And the day you stop fucking so you can *talk* about fucking instead is the day you've thrown in the towel.

Enolah Gaye Taylor made her living as a dominatrix. Men and women pay her to be told they're worthless. They pay her to humiliate and debase them, to whip them and cut and scar them. She punishes them for what their hippie parents allowed them to become. Daddy beat them either too much or not enough, and Mommy didn't care.

The art of it is when you know what people hide in their secret places, and you touch that nerve to sting their real tears out. When you cross the line from the psychosomatic crap and "Yes, Mistress" groveling to real emotional cruelty, you have the ability to mess someone's life up forever.

Barbeque their sacred cows, so to speak. Throw open that trapdoor covering the oubliette of their subconscious, and take a good long piss into the hole. They all view themselves from that framework of early experience, and once they have that view dashed to smithereens it is impossible for them to pick up the pieces on their own.

A madman once said that a moment of self-realization is worth a thousand prayers. Once you see yourself from a distance, peripherally, the way you look at the side of a thing to see it in the dark, you can never feel the same way about yourself again. My favorites were the women with no inner confidence, who measured themselves only by their reflections in other people's eyes. Swing the mirror on that fact, the key to their every motivation, and confront them with themselves, and you dash them to bits at your feet. Sex is where we find out things about ourselves we would rather not know, good things and bad. Vulnerable need, humiliation, pain, rejection and acceptance. Who we *really* are comes out.

Of course, that gets old too.

The real fun begins when you delicately pick them up and praise them for what they are underneath their façades. You dust them off, you dry their tears, and you put them back together again, telling them they are stronger than before. You become their God.

And you can shatter them again, any time you want.

When I met Enolah, she was so calm and self-assured. She had the cold, calculating predatory cunning of a snake, and I thought, "Here is my equal." Then I broke her in half. It was disappointing to see her tears, the blood of the soul, stream down her quivering cheeks.

At the core of her being is a little girl who wants to be respected, loved, and eventually worshipped, and can't accept the fact that she's human and incapable of what she thinks she sees in other women. She sees their disguise and, like men, is deceived. So, she worries over the nails, the skin, the hair, the makeup, and the clothes. She studies the fashion magazines for the latest trendy way to decorate her shell. She sees her idol, rival, and nemesis, my sister, with gold piercings. So, she got platinum. If Ana cut one of her tits off, Enolah would cut off both. I despise that in a person.

While I insist on looking good myself, I refuse to suffer the slings and arrows of outrageous fashion, but I cannot find the resolve to leave her and stay gone. Why? Simple.

Because she's hot, and can fuck like a dream.

She can suck the paint off a car door. She rides the Meat Boat all the way to Gravy Town. Which are all highly admirable qualities, no matter who you are. But I know her better than she knows herself, and that is the deep dark secret a bride of God cannot have. It was her presumption to even try competing with my sister that led me to first hold her in contempt.

But now, I recognize her right to respect herself. Now I recognize the sanctity of all life and everyone's right to pursue completion. I know, as only a saved individual can, that peace and completion are unattainable without Jesus Christ, and am determined to share that with my girlfriend. Of course, I have to do it in my own perverse way. And there's a very influential voice in my head that tells me not to bother. That's not the "Devil" in any literal sense, but it is a demon, the shadow in my head, that is very real and very persuasive. The Christians' Bible is correct in the gospel according to some guy Matthew, the twelfth chapter I think:

"When the unclean spirit is gone out of a man, it walketh through dry places, seeking rest, and findeth none." So, it says Screw this, and goes back to the home he'd been evicted from, finding it "empty, swept, and garnished. Then goeth he, taketh with him seven other spirits more wicked than himself, and they enter in and dwell there: and the last state of that man is worse than the first." Anyone who's ever driven out a personal demon—smoking, drinking, drugs, masturbating, whatever— knows that when it comes back, it always comes back seven times stronger. If you diet for six months, you'll overeat when you take a break. If you're a fat cow and you diet all the time, now you know why.

I've begun writing a self-help book. It will not be a bunch of feelgood bullshit that makes you think you are beautiful and special the way you are without changing any of the bad habits that make you ugly and mundane. Do not expect an 18-carat, 200 proof, matured in oak and 97% fat free life management course of six cassettes for the low, low price of $49.94 plus $3.50 shipping and handling. Do not expect to receive in six to eight weeks what you would assume a Satanist would—and often does—try to sell you.

It will give the advice all of America needs to hear, but until now, the writers have been too chickenshit to give. I'm going alphabetically, and I'm going to save people's lives by self-destructing them. I'm starting with Alcohol, by which the miracle of self-realization is possible and I'm going to leave out any disclaimer about abusing it.

Alcohol is magic.

Alcohol is the vehicle by which people get past grudges, pride, prejudice, and fear. Honest connections are made between people, through which enemies become friends, masquerades end, and hidden love is made known.

Alcohol heightens the senses and gets one in touch with his own secret feelings—the ones he hides even from himself. The tears and the laughter, both highly therapeutic, would remain locked away if not for the divine power of Drink.

Why does this need to be mentioned? Because our culture has taught us how to lie to each other—and ourselves—about everything, and the only thing that will make us speak honestly is drunkenness. "Out of the mouth of babes" can only happen after multiple shots. Then, and only then, can

614

we break things down to their true essence. Like, So-and-so isn't a sadist with father issues and a Napoleonic persecution complex. He's a prick. Notice that? There are no simple descriptions anymore.

You can't just be a daydreamer anymore. You are suffering from Attention-Deficit Disorder. You can't be angry, offended, or even righteously indignant. You have repressed mental anguish over pre-adolescent trauma that has developed into Borderline Personality Disorder with possible resentment of latent homosexuality and an Oedipus complex that needs to be dealt with.

And you're in Denial about it.

What we all need is medication. What we all need is our individuality, in whatever form it takes, pruned. Trim this, amputate that, until we are all distinguishable from each other by outward appearances only. Psychotropic drugs for everybody. Bend the populace to fit into this mold, that cookie-cutter shape, a generation of milquetoasts who meet with "sharing groups" to discuss their "feelings". According to the experts, this is what America needs.

Bullshit, you cocksuckers.

Subject A is a class clown.

Subject B is a bully.

Subject C is a daydreamer.

Subject D is a fag.

And until this is all out in the open, I prescribe them alcohol to help maintain their personality.

We are told to be comforted in that we're unique, but then the very differences in us are catalogued and labeled with euphemistic pomposity, followed by the surname Disorder. I've apparently got Intermittent Explosive Personality Disorder. My victims have Post-Traumatic Stress Disorder. As if whatever the "proper" Order is, that's what we should strive to be through medication and counseling—to what end?

To all be *alike?* Uniform?

It's okay everybody! You don't have to be unique anymore! There's a McDonald's on every block nowadays, and a one-night-stand in Rio de Janeiro is no different from masturbating at home! Only one flavor of jellybean from now on!

If *this* is the Utopia they're shooting for, I expect they'll have assisted suicide in package deals before too long.

It was Gallegher, surprise surprise, who had a few things to say about psychiatry's open-ended, fictitious diagnoses and resultant prescriptions to make all of this more concrete in my mind. It turns out he used to be a psychiatrist, and eventually couldn't look at himself in the mirror anymore. He told me, and I quote:

"Psychiatry is one of the biggest scams in history, causing more damage to the people of America and, these days, the world, than even orga-

615

nized religion. The American Psychiatric Association's Diagnostic & Statistical Manual has grown from 7 mental disorders in 1880 to 112 in the 1952 edition, to 374 in the 1994 DSM-IV, and not because more was learned about the human brain, but because charlatans like me became more creative.

"By 1970, psychiatrists and the pharmaceutical industry had agreed upon a joint marketplace strategy. They would call all things emotional and behavioral "psychiatric disorders" or "brain diseases" and claim that each and every human attribute was due to a "chemical imbalance" of the brain. They then launched a propaganda campaign, so intense and persistent that the public soon believed that pills would cure you of the horror of being you.

"Pharmaceutical companies invited me to Hawaii for conferences, paid my way there and treated me to a fine bit of R&R, also sponsored my research, and paid me handsomely every time they wanted me to parrot whatever they had to say as a speaker or consultant. I got the royal treatment from the good people who make Ritalin. You want to hear something disturbing?

"NIMH, the National Institute of Mental Health, invented what they call Attention Deficit Hyperactivity Disorder. You might've heard of it. It's the most successful invented disease ever. They revise its diagnostic criteria fairly regularly, not for any medical or altruistic scientific purposes, but really just to cast a wider marketplace net. The US Department of Education Children and Adults with Attention Deficit Disorders call ADHD a "disease" so real and terrible that a parent who dares not believe in it, or allow its treatment, is likely to be deemed negligent, and no longer deserving of custody of their child. This is happening in family courts across the country by the hundreds of thousands.

"As if drugging more than eight million kids with Ritalin wasn't enough, we doubled and almost tripled the psychiatric diagnosing and drugging of normal infants, toddlers and preschoolers between 1990 and 1995. We knew these drugs were addictive, dangerous and even deadly. We know that Ritalin and all amphetamines cause growth retardation, brain atrophy, seizures, psychosis, tics, and Tourette's. But we did it anyway.

"I was consulted in three cases where there appeared to have been deaths due to Ritalin or amphetamine treatment for ADHD. There was Stephanie Hall, eleven years old, of Canton, Ohio, who died in her sleep the day she started an increased dose of Ritalin. In March 21, 2000, Matthew Smith, fourteen, of Clawson, Michigan, fell off his skateboard, turned blue and died. His myocardium was diffusely scarred, its coronary arteries diffusely narrowed. Ritalin was, indisputably, the cause of death. Randy Steele, a nine-year-old boy from Bexar County, in Texas, became unresponsive without a pulse while being restrained in a psychiatric facility. His heart was found to be 'enlarged.' He'd had ADHD and had been on Dexedrine; d-amphetamine. Of the 2,993 adverse reactions to Ritalin, at least the ones that were reported to the FDA, from 1990 to 1997, there were 160 deaths and 569 hospitalizations. You can look all this up.

"The fact is, all those kids were normal, at least until the amphetamines they were given caused brain atrophy, making their little noggins shrink about ten percent smaller. Just like everybody else we diagnosed and then unnecessarily drugged.

"For the vast majority of drugs we used to combat mental illnesses—especially depression—we have no idea how they work, yet pretend we do. Patients are regularly told, when prescribed antidepressants like SSRIs, that their depression is due to a chemical imbalance in the brain. SSRIs, like Prozac, for example, increase the amount of serotonin in the synapses between neurons by preventing its re-absorption by the neurons. Because these drugs seemed to work, doctors and pharmaceutical companies decided that depression resulted from a deficit of serotonin. But that's stupid, because a drug alleviating a symptom doesn't mean you can conclude the symptom was due to the deficit of that drug. It's like saying headaches are caused by not enough aspirin in your system.

"Basically, instead of developing drugs to treat abnormality, abnormalities are postulated to fit the drugs. Doctors make a lot more money prescribing drugs than talking, so during the hour occupied by a talk therapy session, a psychiatrist can see and prescribe meds to three or four patients, and pharmaceutical companies make millions by prescribing drugs for mental illnesses, so they're continually trying to expand the range of imaginary conditions that count as drug-requiring "illnesses," including obsessive-compulsive disorder, ADHD, you name it. Medical students are now given minimal training in talk therapy and *lots* of training in how to prescribe drugs.

"Of course, we also have adverinfotainment masquerading as news to help us. Take CNN, for example. They did a spot for Strattera, yet another drug for ADHD, and they were all laughing about the diagnostic questions on the drug's website. "Do you feel unfocused, disorganized, or restless?" Why, yes! "Do you feel unable to concentrate?" Of course, I do! All the while, the crawl along the bottom of the screen is keeping us updated about Laci Peterson, and sports scores and temperatures are flashing, along with blips and blurbs and graphics all competing for our attention. How are you going to focus on anything after that? Now that we're all accustomed to absorbing all that information simultaneously, trying to focus on any one thing bores us quickly.

"There's a book called *Your Call is Important to Us*. You've got to find that book. It'll change your life," he added. "I just paraphrased that last part from it, but don't tell anyone."

"Your secret is safe with me," I said.

"You know what else doesn't help? All that fluoride you've been gargling and swishing since you were little. Did they give you free bottles of fluoride in school, ostensibly to help with your teeth?"

I thought for a second, remembering, and with a crawling fear, nodded my head.

"Well, news flash, buddy boy. Fluoride doesn't do a damn thing for your teeth. There's nothing good for you about it. The reason they tell you to put it in your mouth is, that's the quickest and surest way to get it into your system. What it'll do is shrink your pineal gland and make you less capable of thinking for yourself, make you more susceptible to suggestion. If you crack open the head of a guru, you'll find his pineal gland is the size of an olive. Have a look in a soldier's head, especially one from here in the US, and his'll be about the size of a pea. Not his fault. It's the fault of the people who want him to follow blindly and without question. They've been putting fluoride in the public water supply for how long now?

"I've found that there are no scientific studies that prove drinking eight glasses of water a day is good for you…at least, no study that was not funded by a *water company*. So, it's arguable that drinking eight glasses of fluoridated water a day is the new opiate of the masses.

"And we're not just making you stupider. Look at all the cold medicines out there, to dry up your mucus, keep you from coughing and sneezing, in fact, keep your body from doing all of the perfectly natural things that expel germs from your body, for no reason other than to weaken your immune system, and make you dependent upon those bullshit pills for the rest of your life. Those pills keep the germs in your system until they've run their course, but you think you're better because you're not naturally expelling them.

"They give you Sudafed so your prostate will swell up, and then they can sell you prostate medication."

I tried not to think about how it was Crowe who had really pushed us all to gargle with fluoride.

"But how do the pharmaceutical companies get away with doing all this? I mean, they have to justify it somehow, right?"

Gallegher got serious then, and leaned forward, putting his hands together. Looked at me deeply.

"Operation Paperclip."

"What?"

"More than sixteen hundred Nazi scientists were brought to the United States after World War II, where they worked for the US government during the Cold War in order to avoid trial. After helping one enemy get an edge over another, they went on to form pharmaceutical companies, creating drugs to poison the minds of the people they once tried to conquer by force. Those people then commit crimes and end up in here."

"You can't be serious."

He nodded. "In concentration camps during the war, they had experimented with psychotropics that the Third Reich had hoped to use for mind control. Now they're calling it 'Cosmetic psychopharmacology,' the reordering of our society through drugs. Personality traits can be eradicated, altered, or enhanced but primarily, their purpose is to make the user complacent, compliant, and open to suggestion. The pills work on the limbic system and frontal lobes of the brain, extinguishing normal emotions, including empathy, and causing memory loss.

"With all the movies and shows about serial killers, all of the constant suggestions that violence is an option, it's just a matter of time for a lot of people. A lot of ticking timebombs. It's well-known among those who control the masses that if something is going to catch on, it has to have what they call a low-ability threshold. It must be something any monkey can do easily, like hula hoops and Tamagotchis. When the opportunity to be a part of something new and trendy is easy as pie, everybody will hop on the band-wagon. Think, the Macarena, or abstract art. If you tell the world that going to all the trouble of learning how to dance well, or painting something realistic, is passé, everybody who wants to dance or be called an artist—while putting forth minimal effort—will jump at the chance.

"So, now the cool thing to be is a serial killer. If you are a failure of an individual, you can get revenge on the world for rejecting you, *and* be part of an exclusive clique by giving in to the voice inside your head. A voice the meds put there in the first place.

"There are subcultures on the internet, grooming kids that take SSRIs to become mass murderers. At least one of these kids has come out and admitted it, that he was in competition with other "players" to see how many people he could kill.

"These subcultures are not discouraged because it is in the interests of a corrupt government to disarm its citizens. It's no secret that widely-broadcast events tend to set precedents and inspire copycats. Not many people knew, for example, about the many people who died in Arkansas, Washington, Alaska, and Mississippi *before* the Columbine shootings, but afterwards, all the world knew. And then an epidemic of copycats, more and more kids following suit because the news kept showing it. Next thing you know, if it hadn't happened in a whole year they'd show the last one again to keep it fresh in everyone's minds so that the next pissed-off kid would consider it a solution. Or even 'Columbine, five years later.' Keep it alive in the minds of the populace, keep it ever present, so those ticking timebombs will remember that re-enacting that atrocity is always an option. That if it ever seems that there is no way out of his predicament, he can always go out with a bang.

"This news coverage popularized such crimes, and in turn called attention to the availability and accessibility of firearms, which helps to tighten the hold on honest citizens and effectively disarm them. So, here we are, killing ourselves and each other, and many of us are calling for the government to ban all firearms. And a bunch of Nazis are behind it, the group who'd seized power in their own country after doing what? Taking everyone's guns.

"Does it sound a little far-fetched?" he asked at last.

I hesitated, wanting to say Yes, but thinking Not at all.

He nodded. "Truth is stranger than fiction."

I seem to have strayed from the original point.

Ah, well, there you have it. That's my roundabout way of explaining Enolah Gaye Taylor.

Oh, for that preadolescent wisdom, when I rightfully knew that girls were both useless and the source of cooties.

XII

Crowe called me to his home and let me in on a little secret.

"I know of a job you can do," he said. "Some very good friends of mine are running a new restaurant in New York City. With my glowing recommendation, they will be more than happy to employ you. You'll have a steady job, and live in a place where you are completely unknown by the police."

"You want me to be a waiter?" I asked, doubting.

"Of course not. I want you to be a valet."

"What?"

"First, you will help out with whatever they need, and then you will stand outside their front door and park people's cars for them."

"Why?" I tried not to sound offended.

"Because while those people are eating, you will have plenty of time to makes copies of their keys. I'll show you how."

"Copies of...?"

"Yes. A little bird told me that many important people will infest this restaurant. Mafiosi. Crooked politicians. Many others of that ilk. And my friends tell me that they will be going to visit some of their customers one day. You will furnish the keys, to make their missions much easier."

"But I don't know the first thing—"

"You will know everything soon, Dwight. That is one of the reasons I picked you: you are a quick study. You make me proud, and I can think of no more suitable candidate than you to do this. It helps that your situation is so temporary here. With all of the trouble in this city, there has been too much vigilance by the lawmen for me to be comfortable about you. Also, there will be a curfew real soon. My own idea.

"Besides, there's also a *personal* mission I want you to carry out. Your altar—" meaning Enolah, "—was very distraught a short while ago. It seems someone raped an ex-girlfriend of hers, a young lady she still had feelings for. In fact, this young lady's mother was even a member of our church for a while. Anyway, Enolah and this girl did some work at the D&S place, and they hit it off. This friend I want you to work for is the mother of Enolah's girlfriend's girlfriend, and I'm sure Miss Taylor would love to find out if everything's okay now."

"...I'll do my best."

"I know you will. You always do. The girl you need to ask about is Maya Macaulay. Sweet girl. I sent off a viriphage to her new boyfriend, and I want to know if it took."

"Viriphage?"

"A synthesized virus that feeds on other viruses, and has a particular liking for HIV. A cannibal."

"You're kidding!"

621

"I shit you not, little brother. But try to keep it under your wig."

"A *cure*? And no one knows about it?"

"*Of course* no one knows. Her boyfriend, another pupil of mine, has administered it to her without her knowledge, the same way I administer it to you."

"What!"

"Oh yes. We do indulge in rather risky sexual behavior at our Masses. Don't you wonder why, somehow, no one ever gets sick?"

"My God!"

"Don't say that, Dark. It's unbecoming."

"Yes, right. Sorry. But—"

"But nothing. I am responsible for everyone in my flock, and I do what I can to protect them. I don't tell anyone, however, because then someone will surely come to me with some sob story about a friend of theirs who needs a dose, and if I were to refuse, that would create unrest. Then, word will get around, and we would be exposed for holding out on the rest of the world."

"But how was is made? And who made it?"

"I have completely forgotten. In fact, I don't even know what you're talking about. Now, what do you say? Will you go to New York?"

"Of course, Brother."

"Good. And if you see a fellow called Rabbit up there, tell him I said Hello, and wish him Good Hunting."

That was my fifth day of freedom.

I packed up what few necessities I had, and said good-bye to this dump, trying to convince myself that I wouldn't miss it.

I used to wander out past the Acreage and look at what this world used to be, kicking pine cones, and constantly picking sandspurs out of my socks and shins, and I wasn't sure whether civilization was an improvement or not. At a canal, I almost didn't notice a harmless log drifting toward me. A harmless, yellow-eyed log. An alligator that lurked in the mud near the bank, camouflaged by a coat of slime and spotted purple snails.

Shit.

Maybe I *was* better off in the City of No Stars.

Maybe the Great Outdoors was home for evicted Indians and Australian Aborigines, like Brother Crowe, but those of us spawned by the safe and homogenized modern world...sadly, we wouldn't last the weekend. Whoever heard of a Bushman in the Namib or the Kalahari or Wherever stopping by the grocery store for more insect repellent?

I have been on adventures out in the 'Glades, but that was with Crowe every time, and country boys who knew what they were doing. Out on an airboat, the noise of its giant fan deafening, skimming at exhilarating speeds over the green water. The heavy air rank with the stench of decay,

622

dragonflies and mosquitoes ricocheting off of my goggles.

Blue herons and swimming snakes scattered from our path into saw-grass, sugarcane, and cannabis. Out here, when the ripples of our wake had faded, you could set a long 2x4 on the floating tussock and walk across it with another in your hands, set it down, pick up the first and keep going. Walking on water.

Out here, under the Spanish moss that garlanded the branches of swamp trees, you can find turtle eggs in alligator nests, where the crafty little bastards have hidden them, knowing that raiding 'coons won't dare to try and steal them.

Out here, as long as the Game Warden's not looking, you can make a fortune off poaching.

Use a baby gator that you're holding hostage to cry out and call for Mama, and adults will come quick, fast, and in a hurry. Don't have a baby gator? Smack the water's surface with your open hand while making loud nasal grunts. They'll come.

After you've either harpooned them, or shot them behind the eye—which isn't always that easy, and missing that spot only makes them mad—you have to skin them up the back and preserve the belly. The back is useless, aside from making into body armor. As armor, it's much lighter weight than metal, not nearly as hot, but the swords and arrows it is capable of turning, people just don't use anymore.

A six-foot hide can fetch up to $500. The young'uns, now, they are the ones you skin the backs of. Horn-backing, they call it, for making boots. People who pretend they know about gators will tell you gator tail is "damn good eating," but that's because they've only ever eaten gator in restaurants. The only reason I'm not one of those people is because Crowe allowed me to—*once*—eat an alligator's jaw muscles. Damn, that's good.

But sometimes, I look at the glorious future some of us anticipate, and I inwardly cringe. Having done a little reading up on Aborigines, trying to get at least a little background on my mentor, I try to envision the return of the "Dreamtime," and the only one of us that I can see surviving is him.

I am always a grease spot in a hoof print.

And Misery…my sister, the Lab Rat…

Part of our vows taken, our pledge of allegiance to the Lord of Opened Eyes, we assure Brother Crowe that there will be No loose talk, No second thoughts.

But it's times like these, when the highway's whining beneath the tires of a car I wouldn't get far without, that I look at the dried-out swamplands flanking the road, and wonder what the hell I'm doing.

That's when it happened.

That's when I finally decided to follow Crowe's advice, and think for myself. I jerked the wheel of my red and white shark, swerving across three lanes and cutting off two cars, sliding onto the upcoming exit ramp in the nick of time. A heartbeat later, and I would've crashed into the guardrail lining the overpass I couldn't bring myself to cross.

I had to know for myself who was right—Crowe, or Gallegher. And the only way to find out was to ditch this overtly conspicuous car, dye my hair yet again, and watch my world from another vantage point. From a distance, peripherally. Treason? I hadn't decided yet. Just curiosity. But I had suddenly realized the sheer stupidity of chanting repetitiously: "Think for yourself, question Authority," as a mantra, and then waiting eagerly for your master's next instructions. The stupidity I'd embraced.

This would be the second chapter of my self-help book, the one entitled *Blasphemy*.

My eyes were Opened.

XIII

Ana stood center stage, in a black tube top and an American flag sarong, a white swastika in place of stars on the blue field. Under that, black knee-length combat boots and nothing else. Her hair was a wild mane that her eyes glared wickedly from behind. The guitarists and drummer looked much the same, and it was difficult to tell whether they were men or women.

"Daddy, why?" she screamed, the crowd screaming along with her. There was none of the gutteral howl that marked all singers of her type. Her voice was a clear, piercing clarion that could hold a note long enough to startle and bewitch an audience. Every body in the bar moved to the catchy but furious riffs, every mouth trying to outlast the other in singing along, but none coming close to Ana.

"Daddy, *why?*"

"Our little secret…" the lead guitarist sang.

> "Be a good girl, now, hush, don't cry.
> Daddy sings a different kind of lullaby.
> This may hurt a little, but just hold still.
> Mommy sure likes it, so I know you will.
> Our little secret, you better not tell.
> Just hush now and get used to Drunk Dad Smell!"

Ana had never been molested as a child, but from the rage in her voice, you couldn't tell. From the tears streaming down singing faces in the audience, though, you could see who had been. And there were way too many.

Chapter Three: Children.

I feel terrible saying this, because I love children, I think children are wonderful and I wish more people could be like them. But as cynical as I've become, I can't help but see the inevitable. The way this world has become, sadly, the chances are pretty good every child I see will grow up like me. I don't know where I picked up this depressing habit, but I envision little Timmy as he will be ten years later, and it isn't pretty.

I hate the idea of that cute little girl with the pigtails trying her first joint, even if she'll someday be old enough to decide for herself. I hate the thought of her on her knees. I hate the probability that Kevin's not going to hug his Dad like that a few years from now, instead stealing money out of the kitchen business drawer to buy a bottle of Mad Dog and drink it with Steve and Bobby behind a convenience store.

Eventually, that little girl Julie on the swing set is going to blow somebody. Now, there's nothing really wrong with that, but somehow, it's sickening.

I grieve for the innocence these kids will lose.

I know they won't miss it at all, and most people will think I'm crazy for hoping Christy would stay a virgin until she got married, but I do grieve for their innocence.

Because I never had any.

Now I finally have to get around to telling this—why I left the county jail when I did, not months earlier or one day later. I've put it off as long as I can.

The minx Enolah once did a stint of submission that surprised us all. She went to one of her clients, making up some bullshit about doing so many hours as a slave as part of her "dominatrix training" and asked—*asked!*—if she could do it for him. Sort of like pro bono prostitution, only there would be no actual sex acts performed, only humiliation. It was practically suicide, and we staged an intervention like when you hear about concerned friends and relatives Baker-Acting someone on a bender. Brother Crowe was worried Enolah had gotten her wires crossed somewhere over karma or something and was on a martyr trip. I didn't think it was that complicated. I thought she'd gone slap out of her mind.

But when we confronted her she reassured us, saying she felt she really didn't know enough about suffering, being that her only experience of it was limited to menstrual cramps and hangovers.

"I had to do a report on the Holocaust for school once," she said. "I found it again just the other day when I was going through some old things. Reading it over, I remembered the descriptions of things those poor people had to go through— Hitler's political enemies, vagrants, the Gypsies, queers, cripples, the brave people who hid the Jews, and the Jews themselves—and I remembered the pictures I'd seen of them at the concentration camps when I was doing my research. I got a little depressed."

"Uh-oh," Crowe said.

"Yeah," Enolah agreed, misunderstanding him. "I realized I didn't know anything about real suffering. As a dominatrix, what do I do besides insult businessmen for a few hours, subjugate them, and rough 'em up a bit? Nothing! When it comes down to inflicting real *misery* I wouldn't know where to begin!"

Our high priest started to relax a little.

"So, I'm going to be doing this," she said. "I'm going to put myself in a position where I'm going to really be tested, and see how far I can go, how much I can take without breaking. Frederick Douglass' owner Mr. Covey would do that, used to work right alongside his slaves so he'd know exactly how much work a man could do before breaking, and that's how much work he'd give his slaves to do. Only since *I'll* know where the breaking point is once I've done what I have to do, I should be able to magnify a hundred times my capacity for cruelty. I want to be able to make a guy like Mengle wince."

"Men-gla?" I asked.

"Josef Mengle. The guy in charge of what went down in concentration camps."

"Oh."

"So, you're sure about this, then?" Crowe asked. "How many hours?

"Am I pretending to serve? Forty."

Crowe whistled.

"Ehh, it'll be nothing. But I'll leave it up to him how those hours are broken up. He might want four sessions of ten hours, though I doubt it. Maybe a week's worth of six, something like that."

The he in this case was, of all people, Chadwick Downey, the black rapper who'd come out of Golgotha calling himself, of all things, Downey Fresh. He was that guy who made Top Ten with his debut album about life in prison, showing the little everyday details instead of broad generalizations like all the other rappers—as if I'd listen to that shit to know. He'd made a good chunk of change off of his three singles "One Time at Da Window," "Dime Square-Board," and "Gunning."

So, wow, what a horrible thing, you might think.

Gee, can it be that bad?

And the answer, according to Enolah, is Fuckin-A Right.

It seems that Chadwick Downey had been glutting his ego with his newfound wealth. Not a surprise. But what was really surprising was one of his new indulgences: da employment of bitches ta do e'ry li'l thang fo' him, such as…

Hot bitch number 1—Calpurnia Davis—$10/hour just to roll blunts for him whenever he wanted to smoke weed, which was fairly often.

Hot bitch number 2—Shaquita Moore—$10/hour to pour his Moet (and he actually pronounced it with the T) when he got thirsty.

Hot bitch number 3—Lunalia Turnquist—$10/hour just to polish his shoes every few hours.

Hot bitch number 4—you get the picture.

And of course, these were his "hoes," his "bitches," his "boos," his concubines, with whom he'd "get down," get "freaky," fuck, whatever. So that should have all the bases covered, right? He had his house cleaned, his laundry done, his knob polished, so what else could there be for a submissive "ho-assed li'l cracka bitch" like Enolah to do for him? In the beginning all he could think of was have her get down on her hands and knees in front of him as he sat in his high-backed red leather armchair, and be his hassock. He put his feet on her back and crossed his ankles for a little while, shoes on, as his stereo blasted deafening bass and savagely-shouted unintelligible lyrics and he toked on a blunt that Calpurnia had rolled for him.

The black girls had, at first, been struck dumb by the arrival of a white girl and throughout the hassock period (which lasted maybe two of those forty hours, tops) they acted very uncomfortable. A lot of hesitancy, whispering amongst each other, and outright staring. Chadwick had a smug grin on his face that Enolah later described to me as "he hadn't swallowed just one canary, but all the canaries in the world, and when he slipped his shoes off and started digging his toes into my side between my ribs, he looked like he was still hungry."

I would see her off when she left for Downey's place, kissing her tenderly and, while hugging her good-bye, telling her she didn't have to do this. She would be wearing baggy sweats over her outfit so she wouldn't attract any unwanted attention on the way there—which she certainly would've, wearing only, say, her blue gingham cotton underbust corset, a strapless lacy picot white bra and similar skirt that only barely covered her perfect ass, white fishnet stockings, and sneakers that she would, of course, change out of when she arrived into red patent leather platform heels, the same blood-red as the cute little bow tied near the end of her long black ponytail.

I personally *loved* this outfit, this sassy getup that Chadwick the Ignorant called her "Cafolick skoo-girl unafome."

She'd tell me she knew she didn't have to go, and give me a final extra squeeze before ending the embrace, then look me squarely in the eye. Those were the moments when I'd feel it for sure, the sad and upsetting admission that I really did care for her, much as I tried to deny it. I'd fear for her, then try to cover it up with suspicion and jealous anger that maybe she was enjoying it, maybe she was even letting that baboon of a rap star fuck her.

And I'd sit alone and drink, take a few halcyons, and fester until she got back. She'd come through her door and look at me in surprise, asking if I'd been there the whole time. And I'd lie to her, saying I'd gone out, shot some pool maybe, and just stopped by a few minutes ago and let myself in. "Just stopped by, eh?" I could almost hear her thinking to herself. "Just stopped by long enough to run me a bath and mull me some wine?" Yeah, I'm a sweetie. And she'd take a glass and have some warm wine, loosening her corset and getting ready to slip into the bath I'd prepared with scented bubbles and sacred oils from India or something. And she'd tell me about the fucked-up evening she'd had.

She'd tell me about how bold the girls at Downey's place had gotten, and how harshly they were mistreating her just because she'd let them, as some kind of revenge for how their ancestors had been treated. And she'd see me get angry and get a look on her face like she was happy I cared so much, and she'd tell me more just to watch me get angrier. She'd do her slow See-What-A-Victim-I-Am striptease, showing me the new bruises and the welts those bitches, those *whores,* had given her, touching them gently with a fingertip and sharply sucking her breath in through her teeth. Then she'd strip off all her clothes and walk naked to the bath, leaving me to stew and dream up murders.

Apparently, the black women who served their black massa without any complaint were taking out everything they ever had against white people on my poor Enolah—listen to me! My poor Enolah! When would anyone ever call her poor? Ah, but here I am, being protective of the poor dear whose spirit was mine and mine alone to break.

Then, one night, Enolah did not come home.

I paced the apartment. I drank. I smoked cigarette after cigarette after cigarette until I was all out and had to go buy more, and then I smoked them all back to back to back.

I popped pills trying to calm myself, but got impatient waiting for them to kick in and so I kept popping another one, and another, until they all ganged up inside of me and a warm darkness crept up my spine into my skull, spreading its fingers until they covered my eyes and I slept.

I slept for the whole next day and all of the following night and I awoke to find a little yellow Post-It note stuck to my forehead. Bright morning sunlight came through the blinds to hatch the opposite wall with stripes. It took a long time of fumbling to find the rod and twist the blinds closed to shut out that awful light. Then it took a long time of blinking to clear the blue afterimages from my eyes so I could read the note she'd left.

"Honey, I'll be gone for a few days. No need to hold my fort down. I love you."

I stared at it, baffled. She'd never said she loved me before, but that wasn't it. It was where the hell she'd gone and where she'd been, and how long since she'd been home to write this note and stick it to my head? The last question—it couldn't have been too long ago because foreheads get greasy and the adhesive was still tacky. So, if she'd be gone a few days, that was starting now, not yesterday, and I knew how long I'd slept because the flowers she kept in a vase on her dresser had already closed, and they hadn't even opened yet the last time I remember looking at them. So, where the hell *was* she?

I went about my ablutions, got dressed, and went out to see what harm I could do, what contributions I could make to the World's Pain. I called Brother Crowe and he comforted me, telling me she was fine and off working up a mischief somewhere, not to worry. For the next two days I sinned up a storm. The details are unnecessary.

When I went to her apartment again on the third day, she opened the door as I was unlocking it. I could see the brownish yellow of what had been really bad shiners around her beautiful blue eyes, and noticed, underneath her flowing black hair, hidden, a hint of a long strip that had been shaven bald. Her upper lip was puffy, giving her a Simpsons-character overbite. I started to reach for the hair that covered her shame and she

629

jerked her head away.

"*What happened?*" I demanded.

"Stitches. I had to get stitches," she said, then paused a moment, and met my eyes again. "Am I pretty?" I blinked at her. "Tell me I'm still pretty, Dark." I just looked at her. My mouth wouldn't work. I don't know what the expression on my face registered, but it must have been anything but what she wanted to see. Her voice took on an urgency that was startling. "Tell me I'm still pretty, Dark!"

I didn't say it. I should've, and I wish I had been able to, but I couldn't speak at all. I get that way sometimes, and I watched her go through something painful inside her. When she finally resigned herself, she looked at me and said "A bottle of Moét."

I was lost for a minute. What, did she want me to go get her one? Then she snorted a mirthless laugh and corrected herself.

"I'm sorry, Mo-*ette*. That's how they say it. With a T. Fucking infidels." Her voice was sharp and hard like a shard of broken glass. "They had a bunch of people over. There was crack, malt liquor, sherm, and they forgot that I wasn't there to fuck anyone."

She grimaced as my hand clamped onto her arm like a vise, but she didn't try to shake herself out of my grip. Instead, she backed into her apartment, pulling me in through the door with her. "Yeah, they tried to take it. How'd they phrase it? Take da pussy, that's right. They said if I wasn't comin' up off dat pussy dey was goan *take* it. Well, they tried. I broke a few noses, fattened a few lips up bigger than they already were. But Shaquita there, she came up behind me with a half-empty bottle of Mo-ette. If it'd been full, she would've killed me, probably. But it did put my lights out for a while. When I came to, the lights were on, Chadwick had a wet towel and a bag of ice on my head here," she indicated the spot where I knew the stitches to be. "All the guys I managed to rough up, they had ice packs too, and were cussing me in muffled voices from underneath them, but he was shouting them down over his shoulder. Saying, "Man, where dis bitch works, dey know me dere!"" She paused for a minute, watching me. "They let me go. I drove to the hospital to get patched up. Stopped by here…"

"Where've you been?" I asked, perhaps a little too gruffly.

"I went to see an old friend. Todd Ferguson. You remember him?"

"Not off the top of my head, no," I growled, *not* wanting to hear she'd gone to see another man.

"Well, he's the chemistry major. Chemistry, shit, *alchemy's* more like it. Anyway, he's got this all-glass miniature 'still that he can make his own perfumes with…or poisons."

My ears perked up, and she laughed at my sudden change of expression.

"You don't say," I said.

"Yeah, and he just happened—just *happened*—to have some things handy. Champak, hovenia, all kinds of things. I asked him to whip me up something."

"Oh, you did, did you?"

"Mm-hmm."

"And did he? Whip you up something?"

"He sure did."

"What?"

"I don't know. He just gave it to me and winked. Said it was just the thing for people who wanna git down, git freeky."

"Well, so how did you…what'd you do with it?"

"I put it in a bottle of Moét. Mo-*ette*. Took it over and gave it to them. Chadwick wasn't home, but Shaquita took it. She took it from me as a sort of peace offering. Had this gloat in her eyes while she was looking at me, like she'd won something. God*damn*, I wanted to break her face right then."

"Waitaminute. Time out," I said. "There's no way they'd ever take an open bottle from you. Just try to give them something with the seal broken and they're going to know something's up. They can't be that stu—"

"When did I say it had been opened?" she asked me, with that cute little enigmatic smile.

"Just now, you told me you put that stuff in a bottle of Mo-ette—shit. Moet! Moét! Now you've got me doing it!"

"Ha! Sweetums, I said I put some in a bottle, but I never said I opened it." She was enjoying this way too much. She broke away from me and reached past to shut the door, then sauntered over to her armchair and plopped down.

"Then, how—" I began, but she cut me off.

"With a syringe. I slowly got it in through the cork and sprayed the stuff in that way."

"And it didn't leave a tiny hole? Wouldn't the wine go flat or something?"

"Of course not. I heated up the wax and plastic that sealed the cork so it would run a little and fill the hole back in again."

I shook my head, grinning. "The alley cats would learn a lot from you, Delilah."

She laughed.

I heard in the news the next week that Chadwick Downey, AKA rap star Downey Fresh, had been arrested for the murders of five women. Witnesses said he'd been jus' chillin', like he always be, drinkin' his champagne, smokin' dat chronic, an' poppin' dem peels when, maaaan, it was like a horra flick or sumpin'. He got to hollerin' at dem bitches, den dey got slick out da mouf back at him, and *bam!* Up he come outta dat chair, swingin' like fer all he was worff.

Calpurnia Davis, Lunalia Turnquist, and Precious Smith were savagely beaten to death. Shakita Moore held him off for a little while with a large knife from a kitchen drawer, until he ran to his bedroom to fetch his nickle-plated AK-47. On the way back he found Chancee Williams hiding behind a curtain, and riddling her with bullets, sent her flying backwards out of the shattered window onto the lawn outside. When Shakita tried to run for it Downey caught her in the waist with a three-round burst just as she was reaching for the knob of the front door. The rest of the magazine was emptied into her face at point blank range.

Experts have surmised that it might have been success that drove him to do such a thing. That or a chemical imbalance caused by the mixture of all the drugs he'd been ingesting. Either would be very likely.

Yeah so, anyway, I bring this up why? Well, it came to mind because Chadwick Downey, Inmate 01041628, was just being led into cellblock M3B for spiritual guidance and possible redemption. He shook off all of the greetings from the younger blacks, the jits in the dorm, saying "Naw, dat ain't me no more," when they called him da Bitch-Hater, da Perpetrator, and insisted that he was ready to give his life to the Lord. A noble intention, to be sure. And of course, as can be expected of jailhouse Christians, his fans called him a sell-out, said he wasn't "real", and they "dissed" him every whicha way. But to his credit, at least from a Christian standpoint, he took it all saying "Praise God...praise God...yes, thank you, Jesus, that I'm not like them anymore." At which time others came over to help him with his mattress and property, led him into one of the four cells that had an open bunk, and offered him support and consolation and even praise for standing up for himself against those who would tear him down. He seemed very humble, and said "Right now, I need God a lot more than my so-called homies. It was runnin' wit dudes like dat an' da Devil in 'em dat got me here."

Sitting out in the day room, I heard a bunch of Amens and watched them clap him on the back, and I felt something, a kind of Attaboy feeling that surprised me. I wanted to wish him luck and urge him to be strong, but I choked it back down to wherever it had come from. I willed myself to hate him like I had before, and to be glad that he was awaiting trial and a probable death sentence...but it wasn't easy.

Only then did I bother to notice one of the other two inmates that had come in with him.

Roosevelt.

Oh Christ. There goes the neighborhood.

Before I could even gnash my teeth I heard the shout of "Church time!" and sagged down in my plastic chair, thinking *Jesus!* How many sermons did we need in one day? We'd already had the George & Everett Show first thing in the morning, Voluntary Harry (Father Harold, who you didn't have to listen to if you didn't want to, but out of respect you had to turn off the TV and stop playing cards) at ten, and that snake-oil bastard not even an hour ago. I'd stopped liking the song and dance routine that he came in with as soon as I actually woke up to the concept of Right and Wrong. He started every visit the same way, with that revival style of hyperventilation, making us shout "I don't mind" as loud as we could for almost ten minutes so that we'd all get light-headed, sweat, go numb, and have chest pains. Respiratory alkalosis, it's called, by those who know. Rapture, it's called, by the suckers they preach to.

He'd faith-heal us individually by boxing our ears, jabbing his thumbs in our eyes, and pushing us over backwards so the those waiting behind could catch us and lay us gently onto the floor. We'd hear a thunderclap, see a flash of white light, and fall down disoriented. That was being touched by God.

I used to appreciate him for doing this, gloating vicariously through him while he fooled the gullible, the sheep. Now I hated him almost as much as I hated myself for liking him.

I looked up at the glass wall to see who it was coming in to waste more of my time, dreading it would be that one fruity minister I call Churchy La Femme, but it wasn't. It was worse. It was the Chaplain himself, bringing a guest speaker.

Hadn't we just seen him yesterday? I thought we were only supposed to see his sanctimonious ass once a week—oh, wait. It *had* been a week since the last time. My, how time flies. The days in this dungeon melt into one another until a week and a month and another month have gone by and you've got nothing to show for it. Not even memories.

Well, shit, it's church time, so I stood up and dragged my chair to its spot on the cold terrazzo floor where the others were lining theirs up. An officer unlocked the cellblock door and slid it open halfway, letting the Chaplain and his guest in, then rolled it shut behind them. It slammed with that harsh *clang!* that used to make me flinch inside—not physically, not visibly, but inside my head, where it was somehow even worse. *Clang!* Church time. Fuck.

The brown-nosers, like some kind of minister-groupies, all crowded the Chaplain as he made his way through them into the middle of the day room. Order was called, men went to their seats, there was scuffling and *ahem*-ing and finally, silence.

"Blah blah blah," the Chaplain said. Or words to that effect. "Blah blah blippity bloo bloggitty bloggitty blook."

Then he stepped aside and his guest speaker, a neat and presentable middle-aged black man, took the helm. I tried not to listen to his preamble, certain that it was going to be more Churchianity bullshit, when suddenly a sentence cut through the fog I'd spun about my brain.

"Back in Africa, before the White Man came, we all lived in perfect harmony."

I tasted bile in the back of my throat. God *damn*, I'd heard that one too many times.

"I *really* believed that once," he continued, redeeming himself immediately in my mind. "And I was an angry, *angry* young man, furious at Whitey for taking my people up out of Utopia, out of Wakanda, and bringing us here. I learned something, though, that changed all of that." He held up the Bible he had brought with him, and there was a collective telepathic buzz of irritation from all of us sitting there. It was invisible, inaudible, but it was there in the air somehow, all of us thinking "Yeah, yeah, yeah, forgiveness, redemption, we've heard it already."

But what he said next made all of our ears perk up.

"According to this book here, that's a buncha bullshit."

The air conditioning vents were suddenly deafeningly loud, and the gray fur growing in the slats rasped against each other.

The man opened his Bible to one of many dog-eared pages. "Genesis 10. Noah had three sons: Shem, Ham, and Japheth. Well, Biblical experts say that when Noah's three sons had to repopulate the entire world after the Great Flood, Japheth's descendants would become the Greeks, the Romans, the Germans and the Russians. Shem's were the Shemites, the Jews. And Ham's sons were Canaan, who became Palestine; Mizraim, who became Egypt; Cush, Ethiopia; and Phut, Libya. Now, there are a few Scriptures I'd like to read to you, Scriptures that prophesied...well, let me get to that in a minute. My brothers—excuse me everybody, I'm only talking to my black brothers here—brothers, we blame the white man for *everything*. Enslaving us, setting us free only to keep us down in a different way, sending us off to die in wars, telling us lies, making sure we stay poor, but remember that we are Ham's sons. We had our time in Egypt, when we were in power for three thousand years. We were scientists, educators, inventors, we built the pyramids and the Sphinx which still stand today as monuments to our greatness."

Here a lot of the "Brothers" were nodding and grinning and slapping each other five.

"But..." the man continued, silencing them all. "That also means we were the first slave masters, doesn't it? We enslaved the Jews. God's chosen people. We enslaved them *for four hundred years*. We were on the top, but we picked a fight with the Most High. Isaiah 19:4—And the Egyptians I will give over to the hand of a cruel lord; and a fierce king shall rule over them. What happened to us, happened for the same reason it'd happened to Israel in the first place, because they turned away from God and He punished them. Didn't the slave trade last about four hundred years? You do the crime, you're gonna do the time.

"Ezekiel 29:5—Just as Nebuchadnezzar was made animal-like and driven into the fields, so the Egyptians were made brutish and driven into the bush land. Then Verse 12—I will scatter the Egyptians among the nations, and I will disperse them through the countries. Ezekiel 30:9—In that day shall messengers go forth from me in ships to make the careless Ethiopians afraid, and great pain shall come upon them, as in the day of Egypt. Two chapters later it says why the white man would come to hate us as he does now. 32:9—I will also vex the hearts of many people, when I shall bring thy destruction among the nations, into the countries that thou hast not known. Deuteronomy 28:15—But it shall come to pass, if thou wilt not hearken unto the voice of the Lord thy God, to observe to do all His commandments and his statutes which I command thee this day; that all these curses shall come upon thee, and overtake thee. Isaiah 19:2—And I will set the Egyptians against the Egyptians: and they shall fight every one against his brother. We know that African tribal chiefs sold their prisoners of war to the slave traders. Some of them traded slaves for firearms, which led to more wars, which led to more prisoners to sell to the white man. And we still fight each other today, don't we? The love one black man feels for another is reflected in those bars we have over our windows.

"The Asians and Hispanics are doing pretty well in this country because they live and work together. They keep a unified front and a financial base, helping each other, and they prosper. But us? A lot of rebellions on slave plantations were thwarted by other slaves telling their masters about them being planned. They betrayed their own fellow slaves because they thought that would be their way to freedom. It's happening right here in this jail right now, and when some of you go up the road, you'll see in every day in the prisons. We will not cooperate. When we were emancipated, the government gave us our own country, Liberia, where we could go back and be free. We just had another civil war there in 1990. In 1994, in Rwanda, the Hutus killed one million Tutsis. Two years later, the Tutsis took over Burundi. One month after that, Tupac was at war with Notorious B.I.G., wasn't he? Death Row Records versus Bad Boy. The West Coast versus New York. Over what? And where are they now? Dead, both of them. We cannot stop fighting each other, and we *will* not until we understand ourselves and our history.

"We make a mockery of ourselves with our gangsta tags. I'll bet at least one of you in here goes by the name Snoop, or Tupac, Flav, Sambo, Rerun, even Big Shirley or Wazoo, but how many of you call yourselves George Washington Carver? How many of you even know who he was? Or you copy the Italians, calling yourselves Gotti or Capone, but never Galileo. We don't care about people who did great things, only degenerates who are dead because of their sin.

"Deuteronomy 28:30—Thou shalt betroth to a wife, and another man shall lie with her. 48—Therefore shalt thou serve thine enemies, which the Lord shall send against thee, in hunger, and in thirst, and in nakedness, and in want of all things: and he shall put a yoke of iron upon thy neck. I got this pointed out to me by the Reverend Earl Carter, a great black man. I'd like to quote him now from this book I'm going to leave with you," he held up another book he'd been holding behind the Bible. The cover said *No Apology Necessary, Just Respect.*

"He says in here that knowing black history is part of our healing, because we can never be healed unless we know who we are. God had to leave some of us there in the bush with a brutish spirit to let us understand the seriousness of our crime. If we couldn't see our relatives over there in the jungle, still scarring their faces and putting dung in their hair, stretching out their lips and sharpening their teeth, putting bones in their noses on the cover of National Geographic, I don't think any of us would believe that's where we came from. Some of you in here today, I'll bet you walk around like a lot of our brothers do, wearing your pants down with the buttocks showing. Look out that window there into the other cells and see them right now, with their butts actually hanging out. In Isaiah 20, this represents the shame of our curse—*So shall the king of Assyria lead away the Egyptians prisoners, and the Ethiopians captives, young and old, naked and barefoot, even with their buttocks uncovered, to the shame of Egypt.* Isaiah 19:14—*The Lord hath mingled a perverse spirit in the midst thereof: and they have caused Egypt to err in every work thereof, as a drunken man staggereth in his own vomit.* The problem isn't us, brothers, it's the prophecy on us. Just like the Jews killing Jesus, the consequences fell on their heads, and the heads of their children, and their children's children's children, the punishment for what we did in Egypt still follows us today. I honestly believe that if we demand reparations from the white man for what happened to our forefathers, we must first give reparations to the Jews for what we did to *their* forefathers. But since we're definitely not going to do that, we ought not to go demanding any for ourselves.

"When a person believes that the system is against him, he is a victim with a victim consciousness. He gets bogged down in excuses, and he's never going to fulfill his God-given potential until he gets up. In Proverbs 22, we're told to make no friendship with an angry man; and with a furious man thou shalt not go, lest thou learn his ways and get a snare to thy soul. Think Farrakhan, my brothers. He's trying to tell us that the white race was created in a botched experiment by a black mad scientist named Yakub. Man, it may make you feel good to believe that, but you're not going to get anywhere with it. Philippians 3—Brethren, I do not count myself to have apprehended; but one thing I do, forgetting those things which are behind, and reaching forth unto those things which are ahead, I press toward the mark for the prize of the high calling of God in Christ Jesus.

"And I can tell you some more about the slave trade that should take some of the edge off. Long before Kunta Kinte, the white man was enslaved in America. Maybe you've heard about Australia starting out as a prison colony for England? Well, they only started sending them there after the ones over *here* rebelled. As many as two-thirds of the immigrants to America from Europe in the 1600s came in chains. Cromwell sent them over after he took all their land, and they weren't fit to work in the hot climate they weren't used to, so they were dropping like flies. There were also 'kid-nabbings' and shanghais of children and drunks. Then there were the scams, people being promised a new opportunity in the New World, and indentured servants, too, both of them suckers because they came over expecting a chance and got put in sweatshops and on plantations instead. The switch didn't happen until the island commissioner in Barbados asked him to send black slaves over instead, because since they cost more, they'd be a better investment and maybe the overseers wouldn't whip and cripple and murder them as much. And America only got about six percent of the black slaves. The rest of our people went to Brazil and the Caribbean—where do you think Haitians and Jamaicans and Dominicans came from? But even when they started bringing us over, they still had cheaper slaves coming from Europe, too. Chances are, everybody in this room, from the brothers to the chicos to the white men, unless they came over from the Old Country on a plane, had some slaves in their family tree.

"For almost all of the 17th Century, white and black slaves lived and worked together, and treated each other as equals, and when they rebelled, they fought together. The slave owners were badly outnumbered, and they would have been overthrown if they hadn't started manipulating whites, blacks, and Indians against one another. Blacks were punished far worse for the same crimes that whites were given a slap on the wrist for, not because they deserved worse, but so they'd resent the white slaves for it. Together, black and white and red could have taken over, but kept apart, they didn't stand a chance. And that's where we are today, men. We hate each other because our fathers hated each other, and they hated because their fathers did, and their fathers hated because they were told to. We need to start remembering that we were once equal in chains, and now that we are all free, we are chained instead by our hate. And we need to re-member that "We Shall Overcome" was sung by white men first."

"Man, whutchoo tryn'a say?" one of the jits snapped, unable to contain himself any longer. Our Chaplain, who'd been leaning back against the wall, rocked himself forward with his shoulder blades, ready to take a step forward, but hesitating.

The guest speaker sighed.

"I'm trying to show you why we can forget about the past and start getting along. Build a new future."

"Uncle Tom," another one muttered.

A chill filled the dorm, and the guest speaker did a slow burn toward a sullen black who sat slumped in his chair, hugging himself. They stared each other down, hard, for a long moment, the speaker opening and closing his mouth in quiet rage, until finally he gave up and dropped Reverend Carter's book on the aluminum table beside him.

"God forgive me," he said, and stalked toward the door. "I quit."

The Chaplain moved to intercept him, but was waved off. He followed him to the door where the guard stood waiting, and whispered with him hurriedly while the keys rattled and the lock clanked sharply. The room was alive with buzzing now, and the Chaplain snapped a loud "Quiet!" but nobody listened. The heavy metal door started to roll and the buzzing grew to a din of everybody talking and nobody listening, except me and Gallegher. We just looked at each other.

Once the Chaplain and his guest where outside the dorm, we could see them talking loudly, but could hear none of it. Several guards were hurrying toward them in the hallway and, behind the glass walls of the other dorms, heads were turning. Rubberneckers wondering what all the fuss was about. M3B was in an uproar now, and guards were filing in through the door. The siren up near the ceiling went off and the lights started to strobe, the order for us to get back in our cells immediately, and the guards had their batons and mace out. The yes-men inmates all hurried into their cells and my guru and I followed, leaving the others to shout at each other unintelligibly. Speaking in tongues, it sounded like.

"What's going to happen?" I asked Gallegher, in a naïve-sounding voice I never would've expected to hear come from my own mouth. He raised a quieting hand and sat down heavily on his bunk, on his ratty, green, flame-retartand mattress.

When the guards had gotten all of us locked down, the debates could be heard roaring from our air vents and vibrating along our plumbing. I tried not to listen, but before too long someone was actually on the vents calling to me.

It was Roosevelt.

"Dark! Hey, man, what *you* say bout all dis?"

And Gallegher was looking at me in surprise.

Another voice, and another. People I had pulled aside and whispered heresies to, now clamoring for my opinion, and the louder they called for it, the more the others heard and wondered why I should be asked. Loose lips started sharing the little Truths I had told, and new debates began, and Gallegher stared at me all the harder. *All* of my cellmates were staring silently. The mask I had worn before and discarded was now held up for everyone to see, and it would never matter that I'd changed my evil ways.

And now the truth, why I had stayed so long here when I could have left any day, and why I would have to leave now.

I was in jail because I *wanted* to be. I was so full of confusion and dismay and rage out there, doing exactly what I had been brought up to do and hating myself for it, and not having a clue why, and this was my Time Out from it all. Jail is another dimension where time stands still and all you have to worry about is That Moment. It's purgatory. It is the waiting room between Heaven and Hell, while the jury deliberates, and for some of us

638

here, it is a sweet relief from the madness we had gotten ourselves into. It's almost like what one of our preachers says, to let our tomb become a womb. A lame cliché from a smarmy white guy in a yellow suit—*and* shoes…but it applies. This is a womb for some of us to crawl back into and escape what we must not have been ready for.

And now this place was about to evict me.

I made my decision. I walked to the toilet, stepped on it and climbed up onto the sink so I could stretch my face to the vent and shout.

"Here it is!"

The noise continued, but was cut here and there with loud shushes and *"Quiet down!"*'s. Like I was the expert now. Me, of all people. Mine was the voice of reason that would settle the argument. The air blowing into my face was cold, and stung my eyes, but I did not blink.

"Ready?" I called. And surprise of all surprises, the shouting subsided.

When I had the undivided attention of the entire dorm, with my heart pounding in my ears, I said "What that guy said was in the Bible! If the Bible is the Word of God, then it must be true…"

Scattered mutterings sprang up from behind the tiny holes in the wall, and I shouted again to quell them.

"But…!"

Silence again. I hesitated for dramatic effect, put one hand behind my back so all my cellmates could see, and crossed my fingers for their benefit. Well, mostly Gallegher's.

"And may God strike me dead tonight if I'm wrong…!" Pause again for suspense's sake. "But it's all *lies!*"

The dorm erupted, fury and exultation blasting from the vent and outside our rolling door, echoing out in the day room and startling the guards outside our supposedly sound-proofed wall. In my own cell behind me, eight out of my nine cellmates were shouting also, asking me if I'd lost my mind, asking if I realized what I had just done, and all the lights in our cellblock went out. The guards outside had plunged us into darkness.

I ignored everyone, groped my way off the sink and went to my bunk, grateful for the darkness, grateful that I didn't have to meet Gallegher's eyes. He just wouldn't understand… at least not until tomorrow.

We were locked down for the rest of the day, and after our dinner trays had been passed in through the door flaps and back out again, I lay down on my bunk and meditated a while, in the *samadhi* fashion until I looked to all the world like a dead man.

XIV

I had dyed my hair red and peppered my face with artificial freckles. Tomorrow, when I had time, I'd get whatever chemicals were necessary to make my hair Irishly curly. After that, only my yellow eyes (honey-colored) would betray me as Dark Geiger. This act of being Dwight Saffron wouldn't be too much of a problem, I'd decided. All I had to do was dress in unimpressive clothes. Every time I looked in a mirror, though, my reflection startled me.

After seeing Ana, I drove up to Strega, stopping only to change my clothes. It was a classy Uptown after-hours bar that went overboard in trying to create its image of Hollywood film noir. Enolah stood with much seductive dignity in the dim lights, crooning an old Ink Spots song with her GQ octet in the shadows behind her. Her blue-black hair was up, her perfect body encased in a skin-tight long dress of shimmering emerald, and to subtly repeat her bright color, the eight Negro musicians wore green feathers in the hatbands of their charcoal fedoras, and boutonnières pinned to the lapels of their double-breasted suit jackets. Gardenias, I think.

Here, although trying their best to look coolly elegant, all the image-obsessed yuppies were enchanted by Enolah. Her job at Strega was just to add to the atmosphere, but there was something about her that dominated the scene, and she could never just be part of a background.

I had no idea how much I'd missed listening to her sing.

That's when I noticed the Interloper.

A young woman, maybe my age, was watching Enolah the way I must have been. Not at all with the male adoration or the female resentment, but with the critical eyes of one there to appraise. And this girl wasn't a talent scout. She had a look in her eyes that I'd seen before in a platoon photo from Vietnam, a bunch of guys with the thousand-yard stare, and one little nerdy kid holding his M16 and looking like he knew he was, for the first time in his life, dangerous.

As if I'd broadcasted my interest, the girl turned her head and looked straight at me. No accusation in her eyes, or reproach, but a strange recognition even though we'd never seen each other before. *Anam Cara,* I think Crowe had called it.

I took my martini over to her table for two, helping myself to the empty seat. Conceited swagger is expected in places like Strega, and as long as I was dressed up, I might as well play the part. Shit, I was even wearing a *vest.*

The look this girl wore, it seemed that her eyes were made to look into rather than out of. Not uncommon these days. This kind of person was always intent on some conception she had created in her own image rather than the truth. But some-where behind those eyes she'd changed her mind about how she saw something

"Who are you?" she asked, neither friendly nor suspicious.

"I'm Dwight." I offered my hand.

"Who are you, Dwight?"

"What?"

"You're not a Dwight, or a Gary, so cut the shit."

"Why can't I be a Dwight?"

"Because nobody in a Tom Sawyer Halloween costume, in a place like this, would try to pass themselves off as a *Dwight*."

"Hallow—what're you talking about?"

"C'mon. Every one of those little dots on your face is the same size, like you dabbed them on with a Q-tip, and some of them are smeared. Plus, your hair looks like you dyed it five times in as many days. There's even a false hairline in there where the dye has stained your scalp. You're trying to act all incognito, looking like a white kid in a gangsta rap bar and I'm not buying it."

"Oh, and you're an expert?"

"Not yet, but I'm learning."

"I'm Gary."

"Jennifer," she said, finally shaking my hand.

"I'd had this weird thought that nobody else in our parish found funny," I said. "If there *was* a Forbidden Fruit, wouldn't the marketing people have jumped on it already?"

"What do you mean?" Jen asked.

"Forbidden Fruit marmalade. Jelly, jam, whatever. Fruit of the Knowledge of Good and Evil flavored Pop Tarts. Where the hell are they?"

"You're right."

"See? Finally, someone who agrees with me."

"No, you're right that it isn't funny."

"Bitch." I dipped my fingers in my drink and flicked them at her. We got in a brief flicking duel until she surrendered.

"Now, I need to know, are there really crucifixions?"

"Who said this?"

"The guy who converted me, in Italy. My boyfriend."

"Yeah. Four times a year: Winter and Summer solstices, and Vernal and Autumnal equinoxes."

"Upside-down?"

"Of course." I fished the cherry out of my soda glass and popped it in my mouth.

"And there's an orgy."

"Pff! There's *always* an orgy. Just had one the other night."

"And what's this I hear about a railroad spike?"

"Ten inches long?"

"Yeah."

"One inch diameter nail head?"

"Uh-huh."

"Never heard of it."

It was her turn to flick Pepsi at me, and I didn't stop her. She pointed at my knuckles, raw and scabbed-over from my scrape with Charles L. Porter, hospital intern extraordinaire.

"What's that?" she asked.

"What? Oh, that? That's from me beating off every time I can't find a rape victim."

"You're sick, Dwight."

"Gary."

"Whatever."

"Look, I try to be the bad guy, fit in with all this Evil bullshit, but as you can see, I'm not really cut out for it."

"According to the news, you've got a real flair for it."

"Well, I have my moments."

We'd left Strega hours ago, after losing all interest in Enolah, and putting our cards on the table. She had hesitantly answered my questions, after noticeably recognizing certain casually-dropped passwords and phrases, and we warmed to each other rather quickly. Before Strega closed, we abandoned ship and went to a Denny's, where I suddenly remembered that I love banana splits. I had three of them, back to back, washing them down with Pepsis, with a blatant disregard for my gastric juices. Jennifer, understanding perfectly after being told that I am Dark Geiger, the Walking Dead, raised no eyebrows at my indulgence. She said I deserved it, which made me like her.

"My boyfriend, when he began instructing me, he really built me up, and I've been looking forward to…"

"Orgies?" I prompted.

"No…see, for a long time, I've been having these fantasies of…not sex, but…torture." She finally came out and said it, averting her eyes, pausing, then darting them back to mine. Deadpan, I just looked at her until I was finished tying the cherry stem into a knot with my tongue. Taking it out, inspecting it, I shrugged and handed it to her.

"And?"

She sighed with relief.

"Whew! I thought you were going to think—"

"Think what? That you're a perfectly normal American?"

"Normal? I've been telling myself I was weird this whole time, saying 'bad thoughts, get out of my head.'"

"Jen, the Hindus—or is it the Buddhists? Whichever. They say something that our religion never bothers to bring up, maybe because *our* church wants to *keep* us mad. But this other creed speaks the two wisest words I've ever been told."

"What are they?"

"Just be."

"Just be?"

"Yep."

She mulled it over for a second, and I did an exaggerated shrug.

"Just be, Jen."

"Thanks."

"Don't mention it. Now, what do you want to do?"

"I want to kidnap someone who deserves to be tortured."

I tried to smile faintly, but it grew into a big Cheshire Cat grin the more I thought about it. The plan that had leapt fully-grown into my head was so absurd that I couldn't resist.

"Jenny? I know just the fella."

I knew Ana would be out all night, so I went with Jennifer to pick up a few of my things. My sisters had both given me back my spare keys, so I could drop by whenever I needed to. Jennifer waited in her car downstairs in the parking lot while I rummaged through the trunk my goodies were stored in: a stun gun, a bottle of ether, a spray can of freon to freeze and easily break door locks with, my radio scanner, three sets of handcuffs, two Kevlar vests, two balaclavas, and Switchblade.

Shoving them all in a duffel bag, I left, saying out habit the ritual Satan-protect-this-home prayer as I locked the door. I had parked my rental car (rented with imaginary money, of course) in a hotel's parking lot, and rode here with my new protégé in her—surprise of all surprises—VW bus. Climbing into the back, I waved at her to move along.

"Home, James."

She started the van, looking like a sore thumb in the bucket seat.

"Are you going to be asking for Grey Poupon next?"

"Silence, wench. Now, giddy-up."

Shrugging off my coat, I strapped Switchblade onto my left forearm and tested the spring once, just to make sure.

Cardinal rule: never go into battle with an untried weapon.

Pope rule: never take for granted that it's loaded. With the proper gesture, suppressed barrel and trigger snapped forward. Good. Still worked.

"What was that sound?" Jennifer asked.

"I farted."

"Jesus! Do you ever quit, Geiger?"

"Never." I slid Switchblade back to click home, and put my coat back on to conceal it.

The plan was to abduct Joshua Buckland and torture him in the way he deserved.

No, we weren't going to hurt him.

We would force-feed him some Forbidden Fruit.
We were going to open his eyes.
But we never made it to his house.

The chatter of machine-gun fire split the night, ricochets whining as holes were torn through the van's side panels. Startled, Jennifer instinctively stomped on the gas pedal, but we only gained a few yards before the starboard tires exploded and the van lurched sideways. I felt it starting to happen, the capsize taking a performer's eon. The instant between finishing a set on stage and the audience's applause—a split second that seems a whole minute—the instant passed when Jen and I knew what was about to happen and only had time to say *Shit.* Her seat belt was on, and she pressed her back hard into her seat, locking her grip on the steering wheel.

I tried to brace myself, but when it happened, there was nothing to hold onto. Thrown backwards onto the floor and a second later, slammed into the ceiling. Flashes of white behind my eyes as my head clanged against metal. Roller coaster nausea and limp, rag-doll flopping around. Then sliding.

The inertia dragged me with it, but all I really needed was a moment to rally myself. Head throbbing, dizzy and battered, I forced myself to be ready anyway. The second we were still, I heard them coming. Jennifer lay limp against the door panel, her cheek resting on pavement. Something scrambled up onto the van to check through the passenger side window for survivors, and I dove, falling on my back across Jennifer just as the masked face peeked through.

Shunk! Switchblade leaped out of my sleeve and my finger was inside the trigger-guard, squeezing. The eyes went wide, but the muffled pop, the recoil, the satisfaction of those eyes suddenly going dull and empty, and the ski-mask head whip-lashed back, gloved hands going limp and dropping an MP-5 submachine gun through the window with a clatter—all this happened before it clicked in my mind that those eyes looked strange to me.

No time for that. It was probably just a trick of the reflected headlights washing through the shattered windshield. Other footsteps hesitated outside, and taking the machine pistol in my right hand, I gathered my feet and launched myself out the jagged hole in the crazed safety glass. The gun was already kicking, spraying the legs of men in black. Men? They squealed with pain. Squealed.

No time for that.

Other figures began firing from cover beyond the sidewalk, but those out in the road were down, writhing in agony. I scurried backwards into the van, chunks kicked out of the asphalt and curb I was just lying on. Jen was conscious, just stunned, lying covered in green pebbles of windshield glass.

Shots clunked through the undercarriage barely missing us, one ripping through my coat, vest, shirt, and skin in a long scrape that somehow only grazed my ribs. *Please don't hit the gas tank,* I prayed silently as I slid along the left side wall—now the floor—toward the rear doors. In a second, they'd be shooting through them.

Not a moment too soon, I kicked them open and emptied the pistol at the ninja-looking people as they hurried over into my sights. The rear doors had been ajar and hanging off their hinges, and I only had a second to shoot before they slammed back, but it seemed to scare away those still standing.

I waited, but they must have all run off to find prey that wouldn't shoot back.

"The fuck was that all about?" Jennifer mumbled, trying to get out of her seat belt.

"You got me, hon." I collapsed, trying desperately to fight off sleep. Jen made noises behind me, and I could hear her getting out of the van. I wanted to tell her she should wait a few minutes, but I couldn't find the effort to do anything but stare at the bullet holes. There was silence for a minute, and then she came to the rear doors with an armful of weapons.

"You're not gonna believe this, Geiger. The one you shot in the face? It's a girl."

"Stranger things have happened."

"But you should see this chick. She's a real freak."

"Fascinating." I didn't have time for this.

"Her eyes are bright red."

645

XV

I don't know where I found the strength to bolt to my feet and tear my way out of that van. I don't know how long I stood over my sister's body, staring down at her pale, dead face. All I can say is that, through all the fog in my brain, all the jumbled confusion, I finally made a decision. Or, rather, a decision made itself for me.

Jennifer had, like a good girl, gathered up all of the guns she could find. Most of the clips were empty, and the rest only half-full, but it was something. We could hear gunfire off in the distance. It was hard to tell which direction.

"Who is she?"

I didn't even realize Jen was standing beside me, holding the now stuffed duffel bag in both arms.

"My sister," I said in a small voice.

"Oh, God…"

I shrugged. "I guess she was enforcing curfew." I tried to force myself not to feel anything, but my heart was broken and there was no fixing it. I tried to tell myself that I hadn't gone berserk again, it was self-defense, that it was Intermittent Explosive Disorder, and Missy wasn't dead, she had passed away, experiencing Irreversible Mortality Syndrome after being a High Velocity Ballistic Recipient.

"See this? You still want to be a Satanist?"

She wisely kept silent.

"Let's go," I muttered, lighting a cigarette.

The street we snuck along the side of now, in the middle of a loud and chaotic night, I snuck cautiously along that side of many moons ago, and every detail was just as sharp now as then. When danger is all around you, and death might come at any moment, you tend to appreciate your surroundings. Every weed squeezing its way heroically up through the cracks in a sidewalk, the slow and remorseless force of its tiny roots rupturing the concrete. The red glow of a traffic light swaying in the breeze somehow the most brilliant red I'd ever seen. Tiny bits of glass embedded in the asphalt glittered Morse code responses to the stars high above us.

Seven months ago, I had skulked down this street, every sense taut and alert, and appreciated these things in as weird a manner as now. I was even feeling a kind of perverse nostalgia for that night. I couldn't say why.

The good Samaritan's face smiling good-naturedly into my window and asking stupidly:

"Car trouble?"

Then, just happening to glance into the back seat and say, just as stupidly:

"Oh dear."

My hand jerked the door's lever back and I rammed the car door into him, knocking him onto the road. I bolted out, wrenching my hand to release the spring for Switchblade to *shunk* out of my sleeve. Before I could shoot the good Samaritan in the face, the suppressed barrel only inches away from his nose, I glanced over at the wide-eyed faces in his car.

Two children, a little girl with her hair tied in ribbons; a little boy, his lower lip trembling. Mom, with both her hands pressed, prayer-like, against her lips, suppressing a scream. I should have killed them all, wiped the stolen car down so no prints would betray me, and driven away in their car, instead, with Joshua Buckland in the trunk.

I couldn't.

I can't explain the complete lack of will I felt then, the lack of courage to do what had to be done. I couldn't do what anyone else in my church would've done in a heartbeat. I failed, because I suddenly knew it was wrong.

I turned and ran.

Down this very street I walked now, I dove into this short hedge, feeling the leaves caress my face, the branches gouge my skin, heard them whisper gently as a police cruiser slowly rolled by. Searchlight blinding.

The low swishing rumble of a helicopter on its way.

Not too far from here was the drainage canal I dove into, the cold water hiding me from the thermal detectors the cops in the chopper could've seen me with, plain as day.

When it passed over me, I followed it instead of making a break the other way, always behind the spotlight and thermals, always where they just had looked.

Eventually, they were called away to help pursue some hobo the police had mistaken for me, and I ran again. But my prints were in the car, and it was only a matter of time.

Now, the situation had changed, but not by much.

We walked all night, always hearing distant sirens and gunfire, not knowing where either were coming from. Many times, we hid in the bushes along the street whenever headlights appeared, not knowing who it could be and not wanting to meet whoever it was. Ana and Enolah were both, probably, somewhere safe, because they would have known about this in advance.

Misery. Shit, dying to be the first soldier over the parapet, the forerunner of the first wave, eager to prove something. I didn't want to cry anymore, and I took it as a sign when we came across St. Francis de Sales at dawn. Its doors were open, and defiled. I wandered in.

The cathedral was quiet and beautiful, even though the early sunlight speared in through holes in all the stained-glass saints along the basilica walls, where rocks had been thrown. The carpet was burgundy, the wooden pews dark and immaculately polished. There were clouds of drifting dust that lazily swam in the multicolored haze of light, mesmerizing me until the cooing of a pigeon broke the spell.

Or was it a dove? Whatever it was, it perched with its family on a statue of a crucified man behind the altar. More sorrow than pain was in the eyes of that dying man, and the gaping emptiness in me slowly started to fill.

Then the bird that spoke hopped off of that great wooden cross and flapped loudly down the aisle toward me. A sign.

Something white dropped from the bird to splat on the burgundy carpet, on the steps that led up onto the dais. How poetic the moment could have been. I may even have walked to the statue and dropped to my knees, praying for forgiveness and guidance and light, but this bird had to go and shit on the floor in the house of my lord and savior.

I raised my hand, Switchblade snapping out of my sleeve, and fired once. The pigeon/dove/whatever exploded in feathers, the rest of the birds flapping in startled confusion, their rustling wings flashing in the colored sunbeams. I aimed again, and shot the statue of Jesus Christ in the face.

This, too, was airbrushed like a centerfold, like everything these days. Inoffensive even though it was depicting a horrible death. No blood. No suffering. No flies and sweat and stench. My lord Jesus was bleeding sawdust.

I knew then what all this Savior bullshit was really about, all that shit with the Antichrist and the plagues and tribulation, yadda yadda yadda. I realized that, if He existed at all, this Christ guy was a loving being who couldn't stop giving people the benefit of the doubt. But the concept of an Antichrist wasn't a being of darkness and evil, spawned in Hell by Satan and bent on destroying the Earth. He would merely be the opposing viewpoint, one who insisted Man would never get the fucking point and didn't deserve another chance. One who said, *No, Man is undeserving. I declare him null and void.*

I decided to side with this guy, now.

I have killed some people, crushed some ants, squashed some worms, and I see no distinction between them. No one would've remembered them anyway. Sure, somebody would, but then they'd die, too, and be forgotten. And even if I was wrong, even if my future wanton slaying of unique and beautiful children of God was the ultimate sin and a horrible crime against Nature, fuck 'em.

I've got a head start, and goddamn it, I'm running with it.

In Misery's living room, with cold beer for breakfast, we watched the mayhem on TV with surround-sound and "earth-shaking realism." Enoch sat in-between us, alert for a change, concerned by the smells we came into his home with. Cordite, blood, and stale fear made him suspicious, and it

648

took some time to calm him down, remind him of who I was, and introduce him to Jen. Now, we sat on the couch with him, each of us scratching him with one hand and quietly praising him for guarding the home while we watched the news.

There were riots in every major city in the country. The news anchors, in-between showing atrocious footage, were interviewing people who claimed to be experts on something or other, via satellite.

"The cause of these riots is still unclear, but racial tension has not been ruled out. Dr. Rosensweig, what do you make of the situation?" Cut to a guy who looked just like Dr. Bunsen Honeydew from The Muppet Show.

"Thank you, Liz. As you know, I'm just a humble rabbi—"

I changed the channel, just in time to see a burning building collapse, raising a cloud of fiery ash and spilling smoldering masonry into the street.

"That's a little more like it," Jennifer said.

I flipped from news station to news station at every commercial break. We saw a man held by four others on the roof of a tall building. He was spread-eagled, a young white man holding each limb, and they were swinging him, shouting a countdown. The way guys would gang up on a smaller kid in school and pretend to throw him out of a window, or off a balcony. The way bigger kids used to terrify me when I was smaller and trying to defend my little sister, the Lab Rat.

A news crew captured this on film, a man screaming, four others laughing and shouting in unison.

Four!

I knew what was coming. It wasn't a joke.

Three!

I couldn't believe it. They *knew* they were being taped.

Two!

Only three stories up, but high enough.

We held our breaths.

One.

And they let him go.

Screaming, clawing at the empty air, trying to grab a hold of anything. Falling onto and destroying an old-fashioned red phone booth. The camera jumped back to the four men on the rooftop, cheering. High-fives. Jesus.

The Barbie and Ken Doll news anchors and reporters with styled hair used words like "shocking" and "tragic" and "inexplicable." They mentioned other incidents from the past few days that were still mysteries, because one right after another made investigation impossible. There was still the rumor of "Delenda Est Rap," whatever the hell that meant, which had happened two days ago and nobody would go into. Perhaps it was this that had sparked it all.

"Did she say…?" Jen leaned forward and stared at the TV.

"What?"

"Delenda Est Rap?"

"Yeah, she did."

"I'll be damned."

"What? Why?"

"The girl in Ibiza was talking about it. It's *her* song. My boyfriend, he's the guy that got her the record deal!"

"So, what the hell did they do with it?"

"I don't know, but I can't wait to find out."

"What's his name?"

"Coniglio. Nick Coniglio. Rabbit, I heard some people call him. I'm not sure why."

Ahh. Good Hunting, Rabbit.

And now it all came together.

Parishes all over the country were out committing horrible atrocities to anger everyone else, make them retaliate against whoever they could blame, and the rabble were all just taking advantage of the confusion. And I wasn't invited to take part. I was asked to leave.

I got up and went to Ana's trunk again.

"What are you doing?" Jennifer asked when I came back with Dagger, several boxes of shells, and two Calico M-960 A mini-submachine guns with extra magazines. I sat down and showed her the break-barrel pistol.

"Not the ideal weapon, but as a last resort, it beats the hell out of pepper spray. Now," I added, holding up one of the Calicos. "Do you know how to use this?"

The news finally admitted that the suits in charge up on Mahogany Row insisted that the Delenda Est Incident be kept under wraps, as even *more* people would be outraged. People speculated that the various acts of terrorism were calculated to provoke these riots, and to report on them any further would cause the most dramatic civil war in history. Not just two factions, but every cultural division in the world's melting pot would turn on each other. It didn't have to be mentioned that all news stations were vying bitterly for the true story, so they could run the exclusive. Even though there would be horrible consequences, whoever it was in each police department who held the actual tapes, would inevitably break down and sell.

And then, total chaos.

But then I remembered Crowe telling us that our church had members in very high places, some who could manipulate the news media and strategically air things to cause unrest. It dawned on me then that they weren't members of our church at all. We were members of *theirs*. We were the willingly enlisted foot soldiers who would enthusiastically do *their* dirty work. They told their underlings, like Crowe, what to do, and then he told us what Satan would appreciate. And we did it.

Like sheep.

For guerrilla missions, all Adamist soldiers are required to carry first aid kits, fully stocked with unorthodox but effective supplies. Besides gauze, sutures, syringes, morphine, Betadyne, and Xylocaine, there are a few things the AMA would disagree with—powdered instant potatoes, for example, is the absolute best way to stop a gushing wound. Coconut milk, a great substitute for blood plasma. A poultice mixture of healthy women's monthly blood, placenta, and eleven herbs and spices, which will accelerate the healing process a gajillion-fold.

A grappling hook, rubber coated to dampen its noise, and a coil of rope. Small spray bottles filled with ammonia, to render any spilled blood untraceable.

The Calicos were very light weight, about five pounds, and a little over two feet in length, capable of firing 750 rounds per minute. When I showed Jen the magazines, she impressed the hell out of me.

"Nine mil Parabellum," she said. "Hundred rounds each."

"Uh, yeah, three of them apiece." I handed her share over.

"Who are we going to kill?"

"A bunch of people."

"Will it bring her back?" she asked, meaning Misery.

"No, but it'll make me feel better."

"So, where are we headed?"

I slapped a clip into the Calico and racked the slide.

"We're going to church," I said.

She stared at me, hard, for a long moment. I don't know what it was in those big, blue eyes, but for some strange reason, I looked away. Cursed, and set the submachine gun down on the top of the Wurlitzer. Stared at the bubbles coursing through the tubes in front of pink and yellow neon. Went over to the bar set, just to be doing something, got a glass, and poured myself a vodka.

She still was staring at me. I drank, watching her over the rim of the glass, and choked on the third gulp. The dog, who'd gone back to sleep, woke suddenly with a start and snapped his jaws, then looked about curiously, puzzling over the air he had bitten. Getting up, he plodded over to his corner by the jukebox and curled up there instead, ignoring me. Stinging, vodka came up through my nose. I hacked, pawing at my nostrils, my face going red from looking like a fool, and gasped out a "What?"

"*What?*" again, when she didn't answer.

"Who was it asked if I still wanted to be a Satanist?" she asked. "You want to go and kill your pastor, now? What happens when the others go defend him? You accidentally kill her too, or she chooses between him and you—worst case scenario—and chooses him, and you are *forced* to kill her?"

"The fuck are you talking about?" I managed.

"Your other sister. Or your girlfriend. You're going to put them in a position they don't want to be in."

"Whatever they do, they do! So be it."

"Sit down a minute and think, Dark."

"Think about what? There's nothing to think about here! I have to do it!"

"I saw the look in your eyes tonight. You can't lose another sister, not that way."

"What are you, a psychiatrist now?"

She sighed. "Pour me a drink, please." She climbed onto one of the barstools.

I waited for her to keep on bullshitting me, but she just looked at her fingers tracing the wood grain on the surface of the bar. I snorted and got another glass, thought a minute, and grabbed the Disarrono, Limon, and cranberry juice. While I poured, she spoke quietly, confessing something.

"I have this weird…process, I guess is the word. Not the right word, but the only one that comes to mind right now. This process I go through in my head. I've done it since, I don't know when. A long time. I'd be in a room with a bunch of friends, hanging out, and this horrible thought would come into my mind. I would try to figure out who was the kindest-hearted person in there, by…" She broke off.

"That's horrible?" I asked, prompting, while handing her the drink.

"Thanks. No, but…okay, here goes. Say I have a gun, and there are six people in the room with me. Six friends. I shoot five of them in the face."

I stared at her, trying to hide my astonishment.

"Then, I toss the gun to the one I've left alive. I make it clear that he or she has to kill me, because I'm going to try my damnedest to kill them. Then, I charge."

She looked up at me for a long moment, and I swallowed. I've heard and done things that make this seem like a pleasant daydream, but coming from her, it was somehow unnerving. I don't know why.

"Why I do this," she continued. "Is to figure out who'd be utterly devastated by seeing all the others die, and then having to kill the killer, all in a few seconds' time. Some people might have no problem with it, aside from the shock. Most might have to go through a little therapy. But who would feel so horrible about it that they carried it heavily inside them for the rest of their life? That's the person who's really good inside. And the look in their eyes that I picture, you had that look tonight. I think you're evil only in your mind. You've been told to be evil and you're just trying to live up to it. You don't have to do this."

"Who the hell are you?" I asked quietly.

"It's a long story."

"You're not here to become an Adamist."

"No." A flat No, immediate.

"Why are you here? Why really?"

"A guy named Rabbit sent me."

Rabbit. Good hunting, Rabbit.

She was part of this, somehow, all this mess. I didn't want to know any more about it, but she kept talking anyway.

"I'm here to do the impossible as a homework assignment. What you told me about being a grain of sand? In some other church's oyster? That's what my boyfriend-mentor told me I had to do. Come into a lion's den and be cunning enough to convince at least one person to change."

"Change? To what?"

"Christianity."

Hypocrite that I am, even though I had tried only the other day to convert Enolah, I exploded.

"There *is* no such thing! It's bullshit! It's *all* bullshit! You'd get yourself killed the second you opened your stupid mouth! Your god wouldn't save you from getting nailed up on our cross, that railroad spike hammered into your screaming mouth like a fucking cock through the back of your head!"

"You'd be surprised," she answered calmly.

"Surprised by *what?*"

"Changing someone's mind isn't as hard as you'd think."

She smiled cryptically, as if at some secret joke. My head cleared abruptly. She'd been up to something, I had no idea what, but she had aces up her sleeve.

"What is that supposed to mean?" I asked.

"Haven't you wondered yet why I was there, at Strega?"

I hesitated, my short hairs standing up.

"Why was I watching your girlfriend? Why did I recognize you and let you come over and sit with me? A known criminal, a wanted man?"

"You were there to meet *me?*"

She laughed. "Of course not, silly. Why would you even be there? I was told to come here *weeks* ago, before you escaped."

"Then who...?"

"Your girlfriend, dummy."

"How did you even know about her? I don't get it."

Jennifer sighed. "Did you ever even bother to wonder why you got arrested? Why your car suddenly stopped working that fateful day? When it never had a problem before?"

Somehow, her words didn't register in my head, and right before I could even make a face—

The phone rang, startling me. I reached over and picked it up uncertainly, wondering if it was my other sister. My living one. But it wasn't. The voice on the other end made my blood run cold.

"Dark," Crowe's deep voice rumbled. "You're supposed to be on the road."

"How..." I stuttered. "How did you know I was here?"

"Because you're predictable, which is why I sent you away, you silly boy. Because I knew what you had in mind. And now you're going to throw a wrench in everything I have worked hard *for years,* to create."

Some of my cockiness came back, and I half-smiled at Jen.

"Oh, you don't know the half of it," I said.

"Don't flatter yourself, kid. I know it all. Listen, I have to tell you something."

"This is the part where you explain your evil plan?"

"If you want to call it that."

"Save the rap."

"Listen to you talking like a jailhouse punk. I thought you were better than that. I thought more of you."

"Oh yeah? Well I thought a lot more of *you,* too. Til today."

Crowe sighed.

"Will you at least listen to my evil plan, then?"

XVI

"Nothing's scarier than darkness, right? There are wolves and sabre-tooth tigers, with their eyes glinting like topaz, and hunting parties of cannibals with bones through their noses, lurking just outside the circle of your campfire's light to grab you and drag you off screaming to your doom. Everyone's afraid of the dark. So, what's everyone love? The *sun*.

"Every day, there it is again, rising, casting out the shadows and the danger. If you're a primitive person, you're not thinking, hey, I'm probably walking around on the surface of a rock that's spinning slowly around a giant ball of flaming gas. You are probably thinking that thing up there is a god, most likely *the* god, giver of all life, that comes to save you every morning. And since you don't have MTV, you'll probably make up stories about it to tell everyone else. And once you figure out that every year, it behaves in the same way, losing power after the Autumnal Equinox, and showing up for less and less time every day, and the dreaded night lasts longer and longer, you'll come up with stories to remind you of it and keep you calm with the knowledge that, without a doubt, it will come back when the season ends."

"I know all this, Jim. You told it to me years ago."

"Not this part."

"I don't have time for this."

"Kid, you have to listen to me. Before you make a grave mistake."

"The grave mistake I already made years ago, by listening to you."

"I know, but I need you to understand why."

"Because you're of the Devil."

"No!"

"What do you mean, *no?*"

"That's what I'm trying to tell you, if you'd just shut the hell up a minute."

I stuttered for a moment, because something just wasn't connecting in my mind.

"Dark," he said quietly, as if hoping someone wouldn't overhear. "I'm a Christian, too."

My mind reeled, as if I'd been on a rollercoaster and was suddenly flung out into space. I reached out desperately for something to grab a hold of, something to literally cling to, and gripped the edge of the counter with a white-knuckled hand. I think he heard me gurgle, and knew I was struggling with this.

All my life, until recently, I've been a Satanist.

All my life, this man has been my teacher. He's been the rock I clung to, steadfast, and here I was trying to sever myself from him, and he comes out with this revelation that shocks me like a bucket of cold water to the face.

It must be a lie.

He was, after all, the High Priest of the *Father* of Lies. He was trying to reel me back in, and would say anything to do it. I mustn't believe him. I had to resist.

"That is why I sent you to New York," he said. "So you would be on the road when all this happened. You'd be in a car on I-95, oblivious to all this until it had happened already and the new age had begun. Which'll happen in three days."

"W...*what?*"

"You ready to listen to me, now?"

I was silent long enough for him to assume that yes, I was and he resumed talking in his hypnotic voice.

"Well, Jesus isn't the Son of God. He is the *Sun*. He has died, he has risen. He's Horus, losing a battle with Set, when the *sun sets,* and he returns to defeat the evil in the morning. Every night, every morning. The darkness won't last forever.

"You know how early civilizations didn't just follow the stars, they personified them with myths to memorize all their movements, and anticipate them. So, in the wintertime every year, Sirius, the brightest star in the sky, aligns with the three stars of Orion's belt. On *December 24th*. Those are the Three Kings that follow the brightest star, not three actual 'kings' that wouldn't have been traveling at night, when the weather sucked. And together, they point east, to where the sun will rise the next day, on the winter solstice, the shortest day of the year. You with me on this?"

I hesitated a moment, then nodded. Not realizing that I was on the phone, and he couldn't hear my nod, but somehow he knew. Because that was Crowe. He continued.

"As it gets colder, the sun moves south and get smaller, more scarce. The days get shorter, the crops wither and die. It makes sense that it symbolized death. By December 22nd, the Sun's death is fully realized, because it moved south continually for six months, arriving at its lowest point in the sky.

"Then, it stops. For three days. It stays by the Southern Cross. *The cross.* Get it? And then, on December 25th, the Sun moves one degree, this time north, foreshadowing longer days, warmth, and Spring.

"And thus it was said: the Sun died on the cross, it was dead for three days, only to be resurrected or born again."

"I just realized why you're wasting my time," I snapped, jumping up off my bar stool. "You're stalling. Keeping me here so someone can arrive to kill me."

"For fuck's sake," Crowe said, and his Australian accent came out thick with his anger. "Don't be an idiot! Listen to me! There's a point to this! Jesus had twelve disciples. Those are the twelve months, the signs of the Zodiac. You remember Moses was furious with his people for worshipping their golden calf? That was Taurus, the Bull. That was the end of the Age of Taurus. Moses represents the ram, and that's why Jews still blow ram's horns. He came down a mountain heralding the beginning of the Age of Aries. Jesus was hanging around with *fishermen,* and magically multiplying *fish,* because he's the Age of Pisces. It's all symbols to remember the story with. That's all.

"An Age lasts about 2150 years. From 4300 BC to 2150, it was the Age of Taurus. 2150 to 1 AD was the Age of Aries the Ram, and from the year 1 to 2150 is the Age of Pisces. But there are forces at work today to make the world enter the next age, the Age of Aquarius, sooner than we're supposed to. They think that if they make a large enough blood sacrifice, they can bring about a new Age where they'll rule the entire world, and make slaves of all the other races.

"And it's working. People are gladly giving up their power to the Beast. They are trading freedom for 'security,' but it's all just an illusion. Their noose is growing tighter and tighter around us. So, I came up with a plan."

I shook my head to clear it. I'd been willing to believe all the mythology he crammed down my throat for years, and I swallowed it gladly, but *this* was absurd.

"I know what it sounds like," he went on. "Because I'm giving you the short version. It all makes perfect sense if you hear the whole thing, but I don't have time for that. Just…I need you to know that this fallen angel I've had you worship all your life? He doesn't exist. And neither did his 'enemy' that I made you hate. The only thing that exists are people who believe in them and do things in their name. I do what I do in the name of Jesus because that is the symbol I work to preserve. And the people I fight worship a much older god."

"Who?" I asked, incredulous. "What god?"

"Moloch."

"Who?"

Crowe sighed.

"Satan is a Scooby-Doo villain in red. Satan is the poor man's Moloch. The truly wealthy people, the ones who control our lives, who run the slave trade under our very noses, who abduct children and murder them and bathe in their blood because they think it'll keep them young, who torture them so they can extract adrenochrome and take it at parties, they worship *Moloch.* And it doesn't matter at all that Moloch doesn't exist either, because they *think* he does, and they are the ones with the money. They own everything, down to the main stream media companies that lie to us every day about the world you think you live in."

He waited a beat, either letting that soak in or catching his breath. I wasn't sure. The silence became oppressive.

"So, where do you come in?" I asked, stuttering.

"Simple. I want to kill them. *All of them.* I want to stamp them out like a nest of cockroaches. But I could never do it alone. So, I created an army."

Jen finished her drink and got a cigarette out of the pack in her jacket pocket. The ring of slamming the phone down in its cradle was fading away when her Zippo clicked open.

"I had nothing to do with that," she said, before lighting it and punctuating her denial with a resounding snap.

For the moment, I'd completely forgotten what she said earlier, right before the call. It was there, nagging at me, in the back of my mind, but my head was throbbing with what I had just heard.

Jen blew smoke at me. "Is my mission accomplished?"

"You know it is," I muttered, misunderstanding her.

"Oh no. That could've just been a coincidence. Life is full of little coincidences to impress the imaginative."

"Ha ha."

She drew on the cigarette, looking at me sideways with her eyes wide while inhaling, a move she did so coolly, I knew she must have spent hours in front of a mirror perfecting it. She blew it back out and smiled.

Oh yeah, she practiced that. Got it down pat, though.

"Whatcha say we run around saving people?" she asked.

"From who?"

"Themselves."

"What if we run into my other sister? Or my girlfriend?"

"I'll convert them, too."

I shook my head, laughed. But she'd managed to convince me, so she must be on to something. We gathered up all of our stuff, fed the dog, and bade him good day. I followed Jennifer out the door, ready to crusade for the cause of Good.

At five o'clock that morning, Anathema Geiger and Enolah Taylor accompanied a squad of fellow parishioners to the jailhouse on Buttonwood Avenue. First creeping up on each of the perimeter booths outside the fence, they killed the guards with suppressed automatic fire, then walked in the front door. The guards at the front looked up in surprise.

The same deer-in-the-headlights expression was on every face they encountered, so swift and silent was their progression up to maximum security, floor by floor.

In the officers' station at the top, the control room, Blake Underhill clicked on the PA system and shouted into the microphone in his most obnoxious voice.

"Rise and shine, sleepyheads!"

Then he started scat-singing reveille.

Anathema hit the lights, bathing the entire top floor. Enolah rolled all of the cell doors open, and confused inmates stumbled, scratching and yawning, out into the day rooms.

"The day of doom is here!" Blake proclaimed.

"What a dipshit," Anathema muttered, shaking her head.

THE
CAMEL'S
BACK

Introduction

I wrote this series many years ago, between 2001 and 2005, while in prison. I had seen first-hand the hatred being stoked between races in the US, and foresaw inevitable consequences. This book was intended as a warning.

Spoiler alert: I had not heard of Barack Obama, and would not for several years to come, so when I wrote about a black president, I never intended this character to be him. Everyone who read this told me there'd *never* be a black president, that it was fantasy, and after there was one, people criticized me for writing this book about him.

I had to take it out of print. But now, in the Age of Covid, what I'd predicted in this book is coming to pass, and I feel it necessary to rerelease it. In earlier publications of this book, there is a lot of racism and unnecessarily foul language. That's the result of living amongst the dregs of society, and especially black men who hated me just because of the color of my skin. Inmates talk like that, all day every day, and it is contagious.

If you have read that book, I apologize. It wasn't me. After detox and years of clean living, I've overcome that anger and cleaned up my language. If you haven't, know that I'm making a serious effort to keep the bulk of this novel intact. I have to try not to overhaul it, because 25-year-old me had something important to say. 43-year-old me would never have been in jail to begin with, much less felt obligated to hold up a mirror to the cesspool of society and scream "Look at yourselves!"

I would happily leave this book unpublished and just pray that every other copy of it has been burned and forgotten, but they haven't. They are out there somewhere, and the world I'd predicted in it has reared its ugly head. I'd never heard of the Rothschilds when I wrote it; the name and the black President were in my head from prophetic visions I had in hospital after coming back to life, explained in *The Hero Mindset*. I may have seen the future, but was still too inexperienced to interpret it.

But nobody would ever believe this book to be prophetic with so many F and N-bombs, unless I made a few changes.

So here goes.

I

"You furnish the pictures, I'll furnish the war."
—William Randolph Hearst
Publisher of the *New York Journal*
January, 1897

The Virginia Declaration of Rights, drafted shortly before, and influencing, the United States' Declaration of Independence, calls upon the citizens to rise up and overthrow their government if ever it becomes corrupt or inadequate, and corrupt and inadequate it became.

In the interests of its self-preservation, a corrupt government is not about to arm its enemy, that enemy being its own citizens looking out for their own rights, and so, at the beginning of the third millennium AD, laws were passed banning the ownership of firearms. Pulling their fangs, so to speak.

One way of doing this was through the news media. It is no secret that widely-broadcast events tend to set precedents and inspire copycats. Not many people knew, for example, about the many people who died in Arkansas, Washington, Alaska, and Mississippi before the Columbine shootings, but afterwards, all the world knew. And then an epidemic of copycats, more and more kids following suit because the news kept showing it.

Next thing you know, if it hadn't happened in a whole year they'd show the last one again to keep it fresh in everyone's minds so that the next pissed-off kid would consider it a solution. Or even "Columbine, five years later." Keep it alive in the minds of the populace, keep it ever present, so the ticking time-bomb of a man will remember that re-enacting that atrocity is always an option. That if it ever seems that there is no way out of his predicament, he can always go out with a bang.

This news coverage popularized such crimes, and in turn called attention to the availability and accessibility of firearms, which helped to tighten the hold on honest citizens and effectively disarm them.

The next step was to poison the people against the soldiers who protected them and their international interests. Politics bred resentment between the soldiers and the civilians, and also the entertainment industry drove a wedge between those civilians and the

662

police.

A people who hates its own guardians makes for a weak nation.

Soldiers, for example, built Rome, and its poets and politicians destroyed it. History repeated itself again and again and again, and will continue to do so, and all that is great will perish because what makes it great is forgotten and supplanted by its opposite.

The second President of the United States said that he'd studied politics and war so that his children could study the sciences and philosophy, so that his grandchildren could be poets and artists.

But then what becomes of the great-grandchildren? They must in turn be warriors themselves or risk becoming someone else's slaves. The beginning of the third millennium marked an era of more supposed artists and poets deciding what was best for a country than ever before, even volunteering to weaken themselves as a whole for the benefit of their enemies in the hopes that said enemies would somehow like them better. Would somehow feel less animosity.

The third President of the United States said that the Tree of Liberty had to be refreshed from time to time with the blood of tyrants and patriots.

And a candidate for the forty-fourth Presidency said that the American people were not smart enough to govern themselves, the implication being that they therefore needed more governing and less freedom.

This solidified the fear in the minds of some very powerful and influential people that the United States were doomed to fall, and quite soon.

The last straw, for them, was the kidnapping and rape of a charming and beautiful young lady named Amanda Rothschild. She had maintained that what would be later called the Ghetto Front did not deserve the bad rap it had gotten, that people whose lifestyles were based upon and revolved around "gangsta rap" were good people that were just misunderstood. She came to be called, when other Rothschilds were not in earshot at least, the new Timothy Treadwell.

She adamantly maintained that it was the media that poisoned the public's mind against fans of rap music, black youth in particular, up until she was seized one night, leaving a Miami club she probably shouldn't have been in. Her reappearance on the sidewalk outside of a hospital a few hours later was taken as a message by her family, and their friends and colleagues, who declared war on the very people they had, effectively, created.

Their original plan, to slowly crush the middle class with mounting debt while pitting the races against one another, to eventually make the people cry out for a new government that would "care" for them, was put on hold. No longer could they wait for the population to vote for their own return to slavery.

Taking as their inspiration the great Italian monk Savonarola, whose "Bonfires of the Vanities" cleansed Florence in the 1490s, these captains of industry felt that humans can be nudged and prodded forward into their graves, but cannot be nudged backwards into righteousness. They have to be seized by the neck and dragged, kicking and screaming, or they won't go.

Ahh, but who must do the seizing and dragging?

"Are we there yet?" Evan asked for the umpteenth time in his cheerfully whiny voice. The Army of Shiva, as he'd dubbed it, had been trickling into Florida. En masse, they would've attracted much unwanted attention, but in this gradual relocation, their passing went unnoticed.

There was nervous restraint still in much of the United States, citizens only seeing the lunatic fringe collapsing from the safety of their living rooms. Fires had been started all over New York City, James Harding's handiwork, drawing the fire departments out in different, far-flung directions, returning to find their headquarters demolished in their absence.

Then, homeless, each fire engine and its platoon wandered about the city, the men afraid to leave their trucks and go home.

The houses that were burned were those of high-ranking Mafiosi, and their bodies were found impaled Vlad Tepes-style in the back yards. Mob wars erupted, each family blaming another. Just as planned. The news media, swamped with strange events, were unsure which of them to have a field day with.

The man everyone called Rabbit refused to explain the mysterious incidents in New York, Chicago, Miami, LA, Atlanta, and Philadelphia, when questioned by his allies. He only smiled his strange smile and shrugged when asked why he'd doubled over laughing the first time the Delenda Est Incident was hinted at on the news.

Much publicized since then in magazines, on TV and the radio, the simultaneous concerts held in those six major cities, all supposedly in honor of rap and hip-hop's finest, were now spoken of in quick, interrupted sound bytes. With no word at all, not a single one of those who attended the concerts came home. Neither did the performers. Music was still blaring from the auditoriums' speakers, but it was not rap. The ominously still buildings, locked and impregnable, kept their neighborhoods awake with constantly deafening music, some of which Evan recognized from his ex-girlfriend Maya's "Shrike" album, and some from concerts by his other friend's band Warpath.

Excited at this one clue, he played the CD for his punk rocker friends, then, pointing at Rabbit, loudly declared its origin. Rabbit refused to comment.

On television, all of their attacks, abductions, and sabotages were confused with rap culture aggression, retaliation by upset friends and family members of missing concert attendees—what some media "expert" dubbed the Ghetto Front on the air. What little was actually reported about the concerts and a few other disasters caused by Salon des Refusés, was by MTV News. Several bands were shown wondering why their music was being broadcasted without their permission, but not actively seeking damages since their subversive lyrics got free publicity.

And this just in, all of the senators and aldermen who were mysteriously stricken dead one night in Washington DC and New York City, suddenly awoke in the morgues and ran about screaming gibberish. Suggestions that it was a voodoo drug that had caused a temporary deathlike paralysis were dismissed and even laughed at, correct though they were.

References were made by speculating experts to the many cases in which voodoo bocors secretly administered a poison that caused temporary, well, for lack of a better word, death, and their victims were reported to awake, panicked in their coffins after lying impotently aware of funeral rites and burial.

Those who managed to claw their way out tried to return home and were then killed by their own terrified families, who called them zombies. These absurd—though correct—explana-tions were discarded as foolishness, attention being turned instead to the zombies' images on anonymously donated 8x10 glossy photographs, engaged in acts of depravity in the basement of the hottest new restaurant in Gotham, the one and only Pecado.

All in the wake of the Army of Shiva, the Destroyer.

As the legion of now inconspicuous-looking punk rockers bled into Florida for their real mission, only a few stupid errors were made. Several trucks full of soldiers accidentally drove to the tiny town of Coquina on the Gulf side, which the developers of the target city hadn't known about when they named it.

The Army of Shiva may not've been a legion of diamonds yet, but not a one of those who came out from under the Bridge in Hollywood was still a coal. Each recruit swelled with pride at the almost immediate changes in their physiques, the pole reversal of their outlooks on life, and the calluses on their flesh and souls.

There was no battle flag for Shiva, but they came up with one by themselves, tattooing the icon on each other when their mentors weren't looking: a horned, muscular man bursting from a cocoon, the slime he had been marinating in spattering off his triumphantly spread arms, the cocoon still bearing the imprint of the skinny fetus it had housed for so long.

Soon after their arrival in Coquina, Florida, Evan Lanthorne and Seth McHale went to one of the safe-houses out in the Acreage, summoned by Pedro Vizcaya.

"Hey, it's the Man with the Flan," Seth laughed, greeting him.

"L'il Moke came through for us," the Basque said, cutting him off. "We got one of the Bacalous' guys behind the guys."

"Outstanding. Where?"

The shadow of an expression that Evan didn't expect and couldn't quite identify passed across his dark features.

"In the kitchen. With Rabbit."

He waved them along, and they went down the corridor, expecting to see something marvelously horrible like the death of a thousand cuts, but were puzzled along the way by a mouth-watering smell, overpowering the odors of dry rot and mildew. The scene they came upon would've startled them a few months earlier, perhaps even horrified them, but Evan was now a diamond and Seth was well on his way.

A slender mulatto sat strapped to a large chair that had been reinforced with extra legs, so it couldn't be tipped over by wild thrashing. His mouth could be seen working underneath a strip of duct tape, and in his eyes, the hopeless, terrified look of a poor damned thing. Across the kitchen table from him, Rabbit sat eating.

On the stove, behind him, were a few pots and pans, covered, simmering, and something was roasting in the oven.

The mulatto had no arms.

Or legs.

"Last chance, Ordell. Are you sure you don't want any? Nope? This is the last bite, now." Rabbit held a morsel up in front of his guest, speared on the tines of his fork, and moved it in a serpentine motion toward his own mouth. "Going, going, going, gone!"

Dramatically rolling his eyes and *"mmm"*-ing like a man in a restaurant commercial, he spoke with his mouth full and was barely understandable.

"Yunno, it was considerate of you not to have exercised much, Ordell. You're very tender. I'd say you were succulent, but that would sound awful gay, wouldn't it? No, tender is the word for you."

"Knock knock," Evan said, interrupting.

"Who's there?"

"Is there more for us?"

"Dinner will be served at eight, and not before."

"Splendid," Seth laughed. "And who's this?"

"A stubborn motherfucker. But I'm sure he'll tell us everything we want to know, soon as he sees his girlfriend about to be butchered. We'll find out soon enough."

"Smells good," Evan said, playing along as if this didn't disgust him. "But our friend doesn't seem to be enjoying himself. What's eating you, Ordell?"

Seth tried not to roll his eyes at the stupid pun, and took over.

"Lookie here, whatever your name is, we don't have all day. If you cooperate, we'll put an end to your suffering. If not, the boss said I could eat what's left of you raw, pulling meat off of you with a goddamned fondue fork." A lie, of course, but he was playing Bad Cop to Rabbit's Good Cop. Or, more accurately, Psychotic Freak Cop and Even Worse Cop.

"It's no good," Rabbit said, shaking his head. "We'll have to make hors d'oeuvres out of Lisa."

Ordell started screaming urgent protests, muffled by the gag.

"Jeeves!" Rabbit called, clapping his hands twice.

Klaus was summoned, wheeling in a white woman on a dolly. She was nude, gorgeous, and trussed up like a turkey, her eyes bulging with terror. The dolly came to a stop next to the table, the

Dutchman reaching over to tear off Ordell's duct tape, and the mulatto hurriedly begged for Lisa to be spared.

"Cut to the chase, please."

"Let her go, man! Do anything you want to me—"

"Oh, we plan to."

"Don't hurt her!"

"It's all up to you, Ordell. Tell us what we want to know, and she's free."

And Ordell sang like a bird.

He gave up the address and typical daily schedule of one Rashawn Bunkley and a squadron was dispatched to fetch him that night. In the late Nestor de Medieros' boat, Bunkley was wrapped in strings of small, twinkling, waterproof lights, then keel-hauled. His kidnappers were very attentive, making sure that he was brought up often enough for air and when his screams became too intense, he was fished back out of the water and dropped into the cockpit.

The sharks had not come yet.

Only the barracudas.

The BL gave them Jean Fleurimond, called Cree-Hole by his friends.

By noon the next day, Fleurimond's two brothers were sitting in front of Teresa de Medieros. Lucien and Ezaque flatly refused to speak, as stoically as their little brother, and the two men before them. Rabbit was not running out of ideas, however, so it was surely just a matter of time.

Teresa asked them all of her questions as patiently as she could, half-hoping they wouldn't be answered, finally arriving at the one she'd been at loath to ask.

"Who gave the order to kill my son and husband, and rape my innocent little daughter?"

Their eyes lit up.

"So, that's what this is all about?" Lucien asked in surprisingly cultured English. He and Ezaque shared a grin. "The little dyke tramp and your faggot son cried like babies, and your spick husband—"

A silver arc flashed and he reeled, toppling over in his chair and cracking his head sharply on the cold terrazzo floor. Abuela pounced on him with savage fury, her bruised hands clawing at his face like talons. The knife she had sliced his face with had spun, ringing, across the floor, but she didn't need it.

The bones standing out sharply underneath her blue veins and translucent skin were all Ezaque could see as he looked for his brother's face, suddenly spattered with blood. Scarlet rivulets streamed from between her fingers, and the slender Haitian shrieked in anguish. Ezaque screamed at her to stop, half in Creole and half pure gibberish, but the fiend that had only moments before been a wispy-haired old grandmother heard nothing.

When asked later, she would shrug and say nothing, and just stare at the mashed pulp of two gouged eyes she wouldn't let go of.

Ezaque, his face twisted in fury, tried to swing his weight in the chair he was strapped to, falling sideways, and he began to inch his way slowly across the floor toward them. Teresa helped. Dragging him by the collar around Lucien's chair, she set him where he could get the best view, and had Calibos Lugo hold him there.

Those two took much longer.

It turned out that the real Guy Behind The Guy Behind The Guys was, of all things, an Asian fellow. A businessman. Who'da thunk it? Just as every radio station on the dial, totally diverse genres of music, were owned by one corporation, several gangs warring upon each other ultimately answered to the same people. As soon as this startling truth was revealed, after all the abductions and bloodshed, Teresa tossed up her hands and said, "Forget it. We tried." Not much sense in getting the Crips, the Bloods, the Folk, the Latin Kings, and whoever else coming after them. Might as well throw in the Triads, Yakusa, and the KKK, at this rate.

"Don't worry," Rabbit said. "They'll all take care of themselves, soon enough."

"What, the concert thing?" Teresa asked.

"The news story is due to break any day, now. It's been festering, slowly coming to a head."

"A pimple. Beautiful metaphor."

"Hey, that's why I make the big bucks."

She sighed despondently, slumping in her chair.

"I got so caught up in this, Jared. The thrill of having something to do with a difference being made."

"It'll happen," he assured her.

"I doubt it. This will all be forgotten by next year. Ever since I arrive to this stupid country, nothing but What's Hot, What's Not, and it changes every month. This will all be old news in no time."

"No. People will finally get the point. I promise."

She shook her head, and stared off into space.

"Descrente," he said in mock accusation. Unbeliever. Infidel.

She didn't answer.

Aside from Salon des Refusés, the Army of Shiva, and the Adamist Satanists, there were many seemingly unrelated splinter groups committing carefully organized atrocities, escalating the chaos. Someone, high above, must have created a symbiotic giant, individual causes unaware of each other that would act in perfectly-timed cooperation. Most of them had waited until today to make their presence known.

Americans have never been in a hurry to enter a war, arguably because they know wars are really just a government's way to keep its own population down. A large population is unwieldy and can rebel more easily than a smaller one, so the herd is periodically thinned with arbitrary wars. Surplus population, they call it. Take the Crusades, for example.

The English really didn't give a shit about Jerusalem back in the first millennium. They all had enough problems of their own. But, one day, the higher-ups said that there were too many peasants and they could be a threat to their maintaining power, so it was decided all the young men who weren't firstborns had to go off and fight for something that they knew nothing about. A lot of them would die, and either way, they'd be out of the picture for many years.

Or take the so-called "Big Push" in the trenches during World War I. Field Marshal Sir Douglas Haig could not have gotten to be a Field Marshal by being a complete idiot. So why would he insist on ordering all his men to walk slowly en masse into the crosshairs of chattering German machine guns, getting mown down pitifully, again and again? Could he really be so dumb?

No.

Occam's Razor—the simplest answer is often the most likely—would suggest he did it on purpose, culling thousands of young men so they wouldn't ever make it home to Blighty. It solves the unemployment problem back home. It helps the economy. It prevents rebellions.

But Americans managed to catch on and tried to stay out of wars that they didn't feel affected them. So, the higher-ups learned to orchestrate atrocities to infuriate common men and make them rush to enlist, like printing false pictures in newspapers of Spanish customs officials in Cuba strip-searching white women without cause, or blowing up the Lusitania and then the Housatonic and blaming it on the German Navy, or sending planes to strafe Pearl Harbor and blaming it on Japan, or crashing planes into the World Trade Center and blaming it on Muslims. For example.

But this time around, Rabbit thought, it was going to take a lot more than one atrocity to make the country rise up and cut its own throat. He had some ideas, but he just wasn't sure what the straw that broke the camel's back would be.

He sat with nineteen other men in front of a small television, all of them watching the news silently, only occasionally nodding their approval of some incident among their better friends. Coincidentally, a Ku Klux Klan parade was scheduled to march through the center of town that day. Every news station mentioned at least once the mounting racial tension that might be amplified by the rally.

Evan Lanthorne stood at the back of the crowd, trying to see past the shoulders of weight-shifting and constantly swaying larger men. He could only hear the first murmurs of apprehension and disapproval, when local news showed something unexpected.

Carefully planned to happen just long enough after another, separate incident for the news reporters and cameramen to arrive, a loud explosion startled the bystanders. Shaking, the camera swung back and forth by its ambitious operator, hoping to capture good footage—and settled on a bright flash, fire and sunlight glinting in the windshield of a school bus that veered to strike the guardrail of a small bridge. Timed perfectly to be seen by parents at home, all over the country.

A terrible metallic shriek.

Retaining posts popped away like matchsticks.

The bus lurched sickeningly.

Evan cursed as all of the backs straightened in his way, the other soldiers startled and leaning forward in horrified disbelief.

The bus tipped. Those watching half-expected it to rock precariously, as it would in a movie, but it didn't. Zooming in, the cameraman caught a glimpse of terrified faces in the windows.

Faces of children.

The image only lasted an instant but it was burned into the minds of everyone watching. Then, with the grating screech of twisted metal, the bus heaved over the side and was gone.

Rabbit was up and shouldering his way through the crowd.

"What?" Evan asked, then choked a startled cry as Rabbit grabbed him by the collar and yanked him out into the hallway with him. "What? What happened?"

"You know how to get to Sandy Pines?" Rabbit asked hurriedly, his voice crimped with fear as he dragged the boy behind him. Evan stumbled to keep up, trying to pry the white-knuckled fist away from his t-shirt. With his free hand, Rabbit snatched up two of the Kevlar vests waiting by the door.

"Of course! Leggo!"

"Lead me there."

Behind them, the others moved in closer for a better view, the image on the screen jerking as the camera man ran with the reporter and the interviewees to the edge of the bridge. Other cars were stopping and their passengers gathering at the mangled rail. Almost sixty feet down, bent sickeningly, the bus lay across a dirty creek at the bottom of a ravine, distant screams barely audible. It was on one side, slowly rolling onto its roof. The two emergency hatches flew open and everyone watching prayed silently that nobody got squashed trying to climb out.

A few of the smaller kids were trying to squirm out of the tiny windows, getting stuck, and screaming anew as the bus heaved over, capsized in the water, and left them hanging upside-down.

Ditching their car a block away to avoid later congestion between a disaster and a KKK rally, they ran the rest of the way. Ignoring all of the disaster voyeurs lining the rail, they vaulted over a concrete abutment and scrambled down through kudzu and poison ivy to the creek, pushing past the handful of rescuers helping children up to safety and blankets. Many were still trapped, half out of the windows, or pinned underwater by yellow steel.

Rabbit paused for a moment after jumping into the water and wading to the wreck, paused to look up at all the spectators, displaying their vulgar curiosity that distinguishes Man from the "lower" animals.

"Do something, you pieces of shit!" he screamed. "What is the matter with you?"

Not one of them moved. There were only a dozen people actually helping, standing on the bus's undercarriage around a huge hole that had no guessable origin, helping the children out, then assembly-line handing them to the side of the ravine. Evan scrambled up the side to join a young man and woman, only a few years older than him.

Through the tears and confusion, Rabbit heard a girl's voice coming from the far side of the bus, close to the water. Wading toward her, he came to the bent end, peeked through a window, and heard her cry out again, closer. Inside, the bus was flooded, and a little red-haired girl was sitting in the aisle, up to her chest in the muddy water.

Backing away, Rabbit reached down into the water, pulling up the hem of his jeans so he could get at one of his asps, strapped to his combat boot in an inverted sheath. Unsnapping the thong that held it, he slid the baton out and shot it open. The first stroke shattered the upper half of the window, the part that slid down. Two more, and the partition bar came off. Flailing desperately, he cleared the rest of the glass away to make enough room for him to crawl through.

"What, are you stuck?" he called, ignoring all the other children.

"I'm stuck!" she wailed, as if he hadn't asked her.

"What can you move?"

"My head hurts." Then he got a clearer view of her as he came through, and saw that her hair was really blonde. He swallowed.

"Well, I'm here now, so you'll be fine. What are you stuck in?"

"The door in the roof. I tried to get out." The emergency hatches. She had tried when the bus was on its side, before it tipped over. She was shivering violently, through the water was warm, and she clutched the side of her bloody head.

"My head hurts," she mumbled again.

"Yeah, you got a bump there. But don't worry. A few aspirin and you'll be good as new. Now just hang on and I'll have you out of there in no time."

"My legs are cold."

"Well, you just sit tight a second, and I'll go out for a swim,

673

okay? I'll get you out."

Crawling back out of the hole he'd made, Rabbit pulled himself under the bent and upturned hulk of the bus. Almost a minute passed, and when he came up out of the murky water, gasping for air, he didn't even try to climb back in. He just stared at the hole he'd made, for much longer than it took to get his breath back. He hadn't been able to get at the roof hatch, but he had found something.

"Hey, what's your name?" he called.

"I'm Julie. I'm eight and a half." She could barely speak, but he had a feeling he needed to keep her talking.

"Julie, are you wearing yellow sweat pants, and white sneakers?"

"Uh-huh." Oh. Shit.

That's what he'd come across down there, too far away from where the emergency hatch should be. Sticking out from under the bus's roof at entirely the wrong angle. And too far away.

Taking a deep breath, he spat, and crawled back into the bus.

"What you want to do when you grow up, Julie?"

She was just barely hanging on, and he couldn't decide whether to hold her hand and talk to her or just brain her with the asp and get it over with. Quick and painless. It was the logical thing that he couldn't bring himself to do.

"I'm going to figure skate. I take classes."

"Oh? Is there a lot of ice down here in Florida?"

"No, but there's a skating rink in town called the Palace. It's got a zambonie there and everything. And I practice in front of my house on my rollerblades."

"What can you do, Julie?"

"Oh, lots. But I tried to do an arabesque the other day and I fell down and skinned my knee."

"It happens."

"Did you just say the S word?"

"No...I said it happens. It. It happens."

"Oh. My feet are cold. Can I have my shoes back?"

Rabbit's grip tightened on the asp, but all he did was stroke her hair and try not to cry as she slowly fell asleep.

When the last of the other children were out, Evan peered over the edge to find Rabbit, just standing in the water and staring off

674

into space. The girl beside him, who'd been giving the seriously injured children some kind of painkiller, curiously joined him, and gasped.

"Nickie!"

Rabbit did not look up. Frowning, the orange-haired man that was with the girl came over. His face was lobster red, sunburned from a long time indoors and then a hard day outside. His rusty and obviously dyed hair was limp and stringy, his eyes yellow.

"Nickie! *Nick!*" the girl called again.

"Rabbit," Evan called, and finally Rabbit looked up, distracted.

"Hey Jen," he said in a hollow voice.

"So, you're Rabbit," Dark Geiger growled. "I have a message for you." Evan and Rabbit both blinked in surprise. "The Woolagaroo says 'good hunting.'" His hands itched for a gun, for his Switchblade. But not in front of all of these witnesses, he told himself. Rabbit looked around him dramatically, raising his arms to encompass the scene, then dropping them and shaking his head.

"So, you too, huh?" Evan asked. "Small world."

"Too small!" Rabbit yelled. "There's not enough room for all of us, so we have to resort to this. This?"

"What are you saying?" Dark asked.

"I'm saying this ain't good hunting. I'm saying—" his face convulsed into a hideous snarl, a throbbing forked vein standing out across his forehead and spit flecking his white lips. He trembled, his hands clenching and unclenching, raised his fists in what turned into a helpless shrug. It was hard to say whether his eyes were shining with tears or creek water.

"And you?" Dark asked, turning on Evan. The teenager looked blankly at him, and suddenly felt like he was just a teenager. He didn't have time to answer, interrupted by the distant sounds of all hell breaking loose.

675

Detective Bancroft waited at the foot of the table while Cooper went through his pre-break ceremony, chalking his cue and peering down the length of it, checking it for straightness. He had no more will to be impatient after six Jack-and-Cokes and the numbing Xanax he'd grown fond of. Whether on duty or off, after all he'd been through in the past few months, he spent as much of his time as he could at Rack-em-Up.

"Been watching the news?" Cooper asked, leaning over the table and sliding the cue way too many times, taking aim.

"Been looking out the window?" Bancroft muttered.

"Bah. It ain't so bad here." He shot, the white scattering the racked balls with a satisfying crack. "Not half as bad as Miami. Not yet, anyway." Nothing fell in. "Still open."

Bancroft bent down, the gut he'd grown spreading against the table, and sank the three. Too much back-English. He was slipping.

"Have you solved any crimes since d'Argent got splattered?"

"No, Coop. And thank you very much for bringing back a painful memory. While you're at it, why don't you give me a nice paper cut on my eyeball?"

"Ooh, touched a nerve there?"

"How many guesses do you need?"

"Rita! Another Whatever for Mr. Sourpuss here!" Cooper called.

"I'm busy!" the plump barmaid with the suicide blonde Peggy Bundy bouffant shouted back. She and everyone sitting at the bar had their eyes glued to the television.

"Christ. Look at them all, obsessed with that depressing garbage. Why can't they turn on some positive garbage?"

Bancroft ignored him and, having sunk two more solids, was examining the table and calculating angles of refraction.

"Six in the corner, off the deuce." He shot, the ball clipping the jutting lip of the middle pocket and clattering into the rest of them.

"Shit."

"Oh, show me the color a' money, Tom."

"Blow me."

"Make that a double, Rita!" Cooper yelled. Bancroft was not yet a devout alcoholic, but he was well on his way, and Cooper's joke had burrowed deep into his brain. D'Argent's death was a touchy subject.

"Shut up! Come here and watch this!" Rita shouted back, not looking at them.

"Is there nudity?"

"No, they blew up a school bus!"

"Christ," he muttered, shaking his head.

"Shoot, Coop. I don't have all day."

Cooper lit a cigarette and walked around the table, trying not to think about what he'd just heard, instead sizing up his chances of banking off the far cushion, pocketing the nine and lining up for the seven.

Bancroft set his cue against the neighboring table and walked over to the bar.

"Hey, I can mix the damned thing myself."

"Man, don't you care about this?" some guy asked him. "Ain't you a damn cop?" It was a regular. Perhaps a Too Regular. The detective reached over and confiscated the bowl of dry-roasted peanuts the guy'd been hogging, and began popping them in his mouth while talking.

"You stop caring once you realize there isn't shit you can do about it. You try being a detective in this town and then come talk to me." Then he glanced up at the television, and froze.

Marcia Something was asking Live on the Scene reporter Laura Delaney-Fitz what else she could tell us about the situation. The pretty blonde started saying something, but Bancroft couldn't hear it. He just stared hard at the screen, hoping for another close-up of the people helping kids out of the wreckage. Instead, just meaningless commentary.

"Banksy! It's your turn, fool!" Cooper called, and was ignored.

More shots surveying the damage.

A quick zoom in and panning of the assembly line passing terrified children to safety.

And now back to you, Marcia.

"How long has this been going on?" he asked Rita.

"About twenty minutes. Some guy down there in the water was shouting something up at the camera, but we couldn't hear it."

"That one guy looked familiar," someone said.

"Yeah, saw him on the news every day for a while back."

And that was enough.

Bancroft listened long enough for the name of the street, rummaging around in his fuzzy memory for the bridge's location, and left the bar. Rita shouted after him to pay his goddamned tab, and Cooper waved his cue at him, asking where the hell he was going, but he heard neither of them.

After picking up Rabbit's omnipotent satellite cell phone, the Kevlar vests, and jackets to conceal them, Rabbit, Dark, Evan, and Jen went to where Dark's sister Anathema's "borrowed" car was parked, unlocked the trunk, and removed two "borrowed" backpacks holding several boxes of ammunition, four MP-5s kept from the night before, two Calico M-960As, and three Molotov cocktails. The bottles had come from Dark's bar in his sister's apartment, two of them half-gallons with the little glass handles up on their necks for easier throwing, and the other one just a liter.

Inside the spare tire compartment was a briefcase that held a broken-down thirty-ought-six with scope, "like Scorpio had in Dirty Harry." Dark told them his sister had jokingly dubbed it "Betsy." Jen already carried his sister's other gun, Dagger, in the inside pocket of her denim jacket along with a handful of fat green shotgun shells, and was ordained the Beast of Burden, the one who had to carry everything. She didn't mind. It made her feel important.

Coquina's biggest commercial district was only a few blocks away, with a seething tide of rage rolling through it. Men and women of all colors fought in the streets, some in ghost costumes, many not, destroying shops and each other. People were being dragged out of their cars and businesses, savagely beaten. But some were fighting back.

The employees of the Cheng Du Chinese Restaurant, for instance, made their stand with machetes, meat cleavers, and butcher knives at the front and back doors. Fat Joe laPaglia and his sons brained several would-be defilers with rolling pins, so far losing only the front window of their pizzeria.

It would not be discovered until late that night that Coquina County Jail had been overtaken, the inmates all freed, just as in almost every major city in the country. The night before, just before dawn, the gates had been thrown open and, coincidentally, the truth about Delenda Est Ghetto had finally been aired the next afternoon.

Only a short time after one school bus in each of those cities suddenly wrecked. Coincidence. On KKK Rally Day.

678

A police helicopter flew over past the group toward the square, and they hurried after it. Ducking into an alley, they clambered up on top of a dumpster, making stirrups of their hands to boost each other onto the Spanish-tiled roof of a small travel agency. As they ran, climbing and jumping from one roof to another, the police arrived in full riot gear beneath them, returning from yet another incident they'd been called away for.

Another helicopter had already arrived, filming for a local news station. Rabbit kept an eye on both of them from under the pagoda-style eave of Cheng Du, where it jutted out over an art gallery. Beside him, out of sight, the other three argued over how to assemble Betsy.

"I'm telling you, *this* snaps into *this!*"

"Who's the sniper here, tough guy? Me or you?"

"I don't know about you, but I'm a goddamn diamond!"

"You're both wrong. It's—"

"Christ!" Rabbit yelled. "Give it here!"

Below them, a line of policemen with shields, helmets and shotguns tried to form a phalanx against the crowd. Screams and gunfire echoed deafeningly between the buildings. Within seconds, Rabbit was crouched back in his spot under the eave, breath held, aligning the crosshairs of the rifle scope, waiting for the police chopper to hold still.

"I'm the goddamn sniper, dammit!" Dark hissed.

Rabbit ignored him, waiting.

Hundreds of people filled the pastel-cobblestoned square, looking from only two stories up like a boiling mass, like a stepped-on anthill.

The news chopper rose to get a better view, a shot including the police helicopter hovering over the crowd.

Rabbit squeezed the trigger. A shower of sparks and a clang, audible even over the small explosions and din of voices. A second shot, this time closer to the hub of the tail rotor, and the chopper swung sideways, out of control, the pilot inside wrestling futilely with it as it whined, tipped, and fell into the crowd. The blades snapped off, spinning away and cutting bloody swaths through the rioters, a second before the cabin exploded. Evan and Jen stepped out onto the ledge with two of the machine pistols and sprayed down the SWAT phalanx, while Dark lit the fuse on a Molotov.

Elbowing them aside, he wound back and swung, launching

679

the liter bottle far out over the square, a perfect throw that seemed to hang forever, then slowly drop. They didn't stop to watch.

Running quickly across the art gallery's roof and leaping an alley to its neighbor, they skirted around the square to the far side. The people who had come to kill, steal, and destroy, and now tried to escape down through a shop via, fell, twisting and jerking as bullets tore through them. Jennifer lit and swung the second Molotov, not getting much distance, but still enough.

Jumping again from one roof to another, then another, they cut off another exit with the last flaming bottle. A blaze exploded from the shattered glass, engulfing a fleeing woman with arms full of plunder, and three men. Above, the news chopper had noticed them and zeroed in. Evan smiled and waved.

"Top of the world, Ma!"

"Idiot," Dark muttered, yanking him back by the sleeve, and they ran across the roofs back to where they'd left Anathema's car. It was demolished.

Turning back, they surveyed the terrain, weighing their options, and tentatively climbed down from the roof onto what Rabbit referred to as "the great tide of humanity."

There was no open floor space beneath them. The crowd of ordinary, middle-class suburbanites stood, cheek by jowl with the dead in the vias, many of them already limp and motionless, supported by the press of those around them. Blood trickled from the mouths and nostrils of many, both living and dead. Here and there were belches of red-frothed air as another person gave up the ghost, squeezed to death, still upright.

Rabbit and his companions dropped carefully onto them and picked their way across the via on their shoulders, being sure to try and use the dead as their stepping stones. Each of them secretly likened it in a way to crowd-surfing, but didn't want to be so crass as to say it aloud. Several times, one of them accidentally stepped on someone with a bit of life still in them, and was bitten on the ankle. They'd stumble and almost lose their balance, but one of the others would grab them by the arm and steady them. They had an uneasy feeling that if they fell, they'd be eaten alive.

When they got to the far side, they all helped one another up onto the roof of an antique store, and made their way to the other side without saying a word, until they found a deserted street.

Climbing down a drainpipe to the ground, they ran to where

Rabbit had parked, a block away from the bridge and the wreck.

It was gone.

"Stolen!" Evan growled.

"What's the world coming to?" Rabbit asked.

They walked, a street away from where they could still hear the riots, Evan cursing up a storm. Giving the square a wide berth, they rounded a corner, and Jennifer laughed.

Two large white-trash types in wifebeaters, cutoffs, and flip-flops were trying to drag a fat Hispanic woman out of the window of her car, and she had gotten stuck. The other three laughed, too. They couldn't help it. It broke the tension.

One of the guys spotted them standing across the street and told them to get lost. Rabbit spat and pulled his gun out from behind his back. Evan and Dark had theirs held close to their legs, but when the one was out in the open, the others were obvious. The guy who'd spoken let go of the fat woman, and the other one panicked.

"The fuck are you doing, Jim? Pull, man, pull!"

Jim tapped his friend on the back and jerked his chin in their direction. The man punched the fat woman hard in the back of her head, stunning her, and let go, turning to face them.

"The fuck do you want?" he yelled.

"I want you down on your knees," Rabbit said quietly.

"Sorry, faggot. My asshole's exit only."

Evan shot the other guy, Jim, in the face.

His buddy didn't handle it well at all.

"Oh, my God! Jim! Jim, oh my God! Fuck! Oh, my God, fuck!"

"He said get down on your knees," Evan reminded him.

The fat woman was staring at the blood on her car.

"We're not going to shoot you," Rabbit said. "I promise."

"Please! Please, I don't want to die! Please don't shoot me!" the man begged.

"Kneel. Kneel before Zod!" Evan ordered. Dark rolled his eyes.

"Please! I'm sorry! I don't want to die!"

"Then get down on your knees, Cletus."

The man was trembling violently, but he managed to kneel. Rabbit called out to the woman.

"Ma'am? What's your name? *Como te llamas?*"

"Camila Vasalo." She seemed remarkably calm.

"Step out of the car, please."

She hesitated, and Rabbit held up one reassuring hand. "Don't be afraid. No one will hurt you."

Squirming back into the car, she opened the door and slowly got out. Cletus, or whatever his name was, had to scoot over and make room for her, and was now blubbering on the pavement to her left. Rabbit nodded.

"Now, do whatever you want to this piece of shit."

The guy started to protest, but she grinned and seized him by the hair, yanking him backwards off of his knees. His head hit the side of the driver's seat, and she stomped a high heel into his throat, stepped aside and slammed the door on him eleven times with all her might. When he slid, limply, out onto the pavement, she kicked him again and again and again until Rabbit stopped her. Her face flushed, she looked up at her saviors and smiled, brushing her curly black hair out of her eyes.

"My car's been stolen," Rabbit told her. "Could you give us a lift?"

Her smile broadened, and she nodded. Here, Jennifer thought, was a fair demonstration of the human spirit. According to psychiatrists and similar charlatans, this woman should have curled up into a fetal position and wept. In the very least she should have gone into shock, equating the situation with some vague and overrated childhood trauma.

Instead, she drove them all across town, talking a mile a minute about the horrible riots and the state of the world, and the gleaming rays of sunshine her four new passengers were in this bleak world. They nodded, unable to reply because none of them could get a word in edgewise. They heard all about her family—all of it—locations, well-being, individual names, everything. Camila Vasalo was a rambler, a jovial one. A lousy storyteller, but a dedicated one. She was so grateful to them for rescuing her that she never once asked them where they needed to go, not until they were eager to get out of the car anywhere.

At five o'clock that morning, Anathema Geiger and Enolah Taylor had accompanied a squad of fellow parishioners to the jailhouse on Buttonwood Avenue. First creeping up on each of the perimeter booths outside the fence, they killed the guards with suppressed automatic fire, then walked in the front door. The guards at the front looked up in surprise.

That same deer-in-the-headlights expression was on every face they encountered, so swift and silent was their progression up to maximum security, floor by floor.

In the officers' station at the top, the control room, Blake Underhill clicked on the PA system and shouted into the microphone in his most obnoxious voice.

"Rise and shine, sleepyheads!"

Then he started scat-singing reveille.

Anathema hit the lights, bathing the entire top floor. Enolah rolled all of the cell doors open, and confused inmates stumbled, scratching and yawning, out into the day rooms.

"The day of doom is here!" Blake proclaimed.

"What a dipshit," Anathema muttered, shaking her head.

III

Han Fei-Tzu stared out of the helicopter window at the city as it shrank away beneath him.

Soon, he thought. Any minute now.

The scene he envisioned he knew he would not see, but he still hoped. The romantic and poetic part of him was already at work composing a song in one of the compartments of his mind, while the more practical concerns dominated his foreground. There should be a bit about fire, the all-destroying element that could not possibly know he was its father, and would turn on him as well if he didn't admire it from afar.

He would have to watch it as his comrades did, alone in privacy, but still together in spirit. The news media, puppets of his partner Donovan, would obey him and show the events, not as they happened, but in an artfully-arranged order for a special effect. The timing Donovan had spent months meticulously planning with his colleagues, was everything.

It would draw out the Powers That Be, who would leave behind only a skeleton crew to hold down the fort. Then, Rothschild would step in, his interference causing a nationwide blackout and a brief intermission in the media's show. Then Fei-Tzu's nephew, and his people, would move in to perform.

In Washington DC.

As he watched the buildings recede below him, he could not help but reflect on all of the modern styles of architecture. How visually boring they were. All erect penises, stabbing at the sky, and not even a single pagoda, shikara, or minaret among them. No ascetically pleasing, harmoniously balanced art. Just clutter. No wonder all these people needed psychiatrists. But that would soon change.

Splinter groups of financially-blessed tree-huggers and environmental terrorists crept with soaring hearts into unattended zoos in every major city. Taking up their carefully assigned positions, they opened up the exhibits in order. Graminivorous animals first: elephants, antelope, giraffes, then exotic birds. They were gently coaxed and herded straight out of the gates to safety (?) and freedom.

Next were the carnivores, the wild cats, their cage doors

opened from a distance with extendable gaffs. They crept out, bewildered and suspicious, into the walkways, glancing uncertainly at their liberators and each other. Suddenly, an explosion spooked them. It was a grenade-like device called a flash-bang, and was non-destructive, for causing diversion. Or panic.

Since all avenues but the main one were blocked off, just by whatever was handy for show, the cats and bears, etc, all ran straight for the front exit. The herbivores, already spooked by the sudden noise, had a head start when they saw the predators coming. All fled in every direction, some making it by chance into the wilderness, the rest into civilization.

Trying to contain themselves, the eco-terrorists waited to release the reptiles, the tenebrous, insensate monsters that would prey upon anything they could reach. All over America, crocodiles, pythons, monitors, and every other conceivable descendant of the dinosaur slithered out of captivity, following the mammals and avians, ready to make office buildings and sewers their home.

"You?" The First Lady demanded, aghast.

The President of the United States sighed, and swallowed the urge to slip a patient Let's-Humor-the-Child tone into it. With a smoothness born of countless practice hours in front of the bathroom mirror, he put on his Hear-Me-Out face and walked around his large rosewood and smoked-glass desk, and plopped down into his throne.

They were in the office of their country house they rarely used anymore, but to which they'd suddenly been evacuated. With one hand, he gestured for her to take a seat, and took a cigar out of his wooden humidor with the other.

The First Lady remained standing in the doorway.

"No, dear," he said, contemplating the cigar. "Not me. I may be in on it, but I'm just one of the many."

"You're supposed to be the *President!* How can you do this to the country you're supposed to *lead?"*

"This country is on its way to Hell, Patricia. If I'm to lead it back to glory, I have to first start by taking part in its reformation."

"Reformation!"

"Yes. It's sorely in need of one."

"You call *this* reforming?"

"You're damned right. It would never happen any other way.

The politicians would never go for it. So, it has to look like the government is not behind it. We have to get back to the pioneer state of mind, and to do that, we need a revolution —not against the government, but against the people."

"But Henry, you're a *Democrat!*"

"Was, and stop talking in italics, dear." He struck a wooden match on the sole of his loafer, puffed at the flame, sat back and chewed meditatively on his cigar.

"Like Communism, this democracy only works on paper. Graft is running rampant, and the masses need to be reminded of what's important in life. It is certainly not which pop star broke up with what air-headed stick-figure socialite, or what this summer's blockbuster movie will be.

"Think about this for a moment: when my grandmother was born, there wasn't even a telephone. Then here comes this wonderful thing called a radio, then moving pictures, then talkies, then television, and before she was as old as I am now, everybody had electricity, running water, and refrigeration in their own home. There's a lot of folks in this world that still don't have any of that to this day, but we lose one of them and our whole day is ruined. Then, we all got personal computers, and soon, no one could function without them. Whole businesses are powerless if the computer is down. Then we got the internet, not too long ago, and as soon as it caught on, nobody could live without that! Take away websites and chat rooms and these imbeciles don't know what to do with themselves! So, we're taking it all away for a bit.

"And rest assured, this was going to happen with or without me. I am not truly in charge here, the military is. And what was it Suskind said back in '96? 'The single greatest fear that America faces today is that its military forces no longer tolerate the continuing incompetence of its civilian leadership.' Remember? Well, General Flanagan pointed that out when he approached me about this. I definitely don't want to be on the wrong side here."

"This is the wrong side! It's wrong wrong wrong."

"Earth to Pat! The only wrong side is the losing side. When the time is right, we will 'regain control' and start over."

The First Lady just stared at him, speechless.

President Henry Tucker, usually called Hank by his wife (except when she was mad at him) took a long pull off of his cigar and puffed out a stream of smoke rings. He watched them spiral away and dissipate, then seemed to be staring off into the distance.

"Besides," he added quietly, "I always wanted to see those pricks die. I could never have pulled that Columbine shit, but I admit I used to fantasize at my desk in school of blowing those coons away."

"Coons?"

President Tucker nodded quietly.

"But, Henry!" Patricia exploded. "You're black!"

"Yes, damn it! But I'm not one of them! I never was! And those sons of bitches could never forgive me for it! I was the one who screwed up the bell curve, and I never let anyone copy the answers off of my tests, and when they'd ambush me on the way home and whup my ass, they called me an Uncle Tom nigga. They punished me for wanting to get out of that awful neighborhood—oh, I'm sorry, I meant *da hood*—when I wanted to get out of da hood and make something of myself, they punished me for it! Well, now it's *my* turn! And when the smoke clears, decent black people like you and me will be truly equal with everybody. The whites, the Indians, everybody will be the same. We'll be judged not by the color of our skin, but by the content of our character. You find your territory, piss on the property lines, and live in peace with whoever is living next door. We, the government, won't use our weapons to establish a totalitarian empire. We'll use them to guard the borders. Make sure no one else tries that. It'll be Utopia, Patti! It'll be what the world should be! Not might makes right, so the bullies can rule, but smart survives. Half of our population will revert to savagery when they lose all their cable TV and running water, and they won't last the night with lions running the street. You know who'll survive? People with courage, brains, and respect and consideration for others. That's it."

Patti Tucker gaped at her husband, then quickly left the room. She hurried upstairs to the bathroom, slammed the door, and leaned her back against it, hugging herself. After a moment passed, she sank to her knees on the tile floor, and prayed for the safety of her country.

"What we're doing is right," Rabbit said firmly. It's just the way—"

"There is no other way," Evan interrupted. "Yes, it's horrible that children got hurt. I am the last person to say that you should

687

hurt children at all, considering what I've seen. But you can't just mutiny because one of the means to your end—"

"—Well, no, you can't. But that was going too far."

"The whole point of this is that we're going too far. This way, it can't blow over in a few weeks and people go back to masturbating their lives away."

"Spoken like a diamond," Dark muttered wryly.

"Lookie here, Zombie. Yeah, you got played. You were a dupe. But it's accomplishing something. Sorry your sister got killed. Sorry you were the one to kill her. But you need to look at it from the proper perspective."

"Hey, let him grieve, will you!" Jennifer snapped.

"No. There's no time for that. You have to accept the fact that people die. Everyone dies. Every last one of us will. It's the living that matter, Zombie. Your kid sister died doing what she always wanted to do. She went out gloriously, and now she's off in Valhalla or somewhere—"

"Watch your mouth!"

"No! Face it! And if we all do our part, we can win this thing! We'll spend the rest of our lives at the top of the food chain, where we belong."

Rabbit had looked away and now stared back at the city while Evan gave his pep talk. Plumes of smoke were blackening the sky over the heart of town, but where they stood, in a grove of overgrown sea grape trees near the beach, all was clear. It seemed symbolic to him at that moment. He felt a strong urge to quit now and get away, get back to Maya. Run. Like the rabbit his long-dead father had named him after. The nickname he perversely hung onto because it pushed him to always be a wolf, instead.

He heard his old man's contemptuous voice then, teasing him for running from the bullies. His father who, according to police reports, killed his wife and then himself.

Leaving poor young Jared an orphan.

And a millionaire. But that's another story.

"The blood's already on our hands, man. It's just a matter of degree," Evan was saying. Rabbit turned back to them.

"Hey."

"What you have to—"

"*Ahem.*" The sternness of his tone cut Evan off.

"I've got a cunning plan," he said

688

Their ears pricked up, their faces questioning.

"All of the airports are closed. We saw to that. But we have a boat. My friend Nestor's boat. We take it to the Bahamas, since Nassau is only four hours away, get on a plane to Europe, and start over."

Jennifer was the first to protest.

"But...! But we can't leave now!"

"Of course, we can. And we should."

"And desert the whole cause?"

"Cause? What cause? It's all bullshit, Jen. The only cause you oughta have in mind is the Self-Preservation Society."

Rabbit was reminded of years ago when, as part of his training, Jim Crowe took him to paradise. Well, it was paradise when seen on postcards or the pages of National Geographics read in the safety of a living room. The jungles of Papua New Guinea, pineapple growing out of the ground underneath cocoa and coffee bushes and banana trees, with coconut, date, and oil palms towering overhead, was a far cry from the produce section at Publix.

Mosquitoes swarmed in a humming fog, their noise subtly driving him insane for the past few days. If it weren't for the one modern convenience Crowe had allowed him to bring along—insect repellent—he would have died either of malaria or heart failure on the first day. He had read that cattle (yaks, water buffalo, whatever they had here) would panic and run, and run, and run until their hearts exploded and they died, and then the mosquitoes they'd run from would catch up and eat them up piranha-fast.

Paradise.

Crowe had read Rabbit's book *A Mind Diseased* and said Oh, the Asmat, eh? You want to be like them, do you? Well, let's go meet them, tough guy.

They watched a village from the trees, hiding in tangles of vines and sweating like fat kids. Outside of huts thatched with palm fronds, women tended a large steaming pot over an open fire. Not one of those gigantic cauldrons the cannibals always had in the B-movies. Just a large pot. And the women weren't sexy supermodels in leopard-skin loincloths. Sure, they were naked, except for these fringes of fibrous rags twisted about the waist, and ringworm scars overlapping on their purplish skin, looking from a distance like wood grain. Their breasts hung down, long and skinny like bananas. At least, Rabbit was pretty sure they were women.

The men returned from a raid on another village with tonight's dinner—two men. They wore pale mud, painted on their skin in strange designs that mingled with their decorative scars they got around puberty. Each one of them had a bone or other strange object shoved sideways through their septum. Shells stuck out of their frizzy hair, and they did not bother to even swat at the flies buzzing around their heads and walking on their faces.

There was a powwow of sorts, a lot of prancing about and shouting, and then some little kids were allowed to spear the hostages. More dancing. The kids were scarred to commemorate their rite of passage, and the women set about butchering the corpses. The heads, severed and emptied, were set in a sweat-box after the lips and eyelids were sewn shut, and the intense heat shrunk them into Christmas tree ornaments. What used to be living, breathing men were now food, bone tools, and little hairy coconut-looking totem decorations. Neither of their livers was eaten with some fava beans and a nice Chianti.

It was during that time that Rabbit had changed his mind about hating civilization, and decided to stop taking some things for granted. Like bug spray, for instance. It was bad enough that the mosquitoes were in earshot, for Christ's sake. He didn't care that some of the vermin here were endangered. If he had his way, they'd be fucking doomed.

And this was what Crowe wanted the world to be.

"Have you lost your *mind?*" Jen was asking him. He shook his head.

"Nope. I've just found it."

"What about everything you taught me? When we were in Florence?"

"All lies. Forget it, I was wrong. I've come to my senses." She gaped at him, speechless. He continued. "I taught you to live for the struggle. Now, we've helped bring it about. This is where we quit, and watch it from safety."

"You coward!"

"No, sensible man. You want to end up like his sister?" he asked, indicating Geiger, who glared at him. Evan, however, had immediately seen what would be in it for him. Another chance with his ex-girlfriend Maya. He didn't care if she did have HIV now, he'd have it with her. Maybe that could make up for how he had failed her before. He jumped at the chance

"We've got passports up the wazoo back at base. I've got mine already, and Zombie, all we need is your photograph—"

"No. Not without Crowe's head."

"Fine," Evan lied. "Come with us to the house so we can at least regroup first. You're low on rounds as it is." He really didn't give a shit about this strange-eyed asshole, but two more guns accompanying him and Rabbit would make the trip a little easier. "It's only a mile or so away."

Dark stared at him for moment, then shrugged.

"Bancroft! It's Smiley. Where the hell are you?"

Evan turned sharply toward Geiger, whose police scanner had been spouting frantic messages since he turned it on.

They were back within the city now, moving a safe distance away from but parallel to Poisonwood Avenue, watching cars fly by in panicked evacuation. Their arsenal had been divided: each carrying a Heckler & Koch MP-5, Dark and Jen holding the AK-47s, Rabbit the 30.06, and Evan his modified, fully-automatic Browning Hi-power.

"Bancroft!"

"Smiley," another voice crackled.

"Dammit, I've been looking everywhere for you!"

"I'm on a mission. That punk kid Lanthorne who shot my partner, remember him? Shot, what? Twenty-something people? He's in town and I'm going to find him."

"How in the...? Detective work's not really appropriate right now, Ward. We need riot guns and men to shoot them, so get your ass back here now."

"No, I'm going to get that brat, and I know how."

"What, his parents? They're both dead."

Evan froze. *Dead?* Since when?

"No, a little chippee he used to go out with. Hot blonde chick named Heather Roma."

Evan's eyes bulged.

"I got ten to one he's on his way to save her, and I'll be there waiting for him. The place she went to work today is right in the line of fire."

"Where? Where's this?"

"Fat Joe's Pizza. It just came to me a minute ago."

Evan yelled "We were just *there!*"

He started running.

"Stupid kid," Dark Geiger muttered.

IV

A prepubescent "redbone" gang-assassin known as Shrike called Pedro Vizcaya, interrupting a heated argument. The Basque was furious that Evan had been allowed to leave without an escort, or even an explanation of where he was going.

"Uncle Pedro," the child said. "I got news. They's talk of real military-type action up in here. All the BLs is mad bout they bosses missin' and they gettin' organized to come getcha. All three motels goan get hit."

"How can they know where we are?"

"Man, ya got people that work there dontcha? You don't think some of 'em don't know somebody, and all yous packed in like Mexicans ain't lookin' a bit funny to 'em?"

"Smart kid. So, when are they coming, and from where?"

Shrike told him, and Pedro gathered his lieutenants together to tell them. He gave them their orders.

"And Seth," the Basque said gravely. "You find our boy and bring him to the Acreage house."

Seth ranked high in Manticore, a division of Shiva. (He, Evan, and the other highest diamonds got a little too creative with the name assigning, for the real mercs' tastes, but Salon des Refusés allowed the silliness. What was once Hollywood Hardcore, a gang of punk rockers, was now broken down into Dragon, Basilisk, Gorgon, Griffon, and Manticore, and they insisted on calling the Grazi Mono assassin/spies the Familiars. Seth McHale was not formally in charge of anything, but all of the soldiers he was grouped with had an intense loyalty to him, so he was present at the meeting with Calibos Lugo, Klaus, Oisin, Henri, and Clive.)

While the heads of Basilisk, Dragon, Gorgon, and Griffon were being assigned their strategic positions, Pedro's cell phone rang. He answered it irritably. Normally, he'd be blissfully happy under these conditions, but the boy who used to be his little brother and was now more like a son, was missing. The Basques are, and have always been, famous for their obligation to duty and family. "Intense" is an understatement.

"What?"

"Rabbit, checking in," Jared Layton's voice said breathlessly.

"Where the fock are you?"

"Chasing your little diamond. He just took off."

"Why did you leave in the first goddamn place? And why did you take him with you?"

"I wasn't thinking—"

"No! You weren't! Now where the hell is he?"

"He's running off to save some damned girl, walking into what he knows is a trap." Rabbit filled him in, explaining the radio scanner conversation. "But none of us but him was paying attention, so we didn't catch where the girl is, and the little punk outran us. But it's some ex-girlfriend of his."

"What's the name?"

"Jenna, Heather, Hannah, I'm not sure. Last name sounded like Rohmer."

Pedro played the various names in his mind's ear, looking for anything familiar. Heather Roma clicked.

"Calibos!" he called excitedly. "Remember when Evan saved the boss's kid at the high school? I sent you off to intimidate the girl who might be a witness. Heather Roma. Remember?"

The hideous man nodded.

"Where did she work?"

"Pizza place downtown. Fat Joe's."

"Fat Joe's," Pedro said into the phone. "A pizza place in town. Does that ring any bells?" There was a pause.

"Yeah, the guy with the scanner says he thinks that's it."

"I don't want 'thinks,' I want 'knows.' Now *is* it?"

"Yes. Yes, the girl says she heard that."

"What girl? Who the hell do you have with you?"

"Long story."

"Well, find the fucking place and get Evan back here!"

"I don't even know where it is. I'm not from here…oh, wait, this guy knows. Okay, we're going."

Shutting the phone off and turning, Pedro started giving new orders to send reinforcements, but came up short.

Calibos had vanished.

Jim Crowe froze the recording he'd hastily made of the school bus footage and turned to Anathema and Enolah.

"You two would know better than I would. Is that him?"

They looked closely. It was from a distance, and the face was badly sunburned, the hair rust-colored, but it might be…

"Let it roll," Ana said. Crowe unpaused it. There were only a few seconds of him handing a child down into someone else's arms, then it cut away several times. Then back to him and the other Good Samaritans. Then away again.

"Hold it," Enolah exclaimed. "Rewind!" Crowe did. The shot played out, and she asked him to rewind again. "And you've got a slow motion feature?"

"And how," the Woolagaroo grunted, nodding, and let the recording scroll forward frame by frame. They watched carefully, and Anathema caught it too.

"There!" Enolah said. "See? He's licking his lips. Look at his tongue." They strained their eyes.

"Good eye," Anathema said grudgingly.

"How many guys you know got a forked tongue?"

Crowe answered Enolah by sticking out his own tongue and wiggling the two tips separately.

"Yeah, but you're the one who taught him how to do it, and nobody else in our parish had the balls."

"That's definitely him," Anathema said. "Why?"

"Why? Why do I care? Because I told him to leave town, and that looks like him right there. So, he disobeyed me."

"When did you tell him to go? I never heard this."

Enolah kept her mouth shut, hoping Brother Crowe wouldn't tell her rival that she'd told on her boyfriend. A demand during sex that she convert to Christianity needed to be reported. It just *needed* to be. So, the priest sent him on a fool's errand just in case the young man was confused and might pose a threat during this most delicate of times. Jim Crowe was far from certain, but it was just a hunch.

"That's none of your business. What should be is that the man on my television who you say is definitely him is acting totally outta character. Now, you can't miss that face, even out there in a rioting town. If Dark is helping the victims of one attack, he's most likely going around helping everyone. If he is a born-again shitwit, he would be doing what all of them do. Crusading around town doing good deeds for strangers."

"You think he's downtown?" Anathema asked.

"Only one way to find out. You take your squad and look for him. If you find him, take him to Nest 5."

"Our squad's exhausted. We did Bastille Day last night," Ana said petulantly.

"Did you just refuse me?" The massive Aborigine glared down at her, his corded muscles rippling.

"...No, Brother."

"Didn't think so. Now get your ass out there. Go!"

It is often the way with adventurous young men that logical consequences to their actions do not apply to them. They are immune to any sexually-transmitted disease, impervious to bullets, and quite capable of beating their enemies to a place where an ambush is planned in time to save the day and then set up an ambush of their own. And if there was anyone that Evan needed to prove his manliness and courage to at that moment, besides Maya, it was Heather Roma.

He had been suddenly overcome (and easily, considering the day he'd already had), with the need to rescue the girl he'd horrified months before in the line of duty, and show her what a good guy he really was. So, he ran.

The developers of Coquina had agreed on a Venice theme to add an Old World charm to the commercial district, with narrow byways paved with pastel cobblestones, bougainvilleas cascading over balconies and climbing latticed windows. There were even some small watercourses, spanned by short stone bridges.

A small group of looters caught sight of him as he darted into the honeycomb of shopping vias that would lead to the pizzeria, and gave chase, howling. Though he had ignored all the other looters, instinct warned him now, and Evan glanced backwards as he rounded a stone fountain, seeing his pursuers through the crook of a faux-marble statue's elbow. Their taunts rose in intensity, thinking he ran because he feared them. They mustn't've noticed the nine-millimeter in his fist. Not wanting to waste bullets he would definitely need later, he only fired once. The forerunner's head whiplashed, spraying a scarlet mist into the faces of those behind him, and they all fell headlong as he stumbled, tripping them.

Evan ran on, following the via of shops to a fretwork arch that he used to climb onto a Spanish-tiled roof as a child, to sneak glimpses of a certain hot-but-lonely woman late at night. The hand- and foot-holds he found with old familiarity, and he quickly scaled the building. The lattice beside him, which was fairly new, made it much easier going. Once on the roof, it was but a short sprint to the tenement building, with the flat and far less treacherous rooftop.

From there, it was not far to Fat Joe's. Behind him, the men who had chased him screamed at their fallen comrade, urging him to get up, man, and stop playing around. Rabbit, Dark, and Jennifer all came barreling through, shouldering them aside. Not knowing about Evan's shortcut, they had come this way to avoid the streets and the greater violence.

When the teenager finally came upon the pizzeria, he saw Joseph LaPaglia fall from a nail-bat blow to the head. It was a young Latino, the handkerchief with a frog painted on it that he wore on his head advertising that he was Boriqua. Two-handing the nail-bat, he hove it up over his head, blood-mad to avenge his fallen brethren. Fat Joe just had time to open his eyes and panic before the Puerto Rican's chest exploded. His two large sons also gaped in surprise as those they held at bay were gunned down.

"Paisan!" Evan shouted down, faking a kinship to earn trust more quickly—even though he was Welsh in his ancestry, he looked Italian enough. Joe LaPaglia searched for the voice. "Up here! Five o'clock!"

"Who're you?" Fat Joe asked, finding him.

"Nevermind. Where's Heather?" He swung one leg over, getting ready to drop down.

"Which Heather? The cashier? She hasn't worked here in months!"

Over the din, two shots rang out, and Evan was thrown over the edge of the roof. His fall was broken by cardboard boxes and dead bodies, but he did not move. Fat Joe stared at the two bullet holes in his rescuer's jacket, stunned, until a sharp blow to the back of his head distracted him.

On the pizzeria's roof, Detective Ward Bancroft emerged from behind a large air-conditioning turret.

"It worked," he said quietly, shaking his head and grinning. "I can't believe it. It worked."

He jogged back to the drainpipe he'd climbed and shimmied awkwardly down. As he ran back the way he'd come, he drew his radio from its clip on his belt and shouted happily into it.

"Smiley! It's Ward. I got the bastard!"

Having seen what looked to be a radio scanner on the belt of some guy on TV, and then that guy leaving the school bus disaster area with Evan Punkass Kid Lanthorne, Bancroft called his new partner on his car phone and outlined his half-baked plan.

"Call me over your radio every ten minutes, asking where I am, just in case Lanthorne misses it."

"But we'll be wasting valuable air time."

"Not if he hears it. And I think he will."

"Where will you be?"

"On the roof, waiting. His old man told me the kid could climb like a monkey, and did all his thinking at the top of a banyan tree. Said if he ever saw us coming, if he had nowhere to run, he would try to hide on the roof."

"His father said this?"

"Yeah. That fella hates his kid more than I do. So, if the kid's as smart as they said he is, he'll be coming by the roofs, where all the rioters won't notice him and slow him down."

Bancroft was lurking in wait already when the police helicopter was shot down, and he saw the distant figures running across the rooftops afterward. He watched them go angrily, knowing they were way out of range, and he couldn't hope to go after them without being outgunned.

So, he waited.

And waited.

Crouched there under the sweltering summer sun.

Belatedly, he wondered why Lanthorne and those other two guys he was with had been wearing jackets on such a hot day, but he quickly dismissed it as irrelevant, and ran on.

Dino laPaglia wasted no time, ran over to Evan's body and took the pistol that lay beside it, turned, and shot four would-be assailants. He was not a violent young man, and he was sure he'd feel terrible about this later. His father was proud though, that Dino had protected him and his business without hesitation.

The young baker now stood half-crouched, waving the gun around with a shaky hand at anyone who came too close. The rioters seemed to have changed their minds about destroying the pizzeria, and turned their attention to other businesses. Dino was just about to turn the gun over to his father when he felt a sharp tug on his ankle, and wheeled about with a yelp.

Evan held on firmly, and extended his other hand, looking up at him. Only surprise stopped Dino from shooting, but it would only take him a moment to remember that he held a weapon, and use it.

"Gimme my damn gun back," Evan said calmly.

At that moment, Dark, Rabbit, and Jennifer came around a rear corner of the restaurant, emerging from the tangle of alleys, and saw what was happening at the mouth of the final one. Thinking Dino a cop, Geiger brought his minisub up, planting the butt against his shoulder. Seeing the movement in the corner of his eye, Dino threw himself backward, Evan still holding fast, and fell onto his back.

The pistol slid free across the cobblestones.

Seeing it, several people in the crowd darted forward to claim it, but were blown apart by a spray of minisub fire as Dark came running.

"Not him!" Evan shouted, waving at Dark to stop. "Don't shoot him! He's all right!"

But Geiger was in the moment, as he usually was, and came to plant one foot on Dino's chest, slamming him back down as he tried to rise, and aimed point blank at the baker's broad nose.

With accuracy born of paternal outrage, Fat Joe flung his rolling pin like a throwing knife and cracked Dark in the face. The sunburned man reeled back, reflexively pulling the trigger as his hands came up, and sprayed a chattering hail of bullets into the crowd, before Rabbit crash-tackled him, knocking the gun out of his hands. Evan hastily snatched the AK.

In the struggle, the older laPaglia son retrieved the nine-millimeter, brandished it, and crept in to grab his brother's hand and pull him to safety. Jennifer stepped out of the alley with her minisub at port arms, surprising the laPaglias. Taking in their red, white, and green aprons, she assessed the situation and held up a reassuring hand while Rabbit and Dark wrestled beside her.

"It's okay. We're here to rescue you."

"...What?" Fat Joe asked incredulously.

She repeated herself in Italian, but they were several generations American, and only spoke their native curse words.

"Look, it's a long story," she told them. "Get inside and I'll watch the door." Her calm authoritative voice—and the fact that she had a gun bewildered them, but they obeyed. She took up a position in front of the open doorway, glaring threateningly around her, and felt important. Evan joined her, and together they watched as Jared "Rabbit" Layton put Geiger to sleep with a carotid artery

699

Vulcan neck pinch.

"Do either of you know these people?" Fat Joe laPaglia asked his sons.

They shook their heads, and so did his female employees when he looked at them questioningly. He was about to ask "Then who the fuck..." when his two defenders stepped aside, letting the Rabbit drag the madman inside.

"Who are you guys?" laPaglia asked suspiciously.

"We're here to save Heather Roma," Rabbit said.

"But I told the other guy a minute ago, she doesn't work here anymore." Fat Joe was nodding and looking around at those who did work there, getting them to nod also.

"That so? Hmmm. Okay, let's go then." Jared bent down to slap Geiger awake. The disavowed Satanist came to rather quickly and bolted to his feet.

"What? What the hell happened?" he shouted.

"You got hit from behind," Jared lied. "But we're safe now."

"Where are we?"

"Perth Amboy," Evan said. "Where the fuck do you think? And when I say don't shoot somebody, don't go ahead and shoot them, or I'll kneecap your stupid ass. *Capisce,* Zombie?"

"And you can talk? We gotta chase you all over—"

"Boys." Jennifer's voice had the tone of a stern schoolteacher.

"We're leaving," Rabbit said flatly.

"Hey," Evan called to Fat Joe's older son. "You going to give me my gun back, or what?" But it wasn't a question.

"Which is the quickest way out of here?" Rabbit asked.

"The quickest ways are probably clogged up right now," Evan replied, shaking his head. "We can either hole up somewhere and wait until much of the panic is over, or—"

"We wouldn't *have* to," Dark growled at him, glaring accusingly. He didn't have to finish saying it.

"So, I got a little nuts. It happens. You know it as well as any of us."

"Boys," Jennifer said witheringly.

Pause, then Evan resumed.

"We could keep traveling the roofs, but I'd rather have a planned route first. My teachers say you should be ready for any contingency; you don't go in with one plan, you go in with ten. So

700

we need to get the best view we can."

"Hey," Dark interjected, his spirits rising. "We've got eight buildings around the city, tall ones, with accessible roofs if you know what you're doing, that we used to do all kinds of things from. They were our observation towers, mostly."

"Where are they?"

"Number Five—we call it Nest Five—is right over there." He pointed at a tall office building nearby, with a few high-end stores on the ground floor, commonly known as Edifice Rex.

Usually, access to the roof required agility and stealth, but today, they could just run on up the stairs.

"Let's go then," Jennifer said.

As they ran through the vias in a zigzagging line toward Edifice Rex, a hideous man with long, black hair braided in a queue, emerged from his hiding place and pursued at a safe distance.

They came again through the vias to the fountain with the marble statue, now dismembered like Venus de Milo, and the grieving looters beyond it. Exchanging looks, the four of them fanned out and advanced on the seven, who all looked up and turned varying shades of red. Rabbit stepped forward, whipping out his asps and unsheathing them with the hard snaps that are almost as unnerving to hear as the racking of a pump-action shotgun.

Dark, not to be outdone, held out his hand and wrenched his wrist to unsling Switchblade. The barrel snapped out of his sleeve and his finger curled around the trigger.

Eating up their startled expressions, Jennifer then turned to Evan expectantly, to see what he would do. Everyone did. He rolled his eyes and shook his head, feeling the pressure, raised the Calico M-960A and mowed the looters down as nonchalantly as he could. The other three looked a trifle disappointed, but he ignored them.

"We don't have all day," he muttered, and kept walking.

Not too far beyond, they came across what looked like a M*A*S*H station—a bunch of Red Cross do-gooders with first aid supplies out the wazoo. They had many gofers, running off to find injured people and bring them back on stretchers. Rabbit made a joke that neither Evan nor Dark paid any attention to. Their eyes were riveted on two of the assistants.

Evan stared at Heather Roma, and Dark at Joshua Buckland.

The Bible thumper felt strange eyes upon him, and glanced in their direction. He wasn't sure who he found himself staring back at, but the other's intensity was alarming. It took a moment for him to notice the guns, and then sheer terror engulfed him as the face registered. Dark surprised him, though, holding up a reassuring hand—the one with Switchblade in it, but the manner was non-threatening.

"It's okay, I just want to talk."

Other people, who had ignored the newcomers in their Hippocratic business, now took note, and either gasped or yelped.

"Just passing through," Rabbit said soothingly.

"Evan!"

The teenager's head came around, startled—every bit as startled as Heather was. The overweight woman who'd called his name was hurrying over with rolls of gauze and medicinal whatevers dropping out of the load in her arms. She looked different, as in Overweight, but he would have recognized her anywhere.

"Mom!" He spread his arms just as she dropped her whole cargo and seized him, roughly affectionate.

"Jesus Christ! You're alive! I've been worried sick about you all this time! Where have you been? And what the hell are you doing with that gun! Haven't you learned yet? The size of it! That thing's huge!"

"Mom, I can't breathe."

"Damn right you can't, baby, I'm going to suffocate you into unconsciousness and take you home!"

"What home? I have no home, Mom. Please let go of me. You're crushing me, for God's sake."

Heather Roma still stared, speechless.

V

On the roof of the dizzyingly tall building, a tall and muscular Australian Aborigine studied the faces far below him with a pair of extremely high-powered binoculars, that were capable of telescopic night vision in total blackness. He could even tell the eye color of the ant-sized people in the commercial district, if he chose to. Sweeping methodically, knowing that who he sought would be avoiding the large, mindlessly violent crowds, he searched the perimeters and less public areas. He finally saw Dark Geiger, and the three accompanying him, as they cast quick glances to all sides before leaving the safety of Via Mizner.

He grinned broadly.

One of the best things about your quarry having been your disciple is that they are so easy to predict. He lifted his CB and spoke authoritatively into it, trying not to let his humor and triumph show.

"Kids, report to Nest Five immediately. I repeat—"

"Copy that, Brother."

The voice that crackled through the speaker was Blake's, but Crowe would be able to tell even if the Dipshit had tried to disguise it. The young man loved to use his CB and all of the code words, the lingo—the patois, he insisted on calling it. "Roger. Our twenty is—"

"Your twenty should be here, Blake. So, come on."

"Wilco. Over."

Crowe followed Geiger's progress until he got into the front entrance, then walked across the roof to what looked like a concrete termite mound with a door in it that opened onto the stairs, put his CB and binoculars away on his somewhat Batmanesque utility belt, and leaned against the concrete on the shady side. From an insulated bag he'd brought, he got out an ice-cold bottle of apple juice, took a long, refreshing draught, and waited.

As they ran up the stairs—what with elevators being notoriously unreliable during crises—Rabbit took out his omnipotent satellite cell phone, about the time they all decided they weren't in that big of a hurry. They had only ascended four flights of stairs when each of them began to seriously regret being smokers. They may have each gotten their second winds long ago, considering all of the running they had already done, but goddamn, stairs were different.

"Pedro!" Rabbit wheezed when the phone clicked.

"*Digame.*"

"We've got Evan back. I thought we ought to check in."

"Good. Where are you now?"

"On our way to the roof of...what's this building called?"

"Esplanade de Something-or-Other," Dark managed to gasp.

"Edifice Rex," Evan put in.

Rabbit blinked at him. "You're kidding."

"Uh, no. Why?"

"Nothin'. Edifice Rex," Rabbit said into the phone.

"Ahh. Manticore is out looking for you, now. I'll send them to pick you up right away. Be in the lobby."

"Jesus. Now we gotta go back down—"

"What did you say? You mumbled."

"Nothing. See you in a few." He hung up, filled the others in, and they started to walk leisurely back down. Below, Calibos Lugo paused, one foot on the next step, listening. There was a shuffling of many rubber soled shoes coming across the roseate marble floor of the lobby, running. Voices.

"Stairs or elevator?"

"Stairs? Hell no, not the stairs. I'm tired!"

"Shit, haven't you seen the movies? Elevators are a frigging deathtrap!"

Lugo rolled his eyes, wondering whatever happened to the good old days. Like back in the jungles of Colombia where he grew up with Los Pepes—People Persecuted by Pablo Escobar—killing actual people instead of these gringos.

"Well, make up your minds."

"I'm taking the elevator."

"I'm taking the stairs."

"And you guys?"

"I'll hold down the lobby. Make sure nobody—"

"Get your ass up those stairs!"

"Hell, no. I'm tired."

"Elevator then, you big wuss."

More of a muffled argument, then the rapid footsteps, half of them, came toward the open door to the stairwell. Alarmed, Calibos shrank back against the wall just a second before Dark peered over the railing above him to investigate the noises.

"Ohhhh shit. Up the stairs!"

They scrambled up to the closed door on the next level, finding it locked. Dark remembered his spray can of Freon, but it would (one) take a minute to get out of the duffel bag and spray into the keyhole, and (two) the whole point of going through that door would be to hide, which the shattered knob would not help. So, they tried the next door. And the next. Rabbit called Pedro again as they ran. And again.

The door in the termite mound flew open, and the four of them spilled out onto the roof, scattering, looking quickly for a place to hide or escape. Before the door swung shut again, Calibos Lugo burst through it with the handful of elevator-takers hot on his heels— just as Jim Crowe stepped out of the shade.

What happened took only a few seconds, if that. Seeing Crowe, Dark swung his arm around and released Switchblade. Seeing Evan, Lugo raised his AMT Hardballer, an automatic pistol ten intimidating inches long. Covering Evan, Rabbit aimed the thirty-ought-six at Calibos's Fu Manchu mustache. Blake (the Dipshit) pointed his Heckler & Koch MP-10 at Dark, covering Crowe, Anathema raised hers at him to cover her brother, and Enolah stuck hers in the hollow of Anathema's cheek, ostensibly to prevent anyone else from preventing a loyal Adamist from preventing a traitor from assassinating her leader. But, more accurately, she'd use any excuse to kill the one bitch in the parish that stood between her and the priestesshood.

Evan stood half-turned, facing Calibos, his gun pointing at the floor. Jennifer didn't know who to point her Calico M-960A at, so she just picked someone. Enolah.

"Put that gun down, you bitch," Ana hissed at Enolah.

"*You* put *yours* down. You trying to mutiny, Geiger?"

"He's pulled a gun on my brother."

"He's protecting our priest. Just like me."

"Ana! Don't point that at me!" Blake whined.

Dark ignored them, staring coldly at Jim Crowe, who ignored him.

"Ah! Good hunting, Br'er Rabbit!" the Aborigine called.

Startled, but trying not to show it, Rabbit nodded in greeting. "Good hunting, Br'er Crowe."

"And it looks like you have become acquainted with Br'er Possum," Crowe said cheerfully, finally acknowledging Dark. "A trio of vermin we seem, don't we? And who's this with the mustache? A goddamned badger, by the looks of him."

"Crowe," Dark said.

"Yes, Dwight?"

"I know what's going on, Crowe."

"Do you?"

"Yes. I know the truth."

"My, what a detective you are. But you don't seem impressed."

"Oh, I'm pretty fucking far from impressed."

"Time out. Blake? Blake! Do you copy, Blake?"

The Dipshit finally looked at his priest. He was trembling ever so slightly. "Stop pointing a gun at our brother Dwight."

"But his sister's pointing a gun at me!"

"Yes, I know that. But she will probably stop if you put yours down, and then we can move on down the line to this other young lady I've never seen before."

Reluctantly, Blake lowered his MP-10.

"Now, Ana. Your turn."

Glaring at Enolah out of the corner of her eye, Anathema lowered hers.

"Enolah?" Crowe prompted. But Enolah was even more reluctant, considering the size of the glove she'd just thrown at a previously unsuspecting enemy.

There would definitely be conflict later.

"Enooooolahhhh."

She finally obeyed, looking away, then feeling Anathema's eyes burning into her, tried to meet them. She couldn't, and when she looked away again, she saw Jennifer still holding her AK, aimed at her head. Saw her for the first time.

"Young lady?" Crowe asked. "Do you have something personal against Miss Taylor?"

"Who's Miss Taylor?" Jennifer asked back.

"The one lined up in your sights."

Jen shrugged. "Nah. I've just acquired a taste for this."

"Ah. Well, carry on, then."

Enolah opened her mouth to protest, but was knocked violently to the ground when Ana rammed the butt of her gun backhand into her grillwork. The dominatrix drooled blood and bits of shattered teeth onto the concrete, then the stunned dizziness passed and the gurgled a choking groan. Anathema spat on her, and Rabbit grunted in appreciation.

"Okay, everybody remain calm," Crowe said sarcastically. He turned his attention back to Calibos, but spoke to Rabbit. "Now, who's the Badger, here?"

"He works with the same people I do."

"But you don't like him?"

"I like my little buddy he wants to kill better."

"All righty, then. You remember that NRK?"

No-Response Kill, a military term, for the eye-level ring around the skull that, when hit, does not allow fingers to tighten reflexively on triggers.

Before Rabbit could reply, or shoot, somebody else did. The stairwell was suddenly deafening with the roar of minisub fire as two groups traded shots—the Adamists on the stairs and Manticore up the first flight of them. One of the ex-punk rockers would step out and fire, then duck back as the shots were returned. One brave soul—a fellow named Radcliffe— said Fuck it, threw himself into the open across the first landing and, with his back against the corner, just started spraying.

Under his cover, two more sprang up the steps, around the corner, and halfway up to the second floor to take up the slack. One of these, who "used to be a chick with liberty spikes," but was "now a soldier," took the last steps up to the door and drove the Satanists back further.

The haze of gunsmoke and the stench of cordite stung their eyes, but they steeled themselves to fight on. Repeating the process as many times as it took, the Manticore division of Shiva pushed their way to the top. It was the ninth floor that the door was blown open on the Law Offices of Scarola, Earhart, Denny, and Shipley.

In a fury of desperation, several Adamists stayed behind to guard the doorway and they held their ground, dropping several of their attackers. As Seth McHale charged up the steps, the bodies of his comrades tumbled backwards and almost took him with them, but he and those following managed to keep their footing. It was the dodging of one falling soldier that saved his life. As he leaped aside, pressing against the balustrade, a bullet that would've cloven through his bared teeth instead punched a hole through his shoulder.

He stumbled, crying out, and the others tore up the last few steps past him.

This part of the ninth floor was all desks, with offices beyond. The Adamists had taken cover behind large desks piled high with clutter, and the Manticores stood on either side of the open door or lay on the floor in between, spraying the room down. Soldiers with more training would have fired in salvos, half of them shooting while the others reloaded so a steady stream of bullets would chew through the desks while the enemy hid.

Many of these soldiers, however, were exactly like average American students in any field, remembering what they were taught only long enough to pass their tests. They were only marginally better than their opponents. But Seth remembered Pedro's cardinal rule: don't ever walk in with one plan. Walk in with ten. There was a guy called Murphy who knew exactly what happened to those one-plan types. If all of your men running out of ammunition at the same instant can happen, bet the farm that it will.

It came as no surprise, then, to Seth when the last shot became an echo. Tattooed and raw-knuckled hands scrambled for spare magazines, but that split second was all that the Adamists wasted. When they popped out from behind the desks, seven of the remaining thirty-something Manticores fell. Many others took hits where they were protected by Kevlar, but those seven were punched backwards, down the stairs, spattering Seth with the mist of their blood.

His ears rang from the thunder of gunfire in the closeness so the screams of the dying seemed to come from far away. His brain was working so fast, though, that what he saw registered in slow-motion. It was as if the whole world was moving by the minute for every second he was. Soldiers came falling towards him, twisting and flinging out flying ropes of scarlet, but he sidestepped like a hummingbird.

He swapped out magazines just to be on the safe side, and when his now-twenty-something comrades drove the enemy back behind shelter, he watched carefully to see where everyone was. From what he'd seen, these soldiers must be wearing Kevlar vests as well, though not uniforms. Leggings also, which was unusual (the night before, when Misery Geiger and several others died, the survivors complained that their legs were easy to hit and, crippled, they were sitting ducks for further volleys). Seth had glimpsed a few of them having no regard for their legs being hidden, the way anyone else would be paranoid about them, so he assumed that they would be lying on their backs behind the desks most of the time, with their knees drawn up. Certainly not crouched with their heads "protected" by mere wood.

Seth pushed past the others and ran low, taking cover in front of one of those desks. They were all arranged catty-corner to each other, progressing up the hall in V-shapes with a walkway in between. The desks were heavy and wooden, the kind that covered up everything the lawyer or executive didn't want you to see, like his secretary or your wife giving him head during a meeting. Seth wondered briefly why the hell that thought was in his head at a time like this.

Papers and glass littered the beige carpeting, glass from bullet-riddled computer monitors, and those office lamps with the green hoods—that Seth always likened to the visors that grim-faced, balding accountants wore—and among all the paper, rubble, chunks of splintered wood and green lampshade glass, were rorschachs of blood, some of it his own.

Reaching up with one hand, he signaled for those at the door to start firing. The chatter of minisub fire seemed a long way off to him, though they were skimming the desktop only a few inches above his head. A shot kicked up a computer keyboard, sending it somersaulting in an arc over him, scattering lettered buttons as he crept along the outer side to peek, gun barrel first, around to where the chair used to be. He fired into a wide-eyed face. His victim had been lying just as he thought she would.

Motioning frantically for the others to follow suit, he slid around and crouched over the young woman's corpse. She had an MP-10 next to one hand, and a .357 Magnum in the other. He relieved her of them both, along with her spare magazines. Screams from the direction of the stairwell cut through the din of the gunfire, and though the sound of shots continued, nothing inside this area was being hit. His people were shooting at something else.

He scurried back around to the other side of the desk, just in time to escape notice when the Satanists rose up to return fire. He had front row seats to watch most of his people get cut down mercilessly from two sides.

"Now, Dark, stay calm, don't get nervous and shoot me."

"Oh, I'm calm, Woolagaroo, and I *am* gonna shoot."

"Well, keep your shirt on. Blake? You're now the referee between Enolah and Anathema. Ana? Could you please run downstairs and shoot whoever's shooting at our people?"

"Oh, shit!" Rabbit exclaimed. "That's probably our guys, coming to pick us up!" Blake didn't care; he hurried away, with Enolah in tow.

"Tsk, tsk, tsk. Friendly fire's a bitch, ain't it?"

"Sure is," Dark said coldly. He waited until Ana was gone to speak again. "Does she know that Missy is dead?"

"No. I have been worried about how to break it to her." Crowe's voice sounded heavy with genuine concern, then curiosity as something registered. "Wait a minute. How do *you* know?"

"Because I'm the one that shot her." Dark's voice actually cracked.

"What? Why in the—"

"How the fuck was I supposed to know? She was wearing a ski mask! And she was shooting at me already!"

"But you weren't even supposed to be here!"

The agitated voices were making Calibos antsy, wanting to shoot Evan but certainly not wanting a rifle slug between his running lights, and Rabbit wanted to go ahead and shoot him, but he was afraid Dark might be startled into shooting Crowe, so...

"Woolagaroo," he called. Crowe looked. "Can you chill the fuck out, please?"

Then, helicopters startled the shit out of them.

They had all been faintly aware of the sweeping noises, but not ready to see the two of them rise up on either side of the roof, packed full of gunmen with the Folk Nation trident spray-painted crimson on their noses. Someone in each of them held a rocket launcher. A *rocket launcher.*

Small missiles, but missiles nonetheless, streaked out of the open doors leaving trails of smoke hanging in their wake, and high-caliber bullets rained down on the populace like a hail of mortar shells. The six people on the roof stared for an instant, and Crowe remembered himself, calling out to the others in a calm tone.

"Time out! Nobody kill anybody! Rabbit, are those your people?" He looked over at Jared, who shook his head.

"No, I was hoping they were yours."

"Okay. Momentary truce. We're going back inside in a calm

and orderly fashion. Slowly, now." He led them to the termite mound, turning his back on all of them confidently, and retrieved his own black duffel bag from the shade. They were all still staring at the commercial helicopters-turned-gun-ships. He whistled sharply to get their attention, crooked his finger, and they followed him again.

Inside, down one flight, he unzipped his bag on the landing and unsheathed a broadsword. Those who didn't know him took a step back, surprised. It was of Scandinavian design, but the blade was forged in the Japanese fashion, folded eight times so that it could cut through a bridge and then a tomato with just as clean a slice, like the knives advertized on TV. The quillons of its hilt curved upward and around like ram's horns, intricately carved, with a pommel shaped like a scallop shell. Sigils were engraved up the channeled blade from the ricasso almost to the tip, a patina of gore filling each of them, as well as the nuchals of the horn quillons and the umbones of the shell pommel. It had been recently used.

"We are all putting our guns away now," Crowe said. No one moved. Lugo was the closest to him, and the only one who wouldn't care if anyone was accidentally killed when he tried to defend himself.

The stairway was still alive with gunfire, and plaster dust fell away from gouges in the ceiling above them. Crowe swung the blade quicker than lightning at Calibos's head, stopping it without even a quiver under the line of his jaw, against the skin. The Colombian flinched belatedly.

"I didn't say to surrender your weapons. But I did say to put them away. All of you."

His eyes wide, free hand fingering the gold-tooth beads of his rosary, Calibos hesitated, then slowly raised his pistol and worked it into the waist of his trousers.

"Now, all of you." Crowe said without taking his eyes off Lugo's. "We have to get out of this building, I think, due to unforeseen developments, and then we can all go our separate ways. On the way down, we will resolve our differences, and no one will shoot anyone else." The steel in his tone made all of them forget that they were holding guns. The sheer power of his voice and bearing were enough to cow each of them, and make them think a mere firearm was useless against him. They obeyed.

The gunfire ceased, and Crowe lifted the blade away from

Badger's neck, leaving a thin pink line for him to rub.

"The hell'd you bring a sword for?" Rabbit asked.

"When the bullets run out, it's much handier than a gun butt to clear space with in a crowd," the devil-devil man said. "If, for some reason, you can't make it back to your people, stop by the church. There are a few there you can use."

Rabbit remembered once horsing around with a bhuj in Crowe's collection, the Indian cousin to the battle axe, a long time ago, and thinking about how much fun it would be in combat. Hacking a bloody swath through a crowd with it in his right fist, maybe a cooper's adze in his left. He would definitely need something. Maybe one of the halberds, and a bhuj and an adze for backup. And a scimitar. Gotta have a scimitar.

He turned to Dark. "You know where the church is, and Evan knows where our base is. You two need to talk. And everybody count your bullets. Calibos, you come with me."

"*Vetes pal infierno.*" Go to Hell.

"I probably will, but not in your lifetime. Now explain to me what your problem is with Evan."

"What, is thees a sharing group?"

Crowe unclasped his radio and called Anathema. Waited. Then Blake. After a pause, Enolah answered.

"Here, Brother." Her voice was muffled by a hurt mouth.

"What's the story, Morning Glory?"

"Ninth floor secure."

"Where are the other two?"

"Blake's fainted. Anathema is around here somewhere." The ice in her voice before she caught herself gave her away, but Dark hadn't heard it.

He was staring over the edge of the railing at the corpses far below.

VI

Across town, Jim Harding had mobilized Gorgon Division, who'd been busily feeding Styrofoam into Fire Marshal-approved containers of gasoline, until the mixture had the consistency of gelatin. He hadn't bothered to add up how many gallons of napalm they had now. Whatever it was, it'd be enough.

He was gazing wistfully at the USMC tattoo on his shriveled arm. He'd thought, in the first year after his parachute didn't open, that he'd be a useless cripple for the rest of his life. These days, though, he felt more alive than he ever had. He closed that hand into a fist around the butt of his Steyr AUG 5.56 Bullpup assault rifle, appraised it, hefted a little, making sure the arm would be able to handle it, and smiled.

"Jim?" Oisin asked.

Harding's eyes began to gleam.

"Jim?"

"Yeah."

"We're ready."

"Cool. Let's get this show on the road."

"Dark?" Enolah said quietly. He turned to face her, but she couldn't sustain eye contact, afraid she might be mesmerized and lose all self control. Such was the power he had over her, the leash he had fastened to her neck when he'd exposed her every vulnerability. She tried to replay the mental mantra she used to reassure herself, the sound of teeth crunching through the scarlet skin of a symbolic apple and into the sweet flesh inside. But it wouldn't come.

Everywhere she looked as she gently stroked her swollen lips, she saw his yellow eyes.

"What, Enolah?"

"Um, the other day, why'd you try to make me renounce Satan? You were kidding, right?"

Now it was Dark's turn to look away and pause.

"I, uh...no, I wasn't kidding."

She slumped slightly, as if the thread she'd been hanging by had broken.

"It didn't sound like it. You sounded serious."

"I was."

"You betrayed us all, then."

"No. No, I didn't. We have already been betrayed, and I've found out the truth. Satan isn't even real."

Her head snapped up and around, her blue-black ponytail whipping around under the bandage she'd fastened.

"What did you fucking say?"

"It was all bullshit, Enolah."

"Are you *stupid?* Look outside!" She gestured at the window with a wide sweep of her hand. "It's chaos! It's the Apocalypse! We brought it about, and now the Christ will have to come, and I'm right here waiting—"

Dark looked her squarely in the eyes, hers blazing, his sympathetic. She held his gaze evenly this time.

"No, baby."

"Don't you fucking baby me!"

"Please, listen. I admit that I never loved you, sometimes I downright loathed you, until I asked Jesus into my heart. No, don't look away when I'm talking to you. Listen. Something's been growing in me. Sometimes I've misplaced it, but it always comes back, and it's love. Enolah, I've started to care for you, finally, and I want you to be happy and safe, far away from all these lies—"

"You piece of shit! I've worshipped you, I knew I wasn't supposed to, but..." Her eyes were bright with tears, and she choked. Either grief, shame, or rage was trying to burst out of her, probably all three. "I...I couldn't help it! I ached for you when you were gone." She shook her head, her face wet and red now. "The whole time you were in jail, I felt dead. I needed you, and now you tell me this shit!"

He tried to hold her but she squirmed violently, beating on him with her fists. He wrestled his way around her and pinned her arms to her sides, and she bucked, snarling like a wildcat.

"Let her go, Dark." Crowe's voice was soft and tender behind them. The last thing Dark wanted to do was let go, but the Australian touched them both on their shoulders, and they crumpled to the floor in agony. "Dark, come with me. Let her cry on her own."

Paralyzed by his fingers digging, talon-like, into clusters of nerves, all they could do was gape in silent screams until he let go and repeated himself.

They lay still on the floor for a moment, feeling the immense pleasure they'd been conditioned to feel in the relief of pain. Crowe crooked his finger at Dark, and the sunburned man got to his feet, hesitantly following his ex-mentor. They walked to a far wall, to the large window overlooking chaos, getting a good view of one of the choppers.

"You're right, of course," Crowe said quietly. "And you have every reason to be angry, but keep in mind how much angrier you would have been if your parents hadn't brought you up in our church. You would have abided by laws, and not just any bullshit laws, Florida laws. It is illegal to act in self defense here. You never would have been able to protect your little sister, and you would never have been able to avenge her when you arrived on the scene too late. Would you have preferred that, Dark? Going mad with eroding guts from impotent rage? Putting all of your hopes and faith in the System and its sorry excuse for justice, and the even less reliable power of God? Both will fail you, I swear it. With me, though, you learned how to take care of your problems on your own."

"Misery's still dead, Crowe. And she was on the wrong side when she...when she died. So now she's in Hell—"

"No, Dark. No, she's not. Listen to me, Dark. All religion is, all it's ever been, is a way to give people hope, and hope is nothing but a refutation of logic. It's anesthetic self-deception. It's denial. And Heaven and Hell are mythology."

"Then why have people accepted it for so long?"

"Ha! Listen to yourself, Dark! Just because an idea is old, it's automatically true? Gee, everyone was convinced the world was flat for an awfully long time, weren't they? The Church, the people of God, they executed people for saying otherwise, didn't they? And they wanted to kill Galileo for saying that the Earth moved, but *eppur si muove*. Yet, it does move. Think, Dark! For how many hundreds of years were blood-sucking leeches considered the cure-all?"

"But Hell, Crowe, that's different."

"No, Brother. Mythology of any kind, my people's Dream - time, the Greeks' Mount Olympus, the Christians' Messiah, all it was for was to help us feel better about death. The rest of it, explanations for natural phenomena like volcanoes erupting and farming methods like fertilization, that's just gravy."

"Fertilization?"

"Yes, offering, say, a fish to the earth god when you sow a seed, and that helps the seed grow. That's what early farmers assumed when their experiments in sacrifice showed different results.

Since we know better, we think that such assumptions are absurd. But they didn't have science. They had gods, and belief in gods and an afterlife of some kind helped them feel better about the inevitable, and it also kept the masses in line. And because we as a species are still so gullible, so unwilling to look the facts in the face, many people still hold onto this while they claim to be atheists. Look at this country in particular. See, in order for Christianity to seem even the least bit credible, it had to disassociate the soul of the individual from the collective body of the people. This is the true origin of America's modern, hyper-individualistic anti-culture. Almost all the modern values are merely secularized Christian patterns of thought.

"Christianity is really just the evolution of a political move made by Constantine in the Fourth Century. He knew Rome was going to fall so he began to transform it into an entity that could continue to rule the world, just in a different way. Think about it. Isn't Rome still the seat of power for most of the people in the world?"

Many people who hadn't heard the Woolagaroo open his mouth would never believe he spoke so well, so eloquently. The man was almost seven feet tall, with mountainous muscle bulging underneath his jet-black skin, and although high-browed with widely spaced eyes, he looked far from scholarly. His bearing was that of a concealed-weapon-carrying-but-not-even-needing evil man, always prepared for instantaneous and thorough violence.

People felt the atmosphere of a room change whenever he entered it, as if suddenly realizing how convenient a place it was for casual discreet homicide, and how vulnerable in it they were. He looked fierce, brutal, and when the rage was upon him, hellishly demonic. He looked like a monster, not a genius. But Dark Geiger had known Brother Crowe since he was a child, and was so ingrained with reverence for the priest that he was hard-put to resist his teaching.

The Australian had been watching the reflections in the window, though, of the others behind them. He had seen that they'd taken interest in what he was saying, and he raised his voice somewhat to be more easily heard. Knowing also that they all must be outcasts, or else they wouldn't be in the situation they were in now, he steered his lecture to reel them in further.

"You want to know how religion was really started, little brother? It's the greatest scam in history, and it was a nerd who conceived it. You know how the primitive tribes were run, don't you? Might made right. The strongest man, the best fighter fought his way to Chief, and whatever he said went until he got old, and someone stronger stepped up to overthrow him. Through many generations, the little guy always got screwed. Until he changed the entire world with this one idea. He went to the chief in secret and said, 'Hey boss, I've got a cunning plan. This'll keep you in power until you die of old age, and even ensure your sons will take over for you.' And the chief 's ears perked up. But he asked what was in it for Poindexter too. 'Status. Food. Power. And women, for a change. All we have to do is convince everyone else that there are Gods, invisible, intangible folks who are in charge of everything.

"One of them decides when the volcano will erupt. One decides when it'll rain. And I know how to talk to them. I've got the scoop, the inside track. And you know what the volcano god says? He wants you to be chief of this tribe, even when you're old. And the gods all told you that everybody ought to respect me, because I'm the high priest. Trust me, I've got a few aces up my sleeve, and I can convince these morons. And when they're hooked, you and I are set up for life.' And they were. And so were their successors, for eons and eons.

"I'll bet you that cunning little nerd came up with the idea of sacrificing virgins to the volcano god, to make sure those stuck-up bitches started putting out. Oh, you can't sacrifice me, High Priest, I'm too young to die! Sorry, cutie, but you're a virgin, and Banthog wants virgins. Well, hey, if I let you hit this real quick, I won't be a virgin anymore, and we'll keep it our little secret. Gee, I dunno. Oh, come on! Tell you what, I'll give you head, too. Hmmm, lemme sleep on it."

He grinned over his shoulder at the others, who were stifling their laughter. Even Dark was warming up a bit, so he continued.

"Yassee? Just a con job. A con job that changed the direction Mankind was headed, that brought about civilization in the first place. And who was responsible? The underdog. The poor square that got pushed around and made fun of, and who handled the problem on his own. Not by violence, and certainly not by prayer, but by using his brain. Just like everyone in this room.

"But now, I need to tell you about the real enemy we are facing. Our own government. There is a plutocratic organized crime syndicate controlling both political parties that gets away with everything, including treason and war crimes. Once in a while, their puppet politicians are thrown under the bus, an occupational hazard they're aware of from the beginning, but the real power players are never held to account. Nor does anyone in the political class, mainstream media, or mainstream academia ever acknowledge the existence of a permanent bipartisan criminal cabal above the level of elected officials.

"Hence this permanent coup, which has been in place ever since the rigged election of 1912 put the bankster stooge Woodrow Wilson into the White House, one of the most disastrous administrations in US history. It's actually more of a rolling coup, consisting of a permanent organized crime syndicate constantly increasing its wealth and power through a series of sequential coups such as Wilson and the fraudulently ratified 16th amendment, the Federal Reserve Act, World War I, the engineered stock market crash of 1929, the Great Depression, World War II, the Cold War, the Kennedy assassinations, 9/11, etc. All of these events were planned and perpetrated by the same cabal, all resulted in huge profits and increased power, and the real perpetrators were never even identified let alone held to account.

"As a matter of fact, this same cabal is still in control to this day, actively planning the next steps in their permanent rolling coup, steps which will result in further asset stripping of the public treasury and further loss of liberties for citizens, regardless of whether we elect Democrats or Republicans.

"The plutocrat goal is to create the deepest divisions possible, to prevent any sort of unity that would focus on them and challenge their power, which they are trying to make absolute and permanent. The easiest way to do this is to fund extremist groups on both the far right and the far left, then instigate conflict between the two extremes. Moderates on both sides will be horrified by the extremists on the other side, and they respond by strengthening bonds with their own side, even to the point of defending the extremists in their own camp. The people behind this divide and conquer operation have obviously been focusing their support on the far left recently, which is only natural since they themselves are revolutionaries—revolution being one of their favorite tools for acquiring wealth, power, and control—and because they've been using Cultural Marxism and identity politics for many decades to build an army of extremists on the far left. Now it's time to use them. The solution is to expose, ridicule, and defeat extremists on both sides, but the worst extremists by far happen to be on the left, and that's likely to be the case for some time, thanks to the army of insane leftists, the pluto-crats who support them, and the media that promotes them.

"I've been working for them for many years, as a wolf in sheep's clothing, gaining their trust and letting them believe I would be instrumental in this coup, so that I could strike at their most vulnerable moment, which is now. And that is why I need you to be on the right side. We have to be somewhere else, right now, and the only reason we aren't is that we are all standing in each other's way."

He paused, allowing this to sink in, and the moment was shat-tered by a slow clap. The eight of them whirled, their guns raised, to see Seth McHale leaning against an office doorjamb in the corridor.

"Braaaaavo," he said, smirking.

Evan and Rabbit sagged in relief, but the Adamists were all eyeing his uniform, the same worn by all of the corpses in the stair-well, and Calibos cursed under his breath.

Seth didn't bother to say what he'd seen from the office he'd hidden in, since he had no idea who'd benefit. He also didn't answer any questions about what he was doing there.

As he'd crouched behind the cover of his desk, his comrades jerking sickeningly from a hail of bullets that blew them apart, he checked the cylinder of the double-action Magnum. Only one car-tridge. Swapping out magazines, though, the MP-10 was full. He turned the revolver's cylinder to just past the one shot, and snapped it shut. And he prayed.

When the last of his friends fell and the gunfire ceased, he began pulling the trigger. Even though his ears were ringing with the echoes, the hollow clicks were startlingly loud. The Satanists all shared a smile and advanced into the walkway. Seth cursed bitterly and heard a few of them chuckle. He rose.

The closest one was only a few yards away, grinning wickedly as the .357's hammer fell on an empty chamber for the fifth time. Seth shrugged and smiled back, pulling the trigger once more. The explosion startled even him, the gun bucking in his fist, his victim blown back off his feet.

Sweeping the MP-10 back and forth, he mowed the others down, and hurrying across the room, stepping over bodies, he went to the hall of offices, the plate glass windows with Venetian blinds. Ducking into the first door on the left, he rushed to the window, closed the blinds further, and crouched at the sill, staring out.

A long moment passed.

A young woman's blonde head darted out from behind the stairwell door and quickly vanished again. Anathema Geiger then risked another glance. Then, another one, longer. Satisfied with at least that much, she ran quietly in, hiding behind the desk across from Seth's earlier hiding place.

Blake came in after her, actually doing that dive and roll that he'd seen guerrillas do in the movies. He made so much noise that Seth almost laughed out loud. Anathema shook her head at him.

Enolah just sauntered in as if she owned the place. Seth blinked at her in surprise, at the way her hips moved, her arms swung, the look of cool confidence on her face. Was that blood on her mouth? A vampire, she looked like to him. She swaggered right up behind Blake, who wasn't looking, and cracked him upside the back of his head with the butt of her minisub. The dipshit went out like a light.

Anathema was on her feet, Enolah in her sights.

"Don't need him watching," the dominatrix said as nonchalantly as she could. "This is just between you and me, Geiger." She set the MP-10 on the desk, across the clutter of plastic computer rubble and a tagliatelli of colored wiring.

"I've wanted to beat your arrogant ass for years. What do you say? No guns. Kung fu. To the death."

Anathema just stared at her, considering it.

"Or are you only tough with a gun?"

That clinched it. Ana tossed her weapon away and they circled each other slowly, bodies cocked. Both of them reached for their side-arms, watching each other carefully, not moving until they were sure of the other. They pointed the pistols out, away from their sides, with their fingers hooked in the trigger guards so they flipped over when the grips were released. A tense moment followed, neither one of them completely comfortable with letting their guns fall, but they did a silent three-count, nodded, and dropped them.

Straightened. Kicked them away. Smiled.

Seth was looking forward to a good catfight, and was startled when both of the girls reached quickly behind their backs, whipping out their smaller backup pieces and unloading at each other. The first few shots staggered them backwards, ricocheting off of their body armor. They never stopped firing, until simultaneously remembering to aim for the heads, realizing that's what the other was thinking, and ducking down into half-crouches.

A bullet tore through Ana's forearm, punching the hand holding the pistol backwards, a split second after one of hers gouged a furrow across the top of Enolah's skull. They both screamed, but Ana's weapon went flying, hit the surface of a desk and bounced like a skipping stone.

They both recovered quickly, helped a bit by the methamphetamine roaring through their veins. They hesitated for only a second, locking eyes bright with hate, but that was long enough.

Seth found himself not wanting to see it, but could not look away. Enolah's arm swung back up and the pistol bucked, a muzzle flash belching out of the barrel, and Ana's head was jerked around, her ponytail jumping up behind her with a splash of red. She hit the floor, suddenly nothing more than a tangle of meat and fluids.

Crying out, Enolah clutched the top of her head, blood running from between her fingers in rivulets over her pale hand. Dropping the pistol, she fished around frantically for her syringe of ketamine. Injecting herself, she sagged with relief for a moment, then bandaged her wound with the first aid kit all of them were required to carry. Then she rose, dragged Anathema's body over to where most of the others were, and pulled another corpse over her to conceal the face.

Crowe's voice was crackling out of the CB on the dead girl's belt, and she answered on her own when her little chore was done. She had told Dark when he asked that his sister was running around the other floors looking for people hiding, and that her radio must have died.

Now she stared in horror at Seth, terrified that he'd give her away. He only glanced at her, though. His eyes were mostly on Evan.

"Sleeping with the enemy, home skillet?" he said.

"No, we're supposed to be allies," Evan answered. "It was just a big mix-up."

The Scourge went cold. "We weren't all supposed to kill each other?"

"No. But who knew?"

"If I find out that anybody *did* know…"

"There is nothing we can do," Dark said. "All we have to do now is find my sister and leave. I don't know where we're going, but there's no point being late when we get there."

"Your sister, eh?" Seth asked. Everyone except Enolah frowned at his tone. She cringed inwardly, and Crowe saw it but chose to say nothing. But Dark could smell it. The way animals smell fear, he sensed the tension coming off of Enolah like the smoke off ice. When he looked up at Seth, he saw a casual but significant glance at the dominatrix.

With his throat crimping, Dark moved forward slowly, stepping over bodies, and advanced down the aisle. Enolah held her breath, afraid that in her haste she might have left some part of Anathema's face uncovered. But she knew she hadn't. She would never slip up like that.

Why the hell had she lied about Ana then? What had possessed her to make up a bullshit story?

Guilt makes people stupid. They make mistakes. And she didn't want to see the look on Dark's face when he found out that some hidden sniper had killed her. But that story wouldn't work anyway, because all the enemy bodies were out on the stairs. So, she panicked. She hid the body and she lied. Dark wouldn't see the face, though.

She saw Dark stop and go rigid, staring down at the spot where his sister lay. *Did he have X-ray vision?* No, he was staring at her hand.

A hand with six fingers.

He wheeled around and looked at Enolah, saw the fear stamped clearly on her face. The scarlet mist began to cloud his eyes.

With a roar, he lunged, slapping the weapon she held out of her hands, elbowed her in the side of the head. Seizing a handful of her hair, he bent her backwards, grabbed her by the belt, and dragged her to a window where he heaved her up, high above him, and flung her forward. The glass exploded and she flew out over the sidewalk nine stories below, screaming, flailing, clawing at the empty air. Tumbling end over end, she fell, her stomach suddenly in her throat, catching brief glimpses of Dark's face leaning out of the window, watching.

But the window was Plexiglas, she remembered. Bullets had punched holes in it, sure, but even that hadn't shattered it.

She looked into Dark's eyes, waiting for him to kill her some other way. He could shoot her, break her neck, hmm, that would be over quickly. Strangle her. Oh, that would suck. Beat her to death…

"I'm sorry," she said quietly.

Dark swallowed, cleared his throat, and turned to Calibos. The Colombian was praying with his rosary and had just gotten to the Glory Be when Dark spoke.

"Uh, hey, Badger."

"Calibos," Evan corrected him.

"Calibos, right." It took a few tries to get the ugly man's attention. "Do you...do you know any prayers for the dead?"

Crowe rolled his eyes. Enolah couldn't believe her ears. The hideous Colombian hesitated, then nodded. Dark beckoned him over, and they crouched over the bodies.

They didn't roll the one covering Ana off of her, because Dark couldn't bear to see her face. He just knelt on one knee and held her hand while Calibos prayed over her in Spanish.

Enolah prayed to Satan, giving thanks for it not even occurring to her victim's brother that she could be the guilty party. Thanks for planting a bullshit idea in his head that her lie was intended to spare him the bad news. But even as she said that to herself, it didn't sit right. She looked at Dark, at his face scrunched up, trying to hold the tears in, at the obvious love for his sister and the pain he was feeling. All emotions she had never once seen him display. And she felt something change inside her, with no idea what it was. Ehh, it was probably the meth she was coming down from.

There followed a moment of silence.

"Can we all go now?" Crowe asked, somehow not sounding callous and mean.

In the lobby, Evan managed to persuade them all, with Dark's help, to check in on his mother and ex-girlfriend, make sure they were still alive after the helicopters had hosed down the square. Outside, parked vehicles had been sawed apart, and lay cross-sectioned in the street, bleeding coolant and oil.

Fires and shattered masonry blocked off exits for many of the rioters, forcing them into bottlenecked vias to trample and crush one another to death. The helicopters had gone, but not until firing their last rockets at the Esplanade, shaking it terribly.

More choppers were on their way.

They stared out of the shattered glass doors at an improbable-seeming heap of corpses jamming up the entrance to a via, getting higher and higher as people crushed each other to death, scrambling over.

"And you want to fight your way through that?" Rabbit asked Evan.

"I have to. My mother is in there somewhere. You don't have to come."

"Yeah, I do. I swore I'd have your back."

"Then we'll either get to Ibiza or Valhalla, but it sure beats waiting here for the building to fall on us."

Rabbit nodded, took out three syringes, and gave one apiece to Jen and Evan. Seth watched a light spark in the teenager's eyes. Crowe saw it too, and understood.

"What's this?" Evan asked, trying to mask his eagerness for it. Jennifer examined it dubiously.

"Ask Todd when we get back."

Evan felt the demon stir within him as he watched Rabbit flick his finger against the cylinder to raise any air bubbles, and depress the plunger slightly to release them. It is said that half of an addiction to intravenous drugs is the ritual of preparing the needle and finding a vein. At that moment, Evan saw the truth in it, and performed the ceremony with undisguised relish.

"Big fan of needles, kid?" Crowe asked.

Seth laughed. "Yeah, he got hooked when we gave him a dose in LA, after he stubbed his toe."

"I didn't stub shit," Evan growled. "I was shot."

"He's lying. I tried to spare him the embarrassment, but since he lied I'll spill the beans. He needed morphine after he caught his dick in his zipper."

"Piss on you!" He slipped the needle into a vein he'd tapped, and gasped as he felt godlike strength pour into him. It was like nothing he'd ever felt. It was something pure and holy. He remembered something he'd heard long ago, and began tearing strips out of his jacket lining. The others stared at him. He shrugged off the jacket, doing it out of order, and used the strips to tie tourniquets about both arms and legs.

"Ya know yer history?" Jen asked, smirking. She hadn't taken her dose, just put it in her pocket for safe-keeping.

Evan nodded. "Them wily Filipinos."

When he was done, Rabbit asked if he was ready. He nodded again, breathless with energy.

"Good. Ibiza or Valhalla."

724

The others grinned and nodded.

"Ibiza or Valhalla."

They charged into the fray, shooting down people that used to be high school students, shopping mall consumers, and American Dreamers, but had become beasts in the space of a single day. Trying to conserve bullets, they clubbed men and women down with the butts of their guns, Crowe hacking through meat and bone with every stroke of his broadsword.

Sweat poured off of them as they ran, and most felt a stomach-heavy fear, but in all of them was the unholy joy of battle. Every time they swung and felt bones crunch, heard a satisfying grunt or scream, the dark thrill roared through them. When numbers congested the narrow vias and they reversed their grips to fire, mowing down the enemy with mere squeezing of a trigger, the bloodlust went up a howling notch, and by the time they reached what had been the Red Cross M*A*S*H station, Rabbit knew what the owners of that discotheque in Ibiza had meant by "Feuer-trunken."

Fire-drunken.

The purely elemental joy of slaughter. Magnified by the sight they burst upon, the men beaten unrecognizable, the women each squirming under the weight of grunting defilers. The thin thread that held Evan's sanity together in that wild moment snapped.

A red haze that had been swimming before his eyes went black, and of what happened next he would remember nothing. Foam spattered from his lips as he screamed, ran forward and field-goaled the head of the man on top of his mother, flipping him over onto his back beside her. The butt of Evan's emptied weapon pistoned down, again, again, and again, until nothing remained but a ghastly ruin where a face used to be.

Jumping to where Heather Roma lay screaming, he swung his minisub by the barrel, coming in low like a golf stroke, and put out the man's eye. The stock splintered the fifth, seventeenth, or thirty-third time he bashed it into the man's head. There was no telling how many times, but he pulped the head like a shattered melon, and kept going. Even Dark stared in amazement, after the last of the rapists was dead, having felt the madness of a berserker but never seeing it.

When sight and sounds finally came back to him, Evan stood, tossing the remains of his Calico behind him, and extended a hand to Heather Roma.

She stared in horror at the blood and gore that dripped from that hand. Impatiently, he jabbed the hand closer to her, and she shrank away. He cursed and stooped, seizing her roughly, lifting her to her feet, and set about rearranging her clothes to cover her. She just stood there, shivering, her shoulders hunched, her eyes squeezed shut and grimacing as if expecting to be struck.

Mrs. Lanthorne had composed herself, and now stared at her son, face spattered with blood, his lips and chin flecked with froth, his eyes glaring white-hot from under twitching brows.

This soft, milder age, which embraced cowardice, could not understand what he felt at that moment, and so the feeling was scorned as bestial and barbaric by those weaker of heart and less willing to do what had to be done. He knew the truth of civilization's poison then, that whatever politicians might say, all men were not created equal. The difference between him and Joshua Buckland was that of a wild grey wolf and a poodle. He laughed harshly at the fear in Heather's eyes. That she could not see him as he was, her savior, her knight, was contemptible. He knew now what he'd always been told, but didn't accept. The meek shall inherit squat.

Dark was seeing something different, though. His mind was on a wooden statue of Jesus hanging on a crucifix, sightless eyes without iris or pupil, legs crooked and fastened to the cross by a single nail through both feet. Ribs sticking out, with a gash carved into them on the right side, and a smoking bullet hole in the forehead, bleeding sawdust. INRI on a scroll above His head. *Iesus Nazarenus Rex Iudaeorum,* whatever that means.

Seeing rage from a distance and realizing what he must have looked like all those times, he didn't know what to think. He looked at all the people he'd just helped to save and realized that he was, theoretically, supposed to be one of those dead on the pavement. One of those doing the raping. He threw his weapons down and helped Joshua Buckland to his feet.

Calibos, who had come along mostly because they were safer in numbers and he had to go this way anyway, was making a stand with Crowe, Blake, Rabbit, and Seth keeping the rest of the rioting people at bay.

"We can't take to the roofs this time," Evan said. "The only thing stopping us is those choppers, though. Whose are they this time? The Crips?"

"Vampire Mexican Raza," Dark laughed.

"Who?"

"It's a joke. Never mind."

"I say we should go back the way everybody else has come," Jennifer suggested. "To the main square. It should be safer there because everyone's killing each other trying to leave."

"Brilliant, Holmes. They're all trying to leave for a reason. Unless..." Dark paused to think, reconsidering. "Well, by now, you're right. It's probably the eye of the storm."

Whoever was in the helicopters now, they were trying damned hard to lumberjack Edifice Rex with their rockets, to bring it down and crush some more people, and make the terrain less pleasant. What Evan wanted to know, but didn't waste time wondering, was where did they get choppers?

His eyes settled on a storm drain, and thought How could I be so stupid?

"Hey," he announced. "Find the nearest manhole cover. We're going underground."

"Through a sewer?" Jen exclaimed, wrinkling her nose. "Hell no!"

"No, not a damned sewer. An aqueduct."

"Same thing. An aqueduct is a sewer."

"No, it isn't."

"Yes, it is."

"Look! You want to get into a semantic argument, wait til we're in the clear."

"Rowr," she said in that sarcastic whiny cat voice he hated so much. His voice grew cold.

"Tell you what. You open your mouth again, and we *won't* look for a manhole. I'll stuff you into that drain right there, headfirst, so your little booty cheeks are sticking out for Tom, Dick, and Harry to sodomize until the buzzards get you."

She made a zipper-closing motion across her lips.

"Well, whatever we're doing, let's do it." It was the first time Enolah had spoken since Dark had spotted his sister. She had taken up a position on top of a righted folding table, next to Seth, where she could pick off anyone that came to close to Rabbit, Lugo, and Crowe's flanks.

Josh Buckland words were burning into Dark as the ex-Satanist ministered to him.

"I want to tell you how sorry I am," Dark had started.

"Don't tell me. Tell God. He's the one who needs to hear it."

"Look, I already went through that bullshit—"

"It looks like you need to go through it again. Where are you going with that gun? Somewhere to kill someone. Maybe get killed, yourself."

"It's something I have to do."

"Is it? Just like what you had to do to me?"

"No, this is different."

"All of our sins are different in one way or another, your motives that you think justify them, but they are all essentially the same. And the wages of sin are death."

"Dark!" Jennifer snapped. "Don't let that candy-ass cast his little spell on you! C'mon, let's go!"

Evan agreed that there was no time for any of that, now, and he shouted his idea for all to hear. The helicopters were too far away and moving too erratically for them to be sniped out of the sky by Betsy the 30.06. Nobody was really into the sewer/aqueduct plan, but nothing else was presenting itself.

Then, the decision was made for them.

The sound under the din of gunshots and screams was so out of place that they all froze. It sounded like rushing water. It couldn't be, though. This wasn't Holland, where the dike could burst. If you were six feet tall, you were six feet above sea level. So, what the...

Ohhhh shit, Evan thought.

"Up on the roof!" he shrieked. The others turned to him, but he wouldn't give them any time to give him funny looks. "Get up on the roof, *now!*" He shoved his nine-millimeter into his belt and seized his mother's arm, dragging her to the wall.

"Climb!" But she couldn't. She was not her son.

The tumult had reached them, and the smell. It was not water. Only Crowe and Seth remained calm. Screaming in horror, the rest of them dropped their weapons and ran for the wall of the via, the demolished front of a jewelry store. Without a thought for anyone else, they scrambled up over the bodies of others that Evan had started heaping. He'd never moved so quickly. There was not more than a few feet's worth of corpses, but for those in shape, it was a step up in their desperate leaps for the roof's eave.

They climbed like crabs in a bag, each one dragged back down by the others grasping at them for handholds. Shaking their heads,

Seth and Crowe got on either end of a folding table and carried it over to the other wall, leaning it on an incline, and did a gentlemanly "You first, old man"—"Oh no, by all means," in goofy British voices, until they realized their boots were getting slippery with gasoline, and walking up the table might actually be a chore.

"Climb, goddamn it!" Evan screamed at his mom. He crouched underneath her, trying to shove her up the wall, but she kept slipping from whatever purchase she could get, until finally Evan collapsed underneath her. They were both soaked in the fuel that had come from God Knew Where.

Enolah was helping Dark up onto the roof, and Rabbit was stabbing his hand over the eave at Evan. Jennifer had clawed her way up already, and was now on the other end of the building, watching a wall of flames fly toward them. To her, it looked almost like the milk running between cobblestones when she'd watched Rabbit feed Taorminan stray cats. The wave was a sheet of blue in the many fronts, which split up and rejoined through alleys around buildings. She stared at it coming in mesmerized horror.

Finally, Evan got on his feet, leaped straight up to catch Rabbit's hand, and was hauled up. Turning quickly, he yelled at Rabbit to hold his feet. When he did, Dark ran over to hold him, and Evan was lowered over the eave with his hands outstretched. His mother jumped, again, and again, but never caught a hold.

From the corner of his eye, Evan saw the flood of flames sweep into the via, and heard the screaming reach a new pitch. Terrified, his mother leaped one last time, missed, and fell again. Evan then heard only dimly the urgent shouts above him. His heart twisted inside of him, and as he felt himself being pulled back up, he saw only his mother getting farther away. Crouching in paralyzed fear, her eyes wide with the look of a car-hit dog on the highway.

The image blurred, his eyes burning from a mixture of tears and stinging sweat. Before he was dragged up onto the roof, he pulled his Browning Hi-Power out of the waistband of his pants, and shot Mrs. Lanthorne twice in the head.

Minus Seth and Crowe, they ran to the far edge of the building, where an area separated by Venetian-style watercourses looked safe from the fire. The girls hesitated, but the men all leaped from the roof and hit the ground rolling. Behind Enolah, Heather, and Jen, a rapidly advancing trail of bullets kicking up concrete dust scared them into jumping. All of them fell into the water, finding it surprisingly deep.

It was quiet in the hazy light, and the bullets plunging down after them sounded like only a light ticking, leaving con-trails of bubbles in their wake. They did not have far enough to travel before hitting the floor, though, and they didn't start slowing down until halfway there. Enolah screamed silently as two bullets tore through her, with bubbles erupting from her gaping mouth instead of sound. She crumpled and slowly sank, wisps of blood arching out of her and hanging.

Jennifer was closer to the bottom, and the single round that spiraled toward her slowed until it only touched her face, still hot. She looked at Enolah as she sank, took the bullet, and put it in her pocket with the needle, for luck.

Above, Joshua and Blake had both been cut down, along with a few other John Does no one knew, and not by accident. Rabbit had shoved them out of the cover they'd found, straight into the path of the gunfire. There just hadn't been enough room under the small art gallery's portico for everyone to take cover. When the chopper came around again, Evan stepped out in the open and gave them the Finger.

The helicopter paused, the men in it laughing at him, and then whimsically flew away.

VII

In several billion living rooms across the circumference of the planet, several billion pairs of eyes were glued to television sets and being the audience of one mousy little man's fifteen minutes of fame.

"Well, Janice," the expert whatever said, using his hands rather often in vague gestures to help explain. "Before we get into that, we have to make it understood that there really isn't any 'White Race.' It's complicated, but we all know that Hispanics will recognize quite a difference between, say, Ladrinos and Indigenas, right?"

"Yes," Janice the Interviewer said, nodding, staring at his milk-stain mustache and trying to look interested. The man started rotating his hands about one another, in the popular interviewee gesture that conveyed little more than the simulation of a raffle cage being spun.

"And even though there's racial hierarchy among African-Americans, in which mulattos are called 'red-bones' and quadroons and octoroons referred to as 'high yellow,' there is still a sense of unity that if you're part black, you're all black. And regardless of the African-American's ethnic origin being Ghana or the Ivory Coast, heritage is expressed by pride for the entire African continent, even though there are actually vast differences between the peoples there."

"Mm-hmm." Janice nodded some more.

"But among those defined officially by the United States government as 'White,' meaning non-Hispanics having racial origins in Europe, North Africa, or the Middle East, there is no unity. This supposed race is completely divided by ethnic groups or ideology. An Anglo-Saxon or Nordic-American does not claim to be one with a Jew or Arab, and vice-versa. The same with Irish and Italian descendants. And the commonly accepted but erroneous title 'Caucasian' really applies to the descendants of those who came from the Caucasus Mountains, among whom are the people of India."

Janice actually frowned. "Really?"

"Really. And not many Indians are white. So, as a 'race,' we are divided, and are only truly united in a commonly-felt, and I realize this will suffer politically correct criticism, negrophobia."

"Negrophobia?" Now her eyes were wide, questioning.

"Yes. I have seen young people of all colors calling each other

731

'nigga' as if it were a synonym for 'comrade,' and when asked to explain, they say that to be a nigga is a state of mind. This state of mind has been, thanks to political correctness, sanctioned and encouraged to spread, further dividing our nation. Our nation, where all of us should drop the first half of our ethnic titles, the subspecies categories we confine ourselves by, and instead be Americans."

Janice stared at him for several moments, until the frantic studio floor director finally got her attention.

"Um, and now a word from our sponsors."

"See?" the expert snapped. "This is exactly what I'm talking about!"

In the control room, the director and all his technicians were so startled by the man's sudden ferocity that they didn't cut to commercial. They listened. Only a few people watching at home were quick enough to wonder why they could see this happening. Why were there cameras in the control room in the first place?

"As a supposed race, we have been poisoned by political correctness to feel unnecessary guilt, and fear we'll be branded racists even though we aren't! Fear that we'll be ostracized and possibly attacked, while every other race is actively encouraged by us to speak openly against us! I've said nothing wrong! But you panic and try to shut me up! This is what I'm talking about. Negrophobia.

"It's not negroes we all fear. It's 'niggaz'. It's that 'state of mind,' that way of life that revolves around mindless violence and depravity, that we've allowed Hollywood and the radio to glamorize. We have cultivated it with our tolerance, and now it's going to cut our throats!"

He had calmed down now, somewhat. He looked straight into Camera Two, and addressed the nation more authoritatively. "Right after World War Two, a man named Clifton Fadiman wrote that the next few decades seemed almost to prove years of wholesale suicide, years that would paralyze the moral and religious sense of mankind, and that civilization would fall forward into a new and unimaginable barbarism. As our planet rolls slowly in the direction of its own eclipse, men's minds will darken with it. Losing faith in themselves, they will look into each others' eyes with hatred, and every man's hand will rest lightly on his dagger. New philosophies of violence and despair will be contrived, and old nihilisms be exhumed.

"Look at the history of our country since then, and tell me that all of our events, even including the Sexual Revolution and Generation X did not help to move us irreversibly in this direction. 'Progressiveness' such as this is a classic symptom of every great nation's decline and fall. Nobody listened when I said this years ago. Maybe you'll all listen now.

"Racism's changed hands these days. Even the Supreme Court was called upon to rule against the University of Michigan recently, with President Bush backing the suit in early 2003. The school's admission policy allowed a whole twelve points for a "perfect" SAT score. If you're white. Or Asian. But there was a handicap granted—twenty points for blacks, Hispanics, or Native Americans. It implied that they are not as intelligent, and deserve a lot of slack. When President Bush denounced this policy, he was called a racist. Even black people who agree, who advocate Equality, who say college admissions should be "based strictly on merit," are shouted down by the lazier of their race. It seems that the only thing that's changed is which side to be on. They who thought people should be accepted, hired, or advanced on the basis of skin color were racists, but *now* are politically correct.

"According to politically-correct history classes as headed by Gary Nash of UCLA, this entire country was founded by the efforts of blacks and Asians, and not because of Western Europeans' triumphs in technology or political institutions. Because of 'dead white European males,' we have steam engines, electrical engines, internal combustion engines, computers, the Constitution, the House and Senate, and the ability to live longer and better than ever before in history. But, no. A 'convergence of peoples' was responsible for our success as a nation, according to him.

"Nash was asked by Jane Pauley on NBC Dateline what was one thing kids ought to know about our first President, George Washington, and he said 'He was a member of a slave-holding aristocracy.' Period. Nevermind that whole overthrow of the greatest military power on Earth with a ragtag militia. Forget his guidance in the early Federal era, keeping his fellow free colonists from swerving into anarchy, just like France and, hell, almost everybody else did following a revolution. Yeah, to hell with that.

"Sure, he had slaves. Jefferson, too. But keep in mind that slavery is not something inherently white. It has always existed, everywhere, and always will. It is happening today under our very noses. But according to Nash, it's 'dead white European males,' all the way. Politically-correct historians have rewritten the past, not just to include others, but to exclude white men, teaching kids feel-good sociology instead of pertinent events and facts—things necessary for them to know because if we don't know about our failures, we are doomed to repeat them.

"In World War II history classes, they're teaching a bit about Hitler, but zilch about Mussolini. Out with Stalin, in with McCarthyism. Nothing about Japanese fascism, the rape of Nanking, the victimization of Korea, destruction of Manila —oh, the Koreans, Chinese, and Filipinos know all about the extreme racism of the Japanese warrior class, but little Timmy and Stephanie don't. Ditto with India and Pakistan versus their respective Muslim and Hindu minorities, or Arab Muslims versus East African blacks, et cetera.

"History must be studied entirely to have a valid understanding of a multipolar world, in context. But no. As of 1994, dead white European males and their descendants are responsible for all that is evil in the United States, and all the good that was done was by Asians, Africans, and Indians. At least, according to Gary Nash and his National History Standards."

"These are our *enemies,* anyone who goes against the grain of what America stands for: equality, freedom of speech, freedom of expression. They want their freedom, but, like you just tried to, they forbid mine. These people prevent speech in the name of defending it. They urge division in the name of unity. They backslide in the name of progress."

Cut to Janice.

"Um...and now a word from our sponsor?"

But there was no commercial break, just like there really was no television interview. All this had been filmed over a year prior, supposedly for a film that had never been finished, scripted to seem like the studio crew were afraid of racial repercussions, for realism. Instead of cutting to a commercial, the screens of every television tuned into that station blanked out.   Then, this:

In time with the pounding bass, strobe lights stabbed the blackness and caught figures dancing in its eerie flash, people thrashing, vanishing, and reappearing. The show had begun. Up on stage, prancing though smoke and slashes of blue light, an entire platoon of rappers roared their unintelligible gibberish before they would break up and wait backstage for their individual sets. There would be an encore of this same group effort at the end of the concert, after the headliner.

734

Supposedly, anyway.

There were ten stars on each stage of six packed arenas— New York's Madison Square Garden, the Los Angeles Forum, and the largest enclosed stadiums in Miami, Chicago, Philadelphia, and Atlanta. Each house was filled with men and women of every race, all of them unified by their love for barbaric rhythms, and all of their pants falling down in varying degrees. It was, perhaps, the largest collection of people who'd call themselves "niggaz" without necessarily being black, all at one event, despite being separated by distance.

They were the ones who called white people crackas, even if they were white themselves. They were the wannabe gangsta punks who glorified violence and destruction, while expecting handouts from the very government they defied. In the eyes of the plutocrats who created them, they were everything that was wrong with society. They were the citizens whose destiny it was to eventually justify the tightening of governmental control, bringing about the gradual transition to communism, but because of Amanda Rothschild's suffering, would instead be the excuse for doing it all at once.

Then, when everyone's blood had gotten up, right before everything was about to take off, the sound abruptly died and the house lights came on. Startled, momentarily blinded, they all looked about bewildered, before taking up a roar of "what the fucks?!"

The lighting and sound technicians were already gone. The whole works were on autopilot. Up on six stages across the nation, sixty rappers glared about in outrage.

Famous rappers such as Will Smith or the Beastie Boys were not invited to participate, even secretly discouraged from attending, which made their blood boil. That is, until they saw why they were snubbed. Any rapper with a positive message was kept from the events because they were entertainment, and exempt.

"You know, if you stop and think about it..." a woman's voice thundered, digitally enhanced and echoing majestically. They all looked around for the source of the voice, even though they knew it was coming out of the speakers. "Every last one of us is a tangle of organs and highly compressed fluids, gases, and acids, held together by two hundred some-odd bones, set in motion by electric synapses distributed to meat. If we keep these intricately-woven symbiotic mechanisms in top condition, we can hold our position at the top of the food chain, thanks to the medical advances our ancestors have made, for longer than any of them ever have, in history. It is this, our ability to adapt, and then change our environments to make them adapt to us, that makes us the most magnificent organism on this planet."

In each of the six arenas, several thousand people saw the face of Maya Macaulay on the giant screen that usually shows close-ups of the performers on stage. Some astounded, some confused, but most enraged, the concert-goers shouted at the gigantic face of the "cracker-assed hoe" as if she were 1984's Goldstein. The music began, the opening of a technopera, the melody rising behind her lecture.

"When they say that we're all the same on the inside," she continued, "That's what they mean. We're all sustained by the same program of synchronized convulsions and inflations, and clenches and pressurized releases. Some people will say that it is only the color of our skin that makes us different. Only the differing degrees of pigmentation in the outer layers of our surface. But noooo..."

Those eyes hardened, glaring down at the masses who weren't really listening anyway.

"You call it a state of mind that gives you natural superiority, and license to preach and practice your philosophies of violence and nihilism. To overthrow thousands of years of rational thought! To spit on civilization! To glorify and emulate the very beasts we outgrew when we chose to crawl up out of the primordial slime! You are not even a healthy organism with a right to live, as by your words and actions you are bent on the destruction of Order, the annihilation of everything unlike you, not only through wanton murder and mayhem, but the breeding out of every other subspecies. You are an infestation that goes beyond Parasite, for even a tick or a tapeworm wants to keep its host alive. You, however, are a plague that will wipe out everything in sight, then spread, until it is only you occupying the entire planet, at which time you will turn upon yourselves. You are cancer. You wear your filth like badges of honor. Well, folks, the food chain's about to be redefined. Fight your way to the top if you can, but beware... I'm already there!"

The giant image of the revolution's spokeswoman blinked out, and compartments in all six stadium ceilings opened up, clouds of gray particles drifting down lazily past the light systems. The music swelled.

In the Nazi concentration camps of World War Two, this

nerve gas was known as Zyklon B. Today, under a different name, it is available as a pesticide to anybody with a chemical license, and that was exactly what it was being used as now.

There are quicker, more efficient nerve gases, and this one was not used out of any perverse nostalgia for Nazism. Instead, it was chosen because it was crude and outdated. It took fifteen minutes to kill the average adult human being.

Which was the length of Delenda Est Ghetto.

A man's voice thundered out of the speakers. Rabbit's, digitally god-like. And rapping.

"I'm not a thug, or OG, or a hustler wannabe,
I'm not a pimp and I will not pretend to be,
My ride is not 'pimped out' or 'fly,'
No beer on the ground cuz mah homies die,
I'm not off the chain, I'm not in your face,
My mind's not confined by a color or race,
I'm not proud of black ink on my hand,
And it wasn't a weapon that made me a man!"

An angry beat pounded at Burning Bush volume, catchy enough for many people to stop, exchange looks, and start bouncing slightly in time to it. At least until the billowing clouds sank low enough to reach them.

"I won't glorify how I came to the Pen,
Or how I got sentenced to life plus ten,
No, I'm not strapped with a coward's gats,
My skin's not stained with jailhouse tats,
Won't brag about the size of my yellow sheet,
Or how many bitches I've got on the street,
I don't wear ice and I don't bling-bling,
'Cause your cubic zirconia don't mean a thing,
Obese is obese, not 'sweet thick-thick,'
And I can go an hour without holding my dick!"

The screaming began, but the audio had been edited so it accentuated the music rather than interfering with it, a fiendish parody of applause. The powder burned just alighting on the skin. Breathed in, it made the body desperate to expel it. Projectile vomiting and instantaneous diarrhea were the two most spectacular of the early effects.

"No pant leg hitched up to my knee,
No SWAT man putting down on me,
I don't limp when I am not hurt,
I got no knuckles dragging in the dirt,
No gold front teeth, no pick in my hair,
No pants down showing my underwear,
No welfare checks, no baby mamas,
No kufis, no mats, no Ah-salaamas,
No chickenhead, no skank swayback,
No selling my soul for a pebble of crack,
No hoochie mamas, no ghetto hood rats,
No jiggy, no word, no dawg, no phats,
No freakin' wit hoes, no ballin', no playin',
And I'll never have to ask if you
know what I'm sayin',
No fist salutes, no black berets,
Old Skool is dead, it's New School's day!"

The music swelled again and Maya's bewitchingly ethereal voice soared to take Rabbit's place, while people were crushed climbing atop heaps of each other, like drowning victims clawing their way to the surface.

"If might made right when God sent His
Apocalyptic flood,
Then might made right when the Vandals came
To drench Rome's streets in blood!
(Delenda Est!)
And it was the same when Reginald Denney
Was beaten and left to die,
As when outside of Pilate's walls
They shouted "Crucify!"
So it's only fair when Gangsta Rap has
To bow to my advance,
Like skeletons of elephants
In the wake of marching ants!"

738

The words "Delenda Est" were wailed by banshees in the background. A few music industry executives actually listened more to the music than the screams of the dying, but most of the great American viewing public stopped watching after this much. Many of them went for their guns. Even teenagers who liked rap music, who carried guns just for the image, grabbed them out from behind their underwear drawer and ran outside to kill anyone who wasn't like them. Men and women who avidly demonstrated their right to keep and bear arms before, now happily went out to use them and defend themselves.

This all happened in the early afternoon, not long after a school bus coincidentally drove off of a bridge in Coquina, and nineteen other cities like it.

For all Americans with good red blood, this was the last straw. Many had expected martial law to be declared, at least somewhere, but the only pretense of any authority in any city was the local law enforcement.

Small towns, the Mayberrys, had emergency town meetings in churches, but their doomsday would be a week or so later. When displaced city slickers had no homes to return to, they would roam in groups for the shelter of others, seeking to drive out peaceful rural landowners.

Enough time had been allowed for people to flee in panic, to evacuate their neighborhoods in the hopes that maybe Grandma's house out in the Boonies was a safe place to stay, before the military finally made its brief appearance.

Fighter jets came screaming out of the smoke-blackened skies with both suburbia and the projects in missile-lock, and the bombs fell.

Expecting his people to still be in Edifice Rex, safe, Pedro Vizcaya had given the go-ahead. Twelve black SUVs, having hooked chains fastened to their trailer hitches, had gone to six different gas stations around the commercial center of Coquina. One soldier at each station had gone inside and flipped the pump switches, gotten back into the trucks, which had been chained to the pumps, and watched what happened excitedly through the rear windows. The trucks were started, and roared forward, yanking the chains taut and uprooting eleven pumps. That should be enough, they thought.

Geysers of fuel erupted from the ground, washing all over the streets and flowing downtown. The gasoline from all the stations met together on the ground like floods of quicksilver, and it was left up to chance for it all to be ignited. It was only a matter of time.

It would not last very long, but it should get the job done, they thought.

VIII

They all sat together, way too tired to dive into the water and swim, and waited for the fire to burn itself out. Heather stared silently at Evan, who was staring off into space. Jen was snuggling against Rabbit, still soaking wet, leaning against a portico pillar. Dark brooded over the deaths of the three girls closest to him in one single day, and eventually, he stood.

"I'm done," he said, dropping his weapons to the ground. He pulled up his sleeve and unstrapped Switchblade, tossing it to Rabbit. "You can use this if you want to, but I'm out. All this is of the Devil."

Rabbit pointed at Joshua Buckland's corpse, his "Yahweh or the Highway" t-shirt soaked with blood.

"That's what he said."

"And he was right."

"Right or wrong, he's still dead."

Dark weighed this.

"Go to Hell."

Heather was crouched over the mortal remains of Joshua Buckland, the late counselor of her youth group, her fingers touching his wounds like Doubting Thomas. She looked up at the sunburned man, then at Rabbit.

"You don't feel bad about any of this?"

Everyone was surprised to hear her finally speak. To all of them, she looked positively ridiculous with her clothes torn, hair a tangled blonde shock, sticky from the blood of someone who had forced himself upon her, and still acting as if some form of guilt should be felt after heroism.

"What is there to feel bad about?" Rabbit asked.

"People have died."

"It happens. People die. Sometimes you have to speed up the process to make sure you live."

"People have suffered."

"Everyone suffers. You either waste your life as a victim, or you fight back."

"No."

"No?"

"To kill another human is murder, period. Thou shalt not kill."

"To everything there's a season, and a time to every purpose

741

under heaven. A time to kill and a time to heal. I'm paraphrasing, though."

"That's just a song."

"It's Ecclesiastes, three-something."

"Whatever. It's murder. And under your system, no matter what the cause was, the guy you killed's family has every right to avenge him. Then, the first murderer's family has the right to avenge *him*. It snowballs until murder breeds murder after murder until God gets tired of us and replaces mankind with a new creature that can understand."

"So, you're upset that Evan killed a man who was raping you? Beat you down and took away from you the only thing you truly have? You forgive the piece of shit who filled you out like a god-damned application form, maybe even gave you AIDS?" He seemed to get a little too angry at this, to some of them, but he managed to snap Evan out his trance, who glared at both Rabbit and Heather, not sure yet who to be mad at. The girl hesitated then, stammered out another scripture with sick desperation to maintain her faith.

"Be angry, and sin not. Let not the sun go down—"

"Then forgive. Forgive the virus that invades your body. Forgive the beasts that eat you alive because you aren't strong enough to stop them, and the worms that eat what's left."

"But—"

"Butbutbutbutbut! Now, thank that kid over there for saving you! He's a man."

Evan's eyes flickered, and he turned to look at Heather, but she could only look at the ground. He studied her for a long moment, then turned to Rabbit.

"I am, aren't I?"

"Damn right."

"Finally. And to think I was going to give up a real woman for her."

Heather's head snapped up, her fangs bared.

"You mean that freak? That hippie dyke?"

Rabbit bolted to his feet, snatching one of his asps out from under his jacket. He cleared the gap between them in a tigerish bound, the steel shaft flicking out as he swung. The force of that stroke would've smashed her skull like an eggshell if Dark had moved an instant later. The two of them were a blur of thrashing limbs too quick for the eye to follow. The asp slid ringing across the cobblestones into the water, the splash drowned out by a resounding crack.

Both men whirled, crouched and ready to spring.

Jennifer held Dagger, smoking in her white fist, pointed into the fire. "Time out."

They paused, eyes shifting nervously between each other.

"Hey, Goldilocks," she said. "Are you glad Dark tried to save you? Don't look at me with your mouth open like that. You're not a goldfish." The other people there, the refugees from the M*A*S*H unit, just shrank away. "She'll never learn, Nick. And *you'll* never learn, Dark." Suddenly, something occurred to her. Hippie dyke...

"Hey," Evan said, interrupting her thoughts. "I've got a great idea. Let's wait peacefully for the world to stop burning, then leave and never see most of each other ever again."

They all looked at each other lamely.

"It'll only take a long time or two before we can go," he continued. "Then we can all go our separate ways, and die like civilized people. This is like too many of those movies, yunno? Where everyone's trapped in a hostage situation, or a blocked mine shaft, something like that. Blah blah blah, tensions run high, blah blah blah, gotta resolve differences. Only the cavalry ain't going to show up and save us the moment that we all go for each other's throats. We gotta be planning how we're not going to die."

They all felt stupid now.

"We will probably get out of this situation and walk right back into another one. Then what? We have almost no weapons now, and no plan. So instead of pontificating, can't we put our heads together and decide what to do?"

No one said anything. Evan sighed.

"Fine. In the meantime, let me amuse myself with your radio scanner, Zombie."

The detective's eyes creaked slowly open, to stare dully at the hand of a dead man an inch or two in front of him. He'd heard something, but he wasn't sure what.

"Bancroft!" There it was again. "Ban-cro-o-oft." Then, in the tune of the old horserace derby song, "Ban-ban-ban *bank*ity bankity bank-bank Ban-croft! Hey! The request lines are now open! Remember me? You shot me in the back a couple hours ago?"

Ward Bancroft groaned, rolling his eyes, and died in the middle of a cul-de-sac where he'd been cornered and sold his life as high as he could.

They say that if you sit in one place long enough, everyone you've ever met will pass by.

Which can be a real bitch when you're an asshole cop.

As the gasoline on the road burned itself out, the handful of Bacalous left who hadn't roasted alive in their cavalcade of gunships prepared to walk. Their tires had long melted, the stink of their burnt rubber mingling with that of hot steel and barbeque seeping in through cracks in the doors and windows and dashboard vents.

The holocaust was short-lived, and only affected the part of the city they were traversing, the eastern main road by the marketplace, but thousands died and some still writhed feebly in the gutter. With nothing else to burn on the asphalt, the flames retreated to smoulder in the tar.

Warily opening their doors, though desperate to leave the stifling heat and get some fresh air, they went about escaping very slowly. The cacophony of stenches swept in on them, and they all hurriedly covered their mouths and noses with their shirts as if that would solve anything. Like jerking a Band-Aid off of a hairy forearm or leg, or plunging into freezing water, it was something best done quickly; but they insisted on easing themselves out inch by inch. These were the herd men, who follow orders, and are brave only when they are many.

Most of them were white or Hispanic, with a few Asians thrown in, and only a smattering of blacks. A large number of the latter had charged impetuously out into the fray after the first few minutes of watching Delenda Est Ghetto. There were many who had stayed behind and waited for organization, but they'd been driving convertibles, and burned quickly, like the whites and Hispanics in the beds of their pimped-out pickup trucks and El Caminos.

All the lowriders of any make or model were ovens, immediately. The only survivors were those in jacked-up monster trucks, or SUVs with hydraulic elevation systems, and as soon as they trickled gingerly out onto the streets, where their shoe soles were instantly cauterized to the asphalt, they became target practice for the operators of napalm catapults.

Positioned high atop distant buildings, well out of firearm

range, Gorgon Army was safe, at least until the jets came.

Rabbit watched the flames sputter out on the ground, and knew the way out would be hard, what with burning buildings having a tendency to collapse, and the many people who had surely survived. No matter how many tanks of gasoline trucks (he assumed that's where the flood had originated) could have been emptied, only a comparatively small part of the city could be affected. So, it wasn't over.

And he had a fifty-fifty chance of getting through the city alive, at least the way he saw it. He felt the same way about surviving situations like this as he did about weather forecasts. Twenty-seven percent chance of rain? Bullshit. It'll either rain, or it won't. I'll either live, or I'll die. 50% chance of anything.

He came to a decision while everyone else planned their movements. His just-in-case. He took out his cell phone, surprised that it still worked, dialed a very long number, and calculated time differences while it rang. A woman's voice answered in Dutch.

"Mr. Van Appin, please," he said in her language.

When a total of four different calls had been placed, and banking instructions given in four different languages, Rabbit finally called Maya Macaulay.

Evan had stared, thinking but still uncertain that he had heard her name spoken several times into the phone.

He thought he might have either hear-lucinated, or just misheard two words in other tongues that sounded alike because he wanted them to. Now that he heard Rabbit say hello to her and ask what time it was at her end, he couldn't decide how to feel. Jennifer could, however.

"I can barely hear you, Maya. Can you hear me? Good. Got something to write with? An eyeliner pencil. Congratulations, honey, way to be prepared. Do this instead. You still have the key to our boat?"

Our boat, the eavesdroppers thought angrily.

"Good. In the companionway, between the master stateroom and the head, pull up the carpet. Carefully. You tear my carpet and you've got genital noogies coming when I get back. Now, lift up the carpet and you'll find a trapdoor...yes, I know, but I've got a thing for trapdoors. Open it and take out all the bank documents. Call the four banks and talk to the people whose names are listed. I've got their numbers in a little book you'll find. Call them and do whatever they tell you, okay? Do that in three days, unless I call you to say otherwise, okay? Just trust me." He listened for a while. "No, I didn't see the news, why? Oh yeah, your song. Hey, it's free publicity, babe. Well, what'd you think it was going to be used for? Anyway, did you ever get that bottle you were looking for? That cask of Amontillado? Well, keep looking. I'm sure it'll be worth it."

Jennifer was fuming.

Evan suppressed his anger, and instead, started planning Rabbit's murder. It would require a good bit of thought, considering he had only a few bullets left, and that fucker could dodge lightning, he moved so fast. Even then, with the man dead, he knew he'd still be wary, probably stand guard over his grave with a sharpened stake and a bucket of holy water.

"That is shock, Maya," Rabbit was saying. "It's surprise at seeing yourself on TV. You'll get over it. Shit, my battery's finally going dead. Look, if I don't call back, you know what to do. *No*, it's not that at all. Look, I gotta go. Keep breathing, kiddo."

He hung up, not noticing that Jennifer stood close to him now, or that she'd put another shell in Dagger. He rolled his eyes, irritated with himself, and thinking aloud.

"Shit! I forgot to tell her that she doesn't have HIV any-more." He started to dial her phone number again, when Jennifer wound back and slapped the phone out of his hand.

Stricken, eyes wide, he watched it fly diagonally across the little canal, rebound off the far side ledge, and splash into the water.

Stunned, Rabbit turned to look down the barrel of Dagger, then into Jennifer's cold blue eyes behind it. The gun shook in her hand, but those eyes did not. No one moved.

"Why?" she asked, her words hissing out from between clenched teeth. "Why am I good enough? What'd I do *wrong?"*

"Do it."

"What?"

"Do it. Pull the trigger."

"You going to kill me if I don't?" she asked in biting sarcasm.

He thought a moment. "No."

"Why, Nickie?" she asked, finding herself fighting to keep her voice steady.

"I'm sorry, Jen."

"Why?" The faintest quavering escaped.

"It wasn't you. It was me."

"Bullshit! They all say that!"

"Jen, it really was me. Look, I was…I was a nerd. I still am. Everything you love is a lie. I'm a piece of shit."

"Don't try to—"

"The fire's out," Evan interrupted, trying to distract her. "Time to go." He bit his tongue, remembering that he was supposed to want Rabbit dead. Oops. It had slipped his mind when Rabbit said something about Maya not having HIV anymore, and he wanted an explanation.

Either way, the fire was down. Time to go.

"It wasn't you," Rabbit said again. "Maya fixed my head for me, when no one else could. It wasn't your fault that you couldn't. It was mine. I shouldn't have needed fixing."

Her face twisted, a sob escaping, and she dropped Dagger and imploded. He caught her and held her close.

"Well, you heard the kid."

Everyone spun sharply, finding Jim Crowe's head sticking out of the water. Seth's head was not too far behind. The Aborigine smiled and gestured onwards with a jerk of his chin.

"It's time to go, he said. So, let's get crackin'." He looked at Dark and frowned. "Damn, your face is red as a three-ball."

It was an unspoken agreement among those not wearing "Yahweh or the Highway" t-shirts that those who *were* wearing them should be walking in front. Crowe's joke of "Onward, Christian soldiers," really meant "take the first bullets for us."

Fires still crackled in blackened buildings where they had been fed by wood, and the cobblestones were hot to the touch but it seemed safe enough now to walk.

To all those that had lived there, it looked like Hell had come, seeing the places that they had taken for granted would last forever, crumbling into black ash. They were so entranced by it that it took them a while to notice the strange chanting.

There was still a distant noise of crowds, surprising them, that meant a large part of the city proper was not even affected by the flames. But this, this was weird.

"*Nyah* nyana *nyah*-nyah!" came drifting to them from every direction, but quietly and illusive. At first, it was just startling, but it became eerie and disturbing, the sound of taunting children in so horrific a place. Eyes darted nervously trying to spot one of the kids, but they were always out of sight. Even Crowe began to frown slightly.

"Where are they?" he finally grumbled.

The worry the others had all been trying to hide began to show. Anywhere else, this would have been ignored, but in the smoldering rubble, amid many businesses wreathed in flame, it was born of nightmare and lunacy.

"*Nyah* nyana *nyah*-nyah!" was now replaced by a mocking cry of "Marco? Maaaarco!"

Then, from somewhere else, "Polo!"

The sounds of a distant riot were coming closer. They did not want to meet it, but there was just one road open to them.

All the "civilians" in the trans-Hell expedition were thinking about how poorly prepared they were for such a day. They had considered themselves rather cunning and adventurous on those nights when they met to play fantasy role-playing games, trying to toughen their image by calling their hobbies "RPGs."

But, sitting up all night arguing over paperwork and decks of cards, strung out on Mountain Dew and Gummi Bears, had proved to be a rather poor indoctrination for acting their fantasies out.

And now, on top of that, "*Nyah* nyanna *nyah*-nyah!"

"Marco? *Marco?*"

"Polo!"

The via they had been picking their way through widened into what everyone called the Hub. It was a spot where six of the honeycombing vias came together like the spokes of a wheel. In the center of the Hub was a faux bronze statue, this one a replica of the Venetian monument outside the Piazza San Marco, of King Victor Emmanuel II, with a warrior woman triumphantly posing next to a roaring winged lion on one side, the lion dying next to the woman slouching in defeat on the other, and King Victor swinging his saber on the top. The horse had one foreleg raised, which meant, in horseman statue symbolism, that whoever he was had died of wounds incurred in whatever battle the monument commemorated.

Vandals had defiled the monument with red, black, and yellow slashes of spray paint. The roar of the crowd was louder here with the other avenues opened up, but it was still unclear which direction they were coming from. It could be either Eeney Meeney Miney Moe, or Due East toward the ocean and comparative safety, but once again, the decision was made for them.

"Marco!" came from all around them. They spun, but still found no one. Then, a little black child stepped out from behind the monument where he had been sitting on the dying woman's lap, and he hopped to the ground.

"Polo."

He held a TEC-9 in his little hands, pointed at them with such confidence that it wasn't a weapon, but an extension of his will. He grinned, almost laughing. Children, being total id, found this kind of thing just a game.

"Moke?" Evan asked, blinking.

"Ah'll be damned. The traita."

"There you are!" Seth called, feigning pleasant surprise and trying to be all buddy-buddy wit' im.

"Shut up, bitch."

"What?"

"You deaf?"

Seth's answer was interrupted by a few startled gasps, and he turned to see at least a dozen children surrounding them, all heavily armed. They had come as silently as the shadows of ghosts. Evan had never seen more than one of them alive, and in his mind he pictured them as a bunch of Road Warrior-type feral children, orphaned at infancy and raised by rats. But the children stared at their prey with a creepy intelligence. One of them spoke up.

"We ain't yo Familiars, pretty boy," Shrike said.

"What the hell is this?" Evan demanded.

"Take a wild guess, cracka. Drop the piece."

"I ain't dropping a goddamned thing!"

All of the guns came up instantly, and the people in their sights knew the children wouldn't hesitate. An uneasy moment passed, then Evan dropped the nine.

"All you. And you with the sword, man, where'd you get a fucken *sword*, mah nigga? S'matter? Cat got your tongue?"

"Drop 'em," Moke said. No one moved. Giggling, Moke squeezed the trigger, mowing down a few of the Christians. Screaming, the rest tried to turn and run, but were brought up short by the other barrels aimed up at them. Moke stopped firing, his grin still splitting his face. "Sorry 'bout dat."

"Drop 'em," Shrike repeated. Slowly, the few who carried weapons obeyed. "We got a phone call for you to make."

"This supposed to be funny?" Evan hissed.

"For us, yeah."

"Who do you want me to talk to?"

"Uncle Pedro. That lying motherfucker."

"What? What happened?"

"We know all about dat Santería house."

"What? That was Nestor's thing! Not—"

"Oh, you wanna lie to us, too?"

Evan was speechless, not knowing what the hell was going on or what to do about it.

Dark, however, was trading telepathic messages through eye signals with Rabbit, the both of them communicating rather well. They knew that going for backup weapons, the few of them who had any, would get them a volley of bullets in the teeth, so there had to be some kind of a diversion, something that would distract the children. Although Dark had, to his immense regret, thrown his Switchblade away, he remembered watching Rabbit pick it up and study it before strapping it on himself. Having heard about symbolism in sculpture from the late Dipshit, was determined to have all of his horse's hooves on the ground if ever he was sculpted.

Shrike was saying something about not seeing any of the older Grazi Mono kids anywhere, and no one he asked having seen them anywhere either. So, he looked into it. But neither Dark nor Rabbit were paying attention, and in a moment, neither were the other kids.

Dark had stuck his tongue out.

The children all stared in wide-eyed surprise and disgust as the two tips of his forked tongue wriggled about, separately. Shrike noticed it first, and his face wrinkled. When he turned to the one next to him, repulsed, they all looked at each other to share their disgust, and the second they did, Rabbit flicked his wrist and Switchblade snapped into his hand, and Geiger dove commando-style for Calibos Lugo's dropped Hardballer. The only child who had not been distracted was Moke, who couldn't see what all the *eeeew!* was about from where he stood.

The sudden movement startled him, and he squeezed the trigger again, but Crowe wheeled about so quickly as to defy reason, and the shuriken he'd thrown thunked into Moke before Evan even hit the ground, his shirt shredded by bullets.

Shrike's face was blown half-apart by Rabbit's first shot, and the boy next to him fell, clutching his throat and choking before

Moke's deafening shots galvanized them all into action. On the ground, Dark fired into the little assassins. There was no place for either group to hide. Jennifer fell, her left collarbone and a chunk of her trapezius shattering in a crimson burst. Evan rolled onto his chest and snatched up his nine, but Moke was already dead, he just hadn't hit the ground yet.

Three ninja throwing stars had killed him where he stood.

Rabbit and Seth also fell, both taking shots on their Kevlar, like Evan, but before the tables had time to turn, all of the Grazi Mono were dead, blasted off their feet and flung backwards. Heather Roma dropped the TEC-9 she'd taken, stared for a moment at what she'd done out of instinctive desperation, and swallowed.

Wasting no time, Rabbit ran to where Jennifer lay and gathered her up in his arms. She was gasping in agony, clutching at the fountain of blood gushing out of her. Digging into her pocket, he fished out her syringe, bit off the needle's cap and spat, and jammed it into her good arm where the jacket had slipped down off her shoulder. He injected half of the dose, and her gasping took on a different tone.

He tried to compress the wound while frantically searching for something to cauterize it with, but there was nothing. Crowe was behind him an instant later, preparing a medicine that was half brilliant chemistry and half Dreamtime magic—a poultice with women's menstrual issue, powdered instant potatoes, and various herbs mixed together into a paste.

The giant pushed his student aside and ministered to the girl, pulling the ingredients out of his Batman utility belt.

"We've got to get her to the church," he mumbled. "She's losing a lot of blood." Apparently, they had blood there. Rabbit was surprised at how quickly the Aborigine had come to help her, without hesitation. Crowe felt nothing for the girl, though, only for his little brother. He had seen Rabbit in fear for this girl and not doing what he needed to do to save her, so he intervened.

"What was this all about?" Heather asked quietly, though in a steady voice. Evan looked at her and tried to answer, but there were no words. "This is horrible," she said. He nodded.

A sudden explosion rocked the ground beneath them.

Two fighter jets shrieked across the sky, white contrails streaming out from under their wings, and it felt to those on the ground that Coquina had been struck by the fist of God. Shock waves, intangible brick walls, passed through their bodies at seven hundred miles per hour as easily as bursts of light through glass, and flung them headlong, shattering the few car windows left intact.

Seeing Jen's body thrown, leaving her jacket behind, Evan crawled to it and shrugged off his own, trading the bullet-chewed leather for her denim. His mind reeled, like on drunken nights when he clawed at the ground desperately, praying not to lose his grip and fly away. Scrambling for the syringe that was half-full—or half-empty in his eyes—he stuffed it back in the pocket with the souvenir bullet, got to his feet, and ran.

He neither knew nor cared which direction he was headed. He just wanted to get away. All he had were a few shots left in his nine, and Dagger. He dimly noticed that Dark Geiger ran beside him, without any guns at all.

Heather Roma snatched up the TEC-9 again and bolted. Crowe and Seth helped Rabbit drag Jennifer along with them in another direction, just as randomly chosen as the others, when all of them were suddenly struck by another blast's concussion and hurled away like chaff. A black wave crashed over most of them, and they slept a dreamless sleep.

IX

"Que dia chato, meu filho," Teresa sighed.
What a rotten day, my son.

This time, like many others recently when she'd intended to pray to her god, she ended up talking to her ghosts. She stopped when Pedro entered the room, held up one hand that asked him to wait, and then crossed herself reverently with the other.

"Em nome do Pai, e do Filho, e Espírito Santo. Amem."

"We have to go see someone."

"What about Evan? Where is our boy?"

"I don't know yet," he half-lied. He didn't want her to know yet that he was sure Evan was dead, because he wasn't sure. Yet. He took her hand in his.

"Where are we going?" she asked, reaching for the bottle of cachaça and another cigarette. He told her.

"Sta brincando," she said, frozen. You're joking.

A young woman in Basilisk Division stood rigidly at attention in front of Jim Harding, swelling with pride at the importance she felt. She had only been living under the Bridge a few weeks before Evan and Pedro came to save her. It was odd to be here in South Florida, having left only a short time ago, hitching rides and stowing away, and sometimes renting out the doorway to her womb, just to get to California. Finding the Bridge and a home, and then miraculously, a future. And now, right back here.

It was she who'd come up with the emblem for Shiva, the man bursting from his cocoon, and tattooed it on her idol, Seth, with impressive skill. She had been welcomed under the Bridge, the most warmly by him, even though her horribly-scarred face repulsed almost everyone else she'd met along the way. The rest of the world either looked away in disgust or shook its head in pity, but she was immediately a sister of the punks in Hollywood Hardcore.

She'd shaved off all of the beautiful red hair she used to be so vain about, letting the California sun bronze her bald scalp, covered her body with tats after she learned to use the jerry-rigged gun, and gave herself to anyone who'd have her out of gratitude. Now, though, her fiery hair had grown out into a boyish style, and she'd found a better way to repay those who'd saved her from the streets. She became the fiercest of all the students, the quickest learner, and

753

the most fanatically loyal.

"Scarlet," Harding said, calling her by the name she had given herself. "We've heard you know some hippies out in the woods who call themselves the Rainbow People."

"There's a lot of 'em, sir. Up by Ocala, around there. And so far outta town they don't see Saturday night 'til Tuesday."

"Good. We'll need an emissary to them when we go out into the woods. See, it's one thing for all of you to study witch craft out of a survivalist book, and quite another thing to live out there in the boonies. We don't know any Miccosukees, so Indians aren't going to help much—"

"Actually, sir," she interrupted. "I met a couple of them too, when I was living out in the 'Glades. And a few that live around here somewhere, I ran into them at powwows."

"Christ, you're even handier than I thought."

"I'm not just another pretty face, sir."

He smiled at her little joke, admiring her for not being touchy about her scar. The way he used to be about all of his. "How do we find them, then?"

"Got a phone book handy?"

"Smartass."

Congratulating himself on the successful day, the business man who was ultimately in charge of almost every widespread gang relaxed in his favorite armchair. The giant screen television flashing scenes of violence and atrocity before him reflected its light off the snifter in his hand, the only thing Pedro Vizcaya and Teresa de Medieros saw of him when they were ushered into the den. It looked to the widow like the bad guy in those cartoons her children used to watch, always seen only by his gauntleted hand stroking a cat. A yellowish-brown hand dangling over the crimson arm of the chair, with amber liquor swirling in the snifter held by its rim with his fingertips.

How appropriate, she thought.

"A beautiful day out there, isn't it?" he murmured.

"It is, father." Pedro never learned the Japanese word for *padron*, so "father" would have to do.

"And who is this with you? The lucky lady?"

"She is Teresa Vizcaya."

"Ahhh, I didn't know that you two were married already. Congratulations to you both. Now what news do you have?"

'There is so much to tell. All is going very well and I have you to thank for it." Facing the window, he signaled subtly.

Teresa knew much less about her lover than she thought, and was quickly discovering that most of her assumptions had been way off base. For example, her romantic imagination had pictured Pedro studying martial arts in a mist-shrouded temple hewn out of the side of an active volcano, in the middle of a jungle haunted by apes and demons. Not in a bare-bones gym alongside an Australian Aborigine, and thirteen others, many years ago.

"We are not married," she said. "Not yet."

"Oh? But you've already taken his name?"

"My name right now is de Medieros."

"Pretty."

"Doesn't ring any bells?"

"Should it?"

Even though the Basque was a pupil of Han Fei-Tzu's, he and Teresa had been thoroughly searched and passed through a metal detector by Han's paranoid henchmen, before being allowed inside. Pedro had foreseen this; which is why the knife Teresa pulled out from inside her, under her skirt, was carved of wood.

X

Hiding under the pagoda-style eave of Cheng-Du Chinese Restaurant & Lunch Buffet, Jim Crowe and Seth McHale had found occasion to talk, and not since the council of Nicæa were so many issues debated. Crowe found the young man to be even more intelligent than many of his protégés, and Seth quickly began to develop a liking for the imposing man.

What he did not mention, however, were the possibilities he saw in an alliance with Crowe. His teachers had not needed to tell him that being a diamond was not enough, that once he reached that level he'd still yearn for the jeweler's carving knife and rough polishing cloth. But it was best to keep such things to himself until he knew what might be around the corner.

Now, as he watched Jim Crowe administer to Jen, holed up in what had once been a clothing store, he made up his mind. For the lost and wandering "civilized" people, the future was bleak and dismal, but to those who'd follow Crowe, it was gloriously bright.

"She's pregnant," the Woolagaroo said, startling both of the men who crouched nearby.

"Wh-huh? What?" Rabbit stammered.

"Knocked up. Bun in the oven. Expecting."

"But…how the hell could you tell *that?*"

Crowe sighed. "The secrets of the earth were lost when men became wise and foolish."

He had Jennifer lying in her bra and panties on the floor, on top of a pile of clothes from the storeroom. Most of the blood had been cleaned off her, and her shoulder was bandaged up with torn designer underwear. There was a slack forward cant to her belly, which Rabbit had just assumed meant she'd abandoned the crunches routine he had forced upon her. Apparently not. She was semiconscious, drifting in and out of lucidity but her eyes fluttered open at the announcement of her secret.

"It's admirable she's not miscarried," the Aborigine continued. "How far along are you, young lady?"

"Few months," she muttered. "Four, maybe."

"Is it…is it mine?" Rabbit asked.

"Who else have I been with? Nobody. It's yours."

There was a long uneasy silence. Crowe was the only one who seemed happy about this, and finally, he broke the stillness with low chuckle.

"It's auspicious," he said cheerfully. "This could be a very beautiful thing. I'm sure the maternity wards are full, or at least were until today. But people have degenerated in the past century to where it's considered barbaric and unheard of to give birth anywhere except in a sterile hospital room. Wimps! There are still places all over the world today where women would laugh at Lamaze class and scorn those who use painkillers during labor. All those displaced by what's happened today will most likely squeeze out stillborns, but *this* woman won't."

"Why do you think?" Rabbit asked, skeptical.

"Because she will be safe, and prepared, and she's tough."

"Sure, long as we can get her to a sterile hospital room."

"What? No. She'll be the first of her kind in a long time to give birth under the naked sky, and it will be beautiful. It is the way things should be done, and are in my world. Didn't you describe the world as you saw it? Jared, this is it. It's coming. And you are ready. Your eyes are perfect, your allergies cured by surgery and my people's medicine. You have made yourself strong. You have adapted, and you will survive. And necessity will demand that your child does too. This is an all-weather girl you've planted your seed inside, and she can cut it. Can't you, little lady? Or are you too contaminated by the world you grew up in?"

Jennifer didn't answer. Her eyes were wide with fear and pain, but with something else as well. Pride.

"You will be the first," Crowe continued. "A brave little man or woman is growing inside of you, someone who will make us all proud. Someone who will be born into the world as it should be, and who will be the first to carry your people back up the evolutionary ladder. Just imagine suckling your baby on a meadow like a she-wolf, where once only golfers were free to go, and raise it the way all the best of us were. Imagine playing with it in the rain, laughing and dancing like a fool, instead of dropping it off at daycare while you hurry to the job you hate. And now imagine a strong and sharp-minded athlete, warrior, and artist nearing his prime, instead of a surly teenager sneaking cigarettes and popping zits. A son or daughter ready to face down a charging wild boar and stop it in full flight, throw it sideways by the tusks, instead of hide out in the john at a high school dance. Which would *you* rather have?"

Again, Jennifer didn't answer. Crowe turned to Rabbit, seeing the same faint but growing gleam in his eyes as in hers.

"How about you, Jared? Are you content with going back to the world you hated? Where you went out dancing because you thought you must, even though you can't, and you got as drunk as you could so you think you look like Travolta? You want to go back to washing machines, insurance policies, and fast food restaurants? Microwave dinners when you are alone and miserable? I thought you were through with fast food and microwave culture—your half hour dating shows, thirty second sound bites, fat free, low sugar, and 'please hold.' Or have you degenerated also? Tell me."

Rabbit was staring at the floor and all was quiet except for Jennifer's breathing. His eyes eventually drifted over to meet hers. She swallowed. Whispering in hoarse, uncertain breaths, she told him that she was going to have his baby.

"Are you okay with that?" he asked softly.

"*Okay?* It's the most wonderful thing ever. I'm going to make another you, even though you really are an asshole."

"I am, aren't I?"

"Yeah, but I love you. And I want to make more of you, and I'll do that anywhere I can."

He looked up at Crowe, who smiled.

"It's up to you, Jared. Either this, or…"

He didn't need to finish, but he wanted to say something more, so he changed it from "a diseased bisexual weirdo with serious emotional baggage" to "It really doesn't get any better than this, kid. You'll never find anything closer to perfect."

Rabbit looked back at Jennifer, and made up his mind.

"Do you miss your phone?" Crowe asked. Rabbit thought for a moment, and shook his head. "Someone else is going to have all your money. That bother you?"

"Money is useless now. At least it is here."

"Damned right. People are going to lay siege to banks all over the nation, but it will accomplish next to nothing. They'll feel like kings, sitting on all the loot they have plundered from First National Bank of East Bumfuck, until they try to buy something. Sure, people might consider their paper money as backed by yellow dirt in Fort Knox, at least for a little while, but bartering will be the custom, and even gold bricks will be just heavy, useless bricks."

"My money was just for moving around freely in places I resented."

"I know it. I feel the same way. We are rich now in what we'll actually need. Weapons, tools, access to subterranean fall out shelters. Completely self-sufficient, for a while anyway. We will be fine."

"We'll be fine," repeated Rabbit, half to himself. He was pondering the end of the easy life, fine clothes, the constant search for mere objects to be seen with that would define him to others as a person. The end of sleeping with one foot on the floor after drinking all night. Jennifer's eyes were burning into him, praying to whoever would listen that he agreed.

Deep down, this was what she'd always dreamed of.

But the silence lasted too long for Seth to bear.

"Then it's settled. How far away is the church?"

"You see, it's because of boredom that we have so degenerated," a talking head on an unwatched television said.

"We're so *organized* and regulated, with property lines and speed limits and suffocating ordinances, exposed and naked because of mandatory recordings and registrations and census-taking, that we have no room to move and have any real excitement in our lives without breaking some law. The only adventure we're allowed to have is taxed! Regulated, safe, and monitored. At least, this is the sob story of the law-abiding and the God-fearing. The only people who refuse to succumb to this cookie cutter monotony and are not incarcerated, are those politically sanctioned to get away with it. John and Jane Doe cannot even climb up onto a park statue and be romantic without offending everyone in sight and catching at least one charge. But certain minority groups can publicly commit hate crimes and disturb the peace with any number of 'demonstrations' that are the height of poor taste and ill breeding. What they do are just proclamations of identity, licensed by politics and tolerated—even applauded—by the public, because any speaking out against them is forbidden. It's the Emperor's New Clothes. But John Q Whitey doesn't dare represent *his* beliefs and heritage, or demonstrate his own ways. Instead, he lives out his boring life taking his nuclear family on the occasional vacation from the mind-numbing rat race to safe, regulated, orderly theme parks, until the monotony finally gets to him and he just decides, out of the blue, that he's a serial killer. Or a wife-swapper. And his children rebel against the homogenized and regulated life they're confined to and embrace anything that's outrageous.

"But even outrageousness gets boring, and the search for something new has strange horizons. The descent is rapid and in every direction, so the pieces cannot all be retrieved, restored. There is no cure for this cultural rot. There is only one outcome. The fall. The complete collapse of society into anarchy, followed by repeats of the Dark Ages, when all are illiterate and flea-bitten and savage for many generations of short, meaningless lives.

"Now, on the governmental side of this bereavement, we have the same problem in a certain area. It is well-known that we are the mightiest nation on the planet. The few times we have had to prove it were a cinch. There's the problem. As a nation, we don't have to invent practical works of genius to survive anymore, because we already hold the top rank in the food chain. So, at the top, we stagnate. We turn our minds to useless pursuits to feed laziness. Salad shooters. Robot lawn mowers. And we take pills that make us feel better about how miserable we are. Pills made by descendants of Nazi scientists who came here courtesy of Operation Paperclip, pills with side effects like Sudden Rage Syndrome, where we go from perfect calm to righteous indignation to homicidal outrage in the blink of an eye. We have people snapping and shooting up schools because the anxiety meds they were taking programmed them to, and now an entire nation is going out into the streets, to take revenge on each other for lies the media told them.

"Because of boredom."

"Mind if I take a shower?" Dark asked.

Shaitan shook her head. "Can't. There's been no running water for hours. Soon, there will be no electricity." She smiled, as if this were a blessing.

"Shit," Dark grumbled.

"You're clean already," she assured him. "I gave you each two sponge baths."

Both of them remembered, suddenly feeling uncomfortable. A tiny bit aroused, but still embarrassed.

"Why two?" Evan asked.

"You were filthy when we brought you here, so I cleaned you off, at least enough to get the ink to stay on your skin, and then again to wash it off."

"We?"

She nodded, not bothering to explain.

A knock on the door startled them all. Evan reached for his nine-millimeter, which wasn't there, and started looking around frantically for it. Shaitan stayed him.

"Think, Evan. Who would knock after a day like this?"

She left the room, walking quietly to the door, and peered through the eye-hole at ten men and women dressed in black, heavily armed. She dimly recognized the short-haired young woman in front, but could not place her. She opened the door and smiled at them.

"Jehovah's Witnesses carry firearms now?"

A few of them chuckled. The scar-faced redhead extended her hand warmly.

"I doubt you'll remember me, but we met some time ago at a Miccosukee powwow. I really loved your music."

"Well, I don't blame you—I mean, thanks."

Scarface smiled at the squaw's joke, then put on a serious expression, silently announcing that the small talk was over.

"We were told you have one of our people in there, that he was brought here earlier."

"Who told you that?"

"Genevieve Bucktooth. Friend of mine."

"Who sent you in the first place?" Shaitan didn't seem to even see their guns, or the authority that came with them.

"Jim Harding." Without hesitation.

"I've heard that name somewhere."

"He runs with Pedro Vizcaya." Pride, this time.

"You're kidding."

"Oh, you know him?"

"Evan!" Shaitan called. The teenager was against the wall next to the door, just out of sight, trying to listen. The voices were too low to make out, so he had been straining his ears. Now, as he came to the doorway, Shaitan stepped aside so he could see.

"Christ!" Evan laughed. "I am one lucky—"

"You're the kid who came under the Bridge to talk to us!" the redhead exclaimed happily.

"And you are, shit, you're in Dragon, aren't you?"

"Basilisk."

"Right. What the hell are you doing here?"

"Well, we were in the neighborhood."

"I mean, how'd you know to come here?"

"There's an underground railroad, and a lady I know said one of us was here."

"Three of you," Shaitan interrupted. Evan looked at her in surprise.

"Three?"

"Well, there's your friend in there—"

"He's not one of us, he was just with me."

She rolled her eyes. "Oh, excuse me. You know each other, though."

"Yeah okay, so that's two, then. Where's the..." his voice trailed off as he saw someone moving on the couch, out of the corner of his eye. He knew before even looking, but he looked anyway.

Calibos Lugo stared silently up at him.

Simone Brennan still felt the old demons deep inside her, but it was different now. She could no longer remember what had possessed her to give in to them before, and what memories she did have were like half-remembered dreams, or stories told by others, things she could imagine but not remember being a part of. Trying to see any connection with who she used to be was like trying to recognize her sister's skeleton.

Either decades, six months, or two years ago—she could not remember which—she crouched in the moonlight over an opened grave, holding Salomé's skull like Hamlet and Yoric. It wasn't her sister. There were no twisted plots swirling about in the cavity behind the vacant eye sockets. There was no way to envision lipstick on the flesh no longer covering those teeth. Those finger bones never plucked at guitar strings.

She felt nothing for this pile of bones, and she felt nothing for her old life of drugs and sex.

Dumping her twin's earthly remains back into the grave, she defaced the tombstone neighboring Salomé's, spray painting "Arch Stanton" in white across R.I.P. Joe Schmo, and left, thumbing rides to California.

But now, ghosts of her old life came howling back as she stood looking into Shaitan's apartment. The words out of Evan's mouth had frozen her in place.

"We can't leave without finding Rabbit."

"He's prolly dead," the hideous man said quietly.

"Rabbit?" Simone asked.

Both men and the Indian looked at her.

"Yeah, an associate of ours," Evan answered.

"Good-looking, green eyes, evil, about yay tall?"

"Uh, yeah, that's him."

Despite her shock and confusion, Simone's wheels were turning. This day just kept getting better. She started talking, making things up on the spot, a plan forming.

"We gotta find him immediately. Harding said if we didn't come back with him, we might as well not come back at all, so try to remember the last place you seen him." It was hard for her to speak, suddenly.

Rabbit...

"C'mon, we'll retrace your steps."

Just to see him one more time. Maybe get him to take her back, out of guilt for abandoning her.

Maybe kill the son of a bitch.

One or the other.

"Well, if he *is* alive, he'll be on his way to that church the others were talking about. Hey, Zombie!" Evan called.

Dark appeared, moving slowly. "Holy shit," he muttered. "It's dark out."

Evan hadn't noticed either until now. "Time is it?"

"Three in the morning," Shaitan said. "Give or take. I've never believed in having a watch, and I can't see the sun from here, so I'm guessing."

Facetious, Simone thought. Smartass.

Pretty cute, though.

"It's three-seventeen," one of the Basilisks said.

"Great," Evan said. "Look, Zombie, we need you to lead us to that church. You gave me directions, but that's all muddled now."

"I'm not going."

"What?"

"Never again. I'll draw you a map, though."

"Great. Peachy fucking keen. Draw us a map."

Evan was still worried about Lugo, felt his eyes burning into him and tried not to look that way. Just ignore him and maybe he'll go away. He saw three handguns on a drop-leaf table nearby: his Browning, the break-barrel Derringer, and Calibos's Hardballer. Before he could even start toward them, Lugo had already guessed his intentions and called to him.

763

"Blanquito."

Evan froze, not meaning to, but couldn't help it.

"These might come in handy."

Evan's eyes closed, knowing just by the Colombian's tone what he held up, but turning around to look just to see. Lugo's smug grin was held back a few times, him trying to suppress it, but it burst forth as if some kind of pressure had built up behind it and needed release. In his hand, fanned out like playing cards, was all the ammunition that had been found on them. Four of the green shotgun shells, the nearly spent clip from the Browning, and the Hardballer's magazine.

Everyone looked curiously at Calibos, then Evan, and back again. Shaitan started for the couch, but the Colombian jerked his hand close to his chest and snarled at her. Evan felt helpless, just standing there numbly, imploding.

"Knock this shit off," Shaitan demanded. "Whatever it is, I don't care, but knock it off."

Dark was staring at Evan, it not taking a rocket scientist to figure out the situation, or at least the basics. All of the Basilisks, too, had guessed as much as they'd needed to.

"Well?" the sunburned man said. "Are you going to grow a spine or what?"

Evan's head snapped around to him, glaring.

"Hey," Dark continued, spreading his hands. "I'm not the one just standing there. Whatever you've got to do, get on with it."

Shaitan had her hand out expectantly, and Simone rolled her eyes.

"Buncha fucking children we've got here. Look, we going or not?"

The tableau held.

Simone was sorely tempted to give gun butt grille-checks all around and abduct the sunburned guy, and make him lead them to this church she kept hearing about. But the kid was important somehow to the boss man, and Guido over there on the couch was an officer in, what? Griffon? Griffon Division, she thought. One or the other. So, no treason.

"Truce," Evan finally said. "You don't know what all had happened that day. You don't understand why I did what I did."

Calibos glared at him, sitting up and leaning forward. The hate came off of him like steam.

"Mira, you little beetch, pussy-boy! I don geeve a *fock* why chew run! I keel chew!"

"You don't know what they did to the kids—"

"Fock the keeds! They were all sheet, an they die like they deserve to!" Lugo's English was falling apart like it always did when he lost his temper. His accent came out to the point that everyone expected him to say "cockaroaches!" or something like that. Say 'allo to my leetle freng, chew cockaroaches! Instead, he spat out something about "focking keeds with gones getting keeled alla tahng." Then, something about da Pussyboy turn sneetch, focking maricon sneetch. His face began to redden, a forked vein snaking across his forehead. The knuckles of his fists whitened, the cartridges and magazines spilling to the floor.

"What kids?" one of the Basilisks asked.

"The Familiars," Evan answered, trying to keep his voice calm, not taking his eyes off Calibos. "They all get sacrificed when they're ten, get chopped up—"

Calibos snapped, coming up off of the couch and leaping, his face twisted with murderous rage. Before Evan even had a chance to take a step back, the Colombian had tackled him to the floor. Rising up on his knees, straddling him, Lugo wound back and started whaling on him, spit foaming about his lips and spraying with every hissing breath.

Turning this way and that to take all of the punches on the top or side of his head, Evan flailed about desperately.

Shaitan and Dark both started forward to help him, but Simone's voice brought them up short, snapping something about letting them go at it. When they looked at her, at the ugly smile splitting her horribly scarred face, and at the appreciative expressions on those behind her, they backed off.

"Let the best man win," Simone said harshly.

She had already made up her mind that Guido, here, or whatever his name was, would get a bullet in his head the second it went too far, but she still wanted to see a good fight. See the kid prove himself. Collect yourself, kid, she thought. C'mon, those punches don't hurt. Act like a diamond.

And Evan did, finally. Planting his feet firmly on the floor, he used them to slide a little bit farther under Lugo, get his center of gravity under his assailant, then rock his legs up and forward, trying to wrap his feet around Lugo's neck and slam him backwards.

Calibos reacted too quickly, though, and leaned forward just in time, his weight steadied by one hand coming down on the carpet. Leaving his armpit exposed. There was no leverage for an angle on the ribs, but Evan brought his fist straight up into the armpit, then outward on the way down.

It doesn't hurt much to be punched there, but the whole arm goes instantly numb, and the arm Lugo was balancing himself on buckled. On the way down, Evan's fist swatted it away, throwing the Colombian off slightly. But not enough. The other hand grabbed at the teenager's head, half to steady, half to twist a handful of his curly black hair. Evan growled, jabbing his extended middle finger up into Lugo's eye, blinding him momentarily.

The hand holding him by the hair let go to press against the stinging eye, the numbed hand coming up after it an instant slower. Rocking upwards from the waist, Evan cupped his own hands and slammed them against the sides of Lugo's head, boxing his ears. The loud clap inside his skull thundered, the fluid in his ears sloshing about sickeningly. He slumped backwards, dizzy.

Again, Evan put his back on the floor and swung his legs up, hooking his feet around Calibos' head and slammed him down. Wriggling out from underneath and bolting to his feet, he kicked Calibos savagely in the crotch, doubling him up like a millipede, stretched him back out with a kick to the face, and fell on top of him, fingers digging into his throat. He got a firm grip on the larynx, dug in farther anyway, squeezed, and tore out Calibos Lugo's throat, splattering Dark Geiger's pants leg with blood.

All of the spectators stared in horrified fascination as the Colombian thrashed weakly about on the beige carpet, at the quickly widening pool of crimson like a growing halo behind his head. The panicked and anguished tears in his wide eyes, and the desperate gulps and chokes for air.

They all stood silently, looking down and watching him die slowly, Evan belatedly realizing that he still held part of the man's pulped throat in one hand, and dropping it quickly.

Not quite a minute passed, but it seemed to take eons for Lugo's eyes to glaze over and stare off into nothing. Still, no one spoke.

Evan looked up and around, briefly at each face, stepped over the corpse on his way to the couch, and snatched up the gold tooth rosary that lay like a coiled snake on the coffee table. The teeth rattled together loudly in the uneasy silence. He raised it with both hands, slipping it over his bowed head, and dropped it down around his neck. Bent down to pick up the ammunition Lugo had dropped, and when he straightened, the look in his eyes was cold and empty.

"Don't we have to be somewhere?" he asked.

XI

Now, on their way to the Church of Adam, Rabbit's mind was alive with thoughts of the future. He made plans to loot one of the larger franchise bookstores, those treasure troves of knowledge, for grimoires of horticulture, since all of the spices and seasonings he would need would no longer be dependably found on supermarket shelves. He had a family to think of.

Damn, he thought. I'll have to learn how to cure ham to make prosciutto. I'll have to learn how to milk a cow and process what I get to make bechamel sauce. Christ, I'll have to find a cow first…well, at least I'll never be bored. Frustrated, but never bored.

It was the dead of night, and the distant roar of anarchy still came to them from all directions. They traveled like rats through a dark house, following the shadows and scurrying across open spaces very quickly and at intervals. One at a time, they would wait with the patience of rocks, surveying every visible nook and cranny before exposing themselves. Tedious, but necessary. Jen may have been showing a great deal of admirable stoicism, but taking to the roofs again would've surely been pushing it.

Once, crouching behind a wreck that may have once been a towncar, Crowe hissed at the other three, and they stiffened. It was times like these that Jennifer was grateful their hideout earlier had been a clothing store, with black garments of her size there for the taking.

Looking about, though, she could see nothing. Neither could Seth or Rabbit, but Crowe made a few gestures to the latter and melted away into the darkness. If the streetlights had been on, maybe they could have seen him glide into an alley nearby and scale the rear wall of the building behind them, but as it was, he had simply vanished. They strained their eyes and ears, not seeing any sign of an enemy, and Jen was just about to slump against the car in exhaustion when she was startled back to vigilance.

A low thunk from somewhere above them and down the road slightly, and a flying rope of blood spattered wetly on the sidewalk. It wasn't until then, when the silence fell, that they realized crickets had been chirping, and now stopped. They sensed movement across the street, half a block down, but it was too subtle to recognize.

Minutes passed, a palpable tension thickening the air, when suddenly the stillness was shattered by a racket of metal garbage cans falling ove. A tall white man appeared out of the gloom of the next alley down, clutching the ribs of his left side and falling against the wall at a bank's corner.

More movement across the street, a starting and a stopping, one man reacting and another's hand restraining him. A second figure came walking out of the alley behind the first, slowly, and with deliberate steps and slumped shoulders. He swayed as if drunk, leaning one way and then too far in the other, overcorrecting himself. In the faint light of the moon a ghastly wound could be seen—his skull had been split to the teeth. He was already dead but still moving, and staggered into the first who was trying to push himself off of the wall and into the street. The two of them collapsed.

Now, from the darkness peeled a figure out across the street; the man who'd shaken off the other's hand now hurried towards the two who'd fallen not too far from Rabbit, Jen, and Seth. Before he was even halfway across Driftwood Avenue, he jerked backwards off his feet, thrashing in agony on the pavement.

The night came suddenly alive with the chatter of gunfire, their muzzle flashes illuminating panicked faces. They sprayed the whole area down with automatic weapons, making themselves perfectly visible, and it was their bad example that made their targets afraid to return fire and give their position away.

But one by one, they fell, screaming.

When the last assault rifle clattered to the sidewalk, Seth and Rabbit hurried over to retrieve the weapons and ammunition. There were four men dying in the gloom from the sting of blowpipe darts, dipped in the deadliest animal toxin known to man, that of the tiny South American "poison arrow" frogs, of which a mere 0.0000004 ounces can kill a human being. Yet not render the meat inedible.

Whoever they were, Rabbit was pulling the darts out of them to salvage whatever juice might be left. Crowe had only been able to get his hands on three frogs, enough to harvest a hundred twenty darts' worth, so as much had to be saved as possible. A fine example of the triumph of low-tech over high.

The Woolagaroo came out of the alley near Jen, stepping over the two bodies, and glanced her way in time to see her slump against the side of the car, slide down it, and crumple to the pavement.

Before they left, Shaitan let the Basilisks all strip off their uniforms from the waist up—jackets, shirts, and Kevlar, all of which were sweltering in the summer heat—and towel themselves off with wet rags. Her fridge had been stocked horse-chokingly full of ice bags from the machine outside the nearby gas station, and with several of those bags now melted in a bucket, the water made for a pleasantly cold whore-bath.

The Basilisk women were unashamed of their nakedness, and the men all honorably pretended not to notice, except for Evan. The teenager found himself staring at the spokeswoman. Scarlet's body was covered with tattoos and cigarette burns. The traditional sacred heart, with fire belching from the aorta and girdled by a crown of thorns, stood out between her shoulder blades. On one side of her neck, chrome dice were wreathed in hotrod flames. On the other side, also ablaze, a green sparkplug. Lavender octopus tentacles writhed up out from behind her belt buckle toward her navel, making Evan wonder what the hell she had below. Some Celtic writing was around the navel itself—*"fighte fuaghte."* Plenty of tribal designs, which is a common tattoo, but isn't of any tribe in particular.

Cigarette burn scars formed constellations in all of the spots undecorated. Evan thought the girl must have been seriously disturbed to mutilate herself like that since the last time he'd seen her.

"Jesus Christ, kid!" one of the Basilisk men exclaimed. All turned to see what he was angry about, then frowned at Evan in disgust.

"Get enough of an eyeful?" another one asked.

Simone glowered, but Evan made no apology.

"You've changed an awful lot, Scarlet."

"What?"

"You used to only have burns on your left hand," he said, pointing at all the scars. "No tattoos, either. It took a while to recognize you, but I remember now."

"From where?"

"You were a model. I saw you on magazine covers, and then once you danced naked at this private party I was at."

"I didn't do kiddie parties, killer." Her voice hardened.

"It wasn't a kiddie party, Scarlet. It was a blooding party. For my best friend, who'd just made his bones. Domingo de Medieros."

She frowned off into space for a moment.

"You came to dance for us, and took D'ingo into the bedroom."

Simone's eyes filled with tears, lips tightening into a thin, down-curving line. She didn't remember that particular party, just like she didn't remember a thousand others, but she knew that they'd happened. Those nights had all run together like ice cubes melting into whiskey. Like coke and heroin mixing in a hot spoon. She shook her head and sniffed.

"I had such a crush on you back then, Scarlet," he continued. "Broke my heart when I finally met you and you went with D'ingo, him bragging to me about it later."

Her eyes shut, squeezing out runnels that coursed down her face like cheetah's tears, and she bowed her head.

"Yunno," Evan kept going, unaware of how much this hurt her. "I killed for the first time the very next day, hoping they'd throw me a party and get you to come again. Well, of course that wasn't the *only* reason I shot the fucker, so don't think I'm—"

"Evan," Shaitan said.

"I saw you in an ad in the back of a magazine, too. What were you doing? Had it gotten that bad?"

"Evan!"

Startled, he looked up at Shaitan.

"Shut up," she said curtly.

He thought for a moment, then it dawned on him. And suddenly he remembered the phone pressed so hard to Simone's face in the picture, that phone sex ad, and saw now the scar that she'd been hiding underneath it. And he realized, yes, it had gotten that bad.

"Shut up," she said again as he opened his mouth.

Simone ground her teeth audibly, then shook her head as if to clear it, putting on a stoic face.

"Those days are long gone," she said. "And they won't ever come again. Ever."

The rest of the Basilisks, who had looked embarrassed for her, took on a new light into their eyes, their own private vows echoing hers.

"Domingo's dead," Shaitan said quietly. "He lived by the sword and he died by the sword. I loved him. But he's dead. Let him stay that way, Evan."

The Basilisk who'd first spoken hastily put his shirt back on and picked up his vest by a shoulder strap, sensing the need to leave soon.

"C'mon guys, we don't have all night."

The others nodded and followed suit, one of them gesturing toward Lugo's corpse.

"You want us to dispose of him for you?" he asked Shaitan, who shook her head.

"No, I need to pray over him, then I'll be leaving anyway. This can be his tomb."

The soldier nodded and pulled on his jacket. Dark, who'd been sitting on the couch, looked curiously at the Iroquois woman. He had already drawn out a map and given it to Evan, and had been wondering what in the hell to do with his life. Now he found himself staring at a woman who practiced ways more backward and primitive than he had ever seen, and he wondered if she might be on to something.

Evan and the soldiers said their goodbyes and left.

"I'll be leaving soon also," Shaitan said to Dark.

"Yeah...I don't have any idea where I'm headed, though."

"If you're smart, out into the woods." She went into the corridor between the bedroom and the bath, opening the two slatted doors of the linen closet. Standing up on her toes, she reached for a bow on the top shelf. It was a plastic and fiberglass bow, of the type sold in the Sporting Goods section, with extremely strong and durable wire strung through wheels at both ends, and a molded grip. Behind it came a quiver full of arrows, synthetically fletched, stainless-steel tipped. Then a jabali knife, sheath, and belt with many pouches.

Dark smiled when she came back with her arsenal.

"Impressive."

"You ain't seen nothing yet."

"I'll bet...hey, can I ask you something."

"Shoot."

"Where do you stand, religion-wise?"

She stared at him a moment, inscrutable.

"I mean, you said something about praying."

"Wishing him well to whoever might listen," she said.

"Oh, not like a god or anything."

"My people believe in a Great Spirit, sure. He's just some entity that's in charge of everything. Why?"

"Well, you could say I'm comparison shopping."

"For a creed?"

"Yes."

"Waste of time. Just live your life right."

"Yeah, but what's right? Everyone has a different opinion of how to live, and I'm trying to find out who comes closest. What do you think?"

"Me? Well, I think that, when you get right down to it, impatience and laziness are the two traits all sins spring from. Work hard, and in everything you do, imagine that the person you respect the most can see you. Imagine having to explain your actions to someone whose opinion of you matters, and that will seriously cut down on your bad habits.

"Religion is to deceive us about what cannot be answered: Death. The truth is, we're screwed by having enough brains to know the Question and be stumped by it. The only thing we can do is accept that we will end, and live the best that we can until then, not be afraid to dance at the party, strive, and fulfill all our dreams, even the most trivial ones. Stop smoking so you can live longer and better, and just in case there is a Heaven and Hell, play by the rules while doing it.

"The only way to live now is to know that your life can be snuffed out at any second, so live as if it will. Be at your best always, never be afraid to live up to the highest standard—but don't do this at the expense of anyone else, just in case there is something after death, because there very well might be. There can't *not* be a God, because we're here, and the stakes are too high to bet against that God not having some Divine Plan, so be good."

"That's what you believe?"

"Mm-hmm. But keep in mind I'm not an educated philosopher. I'm probably not qualified to tell you what to do or how to think. I'm just a woman. A savage. I work hard, doing honest manual labor when I'm not singing for my band, and I am happy. I don't drink, gamble, take drugs, fight without reason, or have wanton sex, and I have a fuller, more satisfying life than most."

"Egad."

"I know. It's hard for many people to wrap their minds around. It seems boring to you."

"Oh, good, cultural stereotyping. My favorite."

"That's not what I mean. I'm sorry it came out that way. I really see no difference between people of other races. It's different cultures, and their ways that seem foolish to me but not to them.

But you want to know about how to live? Don't kill if you don't have to. Don't steal. Don't rape. Work hard, deal honestly with other people, and whatever you do, do it bravely and with your whole heart. Those are rules that people of all faiths can live by. How's that?"

"It'll do."

"Good."

A quick search around the immediate area and Seth found three pickup trucks, all of them the type used for towing locomotives or pulling moons out of orbit. They were locked, but he didn't waste any time running back to fish keys out of dead men's pockets.

Backhanding the butt of his gun through one of the driver's side windows, he reached in to unlock the door, climbed in, and pried the cover off the steering column. Cutting and crossing the proper wires, he turned the engine over and jammed it into First.

With no regard for quiet anymore, he screeched around a corner onto Driftwood Avenue and charged up the street to where Crowe was chanting some kind of barbaric shit over Jennifer's prostrate body. Rabbit didn't know what the hell his mentor was up to, but if the devil-devil man was right about everything else, he at least deserved the benefit of the doubt on stuff like this. The Fordzilla pickup jarred angrily to a stop beside them, and Seth leaned over to fling the passenger side door open. Gathering up his woman, Rabbit placed her gently inside the cab, and vaulted up over the side into the back.

Crowe hurried around to take Seth's place, and a moment later they were howling down the stygian streets toward the church.

At that same moment, dark shapes were melting out of the forest and into the parking lot of the Church of Adam. Besides the chirping of crickets and the distant mayhem, the only sounds were the hisses and rattles of spray paint cans, the marbles inside of them knocking around to loosen more color, short and long hisses sounding like Morse code as one shape after another came out of the dark between the trees.

A group of young men, possibly teenagers, put their nicknames and attempts at art on the white walls of the Church of Adam. Six of them, with their oversized pants sagging, held up by one hand while the other defaced a church. Be it a cathedral, mosque, temple, or den of filth and evil, it didn't matter; they thought it was a church, and even though two of the six vandals actually showed talent, the quick-drying paint on the wall would never show their immortal mark, mixed as it suddenly was by their blood, chunks of brain matter, and shards of bone.

One of their killers, a young woman, muttered something about Ozymandias, but was interrupted by sharp cries of terror. The others had recoiled as if stricken, gaping wide-eyed at the red spots of lights that played about on their chests.

They crouched, weapons at the ready, heads darting about trying to find their enemies. The one who'd begun to speak kept her head and decided the Picassos at her feet would not have had friends with laser scopes on their "gats."

"C'mout, c'mout, wherever you are," she called.

Another young woman's voice answered from above.

"Will the real Warren Haggerty please stand up?"

And the Satanist on the ground went still.

"...Is Rabbit not down there?" the sniper asked.

"Who...uh, who wants to know?"

"Who wants to know who wants to know?"

"Fuck, who are you goddamned people?"

"We'll ask the questions. And we already have."

"Shit." The girl looked helplessly around her.

"Look," Evan's voice called down. "Do you all go to this church? Are you down there with Wooly-guru, or whatever his name is? Or are you just wandering around shooting people?"

"We're Adamists!" one of the men shouted, a challenge.

"Okay, we're getting somewhere. Yahoo. Have you heard from Crowe lately, and is Rabbit still with him?" he asked with a patronizingly patient tone.

"None of your business!"

'Okay, we gonna have to kill that one," the woman said.

"No!" Evan shouted. He had seen enough blood for one day, drawn by friendly fire. To the figures below him on the ground, he called urgently. "Christ! We need to find our goddamned friend, okay? Can we cut the bullshit for once? Is our buddy coming, or are we getting eaten alive by mosquitoes for nothing?"

Audrey Gray called up to them.

"Let me get this straight. *Rabbit,* as in Warren Haggerty, is with Brother Crowe, and you, his friends, are waiting for them to come here? I got that right?"

"Yeah."

"Nobody has to kill anybody?"

"I don't think so. But don't quote me on that."

The noise of a speeding truck came in the distance, getting closer very quickly.

"We haven't heard from Brother Crowe since this afternoon, and we don't know anything about—"

"Waitaminute!" the sniper woman's voice shouted. "Who is that down there?"

"We're Adamists. We already established that."

"No, I mean..." The roar of the truck changed as it downshifted into a turn, and came toward them. The wash of headlights swung along the hedge that lined the driveway into the parking lot, and a moment later, Fordzilla swerved into sight with two men in black hanging onto the floodlights from behind. The truck screeched to a halt, and the two leaped to the ground, noticing the situation belatedly.

"Halt! Who goes there?" a Basilisk called out as the engine died and the driver door swung open.

"Shut the fuck up, that's who!" Crowe roared as he glared up at the snipers. "I got no time for bullshit right now!" He turned around and scooped Jennifer's limp body out of the cab, throwing her over his shoulder. "The door better be open when I get to it, or I'm—"

A dozen parishioners scrambled toward the back door of the vestry, eager to roll out the red carpet and appease their lord. The snipers all turned to Evan, who grinned and nodded. Seth was staring up at them, until one of the Basilisks shouted "Shiva!" and brandished his minisub. Seth raised his own in acknowledgement, rather casually, and followed Crowe and Rabbit inside.

"All right," Simone said to Evan. "How the fuck do we get back down from here?"

There was no electricity, so the Adamists swept into the church with their lighters flickering at the candles while Crowe carried Jen down the aisle. He laid her gently but with haste upon the altar, underneath the inverted cross, and barked orders at his flock. The Basilisks came in to frown at the scene before them, eyes straining to pierce the gloom.

"Rabbit?" Evan said, unconsciously being quiet.

One of the figures by the altar turned and was silent for a long moment. "Who's calling?"

"It's Evan."

"Whew! Good, you made it. Is that all our people with you?"

"Yeah, they were sent to find us."

"Good. Mission accomplished. Now go home."

"What?"

"I've got more important things to do, now you all just run along." There was a nervous edge to his voice.

Somebody pushed his way through the crowd of Basilisks with an armload of cold plastic containers, the blood of unwilling donors. Behind him came two more carrying an IV set carried between them.

"Hey, Rabbit," Simone said. "Long time no see."

Rabbit frowned, unable to recognize the voice.

"My name's Jared," he said, correcting her for his own sake. He didn't want to be "Rabbit" anymore.

"And mine's not Salomé," she answered.

Audrey turned slowly from her spot at a cluster of candles. Jared rummaged through his memory.

"Did you miss me?" Simone asked.

He was sure he'd heard that name some...where.

"How have you been?" Simone asked, her voice thick. In her Man-hating phase, especially under the Bridge, she loved to quote Jiang Qing, Evil Bitch-whore Wife of Mao Tse-Tung: "Man's contribution to human history is nothing more than a drop of sperm." Truth was, she'd hated men only because she couldn't have one of them, and that very one now stood before her. And he didn't even remember who she was.

"Salomé...?"

Audrey Gray was making her way between two pews toward the aisle. Evan stared at his former crush. Jared's mind clicked, and he straightened. Sneered wryly.

"Figures."

Simone's mind was made up right then by the tone of his voice, and she stepped forward into the vaulted hall, her Calico coming up.

"Sam?"

She glanced at the shape coming toward her.

Jared's raised left arm halted, hand empty.

"Who's that?" Simone asked.

Audrey didn't answer. Just kept coming. Thrown caution to the wind and was about to blow her cover. Seeing red.

Some other Adamist elbowed his way through and started down the aisle with his arms full of first aid shit, bumped into Simone, and she wound up with her Calico to grill-check him savagely.

It happened so suddenly, in the darkness, that no one was sure afterwards who fired first.

Seeing Simone's gun move quickly, deep-cover operative Audrey Gray squeezed a double-tap, hitting her former lover in the armored midsection. Punched backwards by the volley, Simone crashed into three of the Basilisks, the other six opening fire, startled. The gloom was split by deafening noise and muzzle flashes, a terrible hail of bullets chewing the wooden pews and walls apart.

Splinters, plaster dust, and chunks of candle wax danced in the strobe as the Adamists dove for cover. They popped up here and there in between benches or against the walls, returning fire.

Jim Crowe, leaned over the altar, paused to glare over his shoulder, his teeth bared. Jared and Seth snatched Jennifer and dragged her onto the dais to the lee of the altar, upsetting the IV stand and the two assistants who manned it. Crowe shook his head in disgust and wonder, joining the others in shelter. Unclasping his binoculars and switching on Night Vision, he saw what was happening to his church.

The flames spitting from gun barrels were blinding in the green light of the lenses, painting bright purple blotches across his retinae, so he only got a quick glimpse. But it was enough.

The plaster volutes atop his decorative columns crumbled apart, leaving clouds of dust to swim down lazily after them. The pendentives were pockmarked with bullet holes. The dark wood pews were chewed up like a horny stallion's stall door, and draped here and there with corpses. He sat back down.

Seth and Jared helped the other two reassemble the IV, and held the bag to compensate for the rig being horizontal now, trying to find the level they needed to siphon the blood into Jennifer. As soon as they had everything situated, Jared had time to turn his head and scowl at the stone altar, trying to see through it, putting together what was going on at the other side.

So, your name's not Salomé...

It had been more than a year, but grudges don't see any length of time. He'd been suspicious then, a nagging doubt in the back of his head whispering that something was seriously amiss. But he'd just suffered catastrophically from a deep betrayal; a whore named Layla, a snitch, a narc, a heartbreaker. He was sorely in need of a rebound. And he'd milked the rebound slut for all she was worth, nipping whatever long-con scheme she had in the bud by manipulating her emotions and turning the tables on her. But she'd come back to haunt him. And it was a thicker plot than he'd known, or even imagined.

All the discrepancies in her stories came flooding back as ricochets whined and rang over his head.

What a narcotics detective had said to her once behind St. Ignatius. The scars on the backs of her hands. Certain expressions, verbal tics, things that identical twins do not share no matter how alike they are. And the familiarity with which she'd held "her sister's" gun.

He snatched the binoculars out of Crowe's hand, felt for the strap that would bind them to his head.

"Since when are _you_ the surgeon?" the Aborigine growled.

Jared ignored him, fastening the headset and lowering it over his eyes. He checked on Jennifer, placing his fingers under her jaw line, saw she was asleep and calm, and plucked an instrument out of his belt. It resembled the little mirror on a stick that dentists use to see the backs of their patients' teeth, only the mirror was convex for a wider view, and the stem was telescopic. His few colleagues used to berate him for carrying such things with him everywhere he went, but experience had shown him often enough that it's not when you plan for shit like this to happen that shit like this tends to happen. Ditto for the telescopic magnet-on-a-stick for retrieving fallen vital tiny components of Whatever in cramped spaces in a pinch. And syringes of adrenaline. All of the "just in cases" that he refused to leave home without.

Using his slightly-convex-mirror-on-an-extendable-stick as a periscope, he carefully examined the scene, figuring out who was who as best he could.

The instant the firing began, Evan had leaped backward, colliding with a Basilisk behind him, and was knocked to the floor by another staggering from three quick shots in the torso. Simone

779

rolled sideways, cursing from the pain of impact, not having any clue that the second time she'd taken bullets with Kevlar on had been from the same person as the first.

The shooter, posing as Deirdre Leigh this time, in total ignorance of the old rules of alias-picking, had leaped sideways to fall between two pews.

Most shots fired by either side were deflected by body armor, since they were all aimed at the spaces where muzzle flashes had just been seen, and many of those were hip shots, but it still took less than a minute for almost everyone shooting to drop. The silence that fell after the last report was long and tense. No one living was anxious to move. Except Jared.

Moving silently along the wall, past tapestries that concealed entrances to other rooms, after carefully stepping over the chancel rail, Jared picked his way to the rear of the hall. Ahead of him, crawling quietly through the wreckage and over the dead and dying, Simone tried to sneak up on him. Between the two of them, inching forward, Audrey/Deirdre/Madeleine /Layla crept perpendicular to them, trying to intercept Simone. All of them half-assuming each other was alive, but hoping they weren't.

Back behind the altar, Seth and both Adamists all sparked their lighters to give Crowe something to see by, and he continued his ministrations. Hearing them, Simone quickened her pace and accidentally put her hand down on a severed six inches of candle stick propped diagonally against a dead man.

The snap of it made Audrey catch her breath and proceed more cautiously.

With Jared watching them both, he arranged to meet with them just a moment after they met. He stepped out of the way to avoid the line of fire, and moved behind the next pew up from Audrey.

Somehow, even over the smells of cordite, blood, and the involuntary farts of the newly dead, the two women recognized each other's body odor, and froze.

"Simone?" Audrey whispered, her mind suddenly changing, as women's sometimes do. The fragrance of her, and her voice in the darkness, completed the thought that had been interrupted earlier.

"Layla?"

Jared twitched, almost imperceptibly, and turned to look even more closely at the longer-haired woman. It was impossible to tell what new color her now-wavy locks were, but the profile was pretty close. The cheeks were a bit chubbier, the nose bent slightly where it must have been broken.

But it was her.

Old feelings welled up inside of him, threatening to steal his sense, corrupt his judgment. But he choked them down, reminding himself that any kind of sentimental hesitation in life or death situations is always fatal. Ditto stupid one-liners. Ditto gloating before execution. Just do it. Shoot them.

But he was interrupted by Layla's voice.

"Small world, eh, Sam?" It made this throat close.

Simone was trying to bring her Calico around as quietly as she could.

"Are we on different sides again, Layla?"

Layla was doing the same thing as Simone.

"I don't think so. Not after what happened today. Is that Rabbit you were talking about really our Rabbit?"

"That's the rumor."

"Where do you stand with him?"

"If he isn't already dead, I'ma kill the fucker."

"You mean it this time?"

"I haven't decided yet."

Jared reached toward Sam's face.

"You lied to me before," Layla reminded her.

"Sorry." She planted one hand and slowly began to rise, and Audrey/Deirdre/Madeline/Layla's Heckler & Koch MP-10 moved the final inch to finally face the direction Simone's voice had come from. Then, she gave in to the temptation that is every movie villain's undoing. She paused long enough to say something coldhearted before firing.

"Sorry's not good enough."

She squeezed the trigger, the minisub bucking and Simone losing her balance trying to get out of the way. The bullet stream passed just underneath her, but the bucking of the gun brought the shots higher. Planting her foot against the wall and pushing hard, she held herself against the edge of the pew, only three feet away from Audrey. With that leverage, she held her Calico over the molded armrest and pointed it down, firing blindly.

The first two bullets hit the back of Audrey's right leg, splattering it, severing the shin a few inches below the knee.

Shrieking horribly, Audrey jerked up and backwards, her gun clattering to the floor, and she collapsed. Doubling up, Simone fell onto the floor and rolled to her feet, aiming at the bloodcurdling screams.

She fired, emptying her magazine into Audrey's head and shoulders. It took less than a second to waste the last few bullets, and in that time she saw Jared standing before her out of the corner of her eye, illuminated by the flames spitting out of her weapon.

His arm extended, his hand was almost touching her face. Then all was black again except for the purple blotches, the afterimages, and she recoiled.

For a fleeting instant, Jared wanted her to see the silenced barrel of Switchblade snap out of the cover of his sleeve and into his hand. He wanted to her to say something like "Yeah, you *would* have a gun like that." Or something. Anything.

She did say, what they always say when they're going for their backup piece: "Wait, listen, I can explain."

At which time, he was supposed to say "You have three seconds. Start talking," and she'd say something slick and get the drop on him. Or he should say something slick instead and shoot her. But then she could beat him to the punch and get him, or the gun would jam, or some shit like that.

So, instead, Jared just shot her in the face.

XII

Following Crowe's directions, Jared searched a room hidden behind one of the tapestries, found the emergency generator, and turned it on. So as not to be blinded when the lights came on, he took off the goggles before even reaching for a light switch. The fluorescents nervously flickered to life, and there was much rejoicing.

Jennifer's condition was stabilized, and Evan had appeared by the time Jared made it back to her side.

"Friendly fire's a bitch, ain't it?" the teen said.

Crowe scowled, shaking his head, and held out his hand to Jared. "Gimme a drink, kiddo."

His pupil brought out a hip flask and tossed it over, leaning heavily against the altar.

"Anybody have a cigarette? Jesus Christ, I don't think I've ever needed one this bad."

"You still smoke?" Crowe asked. "Uh-unh. You're quitting as of now. We're not going traipsing all over the countryside looking for cigarettes every time you start nicking."

"No, we're not. Because we're going to be packing a dozen cartons with us. Now, who has a goddamned smoke?"

"Cigarettes are for the civilized. They're for people who *don't* have to run for their lives every day in the real world, where coming in second means ending up as dinner for someone who doesn't smoke. Because there is no more civilization, there will be no more stores to buy cigarettes, and when you run out you will become a psycho in search of them, and even if you find them, there's no room for weakness. Anybody lets him have a cigarette will get kneecapped."

"Don't listen to him—"

"Boys," Jennifer said sternly, and they both smiled down at her.

In Crowe's cottage, they all took weapons down from the walls and swung them at invisible enemies. Jared played with the Indian bhuj and the cooper's adze, and Seth chose a kitana and the shorter sword that went with it, helping himself also to the pair of sai even though he didn't know shit about how to use them. The two looked like kids in a candy store.

More Adamists were showing up, congregating out in the parking lot and sharing accounts of their adventures, and Evan was antsy about getting home. He'd already been disappointed —again—by people deciding not to accompany him, and could think of nothing to do but curse at them until Crowe told him to get lost.

"And no, you can't have any of our guns, kid."

Evan ended up leaving alone with one reloaded Calico that had belonged to a Basilisk, his good ol' trusty Browning, and Dagger with four measly shells.

He walked through the shattered city, marveling at how it had changed in just one night, until the sun came up. He was halfway to the motel that served as Base when a kid his age stepped out from behind a corner store; a black dude in a Coquina County Jail suit of orange coveralls, with hotdog rolls of fat stacked up on the back of his neck, his shaven head grotesquely wrinkled as a sharpei's.

The guy from a year ago, behind the Git n' Split, who had chased him down in a Cadillac.

The guy who'd gotten away.

Before Evan could bring the Calico down from where it rested on his shoulder, and get his finger in the trigger guard, a dozen more Bacalous appeared behind Sharpei.

Seeing him, they whooped like hounds catching sight of a rabbit. Wide-eyed, Evan swung the Calico around to aim it at them, seeing more come out of the woodwork. Blacks, whites, cholos, two Asians, several girls of different colors. All armed. Heavily.

Evan squeezed the trigger at the crowd.

Sharpei's teeth were bared as he side-stepped, his sawed-off pump shotgun coming up, when the first of Evan's bullets glanced off of his hip, shattering it. The jailbird was yanked around by the shot, twisting in the air as he fell. The bullet rebounded into another one's crotch. The second bullet got that same guy in the belly. And that was the last of them.

The gun jammed like an engine seizing.

Terror gripped Evan, filling his bowels with ice.

He turned and ran.

Teresa jumped nervously when her phone rang, and her glass of cachaça fell from her nerveless fingers. She had replayed the scene in her head a hundred times, the look on Han Fei-Tzu's face as she cut his throat.

The squadron of bodyguards gunned down outside. Her reaching into the wound to tug the gurgling man's tongue out in a Colombian necktie. Pedro beside her.

"Sorry, father," he said. "But I had to draw the line."

She answered the phone, fishing another cigarette out of her pack.

"*Mamãe?*" her daughter's voice asked.

"*Colmeia,*" she answered. "Beehive," the nickname Abuela had given her granddaughter after she'd returned from Ibiza, a whirlwind of activity.

"*Mamãe,* I had to get out of town, things got so crazy up here. People are rioting!"

"I know. Where are you at now?"

"I'm at a boarding house in the middle of nowhere. The power's out, so I can't watch the news. The radio, all it's playing is this one song Maya did, over and over, it's weird. *Mamãe,* what's going on?"

"Honey, stay right where you are. Pedrito has a helicopter and will come and get you. Now, give me directions."

Mariana did, and before she hung up, she asked if everything was all right down there. Teresa paused.

"...Yes, baby. Finally. Everything is great."

She hung up, put the cigarette back in its pack, and twisted the cork back into the bottle.

XIII

In the Coquina Mall, trapped inside of a designer clothing store, a small child stared up at the plate glass front wall, as if at a mural. On the other side, cheeks ballooning from mouths pressed against the glass—which fogged here and there from the breath of those still living—was a frozen collage of people, either dead or dying from suffocation, crushing, or trampling, some with their ribcages slowly giving way and cracking with a long-awaited but still sudden violence.

The glass creaked, and it creaked again with the strain, but still the child stared in speechless wonder.

I-95 was congested from the consequences of the crazed driving of people trying not only to escape the city, but enter it, coming by the thousands to loot and pillage, or at least just see the sights and experience a city in murderous chaos.

Downtown, buzzards browsed among the dead.

Somewhere, in the haze of the stench and drifting smoke, dogs growled at one another viciously over a ripe dish.

A woman lay whimpering next to the broken body of her child, blood drying from her ears and nostrils, her head twisted at a grotesque angle. The baby's greenish skin was swelling from bacterial gas, eyes bulging from pressure inside his skull, tongue lolling out of bluish lips, and purge fluid draining from his nose and mouth. The miniature Ku Klux Klan hood he'd worn that morning lay crumpled and stained beneath him.

Blood pooled underneath the body of a man next to her, snaking its way between the cobblestones.

Bloody hands grasped at the thick air, and unseen mouths groaned sprays of scarlet mist.

With the heat of stagnant dying breath on the back of her neck, Heather Roma awoke in a sea of corpses, gagging on the stench, raised herself, and leaned back against a plastic police riot shield propped up by a dead man. She tugged a broomstick out from under him, one that had been sharpened into a makeshift spear, planted the butt of it firmly, and climbed up it, struggling to her feet. Taking shallow, aching breaths, she surveyed the town square, looking vainly for survivors.

All about her, the blood of many different races ran together and dried under the summer sun. In the distance rang a *tink-tink-tink* of a lanyard clip battered by the wind against a flagpole, the Star-Spangled Banner wafting lazily above it.

"So, this is war," she muttered.

Evan made a sharp detour through a parking lot and ran down the walkway between Cowabunga Surf Shop and Sprinkles Ice Cream, between the tables with umbrellas, tasting the fresh salty air. On the other side of the strip mall was a board-walk and the beach. He ran sideways a few steps, to get out of the line of sight, and ran straight at the railing of the boardwalk, hurdling it and falling twenty-three feet to the sand below. He tried to land on his feet but belly-flopped instead.

Above, his pursuers burst from between the shops and looked both ways, not having seen him go over the rail. They split up, one group going the way they agreed he went, and the other to the boardwalk. He had just tossed hands full of sand and seaweed on the Evan-shaped impression he'd made, trying to fill it in, and was now pressed back against the sea wall, staring up at the slits between the planks and the people visible through them.

There were many paths between the Ocean Mall's clusters of shops, many that Evan could now be zigzagging through to shake them off, and abandoned shops with shattered front windows that he could try to hide in. While they debated this above him, he braced his feet against one wooden support and his back against the sea wall, and walked himself up. At the top, he splayed his feet out against the joists and pushed hard, pulling himself up as close as he could to the boardwalk's underside.

A few of his pursuers got down on their knees and leaned out between the balusters to look underneath. His legs trembling after all that he'd already put them through, Evan only had sheer terror to help him hang on. He held his breath for as long as he could, letting it out slowly when he had to, then forced himself to take the next one just as slowly. They looked as far as they could either way, and were in too much of a hurry to study the sand in more than just a perfunctory sweep for tracks. Satisfied, they got up and ran off to catch up with the others.

Always careful, though, Evan forced himself to wait. The feeling of déjà vu made him shake his head. It wasn't too long since he was doing the same underneath the floor of a crackhouse. Holding on just another minute longer, in case those chasing him had gone only a short distance, then hid to see if he'd come out. And then again, under a kitchen sink.

The seconds ticked by, each one taking minutes. Squinting up against the sunshine that painted bars of light across his body, he prayed silently, with only his lips moving.

"I know I said this before, God, but get me outta this and I promise I'll go straight. The marina's right over there. Just let me get to that boat and I can take it from there. I'll open up a Pecado in Ibiza with Maya, but a legitimate one. Just food. No drugs, no guns, nothing bad. Just veal with fried plantains and cherimoya and Orizaba and batidos. I swear. Just help me, please. Help me."

When he was sure he'd waited long enough, he let his legs swing down and he dropped. Pausing another minute to catch his breath and give his legs a much-needed rest, he listened to the waves crash a few dozen feet away.

Soon, he thought.

Sipping umbrella drinks in a hammock under the hot sun, soothed by the rhythmic crashing of Ibizan shore break. The marina was only half a mile away, nestled in the crook of an artificial harbor. The late Nestor de Medieros' yacht, with its secret caches of weapons and money under the steps from the salon to the companionway, awaiting him.

Taking one more breath after the last one he felt he needed, he got to his feet and stagger-ran under the boardwalk.

Each step, having to push off of sand, sapped even more of his strength, and a few times he landed on a half-buried conch shell or starfish, one of the imported lies that the Town Council upheld their image with.

He had gotten a quarter mile when his frustrated pursuers split up again, one division coming back to recheck the beach. Seeing the footprints in the sand, and where they started, they cursed each other viciously and hurried to the nearest flight of stairs, taking the steps five at a time. Baying like a pack of dogs when they spotted him, they gave chase.

Evan moaned, sagging against the concrete wall. Looking back, he saw them well out of range, but coming fast. Then, remembering the syringe in his pocket, he dug it out, tore off the makeshift cap that had kept the needle straight, and stuck it into the blue vein in the hollow of his elbow. A second wind flooded into him as he depressed the plunger, and he dashed off when it was emptied, throwing it away. When he came to the next stairway, he looked back.

They were coming a bit slower now, hampered as he had been by the sand giving way beneath them. They'd just passed their flight of stairs and were closing in. He waited a moment, then scampered up the steps to firmer ground. Cursing, they had to turn around and run back to their own stairs to follow him, while Evan gained a good distance on the boardwalk. It also helped that the idiots were wearing oversized pants with no belt, and were constantly having to tug them back up when they slipped down. Evan could finally find a reason to appreciate that trend.

He came to a taller wall that girded private property, carefully skirted the agave plants and Spanish bayonets that guarded it, and hauled himself up. The mansion that perched atop it was abandoned, its residents having evacuated earlier, but he ignored it, wanting to put as much space between him and the gunmen instead. Crossing two property lines, he could see the bristling forest of sailboat masts, outriggers, and tuna towers not far away. A grove of sea grape trees shrouded one lawn's border, and beyond that, a long stretch of picket-fenced, manicured lawns with beach houses and shade huts.

One more backward glance to make sure he wasn't seen, and he melted into a wall of overhanging branches and broad, round leaves, careful not to disrupt them. Sea grapes are very easy to climb, with thick trunks that bend, usually before forking off into limbs, even the weakest of which are rather sturdy. A small forest of them can be almost as much fun for an avid tree climber as a single banyan.

Evan had plenty of room to move once he got in past the heavy foliage, and he quickly checked for the best of the trees. Deciding, he scampered up the trunk and walked, casually and comfortably, along the lowest branch to where the concealing leaves swayed in the salty wind. To see out of them was easy; to see inside, those chasing him would have to know where to look, especially considering his dark clothes. He watched them climb onto the private wall, trying to ignore the hanging clusters of ripe purple berries. He used to love them, as a kid.

Seven figures came running along the wall, slowing down to do

789

a cursory look at each house. None of the windows were broken—yet—and it was easy to see that no one had gotten in.

Evan waited impatiently for them to pass by. The feeling of power surging through him made him want to pounce out of the tree and tear them apart with his bare hands, but he wrestled the temptation down.

"Come on," he whispered. "Come on. Thaaat's it. Come right by here." Dagger was out, a fat green shotgun shell in its break-barrel, and another one in his fist, ready to replace the first. He waited. The Browning he had emptied and dropped over an hour ago, but it didn't matter, he told himself. These weren't soldiers. They were just guys with guns. Eventually, they came jogging along, saw that the stretch ahead allowed no place to hide, and looked straight into the grove. Evan felt his throat crimp, thinking Ohhh shit, waitaminute! You gotta give me a second!

Maybe the face that he watched most sensed his eyes upon him, or maybe it was just chance that the face went cold, paused for a moment, and slowly tilted up, following the eyes and meeting Evan's stare evenly. Before he could shout, Evan erupted from the bushy cluster of leaves, tackling the guy with his arms while he also swung his legs around to catch the guy next to him. Both of the thugs were caught off balance, the second brought down when the first one instinctively reached out and grabbed a hold of him.

Evan hit the pavement where they had just stood, not bothering to watch them fall backwards, screaming, off the sea wall. He didn't expect the fall to kill them. Just break their necks or something. The spare shell bounced away.

The two on either side, Hispanics of some kind, came at him, and he spun around into the complicated capoeira stunt that looks like a breakdancing windmill move, his legs lashing out as he twisted, catching one of them in the knee and tripping him, then planted one hand, pushed off with a foot, and swung his lower body up over him to kick the other fellow in the gut. He hit neither of them very hard, but hard enough to make the second of the two thugs drop his Glock.

When his feet came back down, before he whipped upright into a crouch, he snatched up the gun and, together with the break-barrel, pistol-whipped the other one across both knees at once. Continuing the arm's motion around to the other gangsta, he fired the Glock point blank into the belly he'd just kicked. Jerking his body around, he fired Dagger between the legs of the stumbling one, aiming a little off so that the scattering shot would hit both of the men on that side.

The closer one's shoulder and neck were shredded, and the face of the one just to the left and behind him looked instantly peppered with measles. Both had been aiming...

As he rose up out of his crouch, the pistol-whipped one coming at him, the one remaining behind him fired, five times. Unloading the last of his clip into Evan's back, throwing him forward into the one trying to grapple with him, the both of them going down, the Glock flying over the edge.

Though it hurt terribly, Evan managed to smile. Dumb bastard actually spared his life by keeping that trigger warm, grouping all of the shots in one area that was guarded by Kevlar. Groaning, he lifted Dagger and slammed the butt of it on the Adam's apple of the thug underneath him, while his other hand fished around in his pocket for another shotgun shell.

The gangsta clawed futilely at his throat, his eyes wide, mouth working like a goldfish's.

"Whut da fuck...?" Evan heard behind him. Rolling over onto his back, he opened the barrel while the last one standing slapped his pockets for a spare magazine, finding none, then frantically dove for one of his fallen comrades' guns.

"Been there before," Evan muttered, but without pity, as he popped a green cartridge into the cylinder, snapped it shut with a flick of his wrist, and aimed. The man looked up and froze, his brown, bloodshot eyes wide. Evan pulled the trigger.

The man's face was blasted into a bloody ruin, a red mist jumping out the back of his do-rag and changing direction as the wind caught it.

Evan sagged with relief, only for an instant forgetting that the one who lay next to him was still alive, and the two he'd shoved off the wall unaccounted for. He got up slowly, achingly, picked up the pistol the other had just been reaching for, and glanced over the edge.

Bam!

A shot grazed the side of his head, burning away part of his ear and digging a trench through his scalp. He jerked back-wards and fell, howling, and lashed out with both legs to kick the gut-shot (and still living) body over the lip of the wall.

Momentarily distracted, the gangsta down on the sand took a step back, involuntarily moving the gun hand farther upwards, and Evan wasted no time rolling to his feet, jamming his own pistol forward and blowing a hole through the chin of the upturned face, the throat behind it.

Growling, enraged, Evan stood and shot the two other bodies, once each, in the head, then the gasping one next to him, and collapsed.

The pain in his head screamed over the aching of his bullet-bruised back and sore limbs, but the adrenaline coursing through his veins gave him the will to stand. Besides, he told himself, it's only pain, and what's pain? It wasn't masochism, it was Krav Maga, hammered by Pedro into his skull. He swayed a moment, the ground rocking beneath his feet. For a second, he had the wild impulse to wind his arm back and hurl the Glock he held out into the ocean, but instead, he released the magazine to check it.

Only three shots left. Every pistol still lying up where he was only held a few bullets, but he emptied them all to fill up one clip halfway, give or take, and started walking.

Then turned back around. Stormed over to the hanging branches of the nearest tree, seizing one of the sea grape clusters and yanking it away.

He was surprised to be hungry, having just shot up what he assumed to be speed, but he felt none of the side effects of uppers. Not the running-on-fumes and paranoia, but power. Indestructibility. And thirst for blood. But sea grapes would do for now.

Popping them in his mouth one at a time, he staggered along the sea wall, his teeth grinding the thin layers of fruit away from the large pits, and spitting the seeds out over the sand, far below.

From a distance, he turned around and looked at the corpses in his wake. Four sprawled on the concrete and the grass, three down in the sand. He laughed, his voice dry like the crackle of footsteps on dead leaves. A bunch of coals, he thought, and wondered if any of them had been in that crack house looking for him while he trembled under the floor, down with the spiders and the roaches and the rats. He hoped so.

He spat the seed he was chewing in their direction, and walked on. He came eventually to the southern side of the inlet, threw the Glock and the Dagger across, where they clattered among the boulders that made up the harbor side, and dove into the water.

The salt tingled in the gash along his head, and he wondered briefly if there were any sharks nearby. But the thought was cast aside by another concern: would Nestor's yacht still be there? Was it intact? What would he do if it wasn't?

Oh, just go back to find Pedro and Teresa. Rejoin the mercenaries. He was a diamond, after all. Spend some more time assassinating people. He gurgled a laugh as he thought of Dark Geiger giving away his weapons and falling in with that God crap. Christ, what an idiot. A man with the world in front of him…

His hand touched a slimy, barnacled rock, and he grabbed it. And the next one nearby. And he hauled himself out of the water, cleansed of the sand and the blood—

He looked up into the barrel of a gun. His own gun. The Glock. And behind it, the grinning face of Cory Walken, who, with his flattened nose, no longer looked too much like a ferret.

"Hey, Lanthorne."

"Put my fucking gun down," Evan snapped as he climbed up onto the rocks. Walken actually backed away a few steps, back up the jetty, before he remembered that he was the one with the gun, and he was the one that did the talking.

"Do you have any idea how long I've waited for a moment like this?"

"You should be used to disappointment by now."

"I want you to apologize," Cory said, shivering with delight. Evan looked around on the boulders for Dagger. Found it, wedged deep between two of the rocks. There was no way he could have dived for it before Walken shot him.

Shit.

I had to be careful, didn't I? I had to make sure the guns didn't get wet. *Shit!* All right God, let's talk this over one more time…

"I want you to say you're sorry," Walken went on. "And I want you to act like you mean it. It better be an award-winning apology, Lanthorne. I want you to apologize to me as if your life depends on it."

The gun was pointed at Evan's face. Not the chest.

But a quick feint to the left and lunge ought to do it. Little pussy didn't have the balls to fire anyway. But keep him talking. Gotta let him really get into this, let him savor it, and close his eyes for a second the way they did in the movies.

"I'm sorry, Walken. I can explain."

"Not good enough."

And Cory Walken shot him in the forehead.

Evan parabolaed backward, cracking the back of his head against the rock he had first touched, his forehead under the water-line, his eyes wide and staring. A billowing cloud of crimson spread out underneath him, the gold-capped rosary teeth and the twenty-four carat crucifix drifting back and forth within it. Shaking, Cory Walken stared down at him.

"Jesus. Christ. Jesus Christ. Oh, my God..."

He dropped the gun, doubled over and vomited, overcome by the feeling he hadn't expected.

"Co-reeee!" A woman's voice called. His mother, on the dock, panicking. "Cory! Where are you?"

"Coming," he choked, stumbling up the wet boulders and running, back to Mother. Back to the sailboat they were getting the hell outta Dodge in.

Evan lay sprawled, his heart no longer beating, the blood that fueled his brain seeping out the back of his skull rather quickly. His last thoughts were not even true thoughts, really.

More like third generation copies of copies. Old, faded, black and white snapshots of impressions, reshuffled and redealt, over and over and over.

Whoa, shit! Rewind!

Karma's a bitch, ain't it?

I guess Shaitan was right.

Whoa. Rewind! Back up a minute!

The waves crashing against the rocks sounded to him for an instant like a studio audience of ghosts, all giving the show, his life's finale, a standing ovation. The fuckers.

I guess Shaitan was right. Live by the sword...

His last pseudo-thought, before black oblivion swallowed him, was that the sharks were probably on their way.

IV

On the other side of town, perched on the rubble of fallen masonry, Shaitan Risingsun stared out over the smoldering ruin that was Coquina, Florida. Behind her, across the street, the button-woods, mahogany, pigeon plums, and casuarinas crawled with unseen things, liberated zoo captives. Smoke blackened the sky, plumes of it twisting up from raging fires. All over the United States, in every major city, this was happening. Buzzards circled over shattered buildings, ready to start dropping as soon as it looked safe.

Several thousand miles away, the President of the United States stepped out of his country home, nodded to the Secret Service men, and took a deep breath of clean air. His henchmen followed at a respectable distance as he went for a walk. His wife watched him through a window, saw him pause under one of the apple trees. Saw him look up, at the serpent hiding in the branches, glaring suspiciously back at him. She saw him burst into a fit of laughter, let out a whoop she could not guess the reason for, and walk on. He'd wanted an apple, but thought better of it.

One of the Secret Service men calmly drew his weapon and shot the snake dead.

Startled, the First Lady watched the limp rope of an animal fall out of the tree, then glanced back at her husband, who still laughed, and shook her head.

In Florida, Shaitan turned her back on what was once her home, dropped down off the ruins, and walked across the street into the woods.

She never looked back.

High above her, past the smoke and the clouds, above the hazy blue of the stratosphere, above even the satellites that kept their eyes on all the world, past the moon, and the planets orbiting our yellow sun, and the gigantic yet still tiny cluster of other suns and solar systems that comprise the Milky Way, and the grayish-blue surface of the molecule that they in turn comprise, and the mitochondria of a cell so large that the mind would collapse merely to envision it, out further than the amoebas that squirmed mindlessly upon the leg hairs of a tiny flea on the back of a dog, whose happy face was in the biting wind outside the window of a fast-moving car on the highway of another world in another solar system of another galaxy that comprised the atoms of a cell of an enormous red crayon in the hands of a child—that child's mother, with her hands full—as well as the tiny philosopher who gazed at the winking stars above him that, combined, made up one of the infinite number of molecules that comprised a fleck of ash that landed upon just one of Shaitan's half-million strands of hair—took no notice of her at all.

President Henry Tucker allowed a year of anarchy to destroy many large cities, before seizing the reins once again and re-establishing some semblance of order. Interestingly, some areas of the United States, such as the South and the Midwest, that are mostly populated by what they call the Silent Majority, did not descend into savagery like the inhabitants of both coasts. Anthropologists and politicians argue the reasons for this back and forth, the world over.

Dark Geiger became the Catholic Church's first saint of the new era, after his conversion, of course, for his selfless acts as wandering missionary and healer of the sick, comforter of the dying, and heroic defender of the weak. His exploits were legendary, and the Christian world praised him and used him as an example long after his death at 72, when he came in second against a Bengal tiger in the wilderness—the granddaughter of a magnificent specimen that had been liberated from the zoo in Chicago so many years before.

Jim Crowe had spent years planning his followers' migration into the Georgia wilderness, where he, with Rabbit as his lieutenant, founded a walled city-state they named New Sparta, modeled after its namesake, which repelled hundreds of attacks from the neo-barbarians and established itself as the first bastion of civilization. Their hitherto under-the-table alliance with the US military helped to rebuild their country and make it once again, truly, the land of the free and the home of the brave.

And Maya Macaulay, well, that's another story.

Afterward

This series was written between the summers of 2001 and 2005, and the message of it was born in coma dreams during a stint in a prison hospital. A black man had called me a cracker before beating me almost to death, and in my light-at-the-end-of-the-tunnel experience (which I explain in *The Hero Mindset*) I saw the world clearly for the very first time. The real world is very different from the one we think we know, and all of what I have to say can easily be dismissed as the fantasy of a crackpot convict who hit his head, except for the inconvenient and disturbing frequency of my predictions coming true.

This is not my definitive work on the subject. In fact, as I mentioned in the introduction, I had unpublished this book. I wrote it during my fifth year in prison, after being a guinea pig for Big Pharma and thinking that my Heresy books needed to become progressively more disturbing throughout the series, if they were going to make any impact on society.

A few years later, I realized how wrong I was, and quietly took it off the shelves. I intended to fix it for years, but never got around to it. Now, however, in the Age of Covid, when I see the events I predicted coming to pass, I have to speak up.

There's a documentary on YouTube about a 1960s experiment called *The Beautiful Ones*, about John Calhoun's research on population density and social pathology in mice. He created what should have been a rodent utopia. It was a two-and-a-half-meter-square tank, with stairs and tunnels leading from a common area to nesting grounds, and it was regularly cleaned and stocked with food. A predator-free, all-you-can-eat-buffet environment without any reason to worry.

It turned into a disaster.

Four dominant mouse couples claimed their nesting areas, and became this idle class, just eating and constantly grooming themselves. Those were 'the Beautiful Ones,' without a care in the world. The others confined themselves to a few places in the common area, not bothering to take advantage of the other available rooms. They lived together and rapidly degenerated into a state of violence, cannibalism, and bisexual rape, all without any need for it. There were no outside threats, no lack of food, no unavailability of mates. Some became sleepwalkers and some became rapists of both sexes, and none of them had any chance of rehabilitating after the experiment was over.

This experiment spawned a new genre of science fiction in which humans have overpopulated the Earth and followed in the footsteps of Calhoun's mice. A lot of people believed it. A lot of influential people also believed Malthusian Theory, even though it has been repeatedly debunked. This gave rise to the fear that, if left unchecked, people would destroy the world by their very existence.

A famous racist named Margaret Sanger pushed an agenda of eugenics and depopulation to cull the black race, calling it Planned Parenthood, and her grandson, Bill Gates, is continuing her work under the guise of "philanthropy." He is accused of using fake vaccines to poison people of color and sterilize women in poverty-stricken nations to prevent them from having children, supposedly for their own good.

Many people do not believe that the US government could be complicit in this horrific plan, but they seem to forget that this same government purposefully infected hundreds of black Tuskegee sharecroppers with syphilis in 1932. Why would the government accused of systematic racism today *not* be guilty of another act of racism? Especially after they already got caught doing it once before?

As explained in the previous book, *Heresy Vol. 4,* the ruling elite created a new system of low-cost expendable labor, and sarcastically called it "welfare." They are effectively breeding a new subculture of people who enter into slavery of their own free will, and are even proud of it. They also, through 'cosmetic psychopharmacology' have convinced white parents to drug their children with pills that make them lose their temper, often in fits of unjustified righteous indignation.

There is a phenomenon in the US where some white people see an injustice and try to make it about themselves. The righteous indignation they are programmed to feel then has a name, and they are presented with a target for their unfounded, groundless aggression—the witch-hunt du jour. After they have been made by the manipulative media to feel guilty about their "privilege," they'll try to undo it by seeking out injustices (real or imagined) and making them their own, virtue-signaling to redeem themselves.

Is there systematic racism? Yes. But the people who have created it, and maintain it, are the very people announcing that it exists, and they are placing the blame on their enemies. They have created the problem, then presented the 'solution,' which is the violent overthrow of the middle class by the lower, and just as they did in the Bolshevik Revolution, they will then line the victorious rebels against a wall and gun them down. There will be no redistribution of wealth, wherein the have-nots will enjoy what they didn't work for, the fruits of the haves' labor.

Watch G. Edward Griffin's 1984 interview of the ex-KGB agent and Soviet defector Yuri Bezmenov. He broke down the stages of the Communist takeover, and there is no doubt it is all going according to plan. The US is destabilized by violence and unrest, a civil war is brewing, and desperate times call for desperate measures. The government will have to take charge, tightening security, abolishing the republic and transitioning to socialism. Then, when the public is disarmed, the culling will continue with forced vaccinations—which are not the same as the ones that cured polio, before anyone pulls that card again.

Of course, there have been good vaccines that saved lives. The problem is that people "default to truth" and assume that *all* vaccines are beneficial, and it is that trust that will be their undoing. This vaccine will sterilize hundreds of thousands.

Now, why would I want to publish this and put a great big target on my forehead? Because I was to be one of these have-nots rioting in the streets. Even though I was born with plenty of bona fide privilege, I fell into the same trap so many others do, and wasted my life, and was ready to take my revenge on a society that *didn't* waste theirs.

The way genocides are planned, a certain demographic—usually it's men who spend most of their time in bars instead of working—is told they're unsuccessful because they are oppressed. People prefer to believe their failure is someone else's fault rather than their own, so they will readily accept it. Then, they are told that the people oppressing them are those who *do* work instead of hanging out in bars. Thus, the ne'er-do-wells are mobilized against the middle class, instead of the wealthy elite who programmed them since birth to be losers in the first place. Angry unemployed people with no prospects go out and burn down small businesses, like we are seeing today.

I have no doubt, and say with great shame, that I might've been one of those Antifa rioters, if my life hadn't taken a turn. I was inspired by *Fight Club* and a selfish urge to condemn and destroy what I was unable to participate in.

I went to prison, where I belonged, and was almost killed, like I deserved to be, when I was miraculously given a second chance. I must not let that chance go to waste.

It is my duty to share this with you before I leave my body a second time, in the hopes that you do not follow in my footsteps, or worse, be the victim of someone else who has.

Look for the first novel in the
Icarus series,

Thy Neighbor's Wife

the early adventures of Rabbit

Available Now

I

Rabbit came bopping out of a store in a shopping center, packing his cigarettes against his palm, and Blue Tick looked down at him and asked "Are you ready?" The little man with the snazzy suit and the moviestar hair grinned. He was nervous and trying not to show it, and anybody else would've been fooled, but Tick had been his henchman for years, and knew better. "When'd you start smoking again?"

"I'm not. I'm just going to have a few because she smokes, and I can't stand the smell or the taste of a smoker if I'm not smoking too."

"Good thinking," the muscle-bound skinhead said, nodding, hoping his sarcasm wasn't too subtle.

Rabbit lit the first cigarette and took a long drag to get into character. His expression grew thoughtful.

"Yunno what I heard someone say a minute ago? It was a bit disturbing. 'The children of single mothers grow up knowing what'll get them laid.' I had to think about that for a bit. But yeah, if Mom's coming home with some new guy all the time, the girls see how she acts and, when they come of age, follow her example, and the boys watch the jackass she comes home with and start to imitate him. The cycle continues—"

He jerked forward suddenly as if elbowed in the gut, his eyes going wide behind his sunglasses.

"What is it?" Tick asked, but then he remembered.

Rabbit felt a horrible sudden coldness inside of him, and gasped out a quick Excuse me. Dropping the cigarette, he turned and hurried toward the long corridor that led to the restrooms. Tick shook his head slowly, thinking If they *always* upset his stomach, why does he always start up again? *Always?*

He nodded slightly to the piped-in muzak he didn't consciously notice was playing, and thought about the sweeping generalization Rabbit had just made, and how it didn't apply to everybody. He made a note to tell him that when he got out.

A moment passed and his cell phone rang. There was only one person it could be, since hardly anyone had these fancy new things yet, except for people like him. He rolled his eyes, expecting to be asked to run go get Imodium.

"Yello?"

"Tick! There's a big guy coming out with a green shirt and a baseball cap on backwards. The shirt says STP. Grab him!"

"What? What do you mean 'grab him'?"

"Grab him and put him in the van and take him to the house in the woods! I'll meet you there!"

"Are you serious? We have a lot to do today."

Blue Tick saw a guy that matched the description coming out of the corridor, and sizing him up quickly, he saw the guy could fight to some extent, but not with any real skill, and he was a bit arrogant. He sighed, thinking Not again. Not now.

Rabbit had already hung up, so Tick followed the guy out to where the cars were parked.

Maybe an hour later, that guy was tied to a chair and telling Tick what would happen if he wasn't let go *this minute*, and the little man with the moviestar hair came in. The guy stared.

"You!"

"Yeah," Rabbit said. "Me."

"What the hell's going on here? You got—"

"Shut up until I'm finished talking, asshole. Since you are officially a captive audience, you're going to listen hard to my question and give me an honest-to-God answer or I'm going to kill you, right now."

"You can't be serious."

"I've got you tied to a chair."

The guy swallowed hard.

"Now, in that bathroom, there were five urinals. Five. And one stall. Why in God's name if there were five urinals did you have to piss, standing up, all over the toilet instead?"

"Is *that* what this is about?"

"Yeah, it is. Because I had to wait for you, I almost made a mess all over myself, and you didn't even need to be there. And when you came out, the entire seat was wet. You couldn't lift the lid? You couldn't clean it off? You left your piss all over the place for me to clean up before I could sit down, and you gave me that little smirk of Go fuck yourself as you were walking out because you knew I was temporarily handicapped and couldn't whup your ass until I got out of that stall. So what is it? Are you a dog marking your territory?"

"Oh my God. I can't believe—"

Rabbit reached behind him up under his jacket and pulled out a James Bond-style Walther PPK with obligatory silencer, and put it to the man's forehead.

"Can you believe it now?"

The man shut up, his eyes crossed looking up at the barrel.

"So think very hard. Why did you do it?"

"I...I don't know."

"That's a child's answer to an angry parent. Act like a man and take responsibility. Act like your life depends on it."

"I...I don't like to go in the urinal. I don't want faggots to see my dick."

Rabbit and Blue Tick both rolled their eyes, and the smaller man backed off with the gun.

"If that's the best you can do, then we'll give you a taste of your own medicine. Tick, pee on him."

"...What?" Blue Tick asked.

"You heard me. Right in his ugly face. And get some in his hair, too. And on his shirt."

"*You* pee on him."

"I already went, remember? I got nothing left."

"Oh, come on."

"I'm serious."

"But why?"

"Because he has to learn, and if I let him off easy, he'll just go and do it again. You know what they say: lessons not learnt in blood are soon forgotten. He has to know that his actions affect other people, and think about how he might just ruin somebody else's day with something as careless as this."

"But we're going to kill him either way."

The captive's eyes went even wider.

"Yeah, but I've been reading this philosopher lately who says that if reincarnation is real, and we die under especially unpleasant circumstances, we will carry that memory into our next life. By that rationale, this guy will enter his next life with an emphatic surety that pissing on toilet seats isn't just wrong, but a really bad idea, without a conscious memory of why, and maybe he will teach his children not to do it, and the world will be a slightly better place."

"Don't we have to be somewhere?"

"Quit trying to change the subject."

805

The giant man heaved a sigh, making a big production of obeying reluctantly, which was comical considering his size in comparison to Rabbit's. Gnashing his teeth, he unzipped his pants. The captive tensed up and held his breath, scrunching his eyes and mouth shut, and braced himself.

The leaves of trees outside rattled against the house, and the ticking of the second hand on Rabbit's watch was suddenly very loud, five ticks going by before the man in the chair's eyes cracked open ever so slightly.

"Well?" Rabbit asked.

"I can't," Tick said quietly.

"What do you mean, you *can't?*"

"What do you think I mean? I can't."

"Why the hell not?"

"He's...he's looking at it."

"Oh, for Christ's sake."

"You can stop looking at it, too, yunno."

"You're three hundred twenty pounds of muscle and you can't pee on a guy because he's looking at you. That's rich."

"I ain't doing this," the big man said, tucking himself hurriedly back in and sulking while Rabbit shook his head.

The guy strapped to the chair was starting to chuckle, until Rabbit put his gun to the sweaty forehead and muttered "This is your lucky day, after all."

And pulled the trigger.

The sound of the exit wound was louder than the *ping!* of the suppressed gunshot, but both were drowned out by the collective gasp from all the other people tied-up in the room.

"I gotta be somewhere," Rabbit said, turning to face five young men whose eyes bulged over the gags that held their mouths shut. "But I'll be back before too long, so don't get too comfortable."

806

After using his considerable wealth to stockpile arms and raise a private army, Alexander Ferrar led an exodus of coed college students into the Amazon rainforest. There his followers have established a sustainable farm/nudist colony and worship him a la Colonel Kurtz. He is scheduled to return after the inevitable collapse of western civilization, at which time he will seize power and usher in the first era of true world peace. In the meantime, he continues to write novels that are delivered to his publisher via drone.

Made in the USA
Columbia, SC
21 December 2023

29307112R00443